THE GLORY: AN APOCALYPSE

BERKELEY BLACKFRIARS • BOOK 3

J.R. MABRY

Apocryphile Press

1700 Shattuck Ave #81, Berkeley, CA 94709

www.apocryphilepress.com

Copyright © 2018 by J.R. Mabry

Printed in the United States of America

ISBN 978-1-947826-60-1

Lyrics from "In the Falling Dark" written by Bruce Cockburn. Used by permission of Rotten Kiddies Music, LLC

CLAIM YOUR FREE BOOK

To find out more about the Berkeley Blackfriar's universe, download your free copy of *The Berkeley Blackfriar's Companion*. Includes short stories set in the Blackfriars' universe, photos of main characters, a complete glossary, a walking tour of the Blackfriars' Berkeley, recipes from Brian's kitchen, a short history of Old Catholicism, a Q & A session with author J.R. Mabry, links to music and videos associated with the books and more!

Click on BookHip.com/DXDCAS
to get your free copy!

REVIEWS

If you enjoy the Blackfriars books, please help other people find them by leaving an honest review on amazon or kobo or wherever you buy books. Thank you!

OTHER BOOKS BY J.R. MABRY

The Berkeley Blackfriars Series:
The Kingdom
The Power
The Glory

The Christmas at Bremmer's Series:
What Child is This?

The Temple of All Worlds Series:
The Worship of Mystery

The glory of God is only conveyed
by the chariot of truth.
—*Rabbi Isaac Bar Baalam of Damascus*

The sun will no longer be your light by day,
nor will the moon shine for illumination by night.
The Lord will be your everlasting light;
your God will be your glory.
—*Isaiah 60:19 CEB*

Wail, for the day of the Lord is near.
Like destruction from the Almighty it will come.
Then all hands will fall limp;
every human heart will melt,
and they will be terrified.
Like a woman writhing in labor,
they will be seized by spasms and agony.
They will look at each other aghast,
their faces blazing.
—*Isaiah 13:6-8 NRSV*

Some [apocalypses], such as *Daniel*, contain an elaborate review of history, presented in the form of a prophesy and culminating in a time of crisis and eschatological upheaval. Others, such as 2 *Enoch*, devote most of their text to accounts of the regions traversed in the otherworldly journey. The revelation of a supernatural world and the activity of supernatural beings are essential to all the apocalypses.

John J. Collins, The Apocalyptic Imagination

ACKNOWLEDGMENTS

The Blackfriars books have always owed much to books that have gone before, and *The Glory* is no different. Larch probably discovered his ascension oil from reading Charles Williams' *War in Heaven*, just as I did.

I want to thank http://www.wiccanway.com/ for guidance on conducting a proper Mabon ritual. I give continued thanks to Josephine McCarthy's *The Exorcist's Handbook* for more creative ideas than I can possibly use. More thanks to my editor, Amanda Noonan, for her encouragement and keen eye.

Grateful thanks to my wife Lisa Fullam, who heard each scene hot off the printer, and who was constantly freaked out by the fact that she was often eager and ready to hear the next scene *and it did not yet exist*. There's a deep philosophical meditation in there somewhere.

Thanks to my old friend Tony Davis, who said, "I enjoy the novels, but can't we see some magickians who aren't assholes? I mean, I want to see someone who looks like me." Tony is a magickian, and definitely has his heart in the right place. I promised him that the third book would contain just such a magickian. Tony, Marco is for you.

About 1/3 of the way through writing this, Marillion's 17th album, *FEAR (F*ck Everyone And Run)* dropped into my lap, and it became the soundtrack for writing the balance of the book, much as their previous CDs have provided the soundtrack to most of my adult life. Thank you, boys—my life would be far less rich without you.

And I know this will be strange, but I want to thank my characters: Richard, Dylan, Susan, Mikael, Kat, Terry and Brian—and hell, even you, Larch—I really love you guys. I have had so much fun hanging out at your house, struggling alongside you, and laughing with you. I never knew what any of you would say until you said it and you constantly surprised and delighted me. This is intended to be the final Blackfriars novel, but you never know. I might just miss you too damn much and will need to come back for a visit, you know?

A QUARTET OF PRELUDES

For not from the east or from the west
and not from the wilderness comes lifting up;
but it is God who executes judgment,
putting down one and lifting up another.
—*Psalm 76:6-7*

PRELUDE 1

Palestine, 1878 BCE

"IF WE TELL him Joseph is alive, it will kill him." Rueben sighed.

It was after breakfast, and Serah the daughter of Asher was cleaning up after her uncles. They barely noticed her as she gathered their plates and carried them to the kitchen, but she took notice of them. Not a word escaped her.

"I agree. He won't survive it. The strain on his heart will be too great," Dan added.

"Then we will have the death of both our brother *and* our father on our souls," Naphtali said, flicking a walnut shell across the room.

Serah dropped the plate she had just picked up. Her uncles looked up at her, their knotty eyebrows raised at her error.

"My Uncle Joseph is...alive?" Her eyes were wide.

The brothers glanced at each other, then looked down. None of them were giving her reproachful looks now.

"How could you have kept this from us? How could you have kept this from grandfather?"

"You don't understand," her father said, with more edge in his voice than usual. She understood his meaning. That edge in his voice meant, *It is not for you to know, and it is not for you to question us.*

"Then perhaps you should explain it," she demanded, putting her hands on her hips. Cool evening air wafted in from the windows, stirring a hanging cluster of bells.

"Asher, control your daughter," Reuben commanded.

Serah ignored him.

"Serah," her father's tone softened. "I will explain it to you...later."

"You will explain it to me *now*."

Her uncles gasped at her impertinence. Wives spoke to their husbands like this in private, but never in public. A daughter never spoke in such a way—not ever. The brothers looked at Asher, expecting him to discipline her. He looked at the rug below his chair. "Serah, I must speak to your uncles in private. Then I shall come and speak to you. Do not shame me in front of my brothers."

Serah looked at her father, then at her ten uncles. Without a word she snatched up the last of the plates and turned, slamming the door to the kitchen behind her with her heel. She handed the plates gently to her mother and put her forefinger to her lips. "Shhhhh." She leaned her head against the kitchen door and listened.

"—is shameful." She couldn't tell who the speaker was.

"Maybe," her father said. "But no daughter could be more precious to me than her. She always tells the truth."

"That is not always a good thing," her Uncle Levi noted.

"It is when she does it."

This made some of them laugh.

"No, I am serious. She's normally a quiet girl, so you may not have noticed. But when she does speak, she says what is true—and when she tells the truth, it somehow...makes things better."

"Is she touched by God, then?" Uncle Simeon asked.

"I believe she is," her father affirmed.

Serah felt her chest swell. Her father had never complimented her that way before, certainly not in front of her. *He's not doing it in front of me now*, she reminded herself. Serah watched her mother tiptoe to the basin, trying to carry on her work without making any noise.

"Asher, are you saying that whenever your daughter speaks what is true, good comes of it rather than evil?"

"That is exactly what I am saying." There was a long silence.

Serah held her breath. She backed off the door a bit, worried that one of her uncles might burst through it and find her eavesdropping. She glanced at her mother and she smiled, unconcerned. It didn't bother her mother one bit that Serah was listening—her mother did it all the time.

When no one opened the door, she leaned closer to it. *Is what father said true?* she wondered. She had always considered telling the truth to simply be a good idea. And in her experience, good always resulted when she did. *But is that not true for everyone?* She had never thought of herself as special in any way.

"This is news indeed," Uncle Reuben finally spoke.

"Asher, your daughter might just prove to be our salvation," her Uncle Zebulun said. He rarely spoke, but when he did, people tended to listen.

"What do you mean?" Uncle Reuben asked.

"When we threw Joseph into that well and left him for dead, we created a deep pool of evil that each one of us drinks from every day. And it is poisonous to us. I fear it will be poisonous to Jacob our father as well."

Sarah's breath caught in her throat. Her uncles had always told her that their brother Joseph had been killed by mountain lions. *Is even my father guilty of this?* It seemed he was. Her mother continued to smile. She was oblivious. Serah longed to tell her mother this awful truth. But...later—she didn't want to miss anything. She kept her ear pressed to the door.

Uncle Zebulun continued: "Every day you send Serah to the well to draw water. This day let her draw healing forth from our poisoned well. Let *her* tell our father Jacob the truth about his son. Let her tell him, so that good and not evil will come of it."

THE SUN WAS SETTING when she slipped into her grandfather's bedchamber. He was standing at prayer, bobbing toward the window, his hands palms up before him, as if to catch the last rays of the sun. It was not unusual for one of his daughters or granddaughters to enter, tidy his room, or remove his soiled clothes from the pile in the corner. Serah gathered up his laundry and set it by the door. She hummed as she worked, as she often did. Her grandfather continued his bobbing, not disturbed by her presence or her song. When she finished humming a verse, she added lyrics.

> *"Joseph is in Egypt*
> *And dangling on his knees*
> *are two of Jacob's grandsons*
> *whom he has never seen.*
>
> *Joseph is in Egypt,*
> *living like a king.*
> *His heart breaks for his father,*
> *whom he would like to bring*
>
> *to Egypt,*
> *to Egypt land,*
> *to Egypt,*
> *to Egypt land."*

When she finished singing, she leaned against the wall and looked at her grandfather. He had stopped bobbing, his eyes were open, and tears streamed down his cheeks. "I cannot tell," he said, his eyes still fixed on the darkening sky, "if you are the messenger of God or if you are simply a cruel, cruel child."

"Grandfather, you know that I love you. Have you ever known me to be cruel?"

"No."

"Have you ever known me to lie to you?"

"Not once."

"Then believe me now, and be glad. Your son, my Uncle Joseph, is alive in Egypt. My father and his brothers met him when they went there for food last month. They were afraid to tell you."

"But he is dead."

She shook her head. "No. They lied to you."

"Wicked children." He turned his face away so she could not see it.

"Yes. They were wicked children. But as men they are contrite."

His face was still turned away, but his fingers reached for her, trembling. "My son, the son of my heart, he is...alive?"

"He is alive."

"He is well?"

"Yes. He is all but king, I hear."

"Glory be to the God of my father, Isaac. Glory be to the God of my grandfather, Abraham. Glory..."

He sank to his knees and clutched at his heart. She rushed to him and held him up. His eyes traveled to the window again. "What is all the noise? What is happening?" he asked her.

"They are readying the wagons. They are going back to Egypt. They are going back to tell Joseph that you...that you *know*."

Jacob staggered to his feet and clutched at the window for support. "I will go to Egypt."

"Go and speak to your sons," Serah told him. "Let them tell you with their own lips about their sin. Let them receive from your own hand their pardon. They have carried the weight of this for twenty years, and it has been heavy indeed."

"They have?" He shook his head in disbelief. "I have carried this grief for twenty years. Has it not been heavy?"

"I know it has, grandfather. I am so sorry."

He looked at her then. He held his arms out to her and she went to him. He embraced her and rocked her as as his tears trickled down his face. "The mouth that sang this wonderful news will never taste death."

Serah felt something catch in her chest. She hugged her grandfather close to her and wondered at his words.

PRELUDE 2

San Francisco, Present Day

CONSUELA WOULD NEVER FORGET the look on her father's face. "She's a witch," he'd said, and there was fear in his eyes. Consuela could never remember seeing fear in his eyes. Never. He was always the one in control, the one who held the power. The one who beat her. But when Mama's mother had come to visit, Consuela saw so many things she'd never seen before—someone who stood up to her father, who gave as good as she got, who made him afraid.

It was a revelation. For the next twenty-four hours she felt like her world had turned upside down. Her Abuelita became her hero. She showed her what was possible in the world. She gave her hope.

And if Abuelita was a witch, then that was what Consuela wanted to be, too. She started by searching the web and was amazed at the wealth of information she found. She wondered if the nuns at school knew about the overwhelming abundance of witchery happening just out of sight, beneath their noses, and around, it seemed, every corner.

Obviously there was much to learn, but where to start? She thought about ordering *Witchcraft for Dummies*, but the truth was, she hated reading, especially in English. No, she needed a tutor, a mentor, a teacher.

She had so many questions, after all. What is *Wicca*? Is it just another word for witch? Did witches go to hell? That was important, because she definitely did not want to go to hell. It was in the middle of her third night of web-surfing about witchery that her laptop pinged at her, signifying she had a message. She did not recognize the person contacting her. Babylon1961? Who in the world was that? She clicked on the message to open it.

Babylon1961: Hey, it looks like you're interested in witchcraft.

Her breath caught in her throat. She brought her hand to her chest and looked around to see if she was being watched. Her stuffed animals stared back placidly, but no one else seemed to be around. She took a deep breath and tried to will herself to be calm.

ConnieQT: Yes. I want to be a witch.

Babylon1961: Do you know why? It is not an easy path. It requires great commitment.

Consuela's thoughts raced. *I want to punish my father. I want to be as powerful as my Abuelita.* That was all too personal. She didn't know this person, after all. *I want to be in control of my own life.* "That's it," she said out loud.

ConnieQT: I want to be in control of my own life.

Babylon1961: There are many answers you could have given. But that is the right one. That is the secret password.

Consuela felt a rush of pride flow through her. She got the right answer! Maybe she could be good at this. Maybe she, too, could make her father afraid.

ConnieQT: I want to learn how to be a witch. I need a teacher. Do you know a good teacher?

Babylon1961: I know several. But I think that I might be a good fit for you. Why don't we meet someplace for coffee? Someplace public, safe for both of us?

This person seemed to know how she thought and what she needed. She or he knew that she might feel unsafe meeting for the first time. A public place, for coffee? That seemed perfect. She began to feel that she could trust this person.

ConnieQT: That sounds good. Where shall we meet?

Babylon1961: There's only one place where witches and other people in the occult community in San Francisco go. It's called The Cloven Hoof.

PRELUDE 3

Berkeley, Present Day

TERRY GLANCED AT HIS SMARTPHONE. The blinking car on the screen indicated that his Ryde driver would arrive in under a minute. He'd never used this app before, but the first all-gay taxi service application had been all the rage in the media in the last few days. *Why not?* he'd thought and downloaded it. After all, he needed to go a bit off the beaten track that day.

He reveled for a moment in the cool breeze, lifting the arms of his cassock to catch the wind. It felt good to just be. He and Brian had fought that morning and he'd had a shitty day after that. *I'm still angry about it,* he realized. Sex was the problem—and sex had never been a problem for them before. Brian seemed to need less of it, which just made Terry want it all the more. He was so horny he was afraid his erection could be seen through his cassock. Terry sighed.

When he opened his eyes, a dark maroon SUV pulled up just in front of him.

The passenger window lowered. "You Terry?" a voice called from inside.

"That's me," he said, snapping out of his reverie and pulling on the door handle. He swung into the passenger seat, turned to face his driver, and melted into his seat.

"Well, aren't you a cutie?" the driver said, offering his hand. "I'm Ben. I'm here to give you a Ryde."

"I...uh...I'm Terry," Terry said, completely lost in the driver's unruly shock of bright red hair, athletic build, and most disarmingly, the dimple square in the middle of his chin.

"I know that, silly," he said. "It's on the app. This your first time?"

"Uh...yeah."

"I love virgins," he said, wiggling his eyebrows. "What are you, some kind of priest?"

"Yes, I am," Terry said as they sped away from the curb.

"So, there's that whole pesky celibacy thing to deal with. How is that?" Ben asked.

"Uh...our Order isn't celibate."

"You don't say?" Ben smiled. His dimple seemed to take up half of his face. "Are you—let me guess—Japanese?"

"Nice guess. Half Japanese. On my father's side."

"Oooh. So you know what that means, right?"

"Uh, no. What does that mean?" Terry asked, relaxing enough to flirt back a little.

"It means that you, Mr. Terry, are just my type."

PRELUDE 4

Oakland, Present Day

WITH A CRACK OF SPLINTERED WOOD, the front door smashed inward, leaving T-Ray and Darnell framed in the doorway, two black silhouettes against the orange curtain of urban twilight. T-Ray glanced behind them to see if anyone had witnessed their crime and saw only a bag lady minding her own business, shuffling away from them toward the 580 freeway overpass. T-Ray gestured for Darnell to enter quickly, and throwing a last glance over his shoulder, Darnell followed. Inside he blinked, waiting for his eyes to adjust.

The foyer was really a hallway, with stairs to the left. T-Ray snapped open the bag he'd brought, and began to cast about for "stealables" as his cousin used to call them, but there was nothing in the hallway except a bunch of old pictures on the wall. T-Ray squinted at them. They were pictures of...nuns? He blinked in confusion, then turned to watch Darnell turn the corner and freeze.

"What?" he whispered. Darnell didn't answer. The hallway doglegged to the left, and T-Ray poked his head around the corner and froze himself. He was looking at a dining room, that was clear. Stretched nearly the length of the room was a dining table, each place set with care. About a dozen old women sat stock still in front of their empty plates.

"There you are!" a cheerful voice called out.

T-Ray and Darnell both jumped.

An old woman spun through the butler door, a large steaming bowl between two potholders in her hands. Her wrinkled face broke into a broad, warm smile at the sight of them. "You, my dears, are just in time for dinner."

Every instinct in T-Ray's body told him to abandon the caper and sprint, but he seemed strangely rooted in place. He licked his lips and nearly vibrated in place from nerves.

"Did you—" the old woman started, ducking past them and peering around the corner at the front door. "Oh, *sugar*! You didn't have to break the door down, sillies. It was open! Tsk..." She waved away her objection. "It's never locked, not here." Walking back toward the dining room, she shooed them inward.

Darnell looked over his shoulder directly into T-Ray's eyes. He'd never seen his homey this scared. Not even when they were being shot at. Then he realized why. None of the old ladies seated around the table were moving, or perhaps *could* move. Then one of them succumbed to gravity and her head pitched face forward into her plate.

Their host tsk-tsked again, and pulled the woman upright again. "Please, have a seat," she said. "We always have a couple of extra seats." T-Ray and Darnell stood as still as the ladies around the table. "Sit!" the old woman commanded. Glancing at one another, they obeyed, each taking a seat between two of the frozen women.

"Everything is hot, so dig in. There's roast beef—it's leftover from last night, but that's when it's best, I think. Mashed potatoes are here," she said, pointing to a covered bowl. T-Ray could see the steam rising off of it. "And carrots, steamed with rosemary, here." She smiled at them with a look of satisfaction. "Please, help yourselves." She grabbed the potatoes and began to serve herself. "So, please tell me your names, young men."

T-Ray blinked and looked at Darnell. He wanted to think of an alias, but he couldn't. Before he could answer, though, the old woman continued. "I'm *fascinated* with the life of crime. You probably wouldn't guess this about me, but I'm a member of the Ellery Queen fan club!"

"Who?" asked Darnell.

"Shut up, fool!" T-Ray whispered.

"Are you gentlemen in the habit of stealing from nuns, then?"

T-Ray looked at the old women. It was only then that they noticed that each of them seemed...well, a little butch. They also had crosses dangling from chains around their necks and were staring, sightless and unblinking, at the feast before them.

"Ya'll are nuns?" T-Ray asked.

"Yes, what did you think? We run the Oakland Food Pantry down the street. Perhaps you know about it? Anyone can get food there, no matter who they are or what time of day it is. Or night." She smiled warmly. "So tell me about yourselves—are your parents living? Do you have siblings? Oh, you haven't touched the roast beef yet! What's wrong with you?"

Darnell reached hesitantly for the platter of meat and looked up into T-Ray's eyes briefly. His hands were shaking as he lifted a slice of roast to his plate.

"You are not going to find much of interest in this house, I can tell you that. We might have some old silver, but we don't wear jewelry. We have a television, but it's the same one we've had for fifteen years —it's not one of those fancy flat screens. How do those work, anyway?" She shook her head and nibbled at a forkful of mashed potatoes. "In any case, you are welcome to anything you find here. And take your time! I won't be calling the police—not that they'd come anyway. This is Oakland, after all! I only have one request, and I ask you to take this very seriously. Please take only what you truly need. And next time, my dears," she flashed them a conspiratorial smile, "just knock."

T-Ray nodded, but his eyes widened as he watched the old lady's head roll back on her neck. Her jaw opened, then opened wider, as if her jawbone had moved out of joint to allow her mouth to stretch and widen unnaturally. Her tongue darted toward the ceiling, then withdrew. A moment later, a thousand ravens erupted out of the old woman's throat and spilled into the air, filling the room with pounding wings, oily feathers, and the hungry screams of scavenger birds.

FRIDAY

I am the Lord, the maker of all,
who alone stretched out the heavens,
who spread out the earth by myself,
who frustrates the omens of diviners
and makes a mockery of magicians,
who turns back the wise
and turns their knowledge into folly.
—*Isaiah 44:24-25 CEB*

1

SUSAN LEANED toward the living room window, and then shrieked and ran to the door.

"What was that?" Dylan asked.

"Your woman seems to be in a state of excitement," Richard noted, not taking his eyes off the chess board. Terry rested on his elbows but was staring off into space, oblivious to the checkered battlefield before him. Tobias reclined next to Richard on the floor, his legs twitching in response to some activity in his dreams.

"Don't you never call her 'yore woman' again, if you value yore fambly jewels, mister."

"What are you gonna do about it?" Richard grinned.

"It ain't me you gotta worry 'bout."

"Marco!" Susan shouted, flinging the door open wide. She rushed outside to meet him.

"Oh, Jeezus!" Dylan buried his face in his hands.

"Marco?" Terry came to, his head popping up.

Tobias opened his eyes and raised his head, looking around, his ears perked for maximum reception.

"Did ya'll know he was coming?" Dylan asked them. His broad Melungeon face darkened.

"I knew he was coming, but I didn't know when," Richard said, standing up. "You know Marco. 'I'll be there soon' can mean anytime between tomorrow and six months from now."

"I'da preferred the six months."

"What do you mean, Dylan?" Terry asked. "Marco is a stand-up guy."

"'Cept that he always wants to stand next to mah wife," Dylan groused, getting to his feet.

Terry looked away and began biting his lip.

"C'mon, be a sport," Richard clapped Dylan on the shoulder. "If she wanted to run off with Marco, she would've done it a long time ago."

"You really know how to comfort a fella."

Richard rose and headed to the door, Tobias trotting at his heels. He stepped out onto the porch just in time to see Susan rush into Marco's arms. Then he glanced across the street and saw the small gathering of paparazzi and onlookers. Cameras flashed and people started waving. *It's good to be famous,* he thought. His pulse quickened a bit. He smiled and waved back before turning his attention to their guest.

Marco was a big man, bigger than Susan, and probably the only person Richard knew who could swing her around like a little girl—which is exactly what he did. Susan giggled and hung onto his neck.

"O, Lord, give me patience," Dylan said, stepping out onto the porch next to Richard. At the sight of him, the crowd across the street gave a cheer. Dylan waved at them with obvious embarrassment. Tobias gave a low woof.

"Courage, my friend," Richard said. It was obvious that Dylan didn't enjoy the attention as much as he did. "The fruits of the Spirit are—say them with me—love, joy, peace, patience, kindness, goodness..."

"You left out faithfulness," Dylan said blackly.

"I was getting to it. And by the way, Susan has never, ever been unfaithful to you. Not even in her dreams."

"Uh...settin' aside how you could possibly know that, Ah would say that she has never been *physically* unfaithful. Emotionally, though...waal, just look at 'em."

"If you were still a toking man, I'd tell you to light up and relax."

"If Ah were still a tokin' man, Ah'd already be high, dude. And this wouldn't bother me nearly as much."

Susan had stopped swinging and had taken Marco's arm. They began walking up to the porch. Marco was a full eight inches taller than Richard, with a barrel chest and great arms the size of industrial canned goods. His skin was the color of burnt caramel, a gift from his Nigerian mother and his Filipino father. A thin excuse for a beard clung to his chin, and he had shaved his head since the last time Richard had seen him.

"You look like the great Beast himself," Richard said, drawing him into a warm, muscular hug. Toby stood by and wagged.

"Ha! You are not the first person to say that!" Marco responded, returning the embrace. "And I am honored by the comparison!"

Marco was a Thelemite, although he had not been an active OTO member for as long as Richard could remember. Marco honored and revered the Great Beast, Alister Crowley, as the revelator of the new Aeon, but he found the company of other Thelemites to be disappointingly erratic. He called himself a "solitary practitioner," but there was nothing solitary about Marco, who was probably the most social, extroverted person Richard had ever met. He was, however, a rover—traveling in his ancient VW van that doubled as his workshop, never staying longer than a few days in any given place. Brian had once called him a professional couch surfer, and Marco did not deny it.

Richard heard the screen door slam and out of the corner of his eye saw Terry step out onto the porch. He smiled when he saw Marco, but it was a sad smile. Marco released Richard from his bear hug and reached for Dylan.

"Dylan, how's my favorite pothead?"

"Cursedly pot-free. Yer lookin' good, though, dude."

"What?" Marco leaned back and studied Dylan's face. "Birds fly, fish swim, Thelemites do sex magick, and Dylan smokes weed. How could you possibly upset the balance of nature that way? Aren't you afraid you'll put a pox on the harvest or something?"

Dylan shrugged. "Ah got allergic. See, there was this little dog—never mind, dude. It's a long story. Ah'm just allergic now—to purty much anythin' fun."

"Really? I brought absinthe," Marco sang, his eyebrows dancing. "Made it myself."

"Hot damn!" Richard said, but Dylan just shook his head.

"Nothin' stronger'n mint tea for me," he said, looking at his shoes.

"Well, buck up, my friend. At least you still got sex," he wiggled his eyebrows at Susan, and she blushed. Dylan turned red, too, but Richard suspected it wasn't from embarrassment.

"Terry, my fey friend," Marco said, stepping up to the porch and catching Terry up in his magnificent arms. He swung him around and put him back down like a child. Terry's smile looked more genuine by the time he was back on the ground, and he gave Marco a fist bump.

"Where's your top half?" Marco asked, kneeling down to give Tobias a nuzzle.

When Terry didn't answer, Susan answered for him. "Brian's fixing dinner."

"You mean I'm on time for *dinner*?" Marco breathed, in mock amazement. "There *is* a God after all."

Richard held the door for them all and they began to stream into the house, to the obvious displeasure of the onlooking crowd. The late afternoon light streamed through the stained glass windows in the chapel, casting a glorious golden glow that extended all the way into the foyer. Marco followed Richard to the kitchen where Brian was standing at the stove, stirring a stew pot.

"Brian!" Marco thundered and coming up behind him, gave him a generous squeeze. Brian accepted the backwards hug, smiling, but then turned away from the stove, catching Marco up in a proper bear hug.

"You look well," Brian said, wiping some mashed potato from his vest and straightening his tallit. A moment later everyone had gathered around the kitchen table, followed by Tobias, who plopped down under the table and began panting loudly. Richard went to the fridge and began pouring iced tea all around.

"Who the fuck is this?" a tinny voice called out, barely audible.

"Dylan, will you turn Randy up?" Brian asked.

Dylan turned the knob on a small guitar amplifier resting on the bench from 3 to 7.

"Who said that?" Marco looked around.

"Kat's brother," Susan said.

"Who's Kat?" Marco asked.

"She's our newest oblate," Richard said. "Wiccan chick—"

"Young woman," Susan corrected.

"She and Mikael are quite the pair."

"And where *is* the spiky-haired one?"

"Can't you guess?" Richard asked.

Marco's face screwed up into a scowl as he thought.

"What's the date?" hinted Richard.

"September twenty-first...Oh, silly me. They're at Mabon!"

"Setting up for it, but yeah. I'm sure the bonfire will start as soon as it gets dark."

"So where is this Randy guy?"

"In the mirror," Dylan said, pointing behind him at the large, framed mirror hanging on the wall.

Marco peered into it, then snapped upright when he saw a person in the reflection who was *not* in the room. "Shit!"

"Close," Dylan said, unkindly. "He did nearly destroy the world."

"I almost rid the world of its dreaded fixation on avocados," Randy said. "Don't be such a drama queen."

"Hi, Randy," Marco said, peering into the mirror again.

"Hey," Randy responded. "So who the fuck are you?"

"I'm Uncle Marco—ceremonial magickian and occult inventor."

"Nice elevator speech. That what it says on your business card?"

"Yes, as a matter of fact. That is exactly what it says."

"I'll bet you're a Thelemite asshole."

"Solitary Thelemite asshole, thank you. I'll bet you're a Golden

Dawn prick."

"How did ya know he was even a magickian?" Dylan asked.

"Just look at him," Marco pointed at the mirror.

"Fuck Golden Dawn," Randy spat. "I've got your Golden Dawn wedged up my ass with a hamster."

"Huh. Hostile son of a bitch. Does he ever stop?" Marco asked Richard.

"He does if you ignore him."

"Done. When is dinner, Brian?"

"Hey!" protested Randy.

"About forty-five minutes," Brian answered. "I just put the pork tenderloin in the oven. Stuffed with sage and blackberries from the garden, by the way."

"Ah am salivatin' on mah cassock, dude," Dylan said.

"Here's some pre-prandials, though." Brian put a plate of figs and whisky-soaked cheddar on the table. A moment later, he set a basket of crackers beside it.

"Sit, Marco, and tell us what you're working on," Susan said, reaching for a fig.

"Oh, do I have a lot to tell you! First, Terry, you'll be pleased to hear I've taken a deep dive into the Enochian rabbit hole," Marco said, lifting a glass of iced tea to his lips.

"Enochian is for pussies," Randy announced.

Marco ignored him. "The language is tricky, but I've got the rudiments of it down pretty well."

Terry seemed to emerge briefly from his reverie. "Marco, I'd be really careful with that, if I were you. If you're going to work Enochian, I strongly suggest amending Dee's prayers."

"Why is that?"

"Because commanding angels isn't nearly as effective as *asking* them."

"That makes sense," Dylan said, "Nobody takes kindly to the imperative mood." He palmed a piece of cheese and passed it under the table to Tobias.

"I saw that!" Brian complained.

"Do you have a grimoire worked up?" Marco asked.

"Sure. I'll email you a Word file."

"I will try it out, and compare my results against Dee's formulations. I'll let you know what I find."

"That right there is the scientific method," Dylan said, putting his arm around Susan.

"Except for the magick bit," Susan said, shrugging free of Dylan's arm.

Marco stood up. "I've got a couple of things to show you," he said, eyes dancing with glee. "Dicky, can you give me a hand?"

Richard leaped up and followed Marco out of the kitchen.

As they walked to the front door, Marco whispered, "That Randy is one friendly guy."

"You don't know the half of it," Richard whispered back.

"Has anyone noticed that he's translucent?"

Richard nodded gravely.

"He's fading, isn't he?"

Richard closed his eyes and nodded again.

Marco opened the front door and held it for Richard. "Does he know?"

"I don't think so."

"How long does he have, do you think?"

"At the rate he's fading? I don't know. A week? Maybe less?"

"And he can't feel it?"

"Honestly, I have no idea what he can feel or can't feel. And from what Kat says, he's kind of autistic. I'm not sure he knew what he was feeling back when he was...in the flesh."

The light was dimming and the breeze was turning cold. Marco slid open the door to his van and with a flourish, invited Richard to enter. Richard stepped up, but there was very little room to navigate. He sat at the small table, overflowing with detritus. Marco knelt on the cushion opposite Richard and, turning his back to him, began digging through a mountain of accumulated odds and ends.

"How do you get any work done in here?" Richard asked.

"Magick," Marco said, dramatically. He apparently had found

what he wanted—a black case about 18-inches long. "Hey, what's with all the people across the street?" he asked.

"Uh...ever since the Republican convention, they just keep coming."

"They got a 'Map to the Stars' or something like that for Berkeley?"

"We're hardly stars."

"Uh-huh. Only three billion people watched Dylan face down that ass-clown Bishop."

"They do seem to really like it when Dylan comes out. You know, just before all that went down, we had another group gathered in that same place—a horde of the possessed."

"Ha!" Marco said. "What's the difference?"

"Well, them we had to kill. These guys, we just *want* to."

Marco fished in one of the overhead cupboards. "There you are, you pork-pecker."

"Pork-pecker?"

"Got it all now. Time for show and tell!"

Inside once more, Marco laid the black case on the kitchen table, along with a carved wooden box about a foot square. Even Terry seemed to surface some interest. "First things first. I know your penchant for spiritual maguffins, so I knew you'd jump at the chance to see these." He touched a spot on the wooden box that Richard couldn't see, and then slid back a panel in its side. He pulled out a small velvet bag—it was a deep navy blue that almost shone. He handed it to Richard.

"What's in it?" Richard asked, pulling open the bag. The velvet was old and slightly faded but still beautiful.

Richard turned the bag over and emptied it into his hand. It looked like a pair of spectacles. And yet somehow, the lenses were wrong. Richard turned them over and frowned. "The lenses aren't clear. You can't actually see through these."

"Those aren't lenses, those are stones," Marco smiled. "These are the magic spectacles that Joseph Smith used to translate the Book of Mormon."

Richard blinked, his eyes wide. "Wait, I thought he used the Urim and Thummim. I've seen those, and they don't look like this. They are...were...in the Jewish museum downtown. So that can't be them."

"Besides, Larch stole 'em," Dylan noted.

Marco shrugged. "Maybe it's not the Urim and Thummim that were used in Jerusalem, but I'll bet it's the same stones Smith *thought* were the Urim and Thummim."

"I guess that could be," Richard held them up to the light. "What happens if you put them on?"

Richard met Marco's eyes, and Marco smiled. "Should I?"

"What's the worst that could happen?" Marco asked.

Richard looked around the room, and everyone seemed to be vibrating with excitement. "Dammit, Dicky, if you don't put them on I'm going to grab them from you and put them on myself," Susan said, gesticulating.

He pulled the spectacles over the bridge of his nose. Instantly he pulled them off. "Okay, that hurt."

"What? What did you see?" Terry asked.

"Light. Just...light. It was so bright it hurt."

"That's pretty much what I found," Marco said. "I haven't tried them at night yet. But the spectacles are just the appetizer. Here's the main course." He opened the wooden box and removed from it what looked to Richard like an ornate censor.

"What is that?" Richard asked.

"Guess," Marco said.

All of them peered at the object, studying it diligently. It appeared to be a globe, about nine inches in diameter, covered with geometric designs in gold, deep crimson, and aqua. The top hemisphere had sections cut out of it, and a leather strap was attached at its crown. Peering inside the cutout sections, Richard saw two dials—like one might see on an old-fashioned compass. It sat upright on a small wooden stand that was obviously carved for it. It reeked of antiquity.

Brian whistled. "That's an oracle of some kind."

"You are correct, sir," Marco said. "But which oracle is it?"

Brian got down on one knee and traced out a caduceus. "This is the bronze serpent. And these are Hebrew letters. This is a Jewish oracle."

"You're getting warmer," Marco said.

"The only Jewish oracles are the Urim and Thummim," Randy called out.

Marco intended to keep ignoring him but couldn't help himself. "That's where you're wrong, my two-dimensional friend. Anyone else?"

Dylan bit at one of his fingers, his brow furrowed in thought. Richard drummed his own fingers on the table, running through his vast store of arcane trivia. Finally, he shook his head. "I give."

"Yeah. Uncle, dude," Dylan agreed. Terry just shook his head. Marco gave Susan a wry smile.

"Don't look at me," Susan said, throwing up her hands.

"It's the Liahona."

"What?" Susan said. "That sounds Hawaiian."

Marco laughed. "It does! But no—"

"Liahona..." Brian straightened up. "*Lee-yah* is the possessive form of the name of God, and *-hona* means 'guidance.' God's guidance. So it's an oracle, all right. Why have I never heard of this?"

"Maybe because you never studied the Book of Mormon."

Brian just blinked but Richard roared with laughter. "Of course! In the book of 1st Nephi, the Liahona was found outside Lehi's tent! It showed him the way that God wanted him to travel—it kept pointing across the Atlantic Ocean until they landed in the New World."

"The very same," Marco beamed with pride.

"How the hell did you get your hands on these?" Richard breathed, his eyes shining.

"I traded them for some secret letters from Joseph Smith to Oliver Cowdery. Let's just say there's some stuff in those letters the Utah church does *not* want coming to light."

"How did you even know they had this—the Liahona?"

"I heard through the grapevine that a Mormon archeological dig in Guatemala had turned it up."

"No shit," Dylan breathed. "Waal, how does it work?"

"I haven't quite figured that out yet. Here's what I've got so far. If you sink into meditation and try to harmonize with it, then you can ask it a question. The dial on the right, there, the one ringed in red, will point in one direction. But the dial on the left, the one ringed in gold, might point in that direction, but might point in another direction." Marco scratched at his newly-bald head. "I can't quite sort it out, yet."

"There are Hebrew letters on the rings around the dials," Brian pointed out. "They're highly stylized, but I'm sure I could figure it out, given some time. Do you want me to see what I can do?"

"I would be very grateful!" Marco said. "I knew you all would be able to sort this puppy out!"

"What you got besides the old globe and the useless glasses?" Randy asked.

"Ah, well, you all put in an order, I believe."

"We did?" Richard asked, draining the last of his iced tea.

Dylan looked a bit sheepish. "Uh, Ah did. While you were...ya know, incommunicado."

"Oh, okay," Richard said. "That's fair. What is it?" What he really wanted to know was how much it was going to cost, but he bit his tongue.

"Can you guess?" Marco asked Richard specifically, his eyebrows comically high on his forehead.

"Dude, ya haven't even taken it out of the case yet."

"Oh, yeah." Marco flipped open the black case and extracted a slim metal box, with a latex tube on one side, and an electronic screen on the other.

"What is it? And do *not* fucking tell me to guess," Richard laughed.

"Would you like to do the honors?" Marco asked Dylan.

"It's a Christometer," Dylan said.

"A whatsit?" asked Richard, scowling.

"No, we talked about this once," Terry said, snapping his fingers. "We were debating the relative validities of different ecclesiastical orders, remember?"

"That's pretty much what Old Catholics do whenever they get together, though," Dylan admitted.

"Yes, but I remember one time Richard said, 'I wish there was a way to measure the presence of Christ in a Eucharist.' You even came up with a unit of measurement."

"Ha! Oh, yeah, the 'christon.' I thought we could measure the level of christons present in a Roman Catholic Eucharist versus an Eastern Orthodox Eucharist verses an Old Catholic Eucharist, versus an Anglican Eucharist—"

"We get the idea," Susan said, rolling her eyes. "That sounds like the kind of conversation you have after three joints and half a bottle of whiskey."

"That's prob'ly accurate," Dylan said, fumbling with the front of his cassock.

"And you authorized Order funds to have Marco actually *build* the thing?" Susan asked.

"Inquirin' minds have been wantin' to know for a very long time, sweetheart," Dylan said, looking sheepish.

"Oh, Christ. Marco, how much do we owe you for this thing?"

"When it's finished, it's gonna set you back $2500. But because it's you, I'll take an even $2000. But you don't owe me anything right now, because I haven't gotten it to work right just yet." He scratched his head. "I'm having a lot of trouble calibrating it. You know, how to set the thing to zero."

"We could take it to a Satanic mass. There's one in Oakland on Friday nights, last Ah heard," Dylan suggested. Susan turned and headed out of the room. "Where you goin', sweet-pea?"

"I have reached my limit of geek absurdity. I've gotta re-think my life," she said. She paused at the door out to the office and flashed them a smile. "Call me for dinner, though."

2

THE SOUND of crickets filled the night sky as Mikael grounded himself and meditated. All around him, members of the coven were doing the same. Through half-open eyes he saw Kat through the leaping flames of the bonfire and couldn't help smiling. Her eyes, too, were half-open, and she swayed slightly as she matched her own interior rhythms with that of the earth. Her head was thrown back, her face turned up to the almost-full moon, a blue cast covering her features, her shoulders, her naked breasts.

Mikael felt the warmth of the bonfire on his back as he sank deeper into trance. Soon, he lost track of time until he was suddenly aware of movement around him. He stood, taking up his candle, as he heard Kat's voice declaring, "Welcome, beloved. It's time to light these candles, festive symbols of this time of abundance and cheer—a time to honor divinity in all her forms, in all his forms. For the Goddess and the God!" Kat held her candle to the one already lit on the altar, then held it out to the person on her left to light her own candle. The flame made its way around the circle until Mikael received the flame from Julia on one side and passed it on to Deb on the other. Before long, all were holding their lit candles high, illuminating the grove and casting dancing shadows over the ground.

Then, one-by-one, they brought their candles together as they linked their fingers and recited, "Hand in hand I cast this circle."

When all were finished, Kat pronounced, "The circle is now cast. Today is not today. This place is not this place. We celebrate now between the worlds."

She then invited them to feel their feet grounded in the soil of their Mother, and to breathe up from her the good energy that would be the fuel for the magick they worked that night. Mikael imagined the energy traveling up his legs, circling momentarily in his loins, then springing up his spine. The energy rushed up then, faster and more intense, until it shot through the top of his head. He felt a little dizzy, and his head ached slightly from a cold kind of fire. Then, according to Kat's instructions, he sent that energy to Deb on his left, even as he received more energy from Julia on his right. As the energy passed around the circle it rose in intensity so that Mikael could feel the hairs on his arms stand up from the electricity of it.

Energy raised, they dropped hands and turned toward the east as Jimmy, the priest for the evening, called the first quarter. In a ringing voice that was only slightly overdramatic, he called out, "Hail, Spirits of the east, Spirits of wind and air, join us now in our celebration. Blow through us, sweep us clean from all the dirt we acquired over the summer. Sweep through our minds, make our thinking clear. Make us ready for autumn, for harvest. So mote it be!"

"So mote it be!" they all called.

After Jimmy called in the other three quarters, Kat stepped forward again, calling out, "Goddess, blessed Lady, harvest Queen, bestow upon us your bounty and joy. We gather tonight to honor you and to give you thanks. Be among us and celebrate with us."

Jimmy stood next to her and called out, "Harvest King, God of riches and abundance, bestow upon us your strength and your joy. Father, we gather tonight to honor you and give you thanks. Be among us and celebrate with us."

"Corn-dollies!" shouted Julia, and Mikael stepped back as the women rushed to the altar to dress several figures laying there with poppies, orange and yellow carnations and other autumnal colors. As

Mikael admired their work, it reminded him of when he was a kid, carving pumpkins or coloring Easter eggs.

As in love with Kat as he was, Mikael discovered it was difficult to watch a dozen naked mostly-young women and not become aroused. So he turned to stare at the bonfire instead, only to find that Jimmy had done the same. They shared an embarrassed laugh.

"No hiding from the wood here," Jimmy said.

"Word," Mikael agreed.

"What's it like being famous?" Jimmy asked.

"You can't be talking about me," Mikael scowled.

"None of the rest of us have been on the front page of the *New York Times*."

"Hm...haven't noticed much difference—except for all the people out in front of the house. Still dirt poor," Mikael confessed.

"But you're happier than I've seen you in years," Jimmy noted.

Mikael smiled at the flames and nodded. "You got that right."

"How is she adjusting? To the whole Christian thing?"

He meant Kat of course. "There's a learning curve. But she's coming along really well. She's on track to be ordained deacon—pretty soon, too. Normally we only do our sabbat work with the Christian pantheon, but I think it's been good for us both to hook up with you guys for the major sabbats. She loves the Order, but some-times...I think she misses her old coven."

"You can never go home again," Jimmy shook his head.

"I don't think she wants to. It's just nostalgic—in a good way."

"Well, we're glad to have you both. You're family."

Mikael put his arm around Jimmy's shoulder and touched his head to Jimmy's as they both stared at the fire. "Deflation achieved, dude."

It was just in time. The corn-dollies having been duly decorated, everyone returned to the circle. The moon loomed above them, even as the last rays of sunlight disappeared below the horizon. Kat shone gold in the flickering firelight. She turned slowly, looking each of them in the eyes as she spoke, "Rejoice, for the time of harvest is here. This is a time for gratitude and celebration. Day and night are now in equal balance. The Sun King has crept into the shadows and sleeps once more in the womb of the Goddess." She held up an ear of corn. "To you, Mother, we offer this fruit of the harvest. All we have is yours, and we return it to you now with thanksgiving." With that, she threw the corn into the fire, and invited them to do the same, naming something they were grateful for.

Jimmy, standing to Kat's left, threw his own ear of corn into the fire, shouting, "I'm grateful for my dog, Benjie."

Luna, next to Jimmy, tossed another ear into the fire, but she mumbled her gratitude, and Mikael couldn't hear it. Julia, though, wasn't shy and declared herself grateful for her cancer. "It woke me up to my own life," she said, radiating authority.

Suddenly, it was Mikael's turn, but he hadn't been thinking ahead. Of course he was grateful for Kat, for his Order mates, for the soulful labor that filled his days. He was grateful for music, for his band, for—

But before he could speak, Mikael felt an unseen force punch him in the chest. He staggered and fell to one knee.

He wasn't the only one. Jimmy clutched at his chest, as did several of the women. A moment later, the attack had passed and they looked around at one another with wild, fearful eyes.

"What...just...happened?" Kat asked.

Mikael struggled to his feet and walked slowly around the circle, testing its edges. His face was grave as he felt the air around him. It was as if someone had opened a hole in their carefully crafted circle and sucked every last electron of energy from it. In Mikael's mind's eye he saw an enormous vacuum cleaner, sucking out the power. But it was probably more like a capacitor—an energy ground from outside that had siphoned it off. But why? And who?

"I'm scared," Luna said, suddenly covering her breasts with her hands.

Why is she suddenly modest? Mikael wondered. But he felt it, too— the feeling of violation. The safety of their worship had been taken from them. The energy they had raised for the healing of the earth and her creatures had been hijacked.

"Should I close the circle?" Kat asked.

"I don't see why," Mikael answered. "The energy is gone."

"Just for the sake of formality, out of respect for the Goddess and the God, I think we should," Jimmy said. He was the priest. He had authority at this sabbat.

Mikael nodded and got back into circle with his brother and sisters. They held hands, but there was no joy. Kat's hands were shaking. They had been robbed.

3

"PHIL? HEY, PHIL."

Detective Philip Cain stared out the window of the service sedan as it wound its way through the forested intestines of Tilden Park.

His partner reached over and slapped his knee. "Hey, Bloodhound. Earth-to-fucking-Phil."

Cain blinked and shot Detective Liz Perry a pained look.

"I need a navigator. The GPS doesn't list picnic sites. Snap out of it."

"Oh. Sorry," he said. He squinted at the signs and clicked on a pen flashlight to check the printout balanced on his lap. "We're looking for a picnic site called 'Fern.' We just passed 'Big Leaf,' so I think we're still going the right way. It should be on our right."

"It's not the end of the world, Phil."

"Huh?"

"Your kid. Jesse. Nothing has changed. He's still your kid. He is still the same kid today that he was yesterday, or even last year. The only thing different now is that he's finally being honest with you."

"I don't even know what 'bisexual' means. Does that mean he has a boyfriend *and* a girlfriend? At the same time? Does he have sex with them *at the same time*?"

"Uh...that's probably something you should ask him, if you really want to know, that is. But uh, newsflash, Phil. I'm bisexual."

"You're married. To Dan."

"Right. But I've dated girls. If I hadn't met Dan, I might be married to a woman right now."

"Does it mean you have a...a...I don't even know how to ask this—"

"Does it mean I have a girlfriend on the side? No. I'm completely monogamous. Not that it's any of your business."

"So...I don't get it."

"Look, Phil, it just means that your boy is equally attracted to men and women. He'll probably settle down with one partner eventually, like most of us do. But it'll be like flipping a coin—you won't know whether it'll be with a man or a woman until you're at the wedding. And then the world will either see him as a straight man or a gay man, but he won't ever be any of those things. He'll always be bi. It'll always be a part of who he is."

"You're not talking about Jesse anymore, are you?"

"I'm just...I'm speaking from experience. And I'm telling you that you'd better not love your kid any less tomorrow than you did yesterday or I'm going to punch you in the fucking teeth."

"Huh," he stared out the window at the dark branches as they passed beneath them. Every now and then a sliver of silver moonlight shone through. "Did I fail him somehow? Maybe I wasn't around enough. Do you think it's a phase?"

"Have you even *talked* to Jesse?"

"What do you mean?"

"*I've* talked to Jesse. The kid is queer as a three-dollar bill. Take off the horse blinders, old man. This isn't about you. It's about him. And it's *not* a fucking phase."

"Fern," Cain said, stabbing his finger toward the sign. He needn't have been looking so carefully, as the place was already lit up by squad cars. Blue strobes panned over the treetops, making them seem like they were in motion—dark, looming persons-of-interest, rushing to make their escape. Stepping out of the car, Cain's nostrils started twitching—wood smoke, dirt, exhaust, and the faint coppery scent of blood.

As he and Perry picked their way to the picnic site, he heard the indistinct chatter of the uniformed officers. He clearly made out the whispered word, "Bloodhound," but he ignored it. He'd gotten the nickname years ago when he'd followed a clue that no one else could discern. No one he knew had as keen a sense of smell as he did. He didn't think too much about it. It was a gift. And he didn't resent he nickname, either. After all, these were cops. He'd heard plenty of nicknames he liked less. There was, at least, respect intended in his.

"What do we have?" Perry asked the uniform guarding the scene. "And why such a wide perimeter?"

Cain hadn't noticed that, but Perry was right. Instead of the immediate area around the body being taped off, the designated area was a radius about 30 feet from the body.

"Couple over there were walking—"

"At night?"

"It's usually safe to walk in Berkeley at night."

"Go on."

"The guy there had to take a leak, walked off into the bushes here, stumbled over the body. Says he checked for a pulse, she was dead. M.E. confirms that. We're getting statements now. There seems to be a large evidence field. Might be nothing, but...might be something, too. We thought it best to wait until you got here before we tracked dirt all over it."

"All over *what*?" Perry asked.

Just then the floodlights popped on and Cain raised his arm to shield his eyes until they could adjust. As they did, he saw the picnic site as clearly as if it were noon—except that the shadows were longer. He saw the fire, complete with still-smoldering embers and a wisp of smoke. He saw the body of a young woman, laying near the fire in a fetal position, and he saw signs drawn in the dirt.

"What the fuck are those?"

"That's what we wanted to preserve. I haven't seen anything like this—I mean, not since I used to play Dungeons and Dragons in High School."

Cain scowled at the uniformed cop. He squinted to see the man's name. *Frey.*

"And what do these kinds of symbols mean in Dungeons and Dragons, Officer Frey?"

"They're...I don't know. Occult symbols. Like, for magical spells and such."

"Magical spells." Cain's eyebrows bunched.

"And such. Yeah."

Cain gave him a curt nod and turned his attention to the scene. He started to step over the tape, but Perry stopped him with a sharp yelp. "Yi! Watch it. Look where you were just about to step."

Cain cocked his head and backed up. Getting down on his knees, he viewed the spot just in front of him from a different angle. Sure enough, someone had created a design in the dirt. He couldn't see it when he stood up, but it was there. The light was bright, but it was tricky.

"Let's get video in here before anything else," Perry called. CSU had just arrived, but Cain hadn't noticed. *This thing with Jesse really has me off my game,* he thought. He kicked himself inwardly and tried to banish his son and the whole confused tangle of feelings and presumptions and disappointments dancing around him. He imagined stuffing the lot of it into a closet and locking it. As he did it he suddenly realized he had just unconsciously negated the symbolism of his son coming out of the closet to him. Cain felt a stab of guilt but took some comfort in knowing that he could never completely close that door again. Not ever. Not even if he wanted to.

And it occurred to him then that he did not want to. He wanted to truly know his son, even if that meant he had to relinquish some cherished ideas about him. That would be okay. There was always a price to pay for authenticity, for intimacy. Illusion was a currency he would not resent parting with—not on his good days, anyway.

The air was turning cold, and he wiped his nose on the back of his hand. "Do we have an ID on the girl?"

"No sir," Frey said.

Cain studied the designs drawn into the dirt. The largest appeared to be a pentagram—a five-pointed star. Cain could clearly see the mash of grass in the center of that star—someone had stood there for some time. The girl's body lay just outside of the star. His nostrils twitched. Perfume? No. "Frankincense," he called out to Perry.

"What? How do you know that?"

He held his palms up as if to say, *What? Are you kidding me?*

"Oh. Right. Okay, we got...frankincense, for Christ's sake. What the hell does that tell us?"

"That this wasn't a bunch of kids playing 'Hail Satan.' Frankincense is expensive. And this was the real stuff. Some myrrh, too. It was also cut with some sandalwood and aloe, but those are cheaper."

"You scare me sometimes." Perry crossed to stand next to Cain. She pointed. "There's something not right about that fire."

"What do you mean?"

"It's ringed with stones, but it's not an official fire pit—there's no grill. It's too small."

Cain nodded. "So where's the official fire pit?"

"Let's find out," Perry said. Cain followed her, as the video guys began to document the scene.

Perry pulled out a flashlight and lit up the road as they walked. About 500 paces further they saw a large picnic site. "So the sign is back there, but the actual site is here."

Cain nodded. "There were people here, too. He pulled out his own flashlight and picked his way over to the large fire pit. "Good citizens. They put out the fire, but I can still smell it. They burned sage, too. And...corn?"

He found a twig and started to pick at the fire. "Yeah. See here? Husks."

"Big deal. A regular picnic."

"Maybe. We should get CSU to document over here, too."

Perry nodded her agreement, but her lips tightened in confusion. Cain shone his flashlight back over toward the crime scene. Were it not for the blue strobes cutting through the trees, he wouldn't know that there were about fifty cops over there. "That little stand of trees is pretty dense," he said. "Good cover."

"So, our killers had a barbecue here, then they stepped out of sight to do the deed?"

"That's one possibility. Another was that they were different groups, and what was going on over there was hidden from the folks here."

"But why be so close? Why risk being seen by the group over here?"

Cain shrugged. He looked up to see the blue-uniformed CSU team walking toward them. "This site, too, please," Cain called.

The team leader nodded and started barking orders. Confident that CSU was on it, Perry and Cain walked back to the murder site. "Sage?" she asked. "Like turkey stuffing?"

"No, more like ritual sage. Burning it for the smell, for the smoke. Like Native Americans do, or those New Age kooks."

"You think they were New Age kooks?"

"Insufficient data," Cain said. "Maybe we had two different occult rituals going on."

"That seems pretty far-fetched to me."

"Maybe. Look, I'm no expert on the occult, but I'm pretty sure that the kinds of groups that burn sage are not the kinds of groups that burn frankincense."

"Hm..." Cain could see that she was mulling it over and didn't like it. "Different groups, huh?"

"Maybe. Definitely different rituals."

"Do we *need* an expert on occult rituals?" Perry asked.

"Maybe. Let's see what turns up first."

Just then Perry's cell phone rang. "Perry."

Cain studied her face as she listened. She wasn't what he would call pretty, although he knew others would disagree. Her hair was reddish brown, without a hint of body—it lay flat against her head like a helmet. And her hips were broader than he liked in a woman. He was glad of it really. He'd had a partner he was attracted to a few years back, and it was hell. He respected Perry. He even liked her. But he didn't want to sleep with her. He realized in that moment that she might just be the best partner he'd ever had. And he felt something new for her, then—affection. The epiphany was uncomfortable, so he wiped his nose again and looked away.

She pocketed her phone. "Kapernacky got the Parks System high mucky-mucks out of bed."

"*She* gets a gold star."

"No shit. This site was reserved for the night."

"We got a name?"

"Yep. East Bay Pagan Assembly."

"Ah. The EBPA," Cain nodded vigorously. "I've seen their bumper stickers."

"You have?"

"Of course not. I'm bullshitting you. Who the fuck is the EBPA?"

"I don't know, but we've got a contact name: James Tomlinson."

"There's a solid British surname. Got a phone number?"

"And an address."

"Let's not call, then. Let's send a squad to pick him up. Now."

SATURDAY

Light pours from a million radiant lives
Off of kids and dogs and the
hard-shelled husbands and wives
All that glory shining around
and we're all caught taking a dive
And all the beasts of the hills around shout,
"Such a waste!
Don't you know that from the first to the last
we're all one in the gift of grace!"

—*Bruce Cockburn, "In the Falling Dark"*

4

―――――

"So I woke up and when I opened my eyes, I saw this enormous black disk hovering over my face. Then it drooled on me," Marco said, picking sleep out of his eyes.

"That's our Toby," Susan gave the dog an affectionate rub.

Brian sat a cup of coffee in front of each of them. "Nothing like the first cup of the morning."

"Thank you, my dear," Susan said. Through the door they could hear the sound of the friars reciting the Venite.

"Then he farted," Marco continued. "So, you know, typical dog stuff. Reminds me of why I'm a cat person." He raised one eyebrow. "So why do I get the spooky sense that this dog could do long division?"

"Because he could probably do calculus," Susan answered.

"I'm not kidding."

"Neither am I." She paused and considered Toby.

"I was standing right here a few months ago," Brian said, gesturing with a spatula. "That dog got up on his rear legs and unlatched the back screen door."

"No shit," Marco said.

"So I followed him outside, and we discovered that an angel had died, and he inhabited Toby at the last moment."

"There's an angel...in your dog?" Marco pointed at the yellow lab. "Is he still in there?"

"As far as I know," Brian said, turning to tend to his bacon.

"Is he conscious?" Marco asked.

"I think so," Brian said.

Marco narrowed his eyes at the dog. "*Nenni trint*," he said. Tobias sat. "*Nenni parmgi*," Marco commanded. Tobias leaped up and ran a circle around the room.

"Did Terry actually train this dog in Enochian?" Marco asked Brian.

"Nope. That dog only knows English commands."

"And not very many of those," Susan said. "This is Dylan's dog, remember?"

"It's the angel that knows Enochian," Brian said, with a broad, wry smile.

"No shit," Marco said, flabbergasted.

"Pretty normal for life around here," Susan admitted.

"Speaking of weirdness, where is that Randy guy?" Marco asked, pointing to the mirror.

"He doesn't get up until about noon. Typical mag—" Brian caught himself.

Marco laughed. "You can say it, man. Typical magickian. It's only funny because it's true."

"Thanks for the grace," Brian said, turning slightly red. "I leave a plate of bacon and maybe some fruit out on the counter for him."

"But how can he reach it?" Marco asked. "He's over there? And he's trapped inside the mirror."

"Watch," Brian said. He finished lifting the last of the bacon from the pan onto a plate and set the plate on the counter. He pointed at the mirror. "What do you see?"

Marco looked in the mirror. "I see...a plate of bacon on the counter."

"Yep. He can reach it."

Marco scowled. "That shouldn't work."

"And yet, the guy in the mirror never complains of being unfed."

"Crazy," Marco said.

"This from a guy who created an animatronic Baphomet," Susan teased.

"Point," Marco agreed.

Susan put a teaspoon of sugar in her coffee and stirred it. "Brian, can I ask you a personal question?"

Brian turned from his stove and cocked his head. "Sure..." he answered, sounding uncertain.

"Does Terry seem a little...I don't know...off to you?"

Brian's mouth opened, then closed. He looked out the kitchen window where the sun was now fully visible. "He's fine," he answered, turning back to the stove without looking at her.

"Bullshit. He's restless. Irritable. He's not acting like Terry."

Brian said nothing. He stabbed at the end of the bacon with a fork and turned it.

Dylan burst through the door and snagged a piece of bacon from the counter before sitting down next to his wife. "Good prayer makes ya hungry!" he announced. Mikael and Kat came into the kitchen next, followed closely by Richard.

"I don't know how good I'd call that prayer," Kat said.

"Whaddaya mean?" Dylan asked, heading for the cupboard to grab a cup.

"I can't stand that Psalm. 'The fear of the Lord is the beginning of wisdom.' What crap."

Richard's eyebrows raised. "It *is* a time-honored Psalm."

"But we shouldn't be *afraid* of God," Kat said, sitting down at the table. "Can't we say, 'reverence for God' or something like that?"

"I'm not sure 'reverence' really captures it." Richard said, a hint of a smile playing at his lips. "We shouldn't cower before the *mysterium tremendum*? Is God not powerful? Is God not terrible? Is not God awesome in the true meaning of that word?"

"Yeah, okay, but how can you really *love* someone you're afraid of?" Kat asked. "I don't think you can."

"Let's ask Dylan," Richard said behind his hand. Everyone burst out laughing.

Susan froze and turned crimson. "That was *not* fair."

"True, though," Dylan said, bobbing his tea bag in his hot water. He was grinning like he'd just won an argument for the first time in months.

"Breakfast is served," Brian said, not looking at Susan. He placed a large bowl of egg scramble on the lazy Susan.

"How was Mabon?" Marco asked.

Kat and Mikael looked at each other before responding. "It was...*kinda* good?" Kat finally said. "I'm so sorry. Pardon my rudeness. I'm Kat."

Mikael smacked his head. "Sorry! Kat, meet Marco. Marco, Kat. Marco's an old friend of the Order. He's a solitary Thelemite. He invents stuff...magickal stuff." Kat reached across and shook his hand.

"I met your brother already," Marco said. "It's a...let's call it a pleasure for now."

"I'm betting it wasn't *much* of a pleasure meeting him," Kat said, steeling a glance at the mirror. Randy had yet to appear.

"So what do you mean 'kinda good'?" Marco asked.

"Kat did great, as usual. She's an ace celebrant," Mikael began.

"Can't wait to hear her say mass," Richard said.

"But just as we were in the middle of it—"

"Tossing our corn thanksgivings on the fire," Kat interjected.

"—something happened."

"What happened?" Richard asked.

"I'm not sure. It was like that moment when you take a swig from a carton of milk and you suddenly realize it's sour," Mikael said. "It was like that, only the whole world seemed sour."

"It felt like a punch in the gut," Kat said.

"Yeah, that too," Mikael agreed. "But after it hit, all of our energy was just...gone."

"You mean personally? You felt lethargic?" Brian asked. He looked relieved and enlivened at the change of subject.

"No, I mean all the energy we'd raised in the circle. Sucked right out."

"I've never heard of such a thing," Richard said.

Marco looked concerned. "I have. This kind of thing doesn't happen by accident. You got sapped."

"What are you saying?" Kat asked.

"I'm saying that this was probably intentional. Someone wanted your ritual energy for...well, for their own devices."

"Who?" asked Mikael.

"I wish I knew. But anyone who would steal someone else's *tapas* was probably not up to any good," Marco drummed absently on the table.

"Eat. Eggs are getting cold," Brian commanded.

"Where's Terry?" Susan asked.

Richard turned around. "Ter!" He sprang up and jogged through the door and saw Terry sitting in the chapel. "Hey, something wrong?" Richard asked, sitting in the short pew next to him. Terry shook his head. "I'm not ready to talk about it."

"Well, you let me know when you are. I mean, if you want to talk to *me* about it."

Terry gave a half smile and rose with a groan. Just then Richard's cell phone buzzed. He fished it out of his pocket as Terry lumbered into the kitchen. "Richard here."

"Is this Father Richard Kinney?"

"The one and only. Who is this?"

"This is Margo Tindall, from CNN."

"CNN, like *the* CNN?"

"The one and only. Is this a good time?"

"Uh...sure. What can I do for you?"

"There's been a lot of interest in you and your Order since the Republican Convention. We'd like to do a human interest piece on you. You know, send a camera crew to follow you around for a couple of days. We especially want to see you perform an exorcism."

"Uh...that can be dangerous. And unpredictable."

"We have insurance, so you won't need to worry about that. We'll also pay you for your trouble. Does $3,000 sound about right for three days?"

"Well...ah, let me talk to my Order mates, but that sounds great to me."

"Fine. If you're on a cell phone you have my number. Text me and let me know. We'd want to start...well, tomorrow if we can."

"Yikes. Uh...I'll let you know later this morning."

"I'm counting on it. Thanks, Father." The phone clicked off, and Richard put it away. He felt a little disoriented as he made his way to the kitchen. "Uh...guys, that was CNN..."

5

It wasn't easy getting a booth at the Cloven Hoof, especially for lunch on a Saturday, and Larch emitted a ululation of triumph as he slid into it. He slumped over his Guinness like a wolf guarding its lair until Frater Purderabo arrived.

A large man, Purderabo scowled at the booth. Larch scowled back, but scooted the table toward himself a couple inches, making more space on the other side. Apparently satisfied with the accommodation, Purderabo sat. Before he could say anything Fraters Turpelo, Eleazar, and Khams arrived, each clutching at pints.

The décor was strictly first-circle Dante, with red and orange lighting and strategically placed fog machines. An unwavering house beat punctuated the air but was not so loud that one could not talk. Larch glanced around at the other clientele. It was the usual crowd, most just rousing from bed at noon and stumbling down for a bit of the hair of the dog. He saw folks he recognized from just about every occult community in San Francisco. Some Wiccans were playing darts in the far corner, looking no worse for wear after their late Mabon festivities. A table nearby held members of the local OTO Lodge, arguing heatedly over something. "As usual," Larch muttered under his breath.

He didn't see any of the Golden Dawners this afternoon, but he did notice some Temple of Set guys playing pool. And then of course there were the wannabe's—the loners brooding over absinthe, the dabblers mooning over the various groups at the bar, and the prostitutes trying to hit them up, looking more tattered than Larch remembered. To complete the scene, waitresses circulated in black fishnets, red teddies, and devil horns stuck on their foreheads with suction cups. It was all great horror show of fun and games, and Larch reveled in the hominess of it.

"Just like old times," Frater Khams bobbed his head. "Still got a shit menu, though."

"Let's make a deal," Larch suggested, "We'll order the most pretentious thing possible and you promise not to complain about it."

Khams narrowed his eyes, but he didn't argue. A moment later, a waitress slunk over to them. "93," she said.

"We're not Thelemites," Larch announced.

"Fuck you, I'm just trying to be pleasant," the waitress said, smacking her gum. "Do you want to order anything or not?"

"We are the illustrious Lodge of the Hawk and Serpent," Frater Eleazar announced.

"I don't care if you're the Lodge of the Smegma and Spittle," the waitress rolled her eyes. "Food? Or no food?"

Khams pointed to the menu. "We'll have the Mediterranean Platter with the hot buttered hummus," he said. "Plus the no-harm, no-fowl vegetarian chicken wings with the spicy tamarind sauce, please."

"Regular panko on those, or gluten-free?"

"Frater Turpelo?" Khams asked, but Turpelo held his hands up and shook his head. "Regular will be fine," he said.

"Aarright. Gotta pay ahead, I'm afraid. New rule. Too many assholes playing dine-and-ditch."

"I'll bet it's those goddam Church of Satan pricks!" Larch asserted.

"I'm not sayin' it's not." The waitress smacked her gum, looking up and away.

"They ruin it for fucking everybody," Larch shook his head and tugged at his wallet.

The others did likewise and threw worn five and ten-dollar bills onto the table until the waitress scooped them up. "That'll do. I'll bring you your change in a minute." Then she spun away.

"A drink to our reunion!" Larch said, holding his ale aloft. He was the only one who took a sip. He noticed the glares. "You gentlemen are looking well."

"No thanks to you," Purderabo said blackly. "Thanks to you we lost our Lodge House, all of our possessions—"

"Including magickal diaries!" Turpelo interjected.

"—and I had to change my identity. Do you know how hard that is to do when you're living off a trust fund?"

Larch opened his mouth to say, "Poor baby," but he reminded himself to be diplomatic. What he ended up saying was, "That is a terrible inconvenience. But magick is an exacting mistress, gentlemen. And we who serve her do it at great personal cost to ourselves."

As he spoke, Larch saw the anger in their faces soften. He saw them sit up straighter in their seats, their shoulders becoming square. They needed to be reminded of the nobility of their calling. And this, Larch knew, was what he was good at. It wasn't that he was a brilliant magickal technician. No. It was that he was a brilliant leader of men.

"And we have all sacrificed a great deal for this Work, have we not? And we should not look back or give up, not when we are so close."

"Um...so close to what?" asked Khams.

"So close to the noble goal that has always been before us."

"Do you mean..." Purderabo breathed.

Larch's lips drew back in a portentous grin as he nodded slowly. "The same. This world groans under tyranny that has prevailed for millennia. But that reign of terror is nearly at its end. And we, gentlemen, are the ones fate has designated to pull the Great Tyrant from his throne."

"You're talking about the overthrow of the Kingdom," Turpelo fumbled at the zipper of his sweater.

"Yes."

"You want to kill the Tyrant?" Khams asked.

"That would be our best-case scenario, yes," Larch answered, looking confident and satisfied.

"You want to kill..." Khams leaned in and whispered the last word, "*God?*"

"Kill is a strong word. I'm not sure we *can* kill God. But we can certainly strip him of his power. We can topple his Kingdom. We can reduce his hierarchy to chaos and rubble. And that is precisely what I aim to do."

Purderabo looked around, as if frightened that they might be overheard. That was impossible, though—the music was loud enough that even the donkey-long ears of a Gunther demon could not hear if more than three feet away.

Turpelo was rubbing his hands together now, clearly salivating. "Oh, how many nights have we spun tales of such an undertaking?" Hopeful light radiated from his eyes.

"How?" Eleazar asked, clearly dubious.

"How what?" Larch's voice betrayed irritation.

"How do you plan to topple the Kingdom?"

Larch leaned in and nearly whispered, "I intend to ascend the Tree of Life, and to destroy the sephirot as I go."

"Like, as in being a terrorist? You're going to what, blow it up? How are you going to ascend with physical bombs?"

"Don't think so literally. The Tree of life hangs together from the top, like a mobile. If you disrupt the sephirot—"

"It throws the other sephirot off balance..." Turpelo nodded.

"And if the sephirot are unbalanced?"

"Chaos," Turpelo grinned, his eyes narrowing.

"But our world is an emanation of the higher sephirot," Khams pointed out. "If they descend into chaos, what will happen here?"

"Anarchy," Larch said calmly, "which is just another way of saying *the end of tyranny.*"

"There's one problem with that," Purderabo pointed a chubby finger at Larch.

"And what might that be?" Larch asked, no longer trying to hide his irritation.

"There are certain friars that, should they catch wind of what is going on—"

"And how could they not, if the sephirot start rocking wildly out of balance?" Turpelo interjected.

"—they will surely try to stop us."

"Do you think I didn't consider that?" Larch leaned back, a self-satisfied look spreading across his wolfish face. "You see, this is the beauty of this plan. It is truly a group effort. Because while I am ascending the Tree of Life, dismantling the spheres, you all are going to be hard at work here on earth."

"Doing what?" Khams asked.

"A little bit of what our stage-magician brethren call 'misdirection.'"

6

RICHARD SAT ON A SHORT, discarded pew in the basement hall of All Saints Episcopal Church and tried to relax. His brain seemed like popcorn ever since the call from CNN. He jumped up and started pacing the linoleum. It occurred to him that he did not have any clean cassocks in reserve. After only seven traverses of the hallway, Mother Maggie slipped her head through the door to her office. "Just give us a second, dear," she said. She closed it again. In a few seconds, it opened wide and a woman about ten years older than Richard emerged, blowing her nose and avoiding his eyes. He recognized her from around town—perhaps he had seen her sitting at one of the tables at the Gallic Hotel, sipping a cappuccino?

She walked briskly to the women's restroom and disappeared inside. Mother Maggie's door gaped, but he waited to hear her call before he entered the sacred space. "I've made tea," she called. He entered and she gestured toward the cups on the table. "Just the way you poor, unrefined Americans like it. No milk." She made a face. "Have a seat, dear."

He did and adjusted his cassock so that it fell properly over his knees and did not reveal the blue jeans underneath. Mother Maggie closed her eyes, and began to sink into contemplation. Richard allowed himself to do the same, noticing the jangliness of his nerves and his industrial-strength monkey mind. He did his best, but to no avail. His mind kept jumping to CNN, to the tremendous opportunity it presented for the Order—the money, the recognition, the *glory*.

The rustle of Maggie's clothes interrupted his fantasies and he opened his eyes to see her leaning across the little table between them, a lit match held aloft in her twisted, arthritic hands. "We light this candle to remind us of all the shit we don't know," Maggie said, lighting a tall candle on the table.

Richard smiled. Maggie was one of a kind. He had been fortunate to have her as his spiritual director for years now, and it was one of the relationships that brought him the most joy. Maggie had been present at every significant event of his life—or for that matter, the life of the friary. He realized how lost he would feel without her, and he squelched the urge to rush over and catch her up in a bear hug.

"Tell me how God is fucking with you," she invited him.

"Uh...huh," Richard passed his hand over his thinning hair and thought. "How do you know God is fucking with me?"

"God is always fucking with all of us," she smiled sweetly at him. "It's what God does."

"What does that *mean*?" Richard asked.

"Don't play coy, you know exactly what I mean," Maggie waved a hand at him. "I want to know how God is punching you in the kidneys, challenging your paradigm, shaking your tree. If you feel safe or secure or satisfied, you can be sure that tree will start shaking before too long. Love doesn't settle for lies, and it isn't interested in appearances or excuses or business-as-usual. Love is always on the move, always poking at us, always threatening us to become more than we are...or else. So. *How is God fucking with you?*"

Richard took a sip of tea.

"Take your time," Maggie said. "I've got plenty."

"We've only got an hour," Richard countered.

"This month, yes," she said, resting her gnarled hands in her lap, waiting.

The implication was that she would sit in silence until he

answered her and would continue that silence into future session unless he relented and answered her question. Richard noted the wide clerical collar that went all the way around her neck, like a halo that had slipped and become a dog collar. *How does she fasten that thing with her hands the way they are?* He wondered. He knew her husband had died years ago. *So how...?* But as intriguing as it was, that was not the question at hand. Internally he slapped himself for dodging. "I don't know," he finally said. "Can I just talk about what's going on, and maybe you'll *notice* how God is fucking with me?"

"Excellent plan!" she announced, pointing at him crookedly. "Tell me a story of Richard."

"Well, our friend Marco came for a visit. He's at the friary now."

"Marco, Marco..." she pursed her lips and looked at the ceiling, obviously trying to retrieve a memory. She found it and looked down again. "He's the inventor chap, yes?"

"Yep, that's the one. He's working on a Christometer, a device to measure the relative amount of christons present in an object or a room or a rite. We hope to compare Eucharists of different denominations to gauge their relative efficacies."

"Do you now?" Maggie's eyes narrowed to tiny slits that Richard did not like one little bit.

"Uh...it's just an experiment," Richard said.

"I'm guessing he has not yet perfected this device?"

"No."

"I'm guessing he's having difficulty calibrating it?" Maggie's mouth stretched into a kind grin. Richard noticed that her lipstick was unevenly applied.

"How in the world could you possibly know that?"

"An educated guess. When he figures it out, I'll tell you."

"Okay, that's a deal."

"What else is happening?"

"There's something up with Terry."

"What do you mean?"

"He's sullen. Maybe depressed. He goes off by himself a lot lately."

"Have you invited him to confide in you?"

"Yeah, but so far he's playing it all pretty close to the vest."

"So what does Jesus say about it?"

"What do you mean?"

"I mean, when you talk to Jesus about Terry, what does Jesus say?"

Richard squirmed in his seat. "Uh...I haven't really talked to Jesus about it."

"Are you nuts?" Maggie snapped.

"Huh?" Richard asked. Even after all this time, Maggie could still unsettle him.

"How dare you bring something to me that you haven't brought to Jesus first? I mean, what do you expect *me* to do about it?"

"Uh...listen?"

"Doesn't it make sense to talk it over with someone who can actually have an impact on the situation?"

"In my experience, God doesn't really work that way."

"Then you, my dear little man, have not been paying attention."

Little man? Richard was nearly twice her height. Perhaps she meant "little in faith" or "little in spirit." The thought caused him to deflate a little.

"From now on, let's make a deal. You bring everything to Jesus before you bring it here."

"What if I forget?"

"Then it's not forgetting. It's resistance." She smiled sweetly at him. "In which case I may have to beat you about the head and shoulders."

"I'm not sure that counts as one of those spiritual direction best practices," Richard said.

"Fuck them, the North American Spiritual Directors Coalition and their fucking rules and regulations," Maggie said, still smiling at him beatifically. "Is it a deal?"

"Okay, I can do that. I'll bring everything to Jesus first." He squirmed. "At least, I'll try to remember to do that."

"And when you don't, then we'll *really* have something to talk about."

"This is the accountability thing, isn't it?"

"It is," she agreed. "The very thing."

"And you're not going to give me a pass on it, are you?"

"I'm going to drill you like a sailor on shore leave."

Richard thought for several moments. "What do you expect Jesus to say about it?"

Maggie's face fell. "Richard! How many years have we been working together? You pray, I know you pray!"

"Yes, I say the hours. But it seems like you're talking about talking to Jesus...like you and I are talking."

"Exactly. Ask him to make you some tea. His tea puts the Queen's to shame." She scrunched her nose. "I love it."

"Would you...would you tell me how *you* pray?" Richard asked.

"Of course, dear!" she said, apparently excited to be asked. "First we walk through the Berkeley Rose Garden together. We hold hands. He's very sweet. I tell him everything I'm thinking about, everything I'm afraid of or worried over. Sometimes I ask for help with something. But mostly I just share my feelings." She leaned forward and shook a crooked finger at Richard. "He's a good fucking listener, he is."

Richard just nodded.

"And then we find a quiet place to sit, and he holds me close while we say the Liturgy of the Hours together. I usually lead, but he reads the responses. I sometimes think he'd be a trifle uncomfortable reading the bits about himself, but it doesn't seem to faze him at all. Then sometimes we make love."

"You make...love?"

"Yes." She bunched her face up looking like one of those wizened apple-core dolls. "He touches me in my giggly place. He's *wonderful*."

"Maggie, it sounds like you pray the way Dylan does shamanic journeys," Richard noted.

"Oh, yes. Same thing. Just with Jesus," she agreed. "It goes back to St. Ignatius, you know."

"St. Ignatius prayed like this?"

"Oh, yes."

"Did he make love with Jesus, too?"

She reached across the table and poked the tip of his nose. "That would be telling!"

Richard started to laugh. "So are you saying that *I* need to...you know, make love?"

"Dicky, why are you uncomfortable? What we're talking about here is *intimacy*."

"Intimacy with Jesus."

"Yes. That's what it's all about."

"What *what's* all about?"

"All of it! The Church, Christian life, prayer, *living*."

Richard thought about that for a moment.

"It scares the willies out of you, doesn't it?" She looked elated at the thought.

"Why are you so pleased?"

"Because God is *fucking* with you! And that means that good, uncomfortable, transformative things are happening in you. Just under the cassock."

"Oh! I forgot the big thing," Richard said.

"Ooo, tell me the *big* thing!" Maggie whispered, conspiratorially.

"CNN called us. They want to follow us for a couple days. Maybe film an exorcism."

He was pleased to see her eyebrows shoot up. "Well, that's flattering."

"It is!" The nervous energy returned, and he got up and paced in the space just behind his chair. "You know, we've toiled just on the edge of poverty for so long. The idea that we might be seeing some light, some recognition, maybe some regular work once people know about us...it gives me hope."

Maggie cocked her head and considered him.

"What?" he asked.

"Chocolate?" she held up a bowl of bonbons.

Richard took one, and then almost immediately choked, as it seemed to be filled with a cayenne cream that made Richard's eyes water.

"Things are not always what they seem," she said.

"Thanks for the object lesson, but—" he choked and slurped at his tea.

"You've 'toiled just on the edge of poverty for so long.'" Maggie quoted him. "Who supported you during that time?"

"Uh—"

"God did," she answered for him. "And when you had success, who got the glory for it?"

"Uh—"

"God did. And when you didn't know where your next gig was coming from, who kept you going?"

"Uh—"

"God did. And here you are on the brink of the undoing of all that support and trust, and *now* you have hope?"

"I...just..." Richard could think of no answer to this.

Maggie looked stern. She leaned forward in her seat and looked him in the eyes. "You listen to me, Richard Kinney. You be careful. Don't you lose sight for a moment whose power casts those demons out. Don't you forget for a second whose work you are doing, or whose name you wear. Glory is a poison if it is placed in the wrong cup."

She reached for a pad of paper and tore off a strip from the bottom of the first page. Then, with a tiny golf pencil, she wrote something on it. "That's our time, Dicky." She put the strip of paper into his hand. "You need to start taking things to Jesus. The big stuff, the little stuff, the stuff that bugs you, and the stuff you think you've got covered. Promise me."

"Okay. I'll give that kind of prayer a try."

"Promise me."

"I promise."

"Good. You're going to fucking need it."

He rose and crossed to the door. "Oh, and Dicky," he paused. "I'll be retiring soon. Probably just at the start of Advent."

"What?" he asked. He opened his mouth to say more, but his tongue was a tangle of protest.

"I'll be praying for you." She smiled sweetly at him. Then she shut the door.

"Holy cow," he said. He felt like someone had just beaned him with a brick. What would he do without Maggie? Intellectually he knew she was advanced in years, that she wouldn't be working forever. But...the idea of continuing his ministry without her constant support, her advice, her transgressive advocacy...he couldn't see it.

He glanced at the scrap of paper in his hand. "Luke 8:17." He didn't need to look it up. He knew what it said, and he muttered it aloud as he set off toward the stairs. "For nothing is hidden that will not be disclosed, nor is anything secret that will not become known and come to light."

7

SUSAN WAS BREATHING HEAVILY as she power-walked beside Kat.

"C'mon, just a little further. We're almost home," Kat said.

"I swear to God, if I had an ounce more energy, I'd beat the spandex off your lean, muscular body."

"That's good. Let the lust for violence fuel your last few blocks."

Susan almost tripped over an uneven sidewalk. Kat caught her elbow. "You okay?"

"Yeah. Just...yeah."

"You don't have to come with me on these every day you know," Kat said. She was striding along without any apparent strain, pumping barbells, while Susan was empty-handed and simply struggling to keep up.

"If I don't, how will we ever share our wardrobes?"

Kat burst out with a laugh but caught herself. She looked sideways at Susan to make sure it was okay. Susan was smiling. Sweating, but smiling. Kat relaxed. The late morning sun was beginning to feel warm on her face, and the wind smelled sweet and vaguely of the bay. "Let's take your mind off it," Kat suggested. "Let's talk about something."

"Okay," Susan agreed. "How do you feel about being ordained?"

"Hm..." Kat looked over and saw someone playing Frisbee on the east lawn of the UC Berkeley campus. "I don't really understand the whole two-step ordination process."

"You and half the Christian world. We did away with it a long time ago."

"We?"

"Lutherans," Susan clarified.

"Right."

"And most Protestants. The transitional diaconate is kind of like a Catholic vestigial organ. Among Protestants, only the Episcopal Church still does it."

"I think being a deacon is a cool thing. I like the whole idea of committing your life to service—to the poor, to the oppressed—that's great. But I don't want to be a deacon. I feel called to be a priest."

"Right. I think that's a good discernment. It's you."

"So why do I have to spend six months as a deacon?"

"Have you asked Richard about it?"

"Uh, yeah, and he gave me a forty-minute lecture on Neo-Platonism, and gradiated spheres of glory and power. I didn't understand a word of it."

"You know, the boys are all theology geeks." Susan took a few deep breaths before continuing. "Mikael is the least bad, so you can thank your lucky stars there. But you *can* tell Richard when he's not making sense. We don't all have PhD's in philosophy, and sometimes he needs to be reminded of that. He's not *trying* to annoy you."

"I know. I think he was genuinely trying to answer my question. I just didn't understand his answer."

"And it's not because you're stupid. It's because, in some ways, *he* is—he doesn't always have the emotional intelligence to know when he's not coming across."

"I didn't want to go there—"

"Go there. He's your bishop. You need to hold him accountable."

"It's not like he did anything wrong."

"No, but he didn't do it *right*. If you tell him that—kindly—you will help him be a better leader."

"He won't take it wrong?"

"I doubt it. And if he does, he'll get over it. Especially if I punch him. He's not *my* fucking bishop."

"Okay, that's scary, but I think I can handle that. But I'm interested in what you think is behind this whole deacon thing."

Susan held up a hand. "Can we just...stop a minute?"

"Nope. Three blocks. This is the burn, baby."

"Oh, holy shit. You're just cruel. Okay. I think the whole ministry ladder is about gradiated levels of responsibility. A deacon has a little bit of responsibility, a priest has more responsibility. And a bishop has the most."

"Okay, I can see that."

"So some people are just called to be deacons. That's fine. But if you're called to be a priest, you don't just jump to a role with enormous responsibility, just like you don't pass the bar and instantly become a partner at a law firm. You gotta work your way up, learn as you go."

"Okay, I can see that, too. But being a deacon is a different role."

"No, that's where I think you've got it wrong. Deacon means 'servant.' Once you're ordained a priest, you'll still be a deacon, a servant. You don't stop being a deacon just because you become a priest. You still serve the needy, you just also teach and administer the sacraments on top of that. It's about *more* responsibility."

"So, you're saying that a bishop is always a deacon *and* a priest, but with the added responsibilities of being a bishop, too."

"Like frosting on a two-layer cake. Vanilla sponge cake, to be exact."

"So this isn't a blind alley that I'll leave behind," Kat said, nodding. It was starting to make sense.

"Nope. It's something you'll spend your whole life living into, even after you become a priest."

"Wow. I can get on board with that," Kat said. "How are you doing?"

"You're right. Talking helped."

"Good. So tell me how Lutherans see the whole ordination thing."

"We think the only ordination worth a damn is baptism."

"Baptism? That's a whole 'nother sacrament!"

"Nope. Baptism makes us all priests—"

"Get out! That's just weird."

"Nope, that's Protestant."

"So don't you ordain pastors?"

"Yeah, but it doesn't put you in a different category of human being. For us it just means, 'Here's this person we trust to do this job. Yay! Do a great job.' But they're no more or less a priest than they were before their ordination."

"I didn't know Protestants were so fucking weird."

"How is that weirder than gradiated levels of glory and power?"

"I see your point."

"I think the big question is why. Why do you want to be ordained? Is God really calling you to it? Or is there some neurotic need in yourself that you think it will speak to, some emptiness you hope it will fill."

"That's a deep fucking question."

"It's the only question, really."

"And what if it's both?"

"What do you mean?"

"I mean what if I want it for some twisted reason of my own, but God really is calling me. I mean, is that possible? Look! Only one more block."

"Oh, shit."

"What?"

Susan pointed, and they both stopped. Kat squinted and saw what she meant. Just in front of the friary she saw people milling about across the street—that was normal, nowadays. But she also saw a black sedan, with two people standing next to it, talking. Both were dressed in suits, and the smaller of them was obviously a woman. "I don't recognize them," Susan said. "They smell like cops."

"Is that a problem?" Kat asked.

"I don't know. Depends on why they're here, I suppose."

"You sound like you don't trust the police."

"Long story. I'll tell you sometime."

"Looking forward to that," Kat said.

Susan started walking again, this time with renewed vigor. She approached the two visitors.

"Hey, I don't recognize you two. We live there," she said, pointing at the friary. "How can we help you?"

Both of them flashed badges. "I'm Detective Perry, this is Detective Cain," the woman said. "Berkeley PD. Is either of you Katherine Webber?"

"I'm Kat." Kat pulled at her leg, stretching into her cool-down.

"Is Mikael Bloemink here?"

"Should be," Kat answered. "I can get him."

"Can we ask what this is about?" Susan asked. She scowled at Kat's stretches.

"Um...why are all those people across the street?" Cain asked.

"Because we're kind of famous. We're the Berkeley Blackfriars," Kat said. There was some pride in her voice.

"Why does that sound familiar?" Cain asked.

"Did you watch the Republican Convention?" Kat asked.

Cain's eyes widened. "That's you guys?"

Kat laughed and winked at Susan. "I'll never get tired of that."

"Been a long time comin', girlfriend."

"Please come in," Kat said to the police officers.

"We just need—" Cain started, but Perry thumped him absently in the chest.

"Thank you," Perry said and followed them up the steps to the house. She motioned with her head for Cain to follow.

"Since when are you taking point?" he asked. She narrowed her eyes at him but said nothing.

Once through the screen door, Susan held it for the detectives. Tobias instantly rushed to them, tail wagging, and stuck his nose in Perry's crotch. "Stop that!" she said, turning away. Undeterred, he stuck his nose in Cain's crotch. Cain squatted and rubbed the dog's neck playfully.

"Mikael!" Kat yelled. She heard steps rumbling above her, and in her mind's eye she saw Mikael rushing to the stairs.

"What?" he called down.

"Big shit happening. Come down!"

She heard the sound of his feet on the wooden stairs. Brian came out of the kitchen, wiping his hands on a towel. "What's going on?" he asked.

"Yeah, what's—" Marco followed Brian, but when he saw the detectives he turned on a dime and headed back for the kitchen, but they were watching the stairs and didn't seem to notice.

Mikael ducked so as not to hit his head on the ceiling as he emerged from the staircase. "What's up?" he asked, his blue-black hair standing straight upright, adding another eight inches to his already six-foot stature.

"Is that the best cassock you've got?" Kat asked.

"What's wrong with...oh," Mikael said, trying to brush away the salsa. Brian crossed over to him and made short work of it with his towel.

"Mikael, this is Officer Cain, and...I'm sorry..." Kat grimaced.

"Perry. *Detectives* Cain and Perry." They showed him their badges.

"Cool!" Mikael said, squinting at them. He straightened up to his full height. "What can we do for you?"

"There was a murder last night at Tilden Park," Cain began, "and we have reason to believe that you were in the vicinity. We're hoping you noticed something."

Kat turned to Mikael. "Was *that* what we felt?"

He didn't answer her, but he nodded at the detectives. "We want to help. That's what we do." He put his arm around Kat and pulled her close to him. Tobias whined in protest at not being part of the intimacy.

"We need you to come down to the station with us. We've got a lot of questions we'd like to ask."

Kat and Mikael looked at each other. Mikael nodded. "Of course."

"Can I get changed?" Kat asked.

"Sure, but...I'll need to come with you," Perry said.

"Oh," Kat said. "So, we're suspects."

"Until we rule you out, everyone is a suspect."

Kat nodded and motioned for Perry to follow. Tobias trotted after them.

"Will you be back for supper?" Brian asked Mikael.

Mikael looked at Cain. Cain shrugged. "Depends how much we have to talk about."

"What's for supper, anyway?"

"Talapia tacos with a chipotle-infused balsamic, flash-fried plantains, and cantaloupe salad."

Cain's mouth dropped open. "Shit. *I* might come back for supper."

"You would be most welcome, detective," Brian smiled and headed back to the kitchen. Just then the phone rang. "Got it!" Brian shouted and made a detour into the office.

Mikael watched Cain and saw his eyes widen at the sight of Brian's hunchback. Cain looked back over at Mikael and blinked. "You all live here?" Cain asked.

"Yes. Kat and I share a room upstairs."

"My husband and I share the room next to theirs," Susan offered. "He's a member of the Order, but I'm not."

"No...cassock," Cain noted.

"Bingo," Susan said.

"The, uh, the cook guy wasn't wearing one, either," Cain mentioned.

"No. He's partnered with Terry, another of our Order members."

"Ah. So, not a *celibate* Order."

"Fuck no," Mikael said.

"But...you're Catholic?" Cain asked.

"Yes," Mikael said, without explaining further. He enjoyed such moments of confusion.

"How does that work?"

Before Mikael could answer, Kat returned, her hair wet from the shower, wearing a newly-pressed lightweight cassock. She grabbed Mikael's hand, and together they headed for the door. "Not you," she said to Tobias, shooing his nose way from the door. Kat shot a last glance at Susan. "Don't wait up."

8

BRIAN PICKED UP THE PHONE. "Holy Apocrypha Friary," he said with an exaggerated professional tone. "How can I help you?"

"Are you one of the friars?"

"No, I...who is this please?"

"This is Monseigneur Bondi of the Diocese of Oakland," the man's voice rang with authority and clipped impatience. "I need to speak to one of the friars, now."

"Everyone's a little busy at the moment. You can go ahead and talk to me. I assure you there will be no delay in our response."

"And what is your role there?"

"I'm..." he didn't know what to say. Resident Talmudic scholar? Jewish esotericism expert? "I'm the cook. And I...consult," he said, a little feebly.

"I—what? I don't want to speak to the-the...cook!" the Monseigneur spluttered. "Now put me on with one of the friars or I'll have your job."

He'll have my job? Brian wondered. *Meaning he'll come over and be the cook? Well, is he a good cook? No, he means he'll get me fired.* That would be hard, since Brian wasn't paid anything. It was just his...role, his place in the household, how he contributed to the mission of the Order.

He believed in the mission, yet the monseigneur's words struck at something deep, something painful, something that he was not aware of until just that moment. *Is that all I am? Just a cook?* His fingers tightened around the telephone's wireless handset. "Wait right here. I'll see if anyone is...if I can find someone."

"What kind of place is this?" Monseigneur Bondi yelled, but Brian removed the phone from his ear and moved, zombie-like, into the chapel—his head swimming and his heart stabbing with pain and regret.

9

"IN HERE, PLEASE," Cain said, holding the door for Mikael.

"You're splitting us up," Mikael said. "That's so biblical."

"It's standard procedure," Cain said, shutting the door behind them. He watched as Mikael surveyed the tiny room. It was painted a pastel gray, barely large enough for the table in its center. "Please have a seat."

Mikael sat, facing a wall dominated by a large mirror. "Just like on TV," Mikael said, pointing at the mirror.

Cain looked behind him. "Oh, yeah. Well...verisimilitude is important to us."

"Will your captain be watching us?"

"If she does, it'll be later on, and through that—" he pointed at the camera near the ceiling, "not through the mirror."

Mikael moved his head in huge, looping nods. Cain was not sure what to make of him. He seemed a little too eager, a little too friendly. Goofy, even. "You're enjoying this, aren't you?" Cain asked.

"Yeah. Well, it's *novel*. I've never been to a police station."

"You're not nervous?" Cain asked.

Mikael shrugged. "Why should I be nervous? I didn't do anything wrong...or at least not that I'm aware of...or at least, nothing *you'd* be interested in." Mikael's mouth moved back into a wide, open grin. "Besides, I kind of like you."

Cain twitched his head to one side. "What did you mean by 'biblical'?"

"Huh?"

"You mentioned it when we split you and your girlfriend up. I said that was standard procedure, and you said that was biblical. How do you mean?"

"You never read the story of Susannah? It's in Daniel—at least in the Catholic Bible it is. In the Protestant Bible it's in the Apocrypha, the Additions to Daniel."

"Let's assume I have not read this story."

"So Susanna is this beautiful Jewish lady, and she's good, too. But there are these two old skeezy guys, and they say, 'Hey baby, sleep with us. No one will ever know.' And she says, 'Fuck you, old skeezy guys.' So they accuse her of trying to seduce them. That's bad, 'cause if they succeed, folks will stone Susannah to death."

"I'm not hearing the splitting up part."

"Oh, yeah. So there's this guy Daniel, who's really young at this point, you know, and he says, 'Separate the two old skeezy guys,' and he questions them separately. And like, their stories don't match, so he knew they were lying. I figure you guys have been taking your cue from Daniel ever since."

"I suppose we have." Cain raised his eyebrows. "Can you summarize any book in the Bible so...eloquently?"

"You bet your boots!" Mikael said. "It's one of my charisms."

"I have no idea what that means," Cain said, shaking his head.

Mikael took a breath and his hands were already gesticulating a reply when Cain held his hand up. "And as interesting as that might be, we have more pressing concerns."

Mikael lowered his hands and smiled cooperatively. "Sure thing."

Cain's nose twitched. "Saffron."

"The color?" Mikael asked.

"Did you have saffron for lunch?" Cain asked.

"Yeah. Saffron rice. With pumpkin tamales."

"Shit, you guys eat good."

"Tell me about it. Brian's a wizard." Mikael leaned across the table. "I mean, not *really*. He isn't an *actual* wizard. He just, you know, his cooking is amazing."

Cain pursed his lips but decided not to pursue it. Instead he opened the file in front of him and laid photos of the crime scene out on the table in front of Mikael. He watched the young man's face intently. He saw Mikael's eyes widen, and his jaw drop open. A wave of distress crossed his face, and his eyes welled up.

"That's...that's terrible," Mikael said.

"It is. It's terrible," Cain agreed. "And that's why I need to talk to you. Tell me what happened the night this happened."

"We were celebrating Mabon with my friend's coven."

"And that friend would be...?"

"Jimmy."

"Do you mean James Tomlinson?"

"Yes."

"You're a Catholic priest?"

"I'm an Old Catholic deacon."

"Doing witchcraft."

"Yeah. Kat and I are both Wiccans, but we usually work with Christian god forms. You know, like you do."

Cain rubbed at his jaw. "Pretend that I *don't*. Explain that to me."

"Wiccans work with a variety of pantheons. Some worship Greek gods like Zeus and Hera, some worship Celtic gods like Bridget and Cernunnos, like that."

"And you?"

"We worship Jesus and Sophia."

"Who the hell is Sophia?"

"That depends on who you ask." Mikael scratched at the back of his head.

"Are you fucking with me?" Cain asked.

"No, no, really. I mean, if you're talking about orthodox Christianity, then Sophia is the pre-incarnate Christ, which has a nice symmetry to it. If you're talking about Gnosticism, then she's Christ's mated syzygy."

"Wait, what was that word?"

"Syzygy? A pair of connected or interdependent things?"

"Okay, yeah, sure, I knew that." Cain slowly shook his head and made a note. He was beginning to wonder just how deep the weirdness could go.

"But we weren't using the Christian pantheon the other night for Mabon. We were visiting our friends' coven, so we used their god-forms."

"And that doesn't create a problem?"

Mikael shrugged. "Why should it? They're just forms."

"And God...or the gods...don't mind that?"

"That would be *awfully* petty," Mikael made a face. "It would be like me going to Mexico and taking offense because someone called me 'Miguel.'"

Cain blinked. "Okay, let's pretend for a moment that I understand that. What's a 'Mabon'?"

"It's a harvest festival, the Autumn equinox."

"And that's a Wiccan holiday?"

"Correct. See, in Wiccan soteriological theory—"

"That sounds fascinating, but let's save it for beer and sausages later," Cain suggested.

"Okay," Mikael brightened, sitting up like a puppy eager for a treat—apparently at the prospect of actually catching a beer with him later. *I don't know if this kid is stupid or bright or just incredibly naïve,* Cain thought.

"Tell me what happens at this Mabon celebration."

"Well, it happens in the context of a normal Wiccan liturgy."

"Pretend I'm not an expert in Wiccan liturgy."

"Okay. First we gather, then we take our clothes off. That's called 'skyclad.' Not all covens work skyclad, but Jimmy's does."

Cain fought to keep his face rigid as he wrote some notes. "So, you get *naked*. What then?"

"Then we cast the circle and raise energy."

"Energy. From where?"

"From the earth, of course."

"Of course. What times was this?"

"Sundown. So...about 7 p.m."

Cain wrote that down. "And then?"

"Then we called in the four directions. Then we made corn-dollies—"

Cain closed his eyes. Then he opened them again and wrote some more, careful to keep his face frozen in place.

"Then we named our gratitudes and threw the corn into the fire as an offering."

"To the god-forms."

"Yeah. And that's when it happened."

"What happened?"

"I felt like someone punched me in the gut. Everyone else said they felt something similar. And all the energy we'd raised, it was just...gone."

"The *energy* was gone?"

"Yeah. Just *gone*." Mikael leaned in and whispered, "We think someone might have stolen it."

"Stolen your *energy*? Uh...did you file a police report?"

Mikael shook his head. "Should we have?"

Cain blinked and cleared his throat. "Okay, then what?"

"Well, we were all pretty shook up. We closed the circle and scattered."

"Scattered?"

Mikael shrugged. "We went home."

"Did you put on your clothes first?"

"Yeah, of course. We put on our clothes, and then Kat and I got in our car, and we came home. And Marco was there!" Mikael brightened up.

"Marco? Who's Marco?"

"He's a friend. He's staying with us for a few days. But he said it sounded like we got sapped."

"Sapped?"

"Yeah. Like, someone stole our energy, our tapas."

"Isn't that a Spanish food thing?"

"No, I mean maybe, in Spanish. But I mean it from the Sanskrit."

"Huh." Cain pointed at the photos. "This happened less than a hundred feet away from your celebration, at exactly the same time. The M.E. puts the time of death at the same time you say you were doing your Mabon thing. Can you tell me anything about this?" He held up one of the photos, showing a girl in the fetal position, ornamented by what looked like blood.

Mikael glanced at it but then looked away. "Please," he said. "We don't know anything about that. I sure don't. I know Kat doesn't." Mikael suddenly looked into Cain's eyes, and light dawned on his face. "Maybe the person who did this was the same one who sapped our energy! Maybe, they did this—" he pointed at the picture without looking at it, "to amplify the energy we raised and to direct it toward..." Mikael trailed off, mouth open. Cain could almost hear his brain churning, trying to work something out.

"Wait, let me be sure I understand your theory of the crime," Cain said. "Whoever did this sapped the energy your group had raised, then murdered this girl in order to amplify that energy?"

Mikael nodded. "I'll bet that's exactly what happened. Like a step-up voltage regulator!"

Cain shook his head. "What?"

"Like in electronics. A step-up voltage regulator."

Cain heard a rap at the mirror. "Excuse me a minute please, son."

Mikael nodded absently, still lost in thought.

Cain stepped through the door and shut it gently behind him. Perry was there, biting her thumb. "What do you think?" she asked.

"I don't understand half of what this kid says, but my gut says he didn't have anything to do with it."

"Same here. Let me see your notes." Cain handed his notes to her and she scanned them. "Well, their stories line up."

"I have to say I'm relieved. This kid is weird, but I kind of like him." He smirked. "He's got good *energy*."

Perry nodded but didn't pick up on his joke. "Yeah, she's sharp as a tack and eager to help. I don't get a whiff of guilt off either one of them."

"What about the Tomlinson kid?"

"He's harmless," Perry opined.

"Do we charge them with public nudity?"

"In Berkeley? Are you going to arrest the dykes-on-bikes with Band-Aids on their nipples next?"

Cain shrugged. "Okay, okay. But what do you think of Bloemink's theory?"

She read from his notes again. "That someone siphoned off their energy and amplified it with the murder?"

"Yeah."

"It sounds crazy."

"I know it does. I'm not saying it's true, I'm just saying that they might *think* it's true."

"I don't follow."

"Look, something like this sounds crazy to us, but it's not crazy to them. And it might not seem crazy to the perp, especially if they come from the same kind of religious community."

"Or at least share some common religious assumptions," Perry said.

"Okay, that works. I'm saying that the perp might have actually done it with the intention of...sapping and amplifying their...energy." He shuffled his feet, realizing how ridiculous he sounded.

"Let's say you're right. What's the motive? The perp amplifies that energy *toward what end*?"

Cain shrugged. "Maybe that's what we need to find out."

10

RICHARD, Dylan, and Terry tumbled out of the Order's beat up Corolla, and straightened their cassocks. Richard looked around, noting the weather-beaten Victorians badly in need of paint, the overgrown weeds in the front yards, the broken cement in the sidewalk, and the rusty, dismantled car at the curb. Tennis shoes hung from their strings from the telephone wires. "There's no getting away from it. This is East Oakland all right," Richard noted. "Hey, I've been here..." He pointed at the Victorian in front of them and his face brightened. "This is the food bank place."

"Actually, Ah think the food bank is *there*," Dylan pointed at a nearby storefront. "It used to be here. Maybe it got too big."

"But this is the address the archdiocese gave us," Richard said, double checking the post-it note stuck to one side of his open wallet.

Terry stared at his shoes.

"Waal, let's knock on the door and see what happens," Dylan said and began climbing the stairs to the faded blue Victorian.

Richard and Terry followed, and Dylan rung the bell. Richard did not hear it ring inside, and apparently Dylan didn't either, because a moment later he pounded a chubby fist on the wooden door. In a few moments they heard approaching footsteps. When the door swung open, they saw a small, dark woman in full habit. "Yes?" she asked.

Richard studied her face and decided that the woman must be Filipino, or from some other Pacific Island nation. She was about his own age, and so slight it looked like the wind might blow her off the landing.

"Hello, Sister. We're the Berkeley Blackfriars," Dylan said, flattening his cowlick unconsciously. He was sweating, even though it was mild out.

"Who?" she asked.

"We're supposed to meet Monseigneur Bondi," Dylan said.

"Oh." She looked down. "Wait here."

She shut the door, and a few minutes later it opened again with a jerk. A tall man in a red cassock glared down at them. As his eyes wandered from one to the other, he softened. "You must be the Blackfriars," he said.

"That'd be us," Dylan affirmed.

The Monseigneur stepped out and looked around, apparently worried he might be seen by someone. "Please come in," he said, holding the door for them. In the foyer he closed the door and offered his hand. Richard took it and introduced himself and his Order mates.

Bondi glowered at them. "I want you to know, I did not approve of the bishop's decision to involve you. I don't understand why involving schismatics in such an unfortunate affair helps us."

"Schismatics is sometimes the best friends you ken have in a sitcheeation like this," Dylan offered cheerfully.

"He's right," Richard acknowledged. "The archdiocese doesn't call us in lightly. But they know that there are certain kinds of...affairs... that we can dispatch without the trouble or embarrassment that might otherwise attend them." Richard smiled gravely. "But I'm grateful for your candor."

"Ken we, uh, take a look at the scene?" Dylan asked.

"Of course. The police have already come and done their thing, and the bodies are gone. But there's still plenty to see." He led them around the corner. The light coming through the living room window cast a warm, golden glow over the room. Just before them was a kitchen table, completely set for dinner—a dinner that must have happened many days ago, as the meat had started to turn a bit green, and flies buzzed around in small swarms.

"Watch your step," the Monseigneur suggested. Richard looked down to see fifty or more dead birds littering the hardwood floor.

"Ravens?" He bent down.

"Or crows," Dylan said. "Ah can't never tell the diff'rence."

"Ravens are bigger," Terry pronounced. "These are crows."

"I'm not so sure about that," Richard said, studying one of the birds. "Look, its feathers aren't articulated. It's like a cheap plastic knockoff of a crow."

"But that's not plastic," Terry knelt down beside him. "That's some kind of organic matter...or something mimicking organic matter."

"Could be an elemental manifestation," Dylan opined.

"I guess we'll find out. If these things fade out or disintegrate over the next few days, we'll know. I think it's a good guess."

"Do you mean they will simply disappear?" The Monseigneur asked.

"Prob'ly," Dylan shrugged. "They're not whatchacall real. Ah mean, they're *real*, but they're not *real* real."

"I'm not following you," the Monseigneur said, cocking his head.

"He's saying that they're probably ectoplasmic, taking temporary solid form. They're made of will, when you come right down to it," Richard explained.

"But I could wish for a crow to appear until I turned blue. Nothing would materialize," the Monseigneur said, looking dubious.

"Waal, that's a relief," Dylan said, not bothering to look at him. "At least we know that yer not a demon."

"He's right," Richard nodded.

"He's *usually* right," Terry added.

"Now you boys'er gonna make me blush," Dylan said.

"Can you lay out the timeline for us?" Richard asked.

"Last Wednesday night, the Sisters of St. Joseph were sitting down to dinner—" the Monseigneur began.

"What time was that?" asked Dylan, gazing at the pictures on the wall.

"About 6:30 p.m. The coroner said that by 7 p.m., they were all dead—all except Sister Timothy Mary. She's at Highland Hospital."

"How did they die?" Richard asked.

"The Medical Examiner said they were poisoned. Rat poison, to be exact. From the box they kept in the laundry room."

"I assume the rat poison was an additive to one of their dinner items?"

"Yes," the small nun answered. "The lumpia." She pointed to a dish, but the police had apparently emptied it of evidence.

"And Sister Timothy Mary?" Richard asked. "How did she survive?"

"It appears that she made the lumpia," the Monseigneur answered.

"That's cold," Dylan said.

"Is there any reason why Sister Timothy might have wanted to kill her sisters?" Richard asked.

"None. By all accounts, it was a very harmonious house."

"Where did the birds come from?" Richard asked. The Monseigneur shrugged.

Richard looked up...and froze. He crossed the room to the far corner and grabbed one of the chairs from the table, swinging it around to face the wall.

"Whatcha doin'?" Dylan asked.

Instead of answering, Richard stepped up on the chair and reached up to where the two walls met the ceiling.

"What is that?" Terry asked, sounding almost interested.

Richard grabbed at a small black sphere set directly in the corner and pulled it loose. He inspected it, then stepped down from the chair. He handed it to the monseigneur. "What is it?" Bondi asked.

"It looks like a camera," Richard said. "Did the sisters have a security system hooked up in the house? I didn't see a sign outside."

"I don't believe so, no. I'll check, however. It doesn't seem like something they would do, though."

Richard pointed at the table. "Someone...someone was watching." He put his hands on his hips indignantly as he thought. "Do you mind if we take a closer look at the house—at the other rooms?"

"Not at all. I was instructed to give you full reign," the Monseigneur said with barely disguised distaste.

Richard ignored it. "Dylan, take the rest of the rooms on this floor. Terry, check out the upstairs. I'll take the garage and whatever's underneath," Richard said. "Shout if you find anything."

With curt nods, they each headed in a different direction.

Richard followed Dylan toward the kitchen, but then swung open a door, revealing a staircase that descended into gloom. Richard toggled the light switch just inside the door and a naked bulb hanging by its cord illuminated the stairs with harsh yellow light. Richard descended without hesitation. At the bottom, he found another light switch and flipped it, revealing a large room with a cement floor and an exposed wood ceiling. Looking up, Richard could see the nails poking through the boards above him. A large, industrial-sized washer and dryer sat against a far wall, looking like they had been in place since the mid-1960s, at least. He backed up and began a systematic search of the room, from left to right. He shivered slightly from the chill. *It's at least ten degrees cooler down here,* he thought. Halfway along the first wall, he saw a door, its blinds drawn and backlit from the outside. Richard pulled on the knob and it swung open easily. He tried to lock the door, but it appeared to be broken. He stepped outside and looked at the outer doorknob—the keyhole was twisted and far too large. It looked like someone had pounded a screwdriver into it.

Stepping inside again, he continued his surveillance around the room. Opposite the stairs he saw a low wall, about two-feet high. The cement floor had been poured up to the wall, but as Richard peered over it, he saw only dirt beyond. The undercroft was completely unfinished—no lights, no floor, and plenty of cobwebs. He pulled out his phone and opened up the flashlight app. A bright blue light popped on, and Richard held it aloft as he stepped over the wall. Waving spider webs away from his face, he turned to begin his surveillance of this room, too. He hadn't gotten far when he whistled.

Two candle-holders had been stuck to the back of the sheetrock with pushpins. The candles were out, but Richard could see where the wax had dripped down onto the dirt. The candle holders were empty, containing only the charred remains of short wicks in the hollows that had held the tapers. But it was what was between the candles that really held his attention. It was a sigil, written in blood, about a yard across.

"Dylan!" he shouted. "Terry!" In moments he heard their feet on the steps. "In here," he shouted, "over the little wall."

Terry's face appeared first and, upon seeing the sigil, froze solid. "Oh, shit," he said.

Dylan strained to clear the wall but finally lumbered over to where Richard and Terry were standing together. "Waal, skin me like a badger, and put me in the pot," Dylan said, seeing the sigil.

"Hold that light steady," Terry instructed and snapped a photo of the sigil. A moment later, Richard heard the whoosh of the photo rushing off into the cyber sphere. "It looks like a sigil from the Lesser Key of Solomon," Terry said, "but Brian can tell us for sure in a minute."

"Good job," Richard said.

"The candles burned out," Terry said, pointing to the trail of wax down the wall, and the small hill of wax on the ground. "You know what? I think it's a timer."

"A timer?" Richard said.

"Yeah. It looks like whatever demon was summoned was only employed so long as the candles kept burning. As soon as they went out, it was manumitted and could go back to...wherever it came from."

"Do ya really think that nun summoned a demon?" Dylan asked. "'Cause that's not a nun-thing, generally."

Richard shook his head. "No. I think that *this*—" he said, pointing to the sigil, "caused the nun to behave in a way she *never* would have, otherwise."

Terry looked at his shoes. Richard noticed and turned to face him, hand on his hips. "Okay, Terry, you're driving me nuts. What's going on?"

Terry looked up at Richard as if he'd struck him. Then he looked over at Dylan. "Yeah, lil' buddy. Yer not yoreself."

Richard saw that Terry's eyes were misting up as he looked from one of them to the other.

"Terry, you and Dylan and me, we've been through hell the last few years. I don't know what's eating you, but you know for sure that the two of us are not going to shame you or abandon you. We're going to be *with* you, no matter what. You've trusted us both with your life more times than I can count. You can trust us with this, *whatever* it is."

Richard could see Terry's mouth working as he thought, but no sound came out. His hands hung straight down his sides, and he seemed paralyzed. Richard stepped over to him and embraced him, and Terry began to sob into Richard's shoulder. Richard held him close and rocked back and forth slightly. He cast a glance over Terry's shoulder at Dylan. Dylan gave him a compassionate look that was half-smile, half-grimace.

After about a minute, Terry's sobs subsided, and he drew back. Dylan was ready with a handkerchief, which Terry gratefully accepted. He blew his nose. "C'mon, Ter, spill it," Richard encouraged him. "Don't carry this alone. We've got your back, no matter what."

Terry didn't meet his eye but nodded. He sniffed and finally said, "I cheated. On Brian."

"Oh, no..." Richard said.

"Now wait, Ah thought gays couples had an *arrangement*—"

Richard cut him off. "There's no cookie-cutter covenant for gay couples any more than there is for straight." He grabbed Terry by the shoulder. "Terry, I've never pried into your private...you know...your sex life before. Do you feel comfortable telling us the details of your covenant with Brian?"

"Sure. We're monogamous, just like Dylan and Susan. We always have been."

"What changed?"

"We used to be once to twice-a-weekers," Terry said. "And then, suddenly, we became twice-a-monthers. And I've...I've got a *crazy* libido."

Richard saw Dylan look at the ceiling, stuffing his hands through the slits in his cassock into his pockets.

Terry started to cry again. "And the Ryde driver was so...cute. *Animalistically* cute. I...I felt like I couldn't stop myself. It was like I was watching myself from a distance." He buried his face in Richard's shoulder again. "Ihmah terr'ble pahsahn," his muffled voice insisted.

"You're not a terrible person," Richard said, holding him again. "You're a weak person, just like we all are. You're a fuckup, just like we all are. You're a sinner, just like we all are."

"Dude, yer supposed to make him feel *better*," Dylan corrected.

Richard ignored him. "You broke your covenant with Brian. But Brian didn't break his covenant with you, so the covenant is still in force. You're still a couple. That's how covenants work. Brian carries you when you're weak, and you carry him when he's weak."

"This is going to kill him," Terry said.

"Terry, I think you learned your lesson here," Richard said. "Wouldn't it do more harm than good to tell Brian about it?"

Terry drew back, surprised. Then he looked down. "I can't live with myself. I can't live with...this...between us. I *have* to tell him."

"Then you have to tell him," Richard shrugged.

"But it's going to kill him," Terry repeated. Just then his phone pinged. Terry looked down at it.

"It's a message...from Brian. The sigil belongs to a wrath demon named Tispis."

"Where is he on the lowerarchy?"

"4th circle," Terry said. "Part of Nuudjal's host."

"Nuudjal...Nuudjal. Why does that ring a bell?"

"Brian's typing something now," Terry said, sniffling. "Here it is: Nuudjal is also known as the Duke of Crows."

"That explains the bird thing," Richard said.

"An' the ready access to elementals," Dylan added.

"So bad, but these boys are not the worst of the worst," Richard said, chewing on his finger.

"Bad enough," Dylan noted.

"Bad enough," Terry agreed.

Richard put his hand on Terry's shoulder. "I think if you tell Brian...and I'm not saying you should...but if you do, yeah, he's going to be hurt."

"Betrayed," Dylan interjected.

"Thank you," Richard said, slightly irritated. "But he loves you. And you love him. You've got more than ten years of building a life together. He's not going to throw that away, not if you're really contrite."

"Do you think...could he really forgive me?" Terry bit his lip as he looked up into Richard's face. It struck Richard that he looked like a forlorn puppy.

"I think he will," Richard assured him. "You're family. He's going to be hurt. He's going to be angry. He may even need some space. But...he'll come around. I know it."

Terry nodded, as if trying to convince himself of it.

"Uh...about the demon?" Dylan suggested.

"Are you good, Ter?" Richard asked.

"No. I have a feeling I'm not going to be good for a while. But... let's move on."

"That's my bean-sprout," Richard said, mussing his hair. "C'mere, I want to show you both something."

He waved them over to the door and pointed out the broken lock.

"So...not an inside job, then," Dylan breathed.

"Nope," Richard said. "My money says that whoever broke in here painted the sigil and summoned Tispis."

"A truly terrible name," Dylan noted.

"For an apparently terrible demon," Richard agreed.

"But why kill a convent full o' nuns?" Dylan asked.

"What do these nuns do again?" Terry asked.

"They run a food pantry," Dylan said. "An' they organize a soup kitchen at St. Denis' a few blocks away, if Ah'm rememb'rin correctly."

"These folks served the poorest of the poor, in the roughest part of Oakland," Richard said.

"Yeah, but they're prob'ly mostly white," Dylan said. "Folks don't take kindly to the white-savior thing anymore."

"True, but they're also mostly elderly and they've been in the neighborhood for years and years. They've built up some cred in this neighborhood."

"The sister here is Filipino," Dylan pointed out.

"She's assisting the monseigneur—she's not of the same order as the nuns who lived here."

"How do ya know that?"

"She's habited. The Sisters of St. Joseph dress like regular people."

"They just wear crosses," Terry added.

Richard shut the door again. He crossed to a dilapidated work-bench and started rummaging through jars filled with what looked like mostly rusty screws. A minute later, he pulled forth a latch and eye-hook. "Found it!" He snatched up a screwdriver and returned to the door. He started screwing in the hook.

"That's not really gonna keep anyone out," Dylan said.

"Not if they really want in, but it'll keep the wind from blowing the door open," Richard said.

"This was the work of a pro," Terry noted. "A serious, experienced magickian. There are a hundred ways this kind of working could have gone sideways."

"Mebbe it did," Dylan said.

"No," Terry said. "I think what went down was exactly what was supposed to go down."

"Agreed," Richard said, turning the eye-hook one final time. He fastened the door closed and stepped back with a satisfied look on his face.

"Why would a magickian want a convent full o' nuns in West Oakland dead?" Dylan asked.

"I can think of two tracks to trace," Richard said, putting the screwdriver back on the workbench. "We look into the nitty-gritty of what these nuns were up to, and we start canvassing all the magickians we know."

"That sounds like a plan," Dylan said.

"You know what bothers me?" Terry asked.

"What's that, lil' buddy?"

"We don't know if the magickian is done here..." Terry began.

"Or if he's just getting started," Richard finished.

SUNDAY

Your light shall break forth like the dawn,
and your healing shall spring up quickly;
your vindicator shall go before you,
the glory of the Lord shall be your rear guard.
Then you shall call, and the Lord will answer;
you shall cry for help, and he will say, Here I am.
—*Isaiah 58:8-9*

11

THE DAY'S first sliver of light intruded upon the cottage, but Terry was already wide awake. He could hear Brian's breathing beside him, but mostly he just heard the pounding of his own heart. He found the waiting excruciating. He kept hoping to find an opening, a good time to bring up his "fling," but there didn't seem to be any "good times." He moved to get out of bed but felt Brian's hand circle his waist and pull him close.

"Hey, baby," his partner's voice sounded groggy. "When are you going to tell me what's eating you?"

Terry buried his head in the pillow and started to cry. "Oh, daddy." He snuggled in closer, spooning with Brian as tight as it was possible to spoon.

Brian rocked him slowly back and forth and whispered encouragements in his ear.

Eventually Terry was cried out. He sniffed. "I did a terrible thing."

"What did you do?"

"You're going to hate me."

"I have shared bodily fluids with you for ten years. I could never hate you. Tell me what's going on with you. It's killing me."

"It's killing me too."

"Just...tell me."

"I fucked the Ryde driver."

"You *what*??"

SUSAN AWOKE to the sound of breaking glass. "What was that?" she asked. Tobias jumped up and started barking.

"Corn flakes," Dylan mumbled, turning over in bed. "Marmalade."

"Dylan, wake up," she said, slapping his shoulder.

"Huh?" He squeezed open one bloodshot eye.

"I just heard something smash."

"It's prob'ly nuh—," he said, not finishing his sentence.

Susan rolled her eyes and then threw back the sheets. Springing to her feet, she felt around for her robe and hastily fastened it around herself. She opened her bedroom door and Tobias ran past her, disappearing down the hall. Susan turned and saw Kat emerge from her room wearing an embarrassingly revealing nighty. "What the fuck?" Kat asked.

Richard's head poked out of his door. "Heard it," he said, noticeably averting his eyes from Kat. "What is it?"

"No clue. Wanna go down together?" Susan asked.

"Sure. Gimme a sec." He closed his door.

Susan turned toward Kat. "Don't you have a bathrobe or something?"

"What?"

"We want the testosterone in this house pointed toward danger, not toward you."

Kat scowled at her but withdrew. A moment later she reappeared in her winter cassock.

"You're just jealous."

"Don't start with me, miss 'I can eat a whole carton of ice cream and still be a size five,'" Susan snipped.

"Jealous."

"I swear to God I'll claw your eyes out," Susan hissed.

"If you didn't love me," Kat grinned. She kissed Susan on the cheek.

"Oh yeah. I forgot about that. Good morning, sweetness."

Richard opened the door, now dressed in his own cassock. His head jerked up when they heard another crash.

The three of them stood looking at each other for a few seconds, listening. It occurred to Susan that if they'd had antennae, they'd all be quivering.

Richard bolted for the stairs, and the women followed closely.

At the bottom of the stairs, Richard looked around the living room but all seemed silent, except for Tobias' distant barking. Then he heard another crash. "Back of the house," he said, and half-ran past the front door, through the chapel, past the hallway leading to the office, into the kitchen. Brian should have been there, beginning breakfast—but he wasn't.

Richard paused as he saw that the back door was already open. Susan caught up to him. "Tobias could have opened that," she said. The sound of barking betrayed that the yellow lab was already in the back yard. Richard flung open the screen door and stood on the wooden steps of the small porch landing. Susan and Kat hovered just inside the doorframe, but they didn't dare step into the backyard.

A three-foot replica of Michelangelo's David was planted upside down in the soft soil of the yard that Brian had just recently been tilling for a new garden. Buried neck-deep, his godlike torso sprouted heavenward from the earth. Susan looked up and saw the shattered plate glass window of the cottage, which must have been destroyed only moments ago by the David-shaped projectile. "Tobias, careful! There's glass everywhere!" For the first time in her life she wished she actually knew some Enochian.

"Ors!" Richard shouted, his teeth clenched. Susan could see he was struggling to remember the language himself. "Tapvin, lvsd!"

"That didn't sound like a complete sentence," Susan noted.

"That's because it wasn't," Richard conceded. But it seemed to do the trick. Tobias gave the house some distance but did not let up barking.

Richard descended the stairs and crossed over to the cottage. He tried the front door, but it was locked. He pounded on it. "Guys, it's Richard. Open up. Now."

Susan could hear Brian and Terry arguing. Every now and then it sounded like a plate smashed against a wall. Susan hoped it was a wall.

"Goddam it," Richard said. He fished the spare key from the top of the doorframe and opened it, disappearing into the house. Susan rushed to the cottage to join him. Just inside the door, she saw Terry in the fetal position in the living room, surrounded by shards of what looked to be the better part of a china set. Brian was in the door of the kitchen, tears streaming from his eyes. In his hand he held a porcelain figurine. "You betrayed me!" Brian shouted, his voice horse. Brian was wearing only dark blue bikini briefs and a t-shirt, his hunched back looming ominously behind his ear. "Mother fucking taxi-fucker!" he said and threw the figurine at Terry. It smashed just inches from Terry's head, sending splinters of porcelain raining down on Terry's flannel pajamas adorned with light blue bunnies.

"I'm sorry!" Terry wailed. "I'm so sorry..." Susan recognized the figurines, then—they were Terry's prized collection of Tom's of Finland porcelain collectables, and Brian had already smashed about half of them.

Brian grabbed another figurine from a shelf that ran around the top of the room and took aim, but Richard stepped in between them and stared hard at Brian, daring him to throw. Brian's eyes lost their crazed look and seemed to sink back into their sockets. His shoulders slumped and he dropped the figurine to the floor. "I'm...I don't know..." but he didn't finish.

Richard walked toward him and embraced him, holding him up as Brian's knees buckled, and he began sobbing. Richard lowered him to the floor gently and then sat cross-legged, tangled up in Brian's limbs while he rocked him gently. He motioned to the women with his head, which Susan took to mean, *Get Terry out of here.*

She knelt by Terry and shook him. Kat grabbed one arm and Susan the other. Together they pulled Terry to his feet and rushed him out of the house. Tobias chased after them as they crossed to the porch, up and into the kitchen. They sat him at the kitchen table and then hovered over him. "Are you all right?" Kat asked.

"What's the fucking racket?" asked Randy's small, tinny voice.

"Not now," Kat said.

"What's wrong with the fag?"

Kat turned the guitar amp to zero.

Terry's hands were trembling. "I fucked up. I fucked up. Oh my God. I so fucked...*I'm* so fucked."

Susan grabbed Terry's hands and squatted down to be at eye level with him. "Terry, what did you do?"

"I...I fucked that Ryde driver," Terry confessed. "Or, I guess to be more accurate, I let him fuck me."

"Don't you guys, I don't know, have some kind of arrangement?" Kat asked, looking confused.

"What is it with you straight people? Some of us are as vanilla as you are!" The momentary flash of anger seemed to actually normalize Terry for a moment.

"Right, of course," Kat fumbled. "I just...assumed...you know."

"You assumed wrong." Terry looked down at his hands and at Susan's hands holding onto them. "I wish you weren't, though."

Just then the doorbell rang. "What the fuck is going on down there?" Marco's voice was barely audible, even though he must have been shouting from upstairs.

Mikael appeared in the doorway with yesterday's cassock thrown on, topped with a jet-black cascade of bed hair. "What *is* going on?"

"Can you get the door, please?" Susan asked, fighting to keep her voice calm and even.

Through the kitchen door Susan heard the front door open, followed by the screen door slamming, the trammeling sound of many shoes, and the clank of unidentifiable equipment. Mikael's face reappeared in the doorway. "Uh...CNN is here, or at least the lighting crew is. They want to know where to set up."

12

"GET IN, QUICK," Larch said, holding the door for Fraters Purderabo and Turpelo. They scurried in and Larch took a quick look around to make sure they were not observed. Satisfied, he slammed the door and shooed them inside.

His apartment was small, as was the norm in San Francisco, but so sparsely furnished that no one felt crowded. Frater Eleazar was seated cross-legged on the floor and appeared to be cleaning his nails with a large hunting knife. Frater Khams turned from the kitchenette with a bowl. "Black bean hummus," he announced. "There's celery and carrot sticks, too." He set the bowl on a low table beside a couple of folding chairs.

Turpelo sniffed at the hummus, made a face, and did not go near it again. He slumped into a chair. "Why all the Skullduggery, Frater Babylon?" he asked.

"There are still warrants out for us, or do I need to remind you of that?" Larch planted himself in a swivel chair next to a large, 27-inch computer display monitor on a solid oak desk—the only substantial piece of furniture in the apartment.

"I've been giving your...ambitions some thought, Babylon,"

Purderabo began, in a tone that was already frosty. "It reeks of arrogant over-reach."

Larch laughed. "Don't beat around the bush, Purderabo. Tell us how you really feel!" He turned to the computer keyboard and navigated his way to a file. "The way I see it, either I lack sense or *you* lack vision."

"It does seem to be one or the other," Eleazar affirmed, not taking sides.

"But look here," Purderabo continued, "we do *not* have a good track record. I mean, when we try to get...ambitious. We're fine for the mundane activities of magickians. Any of us can assert our will on the world—in small ways. But whenever we try to do something of consequence...what I'm saying is perhaps we ought to take a hint."

"Do you know how many times Edison failed before he succeeded at the light bulb?" Larch asked, without turning his face from the screen.

"Edison was not a magickian," Purderabo noted.

Larch turned and narrowed his eyes at him. "I wouldn't be so certain of that, if I were you."

Purderabo's eyebrows raised. "Edison was a magickian?"

"He was a Mason—*and* a member of the Golden Dawn," Larch said. "And the principals upon which electricity work? It's not all physics, gentlemen. Edison set in motion a force that *permitted* electricity to work as it does, and that was a magickal working that is still in effect."

"No shit," Khams breathed, his mouth full of hummus.

"Would you like me to name another alleged failure?" Larch asked.

"Try me..." Purderabo raised a skeptical eyebrow.

"Amelia Earhart," Larch said. "Did she fail in her around the world flight?"

"She did crash."

"She did not crash—which is why no one has found the wreckage of her plane. Instead of crashing, she translated. 'And Enoch walked with God, and suddenly he was not, because God took him.' She was BOTA, by the way."

"The Builders of the Atydum aren't magickians," Turpelo objected.

"They are in their upper grades," Larch said. "Anyway, the point is that she was not a failure, either—she succeeded beyond our ability to imagine. She is a hero."

"But nobody knows about it," Turpelo pointed out.

"Fame is not our object," Larch said.

"Speak for yourself," Purderabo smiled.

"When I was a boy," Eleazar said, gesturing with the knife as if it were no more dangerous than a teaspoon, "my father told me that success was measured not by how many people liked me, but whether *I* liked me."

"You've succeeded, then, Eleazar," Turpelo said with a smirk. "No one likes you."

"*My* father told me that there was nothing more important than my reputation," Purderabo countered.

"Well, you fucked that up, didn't you?" Khams smiled.

"No thanks to present company," Purderabo conceded. "How about you, Babylon? What timeless wisdom did your father pass on to little Babylon—"

He stopped when he noticed that Larch's eyes had grown small and hard. He seemed to have withdrawn within himself, like a cornered animal that might spring an attack at any moment. "We will *not* discuss my father," he said, his voice quiet, hoarse, and cold as quicksilver. "Not ever."

"But Babylon, I was only—"

Larch sprung from his chair and took Purderabo by the lapels, lowering his face so that their noses were almost touching. "Not. Ever."

"I get it, Stanis," Purderabo said, his voice wavering. "You can let go of me now."

Larch released his coat but continued his awful eye contact.

Finally, he looked away and slunk back to his chair. The room was silent as the fraters feared to breathe.

"What were we talking about?" Khams asked.

"Paternal wisdom," Eleazar said helpfully.

"*Before* that," Khams said, scowling at Eleazar.

"Uh...Amelia Earhart?"

"We were talking about Babylon's *ambitious* proposal," Purderabo said, his voice commanding such sufficient authority that the others fell silent. Purderabo set down his teacup and leaned forward toward Larch. "I understand why the scope of the...project...is attractive to you, Babylon. It appeals to your flair for the dramatic."

Larch was about to object, but Purderabo held up his hand and continued. "But you could just as well change global weather patterns or cultural gender norms or any other grand scheme we might concoct. What I don't understand is your passion for *this* project. Just what *are* you after, Babylon?"

Larch looked down at his hands. His jaw tightened. "Justice."

"Justice," Purderabo repeated, a bit sarcastically. "Because you are a *champion* of justice." He turned to the others. "This is the reason we never get any magick done anymore—Babylon is out on the protest lines, picketing for justice." This elicited a few nervous laughs from the others. "Don't bullshit me, Babylon. You've never graced a candle-light vigil with your presence in the whole of your shoddy little life."

"I have never involved myself in a protest because I do not engage in futile activities," Larch's eyes remained hard, and he was grinding his teeth. "But this...this is something I can do, something that is within my power. I can pull tyrants from their thrones—" he leaned forward in his seat and spoke so low that everyone held their breath to hear it. "And I *will*."

"Yes, yes, the downfall of God." Purderabo rolled his eyes. "As I said, ambitious. But...Larch—"

"Magickal names only!" Eleazar objected.

"Fine. *Babylon*," Purderabo conceded. "Listen...*if* you do away with...with the Tyrant...what will happen to us?"

"What do you mean?" Larch blinked. "We'll be heroes. We'll be hailed as liberators. We'll be showered with glory."

"Yes, that's all lovely," Purderabo waved his grand vision away. "But just suppose the Neoplatonists are correct, and the universe is contingent—"

"Not just the Neoplatonists," Turpelo interjected catching his drift, "but the Vedantists and the Hermeticists and the...well, the entire Western Mystery tradition that we uphold and carry on. *Everyone* says the universe is contingent."

"If you do away with the One upon whom the universe is contingent, won't the universe simply cease to be?" asked Purderabo. "I mean, I'm all for an end to tyranny, but not at the cost of existence itself."

"Yes," Khams agreed. "I'd rather put up with a little tyranny and continue to exist. Wouldn't you?"

"Has the meeting begun?" Eleazar asked. "Should I be taking notes now?"

"Have you learned nothing in all your studies?" Larch asked. "The one that everyone calls 'God,' the being that has jurisdiction over this *particular* universe, is not the Ground of All Being."

Purderabo moaned. "Must you bring Tillich into this?"

Larch ignored him. "The Creator is a demiurge. No less an authority than the Gnostics mapped out the basic celestial hierarchy in great detail. Not just the angelic hosts, not just the Tyrant, but what was above that—the Godhead, the *Pleroma*."

"The Fullness," Purderabo translated, awe sounding in his voice.

"Precisely," Larch said. "The *Pleroma* is the Ground of All Being. This being the common folk call 'God'—the Gnostics named him Samael, by the way—he may have made this world, but he himself is supported and contingent on the Pleroma."

"So if we defeat the Tyrant Samael," Purderabo reasoned, "the universe will *not* wink out of existence?"

"No more than England ceased to be simply because the tyrant Charles the First was deposed," Larch affirmed.

"And you're...*sure* of this?" Eleazar asked, a little nervously. He had found a notebook and a single periwinkle crayon but had not yet started writing.

"Were the allies sure that the entire universe would not implode when they set off the first atomic bomb?" Larch asked, a little impatience creeping into his voice.

"I would hope so," Khams said.

"No, they were not. But they deemed the risk worthwhile." He leaned over and peered into each of their eyes in turn. "So. Do. I."

Purderabo stuck out his lower lip and nodded as he thought. "You make a compelling argument, Babylon. But you said some misdirection would be in order, if we were not to be thwarted."

"Yes. That is why I called us together," Larch said. His black mood seemed to have passed and he turned up the corners of his mouth in the beginning of a proud grin. "Take a look at this." He pressed a button on the keyboard and a video sprang to life on the computer screen. Purderabo rose and lumbered over to where Larch was sitting. The others also crowded around for a closer view.

"What are we looking at?" Turpelo asked.

"This is a convent in West Oakland, about two blocks from the 580 overpass into Emeryville," Larch said. "The godly women have just sat down for dinner. Aaaand, there we go." They watched as one of the old women pitched forward into her plate.

"They're not moving," Khams pointed out.

"No," Larch said, stroking his chin.

"They're still as stones," Purderabo noted.

"Lifeless as cow-patties," Larch agreed.

"That's not even a saying," Eleazar protested.

"Wait, that one's moving," Khams said, pointing to one of the nuns.

"Yes. She's the one who poisoned them," Larch said. "At least, that's my theory. Now...*watch*."

They held their breaths as two young African American men entered from the hallway.

"Who are *they*? They look scared out of their skulls." Purderabo sounded delighted.

Their eyes widened as the living nun's head pulled back, her jaw distended, and black birds poured out of her throat, filling the room with the frantic beating of wings.

"Splendid!" Turpelo breathed. "Let's watch that again!"

"I'm way ahead of you. I've already edited the last fifteen seconds into an endless loop for my ongoing amusement," Larch said, sounding a little giddy. He clacked on his keyboard and pulled up another file. Once launched, the murder of crows erupted from the old woman's throat perpetually.

"Where did you get this footage?" Purderabo asked. His eyes were shining, and it was clear that he was, once again, in awe of Larch.

"I made it myself. I planted the camera in the convent, posing as a PG&E technician—'Just here to check for gas leakage, ma'am.' Nobody watches you as you scurry here and there, you know. And after that was in place, I captured the footage on a laptop set up in their undercroft, where I also placed *this* sigil." He pointed to a sigil on the screen.

Larch noted the gaping jaws of his fellows. "Who...is that? Tisspis?" asked Turpelo.

"Very good, my friend." Larch patted Turpelo on his hip. "Nice to see that you are up on your sigils."

Turpelo shrugged. "I like to think of it as my *expertise*."

"You're going to need it," Larch said, smiling up at him.

"What did you do to activate it?" Purderabo asked, still not able to peel his eyes away from the video.

"I sacrificed a cat," Larch said. The others took a step back, clearly shocked.

"It was a mangy stray," Larch waved them on. "And it's not like there aren't a million of them in Oakland. I gave him the privilege of spending his useless life on something worthwhile and grand."

The others did not look convinced. Larch pulled out a large leather satchel covered with post-it notes, each with spells scrawled on them. "Careful not to let those notes fall away until we're ready for them." He handed it to Purderabo.

"What's in here?" Purderabo asked, taking the satchel from Larch gingerly.

"Sigils," Larch said.

"For what?" Khams asked.

Larch clacked on his keyboard, and the video shrunk to the size of a thumbnail, but a new file sprung to life and quickly filled the screen. It was a map.

"That's Oakland," Turpelo said, leaning in again.

"It is," Larch agreed.

"I hate Oakland," Purderabo sighed. "It's so...common."

"Dirty," Eleazar agreed.

"It's no dirtier than parts of San Francisco," Turpelo challenged. "And may I point out that those are your *favorite* parts of San Francisco, Eleazar?"

"I used to live in Oakland," Khams offered. "It's not so bad. Wait, are those watermarks?" Khams peered even more intently at the map.

"They are, after a fashion." Larch eyed Khams closely, hoping he was catching on.

"There's a watermark etched over each neighborhood," Khams said, pointing at the screen. "There's one over Millsmont. There's another over Laurel, and another over the Dimond district..."

"Those watermarks—Babylon, can you highlight those?"

"Glad you asked," Larch said. At the touch of a button, the watermarks began to glow.

"Sigils," Turpelo breathed.

"And do those sigils correspond to the ones in this satchel?" Purderabo asked.

"They do. This," he said, motioning toward the screen, "is the plan. Your job is to carry these sigils into the heart of the neighborhoods indicated and post them where they are visible but not accessible. We don't want the wind blowing them off or anyone tearing them down. Then you'll mark the boundaries of the neighborhoods with like sigils using spray paint."

"You want us doing graffiti?"

"I want you tagging."

"For demons."

"Yesssss..." Larch grinned. "And not just Oakland." He pushed the forward button on his keyboard. Another map appeared, this one of Berkeley, and another of Emeryville. "Oakland first, then Emeryville, then Berkeley. It will be a couple of long, hard days, but by my calculations, we can mine the whole area in, oh, thirty-six hours, give or take."

"Mine?"

"Like land-mines." Larch grinned. "But with demons."

"Fucking brilliant," Purderabo breathed. "So, how do we activate them?"

"I'm not killing any cats," Khams crossed his arms.

"There are demons on this screen that wouldn't pay attention if you just killed a cat," Turpelo pointed out.

"No need to concern yourselves, my friends." Larch held his hand up. "These sigils are pre-activated." Purderabo almost dropped the satchel, but Larch was ready, holding the bottom of it. "That's why you must be sure that none of the warding spells drop off," he said, pointing to the post-it notes.

"How dare you endanger us by calling us into the same room with...with..." Purderabo held the satchel as far away from his corpulent frame as he possibly could.

"I assure you, it is adequately warded." Larch's confidence was convincing. They all relaxed.

"So...and I hesitate to ask," Turpelo started, running his fingers nervously through his hair, "but, um, *how* did you activate them?"

Larch smiled. "With a little help from my friends. My Wiccan friends, that is."

13

RICHARD SAW the lighting crews setting up near the chapel and froze. "Oh shit," he said out loud.

"Are you one of the monks here?" A severe, angular woman in her early 40s approached him. She hugged a clipboard to her chest and flashed him a smile that was all teeth. "I'm Tapper Alexander. I'm looking for Father...Richard Kinney?"

"That's me," Richard said, trying to collect his thoughts, which seemed to be running in circles and screaming. "And we're friars, not monks."

"Oh, how interesting," Tapper said in a tone that revealed that it wasn't the slightest bit interesting to her. "It's Sunday morning, so I assume you'll be having a service. Is that right?"

"Yes. Mass is at 11 a.m."

"I thought so. Okay if we set up here in the chapel then?"

"Perfect," Richard said, moving his head from side-to-side rather than up-and-down.

"Are you...all right?" Tapper asked him, cocking her head.

"I'm...fine. We're just...juggling a lot this morning," Richard said.

"Oh. Well, is it okay to bother you with questions?"

"It isn't a bother at all." Richard flashed a smile. "We're glad you're here."

"Okay, then," Tapper said, shooting him a look that said that she was not so sure.

Richard turned on his heel and went back to the kitchen. He pressed both hands on either side of the doorway, barring any motion in or out. "Listen up!" he whispered. Everyone stopped and faced him. "This is an emergency situation, so I'm going to start giving orders. Any problems with that?" Everyone shook their heads, a little stunned. "Good. Mikael, make sure that guitar amp is turned off. Not down, off. No one will notice Randy in there as long as he's not screaming expletives at people." Mikael rushed over to the guitar amp and unplugged it. "Kat, please take Terry upstairs and put him in one of your cassocks. You look like you're about the same size. Susan, wake Dylan up and pour about two pots of tea into him before he sets foot downstairs. Also, make sure Marco is presentable, and ask him if he can come down and start breakfast. He loves to cook."

"What are you going to do?" Susan asked.

"I'm going to go take care of Brian," Richard said. He glanced at his watch. "We've got just a little over an hour before mass, and I want everyone calm and in their places at 11 sharp. We've got to get a lid on the chaos so that the cameras don't pick any of it up. Everyone clear?" Nods all around. "Okay, let's move."

RICHARD RAN his fingers through his hair and squared his shoulders before heading out to the cottage. Tobias was underfoot and almost tripped Richard in his rush to get through the back door. Richard rolled his eyes at the big yellow dog's exuberance. Richard took all three stairs to the ground at once, crossed the narrow patch where the new garden had been planted, and bounded up onto the porch. He didn't bother to knock. "Brian," he called.

The living room looked like a tornado had hit it. Richard peeked into the kitchen and, not finding Brian there, headed for the bedroom. He knocked on the door, but there was no answer. "Brian!"

he shouted, before pushing open the door. He stepped inside and looked around, but Brian was nowhere to be seen. He spun around and headed for the bathroom. It, too, was empty. "Brian!" he shouted again, but no one answered.

"Goddam it, Brian," Richard said, slipping down onto the couch. Everything seemed suddenly very, very much out of control. *If only CNN weren't here,* he thought. *Things would be bad, but they wouldn't be…dangerous.* Just then, Brian walked through the front door holding a suitcase.

"Oh, hey," he said. He walked past Richard into the bedroom, and Richard got up off the couch and followed him. He sat on the bed as Brian threw clothes into the suitcase. "Did you know?"

"What? Oh, about Terry? He told me yesterday—me and Dylan."

"Just yesterday?"

Richard nodded. Brian grunted and turned to the chest of drawers, gathering up a heap of socks.

"I'm really sorry, Brian. I wish it didn't happen. And I think Terry wishes it hadn't either. He loves you desperately."

"Apparently not enough to keep it in his pants," Brian said.

"He seems truly penitent to me."

Brian paused and looked at the suitcase. "It's not enough."

"I get it. You're angry. You're hurt. But just because Terry did something he regrets doesn't mean you have to. It's not a contest."

"I'm not trying to hurt him. I'm just…I need some space."

"Where are you going to go?"

"I have a rabbi friend in San Francisco. She has a guest room. I already called her."

"Is she the rabbi at the Gay and Lesbian synagogue over there?"

"Yeah. Well, associate rabbi."

"Can we call you when we need your expertise?"

"You can call me. Dylan can call me. *He* can call me when hell freezes over."

"I'll tell him not to try you for a few days," Richard smiled.

Brian nodded. "That will work, too."

"You're going to miss all the excitement. CNN is here."

"Oh, joy. I'm actually kind of relieved. I'm not...photogenic."

"You are part of our family."

"Terry is part of your family. I'm...I'm the cook." Brian's face screwed up as if he were fighting back tears. He mastered it and walked out of the bedroom. A moment later he came back with a handful of items from the bathroom. "At best, I'm an appendage."

"That is not true. Everyone loves you. *I* love you. You have lived with us for what—five years, now? That's like, what? Thirty-five years in gay years."

Brian let out a weak laugh. "I love you, too. All of you. I just...I need..." He sat down on the bed next to Richard, his shoulders sagging. "Ten years ago, if you asked me where I'd be, it wouldn't be here...cooking. I had dreams of being a Talmudic scholar, of teaching, of doing something important with my life."

"You don't think what we do here is important?" Richard asked.

"I do. It is. I'm just...I'm just not sure that it's *mine*. I'm not sure that what I'm doing is what I'm supposed to be doing. I mean, is this the best use of the skills and the gifts that HaShem has given me?"

"That's an important discernment."

"Yeah, so I just need to...I need some space."

"I get it." Richard put his arm around his shoulder. "We're going to miss you."

"You're going to miss my cooking."

"Also true." Richard stood up, and so did Brian. Richard gave him a long hug. "Are you taking BART over?"

"Yeah."

"Do you want a lift to the station?"

"No. I can walk. Thanks, though."

"You sure?"

"Yeah."

"I'll pray for you."

"Please do."

Richard released him. He felt awkward and didn't know what else to say, so he hugged him again and then turned to go back in the house.

14

RICHARD SAT QUIETLY, waiting for the others to take their places in the chapel. He found it hard to focus, hard to pray. He was distracted by Brian's departure, and he was too keenly aware of the bright lights and the camera, and of Tapper rushing back and forth and whispering to the cameraman, the sound engineer and her assistant. He finally just gave up and opened his eyes, watching as the camera panned over the wall-sized collage assembled from a random assortment of photos cut from magazines: people of all ages and colors, breathtaking scenes from nature, and even architectural marvels. When you stood back from it, though, the pictures resolved into a stylized version of Jesus' face, eyebrows high as if he were merry, mouth open as if he were about to speak.

Kat was always adding pictures to it—he resolved to ask her if she had any ready to go. It would be a good shot for the feature on them. But, he realized, Kat was not there to ask. No one was there. He glanced at his watch. 10:59. He was wondering if he should go upstairs and see where everyone was when Susan entered the chapel and took a seat next to him. He leaned over and whispered, "Where the hell is everyone?"

"Dylan's coming. Terry won't come downstairs—he's a wreck. He tried to put on mascara, but his hands were shaking. And then he cried. He looks like he has some kind of venous condition."

"Venous?"

"You know, like he has black veins running through his face. If we were shooting a horror film, he'd be ready to go."

"Jesus. Kat and Mikael?"

"They're trying to talk him down."

"And Marco?"

"I wasn't able to rouse him. He's sawing logs in the guest room. Mikael said he had a bit of a breakthrough last night and was up until three in the morning working out in his shop." She meant his van, of course.

"It's going to be embarrassing if we start mass and there's no one here."

"Where two or three are gathered..."

"Yeah."

Just then Dylan lumbered in and took a seat across from Richard and Susan. A moment later Tobias trotted in after him and plopped down by his master's feet.

"Time to pray," he said, and smiled. "Uh...who's sayin' mass today?"

"I'm presiding. You're supposed to preach."

"Ah am? Shit. Forgot 'bout that."

Richard rolled his eyes and gritted his teeth. Susan patted his leg.

"Waal, Ah'll think of somethin' to say."

"I'm sure you will, dear," Susan smiled patiently at him.

Richard sighed and stood up. "Let us begin our worship this morning by singing the 77th Psalm, using chant tone nine." Then, in a sonorous tenor, he sang, "I will cry aloud to God."

Dylan and Susan responded, singing, "I will cry aloud and God will hear me."

Richard sang, "In the day of my trouble, I sought the Holy One."

The response came back, "My hands were stretched out by night and did not tire. I refused to be comforted."

Richard heard steps on the stairs, and before the Psalm was

finished, Mikael and Kat had joined in. Richard squinted against the harsh light and tried to ignore the camera.

The Gospel was the dishonest manager, from Luke chapter 16. After the reading of the Gospel, Dylan got up to preach. "Uh... Ah've never understood that parable. You got this guy who's running his boss's business, and he screws it up, and his boss fires him. But he's made a lot of enemies, and he figgers when he's kicked out into the street and homeless, no one is gonna let him sleep on their couch. So he takes everyone's invoices and cuts them in half, cheating his boss, but now everyone loves him and they'll let him sleep on their couch. And the boss isn't even mad. Ah don't get it." He sat down.

The cameras were rolling, of course. Richard wanted to bang his head on the pew.

Susan spoke up. "St. Augustine said he didn't believe Jesus ever spoke that parable. I read that once."

"It's a weird-ass story," Kat said. "How is it good news?"

Mikael stroked his chin as he thought. "Well, you know, the manager *did* forgive the people their debts."

"But he didn't have any right to," Dylan pointed out. "It wasn't *his* money."

"But we who are ordained forgive people's sins all the time," Richard noted. "Do we have the right to do that? No, they aren't sins against us. We forgive sins against God—which is God's to forgive. But God is like the boss in the story, he doesn't get mad."

"Maybe," Kat said, speaking slowly, "It's never wrong to forgive, even if you don't have the 'right' to do it. And whether it's sin or money or...whatever."

Richard felt cut to the quick. He felt his throat tightening up. He knew he should forgive Terry for causing all this upset—today, for God's sake! And he should forgive Dylan for not being prepared with a sermon. He clutched at the seat of the pew until his hands hurt.

There were a few more minutes of discussion, but Richard didn't really hear them. They said the Prayers of the People and brought forward the gifts of bread and wine at the Offertory. Richard stood behind the altar and bid them all rise. "The Lord be with you," he announced.

"And also with you," they responded.

About halfway through the Eucharistic Prayer, as Richard held the chalice aloft, he was distracted by Tapper's wave. He faltered and blinked.

"Father Richard," Tapper shouted. "We'd like to get a different angle on you raising that chalice. Can you back up a bit and do this again?"

"Are you fucking kidding me?" Richard said.

"Uh...no. Do you mind?"

"Yes, I fucking mind. We're not doing some kind of performance for you here. We're praying. If you want to be unobtrusive and document us at prayer, you have our permission to do that, but you do not have our permission to *interrupt* our prayer!"

"Okay, okay. Sorry about that." She tapped the cameraman's shoulder. "Just keep rolling. We'll fix it in editing."

The cameraman nodded without taking his eyes off his viewfinder.

Richard felt derailed. Susan came up to the altar and pointed to the liturgy. "You're right there, sweetie."

Richard let out a long sigh. He closed his eyes, and then he continued the mass. Somehow they got through the Eucharistic prayer without further incident. Richard was giving Kat communion when Marco walked through the chapel on his way to the kitchen. He was naked except for a pair of briefs with a picture of Darth Vader printed on the fly. He was momentarily arrested by the lights.

"Hey, there's a camera crew here," he said. He reached into his underwear and began to scratch his ass.

Suddenly, a howl erupted from upstairs. Richard realized it was the sound of Terry keening.

"What the hell is that?" Tapper whispered, looking at the ceiling.

Tobias lifted up his yellow muzzle and let loose a howl of sympathy.

"Christ," Richard said under his breath.

The phone rang. "I'll get it," Marco yelled from the kitchen. Richard heard his bare feet padding down the short hallway into the office. "Yyyellooooo," he said.

Richard bit his lip so hard it started bleeding. "This is the bread of life," he said, breaking off a bit of bread for Susan.

"Amen," she said, trying not to laugh and failing.

The rest of the mass went quickly. No sooner had Richard pronounced the final blessing than Marco poked his head out of the kitchen doorway. "Hey, you got a gig. I left the address for you on the notepad. They want you to come ASAP."

"It *is* Sunday," Richard protested, taking off his stole.

"No time to lose was how it sounded to me," Marco tossed over his shoulder as he went back into the kitchen.

"What's the case?" Dylan called.

"I don't know, but it sounded urgent. Something about a possessed dog."

15

PERRY PUNCHED him on the right shoulder and then dodged left. Cain fell for it, looking first to the right side of their office, then to the left. "What are you, in fifth grade?" Cain asked. The room was large, with three rows of facing desks contained within cinderblock walls painted a pastel aquamarine. Scuff marks and bits of old masking tape were the chief ornamentations, save for crime scene photos and maps. "You're here on a Sunday," he noted.

"So'er you."

Cain nodded and indicated the photos from the Tilden park crime scene spread out on his desk. "I can't stop thinking about it."

"What's Sally have to say about that?"

"She's at a dog show. She won't know I'm gone."

"That's a weird-ass hobby. It's like signing up to be around obsessives. Why would you do that?"

"Um...*I'm* an obsessive. And as I already pointed out, *you are also here.*"

"Less fur, though."

"Speak for yourself."

Perry smiled and took a seat at her desk, which was arranged opposite his. She interlaced her fingers and stared at him.

"What?" he asked.

"I know who she is," Perry said.

"The girl?"

"The dead girl."

"How?" Cain looked up.

"I was here until 2 a.m. looking at missing persons reports for the greater Bay Area." She fished a photo out of her desk drawer and threw it at him. "Consuelo Hernandez, from South San Francisco. Went missing four days ago, reported yesterday."

"72-hour rule..."

"Exactly."

Cain looked at the photo—a posed photo from school, complete with a fuzzy blue background. She was smiling, but there was a hint of distaste in her brown eyes. He put the photo side-by-side with the crime scene photo of the victim. He had to study them for a minute or so, but he finally had to agree that if it wasn't her, it was her twin sister. "Any connection with our witch cult?"

Perry shrugged. "Let's go find out."

"I'm driving." Cain stood up and shuffled all the photos into the file.

"You don't like my driving?" Perry stood and pushed in her chair.

"You scare the shit out of me."

"You've never mentioned it before."

"My feelings are close to the surface today."

"You heard that on Oprah."

"You think I watch fucking Oprah?"

"I know you watch Oprah, because I've heard it in the background when I talk to you on the phone."

"Fucking Oprah," Cain said, heading to the elevator.

THIRTY MINUTES LATER, they crossed the Bay Bride and were exiting Highway 280. "Should we ask for SF backup?" Perry asked.

"We're not making any arrests," Cain said. "We're just asking some questions. Besides, who's gonna be at work?"

"Only obsessives."

"We sure as hell don't want any of *them* with us."

"Turn there. No, left."

Cain jerked the car to the left and made the turn.

"That was close."

"A little warning would be nice."

"Aren't we irritable today?"

Cain said nothing, keeping his eyes glued to the road.

"This is it. Slow down. We're looking for two-one-zero-five. Should be on the right."

Cain slowed the car to a crawl as they looked for house numbers. Cain caught one and sped up again. A couple houses later, he parked beside a small ranch with a neatly kept yard. Cain got out of the car and looked up. "Overcast. It never ceases to amaze me how different the weather can be from one side of the Bay to another."

"Ever thought of moving to this side? Get some actual weather?"

"I think I'd slit my wrists."

"I kind of like it."

"You kind of would."

"Who's taking the lead on this one?" Perry asked.

Cain stopped up short. "You know, the whole way over I was only thinking about investigating this case. It just hit me—"

"We have to do a notification." Perry stared at him, her mouth open. "Oh, God."

"Or...can we say with a hundred percent certainty that Consuela is our girl?"

"We should probably collect some DNA."

"And we can still ask some questions."

"We can be here investigating the disappearance," Perry nodded.

Cain shrugged. "Why not?"

"Okay, I like it. You take lead."

Cain nodded and headed for the porch. He punched at the doorbell.

"You smell like garlic," Perry waved at his face. "How does Sally deal with you?"

"She loves garlic."

The door swung inward, and Cain saw a woman who looked a little younger than himself clutching tentatively at the door. It was clear she'd been crying. "Are you Mrs. Hernandez?"

The woman nodded.

Cain and Perry both held up their badges. "I'm Detective Cain, this is Detective Perry. We're from the Major Crimes Division over in Berkeley. We're investigating a crime that we think might be connected to your daughter's disappearance."

Cain saw her eyes widen with hope.

"Can we come in and ask you some questions?"

She looked nervous.

"Mrs. Hernandez, we're the good guys. If you have naturalization issues, we don't care about that. We want what you want."

She nodded, still uncertain, but swung the door open for them. Cain gestured Perry inside and then shut the door behind himself.

The room was dim but neat. A stack of Spanish language magazines was on the coffee table, along with a pack of rolling papers. There were posters taped to the wall. They had not been hung entirely straight. Small tears were visible near the yellowing tape.

Cain indicated the couch. "May I?"

Mrs. Hernandez nodded. Cain and Perry sat down next to one another and smiled grimly.

"Mrs. Hernandez," Perry began, "Can you tell us anything about your daughter's interests? Her friends? Did you notice anything different in her behavior lately?"

"Connie is a good girl. She has never been in trouble a single day in her life!"

She seems unnecessarily adamant, Cain thought. "No one is suggesting otherwise," he said. "We are trying to help."

"Why are the Berkeley cops here?" Mrs. Hernandez asked.

"We're investigating a lead in another case, and it led us to your daughter. If you can help us, we might solve both cases."

Mrs. Hernandez nodded.

"Is Connie still in high school?" Perry asked.

Mrs. Hernandez nodded.

"Where?"

"Burlingame, with the Sisters of Mercy" she answered.

"I hear that's a good school," Perry nodded.

Cain kicked her shin, by which he meant "Bullshitter." She didn't know the first thing about that school.

She kicked him back. "What year is she?"

"She is supposed to graduate next June," Mrs. Hernandez said.

"Was she having any problems, or hanging around with anyone new?"

"No, no problems," Mrs. Hernandez said. "Except that she's been sassing the sister in her religion class."

Cain took a note of this, scrawling on a small moleskin pad. "How so?"

"I got a call from the headmistress, Sr. Angelica. Nothing bad, just —too many questions. You know, challenging the sister's teaching."

"Is that unusual for Connie?"

"It's the first time I've heard about it."

"Any new friends?"

"Yes. One girl—Dani. I guess it's short for Danielle or something."

"What's your impression of Dani?"

"She seemed nice. Wears a lot of black, though. Seems depressed if you ask me." Mrs. Hernandez shrugged. "I try not to judge."

"Of course. Did Connie have any hobbies? Or any new interests that you've noticed?"

"She loves karaoke," Mrs. Hernandez smiled sadly. "She's terrible at it, but she loves it." She swallowed. "I'd do anything to hear her sing again."

Cain nodded. He felt incredibly sad but fought to keep a stoic expression. "Mrs. Hernandez, would you mind if we took a look at her room?"

Mrs. Hernandez shook her head, then she stood up and walked to the hall. Cain and Perry followed. She led them to what seemed a typical teenage girl's bedroom. The bed was unmade, and the carpet on the floor was strewn with socks and underwear. A boy-band poster hung above her bed, and My Little Ponies of various hue adorned her bookshelves.

There was a low table that seemed to be used as a desk. An ancient PC was dark and silent. Cain touched the mouse and the screen lit. "Do you know the password to this?" he asked.

Mrs. Hernandez walked up and punched in a short string of letters. Cain stepped in and found the girl's email, searching the message lines.

Perry looked under the bed, then under the mattress. "Jackpot," she said.

She pulled out a copy of *Wicca for Dummies* and held it up. "Mrs. Hernandez, did you know that your daughter was into witchcraft?"

Mrs. Hernandez' eyes went wide, and she shook her head.

Perry thumbed through the book and found a bookmark. "This could be something."

"Whatcha got?"

"Place called The Cloven Hoof. It's in San Francisco."

"What is it? A bookstore?"

"I can't tell. There's an address, though. And hours. It's open."

"I think I might have something here, too. Connie answered a Craigslist ad, offering a free tutorial in Wicca."

"Is there an email address?"

"Nope, it's one of those anonymous thingies—some random string of letters and numbers."

"Take a shot of her screen, and let's check it out."

Cain nodded.

"There's probably more here," he said. There was a lot to go through.

"Mrs. Hernandez, we need to take Connie's computer to a lab so we can do a more thorough search." Perry touched her arm compassionately. "Will that be all right?"

Cain knew it didn't matter whether it was all right or not. A warrant would not be hard to come by in a case like this, and if need be they could stay put until it arrived.

But it didn't come to that. Mrs. Hernandez nodded. She looked utterly beaten. Cain stifled an instinct to give her a hug. Perry could afford to be less cautious. She grabbed the woman's hands in her own and squeezed them. "We're going to do everything we can for Connie," she said. "Do you believe me?"

Mrs. Hernandez nodded, but she didn't look up.

16

BRIAN SET his suitcase down and rang the doorbell. He couldn't hear it go off and realized that he would simply have to trust it. A moment later the security door buzzed, and he was able to push it open. He took the stairs two at a time, and as he stepped out onto the landing, Chava's door opened, and there she was, cooing and embracing him. He let his bag drop the last few inches to the floor and buried his head in her neck. Then he lost it. She held him while he sobbed, rocking him back and forth gently. "I'm so sorry, *achi*." She held him until he was cried out. She picked up his suitcase and, taking his hand, led him inside.

"You need a drink," she said.

"No, I don't," he answered.

"Well, *I* need a drink, and it's rude to make me drink alone."

"It's two o'clock in the afternoon," Brian argued, blowing his nose.

"Then we have no time to lose," she said, her voice filled with mock gravity.

She poured herself a glass of wine, and him half a glass, and set them both on the coffee table. Chava was about six inches shorter than Brian, with wiry, dark brown hair. She wore it long, tied at the back, with a kippah at the crown of her head. Bookshelves lined every square inch of the living room, creating a cozy but slightly claustrophobic atmosphere.

"Thank you," he said.

"You know you're welcome here anytime," she said. "And for as long as you need."

He nodded, tears welling up in his eyes again. "I'm sorry," he said.

"For what?" she asked. Her face twisted up in a sad, compassionate smile. "And why would being told you were welcome make you cry?"

"It's not just being welcome. I guess it's being welcome *here*. In a... a Jewish place."

"Brian, the Hasidim might have expelled you, but there are plenty of places in Jacob that will love you and embrace you."

She moved to sit beside him on the couch and clutched at his hands. "Surely you never felt out of place at our synagogue?"

"No, it's just...it isn't home, I guess."

"And living with those Christians is home?"

"Living with Terry is ho—" His voice caught in his throat and he leaned his head on her shoulder and sobbed again. She held and shushed him until his shaking subsided. "Drink," she said, moving his wine glass closer to him. "Don't refuse HaShem's medicine."

He sniffed and laughed and took a sip. "That's not what's really bothering me."

"It sure seems to be bothering you," she said.

"It just...came up. I didn't expect it."

"That's...normal," she said, putting her own head on his shoulder. "Terry cheated on you. I get it. It's terrible."

"Thank you. And...it's more than that," he said. "I feel like Terry's betrayal kind of woke me up. Like I've been sleeping for years. I mean, all these years have gone by, and what have I really done?" His voice trailed off. "I don't know what I'm supposed to *do*."

"Have you prayed about it?"

"No, it's..." He was going to say it was too soon, but that sounded stupid. The truth was, it simply hadn't occurred to him to pray about it yet. He changed the subject. "Maybe it's good."

"What's good?"

"Maybe there's a blessing hidden underneath his betrayal."

"Maybe so. But, my dear...please don't rush to that kind of opinion. That's like slapping an emotional band aid on it before the wound has really revealed what it's about. I suggest really feeling the pain, really grieving the loss, and letting its meaning unfold over time."

Brian nodded. That sounded like wisdom. "It just...hurts. And I want it to stop hurting."

"I know. That's what wine is for." She took a long pull at her glass then rose and picked up his suitcase. "I'm going to take this to the guest room. C'mon, I'll show you where the towels are."

He nodded and followed her to the narrow hallway so typical of San Francisco flats. She paused by a closed door. "Um...you should be prepared for something."

"What's that?"

"This is my guest room, so that's where you're sleeping." She looked tentative, as if afraid of his reaction. Was it messy? He could deal with that. Was it decorated in some wild way? Was it festooned with bondage paraphernalia? He couldn't quite see it. Chava was a fairly typical liberal rabbi. She and her partner Elsa had never even hinted at any S&M proclivities. "And when no one is here, it's where I do my research." Brian steeled himself for piles of books and stacks of disorganized papers. He could deal with that, too. "Just, don't think I'm too weird, okay?"

"You *have* met the people I live with, right?" Brian asked.

She opened the door and turned on the light, then she stepped to the window and drew aside the blackout curtains. Sunlight flooded the small room, and Brian gasped. Stepping into it, he turned completely around, taking in the photos and papers tacked to every wall, many of which were connected by strands of different-colored yarn stretched between pushpins. Brian could see barely a foot of white wall space, no matter where he looked. On one wall, strands of yarn fanned out in every direction, like the rays of the sun.

"Welcome to my secret obsession," she said. "I don't let very many people know about this, but if you're going to be staying here, I don't see how I can keep it from you."

"What is this all about?" Brian asked, relaxing a bit.

"You know who Serah Bat Asher is, right?" Chava asked.

"Sure. She's the one who recognized that Moses would be the deliverer of Israel."

"You also know that she can never die, right?"

"I vaguely remember a midrash about her being the only person allowed into Eden after the expulsion."

"Well, I'm kind of obsessed with her. In fact, I've been tracking her down for years." She traced one of the strands of yarn back to where it met all the others—directly below a photo of an old woman, smiling a mischievous smile, her eyes filled with laughter and terrible knowledge.

"Oh, fuck," Brian said.

"What?" Chava inquired. "Did you forget something?"

"No, no. I'm just...Chava, I *know* her."

17

"Let's go! Let's go!" Richard shouted from the front door.

"Just a few more minutes!" Tapper responded with forced cheerfulness. "We have a lot of equipment to move."

"Yeah, but we have no idea what these folks are dealing with. We don't want to show up when...when it's too late."

Tapper walked over to him. "Look, it won't be news until we're there to record it. So relax."

Richard scowled. "Um...are you aware of how solipsistic that is?"

Tapper's head twitched, but her smile remained constant. "I have no idea what you just said, but give us a few more minutes, and we'll be right there."

As she walked away toward her lighting technician, Richard pretended that he didn't see her mouth the words, "Whoo-boy."

"Here, Dicky," Susan said, handing him a soft-sided cooler. "None of us got breakfast. Marco and I threw together some sandwiches for you guys."

"For the CNN crew, too?" Richard asked.

"Uh...no, just for you exorcists. I assumed they were smart enough to eat before they showed up."

"Yeah, but it's nearly lunch time."

Susan scowled at him. "Marco, did you start in on your own sandwich yet?" Without another word she turned her back on him and went back into the kitchen.

"Sorry," Richard said to no one.

WITHIN TEN MINUTES, the kit bags were loaded, sandwiches were hastily made and given to the CNN crew, and a convoy consisting of a battered Corolla and a news van wound its way through the Albany tunnel. "Left," said Mikael, navigating. Richard turned left. Their car was packed with all five of the Blackfriars, plus Tobias. He thought about leaving Terry home, but since this was a case involving dogs, it seemed wise to bring both Tobias and Terry—the one who could most easily communicate with the big yellow lab. Richard hoped Terry would be able to hold it together, and he uttered a silent prayer to that effect.

A few minutes later, they pulled up at a modest, sedate-looking house on an idyllic, tree-lined street.

"Don't look like a demonic haunt," Dylan noted.

"Are Ozzie and Harriet here?" Kat asked, climbing out of the car.

A harried woman rushed out of the house to meet them. "Thank you so much for coming. I...I don't know what to do." She was young, maybe thirty, with strawberry hair and freckles. Richard noted that she was about Kat's size, but built more like Susan. "What's this?" she said as the CNN van pulled up.

"CNN is following us for a couple of days," Richard explained. "Will that be okay?"

The woman looked nervous. "I...I guess so. I just wasn't expecting it."

"Just ignore them," Richard said, giving her a wink. "That's my plan."

"I didn't know who to call," the woman said, "I talked to my pastor first and she gave me your number."

"If it's really a deliverance case, you called the right folks. And if we're not the right folks, we can assess the situation and get in touch with the person you need."

"Thank you."

The cameraman rushed up and raised his lens. A moment later the lights started blaring.

"Is that really necessary?" Richard asked. "It's full daylight."

"Just pretend like we're not here," Tapper said from behind the cameraman.

"What is yore name, ma'am?" Dylan asked, notebook at the ready.

"Elizabeth. Barker. My husband is away on business. My son is Teddy. He's thirteen."

You've got a dog problem, and your name is Barker, Richard thought. But he kept his mouth shut.

"And yore dog, ma'am?" Dylan asked. "Tell us about yore dog."

"He's seven. A Dachshund-Beagle mix. His name is Barney."

"Where is Teddy?" Kat asked.

"He's...I put him in the closet."

Richard blinked. "Why did you put him in the closet?"

"To keep him from running to that dog!"

"Where is the dog?"

"In the back yard. In the dog run."

"Okay. First thing, I think you should get your son out of the closet and bring him here," Richard said. "He might have some useful information."

"Oh, okay. Please, come in," she said, gesturing toward the front door.

"We, uh, brought our dog," Richard said. "I know this will sound weird, but we think he might be able to help."

Mrs. Barker looked at him like he was out of his mind, but she didn't object. Richard followed her up the few stairs of the arts-and-crafts bungalow and into the front room. Houses in Albany are typically gorgeous but on the tiny side, and Richard was not surprised to find that the place was crowded before half of them had filed in. He kept walking into the dining room to make space. The place was immaculately kept, he noted, with tasteful, original art on the walls—

blotchy, impressionistic landscapes that reminded Richard of Umbria. A bright light erupted, searing Richard's vision, and he held his arm up to shield his eyes. "Holy shit, you guys," he said in the general direction of the lighting technician.

Dylan and Terry set kit bags down on the floor, and a moment later Kat and Mikael did the same, with Tobias in tow. "I'm not sure we all need to be here," Mikael said.

Richard shrugged. "Don't know what we're dealing with yet, either. We may need Kat as bait." Kat punched him in the stomach.

Dylan jerked his head toward the kitchen and Richard followed him in. When they were out of earshot, Dylan whispered, "You gonna let Kat take this one?"

Richard blinked. "Well, sure, but...CNN."

"You don't trust her?"

"I trust her."

"It's time, dude. If you really trust her, I say let'r shine. You don't need to hog all the glory, do you?"

Richard scowled at him, but it was hard to take offense. He was right. Richard nodded and turned toward the kitchen window. He stood on tip-toe and surveyed what little of the back yard he could see. He didn't see any dog. When he turned around again, Mrs. Barker was leading a teenager who must have been Teddy into the living room, dragging him by the elbow. Richard and Dylan walked over to meet him.

"This is Teddy. Teddy, tell the monks what you did."

"Friars," Terry objected, but his heart wasn't really in it.

"Barney died," Teddy said. The kid had a sullen demeanor and brown hair that hung down over his eyes. He wore a sleeveless black concert tee and ripped black jeans. He looked exactly like what Richard imagined Mikael must have looked like ten years ago.

"Uh-huh. An' then?" asked Dylan, squatting down to be more at eye level with the kid. Dylan lost his balance and rolled onto the floor, and Richard rolled his eyes. The cameras, after all, were also rolling.

"So I wanted to bring him back to life." He looked ready to cut and run—as if he knew he'd done something wrong but was ready to defend his actions just the same. Richard knew the feeling.

"That's something I understand," Richard said, sitting down on the arm of the couch. "A couple of my dogs have died over the years. I'd have done anything to bring them back." The kid looked at him with something approaching hope. "So what did you do?" Richard asked him.

Teddy turned on his heel and ran to the hallway. His mother yelled and started to go after him, but Richard held up his hand. "Give him a minute." Mrs. Barker stood down, her eyes moving back and forth, uncertain.

A few seconds later Teddy returned and thrust an iPad at Richard. Richard turned it around and looked at the screen. Dylan peered over his shoulder and whistled. "Reanimation spell. That's some powerful bad mojo there, lil' buddy."

Richard scanned the spell quickly. "Do you know how this works, Teddy?"

"Yeah, you say the magic words, and people come back to life. Dogs, too, I guess."

"The magic words have meaning. They're not just nonsense sylla-bles. Did you do this *exactly* as it's written? Including the pentagram?"

"Yeah. I did it in the garage."

"Show me," Richard said. He followed the kid through the kitchen into a single-car garage, and everyone followed like the cars of a freight train. Richard saw a pentagram erratically sketched on the floor—running over oil spots and cracks in the cement. He pulled out his phone and called up the compass app. The pentagram was facing roughly the right direction. "Did you stand inside the penta-gram when you said these words?"

Teddy nodded.

"Show me the sigil you drew."

"I copied it from the website," Teddy handed a large sheet of drawing paper to Richard. The sigil was rendered in purple crayon and embellished with guitars and rocket ships.

"Wow," Richard said before he caught himself. "Okay, Teddy, let me tell you what happened. First, you did everything right, which is the only reason you are alive."

Mrs. Barker's hand went to her mouth.

"Second, your dog is *not* alive again."

"He's outside walking around," Teddy objected.

"But he's not *alive*," Richard said. "He's still dead. You just called a demon—a demon named Tenalphador, by the way—"

"Third level, Tenalpier's host," Terry said mechanically.

"—and now that demon is wearing Barney's body, the same way you wear a coat. Barney's body is walking around out there, but it's not Barney."

The child nodded then looked at his shoes. "He doesn't act like Barney."

"No. My guess is that he wants to rip your throat out."

"He tried."

"So you know you almost died twice today, right?"

"Oh my God!" Mrs. Barker nearly shrieked.

"Are you catching all this?" Tapper whispered to the sound man. He nodded.

"Teddy, this is our dog, Toby. He has a spirit in him, too. An angel."

"Is he dead, too?"

"No. He and the angel are kind of...buddies. They're *sharing* the body."

Teddy made a face but brightened up when he saw the dog approach him. Richard noted Terry behind Tobias whispering instructions, no doubt in Enochian.

"The angel in Toby is as powerful as the demon in Barney. So Toby is going to stick to you like glue and he's not going to let anything happen to you."

"Teddy is *not* going back there," Mrs. Barker said emphatically.

"Except that he kind of needs to," Richard said. "We may need answers about the ritual, or the demon's behavior that only Teddy here is going to know." He turned and faced the boy again. "What do you say, Teddy? Can you be brave and face Barney again?"

"Do I have to watch him die again?" Suddenly all the teenage bluster was gone. Teddy looked like he might cry.

"You'll see him return to peace. He's not very peaceful right now, is he?"

Teddy shook his head. Richard placed a hand on his shoulder. "Okay, let's go then."

Teddy nodded curtly, squared his shoulders, and headed for the door at the rear of the garage. It led directly to the backyard, and Richard heard the snarls as soon as it was opened.

"Kat, why don't you take point on this one?" Richard said.

Kat looked surprised.

"Gotta happen sometime, baby," Mikael said. She, too, squared her shoulders and headed out the door.

Richard followed closely after and saw the dog. When he had tried to picture a Dachshund-Beagle mix in his head, the result was slightly comical—a large, tubby sausage-dog with a ridiculous name. And in life, he might have indeed been amusing.

Not anymore.

Fortunately for everyone involved, he was locked in a chain-link dog run, roughly six feet by nine feet, with a small dog house resting on a cement slab. "Teddy, tell me how you got Barney from the garage to the dog run."

"The website said it could take a few minutes for it to take effect. Mom was calling me for dinner. So I put him out in the run and went to eat."

"Do you always padlock the run?"

"Not if we're home. I kind of did that on autopilot."

Richard turned to the boy. "Your mom calling you for dinner? That saved your life. Your reflex to padlock the run? That saved your life. You do understand how close you came to dying today, right?"

The boy nodded, his eyes wide. "Are you getting how dangerous magick is?" Teddy nodded again. "Let me give you a bit of advice, Teddy," Richard said. "I have known a lot of magickians in my time.

Some of them are nice guys, good friends, and they do okay in life. But they're the exception. Most magickians end up crazy or sick or dead. Do you understand why that might be?"

Teddy nodded.

"There are other ways to be powerful," Richard said. "Ways that are much, much safer. And more productive, too." He looked back at Barney. The dog was drooling, and his eyes were cloudy and wild. He growled aggressively, and every now and then he released a barrage of barking so loud and raw that it must have hurt.

"If he's really dead, how is he moving?" Teddy asked.

"The demon you summoned is manipulating his body, just like a puppeteer does when he pulls the strings of a puppet. You've seen that kind of puppet, right?"

"Yeah, but it seems like it's more like the kind you put your hand into. The demon is inside Barney, right?"

"Barney is gone," Richard said. "What we have to do will be a lot easier for you if you remember that. The demon is inside the corpse."

Dylan leaned over and whispered, "That's harsh." Richard ignored him.

Kat had opened her kit bag and was setting items out on the grass.

"What is your first move, Kat?"

"I think there's two ways I could approach this," she said, wiping a lock of hair out of her eyes.

"We could do the full-on frontal, 'I-command-you-in-the-name-of-Jesus' assault," she started.

"Now yore talkin'!" Dylan said. "Ah'm all about that."

"And it works great for you," Kat smiled. "But I'd like to try something else. Something more...subtle."

"Let me guess, something involving angels?" Richard asked.

"Yeah."

"It's not going to be great for the cameras," Richard noted. Tapper frowned.

"I'm not terribly concerned about that," Kat said. "I'm concerned with getting the demon out of the dog body without anyone else getting hurt—or possessed."

"I am behind you one hundred percent," Richard said. "Go for it."

Kat nodded. Reaching into her kit bag, she pulled forth a hand-held censor and charcoal. She lit the charcoal and, as it was warming up, took a small box of salt and made a circle in the dirt around the dog run.

"What's she doing?" Tapper edged in close to Richard.

"She's making a salt line. Evil spirits don't like salt."

"You mean, the demon can't cross over?"

"*Can't* is a strong word. He could, but it won't be pleasant for him. He'll avoid it if he can."

"So where will he go?"

"Two options," Richard said. "Up or down."

"Is this all *normal*?"

Richard shrugged. "It's a particular way of working. It's not our M.O., but I respect the form, which has its origins in British occult circles. I am particularly interested in seeing if Kat has mastered its minutiae."

"How is it different from what you usually do?"

"Uh...our way of working is like a sledgehammer. This method is more like surgery."

Kat sprinkled a few grains of frankincense on the charcoal and properly censed the corners of the yard. Barney watched intently, but without apparent alarm. Richard noted that he was beginning to list to the left, evidence that rigor was setting in and the demon was losing motor control.

Kat raised her hands into the orans position and prayed loudly and from memory: "In the name which is above every other name, and in the power of the Almighty, I exorcise all influences and seeds of evil from this yard. I exorcise all demons, parasites, ghosts, curses, spells, and bindings from this yard. I exorcise all thought forms, magical spirits, and bound angels from this yard. I cast upon them the spell chains and cast them into the outer darkness of the Abyss where they will not trouble the servants of God. Amen."

Satisfied with this, she walked over to Terry and whispered in his ear. He nodded and knelt down to whisper to Tobias. Kat stepped over to Richard and said, "Get everyone on the east side of the yard, as far away from the run as possible. I need them to either be still and quiet, or to go back in the house now. And for God's sake, don't let anyone make eye contact with Barney."

"Why not?" Tapper asked. She was almost spooning Richard.

"Entry point. The demon could leap from the dog into you."

Her eyes went wide. "Even over the salt?"

"Even over the salt. Just don't look him in the eye." Richard turned and passed Kat's instructions along. Then, silently, he waved them all over to the east side of the yard. Barney began to follow them to the east side of the dog run, when Tobias let loose with a deafening barrage of barking. Running back and forth along the west edge of the dog run, Tobias drew Barney's attention, and soon the two were snapping at each other, snarling aggressively.

CONTENT THAT TOBIAS had things well in hand, Kat sat cross-legged about three yards from the dog run and closed her eyes. She saw the black wedge shimmering before her and stepped up and into it. On the other side, she stepped down into the Void. It was warm and desert-like, dimmer than the bright California afternoon she'd just stepped out of. A few tumbleweeds blew by, which Kat knew were not tumbleweeds at all but bound spirits. She saw mountains in the distance in one direction and knew it was just a short journey to the Abyss in the other. She looked around for Sandalphon but didn't see any. "Aunt Beast!" she shouted. Mere moments later, she heard the rumble of large, heavy feet.

TOBIAS AND BARNEY'S barking and snarling continued unabated.

"What's she doing?" Tapper asked Richard. "She's just sitting there with her eyes closed."

"Hard to tell. My guess is that she's just stepped into the Void and is enlisting the help of some Sandalphon."

"What the fuck is a Sandal...whatsit?"

"It's a creature—an angel of sorts. It helps."

"That's fucking weird, and I'll take your word for it. But *this* is not good television."

"Maybe later I can do a voice-over explaining what's going on. Or you could insert a cartoon of what is actually happening in her head."

Tapper blinked and started to chew on her lower lip, and Richard could almost see the wheels spinning in her brain.

———

KAT SMOTHERED her face in Aunt Beast's fur, feeling her soft solidity, delighting in the smell of her otherworldly musk. She felt the great beast lower her head affectionately. Emerging from her hug, she saw that there were four of the beings surrounding her like the points of a compass. The Sandalphon were tall, nearly nine feet as close as Kat could estimate. Their bodies were curved, and they seemed to loom and sway above her in time to some lugubrious music she could not hear. They appeared to have no arms, and their heavy feet were elephantine. Their fur was dark brown, soft and prodigious. "Are you here to protect me?" she asked, but she knew the answer. The Sandalphon did not speak, but they certainly communicated. Feeling supported, empowered—certainly encouraged—Kat cried out again with authority. "I call out to the Angel of the Air. Come quickly, I beg you. I need your help!"

The answer to her plea was swift. The air around her whipped up into a whirlwind. She felt herself being bolstered by Aunt Beast behind her, and she clutched at a handful of fur to steady herself against the buffeting air. She forced her eyes open and saw a being emerge from the tempest—a being composed of a thousand eyes, a corona of radiant hair extending in every direction, and a thousand swords held aloft and ready to strike in every conceivable direction. The Angel was breathtaking, and the air around it crackled with energy. Despite knowing what to expect, Kat felt terrified, and she took an involuntary step backwards. Aunt Beast pressed gently against her back and nudged her toward the shining being. Kat understood her encouragement. Closing her eyes, she took a deep breath, screwed up her courage, and stepped forward. She strode directly toward the angel, ignoring the shimmering, flashing swords swishing perilously close to her. Then she took a final step forward, directly *into* the angel, merging with it, appropriating it into herself—or perhaps losing herself in it. She felt a great inrushing of energy and experienced several moments of vertigo. She was both small and inconceivably large, ancient yet young, many but one.

Opening her eyes, she saw the landscape of the Void and the Sandalphon shimmering with light that seemed to come from within rather than reflected out—radiating from them and yet somehow from beyond them. "That is *glory*," she breathed. She realized that now she was seeing not just through two human eyes, but through a thousand angelic eyes—and the view was kaleidoscopic, even psychedelic. She wondered if perhaps what she was seeing was closer to what God sees.

Looking down she saw that she and the Angel of the Air were indeed one, and yet smaller versions of the Angel were buzzing all around her, preparing her. A breastplate was fastened to her chest by a flock of them. Gauntlets were fastened to her forearms and grieves to her shins. Several others brought to her hand a sword. She wondered if these were metaphorical or real. Then she wondered if it mattered. The hilt of the sword was solid in her hand, the grip was sure and firm. It was heavy but felt well-balanced in her grip, as if it had been crafted specifically for her height and weight. It didn't bother her at all that she didn't know how to use a sword—she instinctively knew how to use *this* one.

Having fully equipped her, the smaller angels dissipated. Kat turned to Aunt Beast and her companions. "Wait for me, please. I should be coming right back."

Aunt Beast bowed. Kat squared her shoulders and strode confidently toward the portal that led in and out of the Void.

———

IN THE OUTER WORLD, Kat leaped from her seated position to her feet. The motion was so sudden, so unexpected, that several people jumped. Kat looked at everyone assembled in the yard and saw Mrs. Barker clutching at her son's shoulders, staring at her anxiously. She saw Richard looking uncertain and even a little frightened. She saw Terry, who smiled at her and winked. *He sees,* she thought. Terry had always been the most sensitive of all the Blackfriars. *If anyone could see what I've become, he can.* She smiled and winked back. "Give 'em hell," Terry shouted. She bowed briefly in his direction, then turned toward the dog run.

Her eyes went wide, because now she could see the dog clearly; not just the puppet corpse that had once been Barney, but the demon coiled up inside him, as well. Kat cocked her head, trying to see it from different angles. She realized this was easier to do if she moved her sight from one set of eyes to another, rather than simply moving her head. The demon had taken the shape of what looked like a large shrimp living inside the dog, sending out feelers like the many feet of a crawdad into its body, connecting with spine and nerves and arteries, bludgeoning it from the inside into something pretending to be life.

She held her arm up, the one with the sword. She wondered if anyone else could see the sword. *Terry can,* she thought. Then she heard Terry's voice, snapping a command in Enochian. Tobias stood down, ceasing his barking. He laid down instantly in the grass, panting and watching with interest. Barney gave Tobias a few more aggressive retorts then looked around as if confused.

"I call upon the demon Tenalphador," Kat announced. "You will answer me."

Barney froze, then slowly turned his head to look at Kat with one mad and ferocious eye.

"Tenalphador, are you willing to leave of your own accord?"

The dog's lips pulled back into a black, malevolent grin. "Hades is coming," the dog breathed in raspy but intelligible English. "And Hell and death are with him."

Kat turned to face Mrs. Barker. "Open the run," she ordered.

Mrs. Barker, eyes wide, turned to face her son. "Stay right here," she commanded. He did not object. She stumbled as she approached the dog run, and her hands shook as she took up the lock. The fur on Barney's haunches stood straight up, and a low growl began again in his throat. Mrs. Barker removed the lock but did not undo the catch. She stepped back toward her son and stood behind him, placing her arm around his chest protectively.

Richard made to intercept Kat, but she held up her gauntleted hand and he stopped. She strode to the door of the run and slid open the catch. The door swung inside, and she moved to fill the doorway before the dog could escape. She swung the door behind her.

Snarling, drooling, and back hunched, Barney backed away from her, poised to spring. Calmly, she fastened the latch and turned toward the dog. She narrowed her eyes. "Last chance, asshole," she said. "Are you willing to leave of your own free will?"

In answer, the dog sprang at her. She raised her left arm protectively, and Barney's teeth sunk themselves into the meat of her arm. With her other hand, she brought the sword to bear, neatly severing the silver cord that tied the demon to the host body of the dog. Tossing the sword aside, she snatched at the crustaceous body of the demon, wresting it free of the dog's spine and nervous system, dragging it backwards...and up...and out.

The body of the dog fell to the ground like a bag of meat, all semblance of life shorn from it in an instant. Holding the demon's body aloft and away from her person, Kat sat down cross-legged, closed her eyes, and leaped through the portal into the Void. Aunt Beast was waiting for her. "To the Abyss," she announced. "Let's toss this motherfucker back to the level of hell where he belongs."

MONDAY

Surrendering to total depravity,
they corrupted, murdered,
or cannibalized each other
and in their madness
prepared for war with God...
trying to fortify earth against heaven
and, in their delirium,
to do battle with the supreme Ruler himself.
—*Eusebius,* The Church History,
translated by Paul L. Maier

18

RICHARD WAS STILL groggy after morning prayer. "Coffee," he said, stumbling into the kitchen. Brian wasn't there with coffee ready, however. Instead, he saw Marco, once again in his underwear, wrestling with something on the stove that was beginning to burn. Tobias was at rapt attention, sniffing up at the stove. "Good God, Marco, whoever informed you that you could cook?"

"I've been cooking for myself since I was seven," he said.

"That is a lack of sufficient modelin', if you ask me," Dylan said, close behind Richard.

"Breakfast will be served in five minutes," Marco announced.

"Whether it's edible or not," Richard warned. He wandered to the back door and looked out the window at the cottage. Dark clouds were starting to gather. "I get worried when Terry isn't at prayer."

"Ah hear ya," Dylan agreed, reaching past Marco to turn on the stove under the kettle. "No one loves prayin' much as the lil' guy."

"Should I check on him?" Richard asked.

"You know, when people are depressed, they sleep," Marco offered.

Richard nodded. "But it's situational, not clinical."

"He's just got to go through it. You gotta *let* him go through it."

"I don't have to like it."

"I don't think any of us do."

"Ah certainly don't. The meals around here are suffrin' somethin' terrible," Dylan opined. He held a piece of bacon out to Tobias, who snatched it up greedily.

"Hey!" Marco objected. "And thanks for the vote of confidence."

Richard noted that his underwear had Chewbacca on the crotch. "Is all of your underwear Star Wars-themed?" he asked.

"Everyone's entitled to their religious denomination," Marco turned back to the stove. "I expect you have Jesus winking out of your pecker-hole."

"I am proud to say that I do not have even one pair of Jesus-themed underwear."

"So you're just jealous," Marco announced.

"Morning," Kat said, emerging from the back stairs. No sooner had she stepped down than she held her hands up to block her own vision. "Holy Christ, Marco, could you put on a bathrobe or something?"

"It's a sin to be ashamed of the glory of man," Marco said, striking a pose that, ironically, accentuated his pronounced beer-belly.

"It's a sin to pretend to represent the glory of man," Kat retorted.

"That's cold, sister," Marco pointed his spatula at her.

"Keep that thing in your underoos, Mister."

They considered each other for a few seconds, which might have gone on longer had Dylan not announced, "Uh, dude, smoke."

Marco turned and rescued what was left of the eggs.

"They'd burn less if you didn't fry the cheese," Dylan pointed out.

"I don't need cooking tips from you."

"Ah'm just sayin'," Dylan poured himself a cup of hot water and snatched a tea bag from one of the containers on the counter. Tobias scuttled under the table.

"You get a pass," Marco said to Kat over his shoulder. "But only because you kicked ass so phenomenally yesterday. Where the fuck did you learn that trick?"

She shrugged. "One reads."

"Have you ever seen anything like it?" Richard asked, clearly proud of her.

"Let's just say there was a lesser banishing ritual with my name on it when I got home," Marco shuddered. "Scared the bejeezus out of me."

"You see, that's what I don't get," Kat said. "You're a magickian, and you're afraid of demons?"

"I'm not a fucking Goetic magickian," Marco objected. "I'm just your ordinary, run-of-the-mill Thelemite. We might traffic in spirits or elementals, but demons? No, no, no. No thank you. I have enough problems without handcuffing myself to pure evil."

"That's actually a pretty apt description," Richard said, his eyebrows bouncing high on his forehead.

"What's burning?" Mikael asked, crouching to clear the ceiling as he came down the back stairs. "Smells like charcoal...and cheese."

"You two can go without," Marco pronounced to Dylan and Mikael.

"What?" Mikael objected. "All I said was—"

"Hey, where's Randy?" Kat asked, looking in the mirror. She turned up the guitar amplifier. "Randy!" She called.

"Maybe he's not up yet," Mikael suggested.

"He's up," Marco said. "He snagged some bacon, so I know." Marco wiped his hands on his apron and leaned over, shoulder-to-shoulder with Kat, staring into the mirror. "See? He's right there—" he pointed at a ghostly, translucent image that was barely visible.

Kat's hand leaped to her mouth. "Oh, God!" she exclaimed. "He's fading!"

"He's been fading fer some time now," Dylan agreed. "Everyone's noticed. Ah think you noticed, too. Ah think you just didn't want to notice."

Kat looked at Dylan and blinked back tears.

"It happens," Richard said, his voice soft. "Spirits aren't supposed to be disembodied. The ectoplasm dissipates over time."

"Did you know this was going to happen?"

Richard moved his head back and forth, "I hoped the mirror

would serve as a body of sorts, that it would stabilize him. But I suspected that this might happen. I just...I didn't want to alarm you."

She nodded, biting her lip. "Randy, can you hear me?"

"Course I can hear you," came a thin response. Kat turned the speaker all the way up, filling the air with static and a sixty-cycle hum.

"Do you know what's happening to you?"

"Yeah. I'm trying to figure out the best way to stab my eyes out so I don't have to watch this fat naked black guy cook my breakfast."

"No, Randy. What does it feel like to be fading out?"

"What the hell are you talking about?"

"Look at your hand," she said. She could barely see him raise it up.

"It's an off day," he dismissed her. "Everyone has an off day."

"Randy, I think you're fooling yourself. I think you're...dying."

"I gotta tell you, little sister, living in this mirror is not really living."

Kat turned and her face contorted as she fought back tears. She looked at Richard. "What will happen to him?"

"He'll just fade out," Richard said. "What happens when smoke gets dissipated in the air?"

"And then he'll just be gone? He won't go anywhere else, like heaven or hell?"

"Spirits need bodies," Richard explained. "Even spiritual bodies. Randy gave up his body to enter an angel's body, remember? And then he left the angel's body. There's no other body for him to enter. Thank God the angels put him in that mirror, or you wouldn't have had the time with him that you have."

"Can he enter another human body, or a dog's body—like the angel that's in Toby?"

"Like who? And you'd need a person's permission."

"I'd give him mine," she said.

"I don't know," Richard said. "At one time, that might have worked. But I think he's too far gone. If we even attempted a transfer, I'm pretty sure he wouldn't make it."

"Are you talking about what I think you're talking about?" Randy asked, his voice strong and loud now, although filled with buzzing and crackling.

"Randy, we're not sure it would work, but do you want to share my body?"

"Does it mean having sex with him?" the ghostly image pointed vaguely at Mikael.

"Uh...yeah, it would."

"Kill me right fucking now."

"You can't mean that."

"He's not putting his dick in *my* mouth."

Kat put her head in her hands. "Randy...do you always have to be so mean? We're trying to help you."

"I think you've helped enough," his image wandered through the mirror-image kitchen, into the office hallway. "I'm going to go surf some porn."

Kat blew air through her cheeks and pushed the hair out of her eyes.

Richard put a hand on her shoulder. "You can't help everyone. You know that."

"But I *want* to help him."

"He's never made that easy."

"No."

"Uh, folks, you have to see something," Susan's head poked around the corner.

"Can it wait?" Marco asked, brandishing a plate full of eggs. "Breakfast is served."

"Why are the eggs black?" Mikael asked.

"Et tu, homie?" Marco asked. "I've had it up to here with the racist bullshit around this place."

"I think you need to see this *now*," Susan said, her voice trailing off as she returned to her computer.

They trotted after her, Marco included, and hovered over her shoulder as she pointed to her computer screen. "Okay, so just for a lark, I decided to check the Oakland Crime Watch Map for the time when our nuns were murdered. Lookie here."

Richard whistled. In a radius of about four blocks, there were seven gray circles with "H" in the middle of them.

"What's the 'H' for?" Marco asked.

"I'm guessing 'H' is for homicide," Richard suggested.

"You would be guessing correctly," Susan said, tapping some keys. The view zoomed out. Although there were numerous multi-colored crime icons, there were only seven gray "H's" in the entire city.

"That's not a coincidence," Richard said.

"No," Susan said. "Your sigil might have been directed toward specific targets, but it wasn't *contained*."

"It has a sphere of influence," Dylan said, moving his finger around the four-block circle.

"Now look at this," Susan moved her mouse around, and a whole new set of crime icons popped up over the Oakland map.

"What are we seeing now?" Richard asked.

"This is from this time yesterday," she said. About a hundred different-colored crime icons dotted the map, seemingly at random. "See any patterns?"

"Not really," Mikael answered.

"So now let's see what the map has to say about *now*," Susan said. "This is being updated in real time. Notice anything different?"

Richard straightened up. "Criminey shit," he breathed.

This time there were about twenty clusters of particular colors, heavy concentrations of crimes of like variety, each centered on a different neighborhood.

"That's not normal," Marco breathed.

"No," Susan agreed.

"We've gotta find out what's causing those," Dylan said.

"Yeah," Richard said, running his hand through his thinning hair. "Let's get our gear. We'll go out in teams. Unless my guess is off, we've got about twenty demons loose on the Oakland public."

19

RICHARD GLANCED over at Terry in the passenger seat. The elfin friar was staring straight ahead, looking at nothing. "Are you mad at me," Richard asked, "because I dragged you out of the cottage and wouldn't let you sulk?"

Terry looked away from him, out the passenger window.

"Fuck you," Richard said. "You know what? We've got demons popping up all over Oakland. Your wallowing in self-pity is a luxury we can't afford right now. So snap the fuck out of it." *That wasn't good,* he thought to himself. *You can't lose your temper like that.*

Terry turned and glared at him. "I did a bad thing. I admit that. How long do I have to be punished for it?"

Richard pursed his lips, thinking of a diplomatic way to respond. "Uh, Terry, it's been about twenty-four hours. How long do you think you *should* be punished for it?"

Terry looked down. "Huh, okay. I guess longer than that."

"There will be plenty of time for you and Brian to make up. You just need to give him some space. He has to miss you enough to forgive you." Richard offered a reassuring smile.

"You want to know what bothers me?" Terry asked, looking out the window again.

"What's that?" Richard pulled onto the on-ramp to Highway 24, positioning the car for a quick transfer to the 980 toward San Leandro.

"That it's somehow all my fault."

"Um...you *did* fuck the Ryde driver," Richard said.

"But I wouldn't have if...if I'd been *getting* any," Terry slouched. "I mean, it's all fun fun fun 'til daddy takes the penis away."

Richard glanced over and blinked. "Meaning?"

"When we were having sex, like twice a day, it was just fine. I didn't need to look anywhere else. I love Brian. He's the best top-dog I've ever had."

"Terry, surely you know that that level of sexual activity is super-human. I can see twice a day when you're in your early twenties and just starting a relationship. But you're both past forty now, and you've been together almost ten years. You know what's normal? Once a week is normal."

"Normal for who? Heteronormative research scientists? *Glamour* magazine reporters?"

"What are you even talking about?"

"It's not normal for *me*! I get horny."

"We all get horny. Susan and Kat get horny."

"But I'm...different."

"*Special*?"

"You say that like it's a bad thing."

"Newsflash—"

"Nobody likes it when people say, 'Newsflash.' So just don't."

"You are *not* special. You're normal."

"I have *super-normal* libido levels!"

"And very normal relationships. And commitments. Your libido doesn't make you special. It doesn't suspend the laws of physics. It doesn't exempt you from the ethical standards that we expect of each other."

"I'm not accountable to you."

"The fuck you're not." Keeping only one eye on the road, Richard turned and shook his finger in Terry's face. "You are fucking accountable to every member of this Order. You are accountable to your part-ner. You are accountable to every person you are in relationship with, to everyone who counts on you, to everyone who fucking *cares* about you."

"So I'll go off to live in a cave."

"You do that. I'll pack you a Bunsen burner and a can opener. Oh, and a teddy bear, so you'll have someone to watch you pout."

"Fuck you," Terry said.

Richard exited at Hegenberger and turned left toward the Coliseum.

"I love you," Richard said. "Even if you *are* being a prick."

"Fuck you."

"I love you."

"FUCK FUCK FUCK you!"

Richard couldn't stop the smile curling up one lip. "Love you," he said as quickly as he could.

Terry stared hard out the passenger window, arms folded.

"Any guesses about who we're dealing with, here?" Richard asked.

"What do you mean?"

"Susan saw a spike in shooting in the Havenscourt/Coliseum neighborhood."

"Shooting?"

"Don't worry, I brought vests."

"They don't fit me very well. Too big."

"You'll make do. Just think, they'll cover your naughty-bits too. Think of it as insurance." Richard turned left at the KFC on International Boulevard. Then he tried again. "Who are we *likely* to be dealing with?"

"Shooting? Gotta be a wrath demon. Could be Tispis again, but I don't think so. I don't think it will even be in Nuudjal's host."

"Why?"

"Guns are another order of wrath. I think it's more likely to be someone in Efrinick's host, or Ludgemin's."

"Care to lay odds on any particular demon, then?"

Terry shook his head. "I can think of about twelve who would be good candidates, and about twenty others who are possible."

"So who do we ask for research on this?"

Terry looked at him for the first time. "I hadn't thought of that." Brian was usually their go-to research person. "Do you think..."

"I think Brian needs space."

"Susan?"

"Susan doesn't have the expertise."

Terry whipped out his phone and his thumbs started flying. "There's an app for sigils," he said. "I just read about it...here it is. Downloading now." He shrugged. "Not as good as Brian, but let's see if it helps."

Richard nodded. "Shoot Dylan a link to that, will you?" Terry nodded.

Richard slowed down and glanced at the address Susan had written down for him. 6249 International. He found it and pulled over. It seemed to be the epicenter for the shooting incidents, or close enough. It was a busy commercial area, although Richard could see residences down one of the side streets.

"All right, let's suit up," Richard said. He reached into the back seat and grabbed the bulletproof vests he'd stowed earlier. He handed the smaller one to Terry and began fastening his own velcro. The vests were black, so they didn't really stand out much over their black cassocks. Mostly they just made their Western clerical garb look exotic, even vaguely Japanese. Richard got out of the car and listened. Sure enough, he heard gunfire.

That wasn't unusual in Oakland. This neighborhood was gritty—a perfect example of the urban blight that had plagued Oakland for decades. Any resident would tell you that they heard gunfire daily, often several times a day. Richard heard another burst, this one coming from another direction and sounding like an automatic weapon. Richard heard screams and waved for Terry to follow. Terry closed the door of the beat up Corolla and jogged after Richard.

"Okay, this is a big neighborhood, and the pattern Susan pulled up was pretty broad. Let's split up and see if we can find a sigil. I'll take the side streets that way," he pointed west, "you take them this way," he said, pointing east. "Call my cell if you find anything. If you don't, let's meet back here in a half hour. Okay?"

Terry nodded and scrambled away from him, perhaps a little too eagerly. *Well, I was pretty tough on him,* Richard thought. He crossed the busy traffic and headed toward one of the side streets. Then he felt a sudden, stinging pain on his ear. He reached up, wondering if he'd been stung by a bee, but when he drew his hand back, he saw it was drenched with blood. It took him a moment to realize what had happened. When he did, Richard dove for the sidewalk. Spread-eagled and faced down, he raised his head and took a look around just in time to see a telephone pole splinter in front of him, torn apart by a barrage of bullets. He strained to catch sight of the shooters. *Surely these can't just be disembodied bullets,* he thought. He couldn't even imagine what kind of magick could produce such an effect. But no, a car zipped past, with a young Hispanic man leaning out the window, firing behind him at a black SUV that had seen better days. Just as it roared out of Richard's sight, he saw a passenger lean out and return fire. He heard another bullet zing over his head. The sound of arguing came from the direction of the residential street just to his left. He had to be close to the sigil—he felt it in his bones, and there was just too much gunplay for it to be otherwise. He rose up into a crouch and, clinging to the cinder-block wall of the mini-mart close by, he inched toward the houses. He ducked into the alley behind the mini-mart and leaned against the wall next to a dumpster, its broad metal side providing decent cover from the street.

Richard heard voices coming close and made himself small, trying to hide completely behind the dumpster. A young, African-American couple came into view. She was slapping him, and he was batting away her arms with one hand, holding a gleaming silver pistol aloft with the other. Richard couldn't figure out what the woman was angry about, but the man wasn't able to get more than a couple words in. The woman was crying now and, with his free hand, he held her at arm's length as she wind milled her own fists toward him ineffectually. There was another sharp crack, and the young woman dropped to the pavement like a stone. The man started shouting, "No, you motherfuckers!" and began shooting at anyone and everything. Richard squeezed himself out of the man's line of sight, putting as much of the dumpster between them as he could. He backed up to the wall of the mini-mart, still crouching, and steadied himself with his hands on the ground. He felt something warm and sticky beneath him and he closed his eyes, fully expecting it to be blood. Slowly he brought his hand up to his face. His eyes widened as he saw not blood, but candle wax.

Barely daring to breathe, he turned and looked up at the wall behind him. Staring down at him was a massive sigil, spray-painted over most of the back wall of the mini-mart. A string of votive candles guttered at the place where the wall met the alley, sending hot wax onto the cement in white rivulets. Richard speed dialed Terry and waited for him to pick up. It rang and rang. Richard's eyes grew wide as the call shunted into voicemail. He dialed a second time and got voicemail again. "Holy fucking shit," he breathed. "Jesus, God, don't let him be dead." Then he closed his eyes, drew a deep breath, and stood up to his full height. "Comin' for you, buddy."

20

LARCH READ the text message and grinned. The last of the Oakland sigils was in place. Purderabo was moving on to Emeryville. "That will keep them busy," he said to himself. "Time to get busy myself." He went into his bedroom and shut the door. He began to unbutton his shirt, and as he did, he wandered almost unconsciously toward the window. It was a muggy, Indian-summer afternoon. The heat was almost unbearable, which made it quite an anomalous day in San Francisco. He drew his shirt off and hung it on the back of a chair. The buzz of traffic blew through the window with the slight breeze. He watched the curtain ripple, a luminous sheet of gossamer. It looked like a beacon, breaking into the gloom of his bedroom—a herald of some rumored glory, a visitation. He pulled off his trousers and hung them on the back of the chair, too. Then he did the same with his briefs.

He sat on the bed and noticed how still everything was. He could just be still, too. He could just breath. And time would stop. He tried it, but the wind blew the curtain again, and it rippled again. Like Heraclitus' river, it reminded him of the relentlessness of time. *The stillness is an illusion,* he thought. *The world is being drawn toward its own tyrannous end. Do not be beguiled.*

He pulled open the night table drawer and withdrew a squat jar. Unscrewing the lid, he held it beneath his nose and breathed deeply. The scent of precious essences and oils wafted up, giving him a chill. The scent of it propelled him back to his childhood, following his father around the sacristy. He remembered pulling the stopper out of a cruet of oil, how the sharp, spicy aroma had intoxicated him—until the back of his father's hand caught him in the temple and send the cruet and himself flying. Both shattered against the sacrarium, the cut glass cruet into a thousand shards, the boy's dignity and safety destroyed as well.

It was a bitter memory, and one he had almost forgotten. It had been one of many times his father had humiliated him, struck him, abandoned him. The boy knew he was an evil thing—born out of wedlock and an embarrassment to both his mother and to his father, the priest, who could never acknowledge him publicly. God might have pronounced that Jesus was his beloved son, but Larch would never hear those words.

He sighed and gathered his thoughts. He reminded himself that his father was not here, that this was not church, that this was not the oil blessed by his father's bishop. It was the ointment of Hashanin, and while many of the spices infused in it were the same, it was consecrated for a very different purpose indeed.

He focused his attention in a single point, infusing the ointment with his magickal intention, then lowered two fingers into the jar. He drew forth a bit of the ointment and began to apply it to his feet, his legs, his thighs, and his genitals. He smeared the ointment on every part of him he could reach, and used a cotton ball fixed to a back scratcher to reach between his shoulder blades.

All the while he chanted the names of the great beings whose power and guidance he sought—the enemies of his Enemy, whom his father had served. He smiled at the thought that his Enemy's enemies were his friends by default. Having anointed his neck, his cheeks, his temples, and the top of his head, he bent low again and began a second anointing. This time he did not cover everything; only certain parts. His incantations changed as well, from greeting to entreaty. He asked the great beings for wisdom, for cunning, for strength and endurance. As he did so, he anointed the soles of his feet, the palms of his hands, his eyelids, and his lips. This completed, he began the third and final anointing. This time his chant became one of praise. The great beings were indeed great. They were worthy of worship. They were worthy of his fealty and service. He traced an inverted pentagram on his chest as he sang.

His body felt strangely cool, despite the afternoon heat wave. He felt as if he were shimmering, as if he were being briefly touched by ice or perhaps by flame—it was hard to tell. When he moved, though, he felt a delicious iciness. His head swam with a potent intoxication, and he quickly sank to the bed. He arranged his pillow and laid back on it, drawing up his legs, and lying flat on the comforter. He watched the curtain ripple again into the room and felt the blessed breeze waft over his naked skin.

Then he ascended.

21

Mikael exited Highway 13 at the main Montclair exit but got no further than the Safeway. "Will you look at that?" Dylan drawled. It looked like a whole fleet of ambulances, zipping one way or the other. Several of them were clustered at a dead stop at a stoplight.

"Can you go around?" Kat asked.

"These streets aren't exactly wide," Mikael said. "But there's a parking spot. Let's just get out and walk."

"Susan marked that corner right over there as the epicenter of all the drug-related crimes," Kat pointed about a block ahead of them. "This is one of the ritziest areas in Oakland. It's not the kind of place I think of as having a drug problem." She got out of the car, shut the door behind herself, and made for the trunk to grab her kit bag.

"Waal, drug problems are no respecter of persons," Dylan shut his own door and waddled to the rear of the car to retrieve his own bag. "Rich or poor, it don't matter none."

"Sometimes different drugs," Mikael added.

"Sometimes, but you'd be surprised," Dylan said. "Ah speak from experience, o' course."

They set out toward one of the ambulances, and Kat stopped. A young man was stretched out on the pavement, his eyes sightlessly looking heavenward. Above him, two paramedics worked feverishly. "Gone," one of them said, feeling at the young man's neck. Wordless, they sat still for a few moments. Then they covered the young man's face and loaded the gurney into the ambulance. Kat could see that there were already other gurneys inside.

"This is terrible," she said. She approached one of the paramedics, a thirty-something woman with her hair pulled back out of her eyes in a tight bun. "What did he die of?"

"Overdose," she said. Kat realized that she probably should not have told her that, but she was grateful that she had. The young woman went on, "They all did. We've got three of them loaded up. And all of these," she waved at the other ambulances, many from competing companies. "All drugs. I don't understand it. We get a couple of calls a day for this kind of shit, but I've never seen it all at once like this. What's going on?" Kat understood that the question was rhetorical. The woman didn't expect Kat to know. Except that she did.

"Can you direct us to where most of them are happening?" Mikael asked.

"They're all over," the paramedic said. "But there's more of them by the sports bar. You know, McGills."

"Right over there. That's the spot Susan indicated," Kat whispered.

"Ah know it," Dylan said. "They got a good whisky selection. Uh... can you tell us what that poor guy OD'd on?"

"Vicodin. Most of them have been. Or Norco, or Oxy, or some other prescription opiates. It's like they all just...emptied their bottles."

"Thank you fer tryin'," Dylan said, placing his hand on her arm. She looked up to see the big bear of a man for the first time. She smiled weakly. He squeezed her arm and set off toward the bar.

"Sounds like some kind of compulsion," Kat said.

"Isn't all drug abuse compulsion?" Mikael asked.

"That's as good a word as Ah ken think of," Dylan said. He stopped and pointed.

At first, Kat only saw two other ambulances, parked at odd angles in the middle of the street. Then she saw people lying on the sidewalks and a young woman staggering out into the middle of the street. *At least there are no cars on the street*, Kat thought, watching the young woman nearly topple over several times as she tried to cross. She was obviously stoned out of her mind, and Kat could guess on what.

"Do you see it?" Dylan asked.

"You mean her? I've got to help her," Kat said.

"Ah mean the sigil. Look!" He pointed at the maroon canvas awning that circled the McGills' exterior.

Kat looked up. "Oh my. Okay, yeah." Spray painted in white on the awning was what was unmistakably a sigil.

Dylan squinted. "An' there's something above it, too."

Kat shrieked as the woman fell and darted across the street toward her. By the time she reached her, the woman was spread-eagled near the waffle house. Kat knelt by her and helped her sit up. "Hey, take it easy. Just sit here. I don't want you to hit your head."

The woman's eyes were barely open slits, and she grinned. "I'm *fiiiiine*," she said.

"You're not fine," Kat said, "Although I'll wager you're not feeling any pain." She prayed that there hadn't been many pills in whatever bottle the woman had savaged. "Sit here, I'm going to go and get you help."

Out of the corner of her eye, she saw Dylan giving Mikael a leg up toward the awning. She frowned, wondering what they were hoping to achieve but didn't stop to ask. Instead, she ran straight toward one of the paramedics. Reaching him, she shook his shoulder but screamed when he fell over onto the street. His head made a sickening "thuck" sound when it hit the pavement. A needle stuck out of his arm at an alarming angle.

"What's wrong?" Dylan called over his shoulder.

Kat blinked, looking around for someone else. There were plenty of ambulances, and plenty of bodies, but frightfully few moving people on the street. The surreality of it rushed over her, and she staggered. "Focus," she said out loud to herself. She jumped up into the nearest ambulance and rummaged around in the cabinet until she found an EpiPen. Kat turned and in the corner of her eye she saw a glass vial that said "morphine." She looked at the EpiPen in her hand then back at the vial.

She started looking for a needle and rummaged through another shelf until she found one. She filled the syringe with morphine, pulling as much into it as she could. She had no idea what the proper dose should be. She just knew that she needed it, more than she had ever needed anything. She had gotten shots before, but she had never given one and had never actually watched that closely. As she tried to position the needle where it might possibly enter her vein, she fumbled it, dropping the syringe onto the ambulance's black rubber floor mat. "Shit," she said out loud. She picked it up and tried again, her tongue stuck out of one side of her mouth as she concentrated. She felt it slide in and experienced a brief pinprick of pain that was quickly relieved.

22

CAPTAIN HERRER BLEW into the room. "Tell me what you've got on the witchcraft murder," she said. Her ever-present coffee mug was in her hand, and her eyes looked baggier than usual.

Cain's nostril's twitched. "That's not coffee from *our* pot."

"No it isn't, Mr. Nose. It's a *cafe au lait* from Tucker's across the street, poured into my cup. Sue me."

He stood up and gave her a grim smile. "We sent an inquiry to that Craigslist ad. No response yet."

"Can I see it?"

Cain nodded and pulled up the Word file he'd used to craft the message. "Posing as the same age and gender as the victim," Herrer noted. "Good. Not race?"

"We figured that would be a little too close to the mark. Besides, Consuela didn't mention being Latino in her initial email to him," he said, pointing to a stack of printouts that the computer lab had produced.

"Were the tech-wizards able to retrieve any of the killer's messages to her?"

"Yep. Looks like they met at a place called the Cloven Hoof in SF."

"Christ, that place draws freaks like a magnet. Where's Perry?"

"She's with the wizards—" Cain started when Perry interrupted him.

"I'm right here, and you've got to see something, Cap. In the lab. You too, Cain."

Cain and Herrer exchanged a look, then Cain shrugged and turned to follow his partner. Less than a minute later they were speed walking into the computer lab, barely able to keep up with Perry. Instead of the pastel walls of the squad room, the computer lab was painted the yellow and purple of UC Berkeley's school colors. "Whatcha got?" Herrer asked.

"Check out this grid," Anastasio said, pointing to a large screen television. Cain wasn't fond of him. He was of that particular breed of computer nerd who eschewed showering and the brushing of teeth and wore clothes that looked like they were made for someone much larger. Maybe other folks could tolerate the man's stench, but Cain's nose was...sensitive. He had to admit that the smelly bastard was good with a hard drive, though.

"What are we looking at?" Herrer asked.

"This is the real-time 911 operator grid in Oakland."

Herrer's eyes narrowed as she looked at it. Across a bright green map of Oakland, little pinpoints of yellow light indicated the approximate location of every caller. Cain had seen these maps for most of the East Bay cities, but usually when used as evidence. He had even seen such maps of Oakland. But he he had never seen anything that looked like this. Oakland saw a lot more crime than Berkeley did, but this activity was of a completely different order. "That can't be real," Cain said.

"It's real," Perry confirmed. "Oakland is completely paralyzed. They're calling on neighboring cities to send them cops."

"I haven't heard anything about this," Herrer said.

"I think that's because they're calling way over your head, and they're getting stonewalled."

"Why would we refuse to send backup?"

"I've got a theory," Anastasio said. He pulled up another screen, this one of the 911 calls in Emeryville. The clusters of calls were smaller than the ones in Oakland, but they were there, and they seemed to be growing. "It's spreading. And Berkeley sure as shit doesn't want it spreading here."

"Or if it does, we're going to need all hands on deck," Herrer nodded.

"My guess is we'll be setting up barriers soon," Perry offered.

"That would be pretty extreme," Herrer countered. "It's not a virus, after all."

"How do you know? What else could cause something like this?"

"A *crime* virus?" Herrer put her hands on her hips. "Are you shitting me?"

"I'm just saying we don't know until we know, so we shouldn't rule anything out."

Herrer harrumphed. "Okay, keep thinking out of the fucking box, Perry. Just don't go down any rabbit holes." Her cell phone buzzed. "Herrer," she said, answering it. She screwed her eyes shut as she listened. "Hey what about—" She lowered her phone. "Asshole."

"Who was that?" Perry asked.

"That was Julabi in the DA's office, calling to bore out my prostate." Cain was about to point out that she didn't have a prostate when she continued. "They want an arrest in this case, and they want it yesterday."

"They'll just have to wait," Perry said. "We're working it as hard as we can."

"Yeah, but now we've got the UC regents breathing down the back of our necks. They want to see some action."

"Who the fuck are they?"

"In case you haven't noticed, they are the not-so-secret cabal that actually runs this town," Herrer said, running her fingers through her hair in exasperation.

"Can we go back to the squad room?" Cain asked. He leaned in to whisper, "You know, some place less...ripe?"

"Sure. Wouldn't want to abuse your sensitive snout." As soon as they'd cleared the door, Herrer said, "I want you to pick up that Wiccan priest guy again."

"Which one?" asked Perry. "The one who's also a Catholic monk?"

"We have a Catholic monk practicing witchcraft?" Herrer asked, stopping in her tracks.

"Yeah, but he seemed pretty clean. Also, he wasn't the leader. That would be the Tomlinson kid. But he seemed clean, too."

Herrer resumed her pace. "There was a time when both of them could have been strung up for witchcraft—especially the monk."

"I hope you're not going to break out into a chorus of 'Happy Days Are Here Again,'" Perry cautioned.

"The charge is murder, and we just need to show that we have a suspect in custody. Don't charge him, just bring him in for questioning."

"We've already questioned him."

"So think of some more questions," Herrer said.

"Begging your pardon, ma'am," Perry said, her voice betraying her irritation. "That's a waste of our time right now."

"If you get the DA off my ass, it's going to *buy* you time. Just do it."

Cain saw Perry literally swallow her expletives. "What the fuck do you think is happening in Oakland?" he asked.

"I've got no frigging idea," Herrer answered. "But trying to figure *that* out would not be a waste of your time." She dismissed them with a fierce look and set off toward her office.

"Let me grab my coat," Cain said.

"You don't need your fucking coat, it's a heat wave out there."

"Oh yeah. The air conditioning in here fools me," Cain said.

"Let's just pick this kid up and get on with it. There's too much bullshit we have to do..."

She was just ranting now, and Cain let her do it for the both of them. He always had more of an even keel than Perry—he didn't get as frustrated or as angry as she did. On the other hand, he didn't have as good a time as she did, either. He was sure of that.

As soon as they cleared the doors of the police station, they were confronted by a gauntlet of reporters. "Shit," Perry said to him out of one side of her mouth as the cameras flashed and people started yelling questions at them.

"Are there any leads in the Occult Killer case?" one woman yelled above the din.

"Does the Occult Killer have anything to do with the sigils popping up all over Oakland?" another reporter asked, squeezing into Perry's personal space. Cain grabbed her hand as she reared back to hit him.

"Don't do it," he whispered. "Don't give them more fodder."

"Do you think it's a coincidence that there are two unsolved occult cases right now?" a third reporter asked.

Perry jerked open the door of their dark blue sedan just moments before Cain reached his side. He quickly scrambled in beside her, and they both slammed their doors. Perry squealed away with no regard for whatever toes might have been unfortunate enough to be between her wheels and the asphalt.

"What the fuck was *that* all about?" she asked. "And what the fuck is a sigil?"

23

RICHARD DUCK-WALKED to the end of the alley then looked up and down the street—it was clear for the moment. Trying to keep his head low, he turned right and scuttled the half block to International Boulevard, careful not to trip on stray trash or the pile of lumber someone had inexplicably dumped on the sidewalk. A bullet struck the cinder block just above his head, and he squatted in reaction. He clung to the corner of a building as he surveyed the street. A few blocks away, he could see pedestrians fleeing. Looking south, he saw a lowrider and a silver SUV parked in the middle of the street, with no apparent sense of order. Huddling for cover behind each were what Richard guessed were rival gang members, waiting for an opportunity to catch the other in the clear. There seemed to be a lull in the shooting at the moment, but he didn't expect that to last. Looking north, he saw the vast urban desert of downtown Oakland, with its prevalent flora—tagged billboards, broken concrete, liquor stores with wrought iron grates over their windows and doors, and a discarded couch legs up on the sidewalk, it's stuffing waving in the wind from a gash in the cushion.

Richard backed up then turned to run back down the alley to the other side of the block. Once he reached the street, he looked around quickly, ready to spring in any direction. No Terry. He squatted again and crept along the side of the mini-mart back to International. Here he got a different view of the feuding gangs, and his attention was drawn to something he had not seen from the other side of the block. Equidistant between the two gangs was—what? Richard squinted, trying to get a clearer view. It might have been a dog, but it was large. It was also draped in red. It could be a piece of furniture.

And then it moved. It reared upright, and Richard clearly saw what was occult to him before—it was a child, maybe four or five years old, wearing a bright red shirt. Richard could not tell for sure whether it was a little boy or girl, but the hair was short, and he? she? looked vaguely Hispanic. "Oh, shit," he said. The gangs seemed to be taking no notice, as they continued their volley of bullets back and forth.

Then from the far side-street, something caught his eye. He was both relieved and alarmed to see that it was Terry. He waved, but Terry didn't seem to see him. His eyes were fixed on the child, and his face was set with grim resolve. He walked upright straight toward the middle of the firefight, straight for the child. Richard could hear that he was talking soothingly but was too far away to make out the words. *I can't leave him out there alone,* Richard thought. *The least I can do is draw fire.* Richard stood up to his full height, pulled the Kevlar vest down as far as it would go, then stepped out into the street. He walked briskly toward Terry, but before he closed even half the distance, he was knocked backward off his feet. He landed on his back and hit his head on the pavement as he fell. A pain like he had never experienced in his life lit up his lower right ribcage and he fought the urge to scream. He forced himself to breathe and explored his ribs with his fingers. He felt a frayed area in the fabric of his vest that had not been there just moments ago. The vest had saved his life, but he had probably also broken a rib. There was no way to know now, and it wasn't important. All that mattered was Terry and that kid.

Richard was not eager to be thrown onto his back again. He moaned involuntarily as he rolled onto his stomach and glanced to both sides. About a hundred yards to the south he saw the order's Corolla, right where they had left it. He dared not stand up. He considered crawling—but the prospect of a bullet in the ass dissuaded him. Instead, he rolled.

He felt ridiculous as he was doing it. *Here I am, a grown man rolling down the middle of the street in downtown Oakland,* he thought, *where I will most likely get either shot or run over.* But neither of those things happened. He reached the car without further incident and, hugging the door, fumbled with the key. He willed his hands to stop shaking long enough to get the key in the lock. He jerked open the door and threw himself in the driver's seat, ducking as he did so.

He scrambled to put the key in the ignition and turned over the engine. Then, keeping his head low, he pulled away from the curb and steered toward Terry. He watched breathlessly as Terry moved forward, taking one deliberate step after another. Richard saw a bullet catch the sleeve of Terry's cassock, knocking his arm to the side with a jerk. But Terry didn't seem to flinch, nor did he stop moving, even for a second. A few steps more and he had reached the child. Terry squatted down, took the child up in his arms, turned, and headed straight for the car.

Richard didn't hesitate. He punched the engine and simultaneously leaned over and popped open the passenger side door. A few feet shy of Terry, he swung the car in an arc to the left. The centrifugal force threw the passenger door open wide and Terry jumped in, still clutching the child close to his chest. Richard gunned it and the tires squealed. He heard a pop and a crash as a bullet took out the back window. The sound made him jump and, for a brief moment, he lost control of the steering wheel. The car fishtailed, but Richard grasped at the wheel with white hands. They dodged an oncoming car, as no one seemed to be obeying traffic laws at the moment. At Hegenberger, Richard threw the wheel to the right, and once again the tires screamed as he accelerated into the turn.

"Are you okay?" he asked Terry as soon as he was sure no one was shooting at them. A passel of police cars passed them on the other side of the street, their lights blazing and sirens in full throat.

"I'm not sure," Terry said. "I'm mostly worried about this one." He loosened his grip, and pulled the child away. Richard could see that it was a little girl, face smudged and eyes wide with fright. She buried her face in Terry's cassock again. "I think she's okay," he said.

"Why didn't you answer your phone?" Richard asked.

"It didn't ring," Terry answered.

"Now is not the time to turn off your ringer, man."

Terry shifted the child on his lap so he could fish into his trouser pocket with his left hand. He pulled out a slim, silver smartphone. "Oh shit," Terry said.

"What?"

Terry held the phone up—there was a circle about the size of quarter cracked into the face of it, and the end of a bullet protruded from the center, as if it were a bullseye.

24

BRIAN HAD no idea where the day had gone. He sat on the edge of his bed in the room filled with Serah Bat Asher memorabilia and stared out the window. It wasn't until the light had begun to mellow into the late afternoon glow that he realized time had been passing. He heard the front door rattle and, a moment later, heard the deadbolt slide. For nearly the first time that day, he ventured out into the hallway. Elsa was struggling with a number of packages, and Brian rushed to help her. With more energy than he'd had all day, he scooped up a grocery bag and bore it quickly to the kitchen, returning a moment later to grab another. Then he joined Elsa in the kitchen as she began to put things away.

"How has your day been?" she asked, turning to the cupboard with a couple cans of black beans.

Brian studied her lean, Nordic features and her long blond hair—different from Chava in almost every possible way—and wondered at how, in this couple anyway, opposites really did seem to attract.

"Quiet," he said.

"That's not a bad thing," she smiled at him but turned away quickly. Brian had always found Elsa a little cool and hard to read. But it was clear how deeply she loved Chava, and that was the important thing. The fact is, he had not had many opportunities to really talk to her, alone anyway. In most events at which they met, she was always kind of Chava's plus one.

"No," he agreed. "I didn't have much energy today, it turned out."

"Are you depressed?" she gave him a slightly concerned look. Elsa was a Marriage and Family Therapist, so her question was not surprising.

"I guess so. But it's not...it seems normal, given the circumstances."

"Yeah. I get it. I know how I'd feel if Chava..." But she just shook her head, as if the thought were too horrible to contemplate.

Brian put the cold cuts in the refrigerator, noting how carefully everything was separated. Chava and Elsa kept a kosher kitchen, and Brian reminded himself to be careful of the rules.

"Want some tea?" Elsa asked.

"Sure," Brian said.

Elsa turned on the stove and then turned to the sink to fill the kettle. "Are you angry?"

Brian sat down at the small table near the window. "Yeah, I guess so. Not as angry as I was. More...hurt now, I guess."

Elsa grabbed two mugs from the cupboard and put a tea bag in each.

"Do you think you can forgive him?"

For a few minutes, Brian couldn't answer. Elsa didn't push him. Instead, she seemed to cherish the silence between them, and Brian didn't feel any pressure to fill up that silence with words. It was refreshing, even healing. Finally, he said, "I think I can. But not yet. I need some time."

The kettle started to sputter, and Brian realized Elsa had not lowered the whistle over its spout. She picked it up and poured steaming water into both of their cups. Then she set one of them in front of Brian and sat across from him. She leaned on her elbow and looked directly into his eyes.

"It's not broken, you know," she said.

"What's not?" he asked.

"Your covenant. With Terry." She took a hesitant sip of the tea. "That's the thing about covenants. They're not like contracts—you know, one party breaks it and it's null-and-void? Covenants are durable. They don't end just because one party fucks up. I mean, where would Israel be now if that were the case? Just think, how many times have we been like Hosea's wife? How many times have we let God down? But our covenant with HaShem is still in effect, because HaShem is faithful to us, even when we are not faithful to HaShem."

Brian considered taking offense. Elsa had converted to Judaism when she and Chava got together and, like many converts, zeal for the faith was strong in her. But a part of him still bristled at being lectured to about his faith by a convert. He chose to let it go. "You're saying that Terry and I are still connected, because *I* am being faithful to *him*, even if he hasn't been faithful to me?"

"Exactly. That's how covenants work. One party fucks up, but the other party stays faithful until the first comes to their senses. You can hold the covenant for both of you. You might not want to, and you might not feel like it, but you can."

"It doesn't seem fair that the one who gets hurt has to work the hardest," Brian looked at his tea.

"No. But since when did fairness enter into it? The question is, what do you want? Do you want to end the covenant you have with Terry? You both have to agree to it in order to set it aside. Or..." she leaned in and waited until he met her eyes, "do you still love him?"

The memories of nearly a decade came flooding over him—of the nights they had slept holding one another tight, of the love they had made, of the life of the Order that he had been thrilled to be part of. He considered the loss of all of that and felt an oily well of despair rise up within him. "Yes," he said, nearly choking on the thickness in his throat. "I still love him."

"Then you'll have to do the work," she leaned back in her chair and took a generous sip from her mug.

"I think it's more complicated than that," he said.

"How so?" she asked. She was patient, kind. It was a side of her he'd never really seen, one that he liked rather a lot.

"It isn't just about Terry. It's about me, too." He looked away. "I feel like I'm just spinning my wheels. I always thought...I always thought I'd do something...important. Not just...cooking. Sometimes I feel like a den mother over there."

Elsa laughed, even though it was clear she tried to stifle it. "What Chava doesn't understand is how you can stand to be with goyim all the time. She doesn't realize how...offensive that is."

"That doesn't bother me," he said. "They're not Jewish, but their love for HaShem is deep. It's real. It's filtered through Jesus, but what are you going to do? They're Christians." He smiled sadly. "And I love them. All of them. They're my family now."

"Are they forcing you to cook?"

"No. I just...do it."

"Are they intentionally keeping you from...whatever it is you want to do?"

Brian thought about it and took a sip of his tea. "Never. I think if I announced I wanted to be a mountain climber tomorrow, Dylan would high-five me, Richard would start researching climbing schools, and Susan would start working out a budget to make sure it happened."

"It sounds like they love you."

"Yeah. They do."

"So if nothing's stopping you from doing what you want to do... what's the problem?"

He didn't know how to answer her. "I don't think I know what it is...what I'm supposed to do."

"Then it isn't really about them, is it?"

Brian felt a strange clarity that was punctuated by a sickness in the pit of his stomach. *Maybe this isn't about the Order or Terry,* he thought. *Maybe this is about me.* It occurred to him that this was about his vocation, his call, his purpose. His cluelessness about his own call frightened him. Several minutes of silence passed between them. "Speaking of call," Brian began.

"Were we?" Elsa smiled.

"Uh...sorry, I think I went a ways down the road without you. Uh...how do you feel about this Serah Bat Asher stuff? I mean, I thought I knew Chava pretty well. But...I didn't know about any of this."

Elsa sighed deeply then leaned over, both elbows on the table. "Oh, God," she said. "Well, I'm not sure I'd speak of that as a *call*, exactly. It's more of a hobby. At least, that's what I tell myself. Between you and me, she's obsessed."

"The guest room feels a little...obsessy," Brian agreed.

"Well, you know, it could be worse," Elsa said, staring into her mug. "She could be a gun nut. Or she could be into dog shows."

Brian shuddered.

"So she spends several hours a week on a global manhunt for a mythical character from the Torah—who she thinks is still alive. Is that crazy?"

"Uh...I thought *you* were the expert on crazy."

"That's what scares me," Elsa said. "If one of my clients was this far gone, I'd be really worried."

"And you're not worried about Chava?"

"Well, except for the time she spends on this, she's pretty normal, don't you think?"

"For a socialist-vegetarian-lesbian-activist rabbi? Yeah, she's your standard brand," Brian deadpanned.

Three beats later, they both burst into laughter. "Good point," Elsa conceded.

"What I don't understand is...well, the picture she has up, of what Serah looks like today? I know that person. I know who the photo is of."

"Did you tell her that?"

"Yeah, but she didn't want to hear it."

Elsa's brows bunched together. "Didn't want to hear it? Why not?"

Brian shrugged. "I don't know. I think maybe she didn't believe me. I mean, what are the odds?"

"You mean the odds of this person she's been chasing all over the globe actually living in her own backyard?"

"Right. In Berkeley, of all places." Brian took a sip. "I think she thinks I'm a little crazy for even suggesting it."

"Ha!" Elsa burst out. "Well, if that isn't the pot calling the kettle *shahor!*"

Brian suddenly felt bad talking about his friend behind her back. He felt his sadness return. "Maybe she doesn't want her quest to end. Maybe she's *afraid* of meeting her idol."

Elsa nodded. "That could be. That could very well be."

"Or it could be that she wasn't prepared to hear what her hero was doing?"

"What? What do you mean? Is she a stripper or something?"

That made Brian smile. "No, although that would probably have been easier for her to hear. No. Sarah Bat Asher is an Episcopal priest."

25

DYLAN STRUGGLED to maintain his footing as he supported not just his own weight, but Mikael's as well. Clutching the tall friar's foot in both hands, he groaned as he tried to hoist Mikael just a little bit higher. "Dude, ken you reach it yet?"

Mikael was straining to reach something hanging just above the maroon awning of McGill's sports bar. "Not...quite."

Dylan did not understand why Mikael sounded out of breath. "Dude, yer *way* heavier then you look."

"Shit," Mikael said. "Hey, I'm going to jump. You okay with that?"

"Yer gonna jump down?"

"No, I'm going to jump up. On three, push me as high as you can."

"An' then what?"

"Uh...I suppose catch me again."

"I was afraid you was gonna say that. Do they do finger-joint replacement surgery?"

"Ready?"

"Ready as Ah'll ever be, Ah reckon," Dylan said. A moment later, Mikael pushed against his hands with unexpected force. Dylan groaned and heaved upward. A moment later, Mikael fell again, and Dylan staggered under the tall friar's weight. "Dude, Ah can't—"

But then Mikael stepped down. "It's fine. You okay?"

Dylan felt at the small of his back. "Ask me tomorrow. What did you find?"

"This." He held out a small square of what looked like parchment. A sigil matching the one spray-painted onto the awning was scrawled on it.

"That's not ink," Dylan pointed out. "That's blood."

Mikael shuddered and dropped it. "What is it?"

Dylan stepped on the tiny scrap of parchment before the wind could catch it. He took a lighter out of his pocket and produced a bright, dancing flame.

"Uh...Dylan, why do you have a lighter?"

"Old habits, Ah guess." He leaned over and picked up the parchment, holding it just above the flame. As the sigil began to burn, it screamed.

"Where is that coming from?" Mikael asked, looking around.

"That is a question fer metaphysical speculation. You mean you never burned a sigil b'fore? Waal, they scream sometimes." He released the parchment just before the flame reached his fingers, and it fell to the ground. Dylan and Mikael watched it as it curled into a black coil and a thin wisp of smoke rose into the air.

"Now, let's paint over that sigil up there," Dylan pointed at the awning.

"Why two sigils?" Mikael asked.

"Waal, Dicky's the expert on demon-magick, but Ah'm guessing the one we just burned was the activator. And that one up there is the amplifier—'cause it's big and you ken see it fer blocks."

"So is it still active?"

"Prob'ly not, but let's not take any chances," Dylan said, handing him a can of spray paint. Mikael took it and Dylan interlaced his fingers, once again creating a step for the tall young man. "Let's get it done while Ah still have some strength in mah hands."

Mikael stepped up, took a moment to gain his balance, and then painted over the sigil without much care for aesthetics. "Someone's going to be pissed."

"If they're alive, we're gonna call 'em lucky, and they ken be as pissed as they want," Dylan called up at him.

Mikael stepped down and looked around. "So...where is Kat?"

SHE JUST FELT the needle enter her arm when it seemed like a great noise suddenly ceased. She looked down at her arm and her eyes went wide. "What the fuck am I doing?" she said aloud, ripping out the needle. Her head felt a little swimmy, and she wondered if that was just due to adrenaline, or if she had actually gotten some of the morphine. It didn't matter. She jumped up and nearly leaped out of the ambulance.

"There you are," Mikael said. She dove for the middle of his torso, planted her face in his belly, and wrapped her arms around his skinny waist. He hugged her back. "What's going on, baby?"

"Uh...nothing. Just...overwhelmed."

Her eyes rolled back into her head, and she crumbled to the street.

TUESDAY

UNTITLED

I will set my face against you,
and you shall be struck down by your enemies;
your foes shall rule over you,
and you shall flee though no one pursues you.
And if in spite of this you will not obey me,
I will continue to punish you sevenfold for your sins.
I will break your proud glory,
and I will make your sky like iron
and your earth like copper.
Your strength shall be spent to no purpose:
your land shall not yield its produce,
and the trees of the land shall not yield their fruit.
—*Leviticus 26:17-20*

26

When Kat opened her eyes, it seemed like everyone she knew was in front of her, looking at her. "Am I hallucinating this?" she asked the sea of familiar faces. "Because it's surreal and I feel really weird. Did I just fall into *The Wizard of Oz*?"

"No, honey, it's really us," Susan said, putting her hand on Kat's arm, just above a purple bruise shaped like Wisconsin.

"What the fuck is that?" Kat jerked her arm up to her face.

"We were hoping you'd remember," Mikael said.

Kat pulled a pillow over her face. "I hate needles," she said in a muffled voice. She could hear Tobias panting beside the bed.

"You collapsed, so we gave you one o' those EpiPen thingies," Dylan said.

"Is that what gave me the hangover?"

"Nah, that was prob'ly the morphine," Dylan answered.

"I feel like a moose parked itself on my head."

Susan pulled the pillow off of her face and held a steaming cup of coffee in front of her eyes. "This will help."

"Ooooh, counter-drugs." Kat sat up, and took the cup willingly. "Did I sleep in my cassock?" she asked between slurps.

"Are you in your cassock now?" Richard asked.

"Uh...yeah," Kat said sarcastically, since everyone could see she had it on.

"You have your answer."

"Damn. Next time—"

"Next time?" Terry asked.

"Yeah, the next time I suffer demonic oppression and it causes me to shoot morphine into my arm..." she glared and waited for any of them to interrupt her, "I give Mikael permission to undress me."

"Noted," Mikael said, smiling weakly but encouragingly.

"Who is that?" Kat pointed.

A little girl had been hiding behind Terry's legs. She looked like she was about five years old, maybe younger.

"Terry rescued her from a gunfight. We don't know her name," Richard said. "In fact, we don't even know if she speaks English."

"Okie-dokie, then," Kat said, cocking her head, apparently not sure how to take in the information. "You want to hop up here with me, honey?" She patted the bed next to her. Tobias jumped up on the bed. "Not you, you big oaf," Kat pushed him back off and gestured to the little girl.

The girl's eyes widened and she leaped on the bed. "Okie-dokie," she squealed, instantly cozying up to Kat, who put her arms around her.

"She's fine," Kat said. "And Toby, too, I guess. But the rest of you...out."

"Fair enough," Dylan said, and turned toward the door. "Time to pray, anyway."

———

AFTER MORNING PRAYER, the smell of bacon lured the remaining friars into the kitchen, where Marco was blessedly dressed and presiding over breakfast with increased confidence. "Coffee is made," he pointed to the Mr. Coffee. "Water is hot," he said to Dylan, "and pancakes are on the way."

"Hot-diggity-damn," Dylan said, pouring hot water over his

teabag. Richard took his seat painfully and sighed loudly as he tenderly held his bruised rib.

"You sure you're okay?" Marco asked as he set a large bowl of fried potatoes on the lazy Susan next to the platter of bacon.

"I had Terry look at it in vision. It's not actually broken, it just feels that way," Richard said. "Besides, I don't want to brave a hospital right now unless I absolutely have to."

"I'll bet they're stuffed to the gills," Marco nodded.

"Ah'm gonna get fat on this kinda fare," Dylan announced.

"I hope that isn't complaining," Marco said without turning around.

"No, suh," Dylan raised his hands. "Not a bit of it."

"Is Kat coming down?" Marco asked.

"I doubt it," Mikael said. "I'll take her up a plate when we're done."

"I'll go ahead and put one together and set it in the microwave. That way you can just give it a blast before you take it up."

"Better make two. The girl's up there with her," Terry said.

"Oh, an' take up a bowl o' kibble fer Toby, too, please," Dylan said.

"It's your dog, take his nasty bowl up yourself," Marco said.

Dylan shrugged.

"We can't just call her 'the girl,'" Richard noted.

"I'd call her by her name, if I knew what it was," Terry said with a slight tone of annoyance.

"Ah'm gonna call her Chicken," Dylan announced.

"What? Why Chicken?" Mikael asked.

"'Cause she's skinny and kinda awkward. Her nose is kinda big. And we found her by the KFC. So...Chicken."

Terry gave Richard a look that he took to mean, *Are you going to let this stand?*

But the fact was, Richard kind of liked the name. "She *is* kind of chicken-like."

Terry looked betrayed, but it only lasted a moment. "She's cute as a button. She's also really traumatized."

"What are we going to do with her?" Mikael asked.

"We should call social services this morning," Richard said. "Although...with all that's going on, I don't expect us to be at the top of their list. We're probably on our own for a while with her."

"We can't just turn her out onto the street," Terry said.

"You've got that 'Daddy, can I keep the puppy?' look," Richard noted. "Stop that."

"Daddy, can I keep the puppy safe—for now?" Terry asked, a little sheepishly.

"Daddy, ken Ah keep the *chicken* safe fer now," Dylan corrected.

"I don't see that we have much choice," Richard said. He took a bite of bacon and his face brightened. "Hey, Marco, you're getting pretty good at this."

"It's been a long time since I cooked for a group," Marco answered. "Took me a couple days to get my sea-legs. But I found 'em. Speaking of which, pancakes are served," Marco said, setting a steaming plate on the lazy Susan.

"Dude, are those pancakes intentionally shaped like unicursal hexagrams?" Dylan pointed at them.

"Hey, when you make pancakes, you can make them into little crosses, okay?" Marco put his hands on his hips.

Dylan shrugged and dug in. "Dude, when is that CNN report supposed to air?"

"I have no idea," Richard said. "Soon, I hope. It's not like we have a lot of gigs right now, and we kind of desperately need the exposure."

Dylan nodded with what looked like satisfaction. "Free advertisin'. Now yer talkin'."

"But you know what's going to mean more to me than that?" Richard asked. "Is finally getting some recognition."

"What do you mean?" Marco asked. "You guys are famous."

"We're well known in a couple of tiny sub-cultures: church hierarchies and the occult community. Those are two pretty small ponds."

"Both full of people who matter—and people who hold you in pretty high esteem," Marco countered.

Richard sighed and sipped at his coffee. "I'm just so fucking tired of toiling in obscurity," he said. "Is that so wrong?"

Susan bolted out of the office holding a few large-format print-outs. She set them on the table and took a seat next to her husband.

"It's not wrong," she answered. "But I'd advise you to be careful what you ask for."

"What's this?" Richard asked.

"It's a printout of the crime stats in Oakland, Emeryville, and Berkeley," she said, spreading them out.

Richard stood up and went to the other side of the table, leaning over Susan's shoulder to see them right-side-up. "Okay, wow. There's a lot more clusters now. And way more in Emeryville."

"Just a few starting in south Berkeley," Susan said. "But they're starting."

"Why isn't this all over the news?" Marco asked.

"It is," Susan said. "Do you even watch or listen to the news?"

"No."

Susan rolled her eyes. "Look here—I've started superimposing the sigils that we've found on the clusters we've investigated."

Richard nodded. "That's good. Boy, do we have a lot of work to do if we want to get our heads around this, though."

"What Ah don't get is how one demon ken wreck so much havoc over an area like that," Dylan said. "You'd need a horde."

Terry leaned over from the side. "Or a host."

"What do you mean?" Richard asked.

"These two aren't just demons," Terry said, pointing at the sigils. "They're both dukes."

"What difference does that make?" Marco asked.

"Both of the sigils we checked out yesterday correspond to demons that aren't in anyone's host." Terry held up his iPad, toggling between the two sigils they'd found.

"How could they not be in a host?" Dylan asked. "All demons are in a host."

"Well, that's not entirely true," Richard said. "Jinn aren't."

"But these aren't in a host because they're the host *commanders*," Terry said.

"Now yer splittin' hairs. They're still part of a host, they're just leadin' it."

"I'm willing to bet that every one of these clusters is being presided over by a duke," Terry said, "with a whole host underneath him, wrecking whatever brand of havoc that duke is known for."

"So you want to know what I noticed?" Susan asked.

"Do tell," Richard said.

"Check out the varieties of crimes for each cluster. Ring any bells?"

Richard scanned the printouts. "They seem like standard-brand crimes to me."

"But notice the gaps."

She was right—there were circles of negative space on the maps. "I just figured they missed a spot."

"I think this was too well planned for that." Susan sat back and drummed her fingers on the table. "What did you notice when you were driving back?"

"You know, the food is getting cold," Marco said testily.

Terry reached for some bacon. "I'm pretty sure we went through a couple blocks that looked like every prostitute and her grandmother was out on the street."

"Good," Susan said. "Well, not good. But good noticing. Can you draw it on the map?"

Terry drew a circle around a section of streets. It bordered a cluster of rape reports.

"Just as I thought," Susan said.

"What?" Richard said. "Spill it. The suspense is killing me."

"Okay, check it out. Shooting—what kind of sin is that?"

"Uh...murder?" Dylan offered.

"No. Think more classically," Susan said.

"Methinks it might-eth be murder?"

Susan scowled at her husband.

"Wrath," Terry said.

"Exactomundo," Susan said. She pulled the cap off a sharpie and wrote "Wrath" over the sigil of Efranadil. Over the circle Terry had just drawn, she wrote "Lust."

"What's the intersection of Wrath and Lust?" Susan asked.

"Rape," Richard said, pointing to the cluster of rape reports. "Shit. Whoever is doing this is summoning the grand dukes of the seven deadly sins."

"And not only that, but we have to contend with hybrid sins as well," Susan said.

"So why the gaps?" Dylan asked.

"Just because something is a sin doesn't make it a crime," Susan said. "There's no crime against gluttony, for instance."

"The intersection of lust and gluttony is promiscuity," Richard said, catching on, "but that wouldn't be reported, either."

"I think we've got this slightly wrong," Terry said. "I think prostitution is the intersection between lust and greed."

"Good, good thinking."

"What about the drug festival Kat and Mikael and Ah came across?" Dylan asked. "Which of the seven deadlies is that?"

"What do you think, Dylan? You might just be the expert on that," Richard said.

Dylan shifted uncomfortably. "Yer one to talk, with yore whisky."

Richard smiled. "I'm a close second, I'll grant you. But what do you think?"

Dylan scratched his head. "It could be an intersection of gluttony, sloth, and wrath."

"But you found a sigil at ground zero," Richard pointed out. "It's not an intersection."

"Right." Dylan looked down at his sizable stomach. "It's a kind of wrath. It's self-wrath, isn't it?"

Terry pointed to the sigil square in the middle of Montclair on the map. "It's Allianatnefar—a hard name to say. A duke primarily associated with suicide and the murder of close relatives."

"That makes a lot of sense," Dylan conceded. "Addiction is slow suicide, after all."

"Good work, Susan. Everyone, this is great stuff," Richard said. Susan gave him a proud but curt nod.

"Terry, you and Susan do what you can to fill these out," Richard continued. "Get us as close as you can to a map of the jurisdictions of the classical sins and their intersections. It'll help us navigate if nothing else. It'll also give us a better sense of who and what we're dealing with. I'm going to go find a list of demonic dukes and the demons in their hosts." He sat up straighter than he had all morning. "We might be on the verge of figuring this out."

"But here's what I don't understand," Mikael asked. "One sigil summons one demon. Even if some wackjob magickian *did* summon a duke, why would the whole host be set loose? Also, the rules are all wrong. There was no pentagram in front of McGills. What stopped the demon—especially a duke—from scarfing up the soul of the magickian as soon as he activated it? There was no way to contain him, no protection."

Richard sat back again, thinking.

"I think I might have an idea," Marco said. They turned to face him. He was leaning against the counter, his bulky arms crossed in front of him and his dark eyebrows knitted in concentration.

"What are you thinking?" Richard asked.

"I'm thinking of the time I was living with you, Dylan, back before you and Susan got married. I was going to the Lutheran seminary at the time—"

"You went to the Lutheran seminary?" Terry asked. "What the fuck?"

"I was doing my doctoral work in the history of magickal theory at the seminary consortium, but you still had to be affiliated with a particular school," Marco said, waving the complication away. "Anyway, Dylan, do you remember that time I came home from the BART station with two black eyes?"

"Yeah, you got mugged!" Dylan said. "That really sucked."

"It did suck, but I only had myself to blame for it."

"How so?" Richard asked.

"Because all day I had been playing with a yo-yo."

Richard narrowed his eyes. "I'm waiting for this to make sense."

"See, I took this yo-yo—I got it from the games store on Shattuck —and I painted the sigil of Mars on both sides of it. I did this in the morning, and all day I played with it. So all day..."

"All day you were summoning *Mars*? Are you fucking nuts?" Terry asked.

"Eh, you live, you learn," Marco shrugged. "The point is, it wasn't a formal summoning. It was a...I don't know...a *luring* of influence."

"Right," Richard said, nodding slowly. "You didn't *formally* summon a particular demon. You *invited* the energy of Mars—of violence, aggression—and by the end of the day, it had caught up to you."

"That's pretty much what happened."

"So these aren't so much summonings as they are...what?" Mikael asked.

"Richard used the word 'jurisdictions' just a few minutes ago," Susan said. "What if it's more like those 'Win a dream house' ads we get in the mail?"

"Huh?" Dylan said. "Ah do not know why you waste yore time on those."

"You won't say that when we win one of them," she countered. "You'll just move right in."

"You betcha! Uh...what'cher point?"

"I'm saying that if you set up a pleasant situation for folks, they don't hesitate to migrate there."

"Ah still don't see where yer steerin' this pickup."

"I think what Susan is saying is that these demons weren't *summoned*, they were *invited*." Richard was nodding. "They're not being forced or compelled to be here, so they're not wrecking this havoc grudgingly. They were *invited*, so they came in willingly and started...well, I guess they just started enjoying themselves."

"It's like when you have a party, you bring all your friends. So, it isn't just one demon—" Susan continued.

"It's the whole host coming to the party," Richard agreed.

"I think that's a useful analogy," Terry said. "But I think it's more complicated than that. I think it's more like the sigils create a thin place where certain energies can come through more easily."

"This is some deadly clever magick," Richard said. "Who in the world would know how to do this?"

"I read an article about a year ago in an online chaos magick journal," Terry said, staring at the ceiling, obviously trying to remember something. "It talked about creating thin places through the use of hierarch sigils. Small stuff, but it's not a huge jump from what the author was suggesting to what we're seeing here."

"Do you remember who it was by?"

Terry shook his head. "No, but I can see if I can find it again."

"Let's put Mikael on that."

Mikael nodded. "Will do."

Just then the doorbell sounded.

"I'll get it," Mikael said, disappearing through the door to the chapel.

A few moments later, he returned, with several people in tow. Richard recognized them—the coven that Mikael and Kat often celebrated sabbats with. But whereas in the past, they had always been a gregarious lot, this morning they were withdrawn. Jimmy stared at his shoes, clearly cowed, Julia had her arm draped over his shoulder protectively, and Luna hovered near them, as if concerned either of them might topple over if she wasn't there to catch them.

"They picked up Jimmy again last night, the bastards," Luna said.

Mikael made quick introductions, as none of them had met Marco before, and the inventor made sure that each of them had a steaming cup of coffee in front of them in quick order. "Tell us what happened," Richard said.

"The detectives came to our house yesterday afternoon," Julia said, holding Jimmy's hand. Jimmy stared at the table. "And they just took him away. No explanation. They just...took him." She shook her head slowly. "There was something strange, though. The man, Detective Cain, I think? He looked straight at me and said, 'I'm sorry,' as if he knew it was bullshit."

"Jimmy, what happened? At the police station, I mean?" Mikael asked.

Jimmy's gaze didn't leave the table. "They just asked me the same questions all over again," he said. "Only this time, they started asking me about sigils. I don't know shit about sigils. I'm not a fucking magickian."

"I heard something about sigils on the news," Luna said, playing with the end of her ponytail nervously. "But we don't do sigils." She shuddered.

Smart girl, Richard thought. He was uncomfortable with any form of magick, even the relatively innocuous spells that Wiccans employed, but he didn't often voice this opinion, especially in the company of Wiccans. "We're working on another case involving sigils," Richard explained. "And I'm sure the police are going crazy because they haven't got a clue what's going on."

"Well, they might ask you to tutor them," Jimmy looked up at Richard for the first time.

"What makes you say that?" Richard asked.

"I...kind of gave them your card," Jimmy said, looking away.

Richard's face softened. "Jimmy, are you ashamed that you referred the police to us?"

Jimmy didn't answer but returned his gaze to the table.

"You don't need to feel bad about that. You didn't rat us out. We like working with the police. Helping the authorities with cases they don't understand is part of how we make our living," Richard said. "I'm surprised these detectives weren't banging on our door before this."

"Yeah, you'd think they would have clued in, when they interviewed us," Mikael said.

Richard shrugged. "I'm sure the brass is uncomfortable about using us, and it's not something they'd broadcast. Still, if the police show up here, we'll be glad to help out. We've found out quite a bit about the sigil business already." He cocked his head. "But how can we help you?"

"We think we're the victims of a magickal attack," Luna said.

"Shit keeps happening," Julia said.

"And you're scared," Susan nodded.

"And shit *keeps* happening," Julia repeated.

"You want the shit to *stop* happening," Susan clarified.

"Yes, please," Julia answered. Jimmy put his head on the table and started to cry. Julia rested her own head on his shoulder blade and just hugged his body until he stopped.

The room was silent, and Richard could see the tension on everyone's faces melt into compassion.

"Jimmy, we promise to do what we can," Richard said. "But my guess is that you were just in the wrong place at the wrong time, not the victims of a sustained attack. Getting picked up again, I think this is just the ripples of that initial violation, when your energy got stolen."

"How could we check to make sure there's no sustained attack?" Mikael asked.

"We could make sure there's no negative energy attached to their house," Marco offered. "I mean, it's easy to tell if it's truly a safe place to be."

"How would you do that?" Susan asked.

"I've got a working narometer."

"A narometer is a device that measures...nar?" Susan screwed up her face in a question.

"Yeah. Nar. Negative energy," Marco said, as if it was something everyone should know. "It's an old cyberpunk term. It works on the same principle as the christometer I was working up for you guys, but it's way easier to calibrate. This place is so well-warded, I'll just set it to zero before we leave. So long as I don't point it at Terry, it should be pretty accurate."

Terry scowled at him.

"Terry, why don't you and Marco go check it out?" Richard said.

"Me? With him?" Terry asked, slightly dismayed.

"He can do a reading...and you can do a subtle reading of your own," Richard explained. "And then you can set some wards."

Terry's shoulders deflated. "Yeah. I guess I can do that."

"Good," he turned to the Wiccans. "There's a lot going on right now. I think the best we can do at the moment is just to make sure you have a safe place to retreat to. But that we can do. And we will."

"Thank you," Jimmy said, grabbing Richard's hands and squeezing them. "And I'm sorry."

"Don't be," Richard said.

Susan pulled out her phone. "Getting a message," she said. She looked up quickly. "The CNN report. It's on."

27

LARCH'S HANDS shook as he sat up. Khams knocked on his door. "Babylon, are you all right?" He peeked in, and then fully entered the room once he saw that Larch was awake. "Uh...you look a little green in the gills."

"Water," Larch said, his voice cracking. The wind tugged at the curtains, causing them to ripple slightly in the morning light. Larch studied his own hands like they were novel alien appendages.

"What did you see?" Khams called over his shoulder as he exited, heading for the kitchen. He returned a moment later with a full glass of water. Larch gulped at it eagerly. Then he handed it back. "Another."

Khams dutifully retrieved another glass. "Thank you," Larch said, and took his time with this one.

"Well, what was it like up in Yesod?"

Larch didn't answer at first. Instead, he flinched as if he just remembered something that frightened him. He lurched toward the window and slid it further up on its frame. He stuck his head out and looked at the sky. Then he relaxed. "Thank gods," he said, his shoulders falling. He laid back on the bed, relaxing.

"Babylon, whatever is the matter with you?" Khams' voice was pitched high with worry.

"I...it wasn't what I thought," Larch confessed.

"How so?" Khams sat next to him on the bed, his eyes shining with wonder.

He didn't look at Khams. But then again, he rarely did. "It isn't a place you would want to go. It was...complete chaos."

Khams frowned. "But I thought...it's *up*."

"Yes, I thought it would be more orderly than...than this place. I thought it was going to be some rarified spiritual environment, where I would transcend the limitations of the mortal world. But instead, those limitations seemed to be strangely...magnified."

"You're revealing the lie," Khams said, pointing a finger at him. "That's what's happening. We always thought that the earth was the lowest place, the place of the most heaviness, the most disorder, the furthest from the divine order. But what if it's just the opposite? Maybe the further up in the Tree of Life you go, the more obvious the tyranny becomes, and the more chaotic his rule!" Khams' eyes were wide and his hands went to his mouth.

"I won't know that until I ascend further," Larch said, swinging his feet to the floor. "But you could well be right. It certainly appears that way so far."

Khams rushed to steady him as he tried to stand. "Careful!" he warned, but it wasn't needed. Larch sat again on the bed.

"I think...a little more time is in order."

"That seems like a good idea."

"I think I'm still slightly intoxicated by the ointment. I need to give it a little time before trying the second ascent."

"If it was this bad, do you think it's a good idea to go further?" Khams wondered aloud.

"It's the *only* idea. And if I have to sacrifice myself for the good of all creatures, so be it." Larch said, laying back. "Tell me what is happening with our little diversion."

"Oakland is burning. Emeryville is exploding." Khams grinned, his eyes shining, his hands mimicking fireworks bursting in air. "And Berkeley is just now catching fire."

"Very poetic. Can you be more specific?"

"We've posted twenty-seven sigils in key neighborhoods across Oakland, and they're all working even better than expected. I've been monitoring cable news, East Bay websites, and police radio, and everything is at a dead standstill over there. You want to talk about chaos? *That's* chaos."

"Go on."

"We've posted fourteen sigils in Emeryville, and those are really swinging into action, now. There's still traffic over the Bay Bridge—but freeways aren't blocked or anything—and on the ground, we've got riots."

"And Berkeley?"

"Nine sigils up, seventeen to go. They take time, though. We don't expect them to be in full swing until tomorrow."

"And any signs of our meddling friars?"

"CNN is advertising an exposé on them," Khams said, smiling.

"Are they?" Larch nodded, a grin tugging at one side of his mouth.

"It's supposed to start...oh, about now," Khams said looking at his watch.

28

IN SECONDS, the kitchen emptied, as everyone streamed past the chapel, past the front door, and into the living room. Richard plopped himself in the easy chair, while Susan and Dylan took the couch. Mikael and Marco hovered behind the couch, leaning their elbows on its back. Terry walked in and squeezed in next to Dylan, while Tobias presided over the gathering from his dog beg in the corner, panting audibly.

Susan grabbed the remote and punched at it. The flat screen faded from black to brilliant color and the sound engaged with a pop. "—police are at a loss to explain what is turning out to be the largest crime spree in Oakland history, a crime spree that seems to be spreading now to nearby communities. San Leandro has already erected barriers and are allowing nothing but foot traffic across their border with Oakland, including the controversial move to shut down the 580 freeway."

Images flashed in quick succession across the screen as the woman's voice spoke: cars on fire, masked drivers speeding through residential streets brandishing semi-automatic weapons, housewives and business people dancing in the street, removing their clothes, seemingly lost in bliss. The camera switched to the on-scene reporter, a pretty blond woman with a pageboy haircut. A house fire raged behind her, and no emergency vehicles were in sight. "The East Bay's gateway-to-the-bay, Emeryville, however, seems to have caught whatever virus is infecting Oakland, as their own crime spree is spinning out of control."

"Annette," said the newscaster, "local news blogs are circulating a rumor about an alleged occult connection. Can you tell us anything about that?"

"Only that people are grasping at straws to explain the sudden and intense outbreak of criminal activity in the city, Chet. In times of heightened stress, people often resort to superstition and religion to make sense of a world that is often scary and chaotic."

The camera cut back to Chet Swanson behind his desk. "Thank you, Annette Chandler, for that on-the-scene report. We will be keeping an eye on events in California's East Bay, and will interrupt with any breaking news there." Chet shifted to face a different camera. "In the meantime, the East Bay is still home to some of the most colorful characters to erupt onto the public stage in recent memory. We're talking, of course, about the Berkeley Blackfriars. Arlene Chin has this report."

Suddenly, the television showed their own house, and a small Chinese woman with a bright smile stepped into view. "This is the Holy Apocrypha Abbey in what is called the Gourmet Ghetto neighborhood of Berkeley, California, where the Berkeley Blackfriars live and—to hear them tell it—fight evil. Just a few months ago, no one had ever heard of this small religious Order, but they became a national headline when they crashed the Republican Convention earlier this year—stealing the spotlight from Governor David Ivory and bringing friends to the party that resulted in the brutal murder of the Episcopal Bishop of California, John Preston, live on nationwide television."

The screen cut to a shaky, hand-held camera that showed Dylan climbing up on a catwalk and just standing there.

"That's my guy," Susan said, hugging his arm.

"It's not mah good side," Dylan complained.

"You have a good side?" Mikael asked.

The scene cut again to a large war horse with a medieval rider, who dismounted and then, in three quick strides, embraced the Bishop as he stood at the podium. A moment later, the rider uttered a pronouncement before slashing the Bishop's throat. Blood spurted into the air.

"There's Terry!" Mikael said, pointing to the screen.

"You didn't even look surprised," Dylan noted.

"Uh...I kind of wasn't," Terry admitted.

The camera tracked as Arlene walked toward Cedar Street. "We decided to find out more about these brave, reclusive Souls. This is what we found."

The scene cut to an establishing shot of the Oakland Cathedral, then a headshot of a white-haired man with prominent jowls.

"Oh, shit, not O'Neil," Richard slapped his forehead.

A caption identified the man as Michael O'Neil, Vicar General of the Archdiocese of Oakland. "Father O'Neil, what can you tell us about the Blackfriars?"

"Nothing good," the man smirked. "They're heretics, schismatics, and from what I hear, unrepentant sinners. They have absolutely no connection to the Archdiocese of Oakland. We neither recommend them nor endorse them."

"And yet, our research indicates that you have employed them no less than fourteen times over the past five years."

Obviously uncomfortable, O'Neil looked down, no longer meeting Chin's gaze. "Let's just say sometimes the best way to defeat Satan is to hire one of his own."

"So you agree that their work is effective?"

O'Neil met her gaze again. "Exorcism is a dangerous job. I've seen more than one exorcist splattered over a bedroom wall," he said. "Better them than us."

"But Episcopal sources are more positive," Chin said. "Episcopal priest Mother Maggie Asher is the Diocesan liaison for occult investigations. She said the Blackfriars are the diocese's first call whenever they encounter a case of demon possession."

"Yay, Maggie!" Terry called.

"Oh, they're dears," Mother Maggie said, looking like she was about to kiss the camera. "They love Jesus, and they know their—." Maggie's last word was bleeped, but her lips plainly said "shit."

"Okay, Maggie," Richard said, beginning to feel a little queasy.

"Not bad so far," Susan said, encouragingly.

Richard got up and moved closer to the television, sitting on the arm of the couch next to Susan.

The scene shifted to Terry, out in the front yard, setting wards. The camera caught his hands in a close up as he put what looked like entrails on a burning censor and then wafted the smoke about the property. "We caught up with Father Terry Milne," said Chin's voice over, "who told us he was burning fish gall bladders in order to ward off evil spirits—"

"That's not exactly what I said," Terry frowned.

"—but when we looked closer, we found out *that* was not the only thing that smelled a little fishy."

The background music took an ominous turn into a minor key, and a still photo of Richard appeared. The camera panned over it, creating the Ken Burns effect, until the sign for The Jizz Factory was revealed in the background. "An anonymous source told us that the monks' leader, Bishop Richard Kinney, is a sexually active bisexual who, just in the past year, has had affairs with women, men, and transgendered persons."

"We're not monks, we're friars!" Terry snapped. "Why is that such a hard concept for people?"

Richard's face drained of color, and he leaned on the couch for support. Susan put her hand around his waist and pulled him close to her and Dylan. "Steady," she whispered.

"Among the monks one has a wife, who sleeps with him in the monastery—"

"Where else should I sleep?" Susan asked the television.

"—two of the monks are reported to be having sex with each other, and one of the monks lives with his gay lover in a backyard bungalow."

"It's not really a bungalow," Terry said. "It's more of a cottage."

"You really can't trust the media to get *anything* right," Marco agreed.

The scene shifted to the chapel, a wide angle in which you could see Richard and Susan sitting in one of the pews, apparently at prayer, but you could also see the doorway into the kitchen. "Despite all the hanky-panky, the monks keep up a pious front, meeting together for both morning and evening prayer in their monastery's small chapel. At least, some of them do." As she was speaking, Marco walked into frame, nearly naked save for his Star Wars underwear. He reached into his underwear and scratched his butt as he headed into the kitchen.

"That black guy is hot," Marco said.

Richard slid off the arm of the couch, and he clutched at it as he sank to the floor. Susan snatched a throw pillow and rushed to his side. "Sit on this," she instructed.

"We got to see the monks in action when we visited their monastery last Sunday. While we were filming, they received a call about a possessed dog in nearby Albany. The dog had been threatening its owners, but had been safely contained in a cage—so far. We expected the Blackfriars to spring into full exorcist action, but that's not what happened. To our surprise, the operation was turned over to a female monk who looked barely out of high school—"

"Oh, for crying out loud! She's 28!" Mikael objected.

"We discovered she is Katherine Webber, a former witch, and the most recent addition to the Order."

"They *are* pretty good at the investigative reporting-thing," Dylan noted, looking impressed.

"Instead of making with the holy water, Katherine—or Kat, as she likes to be called—proceeded with her exorcism simply by sitting down and meditating, or was she having a quick nap? It was hard to tell. About ten minutes later, apparently rested, she got up, and unwisely entered the cage with the vicious Dachshund.

"It looked like the dog bit her arm, but Katherine didn't seem phased. Instead, she actually reached *over* the dog and appeared to scratch its back. Watch what happens on our slow motion video: Here she is, scratching the back of the dog, then she executes what looks like a quick grab, or even a karate chop, and the dog falls to the ground, dead. The demon dog is no longer threatening anyone, but pet lovers might want to keep a wide berth of the Berkeley Blackfriars."

"Oh, I'm so glad Kat isn't watching this right now. She is going to *hate* this," Mikael breathed.

"Kat isn't the only one," Susan added.

The screen cut to the talking head of a public health officer saying, "Because the Berkeley Blackfriars did not properly dispose of the dog, the entire family has been ordered to report for a full round of rabies prophylaxis."

The next thing they saw was the strained, angry face of Mrs. Barker. "I curse the moment I ever set eyes on them."

The report seemed to be over, because the scene shifted back to the anchorman, who sat across from Arlene Chin. "Arlene, isn't there some kind of church body that can hold renegade groups like these accountable?"

"Normally yes, Chet, but the Blackfriars are Old Catholics, and from what I gather, here in the United States that is a very chaotic group without a nationwide organizational system. They call themselves 'autocephalous,' which means 'self-headed.' So there's no one who can keep them in check."

"Buyer beware," Chet said, raising his eyebrows and straightening the small stack of papers in his hands against the desk with a tap.

"Indeed," Arlene Chin answered.

"Next: Goats in the wild found wearing hockey jerseys —after this."

Susan turned off the television. Richard moaned. Dylan, Terry, and Mikael just looked at each other.

Marco just kept staring at the empty television screen. "I'm so sorry," he finally said.

Kat stumbled downstairs with the little girl close behind. "Sorry? What? What did I miss?"

Mikael turned. "Uh...you were better off not seeing it."

"Okay," she said, walking past them all on the way to the kitchen. "I gotta piss like a racehorse. And I'm thirsty." The little girl looked back at all of them, her enormous brown eyes cautious but curious, then she continued following Kat.

Mikael opened his mouth but then thought better of it.

Susan knelt by Richard. "I'm sorry it wasn't what you had hoped for."

Richard seemed disoriented, but he latched on to Susan's hand and held it.

"What's going on?" Susan asked. "Tell me what you're feeling."

"I'm having a shame attack," Richard said. He leaned over onto her shoulder and began to cry.

Dylan sighed. "Ah'm not really the right person to say this, but Ah think it might be time fer a whisky."

Terry shot him a look.

"Fer Dicky, Ah mean," Dylan clarified.

Terry nodded. "I think you might be right. I think it might be time for whisky all around."

"An' a chamomile tea fer me," Dylan said, heading toward the kitchen.

"Dicky, I know you're embarrassed," Susan said. "But we're going to survive this. The Catholic and Episcopal Dioceses are not going to stop employing us. Our friends know we're not charlatans. A week from now, no one will even remember that report."

"I just want to crawl under a rock and die."

"I know, honey."

"I just..." his face screwed up as he fought back tears. "I just wanted to *be* someone."

"I know. It was supposed to be your moment of glory. And now it's just been yanked away from you."

Dylan walked up holding out a glass. Richard had his back turned to him and didn't see him, so Susan motioned Dylan back to the kitchen. Dylan raised his eyebrows and turned on his heel. "Dicky, what would Mother Maggie tell you to do if she were here right now?" Susan asked him.

Richard considered for a minute. "She'd tell me to take my feelings to Jesus. She's been trying to get me to do that for a couple months now."

"Hmm...I smell resistance. So why don't you break through it and finally take Maggie up on her advice? What are you paying her for, anyway, if you're just going to ignore her?" Richard didn't say anything, so Susan continued. "Dicky, listen to me. Why don't you go sit in the chapel and have a chat with Jesus? Just tell him exactly what you're feeling right now. You don't need him to make it better or fix anything. All you need to do is tell him how you feel. That is your only agenda. Can you handle that?"

Richard gave her a quick nod.

Susan stood and helped him to his feet. "After you pray, if you still want it, you can have a whisky."

"Maybe Jesus would like a whisky," Richard said. "Maybe Jesus would like to have a whisky with me."

"Don't try my patience," Susan warned him.

"Yes, ma'am," Richard said, and he hugged her.

She held him tight, for many long seconds. Then she stood back and pointed to the chapel. "Jesus. Now."

29

"Boss, I'm all for putting ourselves in harm's way when it's needed," Perry said, hovering at the door. "And I'm sure we could get across the Bay Bridge right now..."

"I hear a 'but' coming," Herrer said.

"But I'm not at all sure we could make it back. This—" she pointed at the Crime Map that was playing on the flat screen in pretty much every room now, "—isn't going away. And it's not getting better. If anything, it's getting worse."

Herrer deflated a bit. "You're right. I was thinking the same thing myself, although I probably wouldn't have stopped you."

"Gee, thanks."

"Cain, what's your assessment?"

"It smells bad, captain. Ordinarily, I'd say yeah, let's go knock some heads together at this Cloven Hoof place. But it's just fishing. Seems like we've got bigger fish to fry over here...I mean, to extend the whole...fish metaphor."

"Yep. Yep." Herrera turned and faced her window. Cain followed her gaze and saw a man across the street smash a shop window and start stuffing his pockets.

"Um, should we be doing this?" Perry asked.

"What? Watching the looters?" Herrer asked. "No. We should probably be stopping them. Someone should stop them."

"No, I mean...it's a matter of triage, I think. Oakland and Emeryville are overrun with killings right now. Shouldn't we be helping them instead of investigating a single killing?" Perry explained.

"Is this an ethics question, Perry?" Herrer didn't turn away from the window. "'Cause ethics questions give me migraines."

"No...I think it's just a question about allocation of resources."

"For me, this is a matter of jurisdiction. For instance, do you know why I'm not rushing out there to stop that looting?"

"Because we're detectives and not street cops?"

"Exactly. Not our job. Oakland and Emeryville, those aren't our job, either. You know what our job is?" She asked, finally turning to face them.

"Solving this crime?"

"Solving this crime."

Cain sighed and looked at his shoes. "You know what I'd like to do?"

"What's that?"

"People are saying there's a link between the crime wave and the appearance of these...sigils. Maybe so. We don't see a lot of crimes with overtly occult themes. Don't you think it's a pretty big coincidence that we have this witchcraft killing and then, just a few days later we start seeing this..." he waved his arms, "major...occult...crime event?"

"Crime event?" Herrer said drolly. "Is that a technical term?"

"Look, boss, I don't have words to describe this, because I've never seen anything like it. But I've got a hunch that these aren't isolated... things. It's too much of a coincidence."

"And you don't believe in coincidence?" she said, raising an eyebrow.

"Do you?" Perry asked.

Cain lowered his voice and forced himself to be calm. "I'd like to go and talk to those Blackfriars—they're supposed to be experts on stuff like this. Maybe they can tell us about the sigils. Maybe they'll tell us something that will help us see a connection."

Herrer looked at him like he was out of his mind. "Don't tell me you buy into that mumbo-jumbo."

Cain shrugged. "I can tell you I don't understand a bit of it. There doesn't have to be an *actual* connection. But if the people involved *think* there's a connection, then it's important. Understanding how the creepy stuff is supposed to work might give us some psychological insight into what the perps are up to, and how they're thinking."

Herrer narrowed her eyes at him. "Dammit, Cain, you're making sense, too. Knock that shit off."

"Sorry, boss."

"Get out of here," she said and turned back to watch the looters.

30

TERRY WALKED into the room just in time to see Chicken on all fours, touching noses with Tobias. Tobias wagged his tail. Chicken did the same. "Why aren't you scary?" she asked the dog in perfect English.

Terry leaned against the doorway, folded his arms, and watched the interaction. Tobias licked Chicken's face. She licked his back. Terry was about to intervene, but Susan was at his elbow and restrained him. "So it's a little unhygienic," she whispered. "It's a bonding moment. That wins out, I think."

Terry nodded. "She spoke English."

Susan's eyebrows raised and she pursed her lips. "So she's just shy."

"She comes from a culture that is normally scared of dogs, but she seems to be doing fine with Toby."

"No surprise there," Susan said. "He may be the first non-pit bull she's ever met."

"*That* is a cultural stereotype," Terry said.

"Sue me," Susan smiled.

Chicken put her arms around Tobias' neck and hugged him, and Tobias kept wagging his tail. Terry sat down cross-legged near them both. "His name is Tobias," Terry said. "But we just call him Toby."

Chicken's eyes went big for a moment, then she relaxed. She faced Terry but kept one hand on the dog.

"Do you have a dog at home?" Terry asked.

Chicken shook her head.

"Well, you have one as long as you're here," Terry said.

"Toby can be *my* dog?" Chicken asked.

"Toby is a part of our family," Terry said. "Officially, he belongs to Dylan, but unofficially, we all kind of belong to him."

Chicken just stared. Terry had no idea whether she followed his logic.

"What's your name?" Terry asked. Chicken just stared.

"If you don't tell us your name, people are just going to call you Chicken. Do you want that?"

"I like chicken."

Terry sighed. "Okay, then. Chicken it is." He looked up at Susan. She shrugged.

"How old are you, Chicken?"

"Five. Why is he crying?" She pointed over toward the chapel where Richard was sitting in one of the pews.

"Um...I think it's because he feels misunderstood. We all do. But Richard is our leader, our *padre*. He's taking it pretty hard."

"Does he hit you?"

Terry jerked upright. He blinked. "Hit us?" Had Chicken's *padre* hit her? "No. Richard never hits us. He protects us. He loves us. He's self-involved and myopic and he's probably an alcoholic, but he would never, ever hurt us. On purpose." He leaned in. "He can be annoying, though."

Chicken looked over at Richard and then back at Terry.

Tobias rolled over on his back and showed them both his tummy. Terry started rubbing it and Tobias squirmed with pleasure. Chicken smiled.

"Do you want to go home, Chicken?" Terry asked.

She looked him in the eyes and shook her head.

"You don't want to see your *madre*?" Terry asked.

Chicken's eyes welled up with tears. "Mi madre se ha ido."

Terry shook his head. "I don't really speak Spanish."

"My mommy is...gone."

"Where did she go?"

Chicken pointed her index finger at Terry, her thumb erect. She closed one eye and made a splashy, exploding sound with her mouth.

"Oh my God," Susan said, covering her mouth. She took a seat next to Chicken and put her arm around her. "Did you see your *madre* get shot?" she asked.

Chicken nodded.

"When did that happen?" Terry asked.

"Before," Chicken said, looking down at Tobias as he wiggled. "Yesterday."

"Who did it?" Terry asked.

"Mi padre."

Terry looked at Susan and shook his head. Susan hugged Chicken to her, and the little girl gratefully threw her arms around her. "You're big, like her," Chicken said.

"Gee, thanks." Terry could see that Susan was trying not to smile at that, but she failed.

"What are you?" Chicken asked.

Susan and Terry looked at each other. "Uh...what do you mean?" Terry asked. "Who are you asking?"

She swooped her hand around. She seemed to be indicating the whole house. "What are you?"

"I'm a man. Susan is a woman. Toby is a dog..."

"No," Chicken insisted. "You don't look like each other. There aren't any *abuelas* or *abuelos*."

"Smart girl," Susan said.

Chicken smiled for the first time. She turned back to Terry. "Are you a family?"

Terry looked at Susan. She smiled warmly at him and put a hand on his leg.

"Yes, little one. That's exactly what we are. We are a family."

31

RICHARD WISHED he could speak to Mother Maggie, but he realized he was only procrastinating. He sat in the short pew in the chapel and closed his eyes, relinquishing control. In his mind's eye, a new scene splashed over him, and he jumped back to avoid the water.

"Careful. It's choppy today," a kind voice said.

Looking around, Richard saw a small skiff pulled up onto a beach, it's stern rising regularly with the incoming waves. There was a small fire, burning away cheerfully, with a pot hanging over it on a clever tripod made of some kind of rough metal. About two paces from the fire a fisherman was mending nets—a pile of nets was on one side, and in the lap of his tunic were a couple spools of thick, black thread. A knife was at his side, sitting next to a steaming cup of what looked like tea. "It's good to see you, Richard," he said. "It's been a while since we talked. *Really* talked, I mean."

There wasn't any blame in his voice. It was just the truth. "Jesus?" Richard breathed.

The man smiled up at him, and Richard could see that it was. He didn't look like the blond, blue-eyed Sunday School pictures Richard remembered, or the sentimental portraits that were so popular. He just looked small and rugged. And very Jewish.

"What's the matter?" Jesus asked.

"Uh...nothing. I just...I guess I've never prayed like this before."

Jesus patted the spot on the beach next to him and waved him over.

Richard sat near him, but not too near.

"I don't bite," Jesus said. "I've been known to spew people out of my mouth, but I never bite."

Richard scooched a bit closer, and Jesus leaned over and kissed him on the cheek. He put his hand on Richard's neck and pulled him closer so that their heads were touching. Then he let him go. "It's so good to see you."

"Uh...yeah. It's good to see you, too." Richard felt awkward, even nervous. "Are you real? Or am I just...generating you in my imagination?"

"The imagination is an organ of perception," Jesus said.

"So...yes to both?"

Jesus just smiled at him. Then he patted Richard's leg. "Tell me what's on your heart."

"I'm not sure there's much you can do—"

"I didn't ask you what I can do, nor did I offer to fix anything. That's not really my concern." He looked down at the net and drew some thread. His fingers danced as he made knots. "I want to know what you're feeling."

Richard looked at his knees and felt himself sink. A new objection rose to the surface. "Don't you already know what I'm feeling?"

"This is what we call resistance. The fact that I already know what you're feeling is not really my concern, either. I'm after something else."

"What's that?"

"Can't you guess?"

Richard said nothing. He felt stupid. Jesus patted his leg. "What I want from you is the same thing that, deep down, you want from me. Intimacy. People who are intimate talk about their feelings with each other. It's kind of the definition of intimacy. So...tell me what you're feeling."

"I feel embarrassed. I feel ashamed. I feel...like I want to die."

"Because of the news report?"

"Did you see that?"

Jesus leaned away and raised an eyebrow. Then he looked back at his knotting. "Well...what did you expect?"

"I don't know. You know what it really is? I don't want to be a failure."

"Do you think you're a failure?" Jesus asked.

"I don't feel like a success."

"What would success look like?"

"I don't know," Richard looked at the waves as they rolled onto the beach and subsided. It was like watching the earth breathing. "To get some recognition? To not have to struggle so much, money-wise? To finally be seen for who we are and what we...contribute, I guess."

"Hmm..." Jesus put one net aside and started to examine another, checking for rips and holes. "Did I get any of that while I was walking around like you are?"

Richard looked down. "Nothing like that."

Jesus put down his net and placed a warm hand on Richard's knee. "Do you intend to follow me?"

"Of course," Richard answered quickly.

"If you follow me and you expect to receive glory from the world, you're deluding yourself. If you follow me, you follow me into ignominy, into scandal, into ridicule."

"Why is that?"

"I make a beeline for those things, every time, because that's where the hurting people really live." Jesus leaned away and smiled broadly. "So if you really follow me, you will, too. And the world will never understand you or give you a lick of credit."

"Because they don't understand what we're doing," Richard said.

"It isn't that they *don't* understand, it's that they *can't*." Jesus tugged at a knot. "They think I'm a myth. They don't know that I'm a living presence in the world. They don't understand that the very things they spend their lives running after are the same things that are making them sick." He let that sink in for a moment. Then he added, more softly, "And because you are a child of this culture, you believe what the culture tells you. So you want the things that make you sick, too. But deep down you know what's real, what's right, what's true. You don't always act like it, but you know it."

"I know it," Richard agreed.

"I invite you to be realistic. Don't expect peanuts from people who only have a bag full of walnuts."

"Is that an old Jewish saying?"

"No I thought of that just now," Jesus smiled. "Okay, it's not great, but you get my meaning."

"I do." Richard thought about it. "But...how do I do that? How do I want the right things or stay focused on what's true? I'm clear on the *what*...I'm just fuzzy on the *how*."

"Lean into me," Jesus said.

Richard froze. "What do you mean?"

Jesus leaned against him, pressing his shoulder into Richard's bicep. Then he rocked back. "Like that. Lean into me." Richard leaned over, until he was resting part of his weight on Jesus' shoulder. "Good. Lean harder."

Richard leaned in more. "Lean harder." Richard's large frame might have smothered the small man, but he held his own.

"I can bear it," Jesus said. "However hard you lean, I can bear it." Jesus leaned away now so that he could look into Richard's eyes. "I want you to really hear me now. *You do not have to be the strong one. That's my job.*"

Jesus turned to look back out toward the sea and leaned once more against his shoulder. Richard could feel the heat radiating from Jesus, he could smell the man's sweat. He rested his head on the top of his head. He felt the solidness of Jesus' body.

"This is what I want for you," Jesus said. "I want you to learn how to do this all the time. You are going to need it."

Richard scowled. "What's *that* supposed to mean?"

32

MARCO'S HANDS were full of equipment, so Terry knocked on the door. "Who is it?" a voice came from inside.

"Terry. And Marco."

"Nice of you to at least give me second billing," Marco said.

"...aaas the Beaver."

"You're lucky my hands are full."

The door opened a crack and Luna looked past them nervously. "Come in," she said, her voice implying haste.

Once inside, Terry took a look around. The living room was haphazardly furnished. Every piece looked like it had been picked up off the street or at a yard sale. An inflatable vinyl moose head adorned the wall. What really caught the eye, however, was an altar off to one side, dressed with an Indian sheet and meticulously decorated with icons and occult objects.

"Jimmy and Julia are napping, but I'll tell them you're here," Luna said.

Terry nodded. "We'll get set up."

Marco knelt and opened the black box he had been holding. Inside was a machine that looked a lot like the Christometer he had been demonstrating a couple days ago. It was larger, though, and clunkier. Marco must have noticed the look on Terry's face. "I built this a few years ago. I've gotten better at making things smaller and... well, prettier, I guess. But it works just fine."

"There's no tube," Terry mentioned, pointing to one side of it.

"No, just a PVC uptake." He plugged the machine into a battery pack, which he attached to a loop on his belt. "The battery is the heavy part," he said. He gingerly lifted the narometer, and flipped a silver toggle switch on the top of it. Terry heard a small whine that rose in pitch as the device came to life. A green light near the switch turned on and what looked like a touchscreen lit up. Marco tapped a few selections on the screen then turned and pointed it at himself. He gave it a couple moments to absorb the molecules of his t-shirt, then pressed a blue button on its side.

"What did you just do?" Terry asked.

"Calibration," Marco said. "No negative energy here," he thumped his own chest. "I'm a glass-is-half-full kind of guy."

"How do you know *you're* not under magickal attack?"

"Um...only good things are happening to me?"

"You know, you irritate the shit out of me sometimes," Terry confessed. "But you *are* a cheerful motherfucker."

"I aspire to nothing much more than that," Marco nodded. "That's how you stay content."

Jimmy announced his arrival with a yawn, and Julia and Luna were right behind him. "Hey," he said.

"Hey," Terry answered.

"Thank you so much for coming," Julia said.

"Glad we can help," Terry said.

"Shall we?" Marco asked, wielding his machine.

Jimmy waved toward the house. "Help yourself."

"You go ahead, Marco," Terry said. "I'm going to feel it out my own way."

Marco nodded. "Good. We can coordinate our results." He began to trace the perimeter of the room, holding the narometer about a yard away from the wall. He watched the tiny screen as he moved deliberately across first one wall and then another, his face a tight mask of concentration.

Terry turned and walked into the kitchen. *As good a place to start as any,* he thought. He held onto the counter and closed his eyes, going lightly into vision. In his mind's eye, he saw the kitchen, but instead of the bright colors he beheld with his eyes open, he saw only the luminous outlines of the counter, the cupboards, the table, and the shelves. They appeared in his vision as a light gray, faintly shining and slightly out of focus. As he turned toward the pantry, he saw through the door at the gray shelves behind it. There were several jars, many of which were simply culinary, but some of which had magickal properties, and those glowed dimly with faint pastel colors emitting from them.

Nothing seemed out of the ordinary, for a house full of witches anyway. Terry moved on to the bedrooms, and both seemed like tiny disaster areas. He shook his head, marveling at how people lived with such squalor. He surveyed the gray outlines of the walls, beds, night stands, and chests-of-drawers, and he inspected the closets. One room had been converted into a dedicated temple—the only room that was tidy. As Terry stepped into it, it emitted a prominent violet glow with rose highlights. *Seems like a healthy temple,* he thought to himself.

The bathroom seemed similarly clean, though certainly not in an antiseptic way. *Most people are not aware of their own mess,* he reminded himself, shutting the bathroom door behind him. When he walked past the foyer toward the garage, he caught a quick glimpse of the others as they followed Marco around, and something in the corner of his eye writhed. He froze and turned his head. He saw tendrils of corruption feeding on Luna. He shook his head and looked again. The gray outlines of the floor and walls framed his vision. In the center of his gaze he saw Marco—radiating a deep indigo as well-meaning magickians often do. Jimmy and Julia radiated rose. But Luna was different. There was rose there—*Not surprising,* he thought, *she is Wiccan*—but there were also hooked, dark paisley patterns that moved both within her and around her, tendrils that rippled out from her with lysergic intensity.

Terry looked away to avoid staring. He did not want to draw attention to her. He continued his visual surveillance of the house, but he saw nothing else. Nor could he think of much else. The only thing he could think about, the only thing he could see was Luna's soul being caressed by dark, putrid tentacles. He shuddered and intentionally came out of vision. He didn't want to see that again.

He rejoined the others, grateful that Luna looked normal to his naked eyes. He sidled up to Marco, close enough to whisper. "Anything?" Terry asked.

"Not yet. We did get a minor hit from the pound cake."

"The pound cake?" Terry looked skeptical.

"I think it's the GMO's," Marco explained.

"I think you listen to a *leeetle* too much NPR."

"Gets lonely out on the road. I needs me some Terry Gross and Ron Elving."

Terry leaned in closer. "Get a read on Luna," he whispered.

"Why?" he whispered back.

"Just do it," Terry insisted.

Marco shrugged and turned around. "We should check your clothes," he said.

"Sure," said Jimmy. Julia held her arms out. But Luna was gone.

33

BRIAN PICKED a bit of fluff off the rug and carried it to the garbage can in the kitchen.

"Will you please sit down?" Chava said, watching him from her recliner. A Torah commentary was balanced on her knees. "You're driving me nuts. I've had a hellish day and I need some peace. You're like a busy fucking bee."

"I can't help it. I can't stand to see...fluff."

"Brian, for God's sake, this place is spotless. If I'd have known you were a human hoover, I'd have asked you to come live with us years ago. No wonder they love you so much at the friary."

"I have other excellent qualities," Brian objected, taking a seat on the couch. He looked around anxiously.

"You think maybe you've got a bit of cabin fever?"

"What do you mean?"

"I mean you should get out. Do you want me to give you a shopping list?"

Brian looked up, cocked his head, then blinked. "I would fucking *love* that."

"So let's get that together," Chava said, scooting off the recliner and heading to the kitchen. "I'll call, you write."

Brian scrambled after her. He grabbed the grocery list off the fridge, along with its little golf pencil dangling from a string.

"Shoot," he said, settling in at the table.

"We need fava beans," Chava called, scouring the pantry.

"Of course we do," Brian said. "Every house needs fava beans."

"We need coffee—get Peets or Blue Bear. Italian Roast, both caf and decaf, please. A pound of each."

"That's a lot of coffee."

"Not around here it isn't."

"Next?"

"Fruit. We need bananas—extra green, please. While you're at it, get some ripe plantains. We'll have them tomorrow."

Brian heard the front door open and then slam. "Shit!" Elsa cried from the living room.

"Uh-oh," Chava said.

"Why is this place so fucking clean?" she asked, coming into the kitchen. "Makes me want to take a dump in the living room just to even things out."

"Please don't do that," Brian said. "I would have to clean that up."

"Why would *you* have to clean that up?" Elsa asked. Brian noted that she had bags under her eyes and stress lines across her forehead.

"Because I would feel an inward compulsion to eradicate feces on the carpet in a common place," Brian said. "Call it an obsession."

"How was your day?" Chava asked.

"How was yours?" Elsa asked. She sounded angry.

"I asked first," Chava put down the can she was holding and faced her partner.

"So the fuck what?" Elsa responded, a little louder than she needed to.

"Um...guys," Brian interjected.

"We're not guys," Elsa said without looking at him.

"No..." Brian conceded.

Elsa and Chava stared at each other.

"What just happened?" Brian asked.

Chava shook her head. "Nothing. It's nothing. Brian and I are making a grocery list because he's got to get out of the house before he goes stir-crazy."

She crossed the kitchen to her partner and kissed her. "Really, tell me about your day."

"It was hell. Double F-grade hell."

"Mine, too," Chava said, turning back to the cupboard. "Why was yours so bad?"

"Can you at least look at me when I'm talking to you?" Elsa asked.

Chava froze. She turned slowly and faced her partner. "Fine." She crossed her arms. "Please tell me why your day was bad."

"Every client I have called me today. Every single one of them. And every single one of them is in a crisis."

"That's not normal," Chava said, looking concerned.

"No shit. Okay, every other day, maybe I get a call. Today, I got sixty calls, at least. Sixty! My voice mail is maxed out."

"So why are you home?" Chava asked.

"You don't want me home?"

"I didn't say that. I just figured with so much going on—"

"If you don't want me home, I can find plenty of other places to go. And plenty of other dykes that think I'm attractive."

Chava opened her mouth to respond, but Brian stepped in between them. "Okay, time out," he said. "Something weird is going on here. No one should speak unless I point to you."

"Who the fuck are you?" Elsa asked.

"He's my friend," Chava said in a defensive voice.

"And not mine?"

"Children, please!" Brian shouted. They both stopped.

"Chava, why did you have a tough day?" he asked.

"Because every five minutes, a different temple member called, complaining about their partner, asking me to mediate. Can you believe it? I got like eighty calls today. I finally just turned off my phone and came home. A rabbi can only do so much, right?"

Elsa looked shocked.

"What?" Brian asked her.

"My clients are all having relationship problems. Every one of them."

"So, whatever is going on with you two, is going on for everyone," Brian pointed out.

"That's not possible," Elsa said.

"And yet, it seems to be happening," Brian said, sitting back down at the table.

"What could possibly cause something like this?" Chava asked.

"It's wrong, whatever it is," Brian said. "It's not violent-wrong, like the East Bay right now, but it's really, really wrong."

"Do you think that it might have something to do with you and Terry?" Chava asked.

"I don't think so. We...split up before this started happening to you."

"Maybe it was the first fruits," Chava suggested.

"Maybe," Brian said. "In any case, let's be really careful to be kind to each other. If you feel tempted to lash out, remember that it's... some kind of influence. It's not actually something between you two."

Chava and Elsa looked at each other and nodded. "I'm sorry, baby," Chava said.

"Me too."

Brian crossed to the living room and put on his coat.

"Where are you going?" Chava asked. "You forgot the shopping list."

"To the library," Brian said. "I've got to figure out what could cause something like this. Can one of you check the television? Let's find out if this is local or...global, I suppose." He rushed back into the kitchen and grabbed the list. "But I'll go to the store on my way back. Promise."

34

KAT HOVERED OVER THE MIRROR, moving first this way, then that. "I don't see him." Her voice was forlorn.

Marco leaned over and pointed. "There."

Kat leaned in closer and squinted. She could barely make out a ghostly outline of a hand. It seemed to be twisting. "What is he doing?" she asked.

Marco shrugged. "Gauging by the distance from the floor... picking his nose?"

Kat sighed. "I'm losing him."

Mikael entered the kitchen and smiled at them. He moved behind Kat, putting his hands on her shoulders. "He's been lost a long time."

"He didn't have to be," she said.

"He made his own choices," Mikael said. "We all do."

"It's just like Charlie," Kat sighed.

"Who's Charlie?" Marco asked.

"He was a magickian who noviced with us for a while. A few months ago Terry led him and Kat on a field trip to Hell and he just... stayed. Said he was comfortable there. He'll eventually fade out, too."

"Like Sheol. Or Hades," Marco nodded. "It's sad."

"You reap what you sow," Mikael said.

"You're being awfully judgmental," Kat said hotly.

"I don't think I am. I'm not saying anything about your brother, or even about Charlie. It's just a fact. If you cultivate community, you get community, on this side of the grave or the other. If you cultivate isolation, you get isolation. It's just a law of the universe," Mikael argued. "And not only isn't it judgmental, it isn't even judgment, because God doesn't make any decisions about people's fates. The decisions are all ours. And we get exactly what we want...always. If we want to be in community, we get it. If we want to isolate ourselves, we get it."

"So where does heaven and hell enter into it?" Marco asked.

"Can't you guess?" Mikael answered. "Community and heaven are the same thing."

"And isolation?" Marco asked. "Oh. That's hell, isn't it?" He nodded, answering his own question. He looked surprised and a little sad. Kat looked back at him. She could see that Mikael had hit a nerve. She smiled at him, a little sadly.

"Exactly. That's why spiritual community is so important."

"Marco, is something up for you?" Kat asked.

Marco didn't answer. Instead, he asked, "Why spiritual community? Why not *any* community? Why not a bowling league?"

"I think it's because most communities are based on commonalities," Mikael answered. "Let's say you're in a bowling league. Yeah, you're in community, but the community is all bowlers—they're a pretty similar demographic. So it's good, I'd even say it's salvific, but it's not *best*."

"Okay. But what about a church? Aren't they all Christians?"

"Sure, but from wildly diverse strata—at church you form community with people that are wildly different from you: people of different races, different sexual orientations, different political leanings, poor people, rich people, mentally ill people, smart people, dumb people, and so on. And every one of them committed to loving each other."

"I don't think I've ever seen a church like that," Marco said.

"That's because Christians generally suck at it," Mikael said, sounding a little sad.

"At what?"

"At being Christians." He looked down for a few moments. "But we *are* trying."

"And other religions, are they trying?"

"I hope so."

"The bowling league still sounds pretty good."

"Knock yourself out," Mikael conceded. "Fewer casseroles, too, I'll wager."

"More beer."

"You don't know Lutherans," Susan called from the office.

"I know one Lutheran," Marco called back.

"I don't like beer!" Susan responded.

"How can you call yourself a Lutheran? Isn't beer a sacrament?"

"Can we get back to what to do about Randy?" Kat asked.

"Honey, I don't think there's anything we *can* do about Randy. I think we're just watching what happens to isolated people. What's happening to Charlie, too."

"Isn't he in community with *us*?" Kat asked. "Why doesn't that save him?"

Mikael hugged her from behind. "Because he chooses *not* to be in community with us. The mirror he lives in happens to be in our house, but he has no desire to be part of us, to love us, to let himself be loved by us. It's love that makes us real. Without it...we stop being real."

Kat knew that was true. She didn't answer but clutched at Mikael's hands and pulled them tight to her breast.

"Doesn't God love him?" she asked.

"Yeah, and that's probably why he's endured so long. But does he love God back? Is that love *growing*?"

She knew the answer to that. She stared at the wisp of a hand in the mirror.

The doorbell rang. "Ah'll get it," they heard Dylan's voice call from the living room.

A few moments later, Dylan was at the kitchen door, followed by Tobias. "Uh, some detectives, ya'll."

Cain and Perry stepped into the kitchen. Kat felt Mikael jump a bit in alarm. "Uh...hi, officers," she said.

"Sorry to intrude," Perry said, looking around. "We just have a few questions we'd like to ask."

"Something smells...interesting," Cain noted.

"I'm reheating beer-soaked spatchcocked quail," Marco informed him.

"Have a seat," Mikael said. "Marco, is there coffee?"

"Coming right up," Marco said, grabbing a fistful of mugs by their handles and carrying them to the table.

"Tea fer me," Dylan said. Toby scuttled under the table and lay down, panting loud and fast.

"I know the drill," Marco rolled his eyes.

"Are we in trouble?" Kat asked.

"If you were in trouble, we'd be talking to you at the station, not here," Perry said.

Cain added, more softly. "Jimmy—Mr. Tomlinson—he told us about your...speciality. We were hoping you might tell us something useful."

Susan emerged from the office and leaned against the doorframe, looking on with her arms folded over her bosoms. "Richard! Terry! Get your asses in here!" she yelled. A few moments later, Richard clomped down the back stairs.

"Where's Terry?" Susan asked.

"He's in the cottage," Marco answered. "I think he's taking a shower."

"What's up?" Richard asked.

Susan pointed toward Cain and Perry with her chin. "Detectives. They want to know if we can tell them something useful."

"Oh, I think we can help you there," Richard said. "Susan, grab those printouts."

OVER THE NEXT HALF HOUR, the friars detailed their activities from the past few days. Kat saw Cain and Perry's eyes get wider, especially when they saw the sigil maps of Oakland, Emeryville, and Berkeley they'd been compiling. "Okay, I keep hearing the word 'sigil,' but I don't understand what that means," Perry said, a note of edgy frustration in her voice.

"This is a sigil," Dylan pointed at the map.

"Yeah, I get that," Perry said. "But what *is* it?"

"It's a signature, of sorts," Richard said, accepting a mug of coffee from Marco. "It is a pictorial 'name' or symbol of a particular demon."

"Or angel," Marco pointed out. "Angels have sigils, too."

"True, but we're not dealing with any angels here," Richard conceded.

"Fair enough," Marco said, putting a quart carton of milk on the table.

"So, what does it *do*?" Cain asked. Kat could see he was trying to keep the conversation on track.

"It serves to connect a magickian to the demon he wants to work with," Richard said.

"Or she," Susan said.

Richard glared at her. "The next time you meet a woman who practices Goetic magick, I'll adjust my pronouns."

"Goetic?" Cain asked. He looked a little lost, and Kat realized he and Perry had just stumbled into Oz—a vast, unexplored territory they didn't know existed.

"Goetic magick, demon magick," Dylan explained. "Goetia means 'the howling.'"

"That's ominous," Perry said.

"You don't know the half of it," Richard said. "So a magickian uses a sigil to bind a demon to himself."

"Why would he want to do that?" Perry asked. "Aren't demons bad?"

"Demons are really, *really* bad," Mikael nodded.

"But a magickian does it to enforce servitude," Richard said.

"Come again?" Cain asked.

"A Goetic magickian—"

"Wait, are there *other* kinds of magickians?" Perry asked.

"Oh yeah," Richard answered. "There's one, now." He pointed at Marco. Marco, leaning against the kitchen counter, waggled his fingers at them.

"But you don't work with demons?" Perry asked Marco.

"Oh, God, no. Do I look like an idiot?"

Perry didn't answer that but looked plenty troubled. "But demons aren't *real*," she said.

"You jus' keep tellin' yoreself that," Dylan said.

"What do demons actually *do*?" Cain asked. "I mean, why would a magickian—a Goetic magickian, sorry—*want* to bind a demon to himself?"

"That depends on the demon," Richard shrugged. "Demons are organized into companies—like the military. We call them 'hosts.' Each host has a commander. So far, all of our sigils have been of commanders—a duke or a marquis or a baron."

"We got one prelate and two presidents, too," Dylan pointed out. "Ah'm holdin' out fer a den mother, but we ain't seen one o' them, yet."

Richard ignored the joke. "So when you summon a commander you might get whatever demons that commander rules, too. Not usually, but that's what we're seeing here."

"Why not usually?" Perry asked.

"Because the servitude is usually forced. So whatever demon is summoned will perform for the magickian grudgingly and will usually try to make the working backfire on the magickian, if it can."

"Payback?" Cain asked.

"Exactly. No one likes being made into a slave. Especially not a prince of hell," Richard said. "But it seems to us that the magickians doing this working are doing something really clever, something we've never seen before. They're *inviting* the demon princes, not compelling them. And the princes, in turn, are inviting their subordinates."

"But inviting them *where*? To do *what*?" Perry asked.

"To do this!" Susan pointed at the maps. "The shootings, the prostitution, the orgies, the theft, the...you name it."

"The demon princes are structured, too," Richard said. "Each of them is ruled by one of the seven deadly sins."

"So they're bringin' their minions out," Dylan said, waving his arms excitedly, "to play, to wreak havoc, to do what demons *do*."

"And by the looks of it, they're bringing them to Berkeley, too," Richard pointed to the map with the least color on it. "It's just starting here, in the south, where it borders Oakland. But it's growing."

"I'm monitoring it in real time in the office," Susan said, with a flip of her head. "It's growing, all right."

Just then the screen door opened, and Terry stepped into the kitchen. He stopped cold when he saw the room was full of people. "Whoa. Okay, sorry I missed the memo."

"Just filling the detectives in on our findings so far," Richard said. "What did you and Marco discover?"

"Didn't Marco tell you?"

"It was your discovery, not mine," Marco said. "I didn't want to get anything wrong."

"Oh, okay. So we went to Jimmy and Julia's."

"Do you mean Jimmy Tomlinson?" Perry asked.

"Yep. They were afraid they were under magickal attack."

"Magical attack?" Perry jerked upright in surprise. "What's— never mind. I can guess. What happened?"

"Marco used his device—"

"The narometer," Marco interjected.

"And?" Richard asked.

Marco shrugged. "I didn't find anything. Some pingy herbs, but you'd expect that."

"Fucking herbs," Mikael said. Kat poked him in the ribs with her elbow.

"Did *you* see anything?" Richard asked Terry.

"Yeah. I did. Marco was right, everything in the house seemed normal."

"But?"

"But Marco didn't point his machine at the people. Jimmy and Julia were fine. But Luna was there. And she was...not okay."

"What did you see?" Richard asked.

"Serious third-order demonic oppression."

"Are we talking pinstripe or paisley?"

"Hardcore paisley. With claws."

Richard nodded, and Kat could tell he was thinking hard. "What did she say when you confronted her?"

"She didn't say anything. The moment we turned our backs she was out of there."

"Like a bat out o' hell," Dylan breathed.

"Where do you think she went?" Richard asked.

Terry shrugged. "No idea. My guess is she went home, or to report to whoever is oppressing her."

"Do you think she knows she's oppressed?" Susan asked.

Richard looked surprised. "That's a very good question." He looked at Terry.

"I don't think so. She might be under a compulsion."

"And whoever is compelling her might also be involved in the killing at Tilden Park," Richard said.

"And this?" Susan waved her arm toward the maps. "Any connection there?"

"I don't know," Richard said. "If there isn't one, it's a big coincidence that it's all happening at once."

"We're not big fans of coincidence," Cain said.

"No. We're not either," Richard admitted.

"Can we get back to the sigils for a moment?" Cain asked.

Richard looked up at him. "Sure."

"Do you have one?"

"We burned 'em all," Dylan said. "It's the only way to deactivate 'em."

Terry froze. He reached into his pocket and pulled out a scrap of parchment.

"I *meant* to burn this, but I forgot when I saw the girl."

"You mean Chicken?" Dylan asked.

"Do we have to call her that?" Terry complained.

"Ah think it's cute," Dylan smiled.

"Where is she?"

"Napping. In the chapel," Susan said.

"Who's this?"

"A little girl that Father Terry rescued from a gunfight," Richard said. "He even took a bullet to save her."

Perry looked alarmed. "Then how—"

"Kevlar," Terry said, fingering the hole in his cassock. "Hurt like hell, though."

Perry held her hand out to Terry, who handed over the parchment.

"Isn't it dangerous to bring that in here?" Kat asked. "I mean, what's to stop the demon from bringing his party to the friary?"

"We're warded against that kind of thing," Terry said. "Well warded."

"What's 'warded' mean?" Cain asked.

"A ward—as we use it—is an angelic invocation against dark magick," Terry answered.

Perry got up and held the scrap of parchment between her eyes and the kitchen window. The sigil almost glowed from the brilliant backlighting. "What...is...*that*?" Perry asked, pointing to something on the parchment.

"It's a sigil," Terry said.

"No, not the sigil," Perry said. "*That.*"

Richard stood next to her and leaned in so that their heads were almost touching. "Uh...huh. That looks like a watermark. Like you see on fine stationary."

"Who uses parchment for stationary?" Mikael asked.

"Magickians," Marco said.

Richard froze. He snatched the parchment out of Perry's hands and held it directly in front of his gaze. "Well, fuck me."

"What?" Susan asked.

"This watermark has two symbols on it. I see a hawk..."

"Let me guess," Terry said. "The other one is a serpent."

"Ah've heard the fiddler play this tune b'fore," Dylan said.

"I can't believe Larch is behind this," Richard shook his head. "It's too..."

"Successful?" Susan asked.

"Yeah. I would have laid odds that something like this would be too ambitious for him."

"Well, we don't know *why* he's doing it," Terry admitted. "So we don't know if he's succeeded at all."

"Luna lives in San Francisco," Kat said. "And the Lodge of the Hawk and Serpent is in San Francisco, too. Is that one of those coincidences you don't believe in?"

"San Francisco is a big place," Richard said. "It *could* be a coincidence."

"Let's find out," Kat said. "Mikael, you up for a trip across the Bay?"

"I'll grab my coat," Mikael said, darting out of the kitchen.

"Grab mine, too, will you?"

"Wait," Richard said.

Mikael poked his head back in.

"The only way to the City is through Emeryville," Richard said. "Can you get there?"

"The freeways were still clear an hour ago," Cain said. "They should be fine."

"And there's nothing like this in SF," Susan said. "They'll actually be safer than we are once they get there."

"Okay," Richard nodded. "Go and see if you can find Luna. See what she knows."

Mikael saluted, and he and Kat made a hasty exit.

"What if Luna doesn't know anything?" Susan asked. "What if she's just a passive participant? What if she really is being oppressed and has no idea why?"

"She may not know anything about *this*," Terry said, indicating the maps.

Marco held out his hand to Richard. Richard cocked his head but handed the parchment to the magickian. Marco studied it. "We know this demon is involved," he said.

"Yeah, so?" Terry asked.

"So whatever your Hawk and Serpent bozos are up to, this demon is a witness."

"Yeah, okay. So?" Terry repeated.

"So let's ask *him*," Marco said.

WEDNESDAY

See, the name of the Lord comes from far away,
burning with his anger, and in thick rising smoke;
his lips are full of indignation,
and his tongue is like a devouring fire;
his breath is like an overflowing stream
that reaches up to the neck—
to sift the nations with the sieve of destruction,
and to place on the jaws of the peoples a bridle that leads them
astray.
—*Isaiah 30:27-28*

35

RICHARD AWOKE to the sound of smashing windows, screaming women, barking dogs, and the soulless madrigal of competing car alarms. He leaped out of bed, threw on a cassock, and rushed into the hallway to find Susan already there. They rushed down the stairs and stood transfixed before the living room window—Berkeley was ablaze.

By the light of the fire filling every window, Richard rushed to the kitchen. "I'm going to get Terry. Find Marco!" he called over his shoulder as he headed out the back door. His gut sank when we saw that the cardboard patch they'd put on the cottage window had been ripped away, and more of the windows had been smashed. The noise outside was a deafening cacophony of voices, alarms, and roaring flames. "Terry!" he called but doubted anyone could hear him. He noticed that the door had been kicked open—splintered wood adorned the place where the deadbolt had been, sticking out at wild angles.

Richard took the stairs in one leap and landed on the porch with enough force to shake the whole cottage. "Terry!" he called again and dashed inside. He didn't bother to turn on a light—there was no need for it. The fires were so close and so bright that everything seemed to be dancing with a bright orange glow, even inside the cottage. Richard was about to head for the bedroom, when a man emerged from the kitchen, holding Terry in a headlock. An icepick was pressed to the side of the friar's head.

Terry looked terrified, still in his bunny pajamas. He was also, however, wild-eyed and cackling. The firelight reflected off the bald pate of his head, and his goatee was dark and slick with...what? Blood? Richard couldn't tell. It could have been molasses for all he knew.

Richard held his hands up. "Listen to me. The voices in your head are not your friends. And you don't have to do what they are telling you to do."

The man didn't answer but only waved the icepick around dramatically, then he held it out as if to lunge at Richard. Richard retreated a couple of steps, and the man shoved Terry in front of him, making for the door. He grabbed Terry by the neck again before the diminutive friar could spin away from him, however, and dragged him down the stairs. Richard followed, feeling helpless. He saw a poker by the fireplace and picked it up. He swung it to get a sense of its heft, and bounded out the door and down the stairs in pursuit of the attacker.

In the back yard, the bearded man had Terry in a choke hold, once again threatening to run the icepick through his temple. They faced Richard but backed up slowly toward the gate that led to the street.

"What's your name?" Richard called to the man. "Tell me—" he paused. *Tell me what?* He remembered Jesus in his prayer yesterday. "Tell me what you're feeling."

But the man seemed too crazed for conversation. His eyes darted about like angry flies, and his lips were drawn back in a maniacal grin. Richard wracked his brain, trying to come up with the name of whatever demon must have this man in his grip. But there were simply too many possibilities. *There are 72 demons in the* Lesser Key of Solomon, *and each of those has countless subordinates under him,* he thought. He fought the urge to despair and clutched at his head in his hands.

Suddenly the man jerked and flailed and fell to the ground in a spasmodic heap. Terry stumbled backwards and caught his balance on the fence, gasping for breath.

"What happened? What did you do?" Richard asked Terry.

Terry held onto the fence and didn't answer.

"It wasn't him," Marco said from behind them. Richard turned to look at him and saw wires extending from a black handle in his hands to the twitching man. "Taser," Marco said. "Hey, I didn't invent it. This is off-the-shelf."

"Will he be okay?" Richard pointed at the man.

"He'll be okay from the taser," Marco answered. "I can't vouch for the demon possession, or oppression, or whatever is going on for him."

Richard rushed to Terry and caught him up in a hug. "Are you okay?"

"Yeah," Terry said, but his voice was rough. "I think so."

Richard could feel him shaking. "Why didn't the wards hold?"

"I don't know," Terry answered. "Anything can be overwhelmed, I guess."

"Damn. None of us are safe, now. Terry, go and grab a cassock, and meet us back here as soon as you can. Go!"

Terry took a second to get a grip on himself but then darted off toward the porch of the cottage.

"Where—?" Richard looked around wildly for Kat and Mikael, but then he remembered. They had gone to San Francisco last night. He breathed, relieved for the moment. Richard turned and saw Dylan and Susan standing close together, with Chicken clinging to Susan's leg. Except for Mikael and Kat, everyone he considered family was in this backyard. "We're not safe here, anymore," he said. "Whatever overtook Oakland and Emeryville, it's here."

Dylan put his arm around Susan and they both nodded. Chicken buried her face in Susan's jeans.

"We have to get someplace safe," Richard continued.

"Albany," Dylan suggested.

"This is creeping north, now," Richard shook his head. "Albany will be next."

"We could go to the City," Marco said, which Richard took to mean San Francisco.

"We could," Richard said. "But that's too far for us to be of any use, don't you think?"

"It's safe," Marco countered.

"Alameda," Susan said. "There's no crime in Alameda."

"There's *never* any crime in Alameda," Dylan noted.

"But there aren't any of these outbreaks there, either," Susan said. "It's the closest safe place."

Richard nodded. "Let's do it. Dylan, you and Susan and Terry pack up your gear—five minutes, no more, and head out. Marco, you should go, too."

"Ain't you comin'?" Dylan asked.

"Yes, but I have to...I have to do something first. I'll follow."

"In what?" Susan asked. "Mikael and Kat have the only other car."

Shit, Richard thought. His mind raced.

"You guys go ahead," Marco said. "I'll take Richard wherever he needs to go in the vanigan. Then we'll be right behind you."

Richard nodded at Marco gratefully. "Thank you, Marco. Let's move, everyone!"

36

RICHARD WATCHED the beat up Corolla wind through the street around piles of burning trash, dodging running pedestrians, some of whom were holding weapons. He still had no idea what was really going on. He only knew it was bad.

"Up, boy," he said to Tobias. The great yellow lab hopped up into the VW van, his ears erect and his eyes shining, ready for adventure.

Marco looked far less excited. "Where are we going?"

"The friary next to All Saints," Richard said.

"Just down the street?"

"Yeah."

"Thank God," Marco said. "We won't be far behind them, then."

"Shouldn't be," Richard stowed his kit bag on the seat next to Tobias, then climbed into the passenger seat. "Let's move."

Marco nodded and pulled out of the drive, navigating around the blazing trash and nearly running over a man chasing someone with a knife. "I'm seeing a pattern here," he said.

"Yeah. I can think of three wrath demons that could be behind it," Richard said.

"Who are we picking up?" Marco asked.

"Mother Maggie. My spiritual director."

"Your spiritual director?" Marco sounded surprised.

"Have you met her?" Richard asked. He didn't bother to wait for an answer. "She's widowed. She lives by herself in one of the friary apartments. She's got no one." He swallowed. "She's got me."

Marco looked over at Richard and nodded as the van rolled to a stop. "This it?"

"Yeah. Back me up, will you?"

"Sure thing." Marco grabbed his taser and hopped out.

"Stay here, Toby," Richard said, closing his own door. Toby lay down on the floorboard and put his head on his paws.

Richard led Marco to a rickety staircase that clung precariously to the side of the crumbling building. "This does not look safe," Marco looked up.

"It hasn't fallen yet. Can you stand guard here?" Richard asked. Without waiting for an answer, he attacked the stairs, two at a time and was winded by the time he got to the top. He pounded on the door. "Maggie! Maggie, it's me, Richard! I know a safe place!"

There was no answer. "Shit!" Richard yelled. He pounded on the door again, but this time he put his ear to the door and listened. The noise outside was so great he couldn't hear anything from the inside. He leaned over the small metal landing and peered into the window to the kitchen. It was dark. Richard ran his fingers through his hair and forced himself to breathe more slowly. Then he kicked in the door.

"What the fuck was that?" Marco called.

Tobias started barking so loudly that even Richard could hear it. He turned and called down to Marco, "Check on Toby!" and then he entered the darkened room. He tried a light switch, but the power was out. He found a candle and lit it from the stove, then held it aloft as he looked around. He had never been in Maggie's apartment before, but it certainly looked like her. The table cloth was ratty, and there was a liberal dusting of toast crumbs across it. A jar of marmite was open on the kitchenette counter.

He strode to the bathroom, but it was empty. He moved to the bedroom. The bed was made, and the closet was open. There was one brightly-colored sock on the floor. Richard blew air through his cheeks and leaned against the wall. "Maggie, where the fuck are you?" he asked.

Just then he heard Marco bellow, "Son of a bitch!" from below. Richard ran to the door, slammed it behind him, and skipped as many stairs as he could manage without falling. He slid down the metal rails the last half of the ground floor. He landed lightly for his weight and ran toward the van. Marco was holding his head and cursing.

"Goddam motherfuckers!" he shouted.

"What?" Richard asked. "What's wrong?"

"What the fuck do you mean, 'What's wrong?' Just look, man!"

Richard first checked to see if Toby was all right. The dog was sitting upright in the front seat, panting. Relieved, he turned his attention to the van. It was tilting at an odd angle. Glancing down, Richard saw that the two driver's side tires had been slashed. Richard circumambulated the van. A third tire had also been punctured. "Crap," he said, fingering the slash.

"That's what I'm saying," Marco almost wailed. "What the fuck do we do now?"

The piles of burning trash were in the distance, but the streetlights were out. Richard felt blind, vulnerable. He tapped Marco's arm. "Have you got those spectacles?" he asked.

"Yeah," Marco said. He opened the sliding door to the van and snatched the velvet bag from the Liahona case. "Here."

Richard turned them over in his hand. The lenses were stones, not ground lenses, and were opaque. They should be impossible to see through, but he put them on anyway. The light was painfully bright, but instead of snatching them off his face, Richard endured the discomfort and waited for his eyes to adjust.

It took longer than he expected it to, and he almost gave up. But images began to emerge out of the brilliant intensity, and he gasped.

"What?" Marco asked. "What do you see?"

Brighter than the light of day, Richard saw an illuminated street. It was Cedar Street, he was sure of that—he knew it well. But it was transformed. The street itself shone, as well as the very air around him, but the shining wasn't coming from the street or the air though —it was as if it were a reflected light, yet he could not discern the source of the brilliance. He could see for what seemed like miles in all directions. It was heartbreakingly beautiful, but at the same moment achingly sad. For in addition to the illumination, he saw neighbors attacking each other up and down both Cedar and Oxford streets—hundreds of them, moving like angry bees, stretching into the far distance. Some were fully dressed, some were in nightclothes, some were in their underwear, and some were completely naked. But all of them were either attacking or being attacked.

But he saw more. Hovering above the people, mounted on terrible steeds, were demonic princes, their scepters extended as they bid their troops to fan out in this direction or that. Their great cruel beaks clacked, their animal heads fierce and terrible to behold. Their mounts were dragons, ostriches, and goats, all nearly three times normal size, and their saddles supported palanquins for the demonic royalty. Their troops scuttled to and fro on every visible street, slinging chains and bringing sword and axe to bear on the terrified, stampeding people of Berkeley. He heard the screams of victims far and near, and he had to look away as one neighbor smashed the skull of another with a hammer.

Richard removed the spectacles and put them in an inside pocket of his cassock.

"What did you see?" Marco asked.

"Too much," Richard answered.

37

CHICKEN CLUNG to Terry's neck most of the drive over. He rocked her and wondered just how much trauma a little girl can take before she sustains permanent damage. She buried her face in his cassock and started humming. *That's it,* he thought. *Sing. 'He who sings prays twice.'*

Highway 80 seemed almost deserted as they sped toward Oakland. The moon was down, streetlights were out, and the dark seemed like a malevolent, smothering presence. "Any idea what Richard had to check on?" Dylan asked, checking his rearview mirror.

"No clue," Susan confessed. "Let's just pray it doesn't set him back. We may not be the only ones having this thought."

"Yer prob'ly right there," Dylan conceded. "What d'ya think? Which way should we go fer Alameda?"

"The tunnel is the closest," Susan said.

"Yeah, but the trickiest to get to, bein' downtown an' all," Dylan said.

"Let's try it," Susan said.

"Okay. Yer the boss," Dylan said, signaling to transfer to the 980.

"I am *not* the boss," Susan said.

"Name one fight you didn't win," Dylan narrowed his eyes at her before returning them to the road.

"Oh for God's sake," she looked out the window.

"Can you guys do this on your own time?" Terry asked. "I have my own nuptial disaster to nurse without watching yours." Chicken started humming louder. "Beside, you're upsetting the...Chicken."

"How's mah lil' *pollo*?" Dylan sat up straighter and strained to see her in the rearview mirror.

"I need to ward this car," Terry said.

"What?" Dylan's eyes flitted to the left to see Terry.

"The car. Let's say we roll through the jurisdiction of an envy demon—what is going to stop us from getting out of the car and going on a looting spree?"

Susan turned to look at him. Her eyes were wide. "Do you...Could that happen? I hadn't thought of that."

"It *could* happen, and we've *got* to think about it," Terry said. "Chicken, honey, can you move?"

"Okie-dokie!" she said, but she stayed where she was.

"She certainly learned that word," Susan said.

"Is that one word or two?" Dylan asked. "Ah mean, it's hyphenated, right?"

Terry moved Chicken onto the seat next to him, despite her protests. "The only thing stopping me and Richard from leveling a fucking rocket launcher at those gang-bangers was the fact that we simply didn't have any guns!"

"An' wasn't nothin' stoppin' Kat from shootin' up that morphine. She'd be at the morgue if we hadn't burned that sigil when we did."

"That's what I'm saying. We're not immune. Even people of faith can come under demonic oppression."

"That's a fact," Dylan acknowledged.

"Will the wards do the job?" Susan asked. "I mean...they didn't... at the friary."

Terry looked down. "I don't know."

"Well, if we go through the jurisdiction of a lust demon and you start humping my leg, I'm going to put a thumb through your eye," Susan told him.

"Noted," Terry answered. "Wait, did you bring those maps?"

"Nope. Sitting on the kitchen table," Susan admitted.

"Damn. We might have been able to navigate around the hot spots."

"I didn't think of it, Terry. I'm sorry."

"It's okay." He opened his kit bag and began to rummage through it. "I'll set the most powerful wards I've got, and we'll just have to hope for the best."

"Fuck hope, Ah'm prayin'," Dylan announced.

"That's not a bad idea, either," Terry said. He looked around and his shoulders slumped.

"What's wrong?" Susan asked.

"This would be easier if I could get *out* of the car," Terry said.

"Feel free to pass us something," Susan said. "You don't need to climb over us physically, do you?"

"Well, it would be better," Terry said. He selected four stones from his kit bag and said a brief prayer, dedicating each of them to a different archangel. "Oh, shit."

"What?" asked Susan.

"We're in a moving car," he said.

"Well, I should hope so!" Susan said.

"No, I mean—how do I do the correspondences?" Terry asked. "Michael is the archangel of the North. I can set a stone for him in what is north now, but as soon as we turn..."

"It won't be north anymore. How important is that kind of...correspondence?"

"It *is* kind of a form of magick," Terry admitted.

"Angel magick," Dylan countered.

"Non-coercive angel magick," Terry clarified.

"Look, I don't care about your no-magick code right now," Susan said, her voice rising with obvious panic. "I want to make sure I won't be compelled by some disembodied entity to disembowel my husband. Without good reason, that is."

"Amen," agreed Dylan.

"Can you say a prayer that will compensate?" Susan asked. "Or can you set four sets of wards, so that each direction simultaneously corresponds to each angel?"

Terry sat up straighter. He looked at Chicken. Chicken looked at him. She touched his nose. "Terry," she said.

"Did you hear that?" Terry asked. "She said my name."

"It's a fucking Kodak moment," Susan admitted, smiling over her shoulder at the little girl. "What about the wards?"

"It's a really good idea, the four stones in each corner idea. I've never heard of it being tried before, but...the problem is, I only have eight stones."

"Does it have to be stones?" Susan asked.

"No, it can be any object," Terry answered. "Stones are just...traditional."

"You are Terry Milne. You are an innovator," she fished around in her purse. "Here are eight tampons," she slapped them in his hand. "Get busy."

Terry gulped. He didn't know how archangels might feel about feminine hygiene products. What were the likely correspondences? Plastic, cotton...his mind reeled.

"Get cracking!" Susan ordered.

"Dude, if ya know what's good fer ya..." Dylan cautioned.

Terry separated the stones and tampons into four piles of four. Chicken picked up one of the tampons and would have put it in her mouth, but Terry snatched it from her. "Not for eating. Just for angels."

"And for bleeding," Susan said with a little too much cheer.

"This is gonna be one scarred child," Dylan noted under his breath. He turned right on Webster. The streets seemed blessedly deserted, although Terry could hear the distant sound of car alarms and sirens. Before they'd gone a block, however, a gang of tough-looking youth stepped into their path, strutting out together into the middle of the road.

"These don't look like gang-bangers," Susan said. "They look like middle-class suburban kids."

"Yeah, but they ain't themselves," Dylan said. "Look at their eyes." Three of the kids were white and two were African American. All of them were dressed in the kind of torn jeans that cost $60 new. Dylan brought the car to a stop.

One of them broke away from the others and sauntered up to the car window. He tossed a cigarette away. "Hey, man."

"Hey," Dylan said, rolling the window down slightly.

"Whatcha doin' out so late?"

"Uh...comin' home from...a party?" Dylan asked.

"You don't sound too sure of that," the youth narrowed his eyes at him.

"It was *kind* of a party," Dylan said. "We were playin' cards and smokin' dope, ya know. And there was pita chips and hummus. That's a party, right?"

"Is that your wife?" the kid peered into the window.

"Yeah," Dylan said.

"She's kind of pudgy, don't you think?"

"Wall, Ah'm kinda pudgy. We're like salt and pepper shakers, ya know, like a matched set."

"You think you're a funny guy?"

"Ah think Ah hold my own," Dylan said.

"Dyl..." Susan whispered.

"What Ah mean is, people *usually* laugh at mah jokes."

"You sure they're not laughing at you?"

"To be honest, no, Ah've never been too sure 'bout that."

This surprised the kid, who straightened up before bending down again. This time he looked at the back seat. "This your little girl?"

"No, we stole her from some gang-bangers," Dylan said. "Her name is Chicken."

"Is that one of your jokes?"

"Yeah. And that's mah buddy Terry. They're playing a game of rocks and tampons. Do ya know that game?"

The kid blinked at him. "I don't like you, fat man," he said. "I think you should get out of the car."

"Ah don't think Ah will," Dylan said.

Terry leaned over and whispered, "Okay, this could be worse. He's a bully. That means we're at the intersection of wrath and hubris demons." Terry handed two rocks and two tampons to Susan. "Put these by the windshield, as far to the right as you can. And give these to Dylan, for the other side," he handed over another set.

"I said, out of the car, fat man," the kid pounded on the hood.

"Uh, young man, Ah've been really patient with you," Dylan said, placing the stones and tampons on the dashboard as far as they could go to his left. "But Ah think you ferget just who's behind the 3,000-pound projectile here."

The young man pulled a gun out of the small of his back. "I think you'll do as I say."

"Aw, shit," Dylan said. "Ya know, honey, Ah ken see the tunnel."

"So can I," Susan said. "Gun it."

"Chicken, down!" Dylan yelled. Terry dove for the floor and pulled the little girl toward him into the wheel well while Dylan stomped on the gas. He steered the car straight toward the youths, who wailed and scattered when they realized he wasn't going to stop. Terry expected the tough kid who approached them to start shooting, but he didn't hear any shots.

"Ah knew it," Dylan said, making a beeline for the tunnel entrance. "That kid was bluffin'." Just then the rear window exploded sending a shower of glass throughout the car.

Chicken screamed, and Terry pulled her tightly against him. "Shhh..." he said. "It's going to be fine."

Dylan watched the tunnel looming before them, only two blocks away, but he pounced on the brakes.

"Why the fuck are you stopping?" Susan almost screamed. Dylan pointed. Looming before them, previously hidden in shadow, was a whole parade of people. As the car's headlights caught them, Terry saw that most of them were shuffling toward them, their faces twisted into malevolent grins. From the sides came dancers, leaping frenetically—desperate harlequins displaying an enforced merriment.

"What the hell?" Dylan breathed.

A taco truck rolled into the middle of the street, blocking their way, and stopped. Red paint had been sloshed over the menu that covered half the side of the truck, like the exit wound from a giant bullet. And fixed in the middle of the red spray was a sigil, it's activation parchment nailed above it. Terry could see it shuddering in the wind.

"Oh, Christ," he said. "That sigil is mobile. They're taking it on the road."

"Can they do that?" Susan asked.

"I don't see why not," Terry answered.

"What demon is it summoning?" Susan asked.

Terry pulled out his phone. "Inviting, not summoning. This working is as successful as it is only because it isn't coercive," he corrected her. Before he could pull up the Demonfinder app, however, a gloved hand reached through the broken window behind him and lifted him into the air.

"Awww, shit!" Dylan said, his eyes growing huge as he watched Terry get plucked from the car. Chicken screamed, and a moment later, her wriggling body was also lifted through the smashed window.

"You put her down!" Susan shouted. A split second later, a baseball bat shattered the passenger-side window. She ducked and covered her eyes, but then another gloved hand reached in, unlocked her door, and dragged her into the street.

Dylan's own window shattered next, and he jerked his head aside as a shard of glass entered his left eye. "Motherfucker!" he howled, grabbing at his eye. A fist punched at his head, causing him to bite his tongue, and he whimpered quietly. An enormous man, big enough to be a longshoreman, forced Dylan to his knees next to Susan. Terry could have reached out to touch them, but he didn't want to draw any attention. Instead, he cradled Chicken and tried to soothe her.

Another vehicle rolled up to the taco truck. This was a flatbed truck, a familiar sight in this area of Oakland. But on the bed of the truck was a man covered with bruises, defiantly upright, on his knees. Thick ropes bound each of his hands to two of the corners of the truck, ensuring that he couldn't move either to the left or to the right, to the front nor the back. A woman leaped up on the flatbed with him, a wild grin slashing across her face. Her eyes were a little too wide, a little too manic. Her dress had been sexy and expensive hours ago, but now hung from her busty frame in tatters. Terry saw a flash in the air, and the woman snatched at it, holding forth the object she had caught—a filleting knife, it's long thin blade shining in the Corolla's headlights. With a wicked cackle, she began to carve at the man's chest.

The man's torso seized up as every muscle in his body tensed, and he threw his head back and issued a howl at the black morning sky. But the cacophony from the revelers was so loud Terry couldn't hear him even though he was less than twenty feet away.

Terry gulped as he realized that she wasn't just cutting him—she was carving the sigil into his chest. "It's a sacrifice," he called to Dylan and Susan. "To whatever demon that sigil belongs to." He didn't know if they heard him. It didn't matter.

Dylan clutched at his wounded eye and bobbed back and forth, as if he were davening. Terry covered Chicken's eyes and stroked her hair, but he couldn't tear his own eyes away from the truck. With a flourish, the woman cut a final stroke into the man's skin. He opened his throat to issue another howl of rage and pain, but she drew the knife across his throat next. A spray of black erupted into the night sky and the man fell forward onto the truck bed.

Terry felt the energy rise around him. The sacrifice had been efficacious and the demon's presence suffused the street corner, oppressing every sentient being within sight. Terry felt his own bloodlust rise within him. He saw Susan howl with a rage that would have terrified him at any other time, but his own terror seemed to have hit its maximum peak. He watched her transformation with an almost scientific detachment.

The woman leaped off the truck and landed on bare feet a yard and a half from them. She marched up to Dylan and pointed her filleting knife at his good eye. "I smell blood on this one. Let's feed him to our master next."

38

RICHARD FELT the wind of a bullet as it grazed his cheek. "Shit, not again!" He wiped at his cheek and wondered at the blood on his hand.

Marco's eyes went wide. "We've got to get to safety, man. Quick, get in the van!"

"But we can't *go* anywhere in the van," Richard protested.

"Just get in. At least we won't get hit by stray bullets while we think."

Richard couldn't argue with that, and when Marco slid the van's side door back, he hopped up onto the seat next to Toby. Toby slathered a kiss on his cheek and looked surprised at the taste of blood. Marco jumped in himself and shut the door after him. "Duck," he said, laying out on the floor. Richard lowered himself to the floor between the first and second seats, pulling Toby down beside him. Richard and Marco stared at each other under the seats.

"What now?" Richard asked. Marco blinked, apparently thinking.

"Let's ask God," Marco said and jumped up, scrambling for something on the seat.

"I've never known you to be a pray-er," Richard said.

"No, not praying," Marco said. "Asking. With this." He held forth the Liahona box.

"Right, the Mormon oracle," Richard said.

"Liahona," Marco corrected him. "And it's Jewish in origin."

"By way of Guatemala."

"Uh...right." Marco lifted the small globe from the box and set it on the van's carpet just below him. A loud "crack" came from the roof.

"I think we just caught a falling bullet," Richard said.

"Or a rock."

"Sounded like a bullet to me."

Toby's ears lowered and he whined, nosing at Richard's hands until he petted him. Richard did, finding himself to be as comforted as Toby seemed to be.

"What should we ask?" Marco asked.

"Does it do yes and no questions?"

"I don't think so. I mean...I don't know. It's not a fucking magic eight ball, though. Brian was going to decipher the stylized Hebrew, but he never got around to it before he took off. I can't make heads or tails of it."

"What good is it going to do us?"

"Look, I don't want to get all quantum theory on you, but perhaps it will answer according to what we understand it to mean."

"I am not going to stake my life on that assumption," Richard said. He and Toby touched noses. A fire truck raced by outside.

"Look, it's a compass, right? So let's assume it's a directional oracle. Let's ask it to point to the safest route to Alameda. By foot, I mean."

Richard nodded. "Okay, let's give that a try."

Marco peeled back the leather strap that covered the cutouts in the ornately etched globe and stared at the twin dials inside. "Which way, O oracle of God—"

"Good Lord," Richard rolled his eyes.

"—is the safest route to Alameda?" Then he hastily added, "By foot?" Marco reared back and studied the dials.

"What?" Richard asked.

"The red one is pointing this way," he pointed toward the van's door.

"Yeah, that's south. Alameda is due south of here, on the other side of Oakland."

"But the other dial—the gold dial—is pointing...this way," he pointed toward the rear tire on the passenger's side.

"Those are two different directions," Richard said.

"No shit."

"So what does that tell us?"

Marco dropped his face into the carpet. "I hab no idea," he said, his voice muffled.

Richard turned onto his back and scratched Toby's chin as the dog panted just above him. "Here's a thought. What if the red dial shows us the answer to our question, but the gold dial shows us what God wants us to do instead?"

Marco turned his face toward Richard, now resting his ear on the carpet. "Huh?" he said.

"No, I mean it. What if the Liahona's purpose isn't so much navigation as it is discernment? Wouldn't that make more sense if it's an oracle?"

Marco blinked but said nothing. Richard could almost see the wheel's turning in the magickian's head. "Think about it. God has two wills—a perfect will and a permissive will. The permissive will is what God will let us get away with, but the perfect will is what God truly desires for us. I know in my own life I often want to know if my will and God's will are running along the same track. The Liahona could show you that. If you asked it a question and both dials are pointing in the same direction, you can be reasonably certain that what you want to do and what God wants you to do are in sync. But if they aren't...then maybe you should reconsider."

"Are you saying we should reconsider going to Alameda?"

Richard shrugged. "It's just a theory. But I think it has merit. We want to go to Alameda, and the dial shows us the direction for that. And God will allow it. We could set out for it now. But I think the gold dial is showing the way God really *wants* us to go."

"I'm not really on intimate terms with your God," Marco said.

"And yet you're using one of the most holy oracles in Jewish history," Richard noted, enjoying the irony. "Or Mormon, for that matter."

"Aren't the Jewish God and the Mormon God different gods?" Marco asked.

"Not according to the Mormons," Richard answered.

"What do you think?"

"Well, Mormon theology isn't monotheistic," Richard said.

"It isn't?" Marco's eyebrows jumped.

"Nope. It's henotheistic."

"I don't have my Bible dictionary on me at the moment, man."

"Sorry. It means that there are lots of gods, but we only deal with the one who has jurisdiction—" Richard sat up. "—here. The demons are jurisdictional, too. Because of the sigils' influential radii."

"In English, professor?"

"It's just...a coincidence. A parallel. Kind of cool, but not terribly helpful, I don't think. We are suffering under kind of a henotheistic attack."

"Don't you mean henodemonic?"

"I guess I do," Richard smiled. "Anyway, what do you want to do?"

"What do *you* want to do?"

"I want what God wants," Richard answered.

Marco sighed. "I was afraid you'd say that."

39

THE MAN who looked like a longshoreman jerked Dylan to his feet and pushed him toward the flatbed truck. Susan heard her husband shout, "Anytime now, Jesus!" He stumbled toward the truck, still holding his eye. She could see blood trailing from it, congealing in his red beard. Her hand went to her mouth and she fought back a cry of rage and anguish. In her mind's eye, she saw herself leaping up, grabbing the filleting knife from the murderous skinny bitch, and slashing her throat with it. She jerked forward to do just that when Terry caught her by the jeans and pulled her back down. "Don't do it," he whispered.

"These are bad people," Chicken said.

"Yes, honey. They are..." Terry trailed off. "Actually, no. They're just like you and me. They're being forced to act this way by evil spirits."

Chicken's eyes went even wider. "Spirits?"

"Yep. That's who we're really fighting."

"Can't you go into vision and come back with...I don't know, help?" Susan asked.

"By the time I get back, Dylan will be toast."

"He's going to be toast if we just sit here."

"We don't have a lot of options, Susan." He looked around. "Pray."

"I *am* praying," she said, sounding defeated. "I think God just went deaf."

The crazed woman inserted her filleting knife under the flap of Dylan's double-breasted cassock. With the flick of her wrist, she cut the button from it and his cassock fell open on one side. She cut the button on the other side, and it opened altogether, revealing to all that Dylan was naked underneath, his prodigious belly obvious in the streetlight. Dylan seemed to have gained an unearthly measure of courage, though. Susan saw him stand up straighter. He still clutched at the ruinous mass of his eye, but he was no longer grimacing. He seemed to have no shame around his nakedness, either. Instead, he stared at the woman defiantly. She held the filleting knife up to his chest. Then she lowered it and touched it to his penis. "Which would you miss more?" she said aloud. "Your heart or your dick?"

Dylan didn't dignify her query with an answer but only stood stock still. Time seemed to have slowed to a crawl. The woman returned the knife to his chest, and with a deft flick, Susan saw a line of blood begin seeping from her husband's chest. Dylan didn't flinch.

She lined the knife up for another cut, but before the tip of the knife touched his skin a flurry of gunfire ripped through the air. Susan felt Terry leap on her. Together they crashed to the ground and looking back, Susan saw that Chicken was already hugging the pavement, her eyes as wide as eggs. Susan paused for a moment, feeling Terry's body weight on top of her, hearing his breathing in her ear. "You okay?" he whispered.

"I think so. You okay?" she asked.

"Yeah."

Susan craned her neck to see what was happening to Dylan. Dylan continued to stand straight and strong, but the woman had collapsed to the street, clutching at a spurting wound in her neck. "Couldn't have happened to a nicer bitch," Susan whispered out loud. She rolled out from under Terry and crawled toward her husband. "Get down, you jackass!" she shouted. Dylan saw her, blinked, then dropped to the pavement beside her. Another round of gunfire caught several of the revelers. Bodies fell all around them, some of them screaming and writhing in distress.

"C'mon," Susan said. It was unexpected, but in that moment she chose to interpret the gunfire as a gift from God. She didn't know who was firing, or why. She only knew that, for a few brief seconds, no one was paying any attention to them. She grabbed Dylan's wrist and jerked him toward the Alameda tunnel. She started crawling as fast as she could. As soon as she saw that Dylan was following her, she glanced back and saw that Terry and Chicken were crawling too, and gaining on them. She crawled underneath the flatbed truck and out the other side.

It was then that she saw their saviors with her own eyes. Emerging from the Alameda tunnel was a line of what looked like soldiers. Their faces were in shadow, but the bright light of the tunnel behind them made them shine with an ethereal glory. Perhaps it was a trick of the light, but Susan could swear they had haloes. She crawled directly toward them, praying fervent, ungrammatical prayers that they would not shoot them. As she crawled closer, her heart leaped to see them part to make a way for them. Tears sprang to her eyes as she crawled into the safety of the tunnel. Once past the line of soldiers, a team of paramedics rushed to them. Susan didn't notice the shredded skin on her elbows and wrists. She was only aware of Dylan's hand in hers, the amber lights of safety buzzing in the tunnel's ceiling, and the busy chatter of her rescuers as they covered her with care.

40

———

KAT HANDED a medium pumpkin latte to Mikael then took a seat across from him. Peets coffee in the lower Haight was filling up with their regular morning clientele, and they had been lucky to find a table. Mikael pointed to a newspaper the previous occupant of their table had left behind. The headline read, "Divorce skyrockets."

"What's new?" asked Kat.

"Divorces," Mikael answered. Then he whistled.

"What is it, something like half of all marriages end in divorce?" Kat said.

"Yes, but not all on the same day," Mikael answered. "According to this, in the past two days 14% of married couples in the US filed for divorce."

"That's insane," Kat grabbed the paper from him.

"Hey, I *was* looking at that," Mikael protested.

Kat ignored him. "And listen to this: 'For the first time in its history, both Disneyland and the four Disneyworld theme parks closed their gates because whole families were breaking out into brawls. Disney officials said the parks were not safe places for families and will remain closed until the situation improves.' That's crazy."

"Who the fuck do you think you are?" cried a woman at the next table.

The man seated with her reared back in shock. He seemed to regain his strength, because a moment later he answered, "I'm your husband, and I have a right to know how you're spending *our* money."

"You can micromanage the fuck out of your minions at the office, asshole, but you won't do that to me!" She threw the rest of her muffin at him, and it bounced off his nose.

His face grew scarlet, and he stood up. "Asking about a $600 charge to our credit card is *not* micromanaging. It's...concern."

"Get concerned about your ass!" she yelled.

He spluttered but finally managed, "What the fuck does that even mean?"

Everyone in the coffee shop was looking at them, except for a lesbian couple in the corner who both sat with their arms folded, not looking at one another or speaking. It was so quiet Kat could hear the barista scraping change out of the register. Then the normal cacophony of sound erupted again in the room, as everyone else resumed their own arguments.

Kat leaned over. "Are you scared?"

"Of what?" Mikael leaned in to hear her.

"Of...all this fighting."

"Of *us* fighting?"

"Yeah."

Mikael leaned back. "We don't really fight."

"No but...whatever is happening here...we could."

Mikael nodded. "Especially since we didn't get any sleep last night."

"What should we do?"

Mikael shrugged. Then he brightened up. "First, we need more coffee. Lots more."

"Agreed. Then what?"

"Then we should make a covenant."

"With whom?"

"With each other. I'll make a promise to you, and hopefully you'll make a promise to me."

"Okay. What shall we promise?"

"I promise to stick with you, no matter what. When I get irritated at you, I promise to remember that it isn't you—it's whatever magickal weirdness is happening."

Kat nodded decisively. "I'm in. I promise the same. What you said."

"Shall we shake on it?"

"I'll do you one better." She leaned over further and touched her lips to his.

When she finally drew away, he smiled. "That seals it."

"What's next on our agenda?"

"Besides the coffee?"

"Besides the coffee."

"Okay, we've been to the old Hawk and Serpent Lodge House."

"Now occupied by a senior memory care facility, apparently," Kat said.

"Right. Where else might those snakes be hiding?"

"Let's ask Luna."

Mikael nodded, and held up his empty coffee cup. "To Luna's!"

41

FRATER KHAMS CREPT QUIETLY into Larch's room. Eleazar was sitting on the side of the bed, gazing at his master who was lying on his back. Khams approached and saw that Larch's eyelids were twitching. There was obviously a lot going on wherever Larch was. His limbs jerked and spasmed in response to something, somewhere. *In another world,* Khams thought.

Khams handed a cup of tea to Eleazar. "How is he?"

Eleazar moved his head from side to side. "Okay, I guess. He's been out for almost twenty-four hours now."

"Are you worried?"

"Of course I'm worried."

Khams pulled a chair away from the wall and set it where he could see Eleazar most easily. His back was to the window, and he could feel the early morning Autumn chill on his neck. "But just what are you worried *about*?"

Eleazar didn't answer.

"He can't get hurt."

"You don't know that. Plus, I didn't exactly say I was worried about *him*."

Khams sat up straighter, his eyebrows bouncing in surprise. "Who are you worried about, then?"

"Okay, I *am* worried about him. Who knows what he's facing...up there?" He looked at the ceiling. "But I'm also worried about whoever it is he's meeting."

"Why are you worried about them? You don't even know them," Khams answered.

"Because I know Babylon. I know he'll stop at nothing to get what he wants, no matter who it hurts. And I don't have to know someone to...not want them to get hurt."

Khams nodded. Together they looked at Larch's twitching face. "You know that's why you and I both suck at being magickians, right?"

Eleazar didn't answer.

"We've always been the weak ones, you and me," Khams went on. "Oh, and Charybdis, too, but look what happened to him." He let that hang on the air for a moment before continuing. "The others are strong, ruthless even. They're in touch with their True Will."

Eleazar nodded almost imperceptibly. "I'm afraid he'll fail. It will crush him. Especially after last time...and the time before that."

"It would," Khams agreed.

"But I'm also worried that he'll...succeed."

Khams nodded. "I know just what you mean. I don't know how he plans on destroying the Almighty. But if he does..."

"Where do you suppose it comes from?"

"What?"

"This...antipathy toward God."

"Daddy issues," Khams said with conviction.

Eleazar cocked his head. "Where did you get that? Babylon has never said two words about his parents."

"Well, don't you think that's odd?" Khams asked. "Besides, I heard him once when he was dreaming. He was cussing out his father, no doubt about it. There's deep, twisted stuff there."

Eleazar nodded, obviously weighing this news. "What do you know about his father?"

"I know he was a Catholic priest who strung his mother along and never acknowledged him as his son."

"Where the fuck are you getting this?" Eleazar asked.

"After I heard the dream, I did some checking. I talked to his mother."

"His mother is alive?"

"She is. Recovering meth addict, lives in a group home in the outer sunset."

"Harsh," Eleazar shook his head. "And his father?"

"Bishop of the Archdiocese of Santa Fe."

"New Mexico?"

"Uh-huh."

"Fuck. No wonder he hates his guts."

"And God's."

They sat in silence for several minutes, watching Larch twitch.

"He's just guessing, you know...about what would happen. He doesn't know," Eleazar said.

"But he's right so far," Khams admitted. "Have you seen the papers? Yesod, the sephirah of relationship—of conjugal love—has been thrown into complete chaos."

"So he's doing it," Eleazar agreed. "It's working."

"So far."

Eleazar stared at his sleeping master. After several minutes of silence, he said, almost whispering, "I heard about this preacher who plotted to kill Hitler during World War II."

"You mean Bonhoeffer?"

"I don't remember the name. Maybe that was it."

"He failed," Khams said simply.

"We wouldn't have to," Eleazar whispered, pointing at the pillow. "We just hold it over his mouth, and...it would be over in seconds."

"We *could* do that," Khams agreed.

"No one would kill God. No one would put the universe in danger."

"We're already in danger."

"We could stop him before he completely destroys the world," Eleazar said.

"We'd be heroes," Khams said, offering a fleeting smile.

"We would be," Eleazar agreed.

They watched as Larch squirmed, his facial features contorting in response to something he was seeing, somewhere else.

"We won't do it though," Khams said.

"No," Eleazar agreed. "Because we're the weak ones."

42

"CAN you run and look at that thing at the same time?" Richard asked, referring to the Liahona. His hand was poised on the handle of the van door. The sky was rose colored as dawn broke. There was an odd quiet, as if the city were catching its breath.

"Is that a trick question?" Marco asked. "'Cause my hand-eye coordination is pretty good."

"No, you prick. I'm asking for real."

"I've never tried to use it while in motion. The way these dials work...they're primitive. I think we should run, then huddle and check it."

"Okay. That's what we'll do. Anyway, I've got a bead on where we should go first. Let's do it."

"Wait," Marco held his hand up. "What happens if we enter one of the demons' spheres of influence?"

Richard blinked. "That's a hell of a good question."

Tobias nudged at his hand, asking for a pet. Richard obliged.

"We need protection," Marco said.

"What did you have in mind? I don't think you can ward a person."

"Not the way you ward a house, no," Marco said. He pulled at his beard as he thought. "We've got to fight fire with fire."

"What do you mean?"

"Sigils got us into this. Sigils will get us out."

"We are *not* invoking demons to keep other demons at bay," Richard said.

"Who said anything about demons?" Marco said. "I'm not the expert in Enochian magick that Terry is, but I hold my own." He rummaged for a pad of paper and fished a pen out of his pocket. "Here," he quickly sketched a sigil and handed it to Richard. Then he sketched another for himself.

"Who's sigil is this?" Richard asked. It didn't look even vaguely familiar to him.

"The Angel of the Air," Marco said. "I figure, he served Kat pretty well. He might as well be watching out for us, too."

"Don't we need to activate these?" Richard asked.

"You're on better terms with such folks," Marco said, grimacing. "I was hoping you'd do that."

Richard shrugged. "Worth a try," he admitted. He closed his eyes and sank into vision. Tobias nudged his hand again. "Shhhh, Toby. Not now." He stepped through the Void and looked around. The change in temperature was substantial—it was much warmer in the Void. He raised his voice, sending out a call to the Sandalphon. He sidestepped some tumbleweeds and marveled at the distant mountains as he waited. Before too long, he saw two Sandalphon approaching from the distance. It took several minutes for them to lumber up to him, but when they arrived, he reached out and touched the fur of the first one to reach him. "I need your help, brothers." He had no idea the gender of the Sandalphon, but he hoped his familial address would be taken in the spirit he intended. "I call upon the Angel of the Air."

Immediately the air before his eyes began to swirl, creating an opening, a vertical vortex. Goose bumps erupted over Richard's arms as a being with a thousand eyes emerged from the portal. A thousand arms wielded a thousand swords, as lightning flashed all around it.

Richard leaned against the Sandalphon and tried not to tremble. He held up the two sigils. "We are going into danger, sir. We're going into territories controlled by demons. We seek your favor and your protection. We wish to wear your sigil. We ask you to own these, to...bind yourself to them...so that you will be with us, so that no harm will come to us while we seek to get to safety."

A thunderbolt erupted from the angel and struck the sigils. Richard jumped back and dropped them. Looking down at where they lay on the ground, Richard saw that they glowed with a golden light that seemed to come from the inside. "I'm going to take that as a yes," Richard said, scooping up the scraps of paper and holding them tightly to his chest.

"Thank you for your time, sir," Richard said, bowing deeply.

One second there was thunder and the buzz of electricity in the air and the sound of whooshing swords, and the next there was nothing—just the gentle stirring of the breeze in that warm place. Richard did not see where the angel had gone, but it was clear that he had gone. He reached up and stroked the fur of the Sandalphon that had been supporting him. "Thank you, dear friends. As always. Thank you."

He raised his leg and stepped though the Void again. He opened his eyes.

"That took a while," Marco said.

"Sandalphon move slow," Richard said. He handed Marco one of the sigils.

"Whoa, this is glowing."

"It's activated," Richard said. "This was a great idea." He stuffed his copy of the sigil into his front right pocket. "Let's go." He swung back the door.

Tobias hopped out first and instantly pissed on the grass.

"Sorry, boy. I should have thought of that."

"Now that you mention it..." Marco said.

They took turns using the toilet at Maggie's place, and then they set out. Richard turned left onto Oxford Street and headed for the University. Marco walked beside him, while Tobias scouted a couple yards ahead. On their right they passed an agricultural field owned and operated by UC Berkeley. "Don't look," Richard said.

"Don't look at wh—oh," Marco stopped and stared. About five yards from them a couple were making love on the ground. Both were completely naked, and although both were moaning, it was clear that it must have been painful for both of them, as there was blood pouring from their union. Richard tried not to look, but it was too late. "That...does not look fun," Marco said.

"It looks like they've been at it for hours. Maybe all night. A lust demon, no doubt. I wonder if they feel the pain."

Beyond them, on the other side of the chain-linked fence, Richard caught sight of others. There were about a dozen people altogether, in various coital combinations. They all looked enraptured, but the rawness of their flesh told another story.

"That looks sooooo painful. Can't we do something about that?" Marco asked.

"We can find the sigil and destroy it," Richard said.

"Can we?"

"Do you know how long we're going to be at this if we stop to dismantle every sigil in the East Bay?"

"Do you have something else on your calendar for today?" Marco asked.

Richard looked at his shoes. He wanted to get to Alameda, to safety, to his friends. But now it seemed like a selfish goal. There were people who needed his help even more right here. "Shit. I guess not. Let's do it."

"Where do we start?"

"Most of them have been on buildings. So let's start where the action is. There's a prefab building near where most of them are fucking."

Richard found the gate, and was relieved to see the lock was off. He waved Tobias through and waited for Marco to pass before going in himself.

"Hey, shouldn't we put a sigil on Toby?" Marco asked.

"No need. He's already possessed by an angel," Richard said.

"Right, I almost forgot about that. How did that happen, anyway?"

"The angel was delivering Kat's brother's soul in a mirror...um, it's a long story actually."

"Sounds complicated."

"Everything is complicated around here." They turned a corner and Richard jerked his head to avoid seeing what he had already seen. Among the rows of seedlings was a full-on orgy—even in his brief glimpse, Richard could see college students, a couple of old people, and others of various ages, all entwined, all jerking limbs and jutting pelvises, the desperate panting of people not under their own control.

And there was blood. Everywhere.

"This is not fucking pretty," Marco said.

"You can say that again. There are some sights you just..."

"Wish you could unsee?"

"Yeah." Richard looked up, scanning the building. "We got to find that fucking thing."

"You wanna split up?" Marco asked.

"Maybe." Richard purposely looked away from the orgy. Instead, he studied the complex. "There's about six small buildings here. One of them is bound to have the sigil."

"So let's find it."

"Okay, but let's stay inside the lot—that way we won't be too far from each other."

"Got it."

Richard expected Tobias to follow him, but he didn't. Instead, the yellow dog took off on his own, between two of the middle buildings. "Gift horse. Mouth," he said aloud. Marco had gone north, so he turned to the buildings on the south side of the lot. At first, Richard couldn't tell what they were for. Being UC property, they might be classrooms, but as he peered into the windows, he saw lab equipment inside. *That makes a lot of sense,* he thought.

He turned and started. Blocking his path was a man about his own age but not as tall or as heavy. He was bearded, and there was blood on his face. His eyes were wild, his mouth open. He was naked, and his penis was swollen but dangling. It was also caked with blood. He grinned wickedly and took a step toward Richard.

"Let's *fuck*," he said, almost yelling the final word.

"Look, under normal circumstances, I'd say yes to a date," Richard said, slowly backing away. "But I've got a feeling you're not looking for a romantic attachment."

"Let's fuck," the man repeated, advancing on him.

"Let's not," Richard said, turning and walking more quickly. He turned a corner—and discovered himself in an "U" created by three of the buildings, with no obvious escape route. "Oh, shit," Richard breathed. "Why does this kind of thing always, always happen to me, God?"

The man's grin widened, his penis stiffened and stood at full attention. His entire pelvic region was almost black with dried blood, dirt, and maybe excrement. It was hard to tell in the dark, and the floodlights that lit the fences were not pointed in Richard's direction. The friar backed up into the U, his shoulders hugging the wall of the prefab building. The man was close enough now that Richard could smell him—a potent mixture of copper, sweat, shit, and B.O. Richard turned his face as the man pushed himself against his cassock and licked his cheek. He started to hump away at Richard, pressing him hard against the wall, and thrusting his hips in a dry frottage lubricated only by the blood seeping from his member.

Richard turned his face away and tried to grab the man's hands, pushing himself off of the wall with one foot. The man proved to be unreasonably strong, however, and slammed him back against the wall. Richard heard something crack in his own head, which he had no choice but to ignore as he put every ounce of strength into shoving the man away. But the man had reached through the front of his cassock now and was already fumbling at his belt. Richard opened his mouth and bit the man's nose, hard.

The man howled, but Richard held on, feeling the gristle of the cartilage slide between his teeth. He brought his knee up with force and caught the man directly in the testicles, after which the man issued a high-pitched howl of pain and crumpled to the ground, writing and clutching at his genitals. Richard lost no time, springing directly over the man and running headlong toward the corner of the building. He heard Tobias bark, and followed the sound of it. He was winded when he saw Marco walking toward the barking dog from the other direction.

Toby was acting like he'd treed a squirrel. He was greatly agitated, pointing with his nose, barking, and walking in a quick circle before starting the cycle again.

"Well, bingo," Marco said as they drew closer.

Richard raised his eyes to where Tobias was pointing. A large sigil, about four feet across, had been spray painted on the building's side. Above it, attached to a nail, was the activated parchment.

"You all right?" Marco asked.

"Don't I look all right?"

"Your hair is messed up and your cassock is smeared with blood exactly over your privates. I think it's a fair question."

Richard ignored his question, fair or not. "Give me a hand up, will you?"

Marco interlaced his fingers and offered his hands to Richard to step into. Tobias continued barking and circling. Balancing himself against the wall, Richard pushed up against Marco's hands and snagged the parchment from off the nail on the first try.

As soon as he hit the ground, Marco was already fishing in his pocket. He pulled out an old-fashioned styled cigarette lighter. He pulled back the silver cover and tuned the flint wheel with his thumb.

Richard caught movement out of the corner of his eye, and he jerked his head to the right, just in time to see his attacker spring out of shadow and lunge at him. He dropped and rolled, kicking at the man's feet, trying to throw him off balance. "Will you hurry up with that thing?" he called to Marco.

It took Marco several desperate tries to light the wick of the lighter. When he finally did, he hastily held it under the scrap of parchment in his other hand. The activated sigil lit quickly, and as it burned a scream escaped it.

The man was hovering over Richard now, about to force himself on him again, when suddenly the ferocity drained from his face, and reason returned to his eyes. "What the fuck...am I doing?" he asked. He looked down at himself, and a look of sheer horror overtook his face. His lower lip began to shiver, and his eyes were wide with shock. He sank to the ground and once more clutched at his genitals, this time whimpering with what Richard took to be an unholy mixture of pain and confusion and grief.

Marco offered his hand. Richard took it and resumed his feet. Tobias was sniffing at the man.

"Toby, give the man some room," Richard snapped. The dog ignored him, sniffing all the more eagerly. Richard finally grabbed his collar and enforced his command.

"That screaming always gives me the willies," Marco said.

"I'd have thought you'd be used to shit like that by now."

"You never get used to shit like that."

Richard turned around and was relieved to see that the writhing in the field had stopped. Instead, people were starting to scream—some with surprise, some with outrage and alarm, but most with pain. Richard stepped to where most of them could see him. "Listen up, everyone!" He said. "I'm sure you feel violated. I'm sure you're in pain. You have all been...well, brainwashed. You've been oppressed by a lust demon. It's not your fault. The spell has been broken. Please don't waste any time blaming yourselves—or each other. None of this is your fault. You are all victims. Instead, please have compassion on each other and take care of each other. The hospitals are overrun, so please help clean each other up. Wash, apply some antibiotic ointment, and put some bandages on. Stay inside and keep your heads low."

"Who are you?" asked one of the young women.

Richard didn't answer her. He only turned back to Marco. "So... where does God want us to go next?"

43

DYLAN'S EYELID FLICKERED. "HEY, BABY," Susan said. "We made it. We're safe."

Dylan opened his eye and looked around. Susan squeezed his hand. "Where are we?"

"We're in the hospital. In Alameda."

"What's—" he reached up to his face, but Susan snatched at his hand and brought it back down.

"Don't touch the bandages," she said.

"Mah eye hurts," he said.

"It should." Susan's face fell. "Honey, your eye was shredded by the glass. They couldn't save it. They...they took it out."

"Whuuut?" Dylan sat up in alarm.

"Shhhh..." Susan pushed him back down. "You need to rest. And...it's not the end of the world. You have another eye, and it's fine. You need to be grateful. You almost died. An eye is...it was a small price to pay."

"Ah lost mah eye?" Dylan said, obviously not quite believing it.

"Yes, honey. And it's okay. You are okay."

"Ah lost mah fuckin' eye..."

"The socket has to heal. That will take a couple of months. Then they can fit you for a glass eye. If you want it. It should look just like your old one."

"'Cept it'll never be lookin' in quite the right direction," Dylan pouted.

"It'll be one more distinctive thing about you," Susan said.

"Ah'm not sure that is a compliment," Dylan said.

"Shhh...no fighting. Everyone's fighting. Even here," Susan said. "I don't get it."

"Mebbe Alameda isn't immune. Mebbe there are sigils up fer...I don't know, filial unrest demons."

"Name one filial unrest demon."

"Uh...you got me. Don't mean there ain't none."

"When you get internet access, you and your good eye can look for one."

This actually brightened Dylan up a bit. "Okay."

"I think the pain medication is working."

"Ah'll say."

"Don't enjoy it too much. You might start reacting to it."

Dylan shrank slightly. "Ah hope not."

Just then a young woman stepped into the room, holding a cup of coffee. She was dressed in blue-gray mechanics overalls and wore a ball cap over her short, dirty blond hair. She was stocky, but still leaner than Susan. She walked with a hint of redneck swagger. "Dylan, this is Casey."

"Hey," Casey said with a genuine smile.

"He's awake," Susan said.

"Hot damn," Casey walked up to the bed. "How you feelin'?"

"Mah eye hurts, but not too bad," Dylan said, his eye widening at the sight of Casey.

"Don't let him drool on you," Susan said. "You're his type."

"That was a cruel thing to say out loud," Dylan said. "True enough, though."

Casey blushed. "You got the wrong plumbing for my liking, boyo."

"S'alright. I'm pretty fuckin' taken," Dylan conceded. "Where's Terry and Chicken?"

"They're at the High School Gymnasium. We have a shelter set up there."

"Turns out we're not the only refugees," Susan said.

"We actually got about a thousand and a half folks, spread out across a couple shelters," Casey said.

Dylan whistled.

"I wouldn't want to be the mayor right now, but I gotta say, he's doin' a great job. Not many people thought he would, but he is."

"Why didn't they think he'd do a good job?" Susan asked.

Dylan tried to scoot up in his hospital bed. Susan helped him and tucked the bedclothes in around his ample frame.

"Before he was mayor, he was a professional clown. Goggles, the Steampunk clown. It was a pretty heated race," Casey said.

Susan's eyes widened. "Can't wait to meet him."

"Oh, you will. Alameda's a small place. Even with all you refugees."

"I hope you won't be overrun," Susan said.

Casey took a swig from her coffee. "Oh, we won't. Ya'll just made it in under the wire. We're gonna seal up the tunnel later today. And we've already raised the drawbridges at High Street and Fruitvale. No one's gettin' in, no one's gettin' out. Unless you're coming or going to San Francisco, that is. Ferry's still running on the sevens."

"What do you mean 'on the sevens?" Susan asked

"Seven a.m. and seven p.m."

"Okay, so it's not a prison island, at least," Susan nodded grimly. "Just...protected."

"Yup. At least until we figure out what's going on."

"Oh. Well, we definitely need to talk to your mayor then. Because we know *exactly* what's going on."

It was Casey's turn for wide eyes. "You do?"

"Oh, yeah. You may not believe it, and you sure won't like it, but...yeah."

"Well then, let's go," Casey said.

"But Dylan—"

"Dylan is gonna be waited on hand and foot while he sips his morphine cocktail. Dylan is goooood."

"Ah'm goooood," Dylan repeated, so relaxed that his Melungeon face seemed flatter than usual.

"Are you sure you don't mind, honey?" Susan said.

"Ah'll miss ya, but...Ah miss mah eye, too."

"I'm...not seeing the analogy."

"Things is what they is."

"Doubtless," Susan agreed. "You know you're not really making sense, right?"

"But Ah love ya," Dylan affirmed.

She kissed his cheek, right under his good eye. "I love you, too."

44

IT TOOK ALMOST an hour to reach the Outer Sunset district by Muni and bus. As they stepped off the bus and onto the pavement, Mikael looked at his 511 app and pointed down a side street. They only brought one kit bag with them on the bus, and Kat lowered it to the ground with a groan. "I've been here before," Kat said. "But we drove. I'm completely lost."

"We're almost there."

"Are you mad at me?" Kat asked.

Mikael stopped. He studied her face but wasn't sure what her expression meant. "Of course not. Why would I be mad at you?"

"I don't know. You're awfully quiet. And...I guess I'm just oversensitive, since everyone seems to be so mad all of the sudden."

"No. I'm just...scared."

"That's fair." She held his hand and gave it a squeeze. He squeezed back and gave her a grim smile.

"Hey," he said. "Do you think this is a job for...the Confessor?"

She narrowed one eye at him. "Are you fucking with me?"

"No, I think—"

"Luna is our friend," Kat said. "She'll know in a heartbeat that it's you. So what good will the mask do?"

"But—"

"Honey," Kat said, pressing his hand. "I love you, but this whole Confessor thing...it's ridiculous. It's embarrassing."

Mikael looked at his shoes. "I don't want you to be embarrassed of me."

"I don't either," she said. "So let's just lose the mask, okay?"

"I'm not making promises for the future."

Kat rolled her eyes. "Mikael, it's stupid. It's just some pre-adolescent superhero wish fulfillment."

"You don't need to pathologize it—"

"I do if it's pathological."

Mikael held his hands up to stop her and closed his eyes to stop himself. "We're fighting."

"We made a covenant."

"We did."

Kat through her arms around his waist. "Sorry, honey."

"It's okay."

"It's still stupid."

"You're not helping."

Kat released him. "Which way?"

"This way," he said and turned again, this time into an alley.

Mikael could see her studying his face, maybe trying to figure out if she had hurt his feelings. He didn't let on.

"This looks familiar," she said. "Here." She walked up to a door.

"Nope," Mikael said. He kept walking.

"But—"

"Here," he said, pointing at a door set just beside an open-air garage.

Kat walked over uncertainly and looked at the door. Then she looked back at the previous one. "They look exactly the same. Are you sure?"

"Of course I'm sure."

"Don't say 'of course' like that, it's insulting." Kat narrowed her eyes.

"I wasn't insulting you, that just wasn't the right house!"

"And you know that *how*?"

"Because I've been here before."

"So have I!"

"Go ahead and knock on the damn door over there. I'll wait here while you apologize."

"We're doing it again, aren't we?"

Mikael deflated. "Yeah. We never do this." He looked up. "Whatever is going on up there, it's some powerful mojo."

"You're sure this is the right house?"

"Yes. Sorry, but yes."

She shrugged. "Okay, let's do this."

Mikael knocked on the door. They waited. About a minute later, they heard clomping on the stairs. "Who is it?" came a voice. Luna's voice.

"Luna, it's Kat. And Mikael. We want to talk to you."

"Go away."

"We're not going to go away. We're going to pound on your door every minute for the next forty-eight hours. And when your neighbors complain, we're going to tell them you're cooking meth. And when you call the police, we're going to tell them you have something to do with what's happening in Oakland."

The door swung open suddenly. "I don't have anything to do with what's going on in Oakland!" she snapped.

"Good," Kat pushed past her and started up the stairs. "Let's talk about that."

"Hey!" Luna protested, following her. Mikael entered, too, and shut the door behind him. He was impressed by Kat's boldness, as he often was.

At the top of the stairs, he followed them into a minuscule living room, with a kitchenette on one side. Luna put a teapot on to boil, but her actions were jerky, petulant. "You didn't need to follow me here."

"We kinda did," Kat said.

Mikael sat unobtrusively on the couch, and reaching into his cassock, clutched at the Talisman of Amitiel hanging around from his neck by a leather thong. The Talisman had been a gift from Prestor John just a few months ago. By feeling its temperature, Mikael could tell if anyone were telling the truth or not.

"Why did you run out on Terry and Marco? At Jimmy's house?" Kat asked.

Luna froze. "I...don't know. I felt scared. So I just...came home."

The Talisman stayed warm. Kat caught his eye. He nodded. She continued. "We think that whatever is going on in the East Bay is...it's being caused by a lodge of black magickians. Do you know any of the guys from the Lodge of the Hawk and Serpent?"

"Hell no!" Luna pulled the kettle off as it began to sputter. "Do I look like I hang out with skanky vermin like that?"

The Talisman was warm. Kat looked at him. He nodded. Kat frowned.

"Have any of them contacted you?"

"No!" she slammed the tea kettle down on the stove. "Why do you think I'm involved with them?"

Kat looked at Mikael. He nodded.

"Because they have unleashed demon magick all over the East Bay. And you're being oppressed by a demon now."

Luna turned to face her, her jaw tight with anger. "How dare you. I don't even believe in demons."

"You don't have to believe in viruses to catch a cold," Mikael offered. "But it's true. You're not possessed, but you're being oppressed. We can help."

"I don't want your help," Luna turned away again.

The Talisman went cold. Mikael shook his head.

"Yes, you do. You're just too stubborn to admit it," Kat said, opening the kit bag and pulling out her liturgy.

"I'll make some holy water," Mikael said, getting up. "Where is your salt?"

45

"ARE YOU SURE?" Richard asked.

"The dial is pointing right there—right fucking there!" Marco was emphatic.

"Do you think maybe it means something on the other side of it?" Richard asked.

"Let's find out." Marco went to the left, around the perimeter of the building. Tobias sniffed at the wind as they walked. Once they reached the other side, Marco checked the Liahona again. "It's pointing this way, now."

"Right at the police station."

"Yep."

Richard shook his head and sighed. "Okay. Let's go. But first, let's see if they made it." Richard pulled out his cell phone and speed-dialed Dylan.

"Good idea," Marco agreed.

Richard pulled the phone away from his head and tried again. He listened, but then shook his head. "No connection. Cell towers must be down."

"Shit," Marco said. "Well?"

"We may just have to trust God that they made it."

"That's your area of specialty, not mine."

"Ready?" Richard asked. Marco nodded. "Let's go then." They marched back to the front of the building and headed toward the front doors.

"Hold it right there," called a not-too-distant voice.

Richard and Marco froze. Tobias whined and circled around Richard. Richard looked up, hoping to find the voice's owner. A man on the roof appeared to have a high-powered rifle cozied into his armpit. The scope was trained directly at them.

"Not moving," Richard said.

"State your business," called the shooter.

"We can't say we're on a mission from God," Marco whispered. "That's been done."

"What was the name of those detectives?" Richard whispered back. "Cain and…"

"Perry?"

"That was it."

"We're here to see Detectives Cain and Perry. We have information about a case they're working on. Urgent information."

"Are you armed?"

"Only with love," Marco smiled up at him.

"Check the love and whatever weapons you might have at the door," the voice called. "Go on in."

"Including the dog?" Richard called.

"Why not?" answered the man.

Just inside the door they found weapons trained on them again, with very much the same exchange. Once they mentioned Cain and Perry, however, their interrogators softened. "Oh, they're here. Down the hall, third room on the left."

"Thanks," Richard said.

"Gotta pat you down, though," said the guard.

"I would think less of you if you didn't," Marco said.

The guard ran his hands over Marco's clothes, but didn't quite know where to start with Richard's cassock. He pulled open the velcro holding the flaps at each side and slipped it off. The guard went through it quickly, then ran his hands over Richard's jeans and t-shirt. "Be sure you check Toby, too," Richard pointed at the dog.

"I'll skip the dog."

Richard pulled his cassock back on and they proceeded down the corridor. It was a lively place. Computer screens and televisions were lit up in every room they passed. There seemed to be much discussion but little action that they could see. Several rooms looked like they were occupied by families. Blankets were spread out on the floor and several children were playing, arguing, or napping. They squealed in delight and pointed at Tobias.

"Officer's families?" Richard asked.

"If I were them, that's what I would do," Marco answered.

"Me too. This is probably the safest place in Berkeley right now."

"Unless someone paints the sigil of a wrath demon on the side of the building," Marco countered.

"But no one has," Richard answered. "Yet. Thank God. And I doubt they will. The whole East Bay has become too dangerous for the Lodge—or whoever is behind this—to come back into it. They've got to do their work on the edge of the wave they're making. They leave chaos in their wake but they never go back."

"You sure about that?"

"No. But that's how I'd do it."

"But you wouldn't do it," Marco said.

"No."

"Rationality doesn't seem to really be their long suit."

"No." Richard agreed.

They reached the door to the third room, and Richard considered knocking. "Don't knock," Marco said. "No one will hear you. It's a madhouse in there. Let's just go in."

Richard nodded and pulled the door open, and the noise hit them in a wave. It had never occurred to Richard how loud a squad room at full tilt could get. He held the door for Marco and then Tobias.

Richard saw Perry first and pointed. They circumambulated several desks and made their way over to where Perry was studying a computer screen. She looked up and jumped a bit in her seat. "Jesus! Just sneak up on a girl!"

"Um...not sneakin', just walkin'," Marco said. He flashed her his most appealing smile.

She looked from one of them to the other. "Aaaand you brought your dog. Wonderful. You know, we're kind of busy around here. What can I do for you?"

Richard shrugged. "We're not sure. We..." he was going to say, *We asked God where we should go and he told us to come here*, but when he rehearsed it, it sounded a little crazy. Then he had an idea. "We know how to stop what's happening, so we thought we'd coordinate our efforts with you. We can train your officers in sigil removal, then we can systematically—"

"We don't have the manpower for anything but maintaining this building," Perry said. "We fended off two attacks yesterday."

"Then why didn't you shoot us on sight when we approached?" Marco asked.

"Because the real danger is the horde. You're not a horde."

Tobias laid down and started licking his paws.

"How bad is it?" Richard asked.

"It's spread through most of Berkeley. It seems to have stopped at Kensington. Nothing in the hills. On the other side of the Albany tunnel...nothing. El Cerrito, Richmond, they all seem clear."

"That's a relief," Richard said. "At least there's a perimeter."

"Yep. National Guard are on the edges of it, too."

"Wow," Marco said.

Tobias turned onto his back and squirmed on the floor.

"You don't think this qualifies as a national emergency?" Perry darted a look at him that could roast kielbasa.

"Believe me, no one is more convinced of that than us," Richard said. "Please tell us how we can help you."

"You'll only be in the way, here. We can give you shelter enough to get yourselves together," Perry said. "But then you'll have to go."

"Fair enough," Richard said.

"Detective Perry!" a voice called.

"Just a minute," she said, and walked over to consult with a uniformed officer.

"I don't think the Liahona is wrong," Marco said.

"You've got a lot of confidence in that thing."

"It's proving itself to me, yeah."

"We've got a short reprieve. What should we do with it?"

"I think we haul up some demon ass and find out who's really behind all this and why."

"I'm pretty sure I'm clear on the who," Richard said.

"But if you don't know the why, you don't really know how to fight it, do you?"

"No." Richard admitted. "You're right. I don't know what their endgame is. And until I do—"

"You're just putting out fires."

"Right."

"So let's ask someone who knows."

"This is on you, man," Richard said.

"I know about your code," Marco narrowed one eye at him. "I also know you break it sometimes."

"I do *not* summon demons," Richard's voice was firm.

"I don't either—normally." Marco squirmed. "But sometimes you just gotta do what you gotta do."

"And you're sure you gotta do this?"

"Aren't you? Don't you want to know?"

"More than anything," Richard said. He could taste it.

"Then let's get to it."

Just then Perry came back to her desk. She sighed and moved a lock of hair out of her eyes. "You guys can clean up and rest, but you can't do it here."

"We have an investigation of our own," Richard said. "And you might be interested in the results. But first we need something."

"Oh, God. Why do I have the feeling I'm not going to like this?"

Cain wandered up. "Blackfriars," he said, a weary smile on his lips. "I thought I smelled brimstone. Good to see you...alive."

"He's a Blackfriar," Marco clarified. "I'm a roving inventor. And magickian."

"Ooookay, sure," Cain said. "Good to get that out in the open."

"They say they're conducting an investigation," Perry said with audible impatience.

"What do you need?" Cain asked.

Perry flashed him a look.

"Do you have chalk?" Marco asked.

"I can scare up some chalk," Cain assured him.

"We need an empty room," Richard said. "Preferably in a basement."

"Does it have to be big?" Cain asked.

"Cain," Perry said, in a tone of voice that Richard took to mean, *Don't encourage them.*

"About 12-foot square should do it," Marco said.

Cain nodded. "Come with me."

46

Terry held Chicken's hand as one of the volunteers led them through the school gymnasium. They picked their way in between blankets and suitcases and brown shopping bags full of clothes and personal belongings. It reminded Terry of crossing the grass at the Greek Theater in search of a place to spread his own blanket. Finally, they reached a jagged border where the blankets stopped and bare linoleum began.

"This spot can be yours," said the volunteer. She was about forty with deep black circles under her eyes. She was also bone thin, and Terry wondered if she was sick—really sick—but had rallied in order to pitch in. He put his own self-pity aside for a moment as he considered her plight.

"Thank you," he said to her, and he meant it. "Um...I'm afraid we don't have any blankets or pillows or anything."

"Sure we do," said Chicken. She pulled a piece of chalk out of her pocket and began to draw a large square. Then she drew two smaller rectangles.

"There's your pillows, right there," said the volunteer, laughing. "Just sit tight. We'll bring some by soon. I think Jason just left for a run up to Bed Bath and Beyond. We're cleaning them out, I'm afraid!"

"Thank you so much," Terry said. "You've all been so kind. I'm Terry, by the way. And this is Chicken. Well, we call her Chicken. She won't tell us her real name."

"Chicken!" Chicken said, pointing to herself.

"Very nice to meet you, Chicken," the woman said, amused. "I'm Nan. Good to meet you Terry. Is it Father Terry?"

"It is, but no need to be formal."

"We're glad you're here." She rested her hand on his shoulder for a moment then turned to go.

Terry sat down cross-legged in the square Chicken had drawn, careful not to smudge the pillows. His shoulders slumped and for a moment he allowed himself to rest his head in his hands.

That didn't last long, because Chicken squirmed her way onto his lap. "Uncle Terry, why are you sad?"

Terry's mouth opened, but he didn't say anything. After all Chicken had been through in the last twenty-four hours, the fact that she noticed his feelings at all stunned him. That she had identified them precisely also surprised him. "Um...because my boyfriend left me. And I miss him."

"You have a boyfriend? Not a girlfriend?"

"Yep."

Chicken looked confused. Terry wondered at the fact that there were still places in the Bay Area where you could grow up and not encounter gay people. Then she brightened. "Why did he go away?"

Terry struggled to keep the emotion from rising in his throat. "Because I fu...because I messed up. I hurt his feelings really bad."

"Did you mean to?"

"No. But I did."

"You could say *pardon*."

"I will."

"You could say it now and then we could go to her house."

Terry smiled, as much as at her confused pronouns as at her naiveté. "I wish it were that simple, little one."

"Don't call me 'little.'"

"You don't want to be called 'little,' but you don't mind being called Chicken?"

She smiled up at him, kissed his chin, and then she laughed.

Terry hugged her and tried not to cry.

"Why don't you call her?"

"Because my phone caught a bul—" he stopped himself. "My phone broke."

"Oh. Ask *him*."

She pointed at an older gentleman about six yards away, leaning back on a rolled up sleeping bag, talking on a cell phone. When he finished and put it in his pocket, Terry lifted Chicken out of his lap and said, "I'm gonna try to call him. Can you wait here?"

Chicken nodded. "Okie-dokie! I'll draw some cookies. Because I want cookies."

"That sounds really great!" Terry said. "Can you draw some chocolate chip with dried cranberries?"

Chicken scrunched her nose. "What's cranberries?"

Terry smiled sadly and picked his way over to where the man with the phone was sitting.

"Hi, sir," Terry began. "I'm afraid my phone was broken yesterday. Actually," he looked over at Chicken, and determining that she was out of earshot, said, "it took a bullet. I'd love to call my partner and let him know I'm okay. And make sure he's okay, too." It hadn't occurred to him that Brian might not be all right until he said it, and it caused him to reel a little.

The older man looked him up and down, frowning. "Are you gay?"

Terry stood up a little straighter. "We...yes. Of course."

The man cocked his head at that. "Of course?"

"Spend five minutes with me and you won't need to ask."

"Hmph. You dressed up like a priest or something?"

Terry was beginning to get impatient. He wanted to say, "Are you going to let me use your phone or not?" but he kept his temper. "I am a priest. I'm Father Terry Milne of the Order of St. Raphael."

"But you have a gay partner?"

"Yes. We're not a celibate order."

The man narrowed his eyes at him. "I don't approve."

Terry gave him a disappointed smile. "You don't need to. I'm only asking you to show some simple human compassion. May I please use your phone for about five minutes?"

"Oh, hell. Okay. But you stay right here. And all I got is AT&T, which is shit reception in Alameda."

"You're not from Alameda, then?"

"Would I be camping out here if I was?"

"No...of course not. Sorry."

The man threw Terry his phone.

"Thank you."

The man waved him away. Terry dialed Brian's number and waited. There was some crackling, but then he heard it ring.

"Hello?" Brian's voice. Terry didn't realize he'd been holding his breath, and he let it all out. "Who is this?"

"Brian, it's Terry. Please baby...don't hang up." Terry heard silence, but at least Brian didn't hang up. "I just...want to know that you are okay."

"I'm fine."

"The house was attacked last night, about three a.m. Dylan, Susan, Chicken and I made it to Alameda, but not before...Dylan lost his eye. He's in the hospital."

"Oh, God. Poor Dylan!" Brian said. The ice had been busted through. Brian might still be mad at him, but their situation was bigger than Brian's grievance. "Um...who is Chicken?"

"Oh. Wow. I forgot you left before we found her. She's a little girl. About four, maybe five years old. Richard and I found her in the middle of a gunfight near the Oakland Coliseum. We brought her back to the friary."

"Huh. How is Richard? And Toby? And Marco?"

"We don't know. They were supposed to follow us...but they never made it."

"Oh, God. How could you abandon them?"

"What? We didn't abandon them. We had to take two cars—Richard had an errand to run."

"In the middle of the night?"

"It's Richard. He makes the call."

"You don't have to obey it. How could you—"

"Brian, this isn't us fighting—"

"It sure the fuck is."

"—it's whatever is making everyone fight."

There was silence on Brian's end of the call. "Brian?"

"I'm just...I'm worried about him. Them."

"Tell me about it. I'm worried sick. Where are you? Are you okay?"

"I'm with Chava and Elsa. I'm fine. They're fighting, too. I wish we were all together so we could...figure this out."

Terry wasn't sure what Brian was referring to, but he decided it didn't matter and took the ambiguity as a gift. "Me too."

"I don't recognize this phone number."

"No. My phone was busted in gunfire. I'm borrowing this from a very nice man at the shelter here in Alameda. Me and Chicken are making our beds...kind of."

"That sounds wonderfully...domestic." Was that a catch in Brian's voice? The reception was poor, so it was hard to tell.

"Have you heard from Mikael and Kat?"

"No. Should I have?"

"I don't know. They went to San Francisco to investigate...it's a long story. Anyway, they might call. They might need a place to bed down."

"There's not a lot of room here, but they can have my room and I'll take the couch. I'm sure Chava and Elsa wouldn't mind."

"Great. Anyway, I have to go, honey. You don't need to say anything back. I just have to say...I love you." Terry hung up before Brian could respond. He handed the phone back.

After the old man took it, Terry realized he had tears in his eyes. "Sorry," he said. "Didn't mean to be listening in. I hope your partner is okay."

"He's okay. Thank you."

"If you want to call again, it's okay with me."

"Thank you. That's very kind." Terry gave a soft smile and picked his way through the checkerboard pattern of blankets toward Chicken. "What have you made for us?"

"Tamales," Chicken said.

"What kind?" Terry asked.

"Chocolate," Chicken said.

"My favorite," Terry said. He sat down and cradled Chicken as she crawled into his lap again. He lowered his face into her hair and wept.

47

FRATER TURPELO RUBBED his hands together in anticipation. He started salivating even before Purderabo arrived with their beer. The Cloven Hoof was about half full, but the atmosphere was bustling and lively as the lunch rush got underway. Turpelo recognized people from nearly every major occult community in San Francisco, either sitting at one of the booths or tables or at the bar.

"Babylon would like this," Purderabo said, setting a frosty pint glass in front of him. Turpelo uttered a heartfelt "thanks" and brought the deep amber beverage to his lips. The hops almost punched him in the teeth. "Oh, that's good. What is it?"

"The Baphomet IPA," Turpelo said. "It'll take your head off."

"But not without putting a smile on it first," Purderabo said, taking another stiff quaff. Purderabo adjusted his ample frame in the booth. "Could we scoot the table a bit, frater?"

"No problem." They edged the table a couple of inches toward Turpelo. Once adjusted, Purderabo sighed.

"To the East Bay," Turpelo said, holding his pint aloft.

Purderabo clinked his own pint to it gently. "To the East Bay. Long may she blaze."

They both chuckled as they drank.

"That was, beyond a shadow of a doubt, the most fun I have had in a very, very long time," Turpelo admitted.

"I have not taken part in so successful a working since...since I can't remember when," Purderabo was almost purring.

"I agree. I don't remember the last time I felt so alive."

"And exhausted. I'm not used to so much running about."

"But it was worth it, eh?"

"Without a doubt," Purderabo conceded.

"And to think we did it all without raising the ire of a single demonic aristocrat," Turpelo shook his head in amazement.

"Say what you will about Babylon—and we have certainly had our differences—but the man *is* a genius," Purderabo said, real admiration in his voice.

"I wouldn't have thought of it," Turpelo said.

"And it was the *only* way to do something on that scale."

"You mean the cooperation rather than compulsion?"

"Exactly. Who would have thought?" Purderabo asked.

"It shows the power of a party invitation if nothing else," Turpelo jested.

"We know our diversion worked," Purderabo said, "but what about the main event?"

"No clue," Turpelo said. "I talked to Khams this morning. Babylon has been out for about thirty hours at this point. He's got to come up for air or he'll slip into a coma."

"Would that be the worst thing in the world?" Purderabo asked.

"That's a terrible thing to say," Turpelo said. "Have you no faith in his plan?"

"Oh, I have faith that he can kick up some trouble in the higher planes. He's good at that. But whether there will be anything habitable left in any of them..."

"Or here?"

"Or here," Purderabo agreed.

"Babylon *is* a bit like a bull in a china factory."

"Don't ever let him hear you say that."

"No."

"Here's what I don't understand," Purderabo played with a wet ring on the table. "Why does Babylon think that destroying the balance of creation will destroy the Tyrant? You can trash my house and crash my car, but you haven't really hurt *me*."

"Perhaps when you come right down to it, Babylon is a monist," Turpelo reasoned. "With no distinction between the Tyrant and Creation."

"I don't think so. Babylon follows after Berkeley—and Crowley—in their doctrine of the monad," Purderabo said.

"*Every man and woman is a star*," Turpelo quoted.

"Just so."

"Perhaps he thinks the Ancient of Days will simply die of a broken heart if he destroys the one thing that the old bully has spent so many millennia building up," Turpelo offered.

"Oh, I wouldn't count on that. The Tyrant is ruthless. He has a soft spot, sure, but he's cunning as steel."

Turpelo drummed his fingers. "He's going to make a right mess of things, no matter what happens."

"It's a temper tantrum of extraordinary degree," Purderabo held aloft a finger, "and it will certainly piss the Tyrant off."

"On the other hand," Turpelo added, cocking his head. "Babylon never takes anyone *wholly* into his confidence. Not even us."

"Especially not us," Purderabo agreed.

"Do you think bringing down the Tyrant is really his aim?"

"Who can know? He seemed sincere. You can see it blazing in his eyes. So yes, I'm convinced he is determined to bring down the Tyrant. I'm not convinced we understand the whole of his method for doing so."

Turpelo nodded. Then he jumped as Mikael slid into the booth beside him. Kat likewise slid into the booth beside Purderabo.

"Hello, assholes," Mikael said. "What's for lunch?"

MARCO DREW the last line of the circle of containment and sat back with satisfaction. Richard looked on, not quite disapproving. He folded his arms. "No credence table?" The light was dim, a naked bulb hanging from a cord by the door. Ducts ran the length of the room, and there was a stack of what looked like a set of canvass pavilions in the corner, their spindly legs retracted and folded toward their centers. Richard's nose twitched from the dust Marco was kicking up.

"You don't actually need a credence table. You can just put the sigil on the floor."

Richard moved his head back and forth. "Okay. It's primitive, but I guess it'll work."

Marco narrowed his eyes. "You want to do this shit? Be my guest."

Richard held his hands up. "No, no. I'll...keep quiet."

Cain stuck his head through the door. "I brought you some sandwiches. Are you hungry?"

"Ravenous," Marco said, brightening up.

"What's all this?" Cain asked.

"This is where Marco plans to summon a demonic lord."

"You can do that?" Cain looked at Marco uncertainly.

"Anyone can. You just have to know what you're doing."

"And do you?"

"No one ever really knows what they're doing when you mess with this shit," Marco said, reaching for one of the sandwiches on the paper plate Cain was holding out.

"That's not terribly encouraging," Cain confessed. He looked unconvinced but playful, as if he were humoring them. "Where's your dog?"

"He saw what we were doing and removed himself. He doesn't approve."

"Your...dog...knows what you're doing and doesn't *approve*?" Cain's face screwed up like he'd just suffered a rapid-onset migraine.

"Right. My guess is that he's upstairs looking for a kid to rub his belly."

"Huh." Cain put his hands on his hips and studied the chalk markings. "How does it...uh...how does it work?"

"This large circle here," Richard pointed out, "is the circle of safety. That's where we're going to stand."

"We?"

"Me and Marco. You, if you want to watch."

Cain's eyebrows shot up.

"That smaller circle is the circle of containment. That's where the demon shoes up. We're going to draw a sigil and set it in the circle. Then we'll compel the demon to appear."

"How?"

"Blood."

Cain blinked. "Do I want to know whose blood?"

"That would be the magickian's blood, generally."

"The things I do for my craft," Marco said, strengthening the wall of the circle of containment with the chalk. He studied it closely to make sure there were no inadvertent cracks in the line that a demon might be able to follow out to liberty—and bedlam.

"Sandwich?" Cain held the plate out for Richard. Richard thanked him and took two.

"So when does this thing start?"

"As soon as I finish my sandwich," Marco said, his mouth full. He put the finishing strokes on the circle and stood up.

"This requires some imagination to understand what's happening," Richard explained, between bites. "See, Marco is going to go into vision—"

"What's that?"

"It means I'm going to see it in my mind's eye," Marco answered.

"You're going to...imagine it?" Cain cocked his head.

"That's right," Richard answered. "He's going to hold the image of the sigil in his head, and send it out."

"Out where?"

"Into the universe, into hell, into...everywhere, I guess. It's like sending out a radio signal. Then he's going to draw it back—"

"What, like fishing?"

"Exactly like fishing, except without the element of chance. He's pretty certain to come back with the demon he's looking for—unless the demon is in consultation with a larger, more powerful nasty who can override the summons."

"What if that happens?"

"I've never heard of it happening," Richard admitted. "It's just lore."

"I'll bring him back," Marco said.

"You do this kind of thing a lot?" Cain asked.

"Never," Marco said. "Are you fucking nuts?"

Cain's brow furrowed. "I don't understand."

Richard swallowed. "Would you know what to do if you found a bomb in a crowded area?"

"Sure. I'd clear the area and call the bomb squad."

"And if it was going to blow in less than a minute?"

Cain shuffled his feet and cleared his throat. "I guess I'd man up and carry it out."

"It's not something that you would do every day though, right?"

"Hell, no! I'm not bomb squad."

"And you wouldn't do it for fun," Richard asserted.

"Of course not."

"Same here. A working like this is extremely dangerous. No one in their right mind would do it for fun. Only idiots would do it to achieve a magickal end. But Marco is a magickian. He knows *how* to do it, even if he doesn't *like* doing it."

Cain nodded, making the connection. "That's helpful. Just how... dangerous is this?"

"The bomb thing is safer," Richard admitted.

Cain whistled, raising his eyebrows.

"You're patronizing us," Richard said.

"Maybe a little," Cain said. "I think everything you're saying is complete nonsense."

"You should *definitely* stay, then," Richard said. "Just make sure you've hit the little boys room before we start."

Marco popped the last bit of sandwich into his mouth and brushed the crumbs off his hands. "I'm ready when you are. Let's get this over with."

Richard shoved a bit too much sandwich into his own mouth and nodded his agreement. He sat cross-legged on the floor and patted the place beside him.

"Which demon should we summon?" Marco asked, readying a pen and paper. "It has to be a sigil, I know."

"Well, what sigils do you know?" Richard asked.

"I know Tephalus—"

"He's a low-level sloth demon," Richard scrunched up his nose. "He won't have any idea what the higher-ups are up to. What do you got higher up on the food chain?"

"Hmm...it's been a long time since I studied the *Lesser Key of Solomon*. What about Carnaris? I can draw that."

Richard frowned. "Who is he?"

"She, actually. She's a vampiric succubus."

"Let's take a pass on her. Why are female demons always succubi?"

"The demonic hierarchy is even more patriarchal than earthly governments these days," Marco opined.

"I think you're right about that," Richard agreed. "Who else? We need someone with *reach*."

"Oh, I got it," Marco snapped his fingers. "Mandrake."

"Mandrake? Like the root?"

"Yep. I used to invoke him—not summon him, mind you, but just, you know, invoke a bit of his energy—back in the nineties when I was young and stupid."

"For what?"

Marco shrugged. "Paying my bills. Balancing the checkbook."

"Mandrake is a...what? An accounting demon?"

"Something like that. He's a bureaucratic functionary. Big on numbers. He doesn't get around much. Has an office in the business district of hell. But he has big ears."

"Like, actual big ears?" Cain asked, an amused smile spreading across his lips.

"No, figurative. He hears things. Lots of things," Marco said.

"What can it hurt?" Richard said. "Let's see what he has to say."

49

"WHO THE FUCK—" Turpelo bellowed.

A hush descended on the Cloven Hoof as people from other tables halted their conversation and looked over.

Turpelo shrank a bit and waited until the ambient noise resumed its former level.

"I surmise by the way the two of you are dressed that you are Blackfriars," Purderabo said calmly with a hint of snootiness in his voice.

"That would be a correct surmissumption," Mikael said.

"Did you just make that up?" Kat asked.

"I did. Like it?"

Kat bopped him on the nose with the tip of her index finger.

"Worse," Purderabo said to Turpelo. "Blackfriars in love. Gods help us."

Mikael slid his hand into his cassock and clutched at the Talisman of Amitiel.

"And why would Father Kinney send two low-levels to see us?"

Kat gave him a mock-pout. "He doesn't think very much of us, Mikael."

"That's all right, since it's mutual," Mikael grinned.

"What do you want?" Turpelo asked.

"Is 'Enjoying your company' so far-fetched?" Kat asked. "Do they have french fries? I'd trade half my liver for a plate of garlic fries."

"They have excellent fries," Mikael said. "I like the sweet potato with the sun-dried aioli with capers."

"That...is good," Purderabo said, raising a chubby finger.

"See?" Mikael said. "We're getting friendlier already."

"What the fuck do you want?" Turpelo asked again, this time with a bit of growl in his voice.

"Well, first," Mikael began, "we're impressed. The whole conversion of the East Bay into the fifth circle of hell was sheer genius. Hats off to you."

"We're kind of proud of that ourselves," Turpelo took a swig of his beer.

"So you claim responsibility for your act of terror?" Kat asked.

Both magickians froze then looked at each other.

"You tricked us," Turpelo shook his finger at Kat.

"You're pretty gullible," Mikael said. Turpelo opened his mouth to protest, but Mikael continued. "What we don't understand is *why*."

"Why what?" Purderabo asked.

"Don't be coy," Mikael said. "Why did you hang activated sigils all over the East Bay? What's it for? It can't just be chaos for the sake of chaos."

"Why can't it be?" Purderabo asked.

"Because Larch is too goal-oriented for that," Mikael said, "and you know it."

Purderabo pursed his lips and drummed his fingers on the table.

"What's it *for*?"

"It's a test," Turpelo said. "We wanted to see if it worked. Now that we know it does, we're going to scale it up."

Mikael felt the talisman grow cold.

"Why would you want to do that?" Kat asked.

Mikael interrupted. "Don't bother answering that. You're lying. You have no intentions of ramping up."

Purderabo and Turpelo exchanged glances. "How—"

"Never mind how," Mikael said. "Is this about money?"

"Yes," Purderabo answered. "Larch thinks—"

"Lie," Mikael said. "So it's not about money. Is this about power?"

"Not really," Turpelo sighed.

"Well, for once you said something true," Mikael said.

"You get a gold star!" Kat clapped.

Turpelo scowled across the table at her.

"Is this about winning someone's affections?"

"Don't be daft," Purderabo almost spat.

Mikael's brain raced. He'd exhausted the usual magickal motivations for mischief. Then he had an idea.

"Did Larch put you up to this at the behest of someone else? Maybe someone with more power? Maybe someone...not human?"

"Not even close, Christian," Purderabo grinned grimly. The talisman was warm, so that was the truth.

"Take a look at this beer," Purderabo held aloft the glass, now nearly drained of the IPA.

Out of the corner of his eye, Mikael caught movement and realized Purderabo was trying to raise the attention of the waitress without being noticed.

"It has such potential for either pleasure or pain," he continued. His other hand flapped wildly like a pinned seal. No waitress seemed to notice.

Mikael sat up straight in the booth, goose bumps erupting on his arm.

"What is it, honey?" Kat asked.

"I know," he said.

"You know what?"

Mikael cocked his head and looked Purderabo straight in the eye. "You're just keeping us busy, aren't you? The whole East Bay thing, it's just a distraction. You're doing something else—something you didn't want us to notice because we'd be too busy..."

He didn't need the talisman then. The smile on Purderabo's face said it all.

50

"NORMALLY, I'D HAVE INCENSE," Marco said.

"You make do with what you have," Richard reminded him.

"Right." Marco took the paper on which he had drawn the sigil of Mandrake and folded it into a triangle. Then he pricked his forefinger with a pushpin and smeared a bit of blood on the paper. Getting on his hands and knees, he placed it carefully within the Circle of Containment.

"Whatever you do," Richard said to Cain. "Don't leave this larger circle. It's the Circle of Protection. As long as you're inside it, the demon can't touch you."

"Aye-aye," Cain said. He looked as if he were enjoying this. Richard sighed. Cain would be the only one.

"Center, everyone," Marco said.

Marco and Richard sat down cross-legged in the Circle of Protection, facing the Circle of Containment.

Richard relaxed and felt himself connect with the slow rhythmic energy of the earth.

He did not look at the sigil, but he knew what Marco was doing. He would be staring at the sigil, softening his gaze, blurring his own vision. In the absence of incense, Marco would need to rely on more

interior methods of visual obfuscation to entice the demon to manifest visibly. It was a transitional thing. Once the manifestation took
hold, the demon would be able to emerge without the use of further
aid. It was getting started that was the hard part.

Within moments, Richard felt the temperature in the room drop
and the hair on his arms stand up straight with static electricity.
Marco was succeeding. Something—someone—was coming through.
Richard opened his eyes and saw an image appearing within the
paper triangle—although he was not able to make it out. Was it a
beaver? A muskrat? A capybara? It was hard to tell, but other things
were happening that commanded his attention. The wall before him
rippling slightly with liminal energy. Wisps of fog drifted into the
room, mingling and coalescing into vapor trails, then into formless
clumps, and then, in a way that Richard would never, ever get used to,
into recognizable shapes.

"Why is it so cold?" Cain asked, his voice higher pitched than it
had been.

"Shhh..." Richard shushed him.

"What the fuck is that?" Cain pointed at the form taking shape in
the Circle of Containment.

"Greetings, Mandrake, master of the numerical arts," Marco
called to the shapeless form before him. "I welcome thee and bid
thee welcome. I command thee by the holy tetragrammaton to
assume thy human form and speak to me."

The shape hovering in the air before them transformed. It took a
while before Richard realized what he was looking at, but gradually
the image made sense. The being before them was a small man
standing with his back to them. He was wearing the robe of a
medieval scribe, and held a quill pen in his hand. *These are all aspects
of his iconography,* Richard thought. *He isn't really holding these things.*
Then Richard reminded himself that the demon didn't really look
like this, either.

As he turned toward them, Richard beheld a small, moleish man,
his face drawn up to a single point at his nose, but his nose was actually quite small in relation to his other features. Tiny spectacles

perched on his concave, diagonal cheeks. He wore a cravat and a waistcoat.

"What the fuck?" Cain breathed. Richard reached over and squeezed his arm reassuringly. The detective was literally shaking.

"I've got year-end reports to prepare for nearly two-dozen departments," the demon said, sounding both bored and annoyed. At first, his words sounded like they were coming from underwater, but by the time he spoke again, they sounded bold and fiery. "So I am *not* grateful for this interruption. What do you stupid ass-clown magickians want *now*?"

"This isn't real," Cain said. "This *can't* be real."

"Oh, faithful Mandrake, we do not summon thee for frivolous purposes," Marco nearly intoned. "Neither do we seek our own advantage."

"Not that I would care if you did," Mandrake rolled his eyes. "What do you want, magickian? I have a stack of papers the size of a refrigerator on my desk, and I have no time for your petty scheming. Is it algebraic alacrity you're looking for? I can grant that and then we can both be on our way."

"We want information," Marco said simply.

The demon cocked his mole-like head. "What *kind* of information?"

"We want to know what the magickian Larch is up to—he and his confederates in the Order of the Hawk and Serpent."

"What they are *up to*?" the demon asked.

"I compel you by the Holy Name to tell me," Marco said forcefully.

Mandrake waved. "No need for threats. I see what you are doing. It is not without nobility. There has been much disruption."

That's an understatement, Richard thought, but he kept his mouth shut and let Marco work.

"Who are these others?" the demon craned his neck to see past the magickian.

"This one is a police detective—" Marco began.

"He looks like a scared rabbit. Boo!" Mandrake jerked forward, stopping just shy of the edge of the Circle of Containment.

Cain jumped, and Richard gripped his hand. Cain squeezed it so tight Richard felt the bones in his hand shift with a pop.

"The other is a Christian friar and a student of the Black Arts."

"He's not afraid of me," Mandrake seemed to find this surprising.

"He has a healthy respect for you," Marco countered.

"That seems...wise," the demon turned his gaze once more on Marco.

"Do I need to compel you?" Marco asked. "Do you really want me to invoke the Name?"

"Gods, no," Mandrake shook his head. He sighed. "What makes you think I know the answer to your query?"

"Because nothing happens in hell without filing a cost analysis report with you. If it's anything of note, happening anywhere, you know something about it," Marco said.

"You flatter me, magickian."

"I say only the truth and no more."

"Hmm..." Mandrake looked like he was considering his options.

"I'm going to start invoking in five...four...three..."

"Oh, all right, all right. No need for the Name to stick it's prickly, painful, intrusive presence into my business."

"What is Larch up to?"

"He intends—and I have this on good authority, since we ran a cost analysis on this six months ago when the Duke Sheradrigan first suggested it—"

"So this—whatever it is—wasn't Larch's idea?"

Mandrake guffawed. "We haven't seen a truly *creative* magickian since Crowley."

"Fine. What was the cost analysis for?"

"The defeat of the Name," Mandrake said simply. The demon even smiled.

"Do you mean that Larch intends to defeat *God*?"

"To destroy him, yes."

"How?"

"By throwing one sephirot into chaos after another."

"Do you mean he is ascending the Tree of Life—"

"And sawing off each branch as he goes." The demon's smile grew more broad than Richard would have thought his face could physically allow.

Just then the door swung open. "Cain, I—what the *fuck*?" Perry stepped into the room, her jaw dropping almost immediately.

With more speed than Richard could follow, the demon transformed into what looked like an oversized possum, all nose and claws and tiny, snapping teeth. Before he could blink he saw the demon lunge at Perry, clawing at her face and upper torso with sharp, four-inch nails, ripping her skin to shreds and sucking her soul into its gullet. Perry's body dropped to the cement floor of the basement with a sickening thud.

51

Kat and Mikael walked to the other side of the bar, out of sight of Fraters Turpelo and Purderabo. "What do you think?" Mikael asked.

"It makes a hell of a lot of sense," Kat answered. "It's sneaky. It's even kind of brilliant."

"Yeah, but what makes me nervous is what we *didn't* find out."

"You mean what they're really up to?" Kat asked.

"Right."

"So...why don't we go ask the man himself?"

"Who? Larch?"

"Yeah. I mean, we can't go home. What else are we going to do?"

"We could get a hotel room," Mikael's eyebrows bounced playfully.

"Are you suggesting we fiddle while Rome burns?" Kat narrowed one eye at him. "That is *very* naughty."

"It would be fun."

"It *would* be fun. It would also be hard to explain to God."

"Uh, there is that." Mikael thought for a minute. "So...how do we find Larch?"

Kat chewed on her lip. "We could follow those bozos," she pointed back at the table.

"We're pretty obvious," Mikael said.

"So let's ditch the cassocks for the time being," Kat said. "God will understand—we're undercover. I'm guessing that the cassocks are mostly what these guys see. We're not people to them, we're Blackfriars. I bet if we walked over to them in our street clothes right now and asked if they'd like to order anything else, they'd just ask for onion rings."

"No..." Mikael said.

"Wanna bet? How much?"

"Are we talking sexual favors?"

"Huh," Kat appeared to be thinking it over. "Okay. One thing...out of the ordinary."

"Anything?"

"Within reason."

"Damn."

"What the fuck were you thinking?" Kat put her hands on her hips.

"You'll see," he leaned down and kissed the end of her nose.

"I'm serious," Kat said. "What were you thinking?" The playfulness was gone, and she looked angry.

"I...uh...I thought we were having fun."

"We...we were..." Kat looked off into space. "You know what? I'm really, really irritable. And if you say anything about the time of the month you will never, ever get another sexual favor again."

"It's the..." Mikael pointed up.

Kat nodded. "Right. It's not me. It's not you. It's up there."

"Are we okay?" Mikael put a hand on her shoulder.

"We're okay," she said, lifting up on tiptoe to kiss him. He still had to lean down a significant distance.

"Okay, watch this." She ripped the velcro from the shoulders of her cassock and handed the long black robe to Mikael. He took his own off and put them both on the corner of the bar where no one was sitting. Then he crossed to where he could just barely see Turpelo and Purderabo. Kat smiled sneakily and snagged an order pad from the bar. Fishing a pen from her pocket, she walked up to the magickians' table, jutted out her hip, and pretended she was chewing gum. Mikael couldn't hear what she said, but he was in awe of her transformation. He watched as she scratched at the pad with her pen, ripped the first sheet off the pad, and laid it on the table. Smiling big, she took her leave of them and swaggered back toward Mikael.

"That is one shit-eating grin," Mikael said.

"Not a hint of recognition," she said.

"I can't believe it."

"Believe, my boy. And you owe *me* one 'out of the ordinary' sexual favor."

"Huh...well, I'm game for anything!"

"We'll see about that!"

"Shall we go?"

Kat hung back. "Well, we want to follow them."

"Right."

"Plus, I want to see what happens."

"What do you mean?"

"That piece of paper I put on their table?"

"Yeah...?"

"It said, 'Lunch is on the house today. Thanks for being such great customers!'"

"Oh, shit."

"Ever see anyone get caught for dine-and-ditch?"

52

Casey opened the door to the mayor's office a crack. "Goggles, you in?"

Through the crack in the door, Susan saw a tall, bald man with round horn-rimmed glasses look up from his desk where he and several other people were studying a map.

"Funny, Casey," he said. "Balloon animals all around—*after* we're out of danger."

"Hey, I got someone you need to meet."

"We're a little busy here—"

"Which is exactly why you need to meet these folks. They have information that is gonna help us out. They know why...you know, all this is happening."

The bald man looked surprised. "Well, then, okay, that could be good."

Casey threw the door open and waved Susan, Terry, and Chicken through. "This is Susan—her husband is in the hospital. Lost his eye in the melee this morning out by the tunnel. This is..." she paused, biting her lip.

"This is Father Terry Milne of the Order of St. Raphael, otherwise known as the Berkley Blackfriars," Susan said. "And this is Chicken. She's...I guess she's our unofficial ward right now."

"I like chicken," Chicken said.

"Who doesn't like chicken?" the mayor said.

"And this is Mayor Betts. We just call him Tom—or Goggles—his secretary Milo Richards and city planner Amanda Hernandez."

A young African-American man in a skinny tie nodded his greeting, as did the middle-aged Hispanic woman at the other end of the desk.

Mayor Betts snapped his fingers. "The Berkeley Blackfriars— weren't you the guys at the Republican convention?"

Milo narrowed his eyes at them. "I just saw an exposé about you on CNN."

Susan put up her hands. "Look, I live with these guys," she said. Betts' and Milo's eyebrows shot up. "CNN, that was a fuckin' hit job."

Betts smiled at the expletive, and Susan sensed that he like her style. Milo looked unconvinced.

"Please, Miss..."

"Susan. Melanchthon."

"Susan it is, 'cause I'm not even going to *try* to pronounce your last name," Betts said. "We'd be grateful for any information that's gonna help us keep our people safe."

Terry cleared his throat. "First, please let me say how grateful we are that you've taken us in. I thought we were goners out there."

"We're not trying to hoard our resources or anything. We really do want to help." Mayor Betts gave him a grim smile.

"I really get that," Terry nodded. "In the Epistle to the Ephesians, St. Paul said, 'For we wrestle not against flesh and blood, but against principalities, against powers, against the rulers of the darkness of this world, against spiritual wickedness in high places.' Well, St. Paul didn't really write that, it was someone writing in his name, probably some—"

Susan, standing behind him, punched him in the kidneys. "This isn't a homily. Get to the point."

Terry turned and scowled at her. He rubbed at his lower back. "Our enemies aren't people. They're demons."

"Demons?" Mayor Betts looked skeptical.

"Mayor, we have *real* work to do here," Hernandez said, not disguising the irritation in her voice.

"Just...hear me out." Terry took a deep breath. "Look, fighting demons—and other spiritual nastiness—is what we do for a living. We're not making it up. It's real. We discovered sigils all over Oakland. Sigils that designate a certain jurisdiction, a neighborhood, to be the domain of a certain kind of demon."

"What the hell is a sigil?"

"Well, it's a symbol. Like a diagram, but simpler. Like letters, but more complex than that. Anyway, a sigil connects the sigil holder to a demonic entity. If it's properly activated, it can act as a portal, a gateway."

Chicken walked up to the desk, which was exactly eye-level to her. She saw a felt marker, and her eyes widened. She grabbed it and trotted over to the wall, pulling the cap off it and tossing it on the floor.

"What, like between here and hell?" Betts asked.

"Exactly. Or wherever the demon happens to be. It's not like they're confined to hell."

"Of course not," said Betts. "That would be silly."

Chicken started drawing on the wall.

"Are you...making fun of us?" Terry asked.

"Of course not, I—"

He stopped because Susan tapped Terry on the shoulder and pointed at the wall where Chicken was at work.

"Hey!" Mayor Betts yelled. "You can't—"

"Mayor Betts," Susan shouted him down. Chicken stepped back to admire her work. "That—" Susan pointed at the drawing, "—is a sigil."

"It's the sigil that was on the truck that was at the mouth of the tunnel," Terry said. "It belongs to a demon named Alianthor. A wrath demon, third level. A duke, no less. Famous for flaying people alive. Nicknamed 'Skin' in infernal circles, although only demons of greater rank call him that."

Chicken was drawing again, quickly sketching out the scene with the man tied to the flatbed truck. The figures were naive, but recognizable. And she was getting details that Susan had forgotten. Susan found herself speechless. Who knew the little girl had such talent?

Terry, however, found his tongue. "That right there, what Chicken is drawing, is what this demon makes people do. Everyone in his orbit of influence—about two or three city blocks, near as I can figure —acts on this demon's primary activity. In this case, filleting and flaying."

"*What*?" Betts seemed to be having trouble taking it in.

"Demons are arranged into hosts, with numerous lesser demons under their lords or commanders. That demon is a duke, with literally hundreds of other demons under his command. When whoever did this called him up, his underlings came too. And they're...just doing what they do. It's a big party for them. And it's like that all over Oakland. And Emeryville. And probably Berkeley by now."

"Definitely Berkeley," Betts admitted.

"Why not here?" Richards asked, his skepticism seeming to lighten a little.

"Because the asshole magickians who did this didn't post any sigils in Alameda," Terry said.

"What about that one?" Betts asked, his face involuntarily registering alarm.

"Don't worry, it's not activated. We'd have to ritually invoke the demon and feed it some blood."

"Who's blood?" Hernandez asked. All three of them had a look of horror on their faces.

Well, at least we're getting through, Susan thought.

"In the case of most of the Bay Area, a young woman was sacrificed as a demonic offering in Tilden Park last Friday night."

"That's terrible," Betts breathed.

"It's powerful. And it activated all the sigils that the magickians hung all over the East Bay. Just thank your lucky stars no one thought to do that in Alameda."

Betts nodded. "Are you saying that these...magickians...control these demons?"

"They *aren't* controlling them, which is why they're having a field day. They're just...inviting them. But yeah, they're magickians—goetic magickians at that. Controlling demons is normally what they do."

Betts shook his head. "I can't believe I'm actually listening to you. This is crazy."

"I know how it sounds," Susan said. "But it happens to be true."

"We removed several of the sigils from different neighborhoods and burned them," Terry said. "And the influence dissipated quickly."

"So, what do you suggest we do?" Betts said.

"I've been giving this some thought," Terry said. "I think we need a dual strategy—both defensive and offensive. First, we need to keep everyone in Alameda safe."

"I thought there wasn't any danger because there aren't any sigils here," Hernandez said.

"True, but in Oakland we discovered that some clever folks transferred the sigils to a truck and took the whole party on the road. All you need is one sigil-bearing truck to get through the tunnel or across one of the bridges, and suddenly you've got mass killings erupting on Park Street."

Betts rubbed his hand along his naked scalp, his eyes moving quickly back and forth behind his horn-rims.

"Or a boat," Susan said.

"Plus, remember the radius," Terry said. "If you have a sigil on a truck near the water, you could have people crossing on skiffs, on rafts—hell, on inner tubes—and slaughtering anyone they come into contact with. And anyone who's near the shore might pick up on the influence, too."

"So we need everyone to stay...what? A block away from the shore?"

"That should limit the local infection where the channel is narrow. But we also need to arm people along the shore, too, in case any people who are...under the influence, let's say...get through."

"Or, God forbid, carries a sigil over," Susan said.

Betts blinked at her. Richards' mouth hung open, and Hernandez looked like she was swaying in the breeze.

Betts stammered. "Y-you said a dual strategy. You just talked about defense. What about offense?"

"I suggest we train teams to cross over, seek out the sigils and destroy them."

"Who is going to train these people?"

"I will. And Dylan, when he gets out of the hospital. He's more knowledgeable about demon magick than I am."

"He'll be out tomorrow," Susan said.

"He will?"

"Count on it. He's not going to want to miss this."

Terry nodded.

"But you're talking about a suicide mission," Betts said.

"We'll take only volunteers. And we'll make sure they're protected. As best we can," Terry said, not sounding terribly convincing.

Betts looked at his staff. They said nothing.

"This is...I've never heard anything like this. Are you sure you're not shitting me? This is crazy," Betts said, pointing at the sigil on his wall.

"This is magick," Terry said.

"I do magic," Betts said. "But—"

"You do stage magic," Terry corrected him. "This is *real* magick. This is the manipulation of the seen world through unseen means. This is the raising of demons to do the will of whatever assholes were stupid enough to open a portal into hell. This is the real shit and it's coming down on you like a rain of flaming turds." Betts' and his staff reared back from the force of Terry's words. But the short friar wasn't finished. He advanced on them, punctuating his point by thrusting his forefinger with every other word. "And you can either stick your heads in the sand and lose every man, woman and child on this island or you can swallow your fucking rationalistic cynicism," he placed both hands on the desk and leaned over it toward them, "and get to work."

53

"PERRY!" Cain leaped up, but Richard tackled him, pinning his arms and making sure that the detective did not cross the boundary of the Circle of Protection. Richard felt the detective's breath heaving and his bones shaking, and he knew the man was just shy of hysteria.

He pressed his full weight onto Cain's chest and spoke to him in calm, reassuring tones. "There's nothing you can do now. Lie still or the demon will go after you, too. Just be calm. Just relax." There was nothing that would convince Cain to relax at that moment, though, and Richard knew it. He kept Cain pinned until the man finally stopped struggling.

"Enough!" Marco shouted. "You are released!" He snatched the sigil from the Circle of Containment and lit it on fire.

Richard didn't notice the ectoplasmic wisps dissipating, but when Marco called the all clear and he rolled off of Cain, the room seemed quiet and normal. Cain leaped up and ran to where Perry's body lay crumpled on the concrete. He held his arms out from his sides, like a gunslinger waiting for his opponent to draw. But Richard could see that he wasn't preparing to draw a weapon—he just didn't know if he should touch his fallen partner. Cain sank to one knee and felt at Perry's neck. Without hesitation, he straightened her body out, swung his legs aside her, and began pushing on her chest with both hands. Richard rushed to help, pinching her nose and breathing into her mouth whenever Cain paused.

They continued for several minutes, then persisted for several more. But when Richard checked, there was still no pulse. He looked up at Cain and shook his head. Cain fell on her and began sobbing, his back jerking from his dry, heaving breaths. Richard tenderly laid a hand on his back.

"That could have gone better," Marco said.

"You did everything right," Richard answered.

"We could have locked the door."

"It doesn't have a lock," Richard pointed out.

"We could have posted a guard."

"We could have assembled a protective circle of tie-dyed ponies, too. Look, we didn't know what we didn't know. We didn't expect her to step in on us. It's tragic, but it was an accident. It wasn't your fault."

Marco looked down at Perry's body. "Maybe."

"You can't beat yourself up."

"Why not?"

"Because we have too much to do. If you let yourself get incapacitated by grief or guilt, then they win."

"Who's 'they'?"

"The Lodge...or whatever dark powers are pulling their strings... Larch." Richard pressed his arm. "You *cannot* let them win. Pull yourself together. If we survive this, you'll have plenty of leisure for self-recrimination and binge drinking."

"Are you talking about me or you now? You know I don't drink."

"Just—" Richard shook Cain's shoulder. "Detective. You need to mourn later. We need to save Berkeley now."

Cain lifted his head and caught Richard's eye. His gaze was wild, his cheeks puffy and red. "Now!" Richard shouted.

"Has anyone ever told you that you have this...*innate authority* thing going on?" Marco asked.

Richard ignored him as he helped Cain to his feet. Cain removed his jacket and laid it over Perry, covering her face. Richard steered him through the door and toward the stairs. "First thing first. Are your landlines working?" Richard asked.

"They were," Cain answered.

"Can you get me an outside line?"

"Why?" Cain asked.

"You heard what the demon said," Richard said. "This is all a distraction, everything that's happening in the East Bay. The real danger is global...universal, even. I need to get someone working on *that* nuclear bomb of a problem—then we can tend to the brush fires here."

"This is a brush fire?"

"By comparison, yes."

"Oh, Lord," Cain said. At the top of the stairs he stopped and clutched at the wall to steady himself.

"It's going to be okay," Richard said. "You just have to get moving and stay moving. I speak from experience."

"It's not okay for Perry," Cain said.

"Or for a lot of people whose lives are getting wrecked out there every moment we delay," Richard said, speaking a little too loud and too close to Cain for human comfort. He was trying to motivate him, but he wondered if he were pushing too hard given what had just happened. What Cain needed, of course, was a week on retreat with a therapist, working through the trauma he had just experienced. But he wasn't going to get that.

Cain led Richard and Marco into the squad room, and, weaving a little, made his way to his desk.

"Cain!" Herrer shouted.

Cain ignored her and sank into his chair as if it were a life raft.

"Phone," Richard said, right behind him.

Cain lifted the receiver and handed it to Richard. He dialed 9, then swung the cradle toward Richard to dial.

Herrer stormed toward the desk. "Where the fuck is Perry?" she demanded.

"Perry is in the basement," Cain said, not looking at her. "She's dead."

"*What*?" Herrer stepped back as if she'd been punched in the chest. "What happened? Did that mob break through? Or did she... did she have a heart attack? 'Cause I know she's on that medication."

"That's for blood pressure," Cain said. "But...no. She was killed by..."

"By who?"

Richard plugged his ears, but it was still hard to hear. "Shush!" he shouted. He punched the button for the speaker phone.

"Who the fuck is this?" Herrer pointed at Richard. "And this?" She pointed at Marco.

"Brian? This is Richard. Are you all right?"

Brian's voice sounded relieved. "You have no idea how glad I am to hear from you, Dicky."

"Listen, I have no time to explain. But everything that's happening over here—it's a red herring. The real action, the real danger...it's celestial. I have it on good authority that Larch is ascending the sephirot. He's trying to destroy them, one at a time."

"Holy shit," Brian said. There was a long pause. Richard could hear him breathing and could almost hear him thinking. "That explains why every couple in the world is fighting right now. He must have upset the order in Yesod."

"It's the seat of romantic relationships," Richard said. "Yes, that makes sense. I had no idea that was going on. Haven't run into many fighting spouses here. Mostly just murderous bands of roving thugs, looters, arsonists...oh, and orgies rubbed raw from lack of lube."

"Huh. I'm gonna take your word on that."

"We've got our work cut out here, but if anyone knows how to stop Larch..." Richard didn't finish the sentence. He didn't need to.

"You want me to...what?"

"What do you think?"

"I have no idea."

"Brian, nobody knows the Tree of Life better than you do. I don't know anyone on earth more prepared for this particular task than you are."

"Go after Larch."

"Yes."

"And stop him."

"Right."

"I think this is a little beyond my pay grade. I look shit up. I cook."

"Brian, if you don't, he's not going to stop with marital discord. He's going to cut the strings of the mobile one at a time until…"

"Until the whole universe comes crashing down," Brian finished.

"Right.

"Brian, listen to me. It isn't just this world that needs saving—it's all of them. And you are the only person I know of who can do it. And saving people…that's what we do."

"But I'm not—"

"Like hell you're not. You might not wear the cassock, but you are every bit as much a part of us as me or Dylan or Terry. We're a team. We've been a team for nearly ten years. You've been an integral part of everything we've done since you came to live with us. I need you to take point on this one."

Silence.

"Brian, just a few days ago you told me you needed to do something important with your life. If saving every world in creation isn't important—"

Richard heard something like a resigned moan.

"What? What does that mean?"

"Okay, okay." Brian breathed. "Just…I'll try."

"You will?" Richard hadn't realized he'd been holding his breath. He let it out, feeling a rush of relief.

"Look…I don't know what to do. I don't know what it's really like up there. I don't know what he's doing or how to stop him, but I'll go. I'll…I'll give it everything I've got."

"That's what I wanted to hear," Richard heaved a sigh of relief. "And be careful. Larch is tricky."

"I will, Dicky. By the way, I heard from Terry. Dylan lost an eye, but otherwise they made it, and they're safe."

"Thanks be to God," Richard said. "Thank you. Listen, I'm at the

Berkeley Police Department. Call me at this number if you find anything, will you?"

"Will do. Be careful. Stay safe."

"You bet. Do you have support there?"

"Yes. Chava and Elsa. I'm not sure how I'll explain it to them, but they'll help. God bless you and keep you, Dicky."

The line went dead. Richard hung up and turned to face Herrer. "I'm sorry," he said. "Who are you?"

54

"Is this what a stakeout is?" Kat asked. "'Cause it's really boring."

"Yep. This is a stakeout," Mikael affirmed. They had followed Turpelo and Purderabo to a bookstore off of Larkin Street. Kat and Mikael had holed up in a coffee shop across the street and were watching through the window.

"On TV, they sit there for about 20 seconds, and then something happens," Kat said. "We've been here for an hour."

"And we might be here for hours more."

"Jesus," Kat said and sighed. "If I have one more latte, my bladder is going to swell up like a balloon."

"There is a bathroom here."

"Nah. I'll suffer ascetically for the good of my soul."

"You don't have to be a fucking martyr about it."

"I'm not a fucking martyr."

"You're acting like a fucking martyr."

"Who are you to call me a fucking martyr?"

Mikael held up his hand. "Breathe," he said. "It's not you, not me."

Kat nodded and blew air out through her cheeks. She pointed at the ceiling.

"Right," Mikael agreed.

"Okay," Kat said, centering herself. "What if Tweedledum and Tweedledee aren't *shopping* at the bookstore?"

"It's an occult specialty shop. What else would they be doing?"

"Maybe they live upstairs, over the bookstore. Maybe Larch is there. Maybe we could be here all night."

Mikael shrugged. "So what if we are?"

She narrowed her eyes at him. "You could make an effort not to get pissy, you know."

"Sorry."

Kat's phone pinged. A split second later, Mikael's did as well. "Must be for the both of us," Mikael said. "I'll watch, you read. What do you say?"

"Okay. It's Brian. And talk about an answered prayer..."

"What?"

"He's offering us a place to bunk down."

"Hot damn!"

"He says it's small, we'll have to share a twin bed."

"We'll snuggle. It'll be fine."

"Sounds great, actually," Kat said.

"Well, 'ask and you shall receive'," Mikael lifted his empty coffee cup as a toast.

"Oh..." Kat's face darkened.

"What?"

"I'm just checking my feed. I'm in the Bay Area Wiccan Network Group."

"Yeah, I'm in BAWN."

"I don't think you've seen this. Posted an hour ago. 'The State's Attorney has opened an investigation against Bay Area Wiccan groups,'" she read.

"What? What for?"

"For inciting and instigating the violence in the East Bay."

"That's crazy."

Kat stared straight ahead. Then she looked back at her phone. "There's a link to an article from *The Chronicle*'s website. It says, 'The SA's office is investigating whether the wave of crime sweeping the

East Bay might be of occult origin. Wiccan groups are being questioned in connection to the violence.'"

"Could they just be talking about us—you know, Jimmy and Luna and such?" Mikael asked.

"I think it's way bigger than that," Kat said, scrolling. "It says here that the leaders of the Reclaiming Community have been detained for questioning, as have leaders from the UU Pagan Alliance and the Church of All Worlds."

"Good lord," Mikael swore. "But what I don't understand is that this isn't news. They *know* it's of occult origin. We told them that."

"We told *Berkeley* Detectives that. This is State. This is happening in Sacramento, San Francisco, and San Jose. My guess is that the Berkeley folks never even passed that info along."

"This is an entirely unrelated investigation?"

"Maybe. I wouldn't call it an investigation, though. Sounds like more of a witch-hunt."

"With real witches."

"Right." Kat's fingers tightened on her phone to the point where her hand went white. She forced herself to relax. She looked back at her phone. "There are protests outside the State Attorney's office in San Francisco demanding their release. And there are counter protests by asshole conservative Christians demanding that all Wiccans be jailed immediately."

"Well, that's a little shit storm," Mikael whistled.

"And it's getting bigger," Kat said. "The police are patrolling the space between the two groups of protestors, but they don't have sufficient manpower. They've called in the National Guard."

"Wow."

"Wow."

Mikael jumped in his seat.

"What?"

He pointed out the window. The door to the bookshop had opened, and they watched as Turpelo exited, followed by Purderabo's lumbering frame. Purderabo wobbled as they walked down the street, side by side, in the middle of a spirited conversation. Without a word,

Mikael and Kat tossed their cups, tucked their folded cassocks under their arms, and exited the coffee shop. They stayed on the opposite side of the street, following from about half a block back. Turpelo turned and looked behind them, but Kat couldn't make out what he was looking at. They continued undetected.

"The whole, 'Let's blame the Wiccans thing,' really chaps my hide," Kat confessed.

"Me too."

"What are we going to do about it?" Kat asked.

"We're doing it," Mikael said. "We're following the people who are *actually* responsible. We're doing what the police *should* be doing, if they had a lick of sense."

"Why do our police not have a lick of sense?" Kat asked.

"Is that rhetorical?" Mikael asked.

"I guess it is. Yeah."

Purderabo and Turpelo turned left, forcing Kat and Mikael to cross. "Let's cross to over there," he pointed to the diagonal corner.

"Why?" Kat asked.

She heard Mikael breathe, obviously trying to control his temper. "Because if we do," he said, measuring his words out slowly, "we can stay on the opposite side of the street from them. It's good cover."

"Okay. Just asking for your rationale is all."

"You don't have to question every word out of my mouth."

"I'm not."

"Seems that way."

"That's the sky talking."

He didn't reply to that. They waited for a break in traffic, then ran for the far corner.

"It's not enough," Kat said.

"What? What do you mean? What's not enough?"

"Just following these guys. It's not enough."

"What the fuck are you talking about?"

"Don't snap at me" Kat snapped. "It just isn't."

"Wait," Mikael said, and turned to look at the garage door to their right.

"Why are we looking at this garage door?" Kat asked.

"Will you stop? Just trust me for once, will you?" Mikael pretended to inspect the door. "I saw them look over here."

"This isn't a shop window in Union Square," Kat noted. "This looks weird."

"Just..." Mikael snuck a look over his shoulder.

"Okay, they're on the move again...wait, no they're not."

Kat turned and looked. Purderabo and Turpelo were looking around, as if they didn't want to be seen entering. Then they climbed the three steps to the grated door of an apartment building and rang the bell. A minute later, the grate swung inward, and they entered the porch. The door beyond swung open a moment later then closed. Mikael pulled out his phone and made a note of the address.

"You think Larch is here?"

"I don't know," Mikael said, looking around for another place to wait.

"There aren't any shops here," Kat said. "Besides, it's getting dark."

"Is that it?"

"What do you mean?"

"You don't have a stone in your shoe? You're not getting a head cold? Planets not in alignment to suit your fancy?"

"Are you saying I'm a whiner?"

"I didn't say that, you did."

Kat held up her hand. Mikael's eyes went wide and he nodded.

"This shit is hard."

"Fucking hard," she agreed.

"I really love you."

"I really love you, too."

"What do you want to do?"

"What do *you* think we should do?"

Mikael indicated with his chin. "I think we should wait at that bus stop over there. It's covered. It has a wind break. One of us can walk back to the street over there for coffee, food, bathroom breaks. It's a good stakeout spot. No one will notice us just sitting there—it's a bus stop. People are supposed to sit there."

"And what happens when the bus comes?" Kat asked as they started to walk toward the stop.

"Look, there's about fifteen buses that stop here," Mikael pointed to the kiosk as they got closer. "No one will think anything if we don't get on a bus. They'll think we're just waiting for a different one."

Kat shrugged. "Okay." She sat down and looked over at the house. "What do you think they're doing in there?"

"I have no idea, but knowing those two, it won't be something my mom would be proud of."

"Is your mom proud of what you're doing now?"

"Ha! Hell no. Mom's an avowed atheist. She thinks I'm crazy."

"Why haven't you introduced me to your mom?"

"Next time we're in Alaska, I'll do that."

"Your mom's in Alaska? Why didn't you ever tell me that?"

"I'm telling you now. My mom lives in Juno."

"What does she do there?"

"She guts fish and chain smokes."

"Huh." Kat nodded toward the apartment building. "Why don't we just see what they're doing?" Kat asked.

"You mean, just knock on the door and say, 'Hey guys, what's up?' Really?"

Kat's shoulders deflated. "I hate just waiting around like this."

"Larch may not be there. Then again he might. But if this is just a stop...they might go elsewhere. We shouldn't give ourselves away just yet."

"It's getting dark. And chilly."

"Whiner," Mikael said.

"Asshole," Kat responded.

"I thought you wanted to get laid?" he said.

"At Brian's? On the twin bed?" Kat rolled her eyes. "I think I have some time to torment you and make up before we have a suitable opportunity for any serious nookie."

"You take me entirely too much for granted."

"Not one little bit," she kissed his nose.

55

BRIAN OPENED the oversized text and stared at the illustration. The Tree of Life filled the page, its ten sephirot hung suspended between heaven and earth like pomegranates, each filled with splendor.

"That's the *Sephir Yetzirah*," Chava said.

"Yes. I've always admired this edition."

"It was my grandfather's."

"It's in beautiful condition."

"It is," she agreed. She looked at the text over his shoulder.

"Chava, I'm going to tell you something incredible, something you won't want to believe."

"Brian, how long have we known each other?"

"Still…"

"Try me."

"You didn't believe me when I told you I know Serah Bat Asher."

Chava turned away. "Only because it is impossible that she would betray her people and become a…"

"A Christian?"

Chava folded her arms over her chest, but she still wouldn't look at him.

"The Christians' greatest and earliest theologian, Paul, said that in Jesus, God was setting up another Israel—not a better one, just a parallel community. Another community full of people who wrestle with God and love God, just as we do. A community specifically set up for gentiles. Okay, we have our doctrinal disagreements, but is that notion of a parallel Israel so far-fetched? Doesn't it sound like the kind of thing HaShem might actually do?"

Chava chewed on her lip, staring into space. "There is a tradition that says Serah was adopted by Asher. That she was *goyim*, brought into the family."

"Well, that's interesting. If she was goyim to begin with, maybe she sees her...affiliation...as more fluid than we do."

Chava didn't answer.

"Chava, if the Christians are right—if God did set up another community to love and save—and if Serah is goyim by birth, might she not feel at liberty to travel back and forth between the two communities?"

"I think living with Christians has poisoned your mind," she said, a little hotly.

"Or opened it."

She didn't answer. Instead, she turned into the kitchen and put on the kettle. "So what's with the *Sephir Yetzirah*?"

"A black magickian is ascending the sephirot and throwing them out of balance. We think he intends to destroy them."

There was a crash from the kitchen.

"Are you okay?" Brian called.

Chava walked back to the doorway, her eyes wide. "Are you shitting me?"

"Nope."

"Is that why..."

"All the fighting? Yeah. It makes sense, don't you think? If you throw Yesod out of balance—"

"You lose marital harmony."

"Right."

"Oh my God." Chava wasn't avoiding his eyes now. "Brian, what do we do?"

"I guess...I have to go after him. None of the Blackfriars know the sephirot, not like I do. And no one else—"

"No one else would believe it," Chava breathed.

"Right. I just..." Brian sank onto the couch. "...don't know if I'm capable of this."

Chava sat down next to him. "I want to tell you a story. When Jacob and his sons returned to Egypt, Joseph prophesied that a redeemer would arise to save the Jewish people. He told them that they would know him by the phrase *'pakod pakadeti.'*"

"*Pakod pakadeti*?" Brian repeated. "I have taken note?"

"Exactly. And Asher told his daughter Serah this secret. So hundreds of years later, when Moses and Aaron were performing their wonders in the sight of our people—to prove they were really from God—the elders of Israel came to Serah and told her about them."

"Wait, hundreds of years later?"

"Serah bat Asher is immortal, remember?"

"Uh...right. Okay, go on."

"So she said, 'I give these wonders no credence.'"

"Wow. Did she later become the book agent that passed up *To Kill a Mockingbird*, too?"

Chava ignored the joke. "So then the elders told her, 'The man called Moses said something odd.' Serah asked them, 'What did he say?' 'He said, "I have taken note of you."' At which point Serah told them, '*That* is the man who will rescue Israel.'"

"That's a great story," Brian said. "But I don't understand why you're telling it to me."

"Because, you idiot," she put her hand on his knee and squeezed it. "You are the man who will save the Tree of Life. I have taken note of *you*. I believe in you. You can do this."

Brian grasped her hand and held it tightly. "I'm unconvinced, but...thank you," he said.

"What do you need?"

"I need to lie around with as few distractions as possible. I'll need a clear path to the bathroom and plenty of fluids."

"I think we can manage that."

"I need someone to run interference for me here in Melkuth—someone to answer the door, my phone, get text messages, etc."

"You need a spotter," Chava said.

"Exactly."

Chava squeezed his hand again. "I'll clear my calendar. When do you want to launch?"

56

"THEY ARE NOT COMING OUT," Kat said. She leaned into him and hugged herself for warmth. She had already donned her cassock again, but it wasn't her winter cassock and its light fabric did little to block out the chill.

Mikael looked at his phone. "It's nearly eleven. I think you might be right."

"He's got to be there."

"Are your teeth chattering?" Mikael asked.

"This bus stop bench is metal. And it's fucking freezing. Don't touch your tongue to it."

"Ew. I don't even want to think about that."

"You've had your tongue is some pretty nasty places," Kat reminded him.

"Now you're just teasing me."

"I'm just trying to stay warm."

Mikael stood up and stretched. "So...how do you want to do this?"

"I'm thinking that just ringing the doorbell and saying, 'Hey, we're Blackfriars. Can we come in?' isn't going to cut it."

"I'm thinking you're right." Mikael stroked his chin as he thought.

Kat admired his angular jaw. The fog was getting thick now, and it gathered around his feet. "I wish I had a camera," Kat said, making a square with her fingers, and looking through it at him. "This is like, the *best* noir romance cover."

"Punk noir romance?"

Kat rolled her eyes. "Oh, all right. Leave it to you to throw us into a genre that doesn't actually exist and can't possibly sell."

"Why do you have to put me in a box?"

"I'm not putting you in a box, you ninny. I'm teasing you."

"Felt like an accusation," Mikael said.

"That's just the...spheres talking, remember? If this thing turns us into people who can't make fun of each other, we're in real trouble."

Mikael nodded. Then he turned and crossed the street to examine the building more closely. Like most San Francisco buildings, it stood impossibly close to its neighbor. Mikael could not even fit his hand in between them. Kat crossed and laid a hand on his belt.

"Sorry I called you a ninny," she said.

"I'm not even sure what a ninny is," he said. "But thank you." He pointed to the apartment building's facade. ""This is straight up—no trellis, no balcony. And no access to the back yard from here," he said.

"We're only three buildings from the edge of the block, though," Kat pointed out. "You could hop some fences."

Mikael started walking toward the corner.

"Hey, slow down," Kat said. "Your legs are like, twice as long as mine."

"Sorry. Just...on the case."

"That's my...friar."

At the corner, Mikael turned right and strode to the middle point of the block. A fence blocked his way, but he was tall enough to see over it.

"What?" Kat asked. "Can you make it?"

"Yeah. The next fence is scalable. I can't see the one beyond that, but I'll cross that bridge when I come to it."

"So to speak. Am I not coming with you?"

"I'll let you in at the front door. Why don't you wait there?"

"Like a good girl, you mean?"

Mikael blinked. "I didn't mean—"

"This is man business, is that it?"

"Kat, it's a simple case of...I'm taller, and these are high fences—"

"Are you seriously going to mansplain complementarianism to me right now?"

"Is that what I was doing?"

"Never mind." Kat looked away. She chewed on her lip as she got a handle on her anger. She turned back to him but didn't meet his eyes. "You want a hand up, Mr. Feminist Icon?"

"No, I got it." Mikael put his cassock under his shirt at the small of his back, then tucked the shirt in. "I'll put this on once I get there. We'll want to be in full Blackfriar's mode, after all." Then he fished a mask out of his front pocket and put that on.

"Oh, Lord," Kat said, her face falling into her hands. "Couldn't you be into the Furry scene or something?"

"This is a job for the Confessor," he said.

"I fuck you in *spite* of this—you know that, right?"

He leaned down and kissed her. She hesitated, then kissed him back with a passion largely displaced from her irritation. Then in a single fluid motion, he swung one leg to the top of the fence, tipped himself over, and was gone.

"...And, he's a gymnast, too," Kat breathed out loud to no one. "That makes me hornier than I want to admit." She sighed and walked back to the front of the apartment building. The quiet descended on her like a blanket. She exhaled and a dozen tightly coiled places in her body relaxed. Now that he wasn't with her, she didn't feel nearly as edgy or angry.

She wondered at this as she walked back to the front of the apartment building. The fog was so thick she could barely see the corner she had just returned from. No cars were on the street—not moving ones anyway. It was as if the world had just...stopped: quiet, holy, shrouded in the smoke of incense.

The buzzer sounded and Kat nearly jumped out of her skin. She snatched at the steel gate handle and yanked on it. She felt the catch give and it swung open toward her. She stepped up onto the tiny porch and clutched at the doorknob. It turned, and she went in.

The landing was completely dark. She let the door close quietly behind her and waited for her eyes to adjust. She heard music playing and the sound of male voices. Occasionally uproarious laughter punctuated the din, and every now and then the sound of a small dog barking.

"Shhh...Kat. Up here." She looked up the stairs, squinting, and saw Mikael crouched at the top, almost invisible in his cassock and mask.

Kat hiked up her cassock and crept silently up the stairs. At the top he started to rise, but she grabbed his cassock and pulled him back down, kissing him long and deep. "Don't talk. You'll just piss me off and it'll ruin everything."

"Okay."

"That's talking."

"Sorry. I'll stop?"

"Do you know what I'm thinking?"

He shook his head.

"I'm thinking *danger* sex."

"Uh...when?"

"How about *now*?"

"Um...where?"

"I don't see anyone." She reached through the fold in his cassock and yanked at his belt.

57

"Boss, I'm heading out." Milo stuck his head in the door.

"Did Amanda head home?" Betts looked up from his computer. He took off his glasses and rubbed at his eyes. They were watering and they hurt. He was sure they were red.

"Yeah, about fifteen minutes ago."

"I'm sorry about this."

"About what?" Milo entered the room fully.

"The late hours, the...craziness."

"It's not your fault, Tom," Milo said. "It's the hand we were dealt. We have to see it through. I'm sure as hell not blaming you."

"I know that," he said, throwing his glasses down onto his desk. "I still feel responsible."

"Let it go." Milo walked over to the desk. "You need to get some sleep."

"Yeah," Betts looked up and gave him a forced smile. "Just as soon as I...oh, Jesus. Do a million fucking things first."

"They'll still be there in the morning."

"They sure as shit will."

"And Tom..." Betts cocked his head. Milo hesitated. "Look, it's not my place to give you advice."

"I beg to differ, you're my chief advisor."

"I mean personal advice."

"Again...Milo, I want you to speak freely."

Milo looked away, as if a thought had just struck him. A troubling thought.

"What?" Betts asked.

"To finish the one conversation," Milo said. "Everything you've got to do will seem less overwhelming once you've had some sleep."

Betts picked up his glasses. "You're probably right about that. I'm just...compulsive."

"You care."

"I do care." He nodded and put his glasses back on. The cartilage over his ears ached from the weight of them. "Now, what was the other thing?"

"I'm not sure it's...anything, but..."

"But what?"

Milo sat in the chair in front of Betts' desk. Betts sat down, too, putting his elbows on his desk and leaning his head on his hands. It suddenly seemed incredibly heavy.

"What if those people we saved last night, that Japanese priest and that fat woman..."

"Yeah?"

"What if they're telling the truth?"

"That demons are destroying the East Bay?"

Milo looked from left to right quickly, as if realizing for the first time how ridiculous he sounded. "Yeeeaaah."

Betts shrugged. "It's the first explanation I've heard that actually accounts for all the weird shit that's been going down."

"Right," Milo looked encouraged.

"Are you thinking we should go along with the priest's plan?"

Milo nodded but didn't answer at first. "In the foreground, yeah."

Betts straightened up, suddenly not feeling so tired. "And in the background?"

Milo chewed on a finger and sat back, thinking, pretty hard and fast it seemed to Betts. "If they're right about those magickians... If demons can be...controlled..."

"That's a lot of power," Betts breathed.

"That's a lot of fucking power," Milo agreed.

58

"THIS IS MADNESS," Herrer said, after Cain had explained everything.

"No. *That* is madness," Richard said, pointing to the outside. "*This* is real."

"I saw it with my own eyes, Captain," Cain said. "And you can go down and see Perry's body for yourself. The claw marks on her face and neck...there is nothing in this building that could have made those."

Herrer turned to Marco. "Whatever you did down there, was it worth it?"

"I don't know the answer to that," Marco said. He shrugged. "We got some very useful information."

"Is it going to stop...all this?" Herrer waved her arm, which Richard took to mean the whole apocalypse that was the East Bay at the moment.

"No," Marco said. "It was about...something else."

Herrer sputtered, unable to even form her next words.

Richard touched her elbow. "This," he indicated everything, just as she had done. "Is small potatoes compared to what we found out."

Herrer's eyes grew big, and she stopped trying to form words. She dropped her hands and looked out the window. "That true, Cain?" she asked, finally.

"Yeah. I'm sorry to say that it is. I don't understand a word of it, but something else is going on, something bigger."

"I...I don't know how to handle this."

"Fortunately, we do," Richard said.

"And who the hell are you?" Herrer asked, shaking her head with pained impatience.

"We're the Order of St. Raphael—"

"He's the Order of St. Raphael," Marco corrected. "I'm just a friend of the family."

"And just what the hell is that?"

"You haven't heard of us?" Richard asked, genuinely surprised.

"No, should I have?"

"We're also known as the Berkeley Blackfriars."

Herrer shook her head.

Richard dropped his gaze, momentarily crestfallen.

"Um...they're world famous demon-fighters," Marco added, apparently trying to be helpful.

"Really? World-famous?" Herrer raised an eyebrow.

"Not really, no," Marco said. "They're more like local celebrities... in small...subcultural, cir—" he trailed off. "Look, they know their shit, okay? *He* knows his shit."

Herrer looked unconvinced but turned to Richard. "Do you have a plan?"

"We do." Richard looked back up, resolute.

"We do?" Marco asked.

"The whole Tree of Life thing is out of our hands—"

"What 'Tree of Life thing'?" Herrer scowled. "What are you talking about?"

"Everything that's happening here is a ruse. To distract us—"

"To distract who?"

"Us. The Blackfriars."

"The apocalypse of the East Bay was orchestrated for your benefit?" Herrer crossed her arms. "Does the word *megalomania* mean anything to you?"

Richard shook his head. "I know how it sounds. Let me back up. There's a lodge of black magickians."

"Er...he means evil magickians," Marco interjected. "I'm black. They're evil."

"Fine," Richard said. "Anyway—"

"We're gonna have to have a talk about intersectionality."

"Do you mind?" Richard snapped.

Marco held his hands up.

"Are they both crazy, or just the white one?" Herrer asked Cain.

"What I'm trying to say is that there is a Lodge of evil magickians in San Francisco. The Lodge of the Hawk and Serpent. We've successfully thwarted them in the past."

"Not all magickians are evil," Marco said.

Richard gave him a look that could turn a beagle to stone. Marco held his hands up again. Richard kept watching him but continued, "They caused all of this. They did it to keep us busy so that we wouldn't notice what they were really up to."

"Okay, I'll play along. And what are they really up to?" Herrer put her hands on her hips.

"They...or at least one of them, probably Larch..." He stroked his chin, thinking.

"Focus," Herrer commanded.

"They are going up to the higher sephirot."

"What is a sephirot?" Herrer asked.

"It's a...a higher plane of existence."

"What the fuck are you talking about?"

"In medieval Jewish mysticism—you might have heard of the Kabbalah?"

"Oh yeah, Madonna is into it," Cain nodded.

Richard rolled his eyes. "Yes, well it's much older than Madonna. The Kabbalists describe ten spheres, or worlds. They call them sephirot, which means 'emanations,' because they radiate out from God. They are manifestations of divine attributes."

"That sounds pretty abstract."

"From what I understand, things get more abstract the further up the Tree you go," Richard agreed. "We live in Malkuth, the lowest emanation."

"No, that would be Oakland," Herrer said.

"Our whole universe is in Malkuth," Richard said. "Every sephirah is a universe."

"You're not making any sense," Herrer said.

"It's hard to give an elevator description of a several-hundred-year-old mystical tradition," Richard said. "There are these worlds, up there," he said, pointing to the sky. "Our is the lowest, but it's fed with higher qualities from the spheres above us."

"And what's at the top of the spheres?" Herrer asked, one eyebrow raised.

Richard blinked. "Why...God, of course."

Herrer turned to Cain. "God. Of course."

"And all of this...abstraction is important why?"

"Because the evil magickian," Richard said, speaking slowly, as if to a child, "is going up to the other spheres intending to destroy them."

"So what?"

"So...we're dependent on them. If they die...we die."

Herrer turned to Cain. "I don't have time for nut jobs."

"Look, Captain, I don't know anything about...spheres. But I do know I just saw a demon kill Perry with my own eyes. They're onto *something* that's real."

Herrer turned back to Richard. "How do you plan to stop this evil magickian."

"I don't. Brian is on it."

"Who is Brian?"

"He's a Talmudic scholar. He's an expert on the Kabbalah. He's the person I'd trust most with this, anyway, so I'm going to do just that—trust him."

"Is he one of your monks?"

"We're friars, not monks," Richard corrected her. "He's the husband of one of our friars. But he's...yes, he's one of us."

"So Brian—whoever he is—is going to take care of the evil magickian. What are you planning to do?"

Richard stood up to his full height and ran his fingers through his thinning hair. "First, I'm going to take my dog out to use the yard."

"And then?" Marco asked, trying not to smile.

"Then we're going to get a good night's sleep."

"Uh-huh...and then?"

"Then we're going to train every officer you have in sigil removal, and we're going to take Berkeley back."

59

"OKAY, SO THAT WAS UNEXPECTED," Mikael said, zipping up his pants and straightening his cassock.

"But overdue and pretty fucking wonderful," Kat said, pulling him down by his cassock and planting a kiss on his lips. "We ought to have danger sex more often."

"That sounds like a subject for a longer discernment," Mikael said. "Maybe when we're out of danger."

"Wimp," Kat said, zipping up her own pants.

"Still sexy," Mikael added.

"Okay, what's next?"

"A cigarette?"

Kat gave him a mock-glare. Uproarious laughter erupted from somewhere down the hall. "I don't know what they're up to, but they're certainly having a good time."

Mikael pulled out his mask. Kat grabbed it and stuffed it down her pants. "No," she said with a firmness that brooked no dissent. He sighed.

"Should we just knock on the door?" Kat asked.

"Hmm...you know, if it's a party, let's just crash it. I'm guessing if we just walk right in like we're supposed to be there, very few people will even notice."

Kat shrugged. "I don't have a better idea."

Together they walked toward the noise and found themselves in front of apartment A2. "Just turn the knob and walk in?" Kat clarified.

"Yep."

"It could be an orgy."

"You really have sex on the brain, don't you? Yeah, it *could* be an orgy, and that would be embarrassing."

"Funny, though. Well, here goes nothing." She turned the knob and the door swung open easily. Kat walked inside, followed closely by Mikael. He closed the door behind him. No one seemed to notice them entering. Kat stood still, trying to get her bearings, trying to process what she was seeing.

"Mikael," she whispered. "What the fuck is this?"

The living room was large for a San Francisco apartment, but it was bisected by an elevated ramp that seemed to be made of gold. It sat on tables that were covered with cloth, complete with bunting. It was hard for Kat to make out the exact color of the cloth, as the room was bathed in colored lighting. A mirrored disco ball hung in the center of the room, projecting silvery flashes in every direction.

The room was filled with about twenty people, lined up on either side of the ramp. *Are all of them men?* she asked herself. No, there were a couple of women, she realized as her eyes adjusted, but they were definitely in the minority. Most of the revelers were middle aged, and most were in various stages of balding and corpulency. They were decked out, however, in their ritual finery—magickian's robes and capes and even the occasional wizard's hat straight out of the movies.

"I don't understand," Mikael whispered.

Just then the room began to chant "The Mange! The Mange! The Mange!"

Purderabo stood up and, grabbing a microphone that didn't seem to actually be connected to anything, shouted, "My friends, I give you Abramalin the Mange!" Another of the revelers lifted a nearly hairless, scabby Italian Greyhound onto the ramp. It was shaking like a leaf and was dressed in an ornate robe with the sign of the sun and moon embroidered on the back. Grabbing a thin lead, the Greyhound's owner walked him down the ramp to the cheers and howls of the crowd. Kat realized that the ramp was actually a catwalk.

"Is this a...fashion show? For what?" she whispered. "Dog magickians?"

The dog's owner walked him back to the starting point. He took a bow, to great cheering and catcalls, and then he lifted the Greyhound to the floor.

All eyes turned to two men and a woman in matching chairs along one wall. After conferring, they held up a card bearing the number "7." More cheering erupted, followed by calls for more beer.

Mikael tugged on Kat's sleeve, and they moved away from the door to an open place where they could lean against a wall. No one seemed to even notice they were there.

Purderabo picked up the fake microphone and held up his hand until the noise died down to a low rumble. "The highest score all night! Splendid! Now, get ready everyone for John Peki-Dee and Edward Kelly!"

Two men lifted a pair of Pekingese onto the ramp. The tiny dogs were dressed in matching Elizabethan collars, and both had long white beards tied to their chins. As the assembly roared their approval, their owners walked them to the edge of the catwalk, then back again. The judges gave the pair a six.

Kat was still trying to figure out what they were witnessing when she saw Turpelo approach Purderabo and whisper in his ear. Purderabo's eyebrows shot up and he looked around the room. Turpelo pointed directly at Kat and Mikael, and Purderabo followed his finger and scowled at the sight of them. Mikael waggled his fingers in their direction. Kat didn't need to look at him to know he was given them his shit-eating grin.

Purderabo's black look didn't lift, but he carried on with his master of ceremonies duties nevertheless. "Just in from Adyar, Helena Puglova Blavatsky!" A small, nearly bald man in a buttoned collar lifted a pug onto the catwalk. Blavatsky's tiny eyes looked like they were ready to bulge out of their sockets. A babushka shawl covered her shoulders and was pulled up over her wrinkled head. The crowd hooted and clapped, although the pug only received a four for her trouble.

"And now, beloved patrons of the canine and occult arts, we will take a half hour intermission, after which our show will continue." He gave Kat and Mikael a dark look, then put the microphone down. Someone turned on some regular lights, although it was still pretty dim, and "Pictures of You" by The Cure began playing on a stereo.

"Shall I get you a drink?" Mikael asked.

"Why not?" Kat shrugged. "We might get tossed out, but until then, I'm having a good time. How about you?"

"I'd have come over to the City just for this, to tell you the truth," Mikael's eyes were goofily large, as if he were saying, *This is crazy great.*

Kat agreed and could only smile. At the same time, though, she was disappointed. She knew what Larch looked like, and she did not see him. Perhaps he was holed up in a bedroom, but she doubted it. There was simply too much noise and distraction in this place for anyone to work in Vision.

"You must be Blackfriars," said a man about Kat's own height and about twice her weight. He was wearing a pinstriped shirt, his cuffs flopping about madly as he moved his hands. He was also wearing suspenders, round glasses, and vintage two-tone sports shoes. Kat smiled at him. It was a great look. "Yes, that's us."

"I'm a real fan," he said, shaking her hand. "Saw the whole Republican convention thing. I've even met Father Dylan on several occasions."

Kat blinked. *This guy is geeking out on meeting me,* she thought, *just because I'm a Blackfriar.* "I'll tell him you said hi. What was your name?"

"Lenny. Valiente."

"I'm Kat Webber."

"Oh my God, your brother is Randy!"

Ouch. Kat winced. She didn't want to think about Randy right now. She didn't want to think about his stupidity, his rudeness, or the fact that he was slowly fading into oblivion. "Yes, that's my brother," she managed.

"How is he?"

"Transparent."

He cocked his head, not sure how to interpret that. "Is this your first time here?"

"Yes," she held her hand out and received the plastic cup Mikael offered to her as he approached. "Lenny, this is my boyfriend Mikael."

"Another Blackfriar. You honor us!"

"How nice!" Mikael said.

"How do you like the show?"

"It's...full of surprises," Kat said. "Do you have a dog in this...pony show?"

"Oh, yes. My boyfriend has him over there." He pointed across the catwalk to a man a little younger than he, but no taller or thinner. In his lap he held a Chinese Crested with a fake, droopy mustache. "And that's our baby, Arthur Edward Waite."

"A remarkable likeness," Mikael said. Kat looked at him to see if he were kidding, but he appeared to be in earnest.

She wouldn't know Arthur Edward Waite from Albert Einstein—whom it also kind of looked like—but it was a very cute dog. "Remarkable," she said simply. "You know, I was hoping to see Larch here."

"Oh he never shows his face since he took that place on Caselli."

Kat shot Mikael a triumphant smile but hardly missed a beat. "That explains why we haven't seen him at the Cloven Hoof."

"Oh, he shows up there now and then. But he's become such a recluse. I think his pride got wounded."

"That'll happen when you're an overreaching asshole," Mikael said.

Lenny snorted. "You got that right!" He looked around quickly, probably to make sure no Hawk and Serpent members heard.

"What did we miss?" Mikael asked.

"Oh, well see that Papillon over there?" he said, pointing to a black and white dog with long pointed ears, wearing a thin tie and goggles. "That's Jack Parsons. He got a four. And back over there—," he said, waving his hand at the far corner. "See the Norfolk Terrier with the thick round glasses? That's Colin Wilson. He only got a three, unfortunately." He leaned in and whispered, "Not a very good likeness, in my opinion."

"I wouldn't have guessed Colin Wilson, but it's a fetching look," Mikael commented.

"I wish you were here last month. There was a tie between Paracelsus—a Pomeranian in a red Swiss beret—and Gerald Gardener."

"Really? Do tell." Mikael's face was glowing with pleasure.

"Gardner was a Bichon Frisé owned by my friend Dana. She'd shaved him so that his little white goatee was *perfect*. He has kennel cough this week, though. But he's worth coming back for."

Just then Purderabo slid up to them, his face full of menace. Turpelo was close behind. "Lenny," Purderabo said.

"Carl," Lenny smiled. "Great job tonight."

"Would you give me a few minutes alone with the Blackfriars?"

"Oh. Sure thing!" He nodded at Kat and Mikael. "I'll catch you two later."

Kat waved at him as he crossed to the kitchen.

"Hey, asshole," Mikael said, beaming a wide smile.

"Did you follow us?" Purderabo asked, narrowing his eyes.

Mikael leaned in, apparently just to get in Purderabo's face. "What makes you think that?"

"I smell pussy breath," Purderabo's nostrils twitched. "Why do I smell pussy breath?"

Mikael straightened up, eyes wide. He looked at the ceiling. "I... have no idea...why that would be."

Purderabo looked at Kat, then back at Mikael. Then back at Kat. "I think you're following us."

Kat punched him playfully in the arm. "C'mon Carl, Lenny invited us."

"You know Lenny? Where do you know Lenny from?"

"From the Cloven Hoof, of course," Kat said. "Dart league, Tuesday nights."

Purderabo looked uncertain.

"We belong here as much as you do," Mikael said. "We have lots of friends in the occult community, as you well know. Richard and Larch are friends, after all."

Purderabo scowled and looked down. "They have been known to play chess now and then." He looked at Turpelo, then back at Mikael. "I still don't trust you."

"Fortunately, you don't need to. The only thing you need to do is get this party going again," Mikael said, raising his glass. "I just met a fox terrier who's a dead ringer for the Great Beast himself as a young man in that cute, silk cravat of his. Let's get moving! I want to see him strut his stuff!"

60

SUSAN AWOKE to the sound of whispers and rustling. Slowly, awareness of where she was dawned on her. She was on the daybed in Dylan's room at the hospital. Chicken was snuggled up to her belly, snoring softly. Susan opened one eye. Several nurses were reattaching lines and IV bags. "What's happening?" Susan asked.

"Nothing to worry about," the nurse said. It was Nurse Melissa, a young African-American woman with whom Susan had commiserated earlier about dieting. Susan liked her. "We're taking him downstairs for some tests."

"Now? It's...what time is it?"

"It's almost midnight. Honey, our labs are running twenty-four seven right now. We'll have him back in a couple of hours. You and Chicken just sleep. We'll wake you if anything happens."

"Promise?" Susan asked, but she didn't wait to hear the answer. She was already drifting off again.

61

RICHARD LEANED against the cinderblock wall of the police station. It was late, and all of the children and most of the adults were asleep. Tobias was snoring and twitching at his side. Marco was propped up next to him, braiding something out of twine.

"What the fuck are you doing?" Richard asked.

"Macramé. It's a hanger, for a planter."

"Oh, yeah, I can see that. That would have been lovely in 1972."

"I'm just trying to relax, man. You ought to try it sometime."

Richard didn't disagree. He'd known Marco a long time, and the magickian had him pegged.

"Kind of puts things into perspective, doesn't it?" Marco asked.

"What does?"

"The fact that we could die tomorrow."

Richard didn't answer.

Marco continued. "I mean, shit man, it makes me wonder what the hell I've been doing with my life. If it was over tomorrow, would it have been worth the effort, you know?"

Richard looked at his fingers and noticed the dirt under his nails for the first time.

"Are you okay?"

"Yeah, yeah. Just...thinking."

"What about?"

Richard didn't answer directly. "For me it isn't about whether it would have been worth the effort. It's more...did I do it right?"

"Do what right?"

"You know. My life. Was I...faithful?"

"Faithful? Where'd you dig that word up from? Your grandma's trunk in the attic?"

Richard smiled. "Still...it's the only thing that haunts me. If I go down tomorrow, the only thought in my brain is going to be 'Was I faithful?'"

"Faithful to what?"

"To God, of course. Did I do what I was supposed to do with my life? Did I make good use of the gifts I was given?"

"Sounds like you're worried Daddy won't be proud of you."

Richard chuckled. "That's one way of putting it, yeah."

"He's not worried about that," Marco pointed at Tobias. The dog's lips pulled back in a grimace while his legs twitched.

"Not at the moment, no," Richard agreed. "But I wonder about the angel. I have this suspicion he's kind of hiding out. And you gotta wonder what he's hiding from, if not God."

"I'm more interested in what Toby is dreaming about. I have this invention, back in the van. You hook it up to someone, you go into vision, and you can see what they're dreaming. I gotta try it out on Toby."

"My guess is you'll see a lot of chasing rabbits, ripping their throats out, and mounds of white fluff pouring out of them."

"White fluff?"

"I don't think he's ever killed a real rabbit. He probably thinks they're just animate stuffed animals."

Marco smiled.

"What about you?" Richard asked.

"What about me?"

"You said it puts things in perspective for you."

"Yeah." Marco tied a knot and unspooled another length of

twine. He cut it with a pair of scissors and started braiding again. "It makes me realize...I don't know, man. I guess I just didn't realize how alone I've been feeling. And today, it just...it hit me like a wrecking ball."

"You do live a peripatetic lifestyle," Richard pursed his lips.

"And I've enjoyed it. But lately I'm thinking maybe it's time to settle down."

"What brought this on?"

"Truth? It's been brewing a long time before I got to the friary," Marco admitted. "Then it really started to ache, like right here in my gut," he pointed to his protruding tummy, "hanging out with you guys. Cooking for you all, after Brian left? That was *so* satisfying. And I did not see that coming. I love the family you all are. I love being a part of it. I guess I...I want that for myself, you know?"

Richard caught his eye and held it. "I do. It's a wonderful thing. To belong to people, to have them belong to you."

Marco sniffed. Richard couldn't remember the last time he'd seen Marco get emotional like this. "Yeah, man. I don't know anything about you being faithful, motherfucker. But you're sure as shit a lucky man."

Richard didn't know what to say. It was true. And he hadn't known it was true until Marco said it. "I am," he said finally. "I spend all this time being miserable, and that's such bullshit, because I really am very, very lucky."

"That's what I'm saying," Marco said. He put two strands of twine in his mouth to hold them as he measured out one length, then another.

"You don't have to start from scratch, you know," Richard said. "We love you. You could join us."

"And I love you guys, but...no. It wouldn't work."

"Why not?"

"Because I don't live inside the same story as you do. That whole huge Christian drama you've got going on, you all inhabit it. It... defines your world. But that's not my story. I love to visit you, but I always feel like I've wandered into someone else's book while I'm there, like I'm living someone else's life. It's great, but I can't live there."

"I understand," Richard said. "But you can borrow us any time you want."

"That's a deal," Marco said, tying a knot. "I just need to start my own family...or find them somehow. If I live long enough, that is."

"That's a good reason to stay alive," Richard said.

Marco threw the mass of macramé on the floor. "Shit, man. 1972. You ruined the whole thing when you said that."

"I'm sorry. There's something to be said for nostalgia, though."

"Do you think you'll ever be nostalgic about this?" He waved his hand around the room of sleeping people.

"I'll tell you what I'm nostalgic for. Brian frying bacon, Dylan lighting up a joint, Terry prancing by in a tiara...Susan putting me in my place." He laughed.

"You'll get it back," Marco promised.

"I can't believe I ever wanted more than that."

"You'll get it back."

"I love them so much." It was Richard's turn to get emotional.

"I know you do. You know what I find helps at a time like this?"

"Don't you dare say macramé."

THURSDAY

Radiant is the World Soul
Full of splendor and beauty,
Full of life,
Of souls hidden,
Of treasures of the holy spirit,
Of fountains of strength,
Of greatness and beauty.
Proudly I ascend
Toward the heights of the world soul
That gives life to the universe.
—*Rabbi Abraham Isaac Kook*

62

It was the busy chatter of people in the hall and the clang of metal trays that woke Susan again. She was cold. The blanket she had pulled over herself and Chicken was on the floor, and Chicken was nowhere to be seen. Susan sat up, rubbed at her eyes and yawned. Then she noticed that Dylan was gone, too.

"Those must have been a lot of tests," she said to her herself out loud. In her mind, she made a to-do list: pee, find Chicken, find Dylan. She wove a bit as she made her way down the hall toward the restroom. She half expected to meet Chicken coming out of one, but she didn't. First things first, she thought, locking the door behind her and loosening her jeans. Sheer relief poured through her, and relieved of her distress, her rational capacity returned.

She washed her hands and ran her fingers through her hair, unclumping the blond locks where they had bunched together during the night. She pronounced her hair, "Sad," shrugged, and unlocked the door. She went first to the nursing station. Melissa was off duty, but an older Filipino woman was there. Her name tag said, "Felicity."

"Hi, I'm Mrs. Melanchthon. My husband is in Room A113. Or...he was. He's supposed to be." *One thing at a time*, she told herself. "Have you seen a little girl? About four years old, Hispanic, goes by Chicken."

"You named your daughter Chicken?" The woman looked vaguely horrified.

"No. She's not my daughter. I'm just...taking care of her. Chicken is what she *wants* to be called."

The woman gave Susan an uncertain look.

"Look, just...have you seen her?"

"No. I have not."

"Oh, God. Okay, can you tell me what has happened to my husband?"

"Dylan Mela...Melan..."

"Melanchthon."

"What kind of name is that?"

"It's German."

"Are you German?"

"No, I'm Swedish. Mostly."

"Hmm..." Nurse Felicity clacked at her keyboard and followed a line on the screen. "Your husband was taken for tests."

"Yes, last night at about midnight. Where is he now?"

"He should be back. The tests are finished."

"He's not back."

"Not back?"

Susan lowered her gaze at the woman. "My husband is not in his room. Did you misplace my husband?"

The woman softened a bit. "I see the problem. Let me ask around. I'll come find you."

"Okay," Susan agreed. She went back to Dylan's empty room. The blanket still lay on the floor, empty, discarded, out of place. Susan stared at it, and a loneliness filled her that she did not understand. She picked the blanket up and wrapped it around her shoulders, hugging herself and trying not to shiver.

63

RICHARD WOKE to the sound of smashing glass. He had been spooning with Toby on the carpet in the squad room that had been converted into a makeshift dormitory, but at the sound he jerked upright and froze, listening intently. Tobias yawned and stretched. "Shhh..." Richard said, ears alert. He heard another crash and sprang to his feet, finding others already awake and congregating in the main hallway of the police station.

"Status," Herrer barked into a walkie-talkie, speed walking down the hallway toward the sound. There was a burst of white noise, then a high male voice responded. "Doors are holding, Captain, but I don't know for how long."

"What's happening?" Richard asked. Marco stumbled into the hallway.

"There's a gang vandalizing the station. Everyone stay in the hall! Keep clear of all windows!"

"Vandals—that means we're at the intersection of a wrath demon and an envy demon," Richard said.

"But according to your theory, these crimes are territorial," Herrer paused and narrowed her eyes at him.

"Yes, but the territory can change if the sigil is moved."

"So we've got two mobile...spheres of evil influence that just happen to overlap at the police station?" Herrer asked.

"Sounds implausible, but it's the best explanation I can muster," Richard said.

"We've got to get rid of those things," Herrer said. She put her hands on her hips and stared at the floor, apparently thinking.

"We've got to be able to get outside safely first," Richard said. "Marco, can you make and activate enough talismans for two teams?"

"Sure. How many people on a team?" Marco asked.

Richard looked at Herrer. "How many?"

"I'm sending four men with you, tops," she said.

"That'll be enough. So...make four, please, Marco."

"Now?"

"We want to hit the street as soon as that crowd moves on," Richard said.

Herrer's attention had been taken by a uniformed officer, so Richard took Marco aside. Before he could say anything, though, Marco asked, "Whose teams are we on?"

"I figure I'll lead one team, you lead the other," Richard said.

"That might not exactly be the power structure the Chief is envisioning. But anyway, how are we going to find the sigils?"

"Between us we have two unstoppable sigil-locating machines."

"We do?"

"You have the Liahona, and I have Toby's nose. Remember how he sniffed out that last sigil we found?"

Marco's eyebrows raised and he tried not to smile. "Those are very different methods."

"Both good, though."

"You know how to say, 'Sniff out the sigil' in Enochian?"

"That's where I was hoping you could help me."

"There's no word in the lexicon for 'smell,' I can tell you that. There's no word for 'find,' either."

"There has to be," Richard scowled.

"Sure, there has to be, but it wasn't revealed to John Dee or Edward Kelly. All we have is what they recorded."

"All right, what *do* we have?"

"Will 'bring down' work?"

Richard scowled. "*Maybe.*"

"Okay, that's 'drix.' Say this with me: 'Drix babalon gah.'"

"What's it mean—I mean, literally?"

"It means 'bring down the wicked spirit.'"

"We can't say 'The symbol of the wicked spirit'?"

"Oh, I guess we could say that," Marco said, his eyebrows raising. "Try, 'Drix aziazor babalon gah.'"

"Drix aziazor babalon gah," Richard practiced.

Marco shrugged. "It's worth a try."

"Let's see which direction the Liahona wants our teams to head out in," Richard said.

"Okay, I'll grab it."

Richard turned to Tobias. "I wish I had some breakfast, boy." The dog's tail thumped twice on the floor.

A moment later, Marco emerged from the room they had slept in, Liahona box in hand. Tobias trotted after them as they headed toward the glass doors at the front of the building.

"I wouldn't go any closer if I were you," the door guard said. He had his hand on his service revolver and looked like he was about to jump out of his skin. Richard looked at the doors and saw why. Near the doors was a small pile of bodies—just beyond them a crowd raged, shouting and jeering and daring the police sniper on the roof to take another shot.

"I'm guessing the dead folks there got a little too close to the doors for the comfort of the officer on the roof?" Richard asked the guard.

The young man nodded.

"Okay, let's ask right here then," Richard said to Marco.

As Marco pulled the Liahona out of its case, Richard jumped at the sound of another crash. Looking toward the doors again, Richard saw the source of the sound. Someone had lit a homeless person's shopping cart on fire and had given it a running start. It had crashed against the doors, and then bounced back a couple of feet—the flames leaping nearly as high as the roof.

Just then a rock burst through the glass doors, sending glass spraying over the linoleum. "Dammit! Toby, stay back!" It wasn't any good. There was no place the dog could step without getting glass in his feet.

Richard could hear the mob outside now, and he could see that it was making the guard more nervous than ever. The young man drew his pistol and trained it out the jagged hole in the plate glass of the door. Richard squatted down and scooped Tobias into his arms, groaning as he stood upright. "Good God, dog, you are fat." Tobias squirmed then panted in his ear.

"Okay, we're sending out two teams to destroy sigils," Marco said, for the Liahona's benefit, it seemed. "Which direction should the first one go in?" Richard and Marco watched as both needles pointed due north.

"That's clear," Richard said. "And the other team?"

"Which direction should the other team go in?" Marco asked. Once again, both needles pointed due north.

"Huh," Richard said.

"Hey, demon-guys," Herrer called from down the hall.

Richard and Marco looked at each other. Marco shrugged. "I don't know about you, but I've been called worse."

Richard panted as he lugged Tobias down the hall. As soon as they got to a patch of linoleum not scattered with broken glass, he set the big yellow dog down with a groan. "When we get through this thing, Toby—diet."

Marco patted Richard's tummy. "You can do it together."

"Jerk."

"Dough-boy."

"Look who's talking."

Herrer stood in the hall with her hands on her hips. "Are you two finished?"

"Uh...yeah," Richard said.

"Good, follow me." She led them into the operations room and pointed to a large map of Berkeley. Before she could open her mouth to speak, the power failed. Groans filled the air for a few seconds, and Richard saw one officer bury his head in his hands.

"Mendel, generator, now!" Herrer shouted.

It was early morning yet, but there was still enough dawn coming through the windows to see by. Marco and Richard stepped closer to the map to see it better. Tobias sat and began licking his balls.

"Here's what I'm thinking," Herrer said. "We got riot gear for six at hand. You'll make two teams of three each. I want you to stay within half a click of each other, if possible. If you're going to get any backup at all, it'll be from each other."

"That's why the Liahona told us to go in the same direction," Marco said.

"The Lia-what?" Hearer's brows knitted together.

"This," Marco held up the Liahona. "It's got a complicated history, but—"

The officer with his head in his hands bolted upright and pointed. "Did you say Liahona?"

Marco smiled. "I did. It's right here. You must be Mormon."

The man nodded and approached them with wonder lighting up his face.

"Ellison, you know about this thing?"

"Yeah. It's legit. I mean, I don't know if this is the one, but it's a real thing."

"What does it do?" Herrer stared at it.

"It does a lot of things, and its complicated," Richard said. "But today, it's going to lead one of our teams to the sigils."

"And the other team?" Herrer asked.

Richard pointed to Tobias.

Herrer looked skeptical. Tobias had one leg stretched out and was biting at one particular stretch of skin, apparently scratching an itch.

"Does he have fleas?"

"He might. I'd think that's the least of our problems at the moment."

"He could have *demon* fleas," Marco said, his voice filled with mock menace.

"Thank you, Vincent Price," Richard punched him in the arm.

"I suggest you head toward the Albany Tunnel—"

"Due north," Marco punched him back.

"—and then head east toward the Marina. Then head west on University, skirt the campus toward Telegraph, then College, until you hit the Claremont, then—"

"That's more than we'll get to in one day," Richard stopped her. "I see what you're doing, cross-hatching the city systematically. It's a good plan. The only problem will be the roving sigils, but there's nothing we can do about them except pick them off as we encounter them."

"I'm going to send everyone out with backpacks," Herrer said. "Including you."

"What's in the backpacks?" Marco asked.

"Mostly ammunition," Herrer said. "We're emptying the armory for this. I hope you realize I'm putting all of our eggs in this basket."

"It's the right basket," Richard said.

"It fucking better be," Herrer brushed a stray lock of hair out of her eyes. "One more thing. Can you shoot?"

64

BRIAN AWOKE to the tickling of feet. He squirmed and jerked his foot away. When he opened his eyes, Kat was smiling at him. "Hey there, sleepy-headed stranger."

Brian raised his eyebrows and turned over on the couch to face the room. He heard clattering in the kitchen and smelled the glorious aroma of coffee. He would have liked to have smelled bacon, too, but reminded himself not to mention that in this house.

Mikael joined Kat and gave Brian's hair a muss. "Mornin', old man."

"Watch who yer callin' old, sonny."

Elsa came out of the bedroom and stopped short. "Uh...full house, I guess."

"Elsa, these are my friends Kat and Mikael. They're Blackfriars—refugees from the East Bay."

Elsa offered her hand. "Well, we can't say no to any refugees."

"They came in after midnight," Brian said. "I gave them my room."

"I wish I could stay and chat," Elsa said, heading to the kitchen. "But I'm going to be late for my first client."

Brian heard her talking to Chava. A moment later, he heard their voices rise in a testy exchange that he couldn't quite make out. Then he heard shushing. Brian and Kat and Mikael shared an awkward moment until Mikael said in a low voice. "I left the talisman in the bedroom."

"The Talisman of Amitiel?" Brian asked.

"Yes. I wrapped it in a pillowcase and put it under the pillow. You might want to check it later."

"What's going on with it?"

"It was too cold to touch. It almost burned me in my sleep, it was so cold."

"Even the leather thong was frosty," Kat noted.

"The talisman only gets cold when people are lying," Brian remembered.

"Right. But neither of us was talking," Mikael said. "We were sleeping."

"What do you think that means?" Brian asked, still whispering.

"I think it means that deceit is so pervasive it's *ambient*."

"Either that or there's a level of wrongness in the world so great that it's just reacting perpetually," Brian reasoned.

Mikael shrugged. "Either way, I can't wear it right now."

Brian nodded, thinking. Elsa breezed out of the kitchen and through the front door with a wave, coffee and coat in hand.

"That was Elsa," Brian said. "Chava's partner." He lowered his voice even more. "They've been fighting a lot."

"Who hasn't?" Kat gave Mikael an apologetic look.

Chava emerged from the kitchen with a tray bearing four steaming mugs along with milk and sugar containers. She set it on the coffee table and took a seat next to Brian. "I'm sure I smell like muskrat," Brian said, leaning away from her.

She waved at him dismissively. "Can you stay for coffee?" she asked Mikael and Kat.

"We were just going to head out," Mikael said. "Sorry."

"Don't worry about it. I'll just pour them back into the Mr. Coffee. So no breakfast, either?"

"We're going to head over to the Hoof for brunch," Kat said.

"There's a strategy meeting for the Bay Area Wiccan Alliance. Forty Wiccan leaders are being detained right now, and the natives are getting restless."

"Rightfully so," Chava exclaimed. "I practiced Wicca for a while, in my misspent youth."

"What pantheon did you work with?" Kat cocked her head, revealing a curious smile.

"Oh, I didn't wander too far from my roots. I mostly invoked HaShem and Ashera."

"A middle-eastern classic," Mikael nodded. "But Kat misspoke— *she's* going to the Hoof. I'm off to the Castro."

Kat shot him a betrayed look, her lips growing thin and rigid.

"What's going on in the Castro?" Brian asked. "I mean, besides the early morning leather bars?"

"We got a lead on Larch last night. I'm going to run it down."

"I didn't misspeak," Kat said.

"What?" Mikael asked.

"I didn't misspeak. I just didn't see the point in getting into that kind of granular detail."

"I wouldn't call that 'granular,'" Mikael said. "You're doing one thing, I'm doing another."

Kat looked away from him. An awkward silence fell over the room.

"Well," Brian said, a little feebly, "be careful. This is Larch we're talking about."

"You too," Mikael said.

Brian nodded gravely. "Chava will be here to spot me."

"It's not what happens in the apartment that I'm worried about," Mikael said.

"Well, onward," Kat said, getting up and heading for the door. She opened it and went through without a glance behind her or a good-bye. Mikael followed, waved, then closed the door behind him. Moments later, a muffled argument broke out in the hall, diminishing in volume as Mikael and Kat descended the stairs.

"That was awkward," Chava said, still looking at the door. "Are they always...you know..."

"No," Brian said. "Never. Ever. I've never seen them fight."

"Then it's the Yesod effect?"

"Same as you and Elsa. But...I think it's actually worse than that," Brian said.

"What do you mean?" Chava asked.

"I've never heard Kat lie before," Brian said.

"I thought she was just keeping it simple."

"Yeah, but that's not really like her, either. I've never even heard her twist the truth—not even a little bit. And she's not defensive, either. Nothing about that exchange seemed like her."

"So...?"

Understanding lit up in Brian's eyes. He nodded slowly. "I think Larch has moved on to Hod."

Chava's mouth dropped open. With swift movements she crossed to the large edition of the *Sephir Yetsirah*. Hod is the sephirah of language—"

"Of representation," Brian corrected. "I mean, language, yes, but more than that—how reality gets abridged and distorted in our communication about it."

"So that makes sense. Kat didn't out-and-out lie..."

"No, but she distorted reality to make it more *manageable*."

"But her judgement was off."

"It was a completely unnecessary distortion. So if that ability to sort out how much to share or not share starts falling apart..."

"Brian, if this becomes widespread, we could be looking at a complete communication breakdown at every level of society."

"That's putting it nicely. I'd say, welcome to a world of completely out-of-control spin."

Chava drew back and clutched at her breast. "You'd tell me if I was blowing this out of proportion, right?"

"God, listen to yourself!" Brian laughed. "If we're not really careful, we won't be able to even talk to each other without second guessing ourselves."

"Maybe second-guessing ourselves is the best thing we can do right now," Chava said.

Brian's smile faded. He looked down at his coffee. "Maybe you're right."

"You've got to get up there," Chava said.

"I didn't think he'd move this quickly," Brian said.

"If he's dismantling a sephirah a day, the end of the world is coming a lot more quickly than we thought," Chava said.

"Maybe I can just zip through Yesod and catch up with him," Brian wondered aloud.

"Do you really think you can move through Yesod without doing anything to...I don't know...fix things?"

"I don't know. I guess I won't know until I get there. Up until now, this has all been pretty theoretical."

"Well, it's about to get real. You just tell me what you need," Chava said, heading toward the kitchen. "Because it's time to get cracking. Whatever is happening in Hod isn't just happening to Mikael and Kat —it's happening on the Stock Market and at the Kremlin and in Washington, too. At the rate we're going, we're about two international diplomatic incidents from World War III."

65

THE CLOVEN HOOF was so packed Kat had to enter it sideways. She slunk her way around the periphery of the bar, trying to get close enough to the stage to see who was speaking. It seemed like every Wiccan in San Francisco had turned out. *Everyone who isn't in jail, that is,* she reminded herself.

She found a nook, just where the bus tub usually sat. It wasn't on its holder, so Kat folded the holder and leaned it against the wall. Turning back toward the stage, she found she still couldn't see anything but only because she was short. She cast about and found a bus tub leaning against the bar. Snagging it, she turned it upside down and stood on it, congratulating herself on her ingenuity.

There was a lot of noise, and the air buzzed with angry voices like a hive of giant bees. Kat tried to get a sense of who was speaking or what was going on, but it appeared to be only chaos. There was nothing she could do, so she just floated with it, allowing herself to feel the successive waves of fear and rage that rocked the cafe. Her mind turned to Mikael, and she felt a new jolt of rage rise up in her. They had tried to talk it through, but they both had realized that whatever was happening in the sephirot made it almost impossible for them to talk about anything with any kind of emotional charge.

He had accused her of "bending the truth." She ground her teeth at the memory of it. *I wasn't bending the truth, you asshole,* she thought. *I was just keeping it simple.*

A shrill, deafening whistle lowered the din to the level of mere murmurs. Gasps went up all around as Kitty Moon took up a microphone and flipped back her kinky hair. Kitty had made a name for herself in the Wicca community in the 1990s, and she continued to reign as one of the religion's primary thealogians and spokespersons. Kat had profound respect for her. She remembered back to a time when she had met her at a party. She knew Kitty would be there, and so had rehearsed a speech in her head, but when they actually met, Kat had dissolved into tears. Kitty had clicked her tongue disapprovingly and moved on to the next supplicant, who had been blessedly more articulate. Kat felt shame at the memory rise up within her. But then she remembered that she'd had a cold the previous week. *That's what happened,* Kat told herself. *I wasn't feeling good. It wasn't that I was just lame. I was...ill.* But as she tried to convince herself, she felt a souring in her stomach.

Kitty started singing. At first, Kat couldn't hear her, but soon the chant had its desired effect. Others started singing, too. The noise level didn't go down, but the chaos resolved into melodic order. Kat knew the song—it was a familiar Mabon chant. She added her voice to the others and felt a rush of belonging and sympathy.

When the chant ended, Kitty held up her hand, and silence descended on the bar.

"We don't know what's happening to the East Bay." Her voice was confident and strong. "From all accounts, it's terrible. I'm willing to bet there isn't a single person in this room that doesn't know and love someone who lives there. Some of you probably live there yourself but were caught elsewhere when the...the chaos began."

There were murmurs of agreement. Every eye was on her. "Many people are saying that the chaos is the result of magick—bad magick. And from what I've seen, they could be right."

Many heads nodded, but there were a few scattered "boo's" at this. "No, listen," she raised one hand again. "We know that not all magick is pure. Not all magick is good. Not all magick is healing. Not everyone holds to our Rede." People were agreeing again. "But the police don't understand that. They don't know us. They don't know our religion. They hear 'magick' and they think of us because we are the biggest group—we're the most visible, the most vocal, the most numerous."

This elicited a cheer. Kat began to feel a bit nostalgic for the Old Religion. *I love you, Jesus,* she prayed silently. *But sometimes I feel homesick, too.*

"And they're still afraid of us!" she raised her voice. "Even though they live beside us, work with us, exercise with us, see the same movies as us—they still fear us, because old prejudices die hard!" There were some cheers at this. It didn't seem entirely appropriate, but Kat understood that they were cheers of agreement, not approval. "And now they're arresting us for something we did not do!" More cheers erupted from the crowd. "We are at the brink of history, sisters and brothers. A new Burning Time is upon us." At the mention of the Burning Times, the crowd fell hush. Kat heard only her own breathing.

In a far corner of Kat's brain, a voice said, *Really? Isn't that a bit much?* But she ignored the voice, caught up in the emotion of the crowd.

"This could start a domino effect. If they are locking us up here in California, what's to stop them from locking us up in the red states—just as a precaution, mind you? Can't let those witchy women get out of hand!"

The audience roared at this. Kat felt her heart rise into her throat.

"But we will not be locked up!"

"No!" shouted the crowd.

"We will not lie down and submit to persecution, not again! Not ever! Never again!"

"Never again!" the crowd echoed.

"And to show them that we are not the enemy, to show them that we are powerful, I call upon you to summon every person who practices the Craft that you know. Sunset is at 6 o'clock tonight. Meet me at the Bay Bridge—"

"But the Bay Bridge is barricaded!" someone yelled above the din.

"The Bay Bridge is barricaded to cars," Kitty countered. "But on foot we can step right over them. Tonight we march across the bridge, hand-in-hand, arm-in-arm. We will be ten thousand strong. We will show the world what our community looks like. We will show the world that we are numerous and strong! We will show the world what we stand for—and what we stand against!"

The crowd cheered wildly. The air in the bar was electric.

"Tonight, we will take back the East Bay from whatever assholes have cursed it! We will turn their curse into blessing. We will raise power and we will direct that power for healing—for the healing of the East Bay!"

The crowd began clapping now, rhythmically. A chant arose, "Take it back, take it back, take it back..."

A part of Kat felt elated and ready to go. But the dissenting corner of her brain spoke words that she mostly ignored, *Oh, that sounds like a baaaad idea.*

66

DYLAN'S EYE FLUTTERED OPEN. He jerked his head forward, intending to sit up, but discovered that he couldn't move. Casting his eye down, he realized that his hands were tied to the frame of a gurney. "Aw shit," he said. "This can't be good." He forced himself to relax and took careful note of his surroundings. He seemed to be in a warehouse of some kind. From the stenciled lettering on the slate-gray walls, he wondered if he might be in a military facility. He moved his head around so his eye could take in everything possible. He couldn't see any windows, and the place was lit only by a naked bulb screwed into a socket mounted high on one wall, surrounded by a wire cage. The place was damp and smelled powerfully of mold.

He could see two doors, but one was more of a sliding barrier. Dylan noted the metal track about eight feet from the floor. The door itself—or was it more of a gate?—was about twelve feet long. At one side of it he saw the arm of a handle pointed toward the ceiling. To his left he saw a regular sized door, with privacy glass set into its upper half. It seemed to be hung inexpertly, as it had swung open into the room.

Dylan looked down at his feet. They were bare, and only then did he realize how cold it was. The thin hospital gown was his only covering, and he noticed the blue diamond pattern on it for the first time. *It's kinda pretty,* he thought. *Why did I never notice that before?*

He didn't dwell on it. He heard a noise and moved his head toward it, but he couldn't see anything. "Mah nuts 'er gonna be shriveled up like prunes in this cold," he said out loud, mostly just to hear an actual sound. But he found the way his voice echoed to be strangely informative. It gave him a sense of how much more of the room there was behind him. "Hey!" he shouted, in a loud, staccato burst. He listened to the echo. He was about to do it again when he felt something on his arm.

He tried to jerk his arm away, but the rope held it fast. Breathing in gulps, he moved his head so that his eye could see what had touched him. Chicken waved at him and smiled. Then she put her finger to her lips and said, "Shhhh."

"Chicken, mah God, what are you doin' here? Ah mean, Ah don't know what *Ah'm* doing here. Hell, Ah don't know where *here* is. How did you get here?"

She took a step back and pointed under his gurney.

"Did you stow away on mah hospital bed?" Dylan whispered.

Chicken smiled and nodded her head with huge, exaggerated movements.

"Where are we, lil' one?"

She shrugged. "Uncle Terry is sad."

"Uh...Ah know Uncle Terry is sad, but Ah got some problems of mah own right now."

"I think his heart hurts."

"Oh boy. Ah don't guess ya know why we're here, or why Ah'm tied up?"

She shook her head.

"I gotta take a whizz," Dylan confessed.

Chicken giggled.

"Chicken, honey, can you do somethin' 'bout these ropes?" He motioned with his chin toward his hands.

Chicken grabbed the rope nearest her and started to pull at it. She hadn't gotten very far when the handle on the long metal gate rotated. A loud clank echoed through the chamber.

Chicken looked up in alarm

"Chicken," Dylan whispered, getting her attention, "there's another door behind you. You gotta be real, real quiet, honey. But you gotta *run*."

67

When Brian opened his eyes, he found himself on a busy city street. Water hit his head and he looked up—more water hit his face. It was raining, but he didn't have a raincoat. People brushed past him, their heads down. No one seemed to notice him. He pushed his hands into his pockets against the chill and shivered. Not far away was a restaurant and beside that a convenience store. He jogged toward it, grateful just to get out of the rain. Then he tripped and hit his head on the pavement.

"Great," Brian said out loud. He felt at his head, but it seemed he hadn't broken the skin. Although the sidewalk was crowded, no one helped him up. He pushed himself to his knees and then to his feet and noticed his shoelaces were untied. He squatted back down and tied them quickly, muttering to himself. Then he crossed the sidewalk to the convenience store.

The doors slid closed behind him and he looked around. The store was not from a chain he knew—nor was it like any chain he had ever seen. It was roomy and brightly lit, yet the effect was ruined by intrusive ductwork snaking down from the ceiling and running the length of the store. People ducked as they moved past it and seemed completely oblivious to the inconvenience. Glancing at the shelves,

Brian noted that the brands of packaged food were mostly unfamiliar. Some candy bars were the same, but other things had bright but completely alien packaging. It was like going to a store in another country. *And that's exactly what I'm doing,* he reminded himself. *This isn't just another country, it's another world.*

Brian wandered the aisles, squatting to avoid hitting his head on the ductwork, pretending to look at the food items, but really just trying to get his bearings. The air was strange, and he found it hard to breathe—it was thin, as if he were at a high altitude, and he found himself laboring to get enough oxygen. *Be calm,* he told himself. *Don't hyperventilate.* Everything seemed to have a slightly purple cast to it, as if he were wearing lilac gels set into a pair of eyeglasses. He had worn a pair of glasses like that once, in a head shop on Haight Street. They were round, like John Lennon's, and the packaging had promised that they would make everything look *groovy.* But the purple cast here just made everything look kind of spooky.

Brian passed his hand over his face and realized that it was as if he were looking through some kind of purple fog or smog. *There is a shadowy aspect to this world*, he thought to himself, and he wondered if those native to this sephirah experienced it the same way, or if it was only because he was an interloper. *After all, sherpas don't experience their air as thin, do they?* he wondered. But he didn't really know.

He kicked himself for not dressing more warmly but just then came across a rack of hoodies. They were purple, with the word *Yesod* written in dynamic script across the front, as if it were a sports team. He shrugged and took a large off the rack. *Don't look a gift horse,* he thought as he laid the sweater over his arm. He found a display of short, folding umbrellas and snatched one up. He couldn't decide if it was black or just really dark purple but realized that the haze could be playing tricks on his eyes.

He got in line and noticed his fellow shoppers for the first time. No one looked happy. No one was talking to one another. They all stood in line with a grim determination that made Brian think they were all just about to go into a quarterly evaluation meeting with their bosses and knew it was not going to go well. Other than that, they looked just like people from his own sephirah, Malkuth. They weren't monopods or sea monsters or energy beings—they were just people. But they were sad people. Lonely, too, it seemed to him.

In a few minutes, Brian had worked his way to the front of the line. A large section of the counter was taken up by a large metal box screwed into the particle board of the counter, a whirring fan recessed into its top. Brian was careful not to drop anything into it. The cashier did not speak to him but just pointed to the digital readout on her cash register. Brian pulled a twenty out and handed it to her. She scowled at it and then looked up at him for the first time. "You've got to be kidding me. Are you a magickian?" she asked, narrowing one eye.

"No, of course not!" The offense in his own voice surprised him.

She scowled at him, clearly suspicious. "Where's Minister Joseph?" she asked. When he didn't answer, she grabbed at his hand and ran her finger along his arm. "Hmmmmm," she said, and then she let it go.

"What was that about?" Brian snatched his hand back.

"You got another form of payment?" she asked.

Glancing into the cash register, Brian saw that all the money was purplish. Different bills were of different hues—periwinkle, lavender, and heather. He fished in his wallet for a debit card. She scrutinized it and handed it back to him, indicating the keypad. He inserted the card and typed in his PIN code. "Cash back?" she asked.

"Sure. Can you give me enough to get by for a day?"

Her eyebrows shot up and she gave him a bemused look. "You'll want about 40,000. Just enter it and hit the green button."

Brian did. His own purchase had come to about a quarter of that, and he realized he had been interpreting the digital readout as if there had been a decimal point. Looking closer, he realized there wasn't. "Thanks," he said. The girl did not look up at him again. He pocketed the cash and ducked under a large pipe, nearly hitting his head on a valve as he headed for the door. When he could straighten up he pulled the hoodie on and freed the umbrella from its packaging. He stepped outside before opening it up.

He felt a swell of pride—having navigated, in so short a time, proper clothes, money, and rain gear. But he also felt a twinge of danger. Why had she grabbed his hand like that? And why had she felt at his arm?

"Don't get a big head," said a voice beside him. "It's trickier than you think here."

He looked down and saw Mother Maggie waddling beside him underneath her own umbrella. She was wearing a clerical collar, as usual, and carrying a bag with a seal that looked similar to the Episcopal seal but wasn't. "Maggie!" he said, turning to her and opening his arms.

She did not embrace him but kept looking straight ahead. "Shh! Eyes front. Pretend we're not talking. Don't draw attention."

"But...I don't understand."

"You will. I'm going to step out ahead. You follow me, but don't speak to me until we get inside and we're alone. Understand?"

"Uh...yeah."

"Good. And don't trip."

"Huh?"

She pointed down. "Shoelaces." She was right. They had become untied again. He knelt and tied them, even tighter this time. Maggie waddled out in front of him, not bothering to even look in his direction.

They waited at a light then crossed a busy street. Looking to his left, Brian saw that they were at an enormous roundabout. In the center, perpetually being circled by an army of trucks and automobiles, was a statue of what looked like Atlas, holding up the world. The globe on his back reached a height of at least three stories. His shoulders were massive, and the corded muscles looked amazingly lifelike. Brian could almost see him trembling under the weight on his back. The figure was naked, his testicles swollen like pomegranates, his legs massive and thick like redwoods. His gaze saw for a hundred miles, and his jaw was set with grim determination.

"This is the soul of Yesod," Brian said out loud to himself, awed by the statue. "This is its avatar."

"Quiet," Maggie shushed him as they waited for another light. They had emerged into what looked like a greenbelt. City stretched on three sides, but ahead of them was a park with vast fields of grass stretching to the horizon. And on that horizon... Brian stopped and stared. "What the..."

"Pssst! Keep moving," Maggie called over her shoulder.

Brian sprang forward to close the distance between them somewhat, still careful to stay a couple yards behind her. But his eyes kept darting to the horizon. His mouth gaped as he took it in. An enormous, alabaster pillar rose from the ground straight into heaven. It wasn't a thin pillar, though, it was massive. Brian flashed on a woodcut of the Tower of Babel in an old Bible Richard had. That was close, but not quite right. As he stared at it, Brian realized what it was like. "It's a lingam," he said out loud.

68

MIKAEL KICKED himself internally as he walked. Why had he called Kat out on such an insignificant, stupid point? He didn't think of himself as a particularly anal kind of guy. He didn't normally strain at gnats.

The sun was just beginning to burn through the fog and, as it did, Mikael felt his mood lighten. It was hard to be truly despondent in San Francisco—the city had more life per square inch than Mikael had ever seen, anywhere, and he soon found himself smiling. The exercise helped, too, and by the time he reached the Castro, the last wisps of his argument with Kat had dissipated, along with the morning's fog.

He checked his phone and followed the directions app to Caselli Avenue. It was a short street, maybe four blocks long. The houses had no space between them, as was usual in San Francisco, but they were beautifully maintained. It occurred to Mikael that even the most modest of these sold for well over a million dollars. The thought of it staggered him, given his own income. He did a quick calculation and realized that there were nearly a hundred houses on this street. He blew air out of his cheeks. Larch could be in any one of these houses. "Where do I even start?" he wondered aloud.

Be systematic, he told himself. He walked to where Caselli dead ended into Douglass Street and walked up to the first house. He knocked on the door. A few moments later, he heard a rustling inside, and the door swung open. An older balding Asian man in a muscle T stood in the doorframe. "Yes?" he asked.

Mikael hadn't rehearsed what he would say, so he just blinked. His mind simply said, "Larch isn't here. Move on to the next house." But propriety prevented him from moving. "Uh, hi!" he said. "My name is Mikael and...I'm taking a survey. Do you own your own home?"

"Yes," the man narrowed his eyes at him, not liking this at all.

"How long have you been in residence here?"

"Twenty years," the man said.

"Have you noticed any strange occurrences in the neighborhood?"

The man cocked his head. "Like what?"

Mikael moved his head back and forth, "Oh, I don't know... anything supernatural? Strange voices, spiritual attacks, ectoplasmic manifestations, you know...the usual...stuff?"

"I think you should go now," the man said, closing the door.

"Going now," Mikael said, stepping off the curb. He walked to the next door. He *did* need a better story. But it wasn't a bad idea to ask neighbors for some clue as to where Larch was. It would be far better, in fact, to have the house pointed out to him by a neighbor than to have the door opened by one of the Hawk and Serpent boys. It preserved the possibility of surprise.

Mikael pulled something up on his phone. Then he knocked on the next door. No one answered. At the next house, a young woman answered who was clearly hung-over. "Hi," Mikael said. "I'm so sorry to bother you. I'm supposed to meet my friend on this street, but...I don't remember the house number."

"Hook up?" the woman asked, lighting a cigarette.

"Yeah," Mikael confessed. "I got the name, and the time, and the street...just not the house number."

"So, does your Mr. Wonderful have a name?"

"Stanis Larch. This is him. I took it last night in the bar." He showed her a photo that he'd pulled down from the Order's dropbox.

"He's a hottie...for an old guy. You into that? Old guys?"

Larch was about Richard's age—in his mid-forties—but Mikael could see how this young woman might think of him as old. "It's kind of a daddy thing," Mikael said sheepishly.

"No need to get all Freudian on me," she said, smiling. "Sorry, honey. Can't help you find your sugar-daddy today."

"Oh, well. Thanks for taking a look," Mikael said.

"You don't swing both ways, do you?" she asked.

"Uh...no, sorry," Mikael said.

"Your loss," she said, shutting the door.

69

RICHARD FELT incongruous with a rifle slung over his back. It wasn't as if he'd never shot a gun before. His father had been a cop, so he'd been to the firing range. They'd gone hunting. He knew how to aim, and he knew to expect the gun to punch him in the shoulder when it fired. He just didn't feel right carrying it while wearing a clerical collar. He thought of taking off the collar, but that seemed like an even greater betrayal.

Live in the ambivalence, Dicky, he told himself. *It's the richest place to be.*

Richard walked between two policemen, one in front of him and another behind him, as Tobias trotted along at his side. He realized he was being "sandwiched" for his own protection, and it pricked at his pride a bit. But he reminded himself that he and Toby were civilians here, and what they didn't know could easily get them killed. The fact that Toby knew infinitely more than either of these policemen provided sufficient irony for him to actually enjoy the situation.

They were walking north on Shattuck, past the Cheese Plank, past the Safeway, past the building on the weird triangle of land where the old Goddess Bookstore used to be. He could see Marco's group about a block and a half ahead of them, heading for the tunnel into Albany. They were about to cross Rose Street to connect with Henry when Tobias whined and darted to the left.

"What is it, boy?" Richard asked. He had given Toby the command, *Drix aziazor babalon gah*, and the dog had not looked confused. Richard tried to have faith and hope for the best. *Leaning on you now, Jesus,* he prayed silently.

Richard turned and followed the yellow lab. The police looked momentarily confused. "Wait, we're following the dog?" one of them asked. Richard tried to remember his name. He couldn't. He stole a glance at the cloth name tag on the officer's black uniform. *Evans.* Officer Evans was as tall as Richard with swarthy skin and short but curly black hair. He seemed nice enough.

"He's a lab, but he must have some bloodhound in him some-where," Richard joked. "He's pretty good at following a scent."

The other officer—Martinez—scowled. "Only dog I ever had was a Chihuahua. Damn dog wasn't good for anything except barking at nothing and pooping on my mom's bed."

"That's the kind of dog that would be good in a stew," Richard said.

"Woulda been a pretty stinky stew," Martinez countered. Martinez seemed to be impossibly short for a policeman, but Richard knew nothing about such regulations. The Hispanic officer's eyes came to about nipple-height to Richard, but he seemed light and fast and had a quick wit.

"So what's he smelling?" Martinez asked.

"Hard to say," Richard answered. "Maybe just the paper that the sigils are drawn on. More likely the blood that activated the sigils. But maybe he's just sniffing out the demonic activity itself."

"You talk like all this shit is real," Evans said.

Richard stopped and faced him. "You ever see anything like this before?" He waved his arm to include all of Berkeley.

"No."

"It's real." Richard continued, walking behind Tobias who had his nose in the air and was snuffling away eagerly.

"But how do you know it's...I can't even make myself say it, it's so ridiculous...but here goes: how do you know it's *demons*?"

"Because that's how we make our living."

"You and the black guy over there?" Evans pointed north toward where Marco was leading the other team.

"No, he's a magickian. I mean my order-mates."

"What do you mean he's a magickian? Like card tricks?"

Richard rolled his eyes. "Yep. Ask him to show you his levitating penis trick sometime."

"Really?" Evans asked.

Richard didn't answer. They were in the thick of affluent, residential North Berkeley, approaching Martin Luther King Jr. Way, when Richard heard a crack and a *zing* by his ear. "Gunfire, down!" he said, dropping to the pavement. Tobias didn't drop, though, and kept going, straight toward where Richard heard the rifle crack come from. "Toby! Wait." Tobias turned to look at Richard and stopped, panting. There was another shot, this one from a slightly different direction.

"Crawl," Evans commanded. He pointed at Richard. "You last."

Richard nodded and fell in behind Martinez as Evans took point. Tobias sprinted out ahead of Evans, seemingly oblivious to the danger. *Jesus, protect our dog—and your angel,* Richard breathed. The yellow dog ran up the steps of a squat, stuccoed arts-and-crafts house and straight through the door.

Evans looked back at Richard, and Richard gave him an exaggerated shrug. Evans seemed to be thinking. Then he started crawling again toward the house's stairs. By the time Richard reached the front door, it was open. He didn't know if Evans had opened it or if it had already been standing ajar, but at this point it didn't matter. Evans and Martinez had already crawled in. Tobias was nowhere to be seen.

Evans stood and so Richard did the same. Evans held his hand out in the universally-recognized "halt" sign. Richard nodded and froze in place. Turning to Martinez, Evans pointed to his own eyes, and then pointed deeper into the house. Martinez gave a quick nod and, rifle at the ready, sprang through the wide door separating the living room from the dining room. "All clear," he shouted, and Evans waved at Richard to follow.

From somewhere, Richard heard Tobias start to bark. *If he's barking, he's breathing,* he thought to himself. *So that's a good report.*

Richard watched Martinez edge toward the kitchen. Between the kitchen and the dining room he saw the kind of door on a spring that swung both ways. Martinez knelt and pushed the door open just a crack. He let it shut then glanced back at Evans, holding up two fingers. Evans nodded and crossed to the edge of the door. He pointed to Martinez, then at the bottom the door; he pointed at himself and then at the top of the door. Martinez gave a curt nod. Then Evans turned to Richard and lowered his hand, flattened toward the floor. Richard crouched and waited. Evans counted on his fingers with exaggerated motions—*one, two...*

On *three*, both officers burst into the kitchen, Evans high and Martinez low. "Berkeley PD! On the ground!" Evans shouted. Richard heard the clatter of what sounded like a handgun hitting the tile. "Both of them!" Evans added. Richard heard the thud of a rifle or a shotgun being set down, then the clatter of it falling to the floor.

Richard scooted through the door himself and saw a thirty-something-ish white couple sitting on the floor with their hands up. There was glass everywhere, and it looked like the man had cut his hand on some of it. Smears of blood punctuated the tile in a truly random pattern. The large, french windows looking out onto the back yard had been mostly shot out—and it looked like the shots had come from the outside, since the glass had fallen *in*, Richard noted.

"Who are you shooting at?" Evans asked, not dropping his weapon for a second.

"At them—" he pointed at the backyard. "The Olivos." The man didn't look scared, he looked determined and frustrated. Richard guessed that the man saw their presence as an annoying distraction from what he really wanted to be doing—shooting at the Olivos, presumably. Richard would have pegged the young man as a typical Silicon Valley hipster, or more likely a Pixar animator. He had straight brown hair that was lopped at an odd angle on one side, in a way that was not unfetching, Richard had to admit. But then there was the ridiculous soul patch. The woman with him, who Richard guessed was his wife or girlfriend, looked more frightened. She wore a blue-patterned print dress that rode just a little bit too high up her thighs for modesty given the way she was sitting on the floor. Her blue sweater had bits of broken glass caught in it that flashed like sequins in the morning sun.

"Where are the Olivos?" Evans asked. "In the back yard?"

"*No*," the young man said impatiently, as if his next word was going to be "stupid," but he thought better of it. "They live behind us. Their house faces MLK."

"Why are you and the Olivos exchanging gunfire?" Martinez asked, as if it were a completely reasonable question.

"Because..." the young man said. Richard though he was going to stop there, implying that the reason for the shooting was self-evident, but after a moment, his eyes moving back and forth rapidly, he continued. "They have this..." he motioned at the air in front of him as if he were pulling salt-water taffy, "...this brewing setup. It's *brilliant*."

"You're shooting at them because they make great beer?" Richard asked.

"No! Don't be an idiot," the man said. "Well, kind of. I mean, why should he have such a great beer-making set up? No one loves beer as much as I do. Do they, Rach?"

The woman nodded. "And...they stole our kids," she added.

"They...the Olivos have your children?" Martinez asked.

"Yes," the woman said. "That's what you get from immigrants. They can't have children in their own country, so they come here and steal ours."

Richard's brows knitted together, and he tried to sort out what he was hearing. "Where are the Olivos from?" he asked.

"Italy," the woman said.

"What do they do...for work, I mean?" Richard asked.

"Visiting professor at the UC," the man said. "Stupid Italians."

"And they have your children?" Evans asked.

"Yes." The man stood up as high as he could on his knees and yelled out one of the broken panes, "Have your own children, fuck-heads!" There was a rifle crack and his head jerked backwards as the bullet entered his brain. He fell over like a log, limbs splayed out over the tile.

70

CHICKEN HID behind the door and tried to listen, but she wasn't close enough to hear. She wrestled with what to do. Should she wait and see if the men would leave? She didn't want to leave Dylan. She faced a long corridor, with several doors on either side leading to mysterious places. And she didn't know where the hallway led to. Outside? *Todo teine un final, y estos pasillos tienen que salir en algún sitio,* she thought. *Everything has an end, and these halls have to go somewhere.*

She thought of Susan. Susan would know what to do. For a moment, the thought of Susan made her want to cry. She was so warm, so squishy, so like what her own *madre* had been like. Yes, she must go to Susan. Careful not to scuff her feet, or trip, or do anything else that might make a noise or give her away, she walked as briskly as possible down the long hallway.

Chicken felt the little hairs on her arms stand up. The coldness of the place, the emptiness, the institutional nature of it—it all gave her the willies. Yet she set her face and walked on. For a minute it looked like the hallway would dead end, but as she got closer, she saw that it just dog-legged to the left about six feet. She turned left, then right, and then discovered something beautiful—at the end of the hallway was what looked like daylight.

She stopped and looked back, but all she could see was the dogleg. She thought of Dylan, and what might be happening to him. A wise part of her said, *The best way to help Uncle Dylan is to get help.*

She started to run. The hallway was long, but there was a window set into the door. The light coming from it seemed impossibly bright. She was tempted to slam into the door at full speed, but at the last minute pulled back, worried about the noise. She pushed it open quietly, then burst into the open air.

The sunlight blinded her momentarily—but she didn't let that deter her. She ran but almost immediately hit an immovable object.

"Woah, that hurt! Watch where you're going, little one!" The man was tall—or he seemed tall to Chicken. He had sunglasses on, and he had a friend with him. They were standing by a Jeep in a parking lot. Both of them had rifles slung over their shoulders. *Should I tell them about Uncle Dylan?* She wondered. There was something about these men. Some internal radar warned her not to trust them.

"Have you seen my dog?" she asked.

"What?" the other man asked.

"Wants to know if we've seen her dog," the man said, a little louder. "Jesus, you got to get your hearing checked."

"It's the tinnitus," the second one said. "Sounds like a fucking freight train in my head twenty-four seven."

"Hey, language—little girl," the man said. He turned to Chicken. "What's your name, honey?"

"Julie."

"What's your dog look like?"

"He's gold-colored. Kinda fat. His name is Toby."

The man pulled a walkie-talkie about the size of a brick from his belt. "Boss, Nathan here. And Fuller."

"I'm in the middle of something, Nathan. Is it important?"

Chicken recognized the voice of the mayor. She cocked her head and listened.

"Found a little girl wandering around the navy base. Just burst out of building 2A."

There was a long silence on the other side. "What's her name?"

"Julie. Says she lost her dog."

More silence followed. Finally, the man said. "Eighty-six her. Do it fast, do it clean."

Both men's eyes widened. They looked at each other. The first man, Nathan, spoke into his walkie-talkie again. "Sir, come again?"

"You heard me. This is a code eighty-six. Now, if you'll excuse me, I have important matters of state to attend to." The radio squelched then was silent.

Chicken didn't know what "86" meant, but from the men's reactions, it couldn't be good. She looked around her. Time seemed to stand still. She could smell the water. She could hear the birds. She noticed the way her chest moved in and out as she breathed. She blinked up at the first man. "What does eighty-six mean?" she asked.

The men were still looking at each other, but now they looked at her.

71

TERRY ARRIVED within sight of the parking lot just in time to see a woman in kakis and a white sleeveless t-shirt deck a taller man holding a rifle. As if in slow motion, the man's face rippled and stretched and a stream of blood leaped into the air above him. He hit the ground like a bag of rocks. The woman wiped blood from her own mouth as she stood over him panting. "You say that one more time, motherfucker. Just give it a go."

Terry's view was obscured as a crowd surrounded the fallen man, cheering the woman on. But Terry heard the man's voice, cutting weakly through the crowd noise. "Marcia, honey, all I said was how good you look in a muscle shirt. But you *do* look good in it!"

"Motherfucker," Marcia said again, raising her fist.

Just then Casey whistled so loud that Terry's ear rang afterward. He inwardly cursed her, but it had the desired effect. The large crowd gathered around the fighting couple quieted down and turned to see who it was. They were assembled in a parking lot near the channel that separated Alameda from Oakland—mostly men, mostly young, many of them armed. The lull wouldn't last long, and Casey didn't hesitate. She put her hands on the hips of her stained blue coveralls.

"Hey, jerkoffs, listen up! You can fight later—we've got important news and an even more important mission. One that could mean the survival of everyone on this island." That got their attention. She adjusted her ball cap over her dirty blond hair and glared at them. One by one, they began to wander over to where Casey and Terry were standing. Marcia even helped her boyfriend up off the pavement. Not only did Casey have the attention of the mayor, but everyone else listened to her, too. Terry began to appreciate just how respected she was and did not wonder why no one wanted to cross her.

"I want to introduce Father Terry," Casey half yelled so everyone could hear. "We pulled Father Terry and his friends out of the tunnel last night just before they bit the big one. And it's a good thing we did, too, because they know what's happening out there, and they know how to stop it!"

"What *is* going on?" one of them called out.

"Demonic oppression," Terry said, stepping forward. His cassock was smudged and his cuff was ripped, but his confidence made him an impressive figure, despite his short stature.

"Did you say possession?" someone asked.

"No, *oppression*," Terry said. "Demons aren't inhabiting people— that would be possession. Instead, they're riding people like horses and making them do things they wouldn't ordinarily do. Think of it as a temporary insanity. Oppression."

Terry could tell from their furrowed brows that they were skeptical.

"I'm sorry, but that sounds like a lot of superstition," one of the young men said. He was better dressed than a lot of them, probably a lawyer or a real estate agent, Terry guessed.

"I understand your skepticism," Terry said, "but there isn't any doubt about it." He unfolded a sigil. "The demons are called by this. It's called a sigil. It opens a narrow place between the worlds where demons can slip through. Think of it as a party invitation."

"I'm waiting for the joke," said one man, a little older, with his arms crossed.

"I think the 'party invitation' line *was* a joke," the man next to him said.

"There's no joke," Terry said. "I'm looking for volunteers to do short missions over to the mainland—to Oakland—to find and destroy these." He waved the sigil.

"Because..."

"Because that will stop the demons. And that will stop the killing and the madness."

There was a low murmur as people shook their heads and discussed it with the people around them.

"I don't want all of you. I don't even want half of you. I don't want anyone who's scared. I don't want anyone who is skeptical. I just need a few volunteers. I need some men—and women—with enough vision to see what's happening to us and enough guts to do something about it."

One man walked up to Terry, his hands on his hips and a shotgun slung over his shoulder. The top of Terry's head was about halfway up his torso. Most people would have been intimidated, but Terry looked straight into his eyes. "You got what it takes?" he asked the tall man.

The man scowled, but then his scowl turned into a wide smile. "The little guy has balls!" he announced to the crowd behind him. Plenty of folks laughed. Then there was the sound of a distant crack, and the man crumpled to the ground. Terry ducked and sprang over to where the man had fallen. A morbid gash ran across his scalp, and blood began to gather in a puddle under his head. Terry felt for his pulse and breathed a sigh of relief. It was strong.

"The bullet just grazed his scalp—a kick to the head. But he's just knocked out, I think," he said to Casey as she crawled over to them.

"Who did that?" called one of the men.

Terry crouched as he ran and made for a gray wooden building near one of the docks. Peering around the corner, he saw a speedboat coming toward them, about to dock. A large sigil was spray-painted in red on the roof of the boat. Squinting, Terry could just make out a fluttering scrap that must be the activated sigil. Crouching again, he ran back to the parking lot. "Okay, that time we've been afraid of? It's here. We're being invaded. We got a mobile sigil and a boat full of frenzied folks with guns. As soon as they dock, they are going to let loose with everything they've got on our civilians here. And if they're successful, more will follow. If you want to save your island, you have to stop them."

Craning their necks, the crowd looked down to the dock, then back at Terry. Instantly, the parking lot erupted with shouts and questions. Terry disentangled the shotgun strap from the shoulder of the downed man and rummaged in his pockets for shells. Finding some, he shoved them through the slits in his cassock and then into the pockets of his jeans. Without standing up again, he yelled back to the parking lot. "Anyone here who wants to save your island, with me!" He ran for the dock.

He didn't look behind him, but he didn't need to. He felt their energy. He knew that at least some were coming. He gritted his teeth and ran full out as he saw the speedboat slide parallel with the dock and saw several of the Oaklanders leap out, waving weapons. Terry dropped to the ground at the edge of the road just before a steep hillside down to the water. He rolled over on his back to allow his arms some freedom while at the same time staying as small a target as possible. He unlatched the break-action double-barreled 20-gauge, checking to make sure there were fresh cartridges in the breach. There were. He snapped it shut again and rolled over, snuggling the stock firmly into his shoulder and taking aim.

In his peripheral vision, he saw others joining him along the same ridge, first to his left and then stretching out to the right. He didn't bother to count. He just hoped there were enough. "Stay low!" he shouted as they readied their weapons.

"Shouldn't we check with the mayor first?" someone asked.

"Before or after they murder, rape, pillage, and maim?" Terry asked.

"Surely not," one woman said. She was young, and sounded vaguely British. "These people are from Oakland, they—" With a sickening "thuck" sound, a bullet penetrated her brain and she fell over like a rag doll.

"Surely not," Terry repeated, sarcastically. "All right, listen up!" he called as the last of the Oaklanders exited the boat. All were running along the wooden dock platform straight toward them. "You don't need to show any mercy, because they won't. Shoot to kill, not to wound, because they're not going to let a flesh wound stop them—they're going to keep coming. As soon as I can, I'm going down there. Cover me if you can. Stay—"

But his words were cut off by the blast of a nearby rifle, a call answered by more. A chorus of gunfire erupted all around him. Terry got one of the Oaklanders in his sights, a lanky white kid with a machete in his hand, and squeezed the trigger. The stock kicked him in the shoulder as the shotgun fired and the kid went down, a red bloom erupting across his chest. Terry aimed again, this time at what looked like a Latino gang-banger, his bandana pulled down over his nose and mouth. He squeezed the trigger, but this time his shot went wide. "Shit!" he yelled and turned over again, unlatching the action and shaking out the spent shells. Smoke rose from the breach and Terry's nostrils twitched at the smell of sulphur. Careful not to burn his fingers on the gun metal, he shoved two fresh shells into the chambers and closed the breach again, turning to aim—but it was too late.

The berserkers were upon them, and Terry had nothing to fight with at close quarters. Few of them did. But most of the attackers were better prepared. They flashed knives, brandished tire irons, and rebar—Terry even caught sight of an ax and a meat cleaver. He shuddered, but there was no time to think. All around him people were standing up and swinging their rifles at the first few Oaklanders to reach the ridge. Instinctively, Terry stayed low, rolling to his left until he was no longer underfoot, then crouching as he ran to the relative safety of the gray wooden out-building.

Strangely, one of the Oaklanders had stayed with the boat. He hadn't expected that. He would have guessed that their bloodlust was high enough to compel all of them into the fray, but no. One skinny black kid, dressed in baggy pants and a hoodie, stood on the dock, rifle at the ready.

Terry snuck around the other side of the out-building and, concealed from everyone for the moment, removed his cassock and folded it. He laid it on the ground, along with his wallet, keys, and shoes. Then he slunk down to the water and soundlessly lowered himself from the edge of the dock. Carefully controlling his breathing and trying to stay calm, Terry edged his way beneath the docks, clinging to the mossy, slime-covered pylons. He drew his hand back too quickly, and blood started seeping into the water. *Barnacles*, he thought. *Damn it.* He refocused and continued to edge to the left until he approached the boat. He swam out to avoid the prop, even though it was still, but then swam toward the short ladder hanging off the port stern. Trying to splash as little as possible, he grasped the metal ladder with one hand. Then, placing the other slightly higher, he pushed off the stern of the boat with his feet and hauled himself up. Getting one foot on the ladder, he looked up, straight into the barrel of a rifle. The skinny kid drew his lips back into a satisfied smile.

72

MARCO STOPPED and checked the Liahona. It pointed in a slightly different direction than they'd been going. But since they couldn't travel as the crow flies in North Berkeley—with its houses stacked on top of one another like sardines—it hardly mattered. They set off again, still heading mostly north along the main road and heading toward the tunnel into Albany.

"How does that thing work?" one of his companions asked. He was gregarious, friendly, and just a little too chatty for Marco's comfort. He was African American, with a lot more swagger and street sensibility than Marco himself possessed. He wasn't a detective, like Cain. Marco assumed he was a beat cop. He strained to remember the man's name. Then it came to him: Madison, like the president.

"Hell if I know," Marco answered. He explained the two dials and briefly recounted Richard's theory about God's perfect and permissive wills. He stopped when Madison's eyes glazed over.

"Technical shit, in other words," Madison said. "Technical God shit."

"Something like that," Marco agreed. He looked up at the too-blue autumn sky. The clouds formed serene, floating palaces, completely unconnected and unconcerned with the chaos that surrounded them.

"So are you a priest?" the cop asked.

Cain laughed. "I'm sorry. I don't know why that's funny. Richard doesn't seem very priest-like either, and he is a priest...isn't he?" Cain looked taller and a little meaner in the dark blue coveralls that accompanied the riot gear.

"He's a bishop," Marco nodded. "But I know what you mean. I'm not even a Christian. I'm a Thelemite. A magickian."

"A what?" Madison asked.

"Thelemite. Have you heard of Aleister Crowley?"

"No," Madison said, making a face.

Cain snapped his fingers. "Isn't he that guy...'the wickedest man alive' guy?"

"That's the one," Marco grinned. "But it's mostly PR. He just wanted to shock everyone out of their Victorian sensibilities, so he sometimes posed as the anti-Christ. Kind of like Marilyn Manson. We consider him the prophet of a new age."

"This whole world is so new to me," Cain confessed. "Until that murder last week, I didn't know half of this existed." He shook his head as they walked. "So...what did this Crowley guy preach, anyway?"

"Hmm...he didn't actually preach much. He did take lot of drugs and have a lot of sex, though."

"Shit, man, you'd think a religion like that would've taken off!" Madison crowed.

"You'd have thought. But Thelma has always been small. And it's not his outrageous behavior that was important—it was what he wrote," Marco continued. "Our scripture says that 'every man and every woman is a star.'"

"So...all humans are bags of burning gas?" Madison teased.

"We interpret that a *little* more poetically," Marco answered, with just a hint of edge to his voice. "It means that each of us is divine, and answerable, ultimately, for our own fates." Down a side street, Marco saw someone pushing a shopping cart about two blocks away. Other-wise, the place seemed deserted.

"That sounds pretty woo-woo to me," Madison said.

"Hey, Madison, haven't you ever had faith in something?" Cain asked.

"I have faith in what I can see with my own two eyes and what I can do with my own two hands. Beyond that, I don't trust the church or the government or anything else that happens behind closed doors."

"You're not alone," Marco said.

"And women. I sure as hell don't trust women."

"That doesn't stop you hitting on them," Cain noted.

"You got to play the game at least as good as they do, or you'll end up with atrophied genitals. You know, use it or lose it."

"That is complete bullshit," Cain said.

"You tell me you never once got it on with Perry."

Cain's face flashed with anger. He pointed at Madison. "Don't you ever. Talk about her. To me."

"You gotta wonder if Mrs. Cain worried about the two of you."

"Am I going to have to turn the hose on you dogs?" Marco asked.

"There's no...Mrs. Cain."

"What? Man, what the fuck are you talking about? I been to your house. I met your wife."

"We're separated."

"Over what?"

"What goddam business is it of yours?" Cain asked with a little venom in his voice.

"Just asking," Madison put his hands up.

Marco was amazed at how deserted the streets were. On the other hand, if he lived there, he'd be holed up, too. Any sane person would be.

"Over what?" Madison repeated.

Cain was silent. "Money troubles," he said finally, looking down.

"Man, your wife is a lawyer. You all ain't got any *money troubles.*"

Cain wouldn't look at him.

"He's lyin'," Madison said to Marco.

"Why would he lie?"

"I don't know. He just is. I'll bet you dinner."

"Where you gonna buy dinner?"

"We'll get dinner *after* the zombie apocalypse, all right? But you're gonna pay for it, 'cause Cain here is lyin' through his ass."

Cain's face was rock hard. He refused to look either of them in the eye. Marco stopped. "You know, it's funny that you should bring this up, because I just caught myself about to lie to you guys, like, three times."

"What for?" Madison asked, putting his hands on his hips.

Marco shrugged. "I have no idea. I chose not to, but it wasn't my first impulse." He took a couple of test sniffs of the air. "This might be nothing, but it might be something, too."

"What? What might be something?"

"The urge to lie...or at least the urge to not tell the whole of the truth."

"None of us ever tell the whole truth," Madison said. "Actually, I don't think it's ever possible to tell the whole truth."

"Why do you say that?"

"Because words are so...lame. You describe anything in words and it's not even close to what you are trying to say. Not ever."

"Maybe your vocabulary just sucks," Cain said.

"Maybe you still waitin' for your balls to drop."

"Let's be on guard," Marco suggested. "Let's be careful with our words, just in case. Something's not right. It might be a magickal attack or something. Or maybe there's a falsehood sigil around."

"Or maybe Cain here just isn't ready to talk about it," Madison said, sounding conciliatory.

"No. There's some kind of compulsion going on," Marco said. Truth was, he liked Cain. The man might have skeletons in his closet, but thus far he'd struck Marco as being fairly open and vulnerable. And Madison's angry jabs were beginning to get on his nerves, so he really wanted to cut Cain some slack.

"Can't you check that with your compass-thingy?" Madison asked.

Marco nodded and pulled out the Liahona again. Holding it firmly in both hands, he asked it, "Take me to the sigil for the nearest falsehood demon." Both arrows moved lazily around their respective dials, not pointing in any particular direction, under no apparent influence or power.

"Let me try something else," Marco said, suddenly inspired. "Take me to the source of the Lie."

Instantly, both needles spun and pointed due south.

Cain looked up. "That's the hills."

"Toward the hills, then," Madison said, shrugging.

They walked uphill to the roundabout, then headed off on Marin. A couple of blocks in, Madison raised his hand. "Somethin's not right," he said.

Marco froze and listened. He didn't hear anything.

"No birds," Cain said.

"Right," Madison agreed.

Then they heard the boots. Not all at once, but slowly, as if someone were turning up a volume knob. "What the fuck is that?" Marco asked.

The three of them instinctively gathered together, standing back-to-back in a triangle, warily watchful on all sides. "There," Madison pointed. Marco and Cain pivoted as the marchers came into view.

It took a few moments for Marco to understand what they were seeing. About a hundred people—men and women, all of them white—were marching in formation, with rifles slung over their shoulders. All were wearing boots of some kind, and although their clothes didn't match, all of them were wearing black with blood-red accessories.

"I am not liking that color-scheme," Cain said. "Not one bit."

Sticking out like a sore thumb on every one of them, however, was a white hat. Again, there seemed to be no rhyme or reason as to exactly what kind of hat it was—Marco saw fishing hats, cowboy hats, baseball caps, and even an Easter bonnet, but all of them were white.

"I am not liking the funky hats," Madison said. "Clashes, don't you think?"

"I am not liking how they're marching," Marco said. He hadn't ever seen a group goose-stepping in real life before, and he didn't like it one bit. Goose bumps crawled up his arms.

Someone acting as a sergeant-at-arms called them to a halt, and every boot hit the ground at exactly the same second. "I don't have a good feeling about this," Marco whispered.

A short, middle-aged man with a pronounced beer belly separated himself from the crowd and approached them. His motions were formal, jerky, unnatural. With a flourish, he came to a rigid parade rest just a few yards from them.

"Citizens," he began, then appeared to notice Madison and Cain's uniforms for the first time. "Officers," he gave a slight deferential nod. "We welcome you to the Republic of Stan."

"The Republic of who?" Madison asked, but the man ignored him.

"The Republic of Stan is the world's youngest sovereign nation, claiming as its jurisdiction most of the Berkeley Hills at present. We welcome you and we promise to keep you safe." He turned and began to pace, still holding himself with an awkward stiffness. "In the Republic of Stan, we have declared martial law in order to put an end to the rampant killing and looting that has plagued most of Berkeley. Here, everyone obeys orders, everyone pulls their weight, and everyone is provided for. Restrictions will be relaxed once the crisis has passed, but until then we do as we're told and we protect our own."

"And who does the telling?" Madison asked warily.

"Stan does, of course," the man smiled paternally. Marco didn't know why, but he already wanted to slug the man.

"We are here to escort you to our quarantine center until your safety can be assessed and you can be properly assigned. Everything you need will be provided. There is no reason for you to fear. You are safe now. We extend the gift of the Pax Stan to you."

"Pax Stan!" everyone in formation repeated.

"I'm afraid that's not possible," Cain said. "We're on patrol with the Berkeley PD. We're trying to keep people safe, too."

"But you are no longer in Berkeley. You are in the jurisdiction of the Republic of Stan and are therefore now subject to the laws and regulations of the Republic. You are, in fact, trespassing on sovereign soil. We could arrest you as spies. Instead, however, we are extending to you the same courtesy that we extend to everyone that wanders over our borders. We offer you our protection, food, shelter, order, and meaningful work. Surely you can see how refusing such hospitality and kindness might be seen as ungrateful, even rude."

"We had no idea we were trespassing. Last we heard, this was still Berkeley," Marco said.

"The world has changed," the little man answered, smiling grimly. "Or perhaps you haven't noticed."

"We apologize for the indiscretion," Marco said. "And we request leave to go back the way we came. You can even escort us to the border if you like. Just...let us carry out our own orders. Surely you can understand why it is important to us to fulfill our duty."

"What you ask is not unreasonable," the man said. He stopped pacing and faced them. "Almost you have convinced me. But no. My orders are clear. You are here, and you must be assessed. Please follow the squirrel."

"The squirrel?" Marco asked.

From the company ranks a young woman stepped forward and processed into the open, raising up a pole. At the top of the pole was the carcass of a dead squirrel, swinging from a length of twine.

"What's with the squirrel?" Madison asked.

"It is the emblem of the Republic," the man said proudly. "Soon, all our uniforms will be adorned with its likeness."

"A dead squirrel?" Marco shook his head.

"Not a dead squirrel, just a squirrel," the man said testily.

"But that's a dead squirrel," Marco pointed out.

"You can't very well keep a live squirrel at the top of a pole," the man said in a tone that clearly warned Marco to stop being silly. "It would never stand still and might become dangerous if it became spooked. Anyway, sergeant-at-arms, to the Quarantine Center!"

A young man who looked very much like he must be in the

marines stepped forward. "Sir! Yes, sir! Squirrel-master, forward march!"

The little man approached them menacingly. "You will follow the squirrel, and you will do it now, or we will resort to some unpleasant persuasion."

Marco looked at his companions.

"We're outgunned here," Madison said.

"This is so wrong," Cain said.

"It'll be more wrong if they shoot us on the spot," Marco said. "I'm going to follow the fucking squirrel. For now."

Marco started walking after the squirrel-bearer and was relieved when the two officers followed. He tried to stay alert for details, for clues to their situation, and to any possible exits.

"Militia, right shoulder, Arms!" the sergeant-at-arms barked behind them. "Forward march!"

With a rising sense of alarm and the sound of tramping boots behind them, Marco followed the emblem of the Hanged Squirrel into the bowels of the Berkeley Hills.

73

"IT'S A LINGAM," Brian said out loud.

Maggie looked back at him, and for the first time, a slight smile escaped her lips. A moment later, Brian was looking at the back of her head again.

A lingam, looming on the horizon, was dwarfing everything else in this shadowy, violet world. Sexual images blasted through Brian's brain, as if they had been building up pressure, and had just been released—like the opening of a firehose or the gush of orgasm. He was staring at the pillar of the world, the organ that rested in the yoni of Malkuth, his own world, and stretched to connect this world, Yesod, with the higher sephirot. It was the connector, the vital pipeline, a rock-hard penis bursting with life and seed and joy, stretching from one world to another, aching to connect.

Brian felt himself getting hard as he watched it, and yet, he reminded himself, there seemed to be precious little joy or connection in this world—at least that he could see so far. They crossed over the greenbelt mall and headed into what looked like a residential area. He was sorry to leave the open plain and the grass. The buildings they passed were crowded too closely together for Brian's liking.

It was depressingly urban, with wet alleys and mangy cats and profane hip hop spilling out from open windows.

And the arguments. Every block they passed seemed to sport one. Brian hunkered down into his new sweatshirt, but it wasn't from the cold. It was an instinctual withdrawal from conflict. Maggie walked up to a rock wall about three feet high. Her hand descended, facing him, flat as a pancake. *Stop.* Brian stopped. Then he stood on tiptoe and tried to see over the wall. They appeared to be at a small river or a canal. Looking to the right, Brian noticed the remains of a bridge. He squinted, trying to see it more clearly. It looked like a truck had hit it and left a tangle of twisted metal and wire and jagged scrapes of paint. Whatever had happened to it, one side of it had fallen short of its moorings, hanging from the far shore at a dangerously diagonal angle. Was it possible to navigate through the wreckage, to climb up to the other side? Maybe, but he wouldn't want to gamble his life on it.

Maggie was negotiating with a man in uniform. She gave him two purple bills and pointed back at Brian. The man gave him a quick glance, then handed her two tickets. She waved him toward her and, as he approached, she handed him a ticket. Then without another word, she turned left and speed-walked along the stone wall to a cut-out section that led to a cement staircase. She turned right and began to descend. Brian followed, still respecting the distance between them. At the bottom, two uniformed officers held a skiff still on a quick-moving river. A third officer was in the boat with a long pole.

"You've got to be kidding me," Brian said out loud.

Maggie didn't reply but held her hand out to one of the officers. He grasped it and held her steady as she stepped into the boat. Brian thought to eschew the offer of help but nearly fell when the boat lurched beneath him. The officer caught his elbow and said, with a hint of reproach in his voice, "You can't do it alone, son. By the way, your shoe is untied."

Brian thanked him but felt the heat rising in his face. He sat and tied his shoe with double knots. He was grateful to sit for a brief moment, realizing just how far they'd walked. The officer with the pole expertly navigated to the other side of the river, and two more officers caught the skiff and helped them as they climbed out.

Brian waited a few seconds for Maggie to get a good lead on him, then set out after her, up another flight of cement stairs, and through a low stone wall identical to the one on the other side. Maggie crossed a street, and Brian was about to follow, when a bus roared by him, passing so close to his nose that he nearly lost his balance. *Did not see that coming,* he thought. *I've got to be more careful.*

He waited for a reasonable break in traffic then darted across the street. A moment later and he would have missed Maggie turning left into an alley. He walked briskly to catch up and turned left himself. He did not see her. He continued to walk quickly down the narrow passage between two blocks of apartment buildings. Every now and then he had to dart sideways to avoid a duct or climb over some apparatus he couldn't identify. The buildings seemed to be cluttered with far more machinery than in Malkuth, of curious design and unidentifiable purposes. In fact, now that he was paying attention, there wasn't a single building that wasn't covered in machinery. Like warts marring every flat surface, there was not a two-square-foot area of wall that was not ornamented by some kind of metal box, fan, duct, or tangle of wires. There seemed to be no rhyme or reason to them, and there was certainly no thought to aesthetics.

Brian heard a sharp "Pssst!" and stopped. A door in the rear of one of the apartment buildings waved open, and he sprinted toward it. He leaped up the steps and entered, looking around. He seemed to have stepped directly into a kitchen, and into yet another, different world. Maggie squeezed past him and shut and bolted the door. Then she yanked on his sweatshirt and drew him down to her eye level. "Hello, you old sod," she said in her thick cockney accent. She planted a kiss on his cheek and released him. "D'ya want some tea, then?"

"Uh...sure." The kitchen was tiny, but cozy. There was barely room for the two of them to navigate in it, so Brian took a seat at the small table set against one wall beneath a lithograph of the Thames in winter. Maggie turned on the burner and set the kettle to boil. She reached up into what would have been a low cupboard for Brian and pulled out two mugs.

"I hope you like chamomile, love. Nothing says 'comfort' like the taste of dirty socks."

She waddled back to the table, and Brian wondered at how she handled the cups in her gnarled, deformed hands. The ravages of arthritis had not been kind to her, but Brian had never really noticed how profoundly misshapen her fingers were. *Perhaps the Maggie of our world is not as badly off?* he wondered. *Or is this the Maggie of our world, crossed over like I am?* But he didn't know what was kosher to talk about and what wasn't. He decided to let her take the lead.

"Oh, Brian, it's good to see your face, love," she said, easing her plump frame into the other kitchen chair. "You have no idea how lonely I've been here—or how ironic that is."

Brian blinked, not sure how to respond. "It's...good to see you, too," he said lamely.

"Oh, don't be such an oinker," she slapped his hand. "It's safe here. You can talk freely." She leaned in and said conspiratorially, "You should have seen the look on your face when you saw the zayin."

Brian blushed. "I was thinking of it as a lingam."

"Then you were right on target," she said, patting his hands.

Brian looked into the cup in front of him. It was chipped and stained a dark brown. He blinked and averted his eyes. *Best not to look,* he thought.

"I never run into this world's Brian," Maggie said. "So you mustn't be from this world."

"No," Brian said. "Are you...from this world?"

"Of course I am." The kettle began to sputter so she lifted it with one twisted hand and filled a teapot.

"Are you okay...I mean, are you alive...in my world, in Malkuth?"

"The me in Malkuth is fine. I'm in Tahoe, playing the slots. Or at least I was. Now I'm watching the news, worrying about you all."

"And...how do you know that?"

"Because we're all just one person, really. Souls have a lot more parts than people imagine. But you should know all about that. We're all just one person, spread out into these different spheres. Most people just aren't aware of their souls. But I've had time to...let's say, get acquainted." She winked at him.

"So if I run into myself here—"

"That won't happen, dear." She waved him away. "You *are* yourself here. Your consciousness just travelled to the part of your soul that lives here. Try one of the biscuits."

Brian blinked, trying to take that in. "Okay, so if the you in Malkuth is in Tahoe, why aren't you in *this world's* Tahoe?"

She lowered one eye at him. "This world doesn't have a Tahoe, dear. Or a Berkeley or a San Francisco. We have entirely different political systems, financial systems—"

"I noticed the money," Brian interjected.

She nodded. "Plus, space and time work differently here. You'll find spatial relationships distorted, at least according to your sensibilities. Things that look small will seem bigger inside and vice versa." She took a bite of a cookie.

"I've noticed there's a lot of machinery here. I've never seen a place with so many ducts and hoses and gears and...little boxes with fans in them and such."

"You're welcome, dear," she smiled. A part of a cookie clung to her lower lip.

Brian tried not to look at it. "Um...welcome for what?"

"They stuff all the machinery that makes Malkuth work up here in Yesod. We barely have room for our own anchovy tins—you know why? Because half of our cupboard space is taken up with *your* electric wiring and chutes and levers and Jesus' pajamas."

"But why is that? How could it—?"

"Do you think electricity just *works*? No. It's all finagled from here. And when the internet went in, good God man, suddenly we had all these government men crawling around our flats installing all this naff ductwork. 'For the good of the Mals,' they say. 'Oh, yes, by all means, for the Mals,' we answer. Bloody ductwork, in through here, through the wall there, up through the floors, bloody ductwork coming out of my twat—all to carry your messages and those stinking Black Friday adverts."

"But that's all just electronic," Brain objected.

"Don't fookin' rub it in," Maggie slammed her fist on the table. She continued in a mocking, sing-song voice, "It's just electronic, nice and neat—nice and neat my scabied ass! The internet is a series of tubes, my son, and where do you think those tubes actually reside? In Yesod!"

Brian wanted to shrink under the table. "Sorry. I didn't know."

Maggie's fury seemed to melt away as quickly as it had risen. "Oh, it's not your fault, dear. You're just clueless."

Brian nodded—because he was, and he didn't know what else to say.

"All that machinery isn't pretty, but it's how we pull our weight," she smiled sweetly at him. "You'll get used to it...if you spend any time here, that is."

"I hope not to," Brian said, a little tentatively. "I'm not here for vacation. I'm looking for someone."

"A magickian?"

"Yes. How did you know?"

"Because it's always a magickian. He was here yesterday. He may still be here. I don't know."

"Did you meet him?"

"No. I didn't need to. I *noticed*."

"So things have been falling apart since yesterday?"

Maggie cocked her head at him. "What do you mean?"

"I mean the bridges, I guess. The fact that no one talks to anyone else. The arguments. The...sterility."

"Oh no, that's just *you*."

Brian drew back. "What do you mean?"

"You aren't seeing this world the way it is. You're seeing it the way you are."

"Anaïs Nin said that."

"And she was right. You are disconnected, so the bridges are out. You aren't communicating well, so people aren't talking to you."

"But they're *not*. They're *not* talking to me. At all."

"Yes, dear." Maggie smiled sweetly, aggravatingly. "I also noticed your shoelaces. Something's going on there. Did you and Terry split up?"

Brian swallowed, and he felt water rise to his eyes. "I...we did. Kind of."

"Oh, dear. I thought as much. I *am* sorry. You were like two bangers in a bun." She sighed. "What is interior reality in your world has an external manifestation in this one. Everything in this world is a little more...rarified than you're used to. It's the outer of the inner, so to speak."

"Meaning?"

"Don't be stupid, dear," she said, waving a gnarled hand at him. "You know very well what I mean."

"So the bridge wasn't really out?"

"It was really out."

Brian shook his head, confused.

"It isn't *all* about you," Maggie scolded him. "Sometimes how you feel and how things actually are line up, you know."

"So how do you tell which is which and where the line is?"

"Hang in there," she patted his hand, "you'll get your sea legs."

Brian wasn't sure he would, but she had given him lot to think about. "So what was it like when Larch was here?"

"Larch? Ah, you must mean the magickian," Maggie nodded. "I imagine he saw it as most magickians see it. Total chaos."

"Because the chaos is inside of them?" Brian asked.

"You get a gold star," she said. "And another biscuit." She reached for a bright red tin on the table and pulled it open, offering it to Brian. He pulled half a broken shortbread cookie out of it and nibbled at it.

"The girl at the store," Brian said. "She asked me if I was a magickian."

"We get a lot of visitors here, more than you might think."

"I would think most of them would be Jews, though."

"Yes. Mostly Jews, but they never make a fuss, and they mostly go to synagogue to pray. The ones flashing money around, getting liquored up, and trying to get laid? *Those* are usually magickians. They're the ones who get into trouble. An unsavory lot, in my opinion."

"She felt at my arm. What was that about?"

"Checking for ointment," Maggie said.

"Ointment?"

"Kelipot ointment. To mask one's intentions," Maggie said. "You don't need it because you're not hiding anything. Your intentions are good. And that," she twisted the end of his nose, "is as clear as the honker on your face."

"Because this is the outer of the inner?" he asked, feeling his nose. She'd given it a good twist.

"Precisely. No one is going to bother you here. But if you were up to no good, that would be obvious, too."

"So I'd want to mask that...if I were up to no good."

"Yes. Kelipot ointment. It's kind of a concealment spell. A glamor."

Brian nodded. "That makes sense. The Kabbalists speak of *kelipot* as a kind of shell that conceals holiness. I suppose it could conceal evil intent just as well. In our world there have been terrible repercussions. The divorce rate has gone through the roof. Couples everywhere are fighting."

"Yes, it's very sad," she said. "Malkuth is displaying the outer of *our* inner, it seems. Very unusual. Oh, well, it will all be over soon."

"What do you mean?" Brian asked, hopeful. "Will these effects just dissipate?"

"What? No, don't be silly," Maggie said. "This whole world is about to collapse, and it will take Malkuth with it."

Brian froze, mid-sip. He set the cup back down. "Maggie, what on earth do you mean by that?"

"Come," she said. She led him to her front door, then smacked at her head. "Damn, I should bring the specs." She went to a bookshelf, stuffed to bursting with much more than books. From a shelf near the bottom, she grabbed a pair of binoculars. Then she waddled over to the front door again, opened it, and waved for him to follow her.

She led him up five flights of stairs. Brian was amazed at her alacrity and embarrassed that he was so quickly winded. At the top, they reached a metal door. Maggie pushed it open and led him onto a roof. The rain seemed to have let up for the moment, but water stood in puddles every couple of feet. Maggie led him to the far edge, stepping over the ducts and boxes with fans in them with far more agility that she should have been able to manage. When they reached the railing they were facing the greenbelt. She handed him the binoculars and pointed. "There. Look there."

He held the binoculars to his eyes and adjusted them. "What am I looking at? The lingam?"

"Yes. Do you see it?"

"I see it."

"Now, very slowly, look down. What do you see when you get near the ground?"

"Um...it looks like a construction crew. It looks like the lingam is still under construction."

"You're half right, dear. It's a demolition crew. They're dismantling the zayin."

"But...why?" Brian lowered the binoculars.

"Why do people ever do stupid, tragic things?" Maggie asked.

"Is that rhetorical?" Brian asked.

"No. Please answer the question."

"Why do people do stupid, tragic things?" Brian repeated. "Because they're bad?"

"Did you get thicker when you crossed the threshold of the worlds?" Maggie asked. "People don't do stupid, tragic things because they're bad, you ninny, they do them because they're *scared*."

"Of course they do," Brian felt like an idiot. "And why are they scared?"

"*Now* you're asking intelligent questions," Maggie said. "They're scared because some asshole magickian got online and started fabricating news stories about an army of magickians in Malkuth full of evil intent crossing over into Yesod with the expressed purpose of disrupting our society with lies about kidnappings and bombings and political scandal and whatnot. Your...Larch, was it? Your Larch took several pages from the terrorist's DIY playbook, not to mention the Russians and right-wing nut jobs, and posted all kinds of fabrications and innuendos, poisoning our society with suspicion and distrust and threats of violence."

Brian felt like his head was spinning. "But there *is* a magickian full of evil intent, he *did* cross over, and he *is* poisoning your society with suspicion and so forth—he's actually talking about himself."

"Yes, his only real distortion, it seems, was suggesting he was legion."

"Online, you can pretend to be anyone else. I guess you can pretend to be more numerous, too."

"Just so."

"So they're dismantling the lingam in order to...what?"

"To sever the connection to Malkuth."

Brian felt like he'd been punched in the gut. "Wait, whoa. If you sever the connection to Malkuth, our world—our universe—just winks out of existence."

"Well, not exactly, but close enough. You'll be cut off from the divine energies that give your universe its contingent existence. Imagine that your world is the pod at the end of an enormous Habitrail. This lingam is the tube through which all your air, all your water, all your light, and all your energy travels to your little pod. Remove the tube and...well, you got not much of anything, do you? No energy, so no suns, no stars, no light. You got no communication—because all symbolic connections, all *meaning* is fed to you from the higher sephirot down through the zayin into Malkuth. Sever that tube and you got nothing but a husk. And even that won't last long."

Brian felt chills run up and down his spine. "But why would Larch do something like that?"

"I'm not sure he intended *that* particular outcome. He just wanted to throw us into chaos, and he did that handily enough—the papers have been filled with 'magickian hysteria' ever since, which must have tickled his testicles delightfully. None of our proper work has gotten done in the past twenty-four hours, which is probably why you're seeing those effects in your world. Yesod is all about connection—the connection between your world and the higher sephirot, the connection between language and meaning, the connection between people at every level of society, but most keenly within families. So if we're not doing the work of connection here, then connection isn't happening *there*."

"And when the connection is broken completely..."

"It's like a heart attack. Right now, you got clogged arteries. When the blockage is complete..."

"We die."

"Bingo!"

Brian felt faint, and he sat down on the roof. He felt water from one of the puddles seep into his jeans. The cold felt good, bracing. "How do we stop it?"

"Well, how do you stop frightened people trying to protect themselves? I don't know the answer to that." Maggie looked at him with profound compassion.

"We could do a press conference, set the story straight," Brian said.

"Sure. The Reformed Catholic priest-lady and her Jewish friend. We might get three of my neighbors to attend, but only if we serve scones."

"I feel so helpless." He leaned over and rested his head on her shoulder.

"I know just how you feel," she said as she caressed his temple with gnarled fingers.

"What do we do?"

"Well, I don't know about you, but I'm going to finish my tea."

74

Rachel screamed. Evans' mouth dropped open and Martinez crossed himself.

Richard swallowed hard. Rachel stood up, still screaming. She seemed to have come completely unglued. Richard sprang at her and knocked her to the floor before a spray of buckshot took out the glass in the cabinet doors behind them. "Stay down," he said, allowing his full weight to pin her to the floor.

"Ben!" she sobbed. "They killed Ben..."

Richard realized that he hadn't known the man's name until just now. He had simply thought of him as the hipster guy. But now he was Ben. And Ben's brains were splattered across the tile. Richard couldn't see either of the policemen, but he knew they could hear him. "Two things: we've gotta distract the Olivos, and we've gotta destroy that sigil."

"How are we going to do that?" Martinez asked.

"I'm thinking that the two of you need to pay them a visit, and let them know that one of their other neighbors has won a prize, but they aren't home. Ask if you can leave notice with the Olivos instead."

"What kind of prize?" Evans asked.

"I don't know, make something up. But it has to be something big —like a house in France or a couple million dollars or something."

"Won it how?"

"Do I have to do everything? Do you guys have a policeman's annual raffle or something?"

"No."

"Well, pretend you do. Make it big. Make it convincing. Make it something that will really spark their envy. Big enough that they'll stop thinking about their backyard neighbors long enough for me and Tobias to find the sigil."

"How will you know that it's safe?"

"We all have radios—can you just hold down your transmit button so that I can hear what's happening?"

"Sure, I can talk and Martinez can hold the line open," Evans said. Richard imagined that Martinez must be nodding his agreement.

"Okay, then let's get moving. Rachel, I'm going to move off you now. Will you stay down?"

Below him he heard snuffling, and then a weak "Yes."

He rolled off onto the floor and sat up, being careful not to put his hand down on any shards. He wondered how Toby was doing with all the glass but saw that the dog had wisely kept to the area just in front of the door that was blessedly glass-free.

"How does a visiting professor get guns?" Martinez asked.

"Maybe he's renting the house," Evans said. "And the owner has a stash of guns."

"Maybe," Martinez agreed. "Not a lot of guns in Berkeley, though."

"More than I ever thought there was," Evans said, shaking his head. Then they were gone, duck-walking past Tobias and keeping their heads low.

Rachel had withdrawn into a corner and had curled nearly into a ball. She stared at what remained of Ben and shivered. Richard wanted to comfort her but didn't know what to say. It wasn't safe to clean anything up, and it wasn't clear to him that a hug was what she needed most right now. Instead, he stayed in leadership mode. "You stay right there," he told her, with as much authority as he could muster. "Whatever you do, don't stand up."

Richard crawled over to the back door and, positioning himself with his back to the wall, he swung it open into the room. The Olivos noticed the motion, and several bullets punched into the far wall. Richard leaned out a bit and saw that just beyond the back door was a porch with a waist-high railing. If he stayed low enough, he could move out onto the porch without being seen. He scuttled out the door and held it open. "Toby, come."

Richard was glad he couldn't see Toby as he made his way across the glass-strewn floor because he'd wince at every step. But Toby must have picked his way carefully through the mess, because he successfully navigated to the porch without trailing any blood from his paws—not even Ben's blood.

"Well done, boy," Richard said in a whisper, although he didn't know why he was whispering. Richard turned to face the house behind them and unslung his rifle, setting it down on the gray painted floor of the porch. Then, steeling himself, he raised up so that just his eyes cleared the railing. To his great relief, the Olivos didn't seem to notice. Just then his radio sprung to scratchy life. He heard a loud, authoritative knock.

He looked at the Olivos house quickly. He half expected to see a sigil spray-painted on the back of their house, but no—it was a well-kept Victorian with nary a demonic tag in sight.

"What do you...officer..." a voice with a thick Italian accent came through the radio.

Richard crouched back down and turned to look up at the house he was in. It was clean, too. *Where the fuck...?* he thought. *There must be a sigil here somewhere.*

"Sir, I'm so sorry to bother you. But we're pleased to inform you that your neighbor, right over there beside you—"

"Miss Lessing?" the man asked.

"Yes, that's her. Miss Lessing. Miss Lessing has won the Berkeley PD Sweepstakes this year."

"She has?"

"Who is it, Arturo?" came another voice, this one higher. His wife, perhaps?

Tobias was sniffing at the wind and seemed to have caught a scent. Richard raised his eyes just above the railing and looked in the direction the dog was sniffing in. And then he saw it. Spray painted on the basketball backboard fixed to the garage was a sigil. It wasn't one that Richard recognized, but then again he'd never spent much time studying envy demons—there didn't seem to be a point. Richard squinted, trying to find the activated scrap—and saw something fluttering, attached to the rim by...what? A clothespin? Maybe. It was too far to see it, and Richard's vision wasn't what it used to be, no matter what he told himself.

The radio crackled and hissed. "Says Caroline won some prize."

"What did she win?" asked the presumed Mrs. Olivo.

"She won a new car. A Tesla," Evans said.

"Nice job," Richard said aloud. Evans was doing well.

"I've...always wanted a Tesla..." Mr. Olivo said. Richard had no idea what Mr. Olivo looked like, but his mind's eye summoned up a picture of a slight, Italian man with full lips, thinning black hair and a pencil-thin mustache, his eyes focusing on the distance, almost trembling at the thought of that new car.

Richard cast about and saw a mop leaning on the railing where it joined the house. He crawled over to it and snatched it up, waving the mop about. No gunshots followed. "It's now or never, Toby. Stay right here."

Richard sprang up, then dashed down the stairs, running full tilt toward the garage. As he ran, he heard Evans' voice, "We have to deliver notice in person, and Miss Lessing doesn't seem to be home. We were wondering if we could leave the notice with you?"

At the basketball net, Richard jumped, snatching the scrap bearing the activated sigil from off the hoop. As he pulled it, a medium binder clip snapped off as well, clattering to the pavement.

"Uh...of course," Mr. Olivo said.

"You know, maybe we could just leave the car with you?" Evans said. "How would that be?"

"Oh, that would be even better," Mr. Olivo said.

Richard raced for the safety of the porch railing again. He dove up the stairs and rolled behind the railing. He turned and rested his back against it. Tobias' tail was pounding against the railing on his side. "Good boy," Richard said. He was afraid that Toby would follow him, but whether due to the dog's innate intelligence, or the loaned intelligence of the angel inside of him, he had stayed put and safe.

Without hesitation Richard pulled a lighter from his pants pocket and held it below the sigil. The scrap of paper caught, curled, and crackled. Richard let go of it when the flame got too high. A howling scream pierced the air. Richard shuddered.

"What...what are we doing?" Richard heard Mr. Olivo say.

Richard breathed a deep sigh of relief. He rose and slung his rifle back over his shoulder. He switched off the radio and walked into the kitchen. He held his hand out to Rachel. Her eyes were brimming and her jaw trembled. "What happened to us?"

Richard was sure that she remembered the events that she had just witnessed. He took her to mean something deeper. Something like, "Whatever could have possessed us?" Richard stood his ground until she reached up and grabbed his hand. He raised her to her feet.

"Rachel, I can't begin to fathom what you have been through or what you are feeling. But this is what we need to do right now. We need a sheet for Ben. Then we need to go over to the Olivos and get your children."

"But they'll shoot us," she said.

"No," he said, trying to sound as certain and reassuring as possible. "No, they won't."

He helped Rachel to her feet, and was taken aback when she threw her arms around his neck and clung to him. He paused long enough to give her a firm hug, even though his brain was screaming for them to hurry, to get on with it. *This little diversion has taken up way too much time,* he thought. *Every minute we delay is another minute we are* not *destroying sigils.*

She let him go, and he put his arm around her shoulders protectively. "Come on, let's go." Richard could hear Tobias trotting after them as they crossed the living room to the front door. Richard pulled the door open and pushed at the screen. Tobias burst past them into the open air, almost tripping Rachel. Richard steadied her, and together they descended the few steps in front of the porch.

Rachel seemed to be in too much shock to walk more quickly than she was—which was little more than a slow shuffle. "I can't," she said, finally slumping to the ground.

"Rachel, we're going to get your children."

"His head just...exploded," she said.

"Yes, I saw it, too."

"It was like the back of his head came off and sprayed itself across the wall."

"It was...just like that, yes."

She started hugging the lawn now. Richard pulled on her arm. "Rachel, we need to..." But she wasn't budging. Instead, she was sobbing, clawing up fistfuls of soil, grinding her head back and forth on the grass. Then she began to wail.

Richard sat back on his haunches and looked at her. Then he looked at Tobias. The dog watched the woman with what seemed to be understanding and sympathy. Then Toby looked at Richard, and his tail swooped back and forth lazily a couple of times. "Okay, Toby, let's go get the kids. Maybe seeing them will help her."

He turned and started walking toward the corner with Toby at his heels. *Am I being insensitive?* he wondered. It seemed to him that he was just focused on what needed to be done. Still, his heart went out to her. She had witnessed a terrible thing, and it would take a long time—perhaps years—to heal from the trauma of it.

They turned right at the corner and Richard saw the Olivo's house for the first time.

The front door was open. Richard sprang up the steps impatiently. He was anxious to put this little diversion behind him and get back to finding more sigils. He was about to cross the threshold when Tobias barked. He stopped and looked over his shoulder at the dog. Toby had stopped about four yards from the door and was sitting down.

Richard nodded and waved for the dog to stay put. Much more cautiously, he approached the door. Toby whined, but he continued. The first thing he saw upon entering was the body of officer Evans. A dark stain on the chest of his uniform was spreading. His eyes were open but sightless. His mouth was open but silent.

Richard unslung his rifle again and checked to make sure the safety was off. "Martinez?" he said tentatively. There was no answer. He stepped carefully over Evans' body and, holding the rifle at the ready, burst suddenly into the living room. He took one glance and ducked again behind the corner in the foyer.

Martinez and an older man had been standing at arm's length from each other, both pointing guns, and a woman was lying on the floor. Richard had not gotten a good look at her, but he assumed that she was dead.

"Okay, guys, I'm going to step out again in just a second," Richard called. "I won't be armed. Don't shoot me, okay? I just want to talk to both of you." He leaned the rifle against the corner where the wall met the door. "Martinez, okay?"

"Yeah, I'm not going to shoot you."

"Mr. Olivo, I'm a priest. I just want to talk to you. Please promise me you won't shoot me."

"A...a priest? Oh...okay, I won't shoot," Mr. Olivo's Italian accent was thick, but he was easy to understand. "I'm not making promises about *him*, though."

Richard assumed he meant Martinez. "Okay, that's fine. I'm coming out now." Richard raised his hands and stepped into the open.

He looked down at the woman. He saw a messy exit wound near her temple, about the size of a quarter. His eyes snapped back to to Martinez and Mr. Olivo. "So, I assume you killed Officer Evans, Mr. Olivo."

"He was going to arrest me!"

"I don't think he was," Richard said.

"And now this one is going to arrest me!" The pitch of Mr. Olivo's voice rose with his level of panic.

"Mr. Olivo, no one is going to arrest you."

"Don't you lie to me. He has to arrest me! I just killed a *polizia*!"

"No, he doesn't. In ordinary times yes, but these aren't ordinary times. Mr. Olivo, please lower your weapon."

"He killed my wife!" Mr. Olivo's face screwed up as he fought back tears.

"Martinez, what happened to Mrs. Olivo?" Richard asked.

"She lunged at me," he said. "I told her to stand still!"

"She didn't lunge at you, she was running away from you!" Mr. Olivo countered.

"You don't run away from someone by running toward them!" Martinez countered.

"There is only one door to this room, and she was trying to go through it. She was trying to go past you, not at you!"

"Could that be possible, Martinez?" Richard asked.

"That's...possible," Martinez said. "But that's sure not what it seemed like in the moment."

"That seems possible, too," Richard said. "Both of you, I want you to listen to me. You have both suffered a terrible loss. Senseless, unnecessary losses. But we don't need to have more of them. I want to see both of you lower your weapons. At the same time now, on the count of three. One...two...three."

Both looked from Richard to the other uncertainly but neither lowered their guns. Richard sighed. "Oh, good lord. Fuck you both, then. Where are the children?"

No one answered, so Richard started toward a dark hallway leading further into the house. He realized he didn't know the children's names—or their genders or ages. *I don't know anything, really,* he thought. That stopped him for a moment, but no longer. He opened the door to a bedroom, but it was empty.

As he closed the door, he heard two shots in rapid succession. "Oh, Jesus," he said out loud, leaning against the hallway wall. "Anyone left?" he called out. No one answered. "Oh, Jesus," he said again.

He opened the door to the next bedroom and stuck his head in.

Two children cowered in the corner of the room, their limbs entangled, clutching at one another for comfort and courage. "Hey," Richard said in a calm voice. Their eyes were wide. The younger child, a little boy, was visibly shaking. The older child, a girl of about seven, clutched his head to her breast protectively.

"The man and woman who took you are gone now. I'm going to take you to your mother. Will that be okay?"

Although it seemed impossible, their eyes got even wider at the mention of their mother, and they began to well up with tears. Richard walked around the bed and squatted down on his haunches a couple feet from them. From behind the little boy's back, the girl raised a gun, her hand shaking so hard it was a blur, it's chamber clacking like a straight key sending tapping out Morse code.

Richard instinctively backed up. The gun exploded.

75

THE LARGE METAL gate rolled back, filling the chamber with the sound of echoing thunder. Dylan jerked upright, his limbs straining against his restraints and his eye bulging. Mayor Betts stepped through the gate, followed by Milo.

"You must be Mr. Melan—Melan—"

"Melanchthon," Milo said.

"Melanchthon...that's an unusual name."

Dylan was about to cuss the men out, but he thought better of it. *Ya catch more varmints with honey than vinegar,* he reminded himself. "Mah wife picked it out," Dylan said to the man. "When we got married."

"Really? Neither of you were born with that name?"

"Nope. We decided to pick a new name fer us both. She wanted to be named after someone she admired. So we took the name of Philip Melanchthon."

"Er...and who was he?"

"Martin Luther's right hand man," Dylan said, his eye moving from one to the other warily.

The man waved his hand dismissively. "No wonder. I never really studied the civil rights movement."

Dylan scowled. "Uh...don't suppose you could let me know why Ah'm here?"

"I certainly can. First, though, I think some introductions are in order. I'm the mayor here in Alameda, Tom Betts. You can just call me Tom. Can I call you Dylan?"

Dylan nodded.

"And this is my secretary, Milo Richards." Milo gave him a curt nod.

"Nice t' meet you both. Ah'd shake yore hands, 'cept mah hands seem to be mysteriously immobile."

"We apologize for that, Dylan. I understand why you might think us inhospitable. But I assure you, it's just a precaution."

"A precaution against what? The likelihood that Ah might need to scratch mah ass?"

Betts smiled weakly but did not answer. "I've been talking to your wife."

"Is she okay?" Dylan jerked up again.

Betts patted the gurney. "She's fine, she's fine. She's consulting with us, along with your colleague, Mr...."

"Father Terry, Ah think you mean," Dylan corrected him.

"Yes, I'm sorry. Father Terry is training some of our volunteers, and your wife, uh..." he said, snapping his fingers.

"Susan," Milo whispered.

"Your wife Susan is taking care of that adorable little girl of yours," Betts said.

"Is she now?" Dylan's eyebrows raised.

"Yes, so please relax. All is well. The people you love are safe. The people on this island are safe...for now. I'd like to keep them that way." Betts took another step closer to Dylan. If he'd wanted to, he could have reached out and touched Dylan's face. "I'd like you to help me with that."

"Ah would do anything Ah ken to help," Dylan said. "An' I would'a done it without the skullduggery or the restraints."

"I understand you know something about demons." The mayor cocked his head and waited.

"Yeah, Ah know about 'em. That's mah job."

"And you know how to control them?"

"Ah'm familiar with the basics of all the major grimoires," Dylan answered, one eyebrow raised. "Goetia is really Richard's speciality, but Ah've got a workman's knowledge of it."

Betts laughed nervously. "You know, until yesterday, I didn't think that demons actually existed. The little meeting I had with your wife and Father Terry was...well, it was quite an eye opener for me."

"I woulda liked to have seen that mahself. Do ya'll have any morphine?"

"Do you need morphine?" Betts' eyebrows raised.

He actually looks concerned, Dylan noted. He lowered his eyes. "Nah, not really. Ah think Ah was just lookin' fer a consolation high."

Betts and Milo exchanged puzzled glances. Betts turned back to Dylan. "Tell me about how powerful demons are."

"Ya got eyes, dontcha?" Dylan said. "Ya got two of 'em! Ya know, Ah don't think Ah was ever properly grateful for mah eyes. You sort of take 'em fer granted. Ah mean, have you ever prayed, 'O Lord, thank you fer mah two good eyes'? Ah'll bet ya haven't."

"Um...I don't suppose I have."

"Well, ya should."

"Yes, well, about the demons?"

"The East Bay is burnin' and yer askin' 'Are they powerful?' Dude, how much more power d'ya wanna see?"

"Are they powerful enough to protect this island?"

Dylan blinked. His mouth opened to speak, but he closed it. Then he looked down at his legs. "Oh, Jesus. D'ya want me to make a list of all the ways that's just wrong?"

"Humor me. Can you summon a demon or two to keep the Oaklanders at bay?"

"First of all, let me point out that you are suggesting we summon a demon to fight other demons."

"All right, I suppose I am. So?"

"Mister, d'ya think they don't talk to each other?"

It was Betts' turn to blink. "I don't understand."

Dylan sighed, not sure where to begin. "Okay, let's get one thing straight. Ain't no demon gonna be yore friend. If you compel a demon to do somethin' fer you, ya better be watchin' yore ass, because the demon is gonna find a thousand and one ways to bite it."

"And why is that?"

"'Cause no one likes to be told what to do," Dylan said, with a tone that implied that Betts was an idiot.

"All right. We have to use precautions. That sounds reasonable anytime you are dealing with a powerful weapon, doesn't it, Richards?" Milo raised his eyebrows and nodded encouragingly.

"Second, demons are a lot better organized than ya think," Dylan continued. "They're military. An' their code is hella strict. So you might get a private to do yore bidding, but you can bet his general knows about it and is workin' that into his overall game plan. And you can bet yore ass that game plan is not gonna work out in yore favor."

"Given that half of me thinks this is nonsense anyway, I'm willing to take that chance," Betts said, standing up a little straighter.

"Ya know who you remind me of?" Dylan asked.

"No. Who?"

"Them crazy Church of Satan motherfuckers," Dylan said. "Ah've known a few of 'em. They get a boner fer raisin' demons, thinkin' how cool they are, raisin' demons and shit. An' the fact is they have almost no idea what they're doin' and it's like they're six years old pokin' the beehive with a stick. 'Let's see what happens if we poke this a little harder' they say, until they get swarmed by bees and swell up like a turnip. Fuckin' turnips."

Betts looked confused. "I think I might have lost the thread of your analogy."

"Never mind. Look, the point is you got no clue what yer dealin' with here, and it's gonna bite you in the ass if yer not careful."

"But you'll do it."

"Like hell Ah will."

"Oh, you *will* do it, Mr. Melanchthon."

"Uh-oh. Are we no longer on a first-name basis?"

"You'll do it because you'll stay here in your present condition until you do. And it does get cold at night. Plus," he leaned over until his nose was almost touching Dylan's own, "it would be unfortunate if something were to happen to that little girl of yours—or your wife."

"You slimy motherfucker."

"You have a salty tongue for a priest."

"You have no idea. Ah have not *begun* to cuss, mister."

"Save it. I suppose you'll need supplies?"

Dylan strained against his restraints, a purple vein bulging on his forehead.

"Ah could actually help you, ya know. In a way that wouldn't put everyone on this island in even more danger than we're in now."

"Good to know. But let's try it my way first." Betts pulled his suit jacket tighter around him. "I've got to get out of this place before I catch cold. Please tell Milo here what you need. I'm going to go enjoy the sunshine. And if you had any sense at all, you could do the same."

76

MIKAEL SAT on the curb to catch his breath. He'd knocked on about fifty doors so far, and along the way he'd honed his technique into an efficient inquiry that solicited very little objection. He looked up and noticed that the sun was starting to descend. The San Francisco fog was beginning to coalesce, lending the street a ghostly cast. *I'm going to have to hurry if I'm going to finish this by sundown*, he thought. He sighed deeply and pushed himself up. His phone pinged, and he took it out.

—Going to march with the Alliance across the Bay Bridge. Candlelight vigil. Going to try to retake the East Bay.

Mikael frowned. "That seems like a baaaad idea," he said out loud. He quickly thumbed in a text.

—Going to retake it with what? Your athames and a bundle of burning sage?

He waited while it sent, then he saw it marked "delivered." The little dots swirled as she wrote.

—You're just jealous. Come with us.

—Are you still mad at me?

—Are you still an asshole?

"Ouch," he said.

—No. I found a waxing place on Castro that does de-assholing as well.

—De-assholed with a Brazilian. Now you're talking.

—Haven't found Larch yet.

—I don't think you will, if he doesn't want to be found.

—So far he doesn't know I'm looking for him.

—Bullshit. His poodle goons know.

That was true. Purderabo and Turpelo were sure to have told him. Unless... He didn't really know the internal politics of the Lodge of the Hawk and Serpent. Who knew how close they were? He noticed that he had relaxed. A lot. He hadn't realized how much stress he had been carrying around about his fight with Kat. Just these few messages put his mind at ease. It was going to be okay between them.

—I'm worried about you. And the bridge.

—The bridge will be fine.

"Ha!" he said out loud. He pocketed his phone and approached the next house.

MIKAEL PREPARED himself mentally as he took the porch and rang the bell. For a few moments, he heard nothing. Then he heard rustling from deep within the house. Then he heard voices. "—not lying to you, I just..." one of them said as he approached, "you didn't let me —" Then the door snatched open and Frater Eleazar was standing before him in boxer shorts and a flowered shirt, an empty frying pan in his hand. His eyes locked on Mikael's, and for a moment, he froze. Then he slammed the door.

Mikael jammed his foot forward and bit back on a howl of pain as the door smashed into it. *Knew I should have worn the Doc Martens*, he thought, but he didn't hesitate for more than a second. He heaved the door back in with his shoulder, throwing Eleazar backwards onto his ass. The frying pan went spinning, landing on the tile with a loud noise that was somewhere in between the sound of a bell and a clatter.

"Where is he?" Mikael said, looming over him. His jet black hair pointed straight up and his tall, angular frame curved down ominously toward where Eleazar had fallen.

"Uh...where is who?"

"You know exactly who, you jackwipe."

"Jackwipe?"

"Where the fuck is Larch?"

"Larch isn't here." Eleazar scowled defiantly but didn't move to get up.

For a moment, Mikael wished he had his talisman with him, but it didn't matter. He knew Eleazar was lying.

"The fuck he isn't."

Mikael began to step over Eleazar. The magickian snatched up the frying pan and rose to one knee. Mikael quickly assumed the *hanmi* aikido position, and tried to decide whether *tantodori*—the defense against knife attacks—would be the appropriate strategy against frying pans. But before he could truly center himself, Eleazar came at him with a full-throated scream, waving the frying pan in a wild, erratic pattern that Mikael couldn't anticipate or repel. It caught him in the collarbone and forced him back against the wall with such force that it knocked the wind from him. Off balance, Mikael flailed, and out of the corner of his eye saw an ornamental blade hanging on the wall nearby. He dove for it, snatched it down, and turned—only to be struck in the groin by Eleazar's frying pan.

Mikael howled. "Greasy mutherfucking asshole!" Holding the knife at the ready in one hand, he snatched the pan out of Eleazar's grip with the other and raised it above his head as if to strike. A long moment passed as Mikael and Eleazar locked eyes. Finally, Mikael threw the pan down, well beyond the magician's reach. This time it landed with a sickening crunch of breaking tile.

"What was that?" called a voice from another room.

Mikael followed the voice and burst into the kitchen. He was disappointed to find Khams there rather than Larch. Khams was wearing a red-checkered apron, holding an electric mixer in one hand and a stick of butter in the other. He dropped the butter at the sight of Mikael wielding the ornamental knife. He looked down at where the butter had landed—squarely on his shoe. "Damn! That was the last of the butter!" He set the mixer on the counter, knelt down, and scooped the butter off his shoe, depositing the mess of it in a mixing bowl. "Don't tell Larch," he said.

"So Larch *is* here," Mikael said.

"Oh, goddam it," Khams said, wincing.

"Where is he?" Mikael asked.

"He is...right here," a familiar, vaguely reptilian voice sounded from the dining room. A moment later, Larch lurched into the kitchen, his eyes sunken and baggy. He was wearing a puffy, linen shirt—Mikael had only really seen people wear such things in swash-buckler movies or at a Renaissance Faire. Larch's hair was a mess, as if he had just rolled out of bed. He had a quilt draped around his shoulders.

"You look like hell," Mikael said as Larch sat down at the small breakfast table.

"You're a vision of loveliness yourself," Larch smiled weakly. "And you can put that down," he gestured at the knife. "It's an eighteenth century Mughal blade, by the way."

"What's the matter with you?" Mikael asked, not dropping the weapon.

"I've been sick," Larch answered.

Icy cold or no, Mikael cursed himself for coming without the Talisman. How could he know if Larch was lying? *Don't be stupid,* Mikael thought. *Of course he's lying.*

"I don't believe you," he said.

Larch shrugged. "Be that way." He turned to Khams. "What are you up to?"

"I thought I'd make a cheesecake—with two layers of graham cracker crumbs and caramel marbling."

"Oh, that sounds decadent. Do you have something a little more substantial and...well, savory I suppose? I mean, for right now? I just woke up and I'm starving for real food."

"A cheesecake isn't real food?"

"Don't take it amiss, Frater. It sounds lovely. But at the moment, I require actual nourishment."

"Cheesecake nourishes the spirit," Khams pointed a spatula at him.

"Undeniably," Larch said. "Is there any soup?"

"None fresh, but we have some Progresso."

"That will do nicely."

"I'll warm it up and pour it over some brown rice for you," Khams said.

"Splendid. Perhaps the Blackfriar would like some as well? I'm sorry, I know your face but I don't remember your name. I only know your first stringers—no offense intended. How is Richard, by the way?"

Mikael ignored the jab. "None for me, thanks." The idea of soup over rice actually sounded wonderful, and it was tempting indeed. But all Mikael could think of was Persephone and her fatal pip. Who knew what Khams might slip into his bowl? *Better to be hungry than poisoned or drugged*, he thought, willing his stomach to be silent and his mouth to stop salivating.

Khams immediately set to preparing the soup. Larch watched him absently for a moment, then turned his attention back to Mikael. "Richard?"

"Richard is...I don't know. He's in Berkeley."

"Ordinarily, I have no great love for the clergy—"

Khams leaned over and whispered. "His father was a priest."

Mikael blinked. "He was?"

"The next person who mentions my father will wake up to find a cluster of Gunther demons gnawing on their femurs," Larch growled.

Mikael had rarely heard a voice charged with such venom. Both Khams and Eleazar looked away, and Khams pretended to be whistling.

Mikael haltingly continued. "He...uh...Richard called Brian yesterday, from the police station, and he seemed fine. But anything can happen over there."

"Hell of a thing," Larch said.

Hell of a thing that you fucking caused, Mikael thought. "Larch, look, I'm sorry if you're not feeling well, but...it doesn't do any good pretending you aren't behind this whole thing. Thousands of people are dead because of what you did. Doesn't that bother you at all?"

"My dear, I have absolutely no idea what you are talking about. And put that thing *down*." Larch pointed at the ornamental blade with his formidable chin.

Mikael slid the blade into his back pocket. "Like hell you don't. We also know what you're up to in the sephirot."

Larch bunched his eyebrows in a display of distaste. "What an entertaining notion. Just what *am* I up to in the sephirot?"

Mikael faltered. He knew that Larch was messing around "up there," Brian had said as much that morning. But he didn't know Larch's endgame. He couldn't even guess at it. "We know you're... putting them out of balance. First the fighting—everybody arguing with their partners. And now the lying." He leaned in toward Larch. "It's not like we're not paying attention."

"And I'm flattered that you think I had something to do with such...cosmic disturbances. But as you can see..." He raised and lowered his quilt-covered shoulders. "I have not been in prime condition for a few days."

"Look, I can't speak to that. Lots of us knock back a dose of DayQuil and power through when we're under the weather. I don't know if you're sick or not, and I don't care. I just want you to..."

"To what?"

"To stop it."

"To stop what?"

"Whatever it is you're doing."

"Listen, Blackfriar—what was your name again?"

"Mikael."

"Thank you. Listen, Mikael, I'm going to play along with you. Let's assume for the moment that everything you just said is correct."

Mikael nodded.

"So what?" Larch asked.

"What do you mean?"

"I mean, let's say I *don't* stop. What do you propose to do about it?"

Mikael blinked. He hadn't thought this far ahead. What *did* he expect to do about it? What leverage did he wield over Larch? None that he could think of. His eyes betrayed his desperation.

"I mean," Larch continued, "do you plan to report me? To whom? To the police? 'Hello, officer, there's a renegade magickian mucking around up in the sephirot.' That's the kind of 911 call that can get you prosecuted for frivolous reporting. 'Please send an FBI agent, I have the person who started the East Bay disaster. He's wrapped in a quilt in his kitchen in the Castro. He has a cold and he's eating cheesecake.'"

"The cheesecake won't be done until tomorrow," Khams noted.

Larch ignored him. "No? Perhaps you plan to call the Ministry of Magic? Good luck. *There is no fucking Ministry of Magic.*"

Mikael felt his neck burning as the heat rose to his face. He clenched his fists into tight balls.

"Or perhaps you plan to threaten me somehow? Do you have a gun? No, I can see that you don't. Will you plan some kind of magickal attack? Oh, I forgot, you poor sods don't *do* magick, you only study it. That puts you at a disadvantage, doesn't it?"

Larch stood up and rose to his full height which seemed taller than Mikael remembered. "Just what do you plan to *do about it*?"

"I...I just wanted to..."

"To *what*?" Larch thundered.

"I'm sorry to have bothered you," Mikael said and turned to go.

"Are you sure you won't have any soup?" Khams called after him. "It's hot."

MOMENTS LATER, Larch heard the door shut, and he sank down again into his chair, slouching. "That was unfortunate," he said.

"You do look like hell," Khams noted, pulling a plate of rice from the microwave. "Are you sure you didn't have a mild stroke?"

"I didn't have a fucking stroke," Larch said.

"What was is like? In Hod?" Eleazar asked.

"It was hell," Larch said. "I wasn't like anything I expected. It is sheer, utter chaos. I thought the universe got more chaotic the more wedded to matter it became, but it seems just the opposite is true. I fear my pride has taken a hit."

Khams ladled a measure of soup onto the rice. It began steaming delightfully. "Ah..." Larch said. "That will be just the thing."

"He *could* do something about it," Eleazar warned. "Now that he knows we're here. You just caught him off guard. The Blackfriars are nothing if not...resourceful. Clever."

"No need to pile praise onto peacocks," Larch said.

"Is that a saying? I like that," Khams said, setting the plate in front of Larch.

"When I'm finished here, we must find some new digs. Call Purderabo. He knows people."

"What about the cheesecake?" Khams asked.

"Oh, for Christ's sake, fuck the cheesecake."

Khams' lower lip began to tremble. With jerky, exaggerated movements he undid his apron and threw it on the floor, storming out of the kitchen. A moment later, the front door slammed.

77

TERRY FROZE, water streaming off of him as he hovered, half-in and half-out of the water. The young man's rifle was trained directly at Terry's chest and his wide lips were pulled back in a triumphant smile. Terry looked above the young man's shoulder. The sigil scrap was so close, yet completely out of reach. Even if he lunged up the stairs, there was no way he could fight his way past the man—he was nearly twice his own size, quick, and lanky to boot. But there was nothing else for it but to try. Terry faked left, then pitched himself up and to the right, head tucked down as he rolled onto the deck. He heard an explosion and felt a punch to his shoulder, as if he had just fired a gun. He ignored it and kept moving, diving for cover as soon as the world stopped spinning. Another explosion rang out and a spray of fiberglass fragments caught him in the face. He wiped at his face and drew his hand back covered with blood. He blinked and was relieved to discover his eyes were uninjured.

His pursuer stepped around the corner he was hiding behind. His smile was tempered by anger now, and he raised his rifle again. Terry looked away and squeezed his eyes closed, anticipating the blast, wondering in a split second what part of his body was about to become hamburger. Once more Terry heard an explosion, but to his surprise it sounded too far away. *I'm dissociating*, Terry thought. He opened his eyes just in time to see the young man drop his gun, waver, and pitch forward, nearly falling on top of him.

Terry dodged his falling body and whirled about in time to see Susan lowering a rifle. "What can't she do?" he said out loud to himself as relief rushed through his body. Gunshots were still ringing out right and left, but the battle had largely descended into hand-to-hand scrabbling. Susan held her rifle at the ready and walked slowly and steadily toward him—not cowering, not taking cover—but striding with unhurried confidence, as if she were in a religious procession.

It wasn't until she stepped down onto the deck of the boat that she began to look worried. "Oh my God," she said, dropping her rifle. "Terry, you're hit!"

Terry looked down and noticed for the first time the sizable pool of blood pooling near his feet. "Oh. God," he said. Then he crumpled to the deck.

———

SUSAN TRIED to catch him but succeeded only in keeping his head from hitting the deck too hard. "First things first," she said aloud, scrambling onto the roof of the speedboat. Leaning over, she snatched up the sigil scrap. "Fire!" she said, wondering in an almost panicked state where she could get some. She ran into the cabin of the boat, straight to the pilot's station, and looked around quickly. And there it was. The cigarette lighter, just like she used to find them in cars. She pushed it in and waited. It seemed to take an eternity to heat up. While the seconds ticked away, she looked around for an accelerant. She noted a gas can bungeed into a hold near the stern. She snatched up a coffee cup from the floor and, twisting the lid off the can, poured half a cup of gas. Then she dipped the sigil scrap in it and threw the cup into the water. When she returned to the pilot's station, she found that the lighter had popped out. She pulled it out, enjoying the sight of the glowing cherry of heat at its end and the acrid smell of hot metal. She set the scrap down on the fiberglass floor and touched the lighter to it.

The scrap lit up with a faint "foom!" sound. As the flames rose over it and licked away at its integrity, a distant scream charged the air with momentary venom. Then it was gone, the scrap nothing more than a black twisted fragile thing shuddering on the deck. She stepped on it, and it disintegrated into thousands of individual ashes.

She rushed back to Terry, holding the wound on his chest with one hand, and trying to get him upright with the other. It wasn't working. Fortunately, he came to. "Hold the wound, Ter," she instructed, "as tightly as you can."

"Don't use adverbs," Terry said. He sounded sleepy, delusional. "Everyone hates adverbs."

"Hang in there. Stay awake. Hold that bullet wound! Stand up." Terry did stand but was wobbly. His knees buckled and he would have gone down again had Susan not already thrown his arm over her neck.

Moving slowly, she eventually got him to the side of the boat. An older black man was waiting on the dock with his hand out, ready to help Terry up. Susan startled at the sight of him—he looked like one of the Oaklanders.

"Ma'am, I don't know what happened, or why I'm here, but I'm not gonna hurt you. Let me help you with the little guy."

"Thank you," Susan said, reminding herself that because the scrap was destroyed, the Oaklanders' minds were once again their own. Another man rushed to join him on the dock and between them, they hauled Terry up. This man, too, seemed to be an Oaklander. He was white and dressed head to toe in faded blue—a truck driver perhaps, or a dock worker. He was big and burly and Susan guessed he could probably out cuss her, but right now he was helping. Once Terry was up, she scrambled onto the dock herself, and pressed on Terry's wound as the men picked him up and began to move him to higher ground.

"Ambulance!" Susan shouted. "Someone call for an ambulance!"

Several people had been simply standing around, lost in mid-fight, confused to find themselves standing in Alameda, and even more confused to be holding guns or knives or blood-encrusted scraps of metal.

"Are you all right?" she heard several Oaklanders say to the Alamedites standing near them. A moment ago they were at each other's throats. Now they were rushing to their aid.

"Call for several ambulances!" she yelled. "Look around you!"

Gradually the Oaklanders became aware of the carnage that surrounded them. As if waking from a dream, their jaws dropped, and Susan saw one of them drop to his knees in grief or guilt or some other form of overwhelming emotion at the realization of what they had just been doing moments before. The Alamedites dropped their weapons, one by one, as soon as they realized no one was fighting them anymore. Several people fished out their cell phones and began dialing. Susan knew that she didn't need twenty people calling—one would do, but she also realized that the simple action of dialing a phone was normalizing, a temporary reprieve from the awkwardness and confusion of the moment.

The men set Terry on a level patch of ground and Susan straddled him to get the best leverage on his shoulder. Terry's eyes blinked open.

"Ride the cowboy," he said. His face screwed up in puzzlement. "*You* are not a cowboy."

"No, honey, I'm your best friend in the fucking world."

"Fucking world," Terry repeated.

"Stay with me, Terry," she said. "You're losing blood, so you have to stay awake."

"Blood?"

"You got shot."

"Oh. Well, that's all right, then."

His eyes snapped open and he seemed suddenly alert. "The sigil!" he said.

"It's okay. I burned it. Stay still."

He relaxed but was much more present, more conscious. *A gift of the adrenalin,* Susan thought.

"Thank God," he muttered.

"What were you thinking, Terry?" Susan scolded. "Were you *trying* to get yourself killed?"

"Maybe," he confessed. For the first time she noticed all the lacerations on his face. She considered trying to clean it up, but there would be time for that later. She kept the pressure up on his shoulder. "I think...I think a part of me wanted to die."

"But *why*?"

He looked her in the face and their eyes met for a few seconds. Then he looked away. "Brian and I were together for a long time."

"Almost eight years," she said.

"Yeah. I think I forgot who I was without him. And when I was... just Terry...the alone Terry...I found I didn't like him very much."

"Are you saying you don't like who you are without him?"

He closed his eyes and nodded. "I didn't know that before. But...I do now."

"Oh, Terry." Susan kissed the top of his head. "Open your eyes, honey. I gotta know you're with me."

Terry did. "I like the me *with* Brian a whole lot better. He's happier. He's easier to be around. He's less bitchy—"

"Well, don't get carried away," Susan smiled.

Just then Casey rushed over and nearly slid into them. "Oh, God, is he all right?"

"He'll be okay if we can get him some help, I think."

"The ambulance is coming," one of the Alamedites volunteered.

"Casey, I can't find Dylan," Susan said.

"What?" Terry asked. He tried to sit up.

Susan pushed him back down. "He's missing. The hospital has no record of him checking out or being released or anything. He's just gone."

"Maybe they just misplaced him," Casey said. "That kind of thing happens. Things are a little chaotic right now."

"Hope he doesn't wake up with a lung missing," Terry said.

"What? Why would he have a lung missing?" Susan asked.

"You know, surgical mix-up?"

"Oh, thanks for that. You can lose consciousness again anytime now."

"We'll find him, Susan," Casey said, placing a hand on her shoulder.

"I can't find Chicken, either," Susan said.

"We'll find them, Susan. As soon as the paramedics get here, we'll go looking. We'll find them."

"No. They disappeared at the hospital. I am not leaving Terry's side."

"I'm touched," Terry said.

"I mean it. I'm not letting what happened to them happen to you."

"We'll find them, Susan," Casey repeated.

Susan fought back tears as she renewed her pressure on Terry's wound, her hands crimson and slick with his blood.

78

Maggie washed her hands and then sprinkled some water on her face. She dried it with a hand towel hanging on a nail as she hummed a little tune from her childhood. She looked at herself in the mirror and pushed a straying lock of gray hair back into place. Satisfied, she opened the bathroom door.

She crossed to the kitchen, but Brian wasn't there. "Brian?" she called. It didn't take long to search the rest of the apartment. He was gone. "Aaron's balls," she swore, and she reached for her coat and hat.

As nimbly as she could manage, she descended the steps to the street and looked both ways. There was no sign of him. She shook her head and turned left, the direction from which they had earlier come.

"Lord, give me patience," she prayed aloud. She waddled as fast as she could. When she reached the intersection, she looked both directions—there was Brian, several blocks away, off to the right. "And thank you for decent eyesight, even after all these many years." She trudged after him.

Despite her best efforts she was not able to gain on him, but at least she wasn't losing ground, either. She could see him walking a block or two ahead of her. "So this, Jesus, is one of those kettles of fish people are always talking about," she continued. "And if you care about your worlds, you'll do something about it. If you don't, then I suppose we'll all just wither away and die because some bloody magickian has authority issues left over from adolescence. Is that what you want? Well, don't mind me, love, they're your fookin' worlds."

She was panting now and noted with relief that he'd stopped. He appeared to be simply staring. He'd reached the edge of the greenbelt and seemed frozen in place, gazing at the zayin. She was well and truly tuckered when she pulled up next to him. "Gettin' all hot and bothered starin' at that thing?" she asked, her cockney accent more pronounced since she was tired.

"Maggie, I'm…" but he didn't finish his sentence. "I have to do something."

"Like what?" She put a hand on the brick wall of the building beside her, steadying herself. "Your shoelaces are untied, dear."

He looked down and swore. As he knelt, he seemed to finally see her. "Maggie, are you all right?"

"I'll be all right, love." She was hyperventilating, she realized. She concentrated on her breath to steady it. "I shouldn't be seen out here with you."

"Why not?"

"You could easily be taken for a magickian, you know. They'll put you in a cell and they'll do the same to me. Conspiracy."

"I'm sorry, I'm putting you at risk."

"Some things are worth risking." She gulped at the air. "Why'd you run just now?"

"I didn't run. I just…I couldn't sit there drinking tea and…do nothing."

She narrowed one eye at him. "*Some things* take planning."

Brian didn't answer. Instead, he looked back at the zayin.

"This is my fault—"

"How in the world is this your fault?"

"I have to fix it."

"How is this your fault?" she asked.

"I know the person who did this," Brian said, his voice sounding slightly hysterical. "I should have been able to stop him."

"Because you're psychic? Because you have a dungeon under the friary where you keep magickal miscreants so they can't offend again? You're talking bullocks."

"I feel responsible," he said.

"Ah, that's different. Now you're talking 'bout feelings. They're mad. They're also ephemeral, love. They'll pass."

"But the danger won't. It's real."

"Yes. It's real."

"And now I'm endangering you. Stay here, Maggie. Pretend you never met me." Without another word, Brian set out across the street, heading straight for the zayin.

"Brian!" Maggie shouted. "Jesus teething on the teats," she swore and set off after him again.

He didn't stop. His gait determined, he strode directly toward the construction machinery gathered around the base of the zayin—bull-dozers and dump trucks and wrecking balls.

"It's not safe, Brian. Brian!" Maggie called to him. "It's not just me in danger. It's you. Listen to me! If they throw you in the gaol and then you won't be able to help anyone or do anything!"

Brain stopped and faced her. "But only the me in this world will be in jail, right? The me in Malkuth will still be in Chava's apartment."

"Well, yes..."

"And the me in Hod will be...wherever I am?"

"Yes, of course."

"Then it's worth the risk." He turned and started walking again.

"But not if you die!" she called.

He stopped again. "What?"

"What are you planning to do? Throw yourself in front of the bulldozer? You think people in this world are as merciful as in your own? You don't know this world, Brian. Efficiency counts for a lot here. Other worlds than ours depend on it. I swear on Peter's testicles they will *run you over*. And then where will you be, eh? You'll be dead. In this world *and in every other*."

Brian blinked. "But...how does that happen?"

"Lots of ways," Maggie was breathing hard again, and she tugged on his arm for support. "Someone gets hit by a bus here in Yesod, doesn't mean they get hit by a bus in Malkuth, but they're dead just the same. In Malkuth they just fall to the floor, dead. Heart attacks. Aneurysms. Spontaneous human combustion, you name it."

"Are you pulling my leg?"

"I'm telling you the truth, lad. Don't do it." She could see that Brian was torn. Desperation flashed in his eyes. Finally, with a look of resignation, he looked down at her and asked. "Do you have another idea?"

"What kind of prophetess would I be if I didn't? Listen, it's going to take them days to sever the link here—this is a big project. But I'm betting your magickian has moved on, which means we don't have time to busy ourselves here. We have to catch up with him and stop him where he is. Water flows downhill and so does grace. We stop him up there, things down here will sort themselves out."

"It will?" He did not sound convinced.

"I'm guessing your bladder in Malkuth is about to burst," Maggie patted his arm. "Get down there and piss yourself silly. Eat something fatty and get some strong black tea in ye. Then meet me in Hod."

"How do I get to Hod?"

"Same way you got here. Except that when you get here, you keep going."

Brian nodded. "And you'll meet me there?"

"Yes."

"But it won't be you—it'll be the you in Hod, right?"

"And the you in Hod, too." She smiled. "Don't worry. We'll recognize each other."

"Will you be okay here?" he asked.

"Love, I'm okay anywhere. I'm the Bat Asher." She pinched his nose.

79

"What do you think we should do?" the shorter man said.

The taller man was driving the van. He looked in the rear view mirror. Chicken waved at him. "I'm sure as hell not going to...obey orders. She's just a little girl, for Christ's sake!"

"But, the boss is the boss."

"He's the fucking mayor—not the pope, not the president, and he's sure as hell not the führer." The tall man looked at his friend. "Would *you* obey an order like that? I mean, if you were alone?"

The shorter man looked out the window. "You should watch your language around the little one."

"Oh, I should watch my language, because it might, what? Harm her somehow? But you wouldn't hesitate to k—to obey an order like that?"

"I don't know, man. I don't know what I would do. I...I follow orders, all right? I'm not a thinker, not like you."

"*I'm* a thinker?"

"Yeah. I mean...yeah. You think."

"Every teacher I ever had would be blowing snot out of their assess laughing at that."

Chicken wished she had some paper and a pencil. She'd like to draw people with snot coming out of their asses. She smiled at the thought of it.

"What are you going to do?" the smaller one asked.

Instead of answering, the man made a quick turn onto McKay.

"What are you doing?"

"There's a park here, by the water."

"You're going to do it, aren't you?" The shorter man's face lit up.

The tall man looked at him and scowled. "No I'm not going to fucking do it, you moron. We're just going to keep her safe."

He pulled up at a small day-use building on the corner. Just beyond the building was a small parking lot and the beginning of a large park. Looming Eucalyptus trees swayed in a ring around a grassy area, while to the south of them six-foot boulders marked the entrance to a beach.

The tall man fished through a large ring of keys. "Okay, little one, come with me."

He opened his door and got out. Crossing to the other side of the van, he opened the sliding door. Chicken hopped out obediently, sporting a playful smile. The tall man led her to the wooden building, which had been painted a deep maroon. He put a key into the padlock on the door, but it didn't seem to work. He tried several more, until eventually, the lock snapped open. The man held the door for her and followed her inside.

After he closed the door he squatted down to her height. His face was worried but kind. "Okay, honey, we're going to leave you here for a little while. I don't know if there's any food in the little fridge, but you can look," he pointed through the doorway at the far side of the room to what must have been a kitchen. "And there's a bathroom, in case you need it. And here's a comfy couch, in case you get sleepy." He slapped the top of a corduroy loveseat. Chicken saw a plume of dust erupt into the air. She smiled encouragingly. "I'm going to lock this door and go away for a little while. Can you stay here and be good until I get back?"

"Okie-dokie." Chicken chirped, trying to look as adorable as possible. She knew it was one of her strengths.

"Good. I'll be back soon." The man tried the switch and a light came on, looking dim in the afternoon sun. He shrugged, smiled at her, and closed the door. A moment later, she heard the lock fasten.

For a few minutes, she looked around her, madly curious about the little house. She was listening to hear the van pull away, but she didn't hear anything yet. Maybe the men were still arguing? While she waited, she went through the door at the far side of the room. There seemed to be nothing else to do, so why not explore the house?

She poked her head into the bathroom and scrunched her nose up at the smell. Definitely something not right there. She went into the kitchen—except it wasn't much of a kitchen. A tiny table hugged one wall, while the other wall held a small sink and some cupboards. A microwave sat on the counter, alongside a stained coffee maker, but there wasn't any stove. A refrigerator was built into the lower cupboards, shorter than her. She opened it and once again made a face at the smell. There was an old carton of milk—very old, given the odor—and a candy bar. She snatched up the candy and unwrapped it. She didn't recognize the brand, but it was covered with chocolate and it had peanuts, and it was delicious.

Chicken heard the van start up and drive away. She wandered back to the front room and peeked through the window. The van was gone, all right. She went back to the kitchen and dragged a chair to the back door. Standing on the chair, she undid the deadbolt. She climbed down, opened the door, and walked out into the park.

No one was in the park, but it didn't occur to her to wonder at that. She didn't really have a destination in mind and kept going farther into the park. She knew she needed to find Aunt Susan or Uncle Terry, but she didn't know where they were. If she met a grown-up, should she trust them? She didn't know. She just followed her nose.

Eventually the park led to some tennis courts. A large, fenced-in area was nearby, but she didn't know what it was for—although there were signs with dogs on them. She walked past this area and started walking past the houses on Otis Drive. She followed Otis for quite a while until she discovered a shopping mall to her right. Ordinarily she would have been plenty hungry, but the candy bar had done its job. Intuitively, she turned left at Park Street and headed for the shops. No one seemed to pay any attention to her. People rushed by, but no one seemed to be actually *shopping*. Most of the stores were closed, and some were boarded up. At Tilden, she noticed how the street jutted off at a strange angle, and this appealed to her. She followed it, and it led directly to a grocery store. She went inside and noted once again that almost no one was shopping. It was open, though, and that was a good sign. She went first to the bread aisle and grabbed a box of chocolate donuts. Then she went to the aisle for household items and found a notebook. She had to look for a while to find one without lines, and it was heavier than the others, but that was okay. Then she found some pencils.

How will I sharpen them? she wondered. She spied a small sharpener above her, but she couldn't reach it. Standing on tiptoe, she swung the pad of paper, but she still couldn't reach it. She threw the box of donuts at it. At first she missed, but the next time she hit it— but it didn't fall down. It took eight more direct hits to knock it off its peg. By that time the donuts were in rough shape, so clutching her paper, pencils, and sharpener, she wandered back to the bread aisle and exchanged the battered box of donuts for a new one. Then she simply walked out into the sunshine.

The grocery store was near a river—at least it looked like a river. Chicken sat down and opened the donuts. She took a huge bite, and realizing no one was watching her, shoved the whole thing into her mouth. Then she choked and spit it out. Taking it more slowly, she ate two of the donuts before opening her pencils.

Unwrapping the sharpener, she held it awkwardly. She fitted one of the pencils into it and twisted. Nothing happened. She pushed the pencil in harder and twisted. A thin wisp of wood began to spiral out of the slit in the top. She kept at it and was amazed at how much work it took to sharpen a pencil from the beginning.

Once she achieved a point to her pencil, though, the pleasure of drawing took over. Every now and then she'd help herself to another donut. She'd eaten six of them by the time she was satisfied with her drawing.

She held it up proudly and smiled at herself. Then she turned it over and started drawing again. When the box of donuts was finished, her drawings were, too. She stood up and brushed the dirt off the butt of her jeans. She picked up her paper and shoved her pencils and sharpener into her pocket and started walking.

A copse of trees led down to the water, but Chicken couldn't see a way to walk through it, so she kept right, skirting the edge of the water's bank along the road. After a while she heard gunshots. She ducked and her pulse began to pound. Images of the shootings a few days ago rushed through her. In her mind's eye, she saw her mama shot all over again—saw the brains explode from her head, saw her crumpled to the ground, saw her *padre* holding the gun, his chest heaving and his low-necked t-shirt splattered with red. He had looked excited and confused all at the same time. Then she opened her eyes and remembered where she was. A little wobbly on her feet, she stood again and continued walking.

After a while she came to a parking lot. Sirens were getting closer, and she might have been shy of them except that she saw a familiar form. "Aunt Susan?" she asked out loud.

As she got closer, she saw Aunt Susan riding Uncle Terry. It might have been fun, but no one looked like they were having any fun. Then Uncle Terry saw her and smiled. Chicken smiled. She walked up to Susan and poked her on the shoulder. Susan whipped around. For a moment, it didn't look like she believed Chicken was really standing there. Then she was nearly knocked off her feet as Susan embraced her and began to cry.

Casey dove for Terry to keep pressure on his wound. The ambulances were in sight now, barreling toward them, plumes of dust rising from the dirt road behind them.

"Oh my God, oh my God," Susan said, her mouth kissing Chicken's hair over and over. "Are you okay?"

Chicken nodded. "I think Uncle Dylan needs you," she said.

Susan pushed her to arm's length and gazed at the little girl's face. "Chicken...do you know where Dylan is?"

She smiled and gave a slow, proud, exaggerated nod.

"Where?"

Chicken opened her sketch pad and tore off the top sheet, handing it to Susan.

"Right here."

80

RICHARD ROLLED to the side a split second before the handgun erupted. The explosion made both children nearly jump out of their skins, and the recoil tossed the gun out of the girl's grip and sent it spinning into her forehead. It hit so hard Richard heard it connect with a sickening "thuck" sound. The girl wailed as much from surprise as from the pain. Richard looked up and saw a gash on her forehead beginning to seep.

Richard lunged for the gun and thrust it through the fold in his cassock, bringing it to rest in the small of his back, held snugly in place by his belt. Then he breathed deep and turned his attention to the children.

"It's okay," he said in as soothing a voice as he could muster. "I'm not going to hurt you. No one is going to hurt you now. I promise."

"Who are you?" the boy asked. The older girl was still clutching at her wounded forehead and sobbing hysterically.

"I'm a friend of your mom's...and dad's." Richard squeezed their shoulders reassuringly. "Your mom is just outside. Do you want me to take you to her?"

The boy nodded. He even had the girl's attention now. She didn't respond, but she stared at him.

"My name is Richard," he said, getting up. "What's yours?"

"Mike," said the boy.

"Isn't that a coincidence?" Richard said. "One of my best friends is named Mikael. It's a good name."

Mike beamed at that.

"And what's your name?" he asked the girl.

"Her name is Sophie."

"Good to meet you, Sophie."

"Why are you wearing a dress?" Sophie asked.

"It does kind of look like a dress, doesn't it?" Richard said. "But it's actually called a cassock, and boys have been wearing them for a thousand years. It's my uniform...for my job."

"What's your job?" Sophie got to her feet, and Mike was already heading for the door.

"Uh...Mike, hold up, please. It's still dangerous out there. We need to stick together."

Mike hung back and Richard waited for Sophie to make her way to the door. She seemed stunned, even lost. He didn't blame her for a moment. "I'm a priest," he said. "Like at church."

"We don't go to church," she said.

"Not many people do anymore," Richard said. He noted a hint of sadness in his own voice. "But we're there every Sunday...just in case you show up."

She stopped and her eyes grew a little wider. "You're waiting for us?"

"No, we start on time. But we always hope you'll come." He smiled. She seemed marvelously impressed by this bit of information, and he allowed himself to enjoy it.

At the door, he paused. "Okay, we're going to go out in single file. I'm going to go first, then Mike. Sophie, you're the oldest sibling, so you have to protect your brother from anything that comes at us from behind, okay?"

She looked stunned again. Richard half expected her to ask, "Protect him with what?" but she didn't think that far ahead. She just nodded her assent.

"Good. Let's go." He snatched the pistol from his belt and held it in front of him as he whipped into the hallway. He didn't see anyone —at least, he didn't see anyone alive. The bodies of Officer Martinez and Mr. and Mrs. Olivo, however, were splayed out on the floor at erratic angles. Richard turned around and faced the children. "Okay, change of plan. I want you both to close your eyes. Mike, grab the back of my cassock and hold on tight. I want you to walk right behind me—"

"With my eyes closed?"

"Yes," Richard said. "With your eyes closed."

"Okay," he said, although he didn't sound too certain about it.

"Sophie, you hold onto the back belt loop in Mike's jeans. Just put your index finger in there and don't let go of it. Okay?"

"You want me to close my eyes, too?" she asked.

"Uh...yes." He thought that went without saying, but he inwardly kicked himself for not being absolutely clear with her. "Okay, eyes closed?"

"Yes," they both answered.

"*Now* let's go," he said, and moved again into the hall. He walked slowly, making sure the children could keep pace with him. The last thing he wanted was for one of them to trip and fall face first onto a dead body. With deliberate steps he made his way to the foyer, then veered right, hugging the wall to avoid stepping on Evans. Then he passed through the front door and onto the porch. He let out a sigh of relief.

"Those people were dead," Sophie said. "The Olivos."

"Sophie, you opened your eyes," Richard said, the disappointment evident in his voice.

"They were mean to us," she said.

"They were...not themselves," Richard said. "If you had met them in a different time, like last week, you might have liked them a lot more."

"I don't think so," Sophie said.

"Can I open my eyes now?" Mike asked.

"Yes. Come on down the stairs. This is my dog, Toby."

Toby wagged profusely, and Mike instantly plunged his hands into the dog's fur.

"We're going to see your mom. She's right..." Richard looked up to where he had left Rachel on the lawn. She wasn't there. "Oh, shit."

"Language," Mike said. "You have to do dishes on a night it's not your turn."

"I guess I'm going to be doing dishes every night," Richard said, but he wasn't really paying attention to the exchange. His mind was spinning around how Rachel could possibly have left her children. Perhaps she had gone back into the house? She wasn't feeling well, after all. "She's probably at home," he said. "Let's go see." The last thing he wanted was for them to see the remains of their dad on the floor. It was true, he had a sheet over him, but kids are curious. The sheet wouldn't shield them for very long.

When they got to the house, he stood in the way of the stairs. "It's still not safe. Wait right here. I'm going to go in and see if your mom is there. I'm sure she is. Then we'll...we'll go up to your rooms and get you cleaned up. Okay?"

They looked uncertain, but nodded. He gave them a reassuring smile and took the steps two at a time. "Rachel!" he called as he ran into the living room. No one. He ran into the kitchen. There was Ben, bleeding through the sheet, but no Rachel. He turned and ran toward the stairs, yelling as he ascended them. Within seconds, he had searched the second floor. Rachel was nowhere to be seen.

"Damn," Richard breathed. Then he scrambled down the stairs again.

"Okay, kids, here's what we're going to do," he began as he burst through the door. But he didn't finish his sentence. The children were gone. So was Toby.

81

"UNCLE DYLAN IS RIGHT HERE," Chicken pointed at the center of her drawing. Susan held it up and saw what looked like a maze at first, but as she studied it she could see the outline of a building—one that must be very large, given the number of hallways Chicken had indicated. To one side was a sketch of a hairy man with one eye, tied to a bed. His mouth was open in an angry scream. Susan's eyes widened as comprehension dawned.

"This is where Uncle Dylan is right now?" Susan asked.

Chicken nodded with huge, loopy motions of her head. She was giggling, enjoying the impact of her drawing on Susan. Then Susan looked away. "I can't leave Terry," she said. "You and Dylan disappeared, and I can't have Terry disappear, too."

"I'll stay with Terry," Casey said. "I promise I won't leave him."

"But you're one of—" Susan caught herself in the middle of her sentence.

"What?" Casey snapped. "One of *them*? Is that what you were going to say? As in 'one of those people from Alameda'?" She looked hurt and angry, and Susan didn't blame her.

"No, I—" She stopped before she could blurt out something that wasn't true. It was so tempting right now, so easy. She struggled with what to say. Finally, she met Casey's gaze and forced herself to say, "Yes. That was what I was going to say. You are from Alameda. And right now I don't know who I can trust."

The heat left Casey's eyes and she deflated a bit. "It's okay. I get it. We're all pretty traumatized. But Susan, I wouldn't betray you. I really like you. And...at some point you have to trust *someone*, don't you?"

Susan wasn't sure what to say to that. The sirens had stopped and she saw the paramedics running toward them. "You promise you won't leave his side?"

"I promise," Casey looked directly into her eyes.

Susan believed her and relaxed. "Terry, I have to go. Dylan...I don't know what's happened to Dylan, but I have to find out. I don't want to leave you, but Casey says she's going to stay with you. I guess I'm asking you if that's okay?"

Terry opened his eyes. "One little lapse in judgment, and look what happens."

"What do you mean? If you don't want me to leave you, I—"

"I'm not talking about you, I'm talking about me."

"Terry, surely you don't think all of this is somehow your fault?"

He looked away. "It must be. I fucked up, and the whole world went to hell."

"Oh, honey." Susan kissed his cheek. "It only *seems* that way. But it *isn't* that way. You can't trust—" She stopped herself again, wondering at the words that were about to leave her mouth, and the flood of thoughts that followed. *You can't trust yourself right now. You can't trust anyone. You can't trust anything.*

She stood up as an ambulance arrived, followed by several more. Teams of paramedics jumped out and ran toward several of the people lying on the ground. One of them headed toward them and dove for Dylan's shoulder, taking over for Casey. Casey stood up and put her arm around Susan. Chicken clung to her leg. Susan watched as they put Terry on a gurney and loaded him into the back of the ambulance. Casey squeezed her hand, then climbed into the ambulance beside him. One of the paramedics started to complain, but she tore into him and he relented. Susan smiled at her ferocity. She looked down at Chicken. "I'm going to choose to trust her. What do you think?"

Chicken grinned at her. "Okie-dokie."

"I'm beginning to wish you never heard that phrase." Susan walked a couple of steps and knelt. She picked up a 12-gauge bolt action shotgun and yanked back on the bolt. A shell was loaded, and she could see the outline of at least one more behind it. She slung it over her forearm and held her left hand out to Chicken. "Let's go get your Uncle Dylan, sweet-pea."

82

"So what is with the squirrel?" Madison asked as they marched deeper into the Berkeley hills.

"Lots of squirrels around here," Marco noted. "I think it's the dominant species."

"Did you notice that it was a *white* squirrel?"

Marco looked up at the standard leading their procession. It was actually more of a light gray, but he took the point. It sure wasn't brown.

"What's your point?" Cain asked.

"Are you napping, Cain?" Madison asked. "You see any black or brown faces under them white hats back there?"

Cain looked over his shoulder.

"You see that?" Madison said to Marco. "This is what I put up with every day at the BPD. Cracker didn't even *notice*—that's how white he is. You noticed though." It wasn't a question.

Of course he had noticed. Marco's skin crawled as the sun descended and the breeze began to cool. The Berkeley Hills were an impossible maze of crazy-quilt streets that snaked and intersected randomly. Marco was turned around and lost almost as soon as they'd set out. Only the setting sun provided a landmark for him to orient by—that and the steep grade of the hill that pointed always east—or would until they crested it. But it was a big hill and they hadn't gone nearly that far yet.

They turned left onto a cul-de-sac that contained only three very large houses sitting on almost impossibly large lots for this neighborhood—a filthy rich enclave in an already rich area.

"I see fences," Madison said, his voice dripping dread.

Marco saw what he meant. Straddling the property of two of the large houses was a warren of incongruous chain-link fencing. Marco could make out several discreet "yards" portioned off by the fences, and several large tents and lean-tos inside a couple of them.

In front of one of the houses the squirrel standard came to rest, and the little man leading them barked some orders to the sergeant-at-arms, who called the militia to attention. The man gave the three of them a respectful nod and said, "Right this way, please." He led them to the side door of a garage, which had the emblem of the squirrel painted over the door. This squirrel wasn't hanging, though. Instead of macabre, this was cartoonish. This squirrel was holding an acorn in its little hands and winking.

"That's one cute squirrel," Madison pointed at it.

"Shhh...keep the Eddie Murphy routine to yourself, unless you want to be lynched next to that other squirrel," Macro whispered.

"Ain't no routine, boss, this is just me."

Marco began to wonder for the first time whether it might be safer to be *separate* from the officers rather than stay with them. He certainly did not want to suffer for Madison's inability to hold his tongue. Just then he had a thought. "The talismans I gave you—"

"The what?"

"The scraps of paper with the drawing on it."

"Oh, yeah, what about it?"

"This is just a feeling, but I think it would be best if you put it in your mouth."

"What?"

"Just do it."

As discreetly as possible, Marco withdrew the paper from his own pocket and rolled it in one hand. *All those years rolling joints have really come in handy*, he thought. He pretended to cough, and when he brought his fist up to his mouth, he inserted the talisman, stashing it between his lower lip and his gums. He couldn't see if the others had done what he told them, but he hoped for the best.

"Please, come in," the small man said to them with exaggerated courtesy as he swung the door inward. "This is where we welcome all our guests. We call it Ellis Island West. It's where we determine who is granted citizenship in the Republic of Stan and who needs to be quarantined."

"Why would anyone need to be quarantined?" Marco asked as he entered. He found himself in a normal, semi-finished garage. Kayaks hung from the ceiling, and a work table ran the length of the far wall. The shiny tools hanging from hooks looked like they had never been used. Marco even saw a tag on one of them.

Filling the center of the room were two folding tables, nine feet by three feet with faux laminate tops. Sitting behind the tables were militia personnel, a man and a woman at each. Stacks of paper nearly obscured them, but they looked up as Marco and the officers entered and waved them over.

"Oh, well, there's lots of unexplained phenomenon going around, or have you not noticed?" the short man answered. "You might be infectious."

"Infectious how?" Cain asked as he entered the room. The small man shut the door behind him and motioned for them to move toward the first table.

"Well, there are several signs of infection: uninhibited violent tendencies, for instance. Or ideological liberalism—advocating for 'multiculturalism' is a sure sign of infection. Tolerance for, or God forbid, open *advocacy* of the homosexual lifestyle is a sure sign. It could also manifest as sympathy for the nanny state."

"We get the idea," Madison said huffily.

"It is precisely this sort of infection that got Berkeley into all this trouble in the first place," the little man explained. "But I will leave you in the capable hands of our Immigration Team. I wish you a pleasant stay in the Republic. Pax Stan!" he shouted.

"Pax Stan!" the four behind the tables responded robotically.

A model-handsome young man motioned to Marco, bidding him approach. Marco walked up to the table.

"Name?"

"Marcus Aurelius Sawyer."

The young man cocked his head. "How do you spell your middle name?"

Marco spelled it for him.

"Cool," the young man said. "I've never heard that one before."

Marco rolled his eyes.

"It *is* a fuckin' weird name," Madison opined.

"Uh-uh! Language!" the young man wagged a finger at Madison. "Foul language demeans your race and ours. We won't be hearing any more of *that* while you are guests of the Republic."

"Wouldn't want to demean anyone's *race*," Madison spat.

"Please put all effects here on the table, in this box," the young man didn't look at Marco as he spoke. The young woman next to him quickly folded a file box and pushed it in front of him. "Empty your pockets. The case you're holding, any hats or gloves—everything in the box, please."

Marco clutched the Liahona case more tightly. There was no way he was going to part with it. "Um...this is just a compass—it has sentimental value."

"We won't lose it. Everything is being catalogued and stored. Everything will be returned to you when you clear quarantine or are deported."

"Deported?" Marco asked. "To where?"

"Back to California, I assume," the young man shrugged.

"Could I be deported now?" Marco asked.

"Not my decision," the young man said. "Now, please. Let's not have any trouble."

"Wouldn't want any *trouble*," Madison snorted from behind him.

Reluctantly, Marco set the Liahona case in the box. He clenched his jaw as he withdrew his hands.

"Pockets."

Absent-mindedly, Marco put the contents of his pockets in the box, including his wallet. His mind was fixed entirely on the Liahona, however. He stared at it as the young woman snatched the box back and put a cardboard lid on it. She whisked it off the table and began to fold another box.

"Please step down to the next table," the young man said, writing on his clipboard.

Marco moved to his right until he stood in the center of the next table, where another young couple sat. They were also fit and attractive. He hated them already.

"Please remove your clothes and put them in this box." The young woman seemed to be calling the shots here. The young man finished folding a box and pushed it toward Marco.

"Now, please," the young woman demanded, reaching for her sidearm.

Slowly, Marco began to unbutton his shirt. As he undressed, the young man laid out a pair of white paper coveralls, the kind of disposable gear that painters often wear. Marco nodded. That made sense. Plenty of hardware stores would have these, and perhaps some of the citizens of the Republic were painters and had a supply? He pulled off his pants and rolled them up, placing the roll in the box. Then he put on the painter's overalls, pulling the cheap plastic zipper up to his throat.

"Wrist, please," the young man said. Marco held out his right hand. "Other wrist, please." Marco held out his other hand. The young man fastened a wristband around it. A number had been scrawled on it in magic marker—J367.

"This way, please," the young woman indicated a door on the other side of the three-car garage. Marco stepped toward it and through it, finding himself in a fenced yard. An armed militia member waved him through and he obeyed, walking toward a chain-link gate.

As he passed through, a flash of red caught his eye. Looking up, he saw an enormous sigil spray-painted on the upper half of the house. The roof was covered with solar panels, shining gold in the late-afternoon sun. And at the pinnacle, where the roofs came together at a "V," he saw a flapping scrap of paper.

83

BRIAN OPENED his eyes to find a bright orange sky presiding over utter chaos. He saw something moving toward him in his peripheral vision and dove for the ground. A car door slammed into the pavement and skittered away, kicking up sparks as it slid.

"Holy—" Brian began, but he fell speechless as he beheld the scene before him. He was in a small city park. On an ordinary day, he would have thought it a place of extraordinary beauty. There was something strange and inviting about the orange light cast over everything. At the end of the block buildings loomed in every direction, sheer faces of gray concrete and glass ascending for what seemed like miles. Following them up with his gaze, he saw something even larger—an enormous statue of the Greek god Mercury, running in place on a pillar larger than any of the buildings that surrounded him. A caduceus was cradled in one arm, his winged feet in motion. Brian let out a whistle.

But Brian didn't have the leisure to admire it. At one edge of the park, street traffic had stopped cold. Instinctively walking toward it, Brian saw the wreckage of two cars, one of which was steaming. The car door that almost hit him hadn't flown off in the accident, though. The drivers were screaming at each other, yanking parts of their cars off and throwing them at each other. One of them flung a steering wheel like a frisbee. It struck the other driver square in the forehead and he went down like a sack of rocks.

But the noise was coming from beyond the traffic jam. Brian followed it and, turning the corner, found traffic interrupted again, this time by what looked like a massive demonstration. A great crowd of people had gathered, standing on two opposing sides, each side yelling at the other. The tension in the air was electric and Brian sensed it was about to explode into violence. He began moving back toward the park as quickly as he could walk without drawing attention. Then he remembered he was supposed to be looking for Maggie. He scanned the crowd without going toward them, but he didn't see her.

Finally, with one final searching gaze, he began to walk the other way.

"Watch it, Brian, you'll run a body down, dear boy."

It was true. He'd almost stepped on Maggie—this world's Maggie, anyway. She was a bit more slender than the Maggie he was used to. And she seemed to have weathered the ravages of age more gracefully, too. The lines of her face were not so severe, her hands not quite as knotted. Her clerical collar was of the pull-out tab variety rather than the neckband that Anglican priests at home favored.

Even though he'd only left her Yesod version a few hours ago, he hugged her.

"Well, that's awfully familiar," she said, a little taken aback.

"Sorry. I'm just...glad we found each other." He moved his hand around to indicate the scene. "I seem to have landed in the midst of some drama."

"It's not just here, my dear, it's *everywhere*. We've gone babel."

"What does that mean?"

"This is Hod, a place of splendor. I'd take off that Yesod sweater if I were you. Dead giveaway that you're a magickian."

"But I'm *not* a magickian."

She rolled her eyes. "Yes, dear. Anyway, you know about Hod, yes?"

"It's the realm of communication—of art, symbols, representation, things that stand for other things."

"Yes, it's a regular field day for metonymy around here. Ordinarily."

"What's going on?"

"What do you *think* is going on?"

"People are fighting a lot. Just like on earth."

"Earth? Oh, you must mean Malkuth."

"Yes, sorry. It's mostly married couples there who can't get along."

"That would be because of the disturbance in Yesod. That's not what's happening here, although it *is* affecting us. But the fact is, you throw *anything* off balance and people fight. So here—"

"Everyone is lying on ea—on Malkuth. Is that because of…of this?"

"Probably. Representation has broken down."

"So people are misrepresenting things?"

"Exactly. I'm guessing it's manifesting as a compulsion?"

"That's a good word for it."

Maggie chewed on her fingernail. Brain cocked his head, watching her. It was a movement that would have looked natural on a younger woman, but Maggie was ordinarily so confident that it looked disarmingly incongruous. "C'mon, then. Your magickian friend has been busy here. We've got a complete communications blackout. The phones don't work. The internet is down. Radio and TV are out. The newspaper presses have jammed. Not even the ham radios—"

She was stopped in her tracks by a small man about her own age walking toward them with brisk steps. His head was bald, wreathed by two scraps of white hair. His hands were shoved into the pockets of his coat, and the fringes of a tallit dangled below it. His face looked grim. He stopped just shy of Maggie. Without bothering to acknowledge Brian he said, "Ducklings turn sour and fret."

"I know, dear. Brian, this is Aaron."

Brian scowled in confusion. He whispered, "Does he have a last name?"

"Bar Amram, I suppose. You know, Moses' brother."

"What? Aaron, like *the* Aaron? The first *cohen*, Aaron?"

"Yes. Don't get too excited. He's a pain in the *tokhes*."

The old man narrowed his eyes at her. "Corpuscular snid!" he yelled.

Maggie put her finger to her lips, shaking her head.

"As I was saying, not only have all of our means of communications gone out, language itself has completely broken down. That's what's filtered down into Malkuth as misrepresentation. Here it's full-on confusion of language."

"You mean, no one can understand each other?"

"Nope. In order to communicate, people have to agree on what words represent. If no one agrees—"

"No one communicates." Brian whistled, and stood up as straight as his hunched back would allow.

"It's the Tower of Babel all over again, only this time with inter-dimensional repercussions," Maggie added.

Brian leaned down to her again, "So how is it *we* can understand each other?"

"I don't know that, dear. Maybe because you're not *from* here, and maybe because I always tell the truth. I suspect that's why *he's* here. He probably thinks I can *do* something."

"And can you?"

"I'm doing it. I'm here to meet you, remember?"

Brian felt strangely honored by her words but also humbled since he had no clue what he could possibly do.

Maggie reached out and grabbed Aaron's hands. She raised them up, moving them in opposite directions, as if she were forcing him to do semaphore code. Aaron snatched his hands away from her, but his countenance brightened as understanding dawned. He pointed to the ground.

"Here," Maggie translated the charades.

Then Aaron stood stock upright, throwing his right arm toward heaven, as if it were holding something thin and round, like a rod. His left hand extended toward the ground, pointing at it with his index finger.

"What does *that* mean?" Brian asked. The crowd behind him roared. He looked over his shoulder to see two middle-aged women in the midst of a catfight, while in the background, a sea of people roiled with confused rage. So much was going on it was hard to look away, but he forced himself to do it.

Maggie cocked her head, thinking. Aaron, frustrated, renewed his pointing with force. Suddenly a gear in Brian's brain clicked into place. "It's the stance of the Magician, the 'I' card of the major arcana in the Rider-Waite tarot deck."

"Of course," Maggie nodded. "The magickian has been here. We know that, dear. Yes." She nodded vigorously.

Aaron moved his right hand back and forth quickly, then pointed at the ground.

"Not here." Maggie thought out loud. "The magickian *was* here, but now the magickian is *not* here. The magickian has moved on?"

Aaron nodded. Brian wasn't sure who actually understood what, but they seemed to be making progress. There was an explosion behind them, and Brian struggled to keep his feet. Maggie and Aaron fell into one another and clung to each other reflexively. Brian whirled back to face the park and saw that one of the cars in the accident was ablaze, bright yellow flames reflected off the glass of the buildings, rising to become one with the orange sky.

Maggie stepped away from Aaron again, urging him with her eyes to continue. Still continuing to ignore Brian, he pointed at Maggie. Then he pointed at the sky.

"Translation?" Brian asked.

"Oh, that's easy. 'Stop dicking about in Hod. The damage has been done and the fucking magickian has moved on.' He's saying, 'Hie yourself to Netzach—and step on it.'"

84

SUSAN FELT ODDLY CALM as she and Chicken traversed the island. It took about an hour to walk from the east side parking lot where Terry had been shot to the west side complex near the old naval shipyard. Even though it was nearly dark, Chicken had made only one wrong turn, and she had quickly righted herself. For the rest of the journey the little girl took point, leading confidently toward the place she had last seen Dylan.

At first Susan wasn't really paying attention to their surroundings —finding Dylan was the sole thought in her mind. But as they walked, and as the sun grew higher and the autumnal air began to warm, Susan began to bask in it, to enjoy it. The shotgun became heavy in her hands, and she realized how thirsty she was. As they crossed Webster Street, it occurred to Susan how strange it was that she was walking down a busy city street carrying a shotgun and no one seemed to notice. True, there weren't many people around, but those that were did not bat an eye. *This is the Bay Area, for God's sake*, she thought to herself. *People generally disapprove of guns here.* And yet here she was, and no one opposed or questioned her.

Perhaps it was her grim, determined demeanor. She was not oblivious to it. And she knew she could be a powerful person.

Normally she worked to keep that in check. It was easy for her to overwhelm people. She had discovered as a younger woman how quickly people jumped to a negative opinion of her—as if her forceful nature was all that there was to her, as if she was not also kind and warm and funny.

She knew she was all of those things, and so did the people who loved her. But she had always been a "business first" kind of person, and that was as true now as ever. She slung the shotgun over her shoulders and hung her arms over it until the blood drained out of them from being so high and she felt the prickly sensation in her fingertips begin.

Chicken was no less determined, but her affect was leavened by adventure and playfulness. She led, but sometimes she led as a galloping horse, skipping head of Susan, and sometimes she led as an airplane, arms stretched out like a bomber, emitting an extended raspberry to simulate the engine noise.

When they reached the shipyard, Chicken "flew" directly to a long, connected string of buildings. They might have been warehouses, except that they were smaller. They might have been army barracks, except that they were bigger. Susan got the sense that they had been built without a plan, assembled like a train with a new building added at the boot of the last one whenever they ran out of space.

There were guards at the doors of the end-building. They seemed curious as Susan and Chicken approached them. Susan didn't stop to chat. As soon as they were in hearing range she raised the shotgun to her waist and emitted a ululation that scared even her a little. Their hands went to their side arms, but she blasted a shell high, over their heads. It would be their one warning. Their hands went up. Susan paused by their SUV, Chicken clung to her leg. Susan ejected the spent shell.

"Do you know these assholes, Chicken?"

"Nope."

"Do you care what happens to them, Chicken?"

"Uh...yes. They might have puppies."

"They might indeed, my dear, I hadn't thought of that. Either of you have puppies?"

The color had drained out of both the guards' faces, and perhaps sensing that a proclivity for young dogs might be their only hope for clemency, they both nodded. "Bullshit. Any of you got families?"

"I do," one of them said.

"Any reason why I shouldn't kill your partner here then?"

"Uh..." the two men looked at each other, the apparently single man's eyes grew wide and pleading.

"He cooks a hell of a chili," the apparently married man suggested.

"Here's what's gonna happen," Susan said. "I'm not going to kill you because I love Jesus and he wouldn't like it and I'm more afraid of him than you."

The men nodded, hands still raised.

"I see you got two radios. You're gonna throw those on the ground. Then you're going to throw your pistols on the ground, and any other guns you might have stashed in your socks or underoos, and Chicken is going to collect them. Then you're going to get in this van of yours—"

"It's a Ford Expedition," one of the men corrected.

She ignored him. "—and you're going to go to the east side of the island where there was just a huge gunfight with the Oaklanders. They need help. Nod if I'm making sense to you."

Both men nodded.

"Okay, radios first."

Susan raised the shotgun to her shoulder and took aim as the men removed walkie talkies from their belts and threw them on the ground. Chicken shouted, "Okie dokie" as she ran in and scooped them up, laying them on the ground near Susan's feet.

"Okay, now guns."

Both men unclipped their side holsters and slid their side arms out. Then they gingerly tossed them onto the pavement. Chicken ran up to collect them. Just as she bent to grab them, one of the men lunged for her. Susan didn't blink or hesitate or protest. She squeezed the trigger and the lunging man's head exploded. His body wavered momentarily, then crumbled in the dust.

Chicken hesitated but only for a moment. She scooped up one gun, then moved the dead man's arm so she could get at the other. She ran back to Susan with both guns, dropping them at her feet like a hound presenting a pheasant.

Susan kept the shotgun trained on the remaining guard. "What, asshole? Did you think I wasn't serious? I'm as serious as a day of bad cramps in the heat of summer—but you penis Americans wouldn't know what that's like, would you?"

The man was visibly shaking and did not respond.

"All right, don't piss your panties. You move slow, you get in your fucking Ford Expedition, and you go to the other side of the island without passing Go! or collecting two-hundred dollars. Are we in agreement or do you need more convincing?"

"No ma'am. I got it."

"Then get the *fuck* out of here and have a blessed goddam day."

"Yes ma'am," the man said weakly, tottering toward the SUV as if his legs were made of jelly. He succeeded in climbing into the driver's seat and a moment later Susan heard the engine roar to life. She aimed the shotgun directly at the driver's side window until he backed up and turned off toward the base entrance. The tires squealed as he punched it.

Susan lowered the shotgun, not feeling its weight anymore. She noticed that Chicken was covered with dots of blood and tiny bits of brain and hair. "You okay, little one?"

Chicken smiled and nodded.

"You are either going to turn into a helluva justice warrior or a sociopath."

Chicken smiled and nodded.

"I'm sorry you had to see that. I had hoped that both of those men would live to pet puppies another day."

"I miss Toby," Chicken said.

"So do I, honey-pie. But until we find out what has happened to him, we just have to trust Jesus that he's okay."

"Who's Jesus?" Chicken asked.

"Oh, you'll like him," Susan said. "He's a cheery cuss."

"Cheery cuss!" Chicken repeated.

"Okay, back on the trail. We're here to find Dylan, remember?"

Without another word, Chicken opened the door the men were guarding and held it for her. Susan ejected the spent shell, made sure there was another lined up in the chamber, then followed Chicken into the building.

Once inside, she felt blind. She could barely make out Chicken walking ahead of her, and she willed her eyes to adjust quickly. She knew it didn't work like that, but they adjusted soon enough. The hallways were dark. There were lights, but they didn't seem to be on and she didn't bother to test any of the switches as they passed.

They walked the length of one long building in silence. Then Chicken ducked to the left, and Susan realized that the connection between one building and the next was jerry-rigged in such a way that the passage doglegged. Before Chicken could turn right into the next hallway, Susan called her back. Placing a hand on the girl's head, Susan directed her behind her as she hugged the wall near the corner. Placing one eye to the wall Susan edged it to the corner and beyond. No one.

"Okay, it's clear. Let's go." Stepping around the corner they resumed their hunt.

They passed what seemed like endless doors on either side. Susan couldn't guess what the purpose of this building had been in its heyday. Offices? Storage? Classrooms? Who could know?

At the end of the building was a door with privacy glass set into the top half of it. Chicken paused before it and held her forefinger to her lips as she pointed to it.

"In there?" Susan asked.

Chicken nodded.

"Okay, behind me," Susan said. Holding the shotgun against her arm she raised her meaty thigh as high as she could manage it. Then she kicked at the door with every ounce of force she had.

85

RICHARD SPUN AROUND WILDLY, almost losing his balance, hoping to catch a glimpse of either children or the dog. "Mike!" he shouted. "Sophie!" He heard nothing but the breeze and the distant crack of gunfire. "Toby!" Nothing.

He felt his knees begin to buckle, and a cold sweat broke out around his neck. He nearly fell down the steps and steadied himself against the porch rail. "O Jesus, what do I do now?"

As if in answer, he heard a vehicle behind him. Turning, he saw a flatbed truck rolling slowly down the middle of the street, followed by several beat up cars. As the truck got closer, he heard distorted music playing from large, boxy stereo speakers clumsily fixed to the roof of the truck.

Transfixed, he wandered out to the street to get a better look. The truck stopped, and Richard's mouth gaped. On the truck was an altar, an upside down pentagram fixed on one side, centered tastefully. Behind the altar, slightly elevated, was a chair. No, it was more than a chair, he realized. It was a throne. And on the throne, sipping from a silver goblet, was a young man—perhaps thirty-five? His hair must have been dyed black, because he had rarely seen such a deep, jet black in nature—although Terry's came close. His sideburns were cut to a point, almost like they were in Star Trek, but even sharper. The effect was striking and slightly creepy. He was flanked by a skinny dreadlocked woman and a much younger man in black jeans and a ripped t-shirt.

The man on the throne was wearing a black ceremonial robe over red velvet and paisley satins. *Very Berkeley,* Richard thought, but there really wasn't much incense and peppermints about him. He was obviously a magickian, but strangely not one that Richard recognized.

"You look like a priest," the man said, holding his goblet forth.

"I am," Richard said. "You look like a magickian."

"What a good guess," the man smiled.

"I'm looking for two children," Richard said. "A girl about seven, and a boy about five."

"Yes, our advance scouts found them. They're safe. For now." He grinned broadly, revealing several blackened teeth.

Good God, thought Richard. *How clichéd is that? Magickians and deplorable oral hygiene.*

"Did you pick up my dog, too?"

The young man feigned a sorrowful response. "Oh, dear. Did you lose your dog, too? You *are* having a bad day."

Richard remained impassive, trying to suss out what kind of demon had the magickian in its grip. Sloth? He certainly knew how to lounge.

"For now?" Richard asked.

"What?"

"You said the children are safe *for now.*"

"Yes. Not to worry." He took another sip from his goblet and held it out to the girl with dreads. She lifted up a box of Merlot and thumbed the spigot, topping off his cup.

"Gosh, I hope you're having Spam and Velveeta for supper, too," Richard commented.

The young man blinked, apparently not getting the joke. "I *like* Spam and Velveeta."

"No doubt. Listen, thanks for keeping the kids safe, but I need to get them back to their mother."

"Blond woman? About thirty-five or so?"

"Yeah. Her name is Rachel."

"Too bad. She's dead."

Richard's teeth clenched and he balled his fists. "What happened?"

"I can't know everything. My scouts came by, and she rushed out into the streets. They thought she was attacking them." He mimed firing a gun at his temple. "Don't worry. It was quick."

In his peripheral vision, Richard saw two figures approaching. He couldn't get a good look at them without turning his head, and he didn't want to give the magickian the satisfaction.

"You amuse me, Mr. Priest. I think you will dine with us tonight."

"Us?"

"That would be the royal 'us,'" he said.

"Are you a king, then?" Richard asked, raising one eyebrow.

"I am. My subjects call me the Goat King. I am Hell's viceroy."

"Nice," Richard said. "Have you been to Hell?"

The young man narrowed his eyes at him. "Of course not."

"I have. You know what it's like?"

"Non-stop partying and orgies, I imagine," he grinned and the kid next to him gave him a thumbs up.

"It's a joyless military bureaucracy," Richard said. "Endless high-rise buildings, office drones, cubicles, ringing phones, Starbucks—you get the picture. You know what I've never seen even once in Hell? A party."

"I think the priest is having us on," the Goat King said.

"Well, at least you watch BBC-America," Richard said, "so you've got some cultcha."

"You will come with us. And you will amuse us at dinner."

"And if I fail to...amuse?"

"Then I suppose you'll never see those children again. Besides," he waved dismissively. "You don't really have a choice."

One of the two goons behind him grabbed his arms, while the other duct-taped his hands together.

"You may walk behind my palanquin."

"This is a flatbed truck."

"Remember, priest, that I suffer you to live only so long as you amuse me. Onward!" He rapped on the cab and the truck began to roll forward again at parade speed.

"Why are we moving so slow?" Richard asked the goon nearest him.

The man was big, with a red beard and a sizable belly, reminding Richard of a Viking or a motorcycle gang member. On the other side of him was an angular woman who seemed almost impossibly tall. She was sturdily built, but not fat. She just seemed...strong.

"The king wants to greet his subjects. Most of them don't know he's king."

"True enough. I didn't," Richard rocked his head back and forth.

"You see? He needs to get out and meet his people."

"So, by what right is he king, anyway? And just what is he king of, exactly?"

"He rules earth on behalf of our Father Below."

"He rules *earth*? Not Berkeley? *Earth*?"

"He does."

"And he's qualified to be king because...?" Richard let the question hang on the air.

"Because he says he is king, and he is the king, so what he says is law."

"Ah. So, one of those circular administrations."

"You ask too many questions. You really a priest?"

"I am. Are you a magickian, too?"

"Nah. I don't mess with that stuff. I just like to be on the winning side."

"I wouldn't play the horses if I were you," Richard said. "How about you?" he asked the woman on the other side of him as he walked. "Are you into the whole hail-Satan thing?"

"Satan never fucked me," she said.

"Huh. That's cryptic," Richard said aloud. "I'm just gonna leave that alone. Where are we going?"

"We got a camp at the Marina. It's nice. You'll see. We'll get dinner as soon as we get there."

"And what's dinner like?" Richard asked.

"It's different every night," the Viking said. "So far we're still raiding the restaurants out there at the point. Gonna have to move to the grocery stores soon."

"Do you know what demon rules out there?"

"Demon?" The man looked confused. "I don't know anything about demons. I just know the king holds a Goat Mass every night after supper.

"And what happens at this Goat Mass?"

"He makes a sacrifice to our Father Below."

Richard felt a watery chill run down his spine. "Aaaand...just what does he sacrifice?"

The man shrugged. "It's different every night. One night it was a businessman. Another time it was a lesbian. Last night we got a shock-jock from the radio station. It was cool to see a real celebrity up there thrashing around."

Richard had to force his feet to keep moving. "How many in your camp?"

"Couple hundred," the man answered.

"And us...he wants us because...?"

"Because I don't think we've ever seen a priest sacrificed. That would be a hoot."

"And the kids?"

The man shrugged. "Relax. They probably won't do you all on the same night."

"That's supposed to make me feel better?"

"Don't really care how you feel, mister. Or is it Father? Is it Father? 'Cause I want to be respectful."

Richard didn't answer him but forced his feet to move, one in front of the other. His brain was spinning, trying to fathom how he had arrived there, what his mistakes were, and how he could manage to turn this around. "Okay. Leaning on you, Jesus," he whispered. In his mind, he saw his hand slipping into Jesus' hand. He felt Jesus' hand tighten around his own. A feeling of comfort flooded through him. He squeezed back.

Darkness was descending on the Berkeley streets. The shadows lengthened and then took over, creeping into every space, filling the sky behind him. In silence, they walked due west, toward the last glowing scrap of light.

86

MIKAEL'S SHOULDERS slumped as he approached Castro Street. He had been walking aimlessly, lost in thought and occasionally cursing himself out loud. Seeing a Peets Coffee shop, he checked his watch and decided that it wasn't too late for double espresso. The line was blessedly short and before long he found himself sitting in a faux leather Victorian armchair before an electric fireplace, looking out a plate glass window at the citizens of the Castro as they hurried past, some of them laughing, but more were clearly arguing with their companions. The sun was out of sight and the sky glowed a foggy orange-gray, the dropping temperature causing many folks to huddle into their coats.

Mikael glanced at a discarded newspaper on the table in front of him. He leaned over to read better. "China vows to go 100% green," the headline read. "*That* can't possibly be true," Mikael whispered to himself. He turned the paper over. "Presidential candidates promise fair fight." Next to that was a boxed feature that said, "Fanged bat-boy elected to State Assembly." Mikael checked to make sure the paper was the *San Francisco Chronicle* and not *Weekly World News*. It was, the late edition. He shook his head and opened to the second page.

"You know my favorite thing about this time of year?" Mikael looked to his left and saw a man sitting in the matching Victorian chair next to him. He sported an eccentrically ornate mustache and was wearing a black leather civil war cap. His eyes were small and dark, nested beneath large, busy eyebrows that sat like caterpillars on his brow. "The pumpkin spice lattes," he gingerly took a sip from his cup and then uttered a satisfied, "Aaahhhh." Mikael wasn't sure who the man was taking to, but then he addressed Mikael directly. "You look glum. You just catch your lover with the masseuse?"

Mikael smiled sadly, politely. "Everything I have touched today has gone to shit."

"One of *those* days."

"Yeah."

"Well, welcome to the club. My partner and I went to bed fighting last night. I mean, we literally fell asleep *while we were arguing.* Woke up and started into it again."

"Yeah, but everyone's doing that," Mikael said.

"It doesn't make it less icky," the man said.

"No."

"And then, when he came home for lunch, he asked me what I was planning for dinner—I cook, you see—and I was so angry with him from earlier in the day that I...I told him I was leaving."

"Like, leaving him?"

"Yeah."

"Do you want to leave him?"

"Hell no. He's the best thing that ever happened to me."

"So why did you say that?"

"I don't know. I guess I just...wanted to hurt him."

"And did you?"

"Oh yeah."

"And how did it feel?"

He sighed and looked at the plastic lid of his cup. "It was exhilarating—for about five seconds. Then I just felt incredibly sad. But I couldn't take it back."

"And you couldn't back down without your pride taking a hit," Mikael said.

The man's small eyes met Mikael's and then danced away. "Sounds like you've been there."

"More than once," Mikael said.

"You're dressed strangely," the man said. "Are you an Orthodox priest?"

"No, a Blackfriar, Order of St. Raphael."

"Oh, yeah. You're the guys that caused such a ruckus at the Republican Convention."

"That was us," Mikael smiled again, more authentically this time.

"I gave up on God a long time ago," he sighed. Then he said, "Catholic," as if that explained everything.

"We're Catholic, and half of the people in our order are queer," Mikael said. "Plus...well, just look at the Roman Catholic priesthood. Half of them—"

"At least," the man agreed. "But I can't lie to myself or the world, not as a way of life."

"Do you know what the Zoroastrian term for Hell is?" Mikael asked.

"I'm not sure I know what a Zoroastrian is," the man responded, his bushy eyebrows raising. "So no, do tell."

"The House of the Lie," Mikael said.

"Holy shit," the man said, visibly squirming in his seat.

"What?" Mikael asked.

"I think that's what's got me so tied up in knots," the man said. "When I came out, I promised myself no more hiding, no more pretending to be someone I wasn't. No more *lies*."

"Yeah?" Mikael prompted.

"I don't lie to my partner. Not ever. If he's having a bad hair day, I tell him."

"I've heard there's nothing sexier than bad hair," Mikael said.

"Well, there is that," the man grinned. "I lied to him today. It was a stupid lie. It was a lie that could completely destroy our future. And I don't even know why I did it."

"I do," Mikael said, his eyes fixed on some distant point only he could see.

"You do?" the man asked.

"It isn't your fault," Mikael put a hand on his arm.

"It sure feels that way," the man said.

"And you may not even be completely honest with me now—" The man started to protest, but Mikael held his hand up. "But that's okay. That's not your fault either. There's something...going on." Mikael paused, uncertain how to explain things in terms the man would understand or believe.

"What kind of things?" the man leaned over, clearly interested.

Mikael realized he liked this man, and was suddenly fearful of losing his trust. He opened his mouth to say something about a tainted water supply, but he closed it again. "I'm afraid to say."

"That sounds like an honest reply," the man smiled.

"Yeah. But it wasn't my first impulse. See, I think there's something happening that is...not forcing people to lie, exactly, but making it way easier. So easy that it seems better than just saying what's true. It's the same with the fighting."

"What could cause that?" the man asked.

"Well, I'm a friar, so if you ask me I'm going to give you a spiritual theory about that," he smiled apologetically. "But if you ask a psychologist, I'm sure you'll get a different take on it."

The man nodded, apparently satisfied with that. "Do you think it's always like this, and we just don't notice?" he asked.

Mikael cocked his head. "What do you mean?"

"I mean, maybe our first impulse is *always* to lie. Maybe that's just part of our nature, part of our DNA. And maybe we don't notice it because we're lying to ourselves all the time, too."

Mikael nodded, not convinced but impressed. *Augustine would have loved this guy,* he thought. "Maybe so," he said. After all, who knew? It was a less crazy explanation than Mikael's would have been had he summoned the courage to speak it aloud.

"It's time to face the music," the man said. He stood and set his cup aside.

"What do you mean?" Mikael asked.

"I mean time to eat some crow. Time to say 'I fucked up' and let the chips fall where they may."

Mikael smiled sadly. "Going to try to patch things up?"

"Going to try. I might fuck it up royally. I might make it worse. I might say or do something I'll regret, but goddam it I have to *try*. If I don't try...I'll never be able to live with myself. You know?"

Mikael stood up, nodding. He did know, actually. "Can I give you a hug?" he asked.

The man's face brightened and twisted up in an effort not to cry. "Oh, sweetness, I'll take a hug anytime."

Mikael felt the prickly wax of the man's mustache stab at his temple as he embraced him. "Be courageous," he said, although he didn't know where that had come from.

"You know what," the man said as he pulled away. "I am courageous every single day of my life. Why should I stop now?" He nodded resolutely, then turned to go.

Mikael watched him as he cleared the door and disappeared into the street. Mikael knocked back the final slug of espresso and then made for the door himself. "I'm going to try," he repeated. "I might fuck it up royally. I might make it worse. I might say or do something I'll regret, but goddam it I have to *try*. If I don't try...I'll never be able to live with myself."

87

BRIAN OPENED his eyes and found himself facing a wall of people in uniform. It seemed to be a platoon of soldiers. He froze but relaxed a bit when he realized that none of them were pointing a weapon at him. In fact, no one seemed to even notice him. A drill sergeant barked a call, and they turned in formation—almost. Several of them turned the wrong way, and one of them started marching and then scrambled to regain her place. *They're newbies,* Brian thought. *They're practicing.* His adrenaline was beginning to wane now, and he began to study them more closely. They all wore the same gray-green jacket, with red epaulets at the shoulders, but their pants were of different colors. He even saw some dresses descending from the jacket on some of the women, and one of the men was actually wearing a kilt. Several of the smaller people looked like they were swimming in their jackets, and on some of the larger ones they seemed too tight. But whether they actually fit or not, Brian got the impression that they were all profoundly uncomfortable in their uniforms.

Having successfully turned, the regiment was now practicing marching away from him. Satisfied that he was not in any danger, he took note of his surroundings. Looking up, he saw a deep emerald sky at twilight. The light lent everything a greenish cast, including his own skin. He turned his hand over and marveled at it. He noticed it was a little pudgier than his hand normally was. He looked down and realized he was suddenly about twenty pounds heavier than he was in his own world. He felt a little uncomfortable in his own skin.

Looking up he noticed that, once again, he was in a park. But it was a much larger park this time. In the distance, surrounded by forest, he saw another gigantic statue that dwarfed everything else in this world. It was Venus—her eyes looked out on the world without pupils, her face a flawless oval, her breasts small, upturned, and perfect. Brian was sure the marble was white, but the light made her glow with an almost fluorescent green.

Brian had never felt an erotic urge toward women before, but he felt something akin to it now as he stared at her. Not a sexual urge so much as a human urge to embrace, to be embraced. Brian swallowed as he thought of Terry. What he wouldn't give to be held by him right now, to hold his hand, to spoon with him. Loss sucked at his heart, and he felt sick.

"There you are. Let's get moving." Brian blinked and looked around. He had been so absorbed in the statue and his own feelings that he'd completely forgotten about his immediate surroundings. He spied the speaker and smiled. It was Maggie, of course—this world's Maggie. She was shorter, a little plumper—but she looked younger, too. Just as in Hod, her fingers were less mangled by arthritis, she seemed in better health. Brian smiled, for in *this* Maggie he caught a glimpse of how pretty she must have been when she was young. She was also wearing the same gray-green coat the platoon had been wearing.

He walked toward her and embraced her eagerly. As he did so, he felt flooded with feelings. He flashed on the last time he had seen his own mother. He heard the echo of Terry's last shuddering orgasm. His heart ached with nostalgia for breakfasts at the friary. Goose bumps rose up on his arms as he felt the rough wool of Maggie's coat.

"He's here," she said in a whisper, pushing him away gently. "Quickly, put this on." She handed him a coat exactly like her own.

"That looks so military," he noted.

"Frighteningly so," she agreed. "Welcome to Netzach, by the way. This is the place of Victory."

"I guess that explains the uniform," Brian said.

"No, it doesn't. Quite the opposite." She looked around to make sure they weren't being observed. The platoon was now about a quarter of a mile away. In the other direction, Brian could see where the skin of the city began. Maggie walked in that direction. Brian assumed she was leading him back to her apartment again. He wondered if it would be in the same place in this world. *I guess I'll find out,* he thought as he fell into step beside her.

"Have you seen him?"

"You mean the magickian?"

"Yes. His name is Larch."

"I don't care to know his name. Yes, he's here. Can't you tell?"

"Um...I've never been here before, so no. I don't know what's in place and what's out of place."

"Oh. Right." Maggie's English accent was still present, but it was less pronounced here. "Well, your guy certainly knows what he's doing. He had the place all figured out before he got here. He knew exactly how to reach the optimum number of people—did you know he was tech savvy?"

"Uh...yeah. I think he was a computer engineer before he retired to go into full-time ass-holism."

Maggie burst out with a short laugh. She stifled it, bringing her hand to her mouth. "Got to be careful right now. Anyway, he knew how to reach people, and he knew how to play on their worst fears. He's got the whole world—"

"This world, you mean? Netzach?"

"Of course I mean Netzach," she said, a little testily. "As I was saying, he's got the whole world acting very much *not* like ourselves."

"How so?" Brian asked as they reached the lip of the greenbelt and stopped to wait for a "walk" signal to cross the street into the city proper.

"This is a place of rampant creativity and productivity. Netzach is a place where everyone is always busy."

"Doing what?"

"Why, generating novelty, of course."

"Novelty?"

"Yes. Art. Stuff that no one has ever seen before. New combinations, new ideas. This is where we make it. Novelty is God's food."

"It is?"

"What do you think God eats? Cucumber sandwiches with marmite? Candied sweet potatoes?"

The light changed and they crossed the street.

"I...I guess I've never thought about it before," Brian was taken aback. "I don't think of God as needing to eat anything."

"That would be a joyless God, then, wouldn't it?" Maggie asked. "And don't you think it strange that God instilled in us such a joy of eating if he didn't enjoy it himself? No, Netzach is the breadbasket of heaven. We're a whole world of artists, of free spirits—you might even call us 'bohemians.' Which means, of course, that nobody dresses alike, no one acts alike, we're not a place where pattern or routine has much caché. Certainly few people get up very early. You might even call us a little naughty." She jabbed her elbow into his ribs.

"Ow," Brian said reflexively.

"Oh, toughen up," Maggie chastened him.

"So what happened?"

"Your magickian planted a couple of news stories in exactly the right places. *Fabricated* news stories, I might add...at least I *think* they're fabricated. They'd better be. Anyway, he told people that heaven was going to start phasing us out. Everyone was going to be out of a job."

"But if this is where you make God's food—"

"Right. What did they think he was going to do? Stock up on TV dinners?"

As they penetrated the city, Brian looked around. They seemed to be the only people walking together. Everyone he passed looked hard, even angry. Several people glanced at them suspiciously. And all of them, every last one, was dressed exactly alike.

"But people freaked out anyway, because they were told they were going to lose their way of life. So then your magickian friend suggested we start organizing militias, grouping ourselves into regiments."

"That was fast," Brian said.

"Time moves differently in each sephirah, dear. Don't be an idiot."

Brian opened his mouth but then closed it. They reached another corner and waited for the light to change. They were in a neighborhood business district, and everyone seemed both grim and busy.

"So you see the irony of course," Maggie said.

"I do?" Brian asked.

"I certainly hope the Brian in other worlds is brighter than the Brian here," Maggie said.

"Sorry," Brian felt heat rise to his ears. "What's the irony?"

The light changed and they stepped off the curb.

"That we were so afraid of losing our way of life that we abandoned it in order to fight for it."

Brian nodded, understanding. "And...who do you intend to fight?"

Maggie looked at him like he was stupid. "Haven't you been listening? We're gearing up to fight Heaven, of course."

"That's...that's what he wants," Brian said. "He wants to fight heaven." It was both a revelation and at the same time, not at all surprising. Brian vaguely recalled Richard talking about Larch's antipathy for God, even calling him "the enemy." "So he's here to raise an army."

"Yes. An army composed of the last people anyone would ever suspect. Artists. *Imagine.*"

"I doubt they'd make very good soldiers," Brian objected.

"You'd be surprised how disciplined and determined people can be when the things they love most are threatened."

"But they're *not* being threatened," Brian said.

"You think what happened in Hod only flowed downhill? Think again. That was deliberate. He had to sabotage accurate representation there in order to make his false stories fly here. And of course, wiping out civility in Yesod was the cornerstone to the whole plan.

And so here in Netzach we're...well, we're falling apart." Maggie stopped and looked back at where they had just come from. "And yet, it's *still* beautiful."

It was a moment's pause, but it seemed like a slice of eternity. Then suddenly Maggie was walking again, turning right and proceeding up a long flight of stairs set into a hillside. Brian could see houses above them, palatial but definitely residential. "You live here?"

"Don't be daft," she called over her shoulder. "I live in a basement apartment half a city away from here."

"So where are we going?"

She didn't answer but just kept climbing.

"Maggie, if all the...creativity stops here, will it affect the other worlds?"

"Of course! Where do you think creativity comes from? Not from *your* sodden plane."

"I was afraid you'd say something like that. Artists are always saying that their ideas come from somewhere else."

"They come from here, naturally," Maggie said.

"You know, this is reminding me of Process Theology," Brian said.

"Oh yes, it would. Alfred North Whitehead visited in a fever dream about a hundred years ago. Oh, he was a hit." She was panting now, but didn't slow her ascent.

"Whitehead was a *hit*?"

"Everyone wanted him at their parties," Maggie said.

"Wait, how long was he here?"

"Time, dear. The time is different."

"Oh yeah. I forgot."

"He got here and he assumed that this was 'the top.' He thought he was seeing God's 'primordial nature,' as he called it, the repository of all potentiality, the source of all creativity. Really, it was just a party at Rena's. Fucking *great* party. Still, it primed his pump and gave him some important ideas."

Brain was winded now, but they were very near the top. "Where are we going?"

"Tea dear. We're going for tea."

"We just passed a dozen Starbucks where we could have gotten—"

"Don't make me smack you," Maggie said without looking at him. "Because I *will* smack you."

"Right. No Starbucks. And *why* is there Starbucks here?"

"It isn't just the Starbucks," Maggie said, her voice softening a bit. "We're going for tea with *him*. And *he* doesn't frequent the bloody Starbucks."

"Him? Him who?"

She didn't answer but headed across the luminescent green lawn of a city park toward another cluster of what looked like mansions.

Brian had an idea. "Serah," Brian said.

"Yes, dear—" She stopped and looked up at him, her face betraying a mixture of admiration and irritation. "Oh, that *was* sneaky. So you know about that, do you?"

"Yes. I know who you really are." He smiled. "And I'm honored to know you."

"You'll pardon me if I'm not too sure about *you* yet."

"The other Serahs seem to like me better."

"They *know* you better, but they certainly think well of you. Are you an artist?"

"I'm a cook. So...yes, I'd say so."

"So that's in your favor. What's your function?"

"What? Besides cook?"

"Yes. What do you *do*?"

"That's a rather painful subject at the moment. I guess I...I study Torah. And I take care of people."

"That's the same thing," Maggie said.

"It *can* be...but I've known people who have spent their whole lives studying Torah and seemed to completely miss the point."

"That's wisdom." She gave him a smile that seemed genuinely warm. "I think we might know some of the same people."

"What's *your* function?" Brian asked.

"Well, that seems a fair question. My title is 'the Forerunner.' In my youth, I walked before the pillar of cloud and the pillar of fire.

When I walked, the pillar of cloud moved. When I stopped, the pillar of fire stood still. I am the herald of God's glory."

"Wow."

She shrugged. "Eh. It's a job."

"But you also tell the truth."

"It's part of the same job. You can't usher forth God's glory with a falsehood, now can you?"

"So you *always* tell the truth?"

"Oh, yes. It's my super-power."

"What if people don't want to hear it?"

"Oh, they mostly don't, sure enough."

"But what if they *refuse* to hear it?"

"I don't know. That hasn't happened yet."

"In 3500 years?"

"Not once."

She stopped and rubbed her chin, considering. "You know, I'm not sure about this, but I don't think they *can* refuse it."

"I would have thought you'd know how that worked by now."

"You'd think so, yes." She stopped in front of an imposing house, it's eaves supported by twelve large pillars. It sported a circular drive and a regal and idiosyncratic architecture that seemed to be one-part Roman basilica and one-part twentieth century arts-and-crafts bungalow. Many tall, vibrant oaks presided over an immaculate garden that surrounded the mansion. It was an incongruous mutt of a building that shouldn't have worked, and yet somehow it did, managing to be at once both intimate and extravagant. It was also strangely reminiscent of a ski lodge Brian had visited near Yosemite once.

"Who lives here?"

"No one. It's a government building."

"Pretty nice for a government building," Brian's eyebrows shot up.

"Of course it is. This is Netzach. We treasure beauty here." She knocked on the door. "At least we do when our heads aren't wedged permanently in our bungholes."

After a few minutes, the massive door swung inward and a taut-lipped woman dressed in the same military coat they were wearing greeted them. Descending from it was a knee-length maroon skirt. Her golden hair was done up in a tight bun and her shoes were flat, sensible business-wear.

"I'm here to see *him*, dear."

"Of course, Serah. Come in."

Maggie stepped up and motioned for Brian to follow. Brian did, his mouth dropping open at the sight of the foyer. The room was paneled in marble with great exposed beams. A wrought-iron chandelier hung from a massive carnelian dome. Gold pomegranates and deer adorned its rim, alternating with globes of greenish light. A staircase spiraled around the periphery of the room leading to a second floor, and perhaps a third—Brian couldn't tell from where he was standing. Several doors led in different directions. Their host walked off toward one of them, her heels clicking against the marble floor. Brian noticed that even the slightest noise was accompanied by an echo.

"This way please," the woman opened a door—fully twice as wide as most doors Brian was used to, and much higher, too.

"Thank you, Bet," Maggie said. "How is your father, dear?"

"Touch and go, now," she said, a shadow of sorrow passing over her face.

"I'm sorry to hear it. He is a dear. Please give him my love, won't you?"

"I will."

Maggie pressed the younger woman's arm warmly, then brushed past her into the room.

Fully entering the room, Brian realized it was a lot smaller than he had anticipated. It was larger than any room in the friary, but still seemed small in comparison with the foyer. Still, the overhead lamps were bright, the ceiling was high, and there were several comfortable-looking leather couches.

"He'll be ready for you shortly," Bet said, and she closed the door.

"Oh. This is a waiting room," Brian said. "That explains it."

"Yes, dear."

"Who are we waiting for?"

"*Him*, of course. Moshe."

"Moshe? *Moses*? We're waiting to see *Moses*? *The* Moses?"

"Yes, dear. Don't get all star-struck. He's not all that."

Brian's head swam and he felt his pulse spike. He ran his hand across his short hair and shook his head. "Uh...wow. Gonna meet Moses."

"You were always going to meet Moses."

"Yeah, but there's a difference between, 'Someday you'll go to heaven and meet Moses' and 'Moses will see you now,' don't you think?"

Maggie shrugged.

"You've known him a long time, haven't you?"

"I knew him when he was no one."

"What was he like back then?"

"He was like a rabbit—a huge, hairy rabbit. Scared of his own shadow. I once came up behind him and said, 'boo,' and he jumped three feet from Tuesday."

"Really?"

"No, not really. That's Hod talking." She paused, smiling. "That's not true, either. I'm just pulling your leg."

"But you *did* know him."

"Yes, and he was a nervous nelly—I'm *not* joking about that. He was just about to go see Pharaoh for the hundredth time—the biblical account is condensed, I hope you know—and it was time for an ultimatum. Poor bugger was shaking in his sandals. He just kept saying, 'I can't do it, I can't do it,' over and over."

"What did you say to him?"

"Well, that was easy. I told him he *could*."

"But how did you *know* that he could?"

"Oh, I don't know. I just know the Truth about people somehow, remember?"

"Do you know the Truth about me?" Brian asked.

"Of course. I know that you're miserable without him."

"Without Terry, you mean?"

"Don't be thick, dear. Of course I mean Terry. And I also know that you won't be whole until you swallow your pride and forgive him."

"But he betrayed me."

"Oh, boo-hoo." She waved him away. "Grow up. People betray each other every day. It doesn't give you license to abandon them or to nurture your resentment until it becomes gangrenous. You have too much work to do."

Brian's eyes widened. "And what is that work?"

She patted his hand and stood up. A moment later a different door opened and Bet poked her head in. "He'll see you now."

88

DYLAN STOOD up and wiped the sweat from his one good eye. He marveled at his own constitution that was somehow, despite the bitter cold in the room, still determined to sweat. It didn't *feel* like a gift, but he chose to hold it that way. He was relieved to be free of his bonds, even if he was still being held prisoner. Just being up and moving about the room was a degree of liberation. He made a final, careful line with his chalk and then sat back on his haunches, surveying his work. "That's it," he said with a note of satisfaction in his voice. "Uh...we just need a few candles and a nekkid girl strung out on meth, and we got us a genuine magick show."

Milo's dark face flashed with anger. "Girl? You didn't say anything about needing a *girl*."

"Easy boy," Dylan said, holding his hands up and rising to his full five feet, eight inches. He pushed at the pain in the small of his back with his left hand. "That there was a joke. Ah guess you never really met a magickian, have you?"

Milo shook his head.

"Waal, they're like most folk, Ah suppose. You got some that're serious, really workin' it as a path. Hard-workin' honest people you'd be proud to call yore friend. Mah friend Marco's like that—although

Ah do wish he'd stop flirtin' with mah wife, but that's another matter. But then ya got folks who'er drawn to the tradition 'cause they're broken somehow."

"Broken how?"

"Diff'rent ways. But it's usually somethin' to do with power. Magick is power, so it attracts folk who feel like they got none."

"What attracts you to magick?" Milo asked.

"Not a damn thing. Ah'm a shaman, which a another thing altogether."

"But you know it—"

"Yeah, you hang around Dicky for twelve years you'd pick this shit up, too."

"Dicky?"

"Our bishop."

"So you *don't* need a girl on meth?"

"Nope. We're ready."

"You don't need to test anything?"

"Demons don't take kindly to dry runs, gen'rally. If ya gotta disturb 'em, best to do it only once. It's not like they *enjoy* havin' their wills bound."

Milo studied him in the dim light. "Hmm...are you talking about the demon or yourself?"

"You ever think of gettin' out of the henchman business? 'Cause you ken make a hell of a lot more money as a psychotherapist."

"I am *not* a henchman," Milo said through clenched teeth.

"Oh, damn, mah mistake. It's just...yer shore *actin'* like a henchman, so..."

"Why aren't you afraid?"

Dylan laughed. "Of you, Milo? You gotta be kidding me. On mah off days Ah've faced demons that would eat you fer breakfast an' still be hungry."

"Well, I guess we'll see about that in a minute."

"Ah guess we will."

"I've texted the Mayor. He's close by."

"Ah'll make some final adjustments, then. You got them candles?"

"In that box, along with some glass holders," Milo pointed.

"Fancy," Dylan said. He opened the box and took out a smaller box of tapers. He began to set them into small, disc-like holders until he had eight of them. Taking two at a time, he moved them to the six points of the Star of David he had chalked out on the cement floor of the building. He set another candle in a circle in the middle of the star, and one in the tip of the point facing west.

"Isn't this supposed to be a five-pointed star?" Milo asked.

"Oh, 'cause yer an expert in the *Clavicula Salomonis Regis* now? Or did you just see that on TV?"

"*Supernatural*, actually."

"Uh. That's a fun show. But no, dude. Don't trust Hollywood to get anythin' right when it comes to religion or magick."

"Why is that?"

"Waal, when it comes to religion, it's just sloppy. They don't bother to look shit up. Ah mean, when Ah'm watchin' one o' them Christmas movies and the minister is wearin' red vestments, Ah jus' turn the damn thing off. It completely ruins the realism fer me. But when it comes to magick, them TV folks know that whatever they show...waal, some stupid kid in a cornfield is gonna try it out. So you can't show anythin' *real* or you'd open yoreself up to all sorts of lawsuits when the demons start eatin' the stupid cusses."

He picked up a folded triangle of paper and put it in the Circle of Containment.

"What's that?" Milo asked.

"That's a sigil. It's a symbol that's tied to a particular demon. Kinda like yore own name is connected to you. If people yell Milo, you come."

"Depends who's doing the yelling," Milo said with a hint of resentment in his voice.

Just then the sliding door rolled back and a sound like thunder filled the cavernous room. Mayor Betts entered, wearing a bulky bomber jacket with a fleece collar.

Dylan stared at it, momentarily covetous. He was so cold that he'd almost forgotten how cold he was.

"This had better work," Betts said.

"Good ev'nin to you, too, Mayor," Dylan said.

"This looks appropriately spooky," Betts surveyed the hexagram and candles. "Can you explain what's going to happen?"

"Are you sure you want to be here when it does? It's not safe," Dylan said.

"I want to be here, because I only half believe what any of you have told me in the first place."

"Waal, Ah guess if we're bein' honest with each other now, Ah think you smell funny. An' Ah suspect Milo has a secret HO train fetish."

Betts narrowed his eyes. "Just explain it."

"Okay, okay. Waal, first, you and Milo gotta stand in this box." Dylan pointed to a rectangle just outside of the hexagram, about six feet by four feet. The word "apertiones" was written inside it in large, blocky letters with the same chalk. "That's yore box o' protection. So long as you stand in that box, the demon can't eat you. Whatever you do, don't leave that box. You understand?"

Betts exchanged a worried look with Milo. They both nodded.

"Good. 'Cause yer demon chow if ya don't. Now Ah stand here, in the center of the hexagram. Ya see that circle just beyond the star? That's the circle of containment. We're gonna do our best not to let the demon out of that circle."

"You're going to do your best?" Betts asked. "Is that going to be good enough?"

"Ya know, this is really not mah area of occult expertise. Ah wish Dicky were here, but he's not. So you got me. Ah'm gonna do mah best, an' either that's good enough or it ain't. And that's yore call, dude."

"All right, all right," Betts shook his head. "What's that paper?"

"That's a sigil," Milo said. "It calls the demon."

"Someone is payin' attention and gets a gold star fer the day," Dylan put his hands on his hips, looking satisfied.

"So who is this demon you're calling up?" Betts asked. "Tell me about him."

"Uh..." Dylan looked up, as if trying to remember something. "His name is Pek."

"His name is *peck*?"

"Yeah, he's a Vietnamese demon, originally. He's been workin' the States ever since the 1970s, though. Came over with the boat people, remember them?"

Betts nodded.

"So Pek is an extreme wrath demon, one of the worst hell has to offer. Wrath demons are usually outrageously violent. Once he's bound to mah will and free to roam the land, there won't be any stoppin' him or controllin' him, either, unfortunately. He's pretty much jus' gonna kill everything in sight in the most horrible, bloodiest, quickest way possible. Ah hope you've got janitors ready, 'cause the whole 'buckets of blood' shit is real, dude."

Betts started to look uncomfortable. "Uh, is there another demon who might not be so..."

"Nuclear?" Dylan offered. "Uh...sure, but Ah thought you wanted a demon who could take care of business."

"Well...I do...I'm just not sure..." Betts unzipped his jacket and Dylan could see that he was beginning to perspire, too.

Dylan fought the urge to grin. "Look, Ah told you this was some serious shit. You call this demon up, yer gonna have bloodshed like you've never seen before, an' there's no tellin' him who to kill and who not to kill, 'cause no one out there is wearing team jerseys."

"Can't you just tell him not to kill anyone on the island?"

"Ah thought you wanted him to patrol the island's perimeter, to keep any Oakland incursion at bay?"

"Yes, but we don't want him killing Alameda residents."

"Ya know, makin' that kind of distinction might be a little tough for a demon. It's not like they're Harvard grads." Dylan cocked his head as he waited for Betts' response. None of it was true, of course. Demons were extraordinarily intelligent and would have no trouble making such a distinction, but Betts didn't know that.

"I don't know," Betts said, running his fingers through his hair.

"Okay, ya know what? Ah could call up a glamor demon instead. What do you think about that?"

"What's a glamor demon?" Milo asked.

"I'm not sure glamor is the look we're going for," Betts said skeptically.

"Nah, dude, that's a technical term. A glamor is an illusion. A certain kind of glamor demon looks big and fierce and scary but doesn't actually hurt anyone. They're just projectin' a glamor, an illusion."

Betts nodded slowly, understanding. "That could be very useful," he said.

"Ah could call up a nest of 'em, if ya like," Dylan offered.

"That sounds like an excellent plan," Betts agreed. "Let's do *that*. Keep the friendly fire to a minimum."

"10-4, good buddy," Dylan said. "All Ah gotta do is swap out this here sigil for a different one and we'll get started."

Dylan pulled a notebook and a pencil out of the box of supplies Milo had provided. He tore off a new sheet and scratched a sigil onto it that looked uncannily like Mickey Mouse. Then he folded the sigil and placed it in the Circle of Containment, tearing up the previous one. Dylan faced Betts. "Waal, Ah'm ready whenever you gentlemen are. D'you pray?"

"What?" asked Milo.

"Pray. To God. Do you pray?"

Milo shook his head. Betts just blinked.

"Well, Ah'm only gonna call up a glamor demon, but we're still dealin' with demons here, and once the opening is made, Ah cannot actually control who comes through. Ah'm just saying, if yer prayin' men, now's a good time."

"Thank you, but I think we're ready," Betts said.

"All right, then. You two need to stand in the apertiones box. That's so the demon will know who you are and won't eat you."

"What does 'apertiones' mean?"

"It's the Latin root of our word 'client,'" Dylan said. "Yer the client, so you stand in the client box."

"Oh. Okay." Betts and Milo both stepped into the box.

Dylan took his place in the middle of the hexagram. "Now Ah'm gonna chant." Dylan bowed low in the direction of the sigil and began, "*Intelligere, O dullest populo; et stulti, quando vos sapiens esse...*" It was a Gregorian chant he remembered from the time a couple of years ago that the Blackfriars had tried to do the Daily Office in Latin. It was a miserable failure, but there were parts of it Dylan had found useful.

As he sang, Dylan stole a glance at Betts and Milo in his peripheral vision, and it seemed to be having the desired effect. But Dylan's own glamor would only work for so long. Nothing about this working was real—not the hexagram, not the sigil, not the ritual. And in a few moments, when no demon appeared and nothing actually happened, Betts and Milo would realize he'd been conning them.

Better make the best of it, Dylan thought, and he raised his voice again in a commanding tone. "Oh, great Pek. By the rules laid down long ago by King Solomon, Ah implore you to appear before me—"

"Not Pek!" Betts shouted.

"Oh, right," Dylan stroked his chin. "Oh, great...Fintin."

"Fintin?"

"Irish demon. Big on the glamor," Dylan assured him. He raised his voice again. "Oh, great Fintin. By the rules laid down long ago by King Solomon, Ah implore you to appear before me. Nay, Ah *command* you to appear before me!"

Then there was silence. And that was it. Dylan's shoulders slumped. His play was at an end. Whatever time he might have bought Susan and the others, it was over. Whatever fun he had been able to wrest from Betts was complete. Dylan sighed.

"What? What's going on? Why isn't it work—"

Then the door exploded open.

89

RICHARD SHIFTED on his seat and felt the tingling of blood returning to his left buttock.

"What's going to happen to us?" Sophie asked. She had her arm around Mike protectively. He'd been crying earlier, and Richard's heart hurt for both of them.

They were all sharing the back seat of a late 70s Oldsmobile, which wouldn't have been uncomfortable for a short stretch, but it was apparently being used as a makeshift holding cell. After three hours, Richard was beginning to feel a variety of bodily needs. "I wish I knew, honey," he answered.

"Where's my mom?" Mike asked.

This one Richard knew the answer to, but he didn't see any reason to cause the children further distress. "I don't know," he lied.

"Who was the man with the horns?"

"He calls himself the Goat King. He's a magickian."

"Is he a good magician?" Mike asked. His face even brightened a little.

Richard knew that Mike wasn't inquiring about the Goat King's morals, but about his skill at stage magic. Feeling tired, he ignored the distinction. "Nope. I'm sorry, he's a very, very bad magickian,"

Richard said. *Actually, he's probably a piss-poor magickian, even by evil magickian standards,* he thought.

"Why are we here?" Sophie asked.

It was a good question. Richard had a good idea, but he certainly wasn't going to tell her. "That's what we're waiting to find out."

Sophie nodded. "It's like that time Mike went to the doctor."

"When I was little?" Mike asked.

"Yes, and Mom and Dad were scared that you might have cancer."

"That's silly," Mike buried his face into his sister's shoulder.

"We were waiting in a little room to find out then, too. I didn't like it then, either."

Richard nodded. Without really thinking he asked, "So what did you do?"

Sophie cocked her head. "I pretended I went to a place where I *did* want to be."

Richard blinked and sat up straighter. "Of course..." he whispered.

"What?" Sophie asked.

Richard stroked at his chin as he reasoned through the idea. "Listen, you guys. What if I could take you someplace safe?"

"Like Lake Barryessa?" Sophie asked.

"Uh...sure. As safe as that," Richard said.

She brightened. "Okay."

"Will Mommy be there?" Mike asked.

"No. But the bad men with horns can't get you there," Richard said.

"Okay then," Mike agreed.

"Close your eyes," Richard said, "and pretend that in front of us—"

"This is just pretend, huh?" Sophie said.

Richard opened his eyes and leaned over to squeeze her hand. "No, honey." He looked her in the eyes so she could see he was sincere. "This is for real. But we have to use our imaginations—like a tool—in order to make it happen."

She scrunched up her nose, clearly dubious.

"It's like this. Do you know how sometimes you want to draw a picture and you don't know what to draw a picture of?"

"Yes," she said. Mike agreed.

"So how do you figure out what to draw?"

"I see something inside, in my head," Sophie said.

"Exactly. And then you draw it," Richard smiled. "We're going to see something in our heads, and then we're going to go there."

"Can you really do that?" Sophie asked.

"I do it all the time. It's part of my job."

Sophie nodded. Richard could see her skepticism lift along with her frown. She still looked deadly serious.

"I have to pee," Mike said.

"So do I, but they didn't let us out the last time we asked, did they?"

Mike looked down.

"Listen, you can pee when we get to where I'm going to take you," Richard said. "Okay?"

He brightened and nodded.

"Okay, close your eyes then, and imagine the exact same scene that you see in front of you when your eyes are open. You see the car, you see the seat in front of us. Over that seat you see the rear-view mirror at the front of the car. And you can see the hood out the window. Can you see all that?"

"Yes," said Sophie.

"Yeah," said Mike.

"Okay then, now imagine that a hole starts to form just above the seat in front of us. The hole is floating in mid-air. The air around it is kind of wavy and weird. The hole is black, but it's kind of shimmering too, like the surface of a puddle of water.

"Now reach your hand into the hole—see how it goes in? Now I'm going to climb into the hole. When I'm through it, I'm going to put my hand back through to this side, and I want you, Mike, to take my hand and let me pull you through. Then I'll pull Sophie through. Can we try that?"

"Yes..." they said in unison, a note of wonder creeping into their whispered voices.

Richard climbed into the Void. He was used to stepping in, but had never accessed it from the back seat of a car before—or from the front seat for that matter. But he climbed through, even if it wasn't the most dignified act of his career. Setting his feet firmly on the ground inside the Void, he put his hand back through and held it ready for Mike. He felt Mike's hand grasp his, and he pulled the little boy up, out of his seat, and though the aperture. He set Mike down with a grunt and quickly stuck his hand through to get Sophie. He felt her hand almost instantly, and pulled—harder this time because she was bigger—and in a moment set her down on the solid, dark earth of the Void.

The children's mouths dropped open and they stared around in wonder.

"I didn't know you could do this," Sophie said.

"The world is full of wonders," Richard said, "His glories to perform."

"What's that, a song?" Sophie asked.

"Not really, I just pulled it out of my a—" Richard swallowed his word. "Um...it's a half-baked aphorism of mutt-like provenance."

"What?" asked Mike.

"Never mind, it's not important," Richard said. "I want to introduce you to some friends. They *are* important. Come this way."

Richard set off across the dry, baked dirt. The sky was dimly red, and Richard could see the familiar mountains in the distance. What looked like tumbleweeds rolled by, although the breeze was faint.

"It's like cowboys," Mike said.

Richard's brow furrowed. "What's like cowboys?"

"He means it looks like it does on TV, on cowboy movies."

"Oh, yeah." Richard got it. The Void *was* a very desert-like place, and it did kind of remind him of Arizona. "But it's a lot bigger than any real desert. It's almost infinite, and you can get to anywhere else from here."

Sophie's eyes got bigger as she looked around. Richard guessed she was trying to figure out how it all worked. *Good luck with that,* Richard thought.

They walked in silence for a few moments when Richard saw movement out of the corner of his eye. He stopped and turned and saw five tall, looming figures—almost like walking bananas, if bananas were nine feet tall and covered with prodigious brown fur. A choir of Sandalphon, and a goodly number—an indication of how seriously they were taking their mission to guide and protect. Five Sandalphon for two children. He was pleased and impressed.

They swayed and lumbered as they walked, and Richard could feel the steps of their heavy feet as they approached. As they drew near, Richard bowed in greeting. In his peripheral vision, he saw Sophie bow in imitation. He looked over at Mike to see him simply gawking, wide eyed.

"They don't have any eyes..." he said.

"They don't need them," Richard said.

"How do they see?" Mike asked.

"I don't know. With their hearts, I guess."

"Can you ask them?"

"They don't speak, either."

"'Cause they don't have mouths?"

"That's right."

"Are they scary?"

"Do they look scary?"

Mike didn't look too sure. Richard smiled, stepped forward, and wrapped his arms around the waist of the nearest Sandalphon, burying his face in its warm, dusty fur.

The fur enveloped him and held him. He was tempted to simply stay there, being held, feeling with the whole of his being the fundamental benevolence of the universe toward him. In that moment, this one Sandalphon became metonymous for the whole of the celestial order, for angels and archangels and all the hosts of heaven, who forever sing around the Throne the hymn of glory proclaimed in his own feeble heart.

Don't go. Richard distinctly heard the words in his head. *You have served enough. Stay here and let us carry you to your reward.*

Richard stopped short. What if he just...stayed? He could just walk away with the Sandalphon. He could stay with Mike and Sophie, help them with their transition. Their bodies would be in comas until they were killed or just...wasted away. But they would never know. They would be safely...elsewhere.

"I can't do that," Richard said. "I'm not finished."

This is Adonai's battle, not yours alone, the voice in his head said with calm detachment. *And you can be sure Adonai will win it.*

Richard wavered.

The voice continued, *You can be gathered to your people. Your father is waiting. Bishop Tom is waiting. And several of his cats.*

Richard laughed. He hadn't known the Sandalphon had a sense of humor—not until now. He stroked his chin and thought hard for several moments. "It's tempting. It is. I'm...tired. But...I'm just not finished."

You are *finished. There is no more room to write on your page.*

Richard stopped to wonder at that information. It meant that he would die soon. "You'll have to use post-its, then, I'm afraid."

He stepped back and saw that Sophie and Mike were no longer beside him. Beneath the cascades of Sandalphon fur he saw them each hugging one of the great angelic beasts. "Keep them safe," he said.

All will be well. None can harm them here. Not ever.

"I'm counting on that. And if their bodies die..."

All will be well. We will take them home.

"Mike has to pee."

All will be well. Do what your heart compels you to do, for the glory of Adonai.

Richard nodded, hugged the beast once more, then turned back toward the Void.

90

WITH DETERMINED VIGOR, Mikael strode away from Castro Street toward Caselli St. once more. He was *this* close to Larch, and what did he do? He just walked away. Mikael felt a pang of guilt, of failure. What kind of Blackfriar was he? Even Susan would have kicked Larch's ass. But he...he had just walked out. "That is *not* going to happen again," he told himself. But what would he say? What would he do? He didn't know, and not knowing sapped his resolve until his feet were dragging and he felt like he was slogging through tar.

He played through the possibilities in his head. He could try to talk Larch out of his quest—but he doubted he would get very far with that. He could do a citizen's arrest, or maybe even tie him up—but the more he contemplated force, the less possible it seemed. There were three of them and only one of him, and he didn't like those odds one bit.

"What would Dicky do?" He asked out loud. He stopped to consider the notion. If anyone had a better chance of talking Larch out of it, it would be Dicky, but Dicky wasn't here. Persuasion seemed unlikely, force seemed doomed to failure, so that left...what? Threats. What did he have on Larch that might provide some kind of leverage?

He'd heard that the police had raided the Lodge of the Hawk and Serpent's house and had found the Urim and Thummim, the consecrated stones originally kept in the Jewish high priest's breastplate only to be taken out to be used as oracles. They had been stolen from the Maccabee Museum of Jewish Art and Life in Berkeley a few months before. Surely the police would still love to know the location of the house's owners.

He didn't really feel the need to turn them in—magickal chotchkies were something the Order collected, too. But they didn't know that. It was a threat he needed, after all, not revenge.

With renewed vigor he set out for the house again. Internally, he rehearsed what he would say when Eleazar or that other weasel opened the door. What if Larch was already ascended? *I'll fucking wake him up*, he said to himself.

He missed Kat and was troubled by how they'd left things. He longed to apologize, to hear her out, to make things right. He felt a gulf between them that was more than just the distance of the several city blocks that actually separated them. He felt further away from her than he had since they'd gotten together. He felt a physical ache in his chest, and he knew it was more than just acid reflux.

Turning the final corner, the house came into view. Mikael strode toward it with a boldness he did not feel and literally had to force one foot to follow the other. The idea of threatening Larch with the theft had sounded great a couple of minutes ago, but now that he had to actually make the threat...he wished he could be *anywhere* else.

He climbed the stairs and punched at the door. The sound from his own fist was thunderous. He waited but heard nothing. He reached for the handle, turned it, and pushed the door open.

There were lights on, but he heard no sound. Mikael turned and looked around at the neighborhood, unconsciously checking to see if anyone would notice him going in. He saw people, but no one was paying any attention to him. He turned back to the door and walked through it.

It looked like a tornado had been through the place. He'd been here only—what, two hours ago? Now the place was stripped bare, void of humans, and as far as he could tell, furniture. He walked into the kitchen where they had just been talking. Everything was gone except the mess—no food, no pots, no pans.

Gone. They were just *gone.*

Mikael sat down on the floor and hugged his large, angular knees.

91

K<small>AT SAW</small> the steam rising from her breath as she walked in procession down Harrison Street. The Bay Bridge entrance loomed before them, and she felt a chill run down her spine that had nothing to do with the autumnal air. All around her were sisters and brothers in the Craft—Wiccans and neo-pagans of various sub-traditions—thousands of them. *Perhaps ten thousand*, she thought, and she felt her heart swell within her. It felt holy, and it was truly a religious procession. Everyone held candles, and everyone was chanting songs of the Goddess.

I<small>F THERE'S FEAR</small>, if there's fear
  Mother be near, be near
  If there's strife, if there's strife
  Mother give life, give life

S<small>EVERAL PEOPLE WERE PLAYING</small> djembe drums to carry the rhythm. She knew the words and the lilting chant rose up within her as if it were singing *her*. As she walked, she struggled with her dual identity.

Yes, she and Mikael were Christians, but they were still Wiccans. They worshipped Christ in their rituals, but they used Wiccan liturgical forms. They were Christo-pagans, part of a small but vocal subtradition in the Wiccan community, one that was not always entirely welcome. That made sense, since some sources say that Christians were responsible for killing as many as nine million witches during the burning times. The number had probably not been that high, but it was quibbling. Kat saw her practice as one that healed the rift between the two communities.

They also worshipped Christ is his pre-incarnate form as the Lady Wisdom, Sophia. For them, the Lady and the Lord were not two gods, but two aspects of the same being: one spiritual and one incarnate, one feminine and the other masculine, one eternal and the other temporal. This succeeded in putting them at odds with some Wiccans and most Christians. It was not a comfortable place to be.

Yet, she felt at home as she walked and sang and held her candle aloft in defiance of the dark. There had not been any traffic across the bridge for many days now, but she stepped easily over the concrete roadblocks CalTrans had placed across the onramp. She stopped to help a couple of the more corpulent practitioners of the Craft cross the barriers. Then she set her face toward Oakland.

One of the women she had helped caught up to her. She was a large, fleshy woman who looked confident in her cronehood. She seemed to be sweating despite the cold. "Thank you for that, back there," she said, her voice raised slightly so that Kat could hear her over the chanting.

"No problem," Kat said.

"Celtic," she said.

"Christo-pagan," Kat answered.

"Oh, one of *those*," the old woman smiled. "Well, goddess bless you for trying."

"We're all about healing, aren't we?"

"We are indeed, child. And there's a lot that needs healing right now. Where's home?"

"Oakland."

"So this is personal?"

"Yes."

The old woman nodded. "We're from Burlingame. I say 'we.' My Carl is at home. Had to have part of his leg amputated last month. Diabetes. He just won't let up on the ice cream."

"Addiction is a bitch." Kat nodded.

"Ha!" The woman's quick laugh added a percussive counterpoint to the song around them. "I like you, girl. Her spirit is in you. My brother Sam would have loved to be here, too. So I guess I'm here for the three of us."

"Where is Sam?" Kat asked.

"Sam died last year."

"I'm so sorry," Kat said, who was beginning to wonder if perhaps this was a healthy conversation for her right now.

"It was horrible. Alzheimer's. Do you know what it's like just watching someone you love fade out?"

Kat stopped, creating a bit of a pileup. The crone grabbed her arm and pulled her forward. "Oh, dear. I hit a nerve, didn't I?"

She had. Kat did indeed know what it was like to watch someone fade out. She knew it all too well. Suddenly her feelings about the old woman shifted, softened. She felt a kind of kinship—the sisterhood of women whose brothers had faded out. "It's okay," she said. "My brother is on his way out, too. Not the same way, but...kind of...the same."

The old woman put her arm around Kat and said, "His memory faded, not mine. I can hold the connection for myself...and for him."

The light from thousands of candles reflected off the girders that held the upper span above them, flickering and making them seem warm and alive. Kat looked around her in wonder. The whole neo-pagan community wasn't there, but it was certainly represented. Some even carried banners indicating their coven, city, or bearing witness to the pantheon they served. The mood was joyous, festive, reverent, and even a little dangerous—much like their rituals. Indeed, it *felt* like a ritual, Kat noted. She was elated by the camaraderie she saw, by the solidarity, by the sacredness of the event.

The leaders ahead of her had reached Treasure Island and were heading into the part of the bridge that bore through the island, enclosed on all sides. *I have to get up there,* Kat thought. *I am the only one who has any clue what we're really stepping into.* She disentangled herself from the crone's arm and gave her a quick hug. "I have to go…" she said, pointing ahead.

"Of course you do, you young and impulsive thing." She gave Kat's hand a final squeeze and waved her on. Emboldened by the old woman's blessing, Kat turned and began to trot past the other marchers, heading for those taking point several hundred yards ahead of her.

She passed Wiccans and pagans of every stripe. She even passed a lodge of magickians, but since they weren't Serpentines, she didn't bother with them. "Golden Dawn, Sacramento" their banner read. She dodged several people and nearly knocked another down. "What's your hurry?" a man called after her, but aside from a quick apology thrown over her shoulder she didn't answer.

What is *my hurry?* she asked herself. She didn't know—she only knew she had to get there quick.

About a hundred feet short of Kitty Moon and her immediate acolytes, Kat stopped jogging and speed walked to catch up with her. No one seemed to take any notice of her as she advanced to the front and fell into step alongside her hero.

"It's demons, you know," she said.

"What?" Kitty Moon asked her, only now noticing Kat's presence.

"The East Bay. It's not some kind of political uprising like you suggested at the rally. It's far worse. It's demonic oppression."

"How do you know?"

"I'm a Blackfriar."

Kitty Moon stopped momentarily and considered Kat. She started walking again almost immediately before someone bumped into her.

"You're a Blackfriar and you're marching with *us*?"

"I'm Wiccan—Christo-pagan."

Moon rolled her eyes. "Goddess help us. She sleeps with the enemy."

"I'm *not* the enemy. I'm a...convert." She'd never thought of herself as a convert before. But as she said it, she knew it was true.

"I don't believe in demons," Moon spat over her shoulder, not bothering to look at Kat.

"That doesn't really matter. You don't have to believe in cancer to die from it."

Moon scowled. "Who invited you?"

"I'm on your list."

"I don't have time for this."

"What are you going to do when you get to Oakland?"

"We're going to overwhelm them with our numbers. We're going to force them to lay down their arms and be part of a beloved community again."

"That sounds wonderful," Kat started, "and commendable. But what if they have weapons and you don't?"

"Weapons are the enemy," Moon countered.

"Okay, yeah...*aaaand* your enemy has weapons."

"We have no enemies," she said.

Oh really? Kat thought. *Didn't you just say* I *was the enemy?*

"We're going to march into Oakland and embrace everyone we see," Moon continued. "And they'll see that their weapons are not necessary, because we're not a threat. And when we're not a threat, they won't be a threat, either. This will be the beginning of the Great Disarming. It will ripple out across the globe."

It was in that moment that Kat realized Kitty Moon was crazy. Maybe even delusional. Or perhaps just so idealistic that she had no realistic grasp of their circumstances.

Kat continued to march as she turned and looked at the unstoppable river of neo-pagans emerging from the Treasure Island tunnel. The lights on the Oakland side of the Bay Bridge were out, and Kat saw the swelling tide of witches, druids, and magickians holding their candles forth defiantly, eager to meet the darkness with the surely unstoppable power of their romantic ideals. They wanted to love the East Bay back into normalcy. Kat's heart broke as she fully grasped the naiveté of it all, the glorious good intentions, the damning futility of the endeavor, the sure and certain slaughter that awaited them.

A moment ago, she herself had been enchanted by the vision. But something had changed. Whatever it was within her that had compelled her to lie to Mikael and had been responsible for her fooling herself had shifted. It wasn't gone, but somehow the critical reasoning part of her brain had peeked out and reminded her that it was there, that this was madness, that they were marching straight into the jaws of real and mortal danger. And Kitty Moon—who had always been her hero—could not or would not hear her. Kat watched as she almost floated serenely toward the Oakland toll plaza.

Kat's mind raced as she sprinted to catch up with Moon again. Then she ran past her, and Kat's eyes widened as she saw the hordes of Oaklanders swarming toward them on the freeway overpasses. She stopped to take them in. There were hundreds of them—no, thousands, maybe even tens of thousands. Many of their clothes were ragged, and Kat could just barely make out the gleeful set of their faces. But what struck her most was their eyes—wet and wide and wild. The moonlight glinted off their weapons—hammers, guns, garden tools, tire irons, scraps of wood or metal.

She turned and watched the river of candlelight streaming down the east span of the bridge, lighting up the sleek modern bridge design with flickering gold. It looked like warmth and hope. It was also completely and utterly mad.

Kat whirled and ran to the counterpoint between the two advancing armies. Having positioned herself, she sat down and closed her eyes. She steadied her breathing, saw the opening to the Void in her imagination, and stepped through.

The Sandalphon were waiting. But whereas before they were comforting and loving, she sensed something else from them this time. *Not hostility, but*...she cocked her head, trying to get a sense of it. *Opposition*, she thought.

They surrounded her and allowed her to go no further, jostling their large, furry bodies in a semi-circle around her, preventing her any advance into the Void. "What's wrong?" she asked them. But the

Sandalphon, as always, were mute. She *felt* them, felt their communi-cation. And what she felt then was, "No further."

"I call to the Angel of the Air," she cried. "Come quickly, I beg you. I need your help!"

The air before her rippled with energy, as lightning appeared out of nowhere and folded back on itself. Its thousand eyes saw into her and through her and comprehended her fully. She made to step toward the Angel, *into* it, to *become* it, to wield its sword, it's power, just as she had before. But its voice thundered in her head with such force that she stumbled. "I do not wish it. *He* does not wish it."

"But they'll die," she said aloud.

"You wish to wield my sword against those already oppressed. I will not permit it."

"I only want to stop them," she pleaded, but it was no good. "So what do we do? What are *you* going to do?"

"I will feel pity." There was a flash of lightning, and the Angel was gone.

92

BRIAN BALLED his fists to keep his hands from shaking as he stood and followed Maggie into Moses' office. Greenish light came from what looked like gas lamps set into the walls. The ceiling was high, and the walls were paneled with fine wood, much like Brian would have expected to see in a posh English country house. But one half of the office surprised him. A tent had been hung from the ceiling, covering half the room, looking like something straight out of a Bedouin camp. Inside were rich tapestries and low couches for reclining in a Middle Eastern fashion. Brian smiled at the sheer nostalgia of it.

Even more commanding, however, was the figure behind the desk. He hadn't looked up at them yet but was studying an open file. He was large and burly, with a black and gray tangle of hair cascading from his head and a large, broad nose set into his face that reminded him of Dylan. If fact, there was much about the man that reminded Brian of Dylan, only...bigger.

The door shut behind them and Maggie walked up to the desk and cleared her throat. Moses continued to study the file. Maggie snatched it from him. "You're being rude, Moshe," she said as she closed the file and threw it down on the desk again.

"I'm not being rude. If you haven't noticed, we've got a bit of a crisis going on here. Electricity is out now, too." He gestured at the gas lamps. "I didn't know if these would still work. Thank heaven for nineteenth century durability."

"I thought it was just for show," Maggie smirked. "I know how you love antiques."

"Serah, when this is all over, if there is still a world to govern, you and I will go antiquing."

"That's a date. Allow me to introduce you to someone. This is Brian Epstein. He's a Talmudic scholar."

"Who isn't?" Moses grumbled but gave Brian a curt nod.

"Um...gentiles?" Maggie's eyebrows raised.

"Oh. I wasn't counting *them*," Moses said, waving her objection away.

"They *are* most of the world," Maggie reminded him.

"Don't rub it in," Moses said. Then he seemed to soften. "Come over to my *mag'ad,* I'll have Bet bring us some tea." He pushed a button, and Brian heard Bet's tinny voice respond. "Tea please, Bet, for two."

"Three, Bet!" Maggie shouted.

"Yes, three, sorry." Moses rolled his eyes. "This way." He led them to the tent and sat down on one of the couches with a weary groan.

Maggie reclined on another, facing him, with an ease that reminded Brian that she had grown up with furniture like this—and had many hundreds of years of practice with it. He sat awkwardly on what looked like an ottoman.

"Can you believe this? We've had destructive magickians before, but nothing like this," Moses sighed.

"You've faced your share of magickians, Moshe," Maggie reminded him.

"Yes, sad court magickians who could make sticks wiggle and call them snakes. Crowley made it here a hundred years ago—"

"He did?" Brian sat ramrod straight.

Moses looked at him as if he were surprised to find him present. "Yes, but, he didn't do any damage. He started a salon, but then went away when he realized that no one was interested in talking about how brilliant he was. Regardie came later, but he was a gentleman and mostly combed the libraries."

"Wait, weren't Crowley and Regardie already here, in some form?"

"Is this your story or mine?" Moses asked.

"I'm just trying to figure out how this works," Brian asked.

"The Crowley here was a ceramics painter and Regardie was a plumber. Neither one had any interest in magick."

"Oh. That's disappointing." Brian looked crestfallen.

"Not nearly as glamorous as being a magickian, eh? Just fifteen times more useful to the common good." Moses turned his attention back to Maggie. "We have to stop him, Serah. This assault on Heaven cannot go forward. We can only assume that he will gain support as he ascends."

"I'm surprised he found support here," Maggie said.

Moses pulled at his silver beard. "People do stupid things when they're scared. As I know very, very well."

"Do you have a plan?" Maggie asked.

The door opened and Bet walked in with a tray of tea. Moses waited until she had served them and then retreated before he answered. "I'd hoped that the media would be back up so I could make a public address. I think the people just need to hear from me. I think if I could just talk to them, I could...ease their fears, let them know that it's going to be okay."

"What's the problem?"

"He's militarized society. He's sabotaged the television stations, the radio stations and the internet. I have ordered them to be repaired, but I'm being actively disobeyed."

"We all know how much you hate that!" Maggie shook her head and took a sip of tea.

"Don't be petulant, Serah. I only ever did what had to be done."

"You only ever did what you thought was expedient, and then blamed it on HaShem."

Moses' faced hardened and he looked away. Maggie had spoken the Truth, and he knew it and could not gainsay it. He set down his teacup and faced her squarely. "We need your help, Serah."

"Well, I'd love to help you, but I've been giving it a lot of thought, and I think it's time for me to retire. I've been meaning to tell you, but you're a hard man to pin down. Plus, I knew you wouldn't be happy about it. And I do hate to watch you sputter."

Moses' mouth hung open and his eyes went wide. "Serah, I fully respect that you might want to take things easier, do something else for a while. But can we talk about that *after* the crisis has passed? You're just giving notice, right? Two weeks from now, you'll clear out your desk, or something of the sort?"

"Yes, all right. I'll hang in while we're sorting this out, but I won't be working myself. I'll be training my successor."

"Your successor?"

"Yes. We can't go without a Forerunner, can we?"

"It is an important job. And you've done it well. I can't imagine anyone else..." Moses trailed off.

"I can," Maggie said. "I have just the person. I've been watching him for a while. He's honest, he's a straight shooter. He's of the tribe."

"Who is it?" Moses asked, skeptical.

"Moshe, I'd like you to meet Brian Epstein. This time, why not act like he's actually here?"

Brian felt the blood drain out of him and gather in a frigid pool around his heels. His hands started shaking again, and he opened his mouth to object. Nothing came out.

Moses blinked, then looked at Brian. Then he looked back at Maggie.

"You've got to be kidding me."

"Nope. He knows the tradition. He's comfortable working in Vision. He won't encounter anything that will surprise him. He's been practicing with a bunch of Christians who know the inner planes like the backs of their hands. He'll do very nicely."

"B-b-but he's a...a hunchback. He's..." he leaned in and whispered, "*unclean.*"

"And you're a camel's festering bunghole. You emit toxic clouds from your backside that would render entire villages unclean before the Lord for a week." She banged her teacup on the metal table so hard that Brian was amazed it didn't shatter. "Unclean my ass."

"But-but-but—"

"Don't you dare be so quick to dismiss him," she said, her voice becoming hard and defiant. "He's not a murderer, like some people I could mention."

Moses sat up and his narrowed his yes. It was a low blow.

"He's also not a stutterer, like some in present company."

"Really, Serah, there's—"

"Nor is he afraid of his own skin, if that rings a fucking bell."

Moses' jaw tightened and he looked ready to spit nails. "I could have your—"

"What? My job?" She grinned at him wickedly, enjoying the irony. "*That* would be lovely."

Moses sighed. "Fine. Just...not until after all this—"

"No. Now. I'll show him the ropes. I'll be there to back him up. But it's Brian that's going to face down this magickian, not me."

Moses swallowed and looked at Brian again. This time, his gaze was searching, as if hoping to find some quality that would allow him some shred of confidence. The hair on Brian's arms bristled with electricity and his head was buzzing. He felt profoundly uncomfortable under the prophet's gaze.

"Moshe, listen to me," Maggie said. Moses broke his gaze and looked at her. "You'll support Brian in this. You'll give him anything he needs to do his job well. And you'll recommend him in every sephirah. And do you know why?"

"No, why?"

"Because *I have taken note of him.*"

93

SUSAN BURST into the room with the force of a hurricane. She fired the shotgun at the ceiling and emitted a high-pitched ululation that echoed through the room until it sounded like it was coming from everywhere. She saw Betts and Milo jump nearly out of their skins. They started edging toward the sliding door, so she made a beeline for a spot between them and it. She held the shotgun at her waist, poised to fire at their chests. They backed away slowly.

Chicken ran straight into Dylan's arms. He scooped her up and planted a kiss on her cheek as he lifted her up and swung her around. "Are you okay?" she asked him.

"Ah am now, darlin'," he said. He turned to Susan. "Honey-pot, you got the best fuckin' timin' on earth."

"You can thank Chicken. She brought me straight here," Susan said. She glanced at the hexagram on the floor. "Since when do you do magick?"

"Uh...since never. Look closer."

"Oh. It's a hexagram, not a pentagram."

"Yup."

She looked up at him with an admiring look on her face. "Apertiones? Did you really make these gentlemen stand in a box labeled 'assholes'?"

"Guilty as charged," Dylan looked down, feigning shame.

Betts bolted and made to run past Susan, but before he got two steps she pulled the trigger again and filled the room with thunder. He stopped. "That one was high. The next one won't be," Susan said, ejecting the spent cartridge.

Out of the corner of her eye, she saw movement from Milo's direction. She swung the shotgun towards him, but not before he'd squeezed off a shot from a revolver. The bullet passed through the soft part of her left arm, feeling like a bee sting. "Son of a bitch," she snarled and blasted a load of buckshot into the secretary's chest. Milo's mouth opened, but no words came. He stumbled backward and then toppled to the floor, clutching at his chest. His revolver hit the floor and skittered a couple feet, placing it in easy reach of Betts. He glanced at it and then glanced at Susan. She raised the shotgun to her shoulder, aimed carefully and blasted the revolver into the outer darkness of the room's periphery—and well beyond the reach of the mayor.

"Don't try it, Goggles," she said. "You won't find it, and the moment you turn your back I'll fill it so full of fucking lead that your girlfriend will be picking BB's out of your ass with tweezers well into your nineties—if you survive it at all."

Betts put his hands up, and Susan saw that he was trembling.

"Yore Aunt Susan really knows how to put on a show, lil' darlin'," Dylan whispered.

"What's the magick charade all about?" Susan asked.

"They told me you an' Terry filled 'em in on the whole demon thing," Dylan said.

"Yes, we were trying to be helpful," Susan said. "Too bad our efforts weren't returned in kind."

"Waal, the mayor and his henchman here—former henchman, looks like—they thought it would be swell if I could just conjure up some demons to fight for their side."

"To what end? Fending off Oaklanders?" Susan asked.

"That's the surface story," Dylan walked over to her and planted a kiss on her cheek. "But Ah think if they'd had a real magickian workin' for 'em and coulda got a taste of that power—we coulda had some pretty lil' tyrants on our hands."

"I think we already do," Susan narrowed her eyes.

Betts gulped.

"You know I'm not above blasting a hole in your chest where you stand just to watch you crumple to your knees and fall on your face, right?"

"I thought you were Christians," Betts said weakly.

"Don't make me shoot you in the penis!" Susan took aim.

Betts covered his crotch with his hands and squirmed.

"I find that most non-religious people have an appalling lack of understanding about religious people," Susan said.

"Ah find that to be true mahself," Dylan agreed, putting Chicken down.

"Just because I follow Jesus doesn't mean I ever stop being a sinner."

"Yer just *his* sinner," Dylan said.

"And O Lord, it would feel good to sin today."

"You'd feel bad about it later, though," Dylan said. "An' you'd wanna eat a whole can of cream cheese frosting. Might even scoop it out with yore fingers. An' that would just be sad."

"You know, ever since you got sober, you've been a real pain in the ass," Susan said, lowering the shotgun.

"Ah'm gonna tell ya what, Mr. Mayor—what did you call him?" Dylan turned back to Susan.

"Goggles. His day job—he's a clown, like for children's parties. Goggles the Steampunk clown."

"Yer fuckin' kiddin' me."

"I am not," Susan said. She'd lowered the weapon to her hip, but it was still trained in Betts' direction.

"Waal, Goggles, Ah'm gonna need you to turn around and kneel. Right now—"

"Oh, God. Don't shoot me!" Betts wailed as he turned.

"Ah ain't gonna fuckin' shoot you, you ignorant piece o' shit. Put yore hands behind yore head and interleave yore fingers."

"Interleave. That's a nice word," Susan said.

"Ah am constantly strivin' to better mahself."

"It's working."

Betts interlocked his fingers and faced the back of the room.

"Chicken, let's you and me find somethin' to incapacitate the clown."

"I'll bet you never expected to utter that sentence even once in your entire life," Susan suggested.

"Ah think when Ah was in college, stoned off mah ass at three in the mornin', Ah aspired to one day be in a situation in which Ah could utter those very words an' it would not seem contrived or inappropriate."

"I think we should live our dreams," Susan said.

"Ah think we should dream our dreams, *then* live them," Dylan said. "How 'bout that tape there, Chicken?"

"Okie-dokie!" Chicken said. She handed a roll of duct tape to Dylan.

"Awww, you found mah duct-tape."

"*Your* duct tape?" Susan asked.

"Waal, Ah mean the roll of duct tape they used on me when Ah was on the gurney."

"Oh, shit. Okay, when we get clear of this, I want to hear the whole story."

"We'll trade stories. How's that?"

"I'm looking forward to exchanging more than that," Susan said, bouncing her eyebrows.

"Now darlin', not in front of Chicken. Or the clown."

94

WITH A HEAVY SIGH, Mikael rose to his feet and shut the door to the empty house behind him. His feet felt like lead as he shuffled through the cold San Francisco fog back toward Castro Street. His mouth felt like it was full of cotton, and he was sure that if he tried to speak, all that he'd be able to manage would be a croak.

A convenience store loomed on the corner, and he went in. He paused at the wall-length refrigerator, mulling over his soda options. Nothing looked good until he hit the beers.

It's been a long time since I've had an eight-ball, he thought and picked up a 20-ounce can of Old English 800. He knew it was horrific stuff, but he didn't care. It was the liquid equivalent of chewing Vicodin—the taste was nasty, but the relief was quick.

As he closed the glass door to the refrigeration unit, he heard a familiar voice and froze.

"I don't care what he wants. I'm not making macaroni and cheese. It's beneath me. You just tell him he's lucky I'm coming back at all. On second thought, don't tell him that. But he *is*. Tell him I'll make him a festive fettuccini alfredo with nutmeg and hazelnuts. It'll be just the thing for when he comes back down to earth."

Mikael held his breath. It was Khams—gathering items for a

victory meal? It certainly sounded like it. Mikael ducked, afraid that his punkish shock of wild black hair might be visible over the store shelf that separated the aisles. He peeked around the corner and confirmed it—Khams was there, as short as Terry, sporting the same ridiculous goatee that seemed to hold a perpetual fascination for magickians everywhere.

"The man is driving me nuts," Khams said into his phone, no doubt complaining about Larch to one of his order mates. "We knock ourselves out to cater to his every whim in order to carry out some obscure plan—which he does not bother to explain to us, by the way, and I can tell you that chaps my hide—but does he thank us? Does he acknowledge our hard work? Our ingenuity? That's right."

So they're still in the neighborhood, Mikael thought, every nerve jangling with hope, possibility, and danger. Quietly, he replaced the malt liquor and, keeping tabs on Khams' location, was careful to stay close but out of sight.

"Just tell Purderabo thanks for getting that team in and out so quickly. I will need to make him a very special dish as a thank you. Note that I *am* saying thank you, unlike some magickians we know."

Khams had nearly a full basket now and was making his way to the checkout stand. "Did he? I don't give a shit—that's just between you and me, of course. Why what?...Oh, I don't know. It's his charisma, I suppose. He says something and you don't really think about questioning it. It seems like the logical thing to do. Afterwards, it might seem daft as taffy cake, but in the moment it sounds completely plausible. It's like a spell, really. No, I don't think it's really a spell. I think it's...I think he's a natural leader is all. What? Not me, good God. People wouldn't follow me to breakfast."

The cashier was scanning his items. Mikael tried to make them out in the curved mirror, but he wasn't close enough and the distortion was too profound. "All right, I'm at the store and I—give her that Ensure and don't worry about it. Just give it to her. It's—it's not moldy. It's in a can...what? Don't listen to her, she's delusional. Listen I really have to go. Give my best to Chuck. Kisses." Khams put his phone in his pocket and with almost the same motion withdrew his wallet.

After he had paid, Mikael watched carefully to see which direction he would head. He waited a few moments then headed for the door himself. He paused at the threshold and peered out in the direction Khams had gone. He saw him crossing the street at a brisk pace, heading away from the old house. Keeping about a block's distance between them, Mikael followed.

Khams carried his brown grocery bag two blocks to the left, then turning right, walked another block and a half. He finally went up to what looked like an apartment building, but as he got closer, Mikael saw that it was a B&B called The Hideaway. "That couldn't be more apt," Mikael said aloud. He let himself in through the side gate and watched the windows in back for activity.

The building only had three floors and only four apartments per floor, Mikael estimated, given the size of the building. There were lights on in two of the rear flats on the second floor and one on the third. Michael drew his coat closer around him as he sat on a picnic table and studied the windows. A young woman walked near the window in one of the second story apartments.

Not that one, he thought, turning his focus to the other two. Just then another light came on, on the third floor. Only for a second, as if...as if someone were checking on someone. His mind raced. It could be a parent checking on a child. Could be, but how likely was that at a Bed and Breakfast? Mikael usually thought of B&B's as romantic establishments, not particularly for families—which would be doubly true in the Castro. The innkeeper probably checked Larch in with his two male companions and thought nothing more of it.

Mikael studied the back of the building, looking for a way up. Scaling the building was a Confessor move, but he was too tired and discouraged to take refuge in his superhero fantasies. This was just him against Larch now. He studied the arbor. *Definitely shimmiable*, he thought. From the arbor, a drainpipe clung to the side of the building and connected to the roof. It was wide—maybe three-and-a-half inches around. He undid his belt, hoping there was space for it between the pipe and the wall. If so, he could loop it around the pipe and use it to lean against. His mind flashed to Adam West standing on the side of a building and just walking up. It wouldn't be *that* easy, but it could be done. The drainpipe passed within two feet of the window. And he could see that the window was cracked a bit—it's frame hovered just above the sill, allowing Mikael to see a sliver of white curtain.

Mikael stood and blew on his hands. Making his way to the arbor, he began to climb to its top. Once there, he balanced on the beams as he crossed to the stucco wall. He tested his belt, but the drainpipe was too close to the wall to allow it. He tsk'ed while he put his belt back on and stopped to think. The brackets holding the pipe in place were spaced about three feet apart, and they were substantial. There was definitely space to get a finger hold in them.

He pulled his shoes off, grasped the lower bracket in his toes, and reached up to the bracket just above his head. Concentrating most of his strength into his arms, he pulled himself up, hand over hand, careful not to scrape or bump the wall. After what seemed like hours —but was, he knew, only a couple of minutes—he clung precariously opposite what he hoped to be Larch's window. Fixing his left middle finger into the space between the pipe and the wall, he reached out with his right hand and caught the window frame. He felt at the space between the frame and the sill and, using all the strength he could project into his fingers, he prized the frame upward until he could grasp the inside sill with his whole hand.

His left hand was aching now, not to mention sweaty, and had begun to shake. Mikael involuntarily cried out when the finger gave way, leaving him swinging from the window frame, his right hand twisted at an uncomfortable angle, still grasping at the inside sill. "Shit," he whispered, then instantly hoped no one had heard his outburst. He hung there for a few seconds, allowing his left hand to rest. He shook it, then brought it up, passed it under his right arm, and grasped at the bottom sill. Letting go with his right hand, he swung it out to his right and also got a good grip on the under sill. Heaving with every ounce of strength left in his body, he pulled his upper torso through the window and hung there for a moment, resting his arms. From there, it was easy to worm his way to the floor.

Doing it without making any noise was another matter. During the whole time, a voice in his head kept shouting, *What if this isn't Larch's room? This is breaking and entering. You're going to jail.*

But as he rose to his feet, the light from the window rested on what looked like a sleeping face. Just below, its body was fully dressed, stretched out on the bed. Mikael leaned in, noting the horse-like contours of the face, the acne scars, and the thin-pressed lips. It was undeniably Larch.

He wanted to do the Snoopy happy dance—and would have, had noise levels allowed—but he heard movement in the hall. Catlike, he flattened himself against the wall near the hinge of the door. When the door swung open, he was hidden. But if anyone closed it...

He prayed silently as someone entered. He could hear someone setting objects down and the clatter of dishes, but he couldn't tell what they were bringing or taking away. Then, just as quickly, the person left and pulled the door shut.

Mikael breathed a deep sigh of relief and stepped toward the bed. "Time to wake this asshole up," he whispered. Mikael took hold of his arm and shook him. He expected Larch to open one lizard-like eye and begin to berate him. Mikael was ready for that. But the reptilian eyes stayed closed. Mikael shook harder. He grasped Larch by both shoulders and jerked him around. Nothing.

He felt at Larch's pulse—it was strong, even a little fast.

Mikael stood back for a moment then leaned down with new resolve and slapped the magickian across the cheek. Nothing. He slapped him harder, again and again until he saw red welts rise up on the man's face.

Mikael was sweating now and more than a little nervous. *If I can't wake him up...what?* he wondered.

A voice in his head said, *You could kill him.*

It was a terrible thought, but was there any other choice? Mikael's thoughts raced, remembering Bonhoeffer's dilemma—cooperating with the German resistance to assassinate Hitler. Was this the same? Was he on solid ground here? Was he justified?

He knew that Larch was responsible for untold deaths in the East

Bay. He knew that the magickian was wrecking cosmic damage in the sephirot—damage he could already see around him, but the full extent of which might be universally catastrophic. *Might.* He didn't know exactly what Larch was up to, and Brian wasn't here to explain it to him. He only knew that it was bad, dangerous, potentially apocalyptic.

How would he do it? Larch was only using one pillow on the queen-sized bed. He could smother him with the other. Larch, being so out of it, wouldn't resist. He would just...die. Mikael felt like cold water was running down his spine at the thought of it. He could pray for strength and later for forgiveness, but he knew in that moment what it would do to him.

You would trade the lives of whoever else is going to die because of him —maybe the whole world—just so that you can have a clean conscience? he asked himself. When he thought of it like that, the choice seemed like the ultimate act of selfishness. Or perhaps it was cowardice? He felt confused, even faint, and began to hyperventilate.

What would Dicky do? he asked himself. Dicky would kill him. He knew that in his bones. Dicky wouldn't hesitate. Even if it meant going to prison. Even if it meant damnation. It was a fair trade, and Dicky would be prepared to make it.

What would Jesus do? he asked himself. In his head he heard, *What does it profit a man to gain the whole world but lose his soul?* He may indeed gain the world—even save the world—but at what price?

At that moment, Mikael knew he couldn't do it. He was doing nothing here but putting himself in danger. Larch certainly wasn't in any danger from him. He didn't know if it was because he was too good, too moral, or too chicken shit, but ultimately it didn't matter. He was not going to kill this man and if that was the case, he had better get the hell out of there.

He swung his leg up and out of the window and heard a clatter behind him. He lowered his leg and spun around, holding his breath and looking for the source of the noise. All he could hear was Larch's steady breathing and the distant din of city traffic coming in through the window. He looked down and could have slapped himself as he saw what had caused the sound: The Mughal knife he had taken from Larch earlier had fallen out of his back pocket when he lifted his leg to the window. Mikael snatched it up and raised his leg again.

But then he froze, a distant memory niggling at the back of his brain—a story about the warrior David and Saul, the king who was trying to kill him. Mikael lowered his leg again and walked back over to Larch. He pulled the short, curved knife from its ornate sheath and stabbed downward, driving its tip deep into the wood of the head-board just inches from Larch's sleeping head. He tossed the sheath onto the bedspread and bolted for the window.

95

Kat stepped out of the Void and into chaos. The march across the Bay Bridge had overtaken her, and her heart fell as she stared eastward toward the advancing line of Wiccans, their candles held up defiantly against the darkness. "No," she managed as she saw saw Kitty Moon's arms open wide to embrace the first of the Oaklanders she encountered, her candle guttering in the wind. The Oakland woman could have been one of their own—maybe was—her face curled up in a smile just as she slashed at Kitty's belly with a long blade that glinted in the candle light.

Kat couldn't see how badly Kitty was hurt. Time stood still as Kitty looked down at herself then crumpled to the deck of the bridge. The Oaklanders howled with glee, raised their weapons in anticipation, and then brought them down as the true slaughter began. Kat's mouth dropped open as she watched in horror. A large Oakland man decapitated a younger Wiccan man with the shiny edge of a chrome fender, beaten flat and sharpened. He swung it with both hands, and the younger man's head had sailed into the air, a banner of blood following behind it, looking like a gush of black ink in the moonlight.

Others saw it, too, and it caused the Wiccans to falter. They stopped advancing and just stood for several seconds, not moving forward or back, even while the Oakland army carved their way through their front line with an accelerating frenzy. Shotgun blasts tore through the air, ripping through the thick bodies of three crones standing defiantly arm-in-arm. They wavered, clutched at one another, and then they went down.

That was the moment the Wiccans faltered. As if the cooling corpse of Kitty Moon had called out an order, they all turned as one, dropped their candles, and ran full-out for the safety of the bridge.

But the Oakland army was faster, and they had the taste of blood-lust on their lips. The Wiccans were just as easy to fell from behind, and the demon-ridden army had no scruples about slaying the fleeing Wiccans. In fact, it seemed their joy and their zeal increased exponentially as the scent of fear ripened the air.

"No, no, no, no," Kat kept repeating. She tried to stand still against the tide of fleeing Wiccans, but the current was too strong and she was swept along in their retreat. Her face was still set toward Oakland, and tears began to brim in her eyes as she watched the army pick away at the slowest Wiccans—the old, the sick, the very young. She watched them as they were overcome. She saw the light leave their eyes when the violence caught them, saw their bodies tumble to the pavement.

Surrendering to the flow of the people carrying her backwards, Kat stepped again into the Void. The Sandalphon were still there, ringed around her in a way that was both protective and oppositional. *It's as if they are trying to protect me from myself,* she thought. And perhaps it wasn't far from truth. But she didn't have time to ponder it. The Sandalphon were a distraction. "Angel of the Air!" she yelled, "Come to me!"

It wasn't an entreaty. It was a demand. She half expected to be ignored, but half a second later, she saw the whirlwind ripple at the air around her, and the angel materialized, flashing lightning from its nether regions, a thousand eyes blinking and a thousand swords flashing.

"I have given you my answer," the angel's voice boomed in her head. "I will not kill those whose will is not their own. Why do you persist?"

What could she say? Kat didn't have an argument. It was sheer terror that drove her—that and helplessness. The Angel was the most powerful being she knew. If the angel could not or would not help people at their greatest moment of distress, she despaired of serving the wrong God. She feared she was—

"That's it," she said, feeling almost faint with the force of her revelation. "I don't wish violence against them," she said with defiance. "I wish wisdom for them."

The Angel spat lightning and fire as it hovered in the air just in front of her eyes. It was waiting for more. "The fear of the Lord is the beginning of wisdom," she said. "I don't want to hurt them. But some appropriate fear? That's right and good, don't you think?"

The Angel's swords flashed and its eyes blinked. Perhaps it was thinking? Kat flashed on a memory of a recent Bible study at the Abbey. "You've done it before," she argued. "When Adam and Even were driven out, who was posted at the Eastern gate of Eden? You were. You didn't want to kill them, but you were there to frighten them, to warn them away, to instill in them the proper fear of the Lord."

The Angel did not respond, unless Kat was to interpret a fart of lighting as a response.

Kat continued. "When Balaam went to curse the Israelites, who was it that stood with your flaming sword to frighten his donkey from going forward? I know that was you. Instilling the fear of the Lord is your job." She took a breath and stamped her foot. "God damn it. Do your fucking job!"

"You may enter," the Angel said.

"Thank God," Kat said as she closed her eyes and stepped forward into the angel, possessing it and being possessed by it, assuming its mantle and its power. When she opened her eyes, her vision was kaleidoscopic—for it was a thousand eyes she saw through, in every direction. When she raised her gauntlet feet, they were the size of King Cabs. She looked down at her body, five stories high, the brightest thing for miles around, for she was flashing fire, and when she raised her arm, the flaming sword lit up the bridge like a beacon.

She knew she could will it to blaze forth, and so she did. A bonfire sprung up from her fist, punching back the night so brightly that her two human eyes would have had to close against its ferocity. She looked below her at the Wiccans as they skittered past her feet.

Harm none, the angel thought—she thought—and it seemed an out-of-place statement of the Wiccan rede. But perhaps not out of place, after all. The rest of the rede spooled out in her mind, *An it hurt none, do what thou wilt.*

Yes. She couldn't hurt anyone, but short of that she could do as she chose. She found a spot of the bridge pavement momentarily free of people, and brought down her foot on it. The sound of thunder overwhelmed the cries of bloodlust and frenzy. The resulting earthquake caused the bridge to shudder and sway.

The Wiccans did not falter in their flight, but the last of them sped past her feet in an all-out scramble for Treasure Island. Kat caused the sword in her right hand to blaze forth again and brought it low, parallel to the ground, creating a great, flaming barrier across the bridge. One or two of the Oakland army had pushed past her in time, but she couldn't worry about them. Presumably they would pursue the Wiccans far enough to be out of range of the sigils' influence soon enough.

It was the rest of them, the hordes of them and the thousands of them before her, that concerned her. She wondered if they could see her, but that question was answered soon enough when the advancing line of them reared back before being consumed by the heat of her sword. She saw that their numbers pushed at them from behind and that they couldn't stop, even as they scrambled backwards, tumbling over their fellows in a frenzied attempt to avoid the sword. She took a step back and retreated the sword a bit to give them room to stop before meeting their doom on its fiery edge.

For a few moments it was like watching waves as they swept up on the sand and then tumbled over itself rushing back into the sea. The Oaklanders in front rushed backwards even as the reserve troops pushed forward, creating an angry melee among their own. Weapons flashed, and Kat felt the angel's ire rise within her.

"Enough!" her voice boomed with the urgency of thunder. She liked the sound of it. It was the sound of Power.

It also did what she hoped to do—the Oakland army stopped what it was doing. It stopped marching, stopped surging, stopped fighting. It just stopped, and she had the satisfaction of watching thousands upon thousands of eyes upon her, frozen in terror. She caught a hint of the thrill that bullies and killers are addicted to—the ability to cause fear. It was delicious in the same way that whiskey was delicious—it was savory with danger. She loved it and at the same time it frightened her, for she saw just how enticing it could be.

She raised the sword, held it over her head, and watched the armies of Oakland cower before her. She flashed it down again and watched it cut through the tar and concrete paving the bridge. She jerked it back, not wanting to do unnecessary damage to the infrastructure. No one seemed to notice her gaffe. The Oaklanders were backing up now. With a flood of relief, she saw their farthest ranks fleeing toward the hills. Others followed. Finally, those in front turned their backs on her and retreated toward the shore.

She stood sentinel for some time afterwards, until she was sure that none would return. None would escape her thousand eyes. None would get past her sword.

96

DYLAN FINISHED FIXING the duct tape to Bett's wrists, finally taping him to a workbench affixed to one wall. He then spread a large piece of the silver tape over the mayor's mouth. "Now, Ah don't expect you'll behave exactly, and you'll prob'ly try to escape, and Ah ken hardly blame you fer that. But Mayor, Ah do hope you'll be on yore best behavior and try to be less of an assbag in the future."

"Are you giving him a good talking to?" Susan asked.

"Ah am," Dylan said, standing up.

Susan kissed his cheek. Dylan handed the duct tape to Chicken. "Yesee, here's what Ah see. Betts here thinks he's the good guy. He thinks he's doing a good thing to help the people of Alameda. In his mind, kidnapping and demon-rustling are justified by the ends. So he doesn't even know that he's evil. That's a form of diminished capacity as far as Ah can tell, and that just makes mah heart bleed."

"This is what I love about you," she said. "Your soft spot for lost causes."

"Ah figure God hasn't given up on 'im yet, so Ah shouldn't."

"Did you tape him up good?"

"He ain't goin' nowhere until the cavalry come over the hill, dress

his pecker up like the pope, an' fall down and worship it singin'
'Hail Barry.'"

"Are you through?"

"Ah am decidedly through."

Betts' eyes flashed wildly from one to the other, and he jerked
against his restraints.

"Take a good look, Goggles," Susan said, jutting out one curva-
ceous hip. "This is what the good guys look like."

"That sounds like one o' them exit lines," Dylan said.

"I'm ready to go."

"You gonna take the shotgun?"

"Chicken took all the shells out of it and put them in her
pocket—"

"What a clever girl," Dylan said, lifting her up and planting a kiss
on her cheek. Chicken giggled.

"—so it's useless. I think it'll attract too much attention if we carry
it around. I got Milo's pistol, though."

"We just gonna let Milo rot here?"

"I don't know what else we should do," Susan said.

"Waal, his presence will provide a poignant object lesson fer Mr.
Goggles here. 'The wages of sin is death,' the apostle tells us. It ain't
gonna hurt 'im none to meditate on his wages."

"Then I think our work is done here," Susan held her hand out to
Chicken. They walked out the way they had come in, since that direction was known to them. In a few minutes, they were at the outer
door, and Susan drew the pistol, holding it at the ready. Dylan peeked
out the door, but the pavement was deserted. The only thing they saw
was the moon hanging heavy over the water, creating silver ripples
that danced as if there were still joy and hope in the world.

"Where to?" Susan asked as they stepped into the moonlight.

"Ah haven't got a clue," Dylan answered. "Ah—oh, looks like you
had a bit o' trouble." He motioned toward the headless corpse of the
guard Susan had shot earlier.

"Nothing I couldn't handle."

"Gotta love a 12-guage," Dylan shook his head and started off across the parking lot. "Uh...where were we? Oh yeah, where to? Ah've been kinda tied up fer a while, so Ah haven't had much time to explore the island."

"I have, and I can't think of any place where Betts' folks won't find us."

"I know," Chicken said, tugging on Susan's hand. "This way."

Susan looked at her husband. "She hasn't been wrong yet."

Dylan shrugged and they followed the little girl.

In silence the three of them walked along the quiet, nearly deserted streets of the west end of the island. They walked past the mothballed USS Hornet then turned left and passed Encinal Junior and Senior High School. Fancy condos along the docks stretched out on their right, and old tiny houses and quaint apartment buildings from the naval shipyard's heyday stretched out to their left. At the Tasty Freeze, Chicken turned toward the water. They found themselves walking beneath a dark canopy of trees, toward a small outbuilding. They followed Chicken to the back door, where she reached up to the doorknob and let herself in.

"Honey, Ah think we're home," Dylan said.

97

Richard was applying epoxy to a thing with feathers under the watchful gaze of his dead father when he heard a thump. He looked up as the feathered thing morphed into a leopard-like beast covered not with fur but with the kind of pull tabs Richard hadn't seen since childhood. The beast jumped down from the table, making a great roaring rattle as it did so. The rattling continued as it slunk off, sounding like a thousand African percussion instruments, all shaking in unison. The rattling was almost like sleigh bells, but heavier, duller, accentuated every now and then by a thump. The thumping was rhythmic, too. As the great cat faded, the thumping remained.

Richard sat upright in his automobile prison, blinking back to consciousness. *Thump, thump, thump.* The moon was high in the sky and cast a calm, blue light over the Marina. Richard couldn't see the water from where he was, but he could see the tops of the masts over some hedges. He turned to look behind him and saw the lights of San Francisco to the west, and another sort of light to the south.

Squinting, he sat up on his knees and tried to figure out what he was seeing. The lights were in motion—some of them waving wildly. It seemed to be a candlelight procession, albeit a frenetic one. But where was it? "The bridge," he said aloud, although he couldn't see it. "I wonder what that's all about?"

When no one answered, he sat back down and looked over at the bodies of Sophie and Mike. They looked like they were sleeping peacefully. Only the dark stain running down the leg of Mike's jeans gave any indication that something was amiss. *Looks like he found a place to pee,* Richard thought. He smiled, sadly.

Thump, thump, thump, thump.

Richard had heard the thumping before—he realized it was probably what woke him up. Snatches of the feathered thing and the percussive cat wisped through his mind, but he couldn't snatch any context from the fleeting images.

Thump, thump, thump.

It seemed to be coming from beneath him, as if someone were striking the bottom of the car with some cloth-covered mallet. As strange and unexpected as it was, the sound was also familiar. Richard frowned and sank back into his seat as he tried to place it.

Whatever it was, it didn't seem to be a source of any danger. Sleep pulled at Richard's eyes again, and he found random images and scenes interjecting themselves into his mind. As he sank deeper, they resolved into a bedroom—Richard's own, at the Abbey. In the dream, Richard felt like shit and coughed, hacking up a lungful of phlegm. His dream-self turned over, trying to sleep, but was interrupted by a loud *thump, thump, thump.*

In the dream, Richard opened his eyes, seeing his bedspread adorned by the crumpled white carnations of spent tissues. Peering over the side of his bed he saw...Tobias.

"Toby," Richard sat up, fully awake now, feeling the cold vinyl of the car seat against his forearm.

Thump, thump, thump.

Tears welled in Richard's eyes. Tobias was right beneath him, his tail thumping against the bottom of the car. It was like getting a Morse code signal from a trusted friend telling you that all would be well. He longed to touch the dog's fur, to bury his face in Toby's mane, to breath in his dusty warmth and goodness.

Raising his foot, he tapped back, mimicking the dog's rhythm. Tobias' thumping stopped momentarily, then resumed again with greater fervor. Richard's mind raced, wanting to tell Toby to run, to get to someplace safe, to be anywhere but here. And at the same time he was profoundly grateful for his friend's presence. Richard wracked his brain for the Enochian word for "run," but he couldn't pull it up, if there even was one.

"If only Terry were here," he said, but he didn't want that, either. Wherever Terry was, he hoped it was safer than here—if his friend was still alive at all, of course. It did no good to think about Terry, but he did pray for him, and for all of his friends and order-mates. And as he began to drift into sleep again, a part of him let go of his need to tell Toby to go away and accepted the simple gift of him.

FRIDAY

You, my child, shall be called
the prophet of the Most High,
for you will go ahead to prepare God's way,
To give the people of God knowledge of salvation
by the forgiveness of their sins.
In the tender compassion of our God
the dawn from on high shall break upon us,
To shine on those who dwell in darkness
and the shadow of death,
and to guide our feet
into the way of peace.
—*Luke 1:76-79*

98

"Rise and shine, dear. The world will either end today or it won't."

The Netzach Maggie hovered over him, moving a stray lock of hair out of his eyes. He sat up, groaning. It had been a long night. Brian had no sooner fallen asleep in Netzach when he had been awakened in Malkuth. At first he was angry, but as soon as he cleared the sleep from his eyes, he became aware of the pain in his bladder and how thirsty he was. He had mustered a "thanks" to Chava and dove for the bathroom. His next stop was the kitchen for water. He'd noticed how much his muscles ached, and it reminded him of a time he'd been bed-ridden for several days. He knew what he was doing was hard on his body. He also knew it needed to be done. He'd fended off Chava's questions and ascended again. And, apparently, slept. But had he slept there or here? Both, probably. He had a body in each place, after all. He shook his head to clear it, but the vagaries of inter-sephirotic travel still eluded him.

There were no lights on in Maggie's place. Soft green light peered in from the small windows near the low ceiling, and there were several candles lit set at strategic locations around the room, but neither did much to alleviate the gloom.

"Everything still down?" Brian asked.

"Yes. I was hoping for a newspaper, but no," Maggie answered. She placed a cup of coffee in front of him.

He slurred at it gratefully, but it was too hot and it stung his tongue. "Even if the presses *were* running, he'd probably be censoring the press by now."

"Probably, yes."

Brian rose and stretched. His muscles did not ache here, and he felt grateful for that. "So how does he plan to get the army from here to Tipharet?"

"My guess is he'll hypnotize them and get them to ascend," Maggie said, sipping from her own cup. She was sitting in a lumpy armchair in her basement apartment—a different apartment than her Yesod counterpart lived in.

"Does everyone who lives here live in every other sephirot?" Brian asked.

"Of course, dear. The you in Malkuth and the you that's here aren't separate people, you know. You're all the same person, just different aspects of the one you."

"If I'm a different aspect, why don't I feel any different?"

"You would if you were paying attention."

"I'm not paying attention?"

"Don't sound so hurt. Attention is a continuum, not a light switch. You pay more or less attention, depending. And you get better at it with practice."

"So he's going to hypnotize this army—"

"And let's assume every other army in Netzach," Maggie interjected.

"How, if the communications are down?"

"This is just my opinion, but I don't think they're *down* down. There hasn't been a wind storm or anything. I think they're being suppressed. They'll be back up when he needs them."

"He certainly gained a lot of power fast," Brian blew on his coffee and tried it again. It was tolerable in both temperature and taste. This version of Maggie was amazing in many ways. But he decided coffee-making was not one of them. He set the cup down. "Maggie, about this...job."

"Yes, dear. It doesn't actually pay, if that's what you're asking. It's more of a vocation, a calling."

"I wasn't...that wasn't my question. I don't know if I can do this."

"That's the spirit," she leaned over and patted his hand. "You just keep that up."

"What? I'm saying I don't think I'm the right person."

"My dear, I am the Forerunner. I see the Truth and say it. I see the Truth about you. And I have said it. You can resist it, you can deny it, you can run away from it, but that won't change the truth."

"Maybe it's not *my* Truth."

"Pish on your California relativism," she waved his objection away. "The Truth is always the Truth."

Brian swallowed. If he believed that she was who she said she was —and he did—then he should trust her about this. *Moses freaking trusts her about this,* he thought. "It just scares me, that's all."

"Why does it scare you?"

"It's a lot of responsibility," he said.

"It is that," she agreed. "But there's no reason to be scared."

"What if I don't do a good job?"

"Ah, I'm sensing some performance anxiety," she grinned and took a sip.

"I guess you could say that," he pursed his lips.

"Listen to me. This is ministry. There is no performance. So there's nothing to be anxious about. See? You can relax."

Brian shook his head. "I don't follow you at all."

"If it were up to you, then yes, you would have something to be anxious about. But this is a sacred calling. You'll be on heaven's payroll—for whatever *that's* worth. This is HaShem's work, not yours. If HaShem wants it done well, then HaShem needs to bloody well show up and do the fucking work."

Brian blinked. "You have completely lost me."

Maggie sighed and leaned back in her chair. "Listen, dear boy, the job is very simple. You show up. You pay attention. You speak what you notice. And you trust HaShem to do the rest. That's it."

"That's it?"

"That's it."

"You make it sound easy."

"It *is* easy."

"So, you don't go in with a plan?"

"Of course not. That's a sure-fire way to muck things up. Then you're just making it about you and what a good job you're going to do. It's not about you. It's about HaShem and the Truth of the situation. Your only job is to be aware of HaShem's presence and to see the situation with clear eyes. And then you just say what you see. That's it."

"This is what makes you such a good spiritual director for Richard, isn't it?"

"It's a very similar set of skills, yes."

"He really loves you," Brian said.

She sighed. "He's a very dear mess."

Brian laughed. "I think he would agree with that assessment."

Maggie smiled, then leaned over and held his eye. "You're still anxious."

"Yes. I'm scared."

"Let me tell you what I see, and you can tell me if I'm on target."

"Okay."

"You haven't always been good at noticing, and now you're worried that you won't be good at it."

"What do you mean?"

"Don't be pig-headed, dear. Did you not notice that things were becoming strained between you and Terry? Didn't you see that he was struggling? The poor libidinous dear, you might even say he was suffering. Did you not notice?"

"I—" He was tempted to lie, and he could chalk that up to a compulsion due to what was happening in Hod, but he knew that wouldn't fly with Maggie. Not with someone who could always see the truth about everything. "I saw, but other things seemed more important. I guess I...chose not to notice."

"That," she slapped his knee, "was a very good answer." She leaned back. "So you see, everything is going to be fine."

"What? I don't follow." Brian's head hurt.

"You noticed. You notice well. You chose not to notice, but that's a different thing. That's being callous, not oblivious. That was *sin*, not blindness."

"Gee, I feel so much better about it since you put it that way."

"Sin, well, that you and HaShem will have to sort out. The important thing is that you have everything you need to be the Forerunner. You are keenly observant. And you must trust HaShem to reveal to you the most important things."

Brian stared at his coffee.

"Listen, dear. I know you're scared, but I want you to hear me now, because I'm about to say something you may not have ever heard before. Whether you do a good job—whatever that means—you have to let go of that. Glory is not yours to achieve or earn or steal—that's where the magickians get it wrong. Glory is something HaShem gives you. It is not something wonderful that you wrap yourself in when you are victorious. It is the gift of hearing 'Well done, my good and faithful servant,' when we have done our best."

She let that sink in for a moment, then continued in a voice so low it was almost a whisper. "But the worst, most terrible part of it all is that it is not my own glory that I am responsible for, but everyone else's. Whether I do well is not something I care two whits about. But whether *you* do well, my dear...that, I fear, is what HaShem and I will discuss when I stand before him at judgment."

"And does that scare you?"

"What do you think?" She held up her hand. "Just stop. Look at me. Notice. Then answer."

Brian paused and studied her face. He saw the twitch around her mouth. He saw the gleam of water in her eyes. He saw the kindness of her soul. He saw her sincerity. As he watched her closely, he saw her inner world unfold before him. He saw her in all her mundanity and profundity. He saw...*her*. The Truth of her. And he knew it.

"You're terrified," he said.

"Yes, dear. HaShem loves desperately, but he is also a hard taskmaster. From those to whom much has been entrusted, much is expected."

"You mean me now, too, don't you?"

"Yes, dear. Does that scare you?"

"Yes."

"Good. That means you're ready."

99

RICHARD CAME TO, feeling a great rush of cool air. He opened his eyes to see the tall, angular woman who had accompanied him into camp looming over the open car door. "Up. The Goat King requires your presence at breakfast."

Richard squinted upwards at her. He tried to move, but a bolt of pain shot through his bladder. Eschewing all propriety, Richard gingerly swung his legs out of the car, peeled back the folds of his cassock, unzipped his fly, and let loose with a powerful stream of piss.

The amazon woman jumped back, her face contorted with disgust. Richard didn't care. Sweet relief poured through him, despite the fact that his bladder was still screaming at him. When the stream finally began to subside, he looked up at her. "Don't give me that," he said. "What were you thinking, not letting us out to use the john? The car already smells like piss because the kid couldn't hold it," he said, indicating Mike over his shoulder with a toss of his chin.

"Not my decision," she explained.

"Great fucking excuse," Richard said, his voice still sharp with recrimination. "Gotta be something in the Geneva Convention about bathroom breaks."

"I don't know what that is."

Richard shook his head. "Nor, apparently, is there any reason you should."

Richard spat in his hands and wiped them both on his cassock. Then he stood up and straightened his clothes. "All right. What's for breakfast?"

"I am not sure you will be eating."

"That's a disappointment. I was looking forward to the cuisine here."

"You are too chatty for a man about to die."

Richard's eyebrows shot up. "That's ominous. You obviously know something I don't."

"Then you are a fool."

"That is beyond dispute. All right, take me away, Xena."

"Who is Xena?"

"When were you born?" Richard shook his head, feeling old. "It doesn't matter. Onward."

"I was ordered to bring you and the children."

"Then you'll have to carry them. I smothered them in their sleep."

He watched her eyes grow wide and her mouth fall open. He slugged her playfully on the arm. "Had you going! They're not dead. But they can't walk. You really will have to carry them."

"They're not dead?"

"No. Far from it."

"Then wake them up."

"I can't do that."

"Then *I'll* wake them up."

"You can try. But you won't be able to do that, either."

"Why not?"

"Because they're not here. They're...well, I don't actually know where they are. I left them in the care of some Sandalphon. So I know they're safe, but I have no idea where they took them."

"You're talking nonsense."

Richard waved toward the children. "Knock yourself out."

The young woman crossed to the driver's side and opened the rear door. Sophie and Mike were curled up together. It looked very much like they were sleeping peacefully. The amazon shook them, but to no avail.

"Told you."

"This is a trick. I will walk away with you and, once we're gone, the children will stop playing like they're asleep and run away."

"Damn!" Richard snapped his fingers. "That would've been a great trick! But no. I do wish I'd thought of it, though."

The tall woman shut the doors, making sure they were locked again. She waved at someone across the camp. Squinting, Richard saw it was the Viking-looking man he had met before. The man picked his way through the camp over to where the car was. "Watch them," she commanded him.

"I was just gonna get break—"

"Watch them," she repeated and, grabbing Richard's arm, jerked him roughly toward the most densely populated part of the camp.

Richard passed literally hundreds of people just now rousing from tents and lean-tos. Many of them were dressed in rags, but even more were decked out in flamboyant costumes pieced together from leather, velvet, silk, and anything else at hand. Some of it reminded Richard of *The Road Warrior,* and some of it looked straight out of a steampunk convention. The Marina park was dotted with campfires as people made coffee and fixed whatever breakfast they could scrounge. Few of them gave Richard even a passing glance. The general mood was high but a little groggy, given the fact that it was morning. One campsite featured two men in a fistfight, surrounded by cheering onlookers goading them on. A festival atmosphere filled the air—as did the pungent aroma of raw sewage. Richard wondered how long the camp would endure before typhoid broke out and crippled it. *It can't happen soon enough,* he thought.

The amazon led Richard to a pavilion—a large canvas tent with a bright red sigil spray painted on its side. Richard looked for an activating sigil but didn't see one. The large sigil was just ornamental then, but Richard didn't doubt that the potent sigils were nearby. The people here were too focused, too compliant, and too eager for violence for there *not* to be demonic influence.

"Wait here," the amazon said. A large, beefy man stood at the entrance of the pavilion, an ax hanging over his back. She nodded at him and he crossed his arms and looked menacingly at Richard. The young woman entered the tent. A few moments later she reemerged. "The Goat King will see you now," she said.

"Excellent," Richard said, and he ducked through the doorway.

The tent was bright, as the morning sun lit up the roof and one whole wall. It was about eighteen feet square and filled with couches. A couple of them were old and losing their stuffing, but others looked like they were straight out of the box from Ikea. Lounging on the nicest—a brown leather couch ornately dotted with brass nails—was the Goat King.

His horned headdress was off, sitting astride the arm of the couch, easily at hand should ridiculous and menacing headgear be required.

"Priest! You are here to amuse me," the Goat King announced, smiling and waving a large turkey leg at him.

"I am here. And I *may* amuse you. But it is not *why* I am here," Richard clarified.

"Why do *you* think you're here?" The Goat King raised an eyebrow.

"I think I'm here because a demon-oppressed lunatic is holding me captive."

"You're in my presence thirty seconds and you insult me?"

"And I wasn't really trying," Richard said. "You should see me when I put some effort into it."

"Don't you know I am your King?"

"I only have one king. Is your name Jesus?"

The Goat King scowled. "Don't you know that I hold your life in my hands?" He brandished his turkey leg for effect.

Richard looked away. "That hardly matters. My page is...filled up anyway," he said. He had been so focused on the magickian that he hadn't really noticed the Goat King's "court." About six people either stood or lounged about the king, all of them looking like they had just stepped out of the Renaissance Faire, and all of them staring at him with wicked, aloof amusement. One couple was even decked out in French Renaissance-style white face with fake moles painted on their chins. *Creepy,* Richard thought.

"Where are the children?" the Goat King asked. "I ordered you to be sent to me together."

"They're not here," Richard said.

"I told you to bring them to me!" the king thundered at the amazon. She lowered her head but spoke in a bold, confident tone. "I could not wake them up. He...must have them under some kind of spell."

"Spell?" The Goat King's face twisted up in confusion. "What kind of spell? Spells aren't *real*."

"You're not much of a magickian, are you?" Richard asked him.

"Bring me the children anyway!" he roared. The amazon bowed slightly then turned and exited the tent.

The Goat King turned back to Richard. "Whatever you did to them, *undo it*."

"Hmm...let me think about that," Richard said, stroking his chin. "No."

"You seem to think this is a joke, priest. Just who do you think is holding the power here?"

"I know exactly who's holding the power. It isn't you."

"Are you delusional? I could give an order and have your head crushed in like *that*!" He snapped his fingers.

Richard shrugged. "So do it."

"You think I won't."

"I don't know if you will or not." Richard's face betrayed nothing. "I'm just not terribly concerned about it."

"I will run you through with a pike!" He threw the turkey leg at Richard.

The friar ducked and watched the leg skitter toward the wall of the tent. "Have you thought about an anger management seminar?" Richard stood back up to his full height. "Why is it so important to you that the children be awake?"

The magickian's mouth turned up in a smile at the question.

"Well, if you must know, they will be the main course at the feast I am preparing for our Father Below."

"Sacrifice 'em!" one of the sycophants exclaimed. The outburst was met by several cheers. A couple of people even held up mugs to toast the notion, but whether they contained liquor or coffee Richard couldn't tell.

"You don't need them awake for that. They'll still sacrifice just fine. Whatever magickal working you're planning, their blood will be just as efficacious unconscious as conscious. Plus...they'll be easier to manage. I mean, who needs all the screaming and thrashing about? I hate it when a victim squirms off the altar in mid-sacrifice, don't you?"

The Goat King's eyes narrowed as he considered Richard. It was obvious that he didn't know what to make of the friar, but he also looked so angry Richard thought he might rupture an internal organ.

"Are you even doing a *real* magickal working?" Richard asked. "Because most magickians I know wouldn't care about whether the victims were conscious, so long as the blood was real and alive and virginal. Or..." Richard cocked his head. "Oh, I get it. It's because you won't get to see the fear in their eyes as you raise the knife." Richard feigned a look of pity. "Poor baby. I wish I could say I feel for you, but that would just be silly."

"When they get here, you will wake them up," the Goat King seethed. "I want them *awake* for our feast."

"I can't walk them up, because they're not asleep. They're truly *elsewhere*."

"Then go and bring them back!"

Richard stroked his chin theatrically again. "Um...No."

"I swear by the god of goats I will kill them right now."

"You do that. But you can't actually *hurt* them. They're *safe*."

"I will kill their bodies!"

Richard shrugged. "They'll get other bodies. Or haven't you ever heard of the resurrection of the dead?"

"Bring them back or I'll kill *you*!"

Richard hesitated. *If I die now, I'll never be famous. I'll never get the glory I deserve.* He felt a wave of shame come over him the moment he had the thought.

"Ah, I see you have something to live for," the Goat King's lip curled up into something between a smile and a grimace. "Bring them back. *Now.*"

Richard struggled. He closed his eyes and saw himself on the beach with Jesus.

Jesus' smile was kind and sad. "This is a fine kettle of fish."

Richard sighed. *You should have warned me about days like these.*

"You wouldn't have believed it."

You're probably right about that.

"But even so...did you think this would be a walk in the park? When I said, 'Pick up your cross and follow me,' did you think that would lead to fame and fortune? Really? I'm sorry to break it to you, but it only leads to a cross."

Jesus' words landed like a blow to the gut. Jesus grasped Richard's hands roughly. "And not a metaphorical cross. Not 'Oh, sometimes life will be hard.' Following me can lead to your death, if you do it right." He chuckled. "I ought to come with a warning sticker."

Jesus lifted Richard's chin so that he was looking into his eyes. "But it doesn't end there. This Goat King, as he calls himself? His name is Jerry. Until last week he lived with his mom. He just got fired from the last remaining video store in Berkeley. He is *ridiculous*. All tyrants are. You have absolutely nothing to be afraid of. Trust me. Lean on me. Lean on me hard, like you've never leaned before. Don't be worried about what to say, just open your mouth and I'll do the rest."

Richard's eyes snapped open. "No."

"Then I will take your life." He snapped his fingers.

"My life doesn't belong to you. You don't have the power to take my life."

"I will kill you where you stand," the tyrant said, raising his voice.

"Then stop flapping your gums and do it! At the resurrection of the dead, we'll see who gets to gloat."

"Surely you don't believe religious nonsense like that. That's just a metaphor, and a metaphor can't bear that kind of weight. Life might go on somewhere in the universe—people might even remember you —but you, sir, will be dead as dust. *Forever*."

"Is that all this is to you?" Richard said, gesturing at the Goat King's court. But his action implied much more. "A metaphor? Is your Father Below just a metaphor? Are the demons you summon just metaphors?"

"Of course," the Goat King's eyes shifted back and forth uncertainly.

"Have you even successfully summoned any demons?"

"I thought I felt a wind once—"

"So not only do you suck as a terrorist leader, you're a crap magickian, too."

"Give me one good reason why I shouldn't run you through right now."

"The bad reason—but the only one that is likely to make any sense to you—is that I have something that you want—the ability to bring these children back so you can bathe first in their fear and then in their blood."

"I hear a good reason coming—one that *won't* mean anything to me, I presume."

"The good reason is that while all this is just a Society for Creative Anachronism playdate for you, I have *been there*. I have *seen it*." He took a step closer.

"Been where? Seen what?"

"I have visited the other worlds—the in-between places. It's where I stashed those kids, so I know how safe they are. I have been to worlds of light and seen glory you cannot even imagine. I have been a tourist in hell—and I am not using that as a metaphor but as a fleshy, physical place. I have seen what happens to people there and I know what awaits them—what awaits *you*."

Richard's voice thundered with authority. The Goat King's eyes grew wide, and the friar at least knew that he had his attention. He took a step closer to the faux sovereign and lowered his voice. "Jerry, God didn't reject you because you're rebellious and cool, you rejected

God because of some pathologically narcissistic need to be *special*. But you're *not* special. You're weak and needy and sad. So listen to me, asshole, and listen good. I have fought with demons—not gusts of wind that might or might not have made your nostril hair twitch, but infernal rulers with crowns and scepters sitting astride great beasts with teeth and claws. I have been visited by a procession of infernal majesties and fed them my own blood. You don't need to ask me if the resurrection is real—*it's all real:* angels and seraphim and Sandalphon —they are all real. Thrones, powers and dominions? Real. The resurrection and the judgment of the dead? It's coming like a fucking freight train. No one alive is going to escape the separation of the sheep and the goats—and you, my friend, are backing the wrong farm animal."

The Goat King's eyes drifted into space. Richard could tell he was reeling a bit. He watched Jerry close his eyes, regroup, and regain his footing. His eyes snapped open again and narrowed. "How do you see this ending, priest?"

"What? The world?"

"No, you apocalyptically-obsessed ass. I'm talking about our little standoff."

"You and your menagerie are going to pull up stakes and move on down the road."

"And why should we?"

"Because you can't win here. You want fear and you are not going to get it. Not from these kids, and not from me."

"I could kill your dog."

"Dog?" Richard said, his voice faltering. He looked down and saw Tobias sitting by his leg. The yellow lab's tail began to thump. "Oh, Christ, Toby, what the fuck are you doing here?"

The dog's mouth opened, and it seemed to Richard that he was eating peanut butter or something sticky. Instead, though, the dog was simply trying to get his mouth around something uncomfortable and unfamiliar—language. "R-r-r-un!" the dog distinctly said, before jumping up and bolting for the door of the tent.

100

SUSAN WOKE before the sun was fully up. There was just enough light to see by, and as she emerged fully into consciousness, the events of the last evening rushed back in, filling her brain with images that would drive her therapy sessions for years to come, and jolted her with adrenaline. She forced herself to relax so as not to disturb Chicken or Dylan before she needed to. They were all sleeping like puppies in a pile on the dusty loveseat in the small parks department cottage. Dylan's head rested on her shoulder, his steady snoring punctuated by an occasional wet blockage explosion. That was probably what had woken her, as it often did. Chicken was spatchcocked across their laps, arms and legs splayed out but bent double at the elbows and knees. It didn't look comfortable, but she was sleeping peacefully.

She took advantage of the silence to pray. Her own ferocity scared her, and in her mind's eye, she brought that fear and laid it before Jesus. They looked at it together, and together they sat in the silence. She had done what had to be done, but it didn't excuse the relish with which a part of her had acted. She had read about the ecstasy that came over warriors in the heat of battle, and perhaps for the first time, she had tasted it. She rolled it on her tongue and decided that it was both sweet and bitter—a flavor not entirely to her liking, but one she suspected she could easily develop a taste for, and because of that it was dangerous. These realizations she gave to Jesus, too. Finally, she confessed to him what she had been circling around in her prayer, but not directly addressing. *I killed a man,* she said to him in her imagination. Jesus appeared sitting on the desk in the corner.

"I know," he said.

I'm sorry, she said. *But not very sorry.*

"I know," he said.

What am I supposed to do with that? she asked.

"You could carry it, or you could give it to me and let me carry it," he said. His eyes were sad, but kind.

I think I need to carry it for a while, she said.

"I'm not surprised," he said, smiling. It was a sad smile.

But only because I think I need to suffer for it somehow, she said.

"I understand."

Do you think I need to suffer for it? she asked. *I mean, I know what Lutheran doctrine says about that, but I know we're not right about everything. So I'm asking you.*

"It's not a simple question," he said, playing with a paper clip. "I want to liberate you from everything that enslaves you or limits you or hurts you. That includes your own guilt and shame. But you have your own relationship to your actions, to your feelings, to your self-image, and you have to work that out yourself. Just know that when you're done with it and you want to stop carrying it around, I'll be ready to take it."

She opened her eyes and felt the moral wound hanging heavily on her soul, dragging at her like the Ancient Mariner's albatross. It was disturbing, but it also felt good in a way she couldn't define. Yes, she needed to carry it. In time she would confess it and give it to Jesus, but for now she needed to confront the reality of who she really was and what she was capable of in the darker pockets of her own heart.

She heard the roar of an engine coming closer. She tensed, waiting for it to pass by on the road, but it didn't. It got closer. And closer, until she thought it might ram the little house. She heard the engine turn off.

"Shit! Up, you two! Now!" She shoved at her husband and stood up, depositing Chicken on the floor with a painful thud. Dylan's eyes flickered and he looked around wildly, trying to figure out where he was and what was happening. Ordinarily she'd feel sympathy for him —giving him grace for the PTSD he would no doubt be experiencing from the events of the past couple of days—but there was no time for that now. Chicken stood and rubbed at her eyes, apparently no worse for having fallen to the floor.

"Someone's coming, hide," Susan said.

"It's those men," Chicken said.

"What men?" Susan asked.

"The guarding men. They brought me here yesterday." She pointed to the kitchen. "I'll talk to them."

Susan grasped what she wanted her to do, and she made a decision to trust her once again. Dylan was still oblivious, so she tugged at his arm and steered him into the kitchen. Once out of sight of the living room, she propped him against a wall and put her finger to her lips. "Shhhh..."

No sooner were they hidden than Susan heard the turn of a latch, followed quickly by the sound of boots on the cracked linoleum that ran throughout the cottage.

"Hey, little one. How are you doing?"

The voice was kind, but that didn't stop Susan from pulling the revolver from her jacket pocket and checking the chambers to see how many bullets she had. Four. She quietly snapped the cylinder into place and held her breath, listening.

"We're sorry we have to keep you here. Have you been terribly bored?"

Susan imagined Chicken shaking her head, flashing them a cheerful smile.

"Wow. You're quite a kid, then. Is the bathroom working okay?"

Susan could almost see Chicken nodding her head with the exaggerated loopiness she so often displayed.

"That's good. That's good. Well, I brought you some pizza. It's cold, but it's only from last night. I'll just put it in the fridge—"

Susan tensed and pulled the hammer back until she heard it click.

"—Oh, shit, okay, it's not going to last that long. I guess you would be hungry. I brought you some candy bars and some string cheese, too. Just...put those in the fridge when you've had enough, okay?"

"Okie-dokie," she heard Chicken say with her mouth full.

"Look, kid, I don't know how long this is going to last, but we need to keep you out of sight. The mayor thinks you're...you know, not alive...and if he sees you we'll be in a lot of trouble for helping you. So you have to lay low here, maybe for several days. As soon as we can get off the island, we'll take you to Oakland. Understand?"

Susan imagined Chicken nodding and stuffing her face with cold pizza. She imagined tomato sauce smeared on her cheek, and suddenly some maternal floodgate in her breast opened up and her heart swelled and gushed. She longed to pick Chicken up, to swing her around, to hold her close, to rest her cheek against hers. Susan swallowed and blinked back a tear.

"Okay, little one, I gotta go to work now. You sure you're okay? Okay then. Uh...be good."

Susan heard the door shut firmly, then the catch of the deadbolt sliding into place. She met Dylan's eye and held it until she heard the vehicle, whatever it was, pull away and disappear.

"Ah'm awake now," Dylan said. "What's fer breakfast?"

"Cold pizza, apparently, if Chicken hasn't eaten it all."

"You all right, honey-pot? 'Cause you look like you got somethin' in yore eye."

"I'm...fine. I'm carrying a lot of things I didn't think I was carrying."

"Give 'em to Jesus, that's what Ah do," he said.

"I will," she took her husband's hand in hers. "In time."

Chicken walked into the kitchen holding a medium pizza box from Mike's Pizza Emporium.

"That's not mushroom, is it?" Dylan said. "'Cause Ah hate mushroom on mah pizza."

"Pepp'roni," Chicken said with her mouth still full.

Chicken tripped and the box flipped into the air, spilling its contents. Dylan dove for the floor and scooped the pizza back into the box. "Five-second rule," he said. "It'll just make it all taste better."

Susan rolled her eyes but was too hungry to pass when Dylan held the box open for her. She picked something unidentifiable off the piece she held and then took a bite. A moment later, she pulled a piece of fuzz out of her mouth.

"Best not to think 'bout the toppins," Dylan said, grinning at her. The lid on his sightless eye drooped, and she realized his lovely, broad, Melungeon face would never be the same. She coughed as her love for him rose up in her like a geyser. *I'm too emotional,* she thought. *It's not safe.* She willed herself to master her feelings.

"You all right?"

Her eyes were shining with tears as she nodded.

"You don't seem all right."

"We've got to get off this island, Dyl."

Dylan cocked his head. "Where we gonna go?"

"There's a ferry to San Francisco that runs twice a day. At 7 a.m. and 7 p.m."

"Ah thought it was more often than that—"

"It used to be, but...that's the emergency schedule."

"How do ya know about this?"

"Casey was talking about it when you were...in the hospital."

"Oh. What about Terry?"

"I'm going to go find Terry," Susan said.

"So who's goin' to San Francisco?" Dylan scratched his head.

"You and Chicken. I want you to get her off this island. You heard those men. And you're in no shape to fight anyone. I want you...I want you to get to safety, too."

"Honey, Ah ain't gonna leave you and Terry—"

"Yes, you are. You are going to let me play the hero this time. And you're going to take Chicken to safety."

"Where am Ah supposed to take her?"

"Cell phones are probably working there. Take her to wherever Kat and Mikael are, or where Brian is. Just...get away from here."

"And what are you an' Terry gonna do?"

"We'll be right behind you as soon as I find him."

"Promise?"

For a moment, she saw his neediness, the desperation of his love for her. She kissed him. "Ah promise," she said, mimicking his accent.

101

TERRY WOKE TO BRIGHT LIGHT, a cool washcloth on his face, and a powerful pain in his shoulder. "Hey, sleepy head," Casey said, removing the washcloth and putting it back in the bowl of water in her lap. She was sitting on the edge of Terry's bed. A hospital bed, he noted.

"What happened?" he asked. His tongue was cottony, and he cast about for water.

"What do you need, big guy?" Casey asked. She was wearing tobacco-colored cargo pants and a red-checkered flannel shirt.

"Water. And call me 'big guy' again at your peril," Terry said.

"So much for the calming effects of morphine," Casey said, pouring a glass of water from the pink plastic pitcher near the bed. "Here you go."

Terry slurped at it greedily and when he had drained it, he held it out again. "More, please."

She smiled and filled the cup again.

This time he was sated and he set the cup on the movable table to his right. "Okay. So what happened?"

"You don't remember getting shot?"

"Is that why my shoulder hurts?"

"Yup. You were in surgery until about two in the morning."

"Wow. Where's Susan?"

"I don't know. They're—" she stopped, as if she had said something she shouldn't have.

"They?" Terry picked up on it. "They who?"

"Susan and Chicken went after Dylan. I don't know what happened."

She didn't look him in the eye as she said this. Terry's suspicion was aroused.

"Terry, I have a favor to ask you. It's a big one."

"Okay."

"Okay you'll do it?"

"Okay, I'm listening." He lowered one eyebrow. He didn't like this already.

"The mayor was going to ask Dylan if he would do magick to help protect the island."

"Ha!" Terry burst out. He hastily covered his mouth with the hand attached to the arm that *didn't* hurt. "Sorry. I couldn't help myself."

"Why is that funny?" Casey asked, sitting back down on the edge of his bed. "We don't have a lot of weapons here. We need all the help we can get. I haven't heard from the mayor but I was wondering if maybe you—"

Terry ran his good hand through his hair and looked out the window. "Okay, let me make a list of everything that's wrong with that. First, you don't summon demons to protect people. That's like using rat poison to cure a chest cold. Second, neither Dylan nor any other Blackfriar would agree to that, because it's in direct violation of our vows. Third, demon magick is not my area of speciality."

Casey leaned back and blinked at all this information. "What *is* your area of speciality?"

"Angel magick."

"Is it against your vows to do angel magick?"

"No...not as such."

"Why is it different?"

"Because demon magick is telling—it's coercive. Angel magick is asking—it's petitionary. It's like praying. Nothing wrong with praying."

"So why did you say 'as such'?"

"You can be pretty sure angels will respond to you, but you can't control *how* they'll respond," Terry said. "Not unlike God, now that I think about it."

"But you'll do it?"

Terry scowled at her. "Okay, I'll do it. But I'll need some supplies."

"Like what?"

"I'll need an Enochian table. You can't just get one of those at the Neiman Marcus. I'll have to make it. Please bring me a round table with a light finish, about two-and-a-half feet across—tall, like a standing table at a bar—and a black permanent marker. I can do the sigils from memory."

"I didn't understand much of that."

"Bar table. Blond wood. Thick black magic marker."

"I can do that," Casey said.

"Then what are you waiting for?" Terry asked.

"Can you do it right here?"

"Why not? There are angels everywhere."

She stood up and gave him a curt nod. "On my way, then." She darted out of the room.

"Holy Christ, how do I get myself into these situations?" Terry asked himself out loud. He needed one thing and one thing only—to get the hell out of this room before she returned with a table. He knew it would do no good trying to impress upon her how volatile angel magick really was. His shoulder hurt, but it wasn't unbearable. He groaned and leaned forward. It was *almost* unbearable, he decided. He swung his legs out of bed and was about to hop the short distance to the floor when a round cheery face appeared at the door.

"Hi there. I'm Chaplain Fran. How're you doin'?" Chaplain Fran was a young woman in her mid-thirties. Her face was as red as an apple and she had yellow hair that looked like her perm was well past its shelf life. She wore a striped green shirt with a clerical band collar. She was stocky, but not overweight, and about Terry's height.

"I'm...I've got a bullet hole in my shoulder that feels like someone just shoved a red-hot poker into my chest. But other than that I'm fine."

"Well, you're alive, and that's something to give thanks for."

Terry cocked his head. "Yes," he answered. "Yes it is. Thank you for pointing that out."

"Would you like to talk?" she asked, sitting down in the only chair in the room.

"Well, actually, I really need to get—"

She was looking at his chart. "Would you call yourself a religious person...Mr. Milne?" She looked straight into his eyes. "Can I call you Terry?"

Terry sighed. *Okay, she's too adorable to turn away,* Terry thought. *And it's going to take Casey a while to find a table anyway. And I might get another dose of morphine if I time it right.* "Terry is fine," he answered. "And I am religious. I'm a friar."

"Are you *really*?" Chaplain Fran's eyes got wide and her face broke out into a look of unfeigned delight.

"And for true," Terry answered.

"What order?"

"The Order of Saint Raphael."

She jerked upright. "No."

"Yes," Terry nodded, a little uncertain.

"You're a Blackfriar. From Berkeley."

It was Terry's turn to grin. "Yes, that's us. You've heard of us, then?"

"Are you kidding? I played that scene from the Republican Convention on a loop for—" She stopped and her eyes grew wide again. "Oh. My. God. You're the guy...you were standing right next to him when he die—when he was killed."

"The Bishop? Yes, that was me."

"Oh. My. God!" she repeated. She reached out to hug him then jerked back, remembering herself. "I am such a fangirl, it's embarrassing."

Terry couldn't help but match her smile.

"You're my heroes," she said.

"You do some pretty heroic work here yourself," Terry said, taking her hand.

She blushed.

"You know, when this is all over," Terry started, "why don't you—and your partner, if you have one—why don't you come over to the friary for dinner one night? Brian—" He was about to praise Brian's cooking, but he couldn't get the words out. The whole recent history with Brian came rushing back to him in that moment and he felt crippled by the grief of it.

"What...is something wrong?" Chaplain Fran asked.

"I just...well, I just woke up from surgery a few minutes ago, and my memory is just coming back. And there's a lot...it was easier when I wasn't remembering it."

Chaplain Fran nodded and squeezed his hand encouragingly.

"In fact, there's a lot I need to do. There are...dark forces afoot." He watched her eyes widen. "Fran, I need your help..."

A few minutes later, he was out of bed, dressed in his own trousers and Fran's clerical shirt, walking right out of the hospital with no one questioning him or stopping him or even paying him the slightest bit of attention. "Gotta love a collar," he said to himself as the door to the main hospital exit slid open for him.

102

MARCO HELD out his bowl and the young blonde guard spooned a ladle full of hot cereal into it. "Have a nice day!" she said, her ponytail bobbing behind her head. "Please come again."

Marco walked over to an empty spot in the yard near the barbed wire fence and pulled his designated spoon out of his underwear. He sniffed at the cereal, uncertain as to what it might actually be. *It's too fine to be oatmeal,* he thought. *It's too dark to be Cream of Wheat.*

Madison sidled up to him, spoon already poised. "I am hungry as a motherfucker," he said, scooping up a spoonful.

Encouraged, Marco tried it. It was brown and course and kind of nutty. "It's not bad," he said, his eyebrows shooting up. He ate more.

Madison made a face. "I'd trade my incisors for a pound of sugar."

Cain joined them. "It's animal feed."

"What?" Marco asked.

"We used to feed this exact stuff to our goats on my grandfather's farm in Nebraska."

"No shit," Marco said between mouthfuls.

"May I?" Cain reached for Marco's bowl. Marco reluctantly allowed him to take it. "Gotta watch out for these fellers though." Cain held up a tiny curled worm. "This stuff is rife with them."

Madison spit his mouthful back into his bowl. "Motherfuckers," he said.

Marco eyed his grain suspiciously. "They can't hurt you, right?"

"It's a protein source," Cain said. He sniffed at the cereal and his grin faded.

"What?" Madison asked.

Cain sniffed again. Then he raised his hand. "Don't eat another bite."

Madison froze in mid-spoon.

"It's spiked." He sniffed some more. "It's faint, but...I think it's scopolamine."

"What's that?" Marco asked.

"It was used by the government as an early truth serum," Cain said. "It's easy to synthesize, and it's been used in a rash of burglaries in Europe. We busted a guy at one the UC Berkeley labs who was making it. It's supposed to be undetectable, but..."

"But you're the fucking Bloodhound." Madison punched him in the arm.

"Why would they be giving that to us?" Marco asked.

"It makes people compliant. Those cases in Europe? The perps used a powder form, they'd blow it in people's faces, then tell them to empty their pockets, give them their ATM cards and codes, empty their safe deposit boxes. People just did what they were told—no argument, no fuss."

"That explains a lot," Marco said, looking around.

"It's a low dose, but you get a steady supply of that?" Cain shook his head. "You got a pretty reliable zombie workforce."

"Shit," Madison swore.

"I'm glad you were able to smell that," Marco said, "but I'm not sure what we're going to do for food."

"It certainly gives us a timeline for escape," Cain said gravely.

Just then someone nearby cried out. There was a flurry of motion, and Marco instinctively backed up until his shoulders touched the barbed wire fence.

"He took my food!" Marco recognized one of the other new

arrivals. The man was calling out to the guards, pointing to another new "guest" who was scarfing up cereal as quickly as possible, completely ignoring everything not contained in his bowl.

A tall, neatly dressed guard stopped serving and wordlessly walked around the table. He pulled a taser from his belt and, without warning, punched the man in the neck with it. Marco heard electricity crackle, smelled the unmistakable odor of ozone, and watched the man plummet to the dirt.

Without emotion the young man grabbed the fallen man's collar and pulled. The fallen man moved a few inches, then the paper jumpsuit tore away from his body, leaving him exposed in his regulation briefs.

Another guard crossed the yard, and together they dragged the man to a gate. They inserted a key card and opened it. Then they dragged him out of the yard.

Marco leaned over to another "guest" who seemed to be taking little notice of the drama. "Where are they taking him?"

"Manners readjustment," the man said without looking at them.

"Manners readjustment," Marco repeated to Madison and Cain.

"I heard," Madison whispered. "Shit. Gotta hold my pinky out when tea-time comes."

Marco laughed. In spite of everything, it felt good.

"Any minute now, they're gonna let you go," Madison said, looking at Cain.

"Why do you say that?"

"Because you're one of *them*."

"What the fuck do you mean by that, Madison?"

"I mean you're white, and you're not Jewish, and you're not poor. They're probably going to give you a job."

Cain chewed on that for a moment. Marco could see that Cain followed the logic. "I won't take it."

"If you don't, you don't have any chance of helping *us*," Marco said.

Cain looked down. "Maybe...maybe I could go and get help."

"Have you forgotten what it's like out there?" Madison said. "This might be an internment camp, or concentration camp, or whatever, but is still safer than *out there*."

"If you want to be drugged into zombiedom," Marco objected.

"So we'll be safe *and* we'll be in no pain," Madison said. "It don't seem like too bad a deal."

"Except for the shit we don't know yet," Marco said. "Like what they ultimately are gonna do with us folk that aren't *like them*."

"I can't leave," Cain said, turning away from them.

"Why the fuck not?" Madison asked.

Cain didn't answer at first. When he did speak, Marco could hear the emotion in his voice. "I can't leave because...if my son were here, he'd be in here, too—for good."

Marco could see that the revelation was hard for him, but he didn't understand. "How so?"

Cain pointed with his chin to two men asleep on the ground, slumped on each other's shoulders. Marco didn't get it at first, then he saw that they were holding hands. "Cain, is your son gay?" Marco asked.

Cain looked down, then away. "Bi," he said, not as a shorthand, but because his voice closed halfway through the word.

"Your son is bisexual? Which means the straight world doesn't understand him, and he's rejected by the gay community to boot," Marco said.

"What?"

"It's a thing," Marco said. "Look...never mind."

"No, I want to know. I might never have the chance to hear it from him."

Marco's eyes softened. He sighed. "A lot of gays discriminate against bisexuals because if they wind up with an opposite sex partner, they can pass as straight. It's just a cluster of sour grapes."

Cain's brows furrowed as he took that in.

"And then a lot of gays also say that bisexuals don't exist—that they're just not being honest with themselves."

"What do you think?" Cain was looked at him now.

"I think people get to say what they are, and no one else's opinion counts for shit." Marco placed a hand on Cain's shoulder. "Look for what it's worth, I have close friends who are bisexual. You've met both of them. Remember Susan? She got married to a great guy, Dylan, and it's true—life is easier for her. And then there's Richard—"

"The leader of your Order—"

"Not my Order. I'm not that crazy. I'm just friends with them. Anyway, Richard...he plays the field. And he gets his heart broke on a pretty regular basis. He's the shit when it comes to Christian stuff and he knows his magick...but in love he's just about the unluckiest son of a bitch I've ever met." He squeezed Cain's shoulder. "So, you know? You never know."

"Cain," a guard's voice called out across the yard.

"See there? That's a job offer right there," Madison said. "Get your ass over there. Make your boy proud by doing something useful with your one miserable life."

"Not gonna happen," Cain said. "It's white privilege."

"Are you delusional?" Madison asked. "This is the one time I officially give you permission to use it if you got it."

"Do it, Cain," Marco said. "You can do more good out there than in here."

103

Just as Brian knocked back the last of his coffee, the lights came back on.

Maggie stood up. "Well, that's our cue to leave the green room. It's show time, dear."

Brian felt a wave of dread wash through him. The fact that the lights were on meant that whatever Larch was preparing to do, he was going to do it soon. Maggie turned on the radio, and a news station filled the air with a staticky stream of commentary. "...*are gathering now at the Hostess Ho Ho's Stadium, where Commander Larch is preparing to address the nation.*"

"And we know where we're going," Maggie said. "Although I might have guessed it."

"How far is that?" Brian asked.

"As the crow flies, maybe three miles. But on surface streets, and with things as they are...maybe five?"

"And we're walking?"

"Maybe we can catch the seventy-nine bus, if it's running. We have to go by that stop anyway. Let's give it a go."

Her style was disarmingly free-wheeling, and it made Brian

nervous. But he didn't balk. Instead, he visited the rest room and put his gray-green jacket on. "Ready," he announced.

———

THEY WEREN'T the only ones on the move. It seemed like the whole neighborhood was slowly migrating in the same direction, some in small groups, some in grim solitude. No one was terribly chatty.

They'd walked about three blocks when they heard the roar of a motor behind them. At first, Brian took no notice—it was a city, after all. But when it screeched to a stop right behind them, he turned.

A white government SUV with darkened windows brooded over them menacingly. Maggie smiled, but that didn't mean anything. Brian was half-sure she was crazy. He froze as the door opened. He was relieved to see that the driver was a large, fleshy, hairy man that he recognized.

"Hello, Moshe," Maggie said.

"Morning, Serah." He looked at Brian, and although it seemed as if he might choke on the words, he managed a weak, "Morning...Brian."

Brian smiled a warm return greeting at him.

He continued. "I thought you might like a ride. To the Stadium, that is."

Maggie wagged her finger at him. "You just want to make sure we get there."

"Of course I do. That's not exactly an ulterior motive. If he ascends—"

"If he ascends we'll stop him there."

"But my intelligence tells me that he seems to gain power with every ascent. Let's stop him *here*."

"Well, then, give me a hand up, love. I need a step ladder to get into these things."

Better than that, Moses gripped her on either side of her rib cage and lifted her into the vehicle.

"That was an example of unnecessary manhandling," she complained.

"File a grievance," he said, slamming the passenger door.

Brian opened the door to the back seat and hopped in.

Moses put the SUV into gear and lurched forward into the street, picking up speed quickly.

"There are oodles of pedestrians about, Moshe. Be careful."

"I'm not going to hit anyone."

"You'd better not."

Moses didn't respond, which relieved Brian as he suspected they could go on like that all day.

Moses slowed as he approached a red light. He looked both ways, then gunned it, running the light. He looked over to Maggie. "What are you going to say?"

"I'm not going to say anything," Serah asked. "This is Brian's gig, remember?"

"What are you going to say?" Moses caught his eye in the rear view mirror. "When you confront the magickian, what are you going to say?"

Brian shrugged. "I dunno."

"Wonderful," Moses groused. He jammed on the brakes to avoid hitting a small family. He laid into his horn.

When it stopped, Maggie said, "HaShem will provide the words, just like he provided the ram to Abraham. Have a little faith."

"You know, there's no one in the ten worlds who can get away with saying something like that to me."

"No one but me, dear."

"Why should I let you get away with that?"

"Because I'd box your ears if you tried to stop me," Maggie said.

They rode in silence for several minutes, and before long Brian saw the looming curved shell of a stadium peeking through the spaces between the buildings they passed. Moses turned at the next light and pulled into the vast desert of the parking lot. It was jammed with cars, however, and soon they were simply stalled. No one was moving anywhere.

"I think this is where we take it on foot," Maggie said, opening the passenger door.

"Let me help you." Moses unfastened his seat belt.

"I can topple to earth all on my own," Maggie announced. Gripping the door handle, she awkwardly lowered herself to the ground. Moses turned off the motor and got out himself.

"You're just going to leave it there?" Brian asked.

"Can't take it anywhere else right now, can I?" Moses asked.

Brian wasn't sure what he wanted. *Do I think he should be able to raise his arms and part the traffic?* he wondered and smiled at the image. As he walked behind the prophet, Brian studied him. He forced himself to stop thinking and just notice. He saw the flaky evidence of seborrhea on the back of his head, the curly hair tufting up through the neck of his shirt. And then he saw...more. He saw the frustration of a man who had given his life to leading people—people who didn't particularly appreciate his sacrifice or his hard work. He saw how everyone around him twisted his every word and action to suit their own ends and how much pain that caused him. He also saw that he'd resigned himself to his fate, his calling, a long time ago. He saw how much he missed his brother... and how angry he was at him. He saw his deep love for God, and how deeply hurt he was and how he felt betrayed by that same God.

Moses turned and caught Brian's eye. A look of vulnerable exposure passed across his face. "Stop that," he said.

Brian blinked and looked away.

They moved with and through the gray-green sea of people until they reached the doors. There was no organization. People were just streaming into the stadium, and Brian, Maggie, and Moses allowed themselves to be swept along with the tide. Every couple of minutes or so, someone would do a double take on seeing Moses, and some of them pointed and remarked to a neighbor. But no one tried to stop them.

Once inside the stadium, the river of people headed for service doors. They went down a concrete and metal staircase and onto the field. Emerging onto the green, Maggie stumbled on the grass. Brian caught her hand. "You all right?" he asked.

"Of course I'm all right. I wore sensible shoes."

He released her hand.

She looked up at him sheepishly. "Thank you," she said in a barely audible voice.

Brian looked around quickly to get his bearings. He felt assaulted by incoming information. People were beginning to gather into rough platoons, vaguely amorphous squares of people spread out across the green. Some held up signs with numbers and letters on them, no doubt indicating some pre-arranged grouping plan. Enormous jumbotrons flashed pictures of a main stage as camera and lighting technicians ran through their tests.

"That's it. That's where he'll be," Maggie pointed at a small stage set up on risers near the far end of the field.

Moses walked in front, almost as if he were running interference. *And that's pretty much what he's doing,* Brian thought to himself.

They were nearly halfway across the field when a fanfare began to play through the loudspeakers. Around them, the amoeba-like platoons of people straightened out into neat squares as they stood at attention. On the jumbotron, Brian saw the cameras swing toward a set of doors. They swung open to the inside and someone he recognized stepped into the greenish light.

Larch.

He had never met the magickian, not in person. He'd seen pictures, and he'd heard plenty of talk. He knew for sure it was him. He was wearing a gray-green jacket, too, along with a matching captain's cap. Brian wasn't sure that was exactly what military dress code would have called for, but it made a striking impression. As they drew closer, Brian saw a team of armed guards pointing toward them. Brian steeled himself, but they walked straight past him...and surrounded Moses.

"Keep walking, dear," Maggie whispered, taking his arm. "Don't look back. Moshe is serving as our decoy. They won't hurt him. He's their rightful head after all."

"This place isn't a democracy?"

"Netzach, a democracy? Don't be daft. It's a benevolent dictatorship and has been for more than two-thousand years."

"Has Moses always been in charge?"

"Always. That's his job. Keep walking. Don't make eye contact with anyone."

Brian obeyed. They walked past innumerable uniformed people. They walked past guards. They walked straight toward the podium. Another fanfare blared, and Larch took the stage.

"My dear friends," the crowd went wild. He held his hand up until they quieted down, smiling indulgently. "My dear friends, you have a sacred way of life here in Netzach."

Another wave of applause and shouting rippled through the stadium. Brian looked at the jumbotron and wondered how many other stadiums like this around the Netzach globe were also full and watching.

"A way of life handed down from your ancestors, a way of life you want to hand on to your children—"

Another roar erupted from the crowd. Larch waited until it had calmed down. "Heaven wants to end that way of life. HaShem wants to wrest it from your grasp. Tell me, is that the action of a loving God?"

The crowd started booing, but Larch leaned closer to his microphone and spoke above it. "A compassionate God? A God who cares about *you*?"

A hundred-thousand voices yelled in unison, "No!"

"No. No it isn't," Larch affirmed. "And when a government has become tyrannous, the only sane course is to topple the tyrant from his throne and restore justice."

"Justice! Justice! Justice!" the crowd began to shout. They also began to stamp their feet. Brian felt the reverberations shake the ground beneath him.

"Who knows what other crimes on what other worlds he has perpetrated? Who knows what other peoples he has betrayed? I trust we soon will know. And we will put a stop to it. *Now*. Today. *Today* is the day of your salvation."

The crowd went wild. Larch held his hand up but the people did not stop. He held both hands up. The roaring continued.

"Now, dear," Maggie whispered. Brian felt a little shove in his back. He saw a little step ladder leading onto the riser and tried to move his feet. He couldn't. He felt completely paralyzed and began hyperventilating.

Maggie noticed and slipped her hand into his, squeezing it firmly. "Do you want to know what I see right now?" she asked, just loud enough that only he could hear.

He did but couldn't make his mouth move.

"I see someone who has always been the support person, the help-meet, the person behind the scenes. It was always Terry and Richard and Dylan who went out to slay the dragon. You stayed at home and carved arrows."

Yes, he thought. *That's true. That's who I am. I am the arrow-carver. I am the researcher. I'm the cook. I took care of them so that they could go and save the world—again and again and again.*

Maggie squeezed his hand again. "The reason you've been feeling so frustrated lately is that you know, deep down, that you are called to something more. You are not destined to be an arrow-carver forever. It's time for you to move out of the shadows—to take center stage. It's time for you to step into your power and to claim your true calling. It's time to stop carving arrows and time to start shooting them. Go. This is what you are *here* for."

As if watching his own body from a distance, Brian watched his foot move. Then the other. Then his whole body was in motion, stepping up onto the riser. Maggie was right behind him. A bodyguard tried to intercept him, but Maggie was too quick. She intercepted the guard and spoke to him, and the man dissolved into tears.

Brian was close enough to Larch to touch him before the magickian noticed.

He covered the microphone with his hand, and a squeal of feedback sliced the air. "Who the fuck are you?" he whispered.

"My name is Brian Epstein. I think you know my partner, Father Terry Milne."

"You're a Blackfriar," Larch narrowed his eyes.

"No, but I live with them," Brian said.

"Ah! Another from the second string, then. And I suppose you're here to stop me?"

"I'm here…I'm here to help you."

Larch lifted his nose skeptically. "Why would you help me?"

"I'm here to…to tell you something."

Larch lifted an eyebrow.

But that was it. That was all Brian had. He might have come to tell Larch something, but he was damned if he knew what that was. *Okay, HaShem, any time now*, he thought desperately.

Larch lifted his other eyebrow. "I'm waiting."

Nothing. Brian began to sweat. He looked over at Maggie, and her eyes closed serenely.

He looked back at Larch. And then it hit him. Maggie had told him what to do—he just wasn't doing it. He closed his eyes and reached out with his intuition. He became aware of HaShem's spirit, filling all things. Brian grasped at it, held it and let himself be held by it. He stopped trying to control the situation. He relaxed. There was nothing to do. All he had to do was notice.

He opened his eyes, and he *saw*.

He saw a little boy, playing with matches, angry and hating himself. He saw the boy's mother, alone. He saw the man who visited her, the man she took into her room. This was the boy's father and he did not acknowledge it or have any time or love for him. Brian saw him again, but this time in vestments, lifting high the consecrated host and putting it on the boy's tongue—his only act of nurture. Time swam and unfolded around Larch's face. Brian saw the boy growing up—he saw the crushing powerlessness of poverty and the sensitivity of the young man's soul. He saw the young Larch try to follow in his father's footsteps—and he saw him rejected by the seminary, by the church. He saw Larch's soul curl into a bitter black thing, shuddering like burning paper. He saw him discover magick, saw how it gave him everything he had longed for—a community that accepted him and gloried in him, a spiritual path to work and grow into, and most of all, *power*.

"If you haven't noticed, I'm in the middle of something," Larch said impatiently. "I've just reached a stirring climax in my speech, and I'm afraid you're—"

Brian held his hand up, and to his astonishment, Larch stopped speaking. Brian opened his mouth and the words tumbled out. Once again, it was as if he were observing himself from someplace above himself. "Stanis, be at peace." Brian's voice took on a confidence he did not feel. "Your father was cruel to you and you deserved better. You needed better. You should have had better."

Larch's eyes went wide. The magickian couldn't have known what he was going to say, but Brian was pretty sure he was not expecting *this*. "The church treated you unfairly. It should have given you mercy instead of judgment. It should have guided you not condemned you. You should have been treated better."

Larch staggered backward a couple of steps. Brian advanced to keep the distance between them the same. "And I'm sorry. I'm sorry you had such a sucky father, and that the church hierarchy were such assholes to you. I can see that you would have been a very fine priest. It wasn't only you who was robbed, it was everyone you might have served."

Brian took another step toward him. "But I want you to hear me now, Stanis. Your father is not God. And the church is not God. Your father was a bastard to you, and yes, he liturgically represents God to his congregation. And in your imagination, the two are all tangled up. That tangledness is the wound of childhood. The work of your adult soul is to untangle the two, to see that they are different." He looked Larch straight in the eye and said, "Your father is not God. Your father was a broken, selfish person who did not represent God in any way in his actions. And the church is not God. The church is made up of broken, selfish people, just like your father. They do not represent God. They may point at him imperfectly, but that is all. That is the Truth."

Brian watched a range of emotions play out on Larch's face in quick succession. The man swallowed and looked around as if searching for some place to hide. Brian closed the distance between them and took Larch's hands into his own, speaking to him tenderly. "Your whole adult life you have been plotting your revenge against God, but your anger is really for your father. Your whole adult life you have led other people into rebellion against the Lord of Heaven, projecting onto HaShem every thoughtless, cruel thing your father or the church ever did to you. But God did *not* do that do you. God loves you and wants to be intimate with your soul. And I know, I know... that is *terrifying*. Let it be for now. But also for now, you must release these people from your own delusion."

Larch was no longer covering the microphone. Everyone in the world had heard the Truth.

104

WITHOUT A MOMENT'S HESITATION, Richard dove for the door of the tent, rolling after Tobias. As soon as he hit the floor, a clanging alarm sounded out in the camp. *That was fast,* Richard thought as he cleared the door. He scrambled to his feet and, catching sight of the lab's retreating tail, ran after him. Had Toby really spoken English just now? Surely, if he—or the angel—could speak, he would have before. Still...it could have been his imagination.

A man in front of him swung a rake, and Richard sidestepped it. It didn't seem like the man was aiming at him, he was just in a hurry and clueless. Although a lot of people were running in every conceivable direction in apparent panic, no one seemed to be paying any attention to *him.*

He was feeling elated at the possibility of making his escape so easily, but the more terrified people he passed, the more concerned he became. Tobias slowed down and looked back every now and then to make sure that Richard was still there. He only stopped when Richard scrambled down the bank into what would have normally been the water of the Bay. The tide was out, however, and Richard found himself stepping on a soft green carpet of seaweed and algae.

He leaned against a large, ornamental cluster of rocks near the frontage road and caught his breath.

The fog had not yet burned off, and it lent the bay a ghostly, mystical atmosphere. Tobias sat and looked up into Richard's face with grave concern. Then the ground beneath them rumbled and Toby's tail sunk beneath his legs as he emitted a soft whimper.

Concerned, Richard turned back toward the camp and peered over the rocks. "I can't see anything, boy," he said. He looked around and saw the pedestrian walkway that stretched over the freeway just a few hundred yards away. "Let's get a better vantage point on this," he said, pointing at it.

Toby looked uncertain, but as there was no one on it or near it, Richard didn't see how it could be any more dangerous than huddling blind in the mud. "C'mon," he called and scrambled up the bank again.

Tobias followed, and Richard heard the din of shouts and clatter from the camp as he ran. He couldn't begin to guess what the rumbling was, but he was determined to find out. He ran full-out toward the concrete ramp that led up to the walkway. As he rounded the corner, an ax fell, passing a fraction of an inch from his face. Richard felt the wind of it on his nose and jumped back. It was Viking guy, the one the amazon had sent back to watch the children. Had he been sent to retrieve him? Or was he simply guarding the walkway from anyone seeking to pass into the camp without authorization? Richard didn't know, and the distinction seemed academic as he stepped back, putting as much distance as he could between himself and the Viking.

"Whoa now, watch that thing," Richard said. "Someone could get hurt."

"Thought you might escape your fate, priest?" The man smiled, his long red beard drawing up on either side as he did so.

"I *had* that thought, yes. But only because something is happening in the camp, and for some reason I don't seem...very important."

A look of concern passed the Viking's face and his smile drooped.

It wasn't a line he had expected to hear, and Richard's response seemed to confuse him. "Well, let's go see what *is* important, then."

"I'm not sure that's a good idea," Richard said. "We..." He looked around. Toby was nowhere to be seen. *Good dog,* Richard thought. "I mean, I thought I might see what was going on from up there." He pointed at the walkway. "Why don't we check it out before going back?"

"Because you're tricky and I don't trust you. Come on, move it. We'll see what the Goat King wants to do with you." He brandished the ax menacingly.

Richard sighed. "Fine. But don't say I didn't warn you."

The Viking scowled and gave a jerk of his head. Richard obeyed, turning back toward the camp.

His limbs felt heavy at first, but as they got closer to the camp, it was clear that something was indeed amiss. People were still running in every direction, alarms were still clanging, but people were beginning to assemble into what looked like platoons.

"It looks like war," the Viking said, as if to himself.

"War?" Richard asked. "Against whom?"

"Oakland, I think. I heard there was an army gathered at the foot of the bridge last night to repel an attack from San Francisco."

"An attack? Who was attacking? Who—" then Richard remembered the lights he'd seen last night. "I think that was a vigil, not an attack. People holding candles don't usually hold weapons."

"It was a slaughter from what I hear," the Viking let a smile escape. Richard shuddered. "I think maybe the Oaklanders are coming for the Goat King's spoils," the Viking said. The troops were facing in the direction of Emeryville, toward the foot of the Bay Bridge.

"Are you saying that the Marina is about to burst out into full-scale medieval battle?" Richard asked. The Viking didn't answer but merely swung his ax as if in gleeful anticipation of the bloodlust that would soon be upon him.

"What did you do before...before everything broke down and you began to serve the Goat King?" Richard asked.

The Viking blinked and looked at Richard as if just waking up from a nap. "Huh? Oh, I was...uh..." he looked down and stroked his beard.

"Can't you remember?" Richard asked.

The Viking held his hand up. "Wait...oh, I got it. I was a home care attendant."

"A home care attendant. Like a nurse?"

"I don't have my RN. I just take care of people."

"With an ax?"

"I didn't used to...no, not with an ax."

"Who did you take care of?"

"Old Mr. Schell, over off San Pablo. Albany. Lovely little house. Little Schnauzer named Teacup. They were great. We would just hang, smoke out, and play cards and video games. It was like free money."

"What happened to old Mr. Schell?" Richard asked.

A dark look passed over the Viking's face. "I...don't want to talk about Mr. Schell."

"What's your name, soldier?" Richard asked.

"Cal."

"Cal the Viking," Richard smiled.

"Don't you forget it."

"Not likely. I'm Richard."

"You seem all right—for a priest, I mean. But that don't make us friends. You're my prisoner."

"Of course. What happens when the fighting begins? Will someone give me a weapon?"

Cal stroked his beard. "I don't know that."

"Who do we ask? I think the Goat King is probably busy."

Cal looked concerned. "I hadn't thought of that."

"You can't just put me in a troop without a weapon. Do you have a jail, or a—" Richard stopped. Marching up the frontage road from Emeryville he saw the vanguard of the Oakland army. And emerging from the midmorning fog were the hordes on their heels. Thousands upon thousands of people emerged from the mist, the ground rumbling as they came.

Richard squinted, trying to see them better. They seemed to be of all ages. He saw children and old people and everything in between. Men and women of every race were well represented and there were people of every conceivable ethnicity. There were people in jeans and hoodies and people in tattered business suits, their sleeves dangling from their elbows like vestigial organs. In their hands they held rifles, crowbars, baseball bats, broken bottles, scraps of wood with nails driven into their tips, and anything and everything else that might prove injurious to human flesh. They waved them in the air and shouted, filling the air with ululations and shrieks and terrible roars.

"There are too many of them..." Cal said, his ax slipping to the ground.

It was true. Already those marching toward them outnumbered the Goat King's army, and every second more were emerging from the fog. And more. And more. Richard watched as the troops in the Marina transformed from fierce to fearful. At first, he saw a few weapons drop from their hands to the dirt, then there was an all-out stampede, heading north toward Albany.

Richard wasn't sure where to go. He heard Toby bark behind him. The dog ran a few feet then stopped, waiting for Richard to follow. Richard reached out and caught Cal's sleeve. "This way," he said.

"But the Goat King—" Cal pointed.

Richard followed his finger and saw that the Goat King had assembled his courtiers outside his tent, arranging their chairs for a prime view of the battle. But his officers were fleeing now along with everyone else, leaving the pitiful king alone and exposed.

"There's nothing we can do, Cal," Richard said. Toby was barking wildly behind him, but Cal couldn't turn away. For that matter, neither could Richard. It was then that he realized that the rumbling he felt beneath his feet was not from the approaching army. It was too sporadic, too lumbering and intermittent.

"Oh my God," Richard said aloud. Cal sank to his knees as the fog parted and a great beast was revealed. Surrounded on every side by the Oakland army, the creature stood at least three stories high, his terrible nose raised to the sky, a shrieking scream emitting from its throat. Step after lumbering step, its feet, each the size of cars, crashed onto the gravel road sending booming shudders through the earth, nearly knocking Richard from his feet. A part of his mind heard Tobias continuing to bark behind him, even felt the dog tugging on his cassock, but he could not look away.

The great beast had the shape of a tyrannosaurus rex, but it was a shoddy and malformed excuse for a dinosaur. As it grew closer, Richard could see that it's skin was not uniform but composed of what looked like patches, all stitched together at sloppy angles. Richard felt his skin crawl and his spine turn to ice water as he realized that the patches were...people...people and animals.

Someone among the Oakland army had sewn and stapled and bolted together a mountain of the dead, stitched together in the rough shape of a giant murderous lizard, animated by demonic power. "Oh my God," Richard whispered again. The beast strode forward in unnatural, jerky motions, crushing everything in its path.

Unable to tear his eyes away, Richard remembered the spectacles in his pocket. He pulled them out and put them on, his eyes instantly stinging and blinking back against the ferocious light.

As his eyes adjusted, he saw the hordes of the Oakland army, as he had expected. He saw the shambling, patchwork dinosaur. But he saw more. He saw the glory of God pervading and animating all things—without which the entire earth would curl up into a wisp of ash and blow away like a burning sigil. He saw with his own, aching eyes the grace and love that supported every living thing, no matter how small or powerful, no matter how wicked or fearful. All breathed it in like air, for it was in the air—or more accurately, the air was in *it*. All fed on it without knowing it, for it was identical with the very moisture that composed all beings. It was the electricity that sparked their neurons. It was the well of emotion that fed their passions. It was inseparable from their flesh, inseparable from their thoughts or feelings or actions. It upheld all that Richard could see, and in it all things lived and moved and had their being.

And in spite of the overwhelming, unstoppable goodness with which the army was surrounded and upheld, the Glory suffered them to continue along their murderous path, undeterred in their intentions as the manifestation of their corruption lumbered toward the Marina, crushing cars and buildings and people beneath the heavy meat of its great patchwork feet.

And astride the great beast, balancing upon its shoulders, Richard clearly saw a duke of Hell, clothed in crimson, a great crown upon its terrible head. Its beak extended at a cruel angle, and its long, sharp claws held the reigns that guided the dinosaur. Its beak opened and emitted a high-pitched scream of glee as it guided the beast toward the fleeing army—and directly toward Richard.

105

MIKAEL WOKE up to a tickling on his cheek. He opened one eye and saw Kat hovering over him, trailing the corner of a handkerchief across his face. He wriggled his nose and raised his head, squinting at her. "You okay?"

"Yeah." She blushed. "My ego is pretty bruised, and I've got a story to tell...but I'm physically unharmed."

He propped himself up on one elbow. He was back in the spare bedroom at Chava and Elsa's. For some reason, he was on the floor. He had only the vaguest memory of having come there in the wee hours of the night. He reached out and scooped Kat's waist, pulling her toward him. "You could say the same for me."

"Oh, good. We can compare our level of shame." She smirked.

"I...found Larch. But I couldn't stop him. And—I didn't know this before, but I do now—I couldn't kill him."

"I'm relieved," she said. "That doesn't sound like anything to be ashamed of."

He sighed. "Part of me agrees with you. And part of me...well—"

"Wishes you could be more like Richard?"

"Yeah."

"Thank *God* you aren't more like Richard. You wouldn't be half as sexy." She bumped noses with him.

"You don't think Richard is sexy?"

"Ew..." she said. "Richard is *old*."

"How are you?" Mikael asked.

She looked away. "I'm so sorry, babe. I don't know what got into me yesterday. It started out with the lying, and then... Look, I lie every day—"

"You do?" he said, his eyes growing wide.

"Shut up, fuckhead," she punched him in the arm. "This is hard enough, you know."

"Sorry. Do go on."

"It's that I got so defensive, so angry, so...combative. I mean I want to be—"

"Like Susan?" Mikael offered.

She met his eyes. "Uh...yeah. More like Susan. But I was so... belligerent. It isn't me. It's just...it was just wrong. I don't know what got into me, and I'm sorry I took it out on you."

He kissed her. "It's okay. It wasn't you. It was," he said, waving his hand toward heaven, "it was all that stuff going on up there."

"You sound like an astrologer I had as a housemate once."

"I mean sephirot stuff."

"I know what you mean." She kissed him back. "I'm still sorry."

"You are forgiven."

"So are you."

"What? What did *I* do?"

"Don't push it, buster." She pushed him back onto the floor, straddled his body, and kissed him deeply.

When she came up for air, Mikael said, "And I'm glad you're not Susan."

"Why not?" Kat asked.

"For one thing, you'd be crushing my rib cage right now."

"That's mean," she said.

"Not any less true, though."

"And then there's the bridge," Kat said, her smile fading quickly.

"What? The march?"

"Yeah. I almost got everyone killed. I think." She briefly relayed what happened.

"Sounds like they were going to march into a trap no matter what you did," Mikael said. "It sounds to me like you saved them. That doesn't sound like anything to be ashamed of either." He kissed her.

"It was too close," she said. "It scared the piss out of me."

"I'm proud of you," he said. "It sounds like you and the Angel of the Air are getting to be buds."

"Yeah, sure, let's have him over for barbecue." She rolled off of him and helped him sit up.

Mikael rose the rest of the way himself. "I have an idea. Let's see what they call 'breakfast' around here."

"I'm guessing bacon is out," Kat said.

"Good bet," Mikael said. They opened the door and walked into the living room. Brian was still comatose on the sofa. Chava was sitting near him, reading from an enormous book that looked very old indeed. She marked her place in the book and closed it, smiling. "You two certainly got in late. Did you get any sleep at all?"

Mikael heard a chopping sound coming from the kitchen and surmised that Elsa must be there. He smelled the intoxicating odor of coffee and had to catch himself before his knees buckled from the sheer wonderfulness of it. "I definitely have some catching up to do," he said, letting a well-timed yawn escape.

"Me too," Kat agreed. She sat down on the edge of the sofa next to Brian. "How's our champion?"

Chava shrugged. "Who can tell? He hasn't emerged for ages. I'm getting seriously worried about his bladder. I'm thinking it might be catheter time."

Mikael shuddered. Just then Elsa came out of the kitchen with a tray full of mugs and a glass of water.

"Coffee?" she asked.

"Yes, God, please," Kat answered, snatching one up and gulping at it without bothering with her usual cream and sugar.

"That's hot," Elsa warned.

"I'll heal," Kat said, taking a breath.

"She always this impulsive?" Elsa asked Mikael.

"You get used to it," he said, winking at Kat.

Elsa jumped when a pounding came at the door and spilled a little of the coffee. She hastened to set it down and then ran to the kitchen for a towel.

"Who could that be?" Chava asked.

Mikael's eyebrows shot up. "Do you want me to get that?"

"No, I'll get it," Chava crossed to the door and looked through the security viewer. Then she stepped back.

"Chava, are you all right?" Kat asked. "You're white as a sheet."

"And you're shaking," Mikael said. He rushed to her side just as she collapsed to the floor. She didn't lose consciousness, she just seemed rattled and a little disoriented. Elsa rushed to her from the kitchen. "Baby, what's wrong?" she asked as she knelt beside her partner.

In answer, Chava only pointed at the door with a shaky finger.

Concerned, Mikael fitted his eye to the viewer and looked. "Oh, it's just Maggie." He threw open the door. "Maggie!" He gave her a bear hug, even picking her off her feet for a second.

"Hello, love," she said. "Took you a bleedin' long time, though." She was dressed in stretch pants and a soccer jersey, with a winter coat and scarf over all.

"What the fuck are you doing here?" he asked, grinning.

"I've just come from Lake Tahoe, where I was running the craps tables—meaning I was *winning*, dear. But I stopped and came here, because *he* needs me," she pointed at Brian. She waddled over to him, snatched up the glass of water, and emptied it over his head.

Brian started, sitting upright. "Maggie! Shit do I gotta piss!" He bolted for the bathroom.

Maggie turned toward them with a wide smile. Then she noticed Chava. "Hello, dear. Are you all right? You seem to have seen a ghost."

"Serah...you're S-S-Serah bat Asher," Chava stuttered.

"Damn! So much for my secret identity." Maggie placed her hands on her hips. "And just how do you know that?"

Elsa pointed toward the spare room. Maggie's eyebrows lifted in curiosity, and she followed when Kat waved her over. Kat opened the door and flipped on the light. Maggie's jaw dropped as she saw she was surrounded by pictures of herself, along with the excruciating minutiae of all her many lives.

Having seen enough, she waddled back into the living room, placing her gnarled fists once more on her hips. "My dear, are you a stalker? Because I have no time or patience for stalkers."

Chava shook her head. "Are you really...an Episcopal priest?"

"What kind of question is that? Of course I'm an Episcopal priest. I'm the Canon for Clergy Formation in the Diocese of California. Why do you seem so..." Her face softened. "Oh. You think I've betrayed our people. No, my dear. I do us—I mean the big 'Us,' Israel —as much service as ever. I just serve gentiles, too. It's all the same God, you know." She leaned down. Mikael figured her knees were probably too arthritic to kneel. "But you...I can see you serve well. Don't judge your gentile sisters and brothers so harshly, though. They have a place in *tikkun olam* as well. You should get out and mix a little."

"What do you mean? I married a *goy*!" she said.

"Yes, and you insisted she convert to be like you," Maggie said.

"I didn't insist," Chava objected.

"Yes, dear, you did." Elsa put her arm around Chava's bosom tenderly. "I said yes, and I embraced the People, but...you really did give me an ultimatum."

Chava looked down.

"Don't feel bad, dear. There's nothing broken that HaShem can't fix," Maggie smiled.

Brian walked into the room, feeling at his back. "Pulled a muscle, I think."

"Well, dear, you'll just have to work it out. No rest for the wicked today."

"Are we the wicked?" he asked. "I thought we were the good guys."

"Sorry. There's my inner Calvinist leaping out again. Get your shoes on, dear, and straighten your tallit. And your hair is screaming for a comb. Can't set the world right with bed hair, can we?"

"No, Ma'am," Brian adjusted his tallit under his vest and squatted, reaching for his oxfords.

"I should think not."

"Maggie, are things okay," Mikael pointed at the ceiling, "up there?"

"On the seventh floor, dear?"

"No, I mean...the sephirot."

"Oh, well, we removed the tumor. There's still a good deal of healing to be done, but things are sorting themselves out. Notice no one is arguing now? And no one is stretching the truth—any more than usual, that is."

Mikael looked at Kat. They both nodded at each other.

"We'll be back to normal in no time. Which is to say, ugly tubes and boxes everywhere just so *you* can have the internet. Don't know whose bloody brilliant idea *that* was."

"Al Gore's, I hear." Brian stood and headed to the bathroom for, presumably, a comb.

"What the fuck are you talking about?" Kat asked.

Maggie waved her question away.

"What are we going to do now?" Brian called from the bathroom.

"Today we get a wee foretaste of judgement day," she said, picking up one of the cups of coffee.

"Judgement day?" Kat asked. "Sounds terrible."

"Oh no, dear, not so bad as you think. God doesn't actually condemn anybody."

"He doesn't?" Kat's eyebrows rose in surprise.

"Oh, heavens no. Not his way. God doesn't reward people or damn them, that's just a horrific little myth."

"So what happens at judgement?" Kat asked.

"He just tells them the truth about themselves. If the soul is too sick, it will slink off into isolation. If the soul is healthy enough, it will embrace community and will be embraced by community. God doesn't decide anyone's fate. People choose what they will do. Always."

"That doesn't seem fair," Kat said. "Wounded people aren't responsible for their condition."

"I didn't say wounded, dear. We're all wounded. Sick souls become sick because of little choices people make day in and day out. If you practice kindness, kindness gets easier, and you heal. If you practice spite, it gets easier to be spiteful, and you get sicker. People choose their fates every day of their lives. Judgement is just a public acknowledgment of the sum of all those cumulative choices. God never sends anyone to hell, not ever. People walk there on their own two feet, a little bit at a time."

"Yes, I've seen that," Kat said, remembering Charlie—who chose to stay in hell when Terry brought them there one day for a field trip.

"So my job is to be a mouthpiece for that kind of truth-telling. And after today, I'll be retired, and Brian will take over." Brian returned from the bathroom as if making an entrance, his hair neatly combed.

"Brian?" Chava asked. "*You* are taking over for Serah bat Asher?"

"He is. I have taken note of him. He's the one. Treat him well." She elbowed Kat.

"You bet," Kat agreed. "Actually, he takes care of us."

"So where are we going?" Brian asked.

"Why, the East Bay of course. There are hundreds of thousands of people there who need to hear the truth about themselves."

"Why?" Kat asked.

"Don't be stupid, dear," Maggie said. "It's the only way to set things right and break the power of those nasty demons."

"How are we going to get there?" Brian asked. "BART's stopped. The bridges are closed. Is the ferry still running?"

"Oh, poop on the ferry," Maggie waved. "We'll go the way we always used to go back in the good old days. We'll walk."

106

AFTER BREAKFAST, the prisoners started lining up in groups. "What's going on?" Madison asked.

"Don't know," Marco whispered. "Work groups?" It seemed a good guess, as it looked like people were separating themselves by body type. Large men and the taller, bulkier women were lining up at one gate, while those of smaller stature headed off to the other side of the yard, toward a different gate. "I'm gonna guess the big ones are agricultural workers."

"What makes you say that?" Madison asked.

"Just a hunch," Marco shrugged. "Physical labor."

"I just see a lot of brown and black people."

"And some gay and lesbian white folk."

"Sure, I'll give you that. Looks like one or two Jewish people, too. Though I can't figure out why *they're* here." Madison pointed to a small cluster of white kids in their late teens.

"I don't know. They look kind of Goth. I think they just put anyone who doesn't fit into Stan's Aryan wet dream in here."

"You mean those kids just aren't Hardy Boys and Nancy Drew enough to wear the squirrel?"

Marco shook his head. "Gotta love that fucking squirrel, man."

"I always thought they were cute. Now I'm going to see them as symbols of racial oppression."

"Just the white ones," Marco smiled gravely.

"Do you have white friends? I mean close friends?" Madison asked.

"Yeah. Sure. Most of my closest friends, in fact."

"Man, that's just weird."

"There aren't many black Thelemites."

"Thele-who?"

"Thele...never mind. It's the name of the religion I belong to."

"Was that religion started by a white person?"

Marco blinked. "Uh...yeah."

Madison shook his head. "Man, I knew it. Meet the new boss, same as the old boss."

"You know that's a Who quote, right? Whitest rock group ever?"

Madison ignored him. "Jesus was a black man. Just give me some black Jesus."

"Jesus was Jewish," Marco countered.

"Now you're a Bible expert?"

"You don't have to be an expert to—"

"Shut up, man. I'm gonna trust my pastor before I trust some Thele-whooey."

"Your pastor said Jesus was black?"

"He was Middle Eastern, wasn't he? Don't you think he was closer to what Arabs look like? I mean, Jews hadn't gone through the whole European distillation yet."

"Diaspora?"

"Shut the fuck up, man. What do you know?"

Marco smiled, enjoying the volley. "There's no way they're going to just let us stand here and wank off all day."

"I think you're right about that. Look." Madison pointed to a tall, blonde, impossibly handsome kid holding a clipboard and walking straight toward them. His black shirt bore the emblem of the white squirrel and a white paper hat sat astride his head at a rakish angle.

"You two look like you have strong legs."

"How the fuck can you see my legs?" Madison scowled.

Marco slapped his arm. "We do. And we're eager to help. Anything for Stan."

The young man's eyebrows jumped in surprise. "That's the spirit, comrade! You can help the cause by providing power duty today."

"Power duty! I like the sound of that!" Marco said.

"Uncle fucking Tom," Madison whispered.

"What's that?" the young man asked.

"Uh...he's my uncle. His name is Tom." Madison managed a forced smile.

The young man looked at his papers. "I thought your name was Marco."

"It is. He's just kidding around. Let's go!" Marco said enthusiastically.

"Sure thing. Follow me." He turned on his heel and made for one of the wire gates near the house.

"Watch your tongue or we'll be on the beating end of a stick," Marco whispered. "These folks might be ridiculous, but they're also holding all the weapons."

"You don't need to remind me 'bout that," Madison whispered back. "I gotta get my digs in somehow."

"Moderate that shit if you want to keep all your teeth, that's all I'm saying."

"You callin' the shots now?"

"I'm stating the obvious, asshole."

Stepping through the gate, they waited while the young man secured it.

"So you think it's demons that made these folks go all Hitler youth on us?" Madison asked. "I mean, I don't think I believe any of that stuff in the first place, but let's say you're right. If the demon power was broken right now, what do you think they'd do? I mean, they have the upper hand now. You think they'd just let go of that?"

"I think the fact that you're talking about 'them' and 'they' is just as horrifying as the fact that we're in here."

"Great. Blame the victim. I didn't put us in here, man."

Marco knew he was right. But he wasn't sure how to think about it all, either. His white friends often mentioned that race was too complex for them to completely get a grip on. He'd never sympathized with that opinion before, but now Marco was inclined to agree.

They passed alongside the white-painted house, and as they came in sight of the backyard, Marco saw Cain standing in a black shirt with a squirrel on it. One of the younger members was instructing him in the use of the rifle. Marco was sure Cain didn't need any instruction in firearms but was probably just playing along. Their eyes met for a second, and Cain gave a quick nod.

The young man led them to the back door to a semi-detached garage. Opening the door, he waved his hand inside, as if grandly inviting them to enter. Marco stepped through and caught his breath. Inside were three rows of exercise machines—treadmills, stationary bikes, and ellipticals—each row containing four machines. Marco was surprised to see the racial diversity among the exercisers and wondered if some of Stan's Youth were among them. But no, as he looked more closely, he saw they were all prisoners.

And labor it certainly seemed to be. No one looked happy, that was for sure. Even the righteous determination he saw on the rare occasions he ventured into a gym was missing from these folks. They seemed slogging and beaten. Marco felt punched in the gut.

Then he noticed the wires. Affixed to every exercise machine seemed to be some sort of generator—copper wires sprung up like weeds from each machine, running like vines in apparently random patterns across the room. Marco followed them with his eyes to a bank of car batteries against the inside wall near a door that probably went into the house.

That suspicion was confirmed a moment later when the door opened, and a middle-aged balding man in a black shirt with a squirrel on it stepped through, conversing briefly with the young man. Behind him, Marco saw what looked like a den. A couch full of Stan Youth were crowded together, jockeying for a video game controller as the sounds of digital explosions and mayhem spilled out of the room.

Marco looked at Madison.

"Ah, hell no," Madison said, a little too loudly. "I am *not* gonna be a human generator just so some white boys can play fuckin' Legend of Zelda. Are you kidding m—"

The young man socked Madison in the jaw with the butt of his rifle and Madison went down like a sack of meat. Marco flinched but kept his mouth shut.

Then he had an idea. He turned to the older man. "Sir, if you will permit me, I have a suggestion for how to increase your power yield by about ten-fold."

The man had opened his mouth to yell but somehow actually heard what Marco was saying. He cocked his head. "Go on."

"You've got solar panels on the roof here," Marco said. "But they're probably rigged up to the PG&E grid so you can't benefit from them. I'm an...well, an electrician among other things. Give me the tools I need and the rest of the morning and I'll have your panels pumping out as much power as your batteries can hold every day."

"We can always get more batteries," he said.

"So much the better," Marco said.

"Son, you've got yourself a job."

107

THE PIZZA BOX WAS EMPTY, and the sun was dim but up. Chicken opened the back door for Dylan and Susan, and they headed out into the Alameda morning. They retraced their steps from the night before, and following Susan's dim recollection of exactly where the Ferry Terminal was, they set off down Central Avenue. After a few blocks it turned into Main Street, and Susan relaxed. They were going the right way.

But she didn't lower her hackles all the way. She clutched at the revolver in her jacket pocket and kept an eagle eye out for anyone who might see them or, God forbid, approach them. They did see people, but not many. Those they saw did not seem to take any notice of them and kept their distance. Susan walked as fast as Chicken's legs could manage.

She felt an overwhelming sense of relief that she'd been able to find Dylan, but she was also keenly aware that he was not yet out of danger—nor was Chicken, for that matter. Their safety was the single point toward which everything in her was focused. It was her tabernacle, her mihrab, her north star.

Dylan kept up, but she could see he was struggling. Her heart ached for him. He'd been through so much and yet here he was, tramping on, putting one foot in front of the other in a forced march that seemed endless, even to her. When would they rest? When would they be able to relax and sleep without one eye propped open? When would they get their lives back? Would they? She was reminded that it would soon be Advent and the prophet's cries of "How long, how long, O Lord, will you watch your people suffer before you rise up in power and bring healing to the earth?" had never seemed so timely, so poignant. She decided that the calendar was wrong—it was Advent in her heart.

As if he were reading her thoughts, Dylan began to chant a Psalm: "O Lord, you God of vengeance, you God of vengeance, shine forth! Rise up, O judge of the earth; give to the proud what they deserve! O Lord, how long shall the wicked, how long shall the wicked exult?"

She stopped and faced him, her lips turned up in a sad smile. His forehead was covered with sweat, and his blind eye seemed puffy this morning. There were still wounds on his temples and cheeks that had not yet healed. He looked like he'd just gone three rounds with an ace boxer.

"Psalm 94," he said. "It's from today's Daily Office."

She slipped her hand into his and turned back toward their destination, resuming her brisk pace. Chicken skipped ahead of them as if she were impatient, as if this kind of thing happened every day and she couldn't wait to see what happened next. Susan wondered where such zeal, such trust came from. She wanted it. No, she needed it.

And then there it was—the ferry terminal. It was a small, squat building covered by a larger free-standing roof that sloped toward the water. A minute later, Susan could make out the dock. She wondered why everyone in Alameda hadn't already high-tailed it for the City, but then she realized that it was their home. They loved it. Hell, she didn't live there and *she* loved Alameda. *If it were home for me, I wouldn't abandon it either,* she thought.

There were a couple of people there, but they looked like they were going to work. Susan marveled at that, and it occurred to her that so long as people could go to work, could pretend that things were normal, they would. They reached the terminal and Susan purchased two tickets. She walked to where Dylan and Chicken were standing and handed both tickets to Dylan.

"Ah don't feel right leavin' you here," Dylan said.

"You're not leaving me, you're getting Chicken to safety," Susan said in a tone that said the matter was ended.

But Dylan persisted. "It ain't right."

"It isn't right according to what? The way the world is right now? No, the world isn't fucking right—"

"Fucking right," Chicken repeated.

"—it isn't right according to your misplaced sense of redneck chivalry that says 'menfolk should save the women and children'?" She mimicked his accent.

"Ya' don't have to be insultin'—"

She stopped herself. "You're right. I'm sorry. Dylan, you're wounded and you need to rest and heal. I'm your wife and it's my job to make sure you take care of yourself when you're too pig-headed to do it yourself."

"This is you not bein' insultin', right?"

A woman screamed, and the few people gathered at the terminal began running. Susan whipped around to see the dock surrounded by boats. Not the ferry, as she expected, but a motley barrage of small craft. She left Chicken with Dylan and walked down toward the water so that she could get a view unobstructed by the terminal building. As she did her eyes widened. "Oh my God," she whispered.

"What is it, darlin'?" Dylan called.

The few boats she had seen were only the advance guard. Scores of boats were close behind. *Hundreds?* she wondered, but perhaps it only seemed like it. *That's just a shitload of boats,* she decided.

Directly in the center of the motley fleet was a large sailboat with a tall mast, and it seemed that all the other boats radiated out from it. On its sail a blood-red sigil flapped and convulsed with the shuddering wind.

Susan gulped. *Why here?* She wondered. *Why now?*

The location question was easily answered. As her eye traveled the length of the aquatic convoy, she saw that they all traced back to the docks at Jack London square. She could barely make out the piers in the morning fog. *That's where all the boats are kept, and this is the closest landing point*, she thought. It occurred to her that the landing also made sense tactically. The place was nearly deserted, so they could land, set up mobile transport for their sigils, and wipe out the island by nightfall.

Dylan moved slowly to her side and grasped her hand. "That's the sigil of Tarnequé, the demon behind the French Revolution," he said. "He's a wrath demon. One of the worst Hell's got. He likes the beheadin'."

Susan's heart sank into her belly, along with her hope. She reached for Chicken's hand and the three of them began to back away just as the first of the boats docked and Oakland berserkers of every color and class and religion leaped ashore, slapped each other on the back, and howled with the thrill of battle.

Susan turned. "Run," she said.

"Run where?" Dylan asked.

"I don't...I don't know..." for the first time since the demonic invasion began, tears of panic and desperation sprung to Susan's eyes. Her bravado was fleeing faster than she could, and without it she felt lost. She tugged on Chicken, urging the child to move faster. Chicken began trotting beside them, not speaking, seeming to comprehend the danger so close on their heels.

Susan turned again to see if they were being followed. They weren't, but before she could give way to relief, she noticed the ferry, out on the water, being boarded by one of the smaller boats. *So now there is truly no escape*, she thought, and her despair ripened within her and began a conquest of its own.

Then motion caught her eye, beyond the ferry, and what she saw made her stop in place. Her mouth dropped open.

"Susan, honey, why—" Dylan began, but then he noticed the direction she was looking and turned his head toward it. "Waal...holy fuckin' shit," he breathed.

She nodded in agreement. There was, truly, nothing else to say.

As they watched, a pillar of cloud that stretched from the surface of the bay to the sky was moving toward them. It seemed to be coming from San Francisco, and while it was not moving fast, it was definitely *moving*. Despite being a meteorological event, despite being made of gaseous water, the pillar held its integrity. It roiled, it buffeted, but it stayed together. Its size was hard to gauge, but it seemed to Susan that the pillar must be nearly a city block in circumference. It moved as a witness to power. Its presence reduced thrones and dominions to quaking jelly. It was the incarnation of Glory.

A few of the possessed pirates—for she could think of no more appropriate way of thinking about them—had noticed, too. They slugged the shoulders of their fellows and pointed. Soon, all of the raiders were standing and gawking at the pillar.

Heedless of the danger, Susan felt herself drawn to the water. It made no sense to go *toward* the pirates, but the part of her brain that objected found no traction. She moved as if compelled toward the pillar even as the pillar moved toward her. Dylan, holding Chicken's hand, followed close behind as she approached the water.

Some part of her watched herself as if from afar, even while her eyes were riveted on the pillar of cloud. It seemed to her that she was gliding over the streets in slow motion. Once she stopped and gazed back at her husband, desperate to share the wonder of the moment with another person. His eye was wet with tears and his mouth was screwed up with emotion. When he noticed her looking at him, he wrestled his mouth into a smile for her benefit. She turned again.

"Who is that?" she asked. There was someone—no, two people— moving across the water just in front of the pillar. And they were walking on the water.

There was no caution in her, now, nor was she conscious of whether Dylan and Chicken were following. As the pillar drew near it was as if her soul were standing naked before her God, and neither the love of family nor the violence of the berserker could intrude upon that intimacy. All other awareness, all peripheral vision was stripped away and the pillar of cloud alone filled her sight.

She reached the shore and a part of her was tempted to step out on the water herself. But she did not. Instead, she waded in until the water covered her shins and fought against an almost maddening urge within her to go closer. Suddenly she was aware of Dylan beside her, and Chicken beside him, but she couldn't tear her eyes away to even glance at them. The pillar of cloud was not the only thing in the universe, but at that moment, it seemed to be the only thing that mattered.

"Uh...honey-pie. Them two whats walkin' on the water? Ah think we know them."

She lowered her gaze from the pillar to the two who walked before it. And by now they were close enough that she could make out their features. The taller of the two was stooped, the smaller was wizened. "Brian," she breathed. "Brian and Maggie."

108

RICHARD WAS FROZEN in place as the patchwork dinosaur stomped its terrible feet, crushing everything in its path. Its sides sagged pathetically as the bolts, ropes, and pulleys holding its meat in place struggled against the tyranny of gravity.

The spectacles he'd gotten from Marco kept slipping down the bridge of his nose, but he pushed them back into place, watching the hosts of Hell as they hovered over the tramping soldiers, driving them on, their ectoplasmic lips pulled back in gleeful, wicked grins. Many of them cracked whips, and some marched behind their troops, goading them on with tridents or pitchforks.

The dinosaur stopped and reared back a bit. Directly beneath its feet stood the pitiful, skinny frame of the Goat King. His horned headdress clung precariously to his brow. In the moment, it no longer seemed ridiculous. It was somehow proper—a badge of allegiance to the very forces that lorded over him so menacingly now. Richard was surprised that he did not cower. He did not shake. And he did not beg for his life. Instead, he seemed almost catatonic—as if he were watching the whole drama play out from afar, or was somehow completely dissociated from what was happening to him.

Then he moved. He reached into his pocket and pulled forth a pocket knife. He opened it, and holding it firmly in his right hand, he slit his left wrist, working the blade up his arm. He turned his wrist downward, shaking his blood out onto the ground—an act of offering. It was a gift to his God, who, no doubt to the Goat King's great surprise, had turned out to be real after all.

But before he could complete his act of self-offering, the great foot of the dinosaur sideswiped him as the beast turned. The Goat King's body went flying, his feet spiraling in the air, his headdress finally falling to the ground. He landed atop a picnic table—and might have survived it—but the great beast's next step crushed the table and everything in its vicinity beneath its terrible, sagging, meaty feet.

Tobias had worked himself into a frenzy, tugging and ripping at Richard's clothes. With great effort, Richard tore his gaze away from the dinosaur and looked at the dog, clearly beholding the image of an angel superimposed over the dog's body. Its face was contorted with anger and urgency, its mouth moving noiselessly in entreaty. Richard nodded, forcing his body to move, clumsily at first. Then with greater speed and alacrity, he sprinted after the dog. The intensity of the light made it impossible to see the details of the terrain, so as he ran, Richard tore the spectacles from his face and placed them once again carefully into the breast pocket of his cassock.

Tobias led him to the dried bed of the bay again, but Richard was determined to see the lay of the land. There was too much destruction to wade through to get back to the pedestrian walkway, so Richard raced north toward the University Avenue overpass. Toby grudgingly followed, snarling and barking his protests as they made for the cloverleaf onramp.

Richard was winded as he made for the center of the overpass. It seemed more solid than the pedestrian walkway, but it was wider, too. Running to the north side of it, Richard saw the tail end of the what had been the Goat King's army in full retreat. Turning back to the south, toward the Bay Bridge, he saw the advancing Oakland army, a hundred thousand strong. Oppressed by forces they did not see or believe in or understand, crazed by an irrational bloodlust, they marched on, their faces contorted into an unnatural conflation of rage, pain, and glee.

The army was beginning to pass to his right, along the frontage road. For a moment, Richard feared the patchwork dinosaur might stomp its way onto the freeway, might tear down the overpass with him on it, but no...it seemed the great beast was hugging the coast, following the frontage road as well. Richard had been prepared to flee, but at the moment, it seemed his perch might be the safest place possible, besides affording him a strategically advantageous view.

He watched as the terrible lizard passed and felt the overpass shudder with every crash of the great, fleshy feet. He felt his stomach turn with revulsion as he saw—closer than ever now—the cadavers sewn, roped, and bolted into its sagging sides. It was a diabolically animated monster of rotting flesh, into which women, men, children, dogs, cats, rats, and God knows what else had all been incorporated. *There might be people I know stitched into that*, he thought, and the hair on the back of his neck stood straight with the sheer horror of it.

The infernal duke was invisible to him now, since he was not wearing the spectacles. He reached into his cassock to pull them out, but his eye was caught by something moving in the east, and he jerked his head in that direction.

He didn't need the spectacles to see the glory of it—a pillar of cloud, stretching from the ground into heaven as far as the eye could see. It seemed like a solid pedestal, rooted firmly in the earth and supporting the heavens. As he watched it, it eventually dawned on Richard that it was not stationary. The pillar was *moving*. In fact, it seemed to be on a collision course with the advancing army. Tobias, also looking in the same direction, whined, and his tail began to wag.

Richard looked back at the dinosaur to the north, then south to the approaching pillar. As it got closer, it appeared less solid. It was, indeed, a cloud, and at points he could nearly see through it. Yet its integrity held as it came. As it passed the Ashby Avenue overpass, Richard saw a human figure walking before it.

"Holy Christ," Richard breathed. He knew that figure. No one on earth he knew walked that way except one man. Richard saw the outline of his hunched back, the loping gait made by two legs that were not of exactly the same length. "It's Brian," Richard said to Toby.

Toby barked—no doubt he could see him now as well. Richard wondered at the sight, as Brian stopped to talk briefly with every person he came across. Most of these were people who had been injured on the march from Oakland and were mystified now that they were beyond the influence of a sigil. Richard watched as Brian drew a woman out of hiding. He put his hand on the back of her neck and spoke directly to her face. The woman dissolved into tears.

"C'mon, boy," Richard said, and dashed for the off-ramp. Toby followed, wagging his tail furiously. Sprinting from the ramp to the frontage road, Richard ran south—the bay shimmering to his right, and the Berkeley hills green and towering in the distance to his left.

Richard didn't stop to speak to people along the way. There weren't many, but those that were there seemed fearful and confused. *No more than me,* Richard thought. He didn't know what Brian was saying to people. Richard himself had no idea what to say to any of them.

He ran directly toward the pillar of cloud. Brian was poised over a man, his hand on his head. The man was kneeling. And weeping. Brian removed his hand and said something to the man Richard couldn't hear. It occurred to Richard that Brian looked like John the Baptist or perhaps Elijah or one of the other Hebrew prophets— albeit with sneakers and a hunched back.

Brian lifted his head and his face broke out into a smile as he saw Richard approach. He opened his arms and circled Richard in a great bear hug. Tears streamed from Richard's eyes as he clutched at his old friend.

"I am so glad to see you safe," Brian said.

"That makes two of us," Richard said, drawing back to get a better look at Brian. "Did you stop him?"

"Larch?" Brian laughed. "Yes. Yes, I did."

Richard wanted details, but they could wait. "What are you doing?" he asked, pointing to the pillar. "I mean—what the fuck?"

"I have this new job," Brian said. "I'm taking over for Maggie."

"Maggie? What does being a spiritual director have with the fucking pillar of cloud?"

Brian slapped his arm. "I think there are some things about Maggie you...well, that you never suspected."

"Like what?"

"Like the fact that she's walking ahead of a pillar of fire on the other side of Grizzly Peak right now, putting things right in Oakland."

"What?"

"Look, we'll have to catch up later. It looks like I have a dinosaur to stop. Whodathunkit? As well as a whole host of demons. I...I have to get to work."

"What, exactly, is your work?" Richard asked. He was struggling to comprehend what was happening, but the surreality of it all vanquished his efforts.

"This is my work," Brian put his hand on the back of Richard's neck and gazed at Richard with his kind, ebony eyes. "Richard, listen to me, because this is the Truth. When the Order got all that attention after the Republican convention, it wasn't good for you. You were content before, but now you crave more and more. Before, you just wanted to help people. Now, you can't rest without the fame. It's making you sick, and it's twisting your soul."

Richard looked away. He felt sweat break out on the back of his neck. Brian placed a hand on his cheek and lifted his head until their eyes met again. "Listen to me, my friend. Your reward is not in this world. You must stop seeking glory for yourself and for the Order— you will not advance the Kingdom that way. Your reward is elsewhere, and glory will be given to you there. But it will be God's glory, not yours. What you have is enough. What you *are* is enough. Be at peace and serve God for however many days you have. Do you understand?"

Richard's knees buckled. His hands ran with sweat and he felt faint. He felt deeply ashamed and strangely liberated at the same time. He nodded blankly.

"Good." Brian touched his forehead to his then kissed him on the nose. "Gotta get to work."

Brian looked down at Toby. He knelt and took the dog's head in his hands. "Gnay ip zodireda paaox hami. Adgt eol ripir."

Richard could tell he was speaking Enochian. *When the fuck did Brian learn Enochian?* he wondered. Then he heard Toby respond, "Ulcinin zir." So Richard hadn't imagined it back there in the Goat King's tent. Toby actually spoke—or more likely, the angel spoke using the unwieldy instrument of Toby's mouth.

"What did you say to him?" Richard asked. The words had gone too fast for him to catch any of them.

"I told him he did not need to stay in Toby's body. A way can be made."

"And what did he say?"

"He says he's good." Brian slapped his shoulder. "Gotta go. I'll catch up with you later."

"Sure," Richard said, and turned to watch Brian as he limped northward. He looked taller, more confident than Richard had ever remembered seeing him. For a long time, Richard watched him as he stopped to speak with every person along his way, saw into their soul, and told them the Truth that both undid them and restored them.

Richard looked down and noticed Toby looking up at him. "C'mon boy," he said. "Time to go pick up the kids."

109

MARCO STEPPED off the ladder onto the roof and, getting his balance, climbed the peak toward the solar panels. He knelt to examine them, conscious that he was putting on a show. There was nothing he actually needed up here. To reroute the power, he'd have to do it at the electrical panel at the rear of the house, but they didn't know that. So he pretended to check wires and plugs, every now and then pulling some wire cutters from the cloth sack full of tools they'd given him. All the while, though, he moved toward the front of the house— toward the sigil scrap fluttering in the breeze at the house's peak.

The problem with this plan, he thought, *is that the panels don't actually extend to the edge of the roof. Once I start making for the sigil, the game is over and my goose is cooked.* The trick would be snagging the sigil and somehow destroying it before he got shot. How *would* he destroy it? He could rip it up, he supposed. That would at least destroy the sigil, if not the paper it was written on. He could eat it, but he dismissed that thought. It could take hours for the sigil to lose its potency that way, and if he died, it would be for nothing.

He wiped the sweat from his brow onto the paper sleeve of his jumpsuit. It was chilly, but that didn't stop a man of his size from sweating whenever physical exertion was involved. He looked down at the two guards holding rifles at the ready. He waved at them. One waved back. He squinted and realized it was Cain. *Well, that's a good sign,* he thought. For a moment he wondered if Cain still had the talisman that protected him from the demon's influence. He felt a moment of panic but then breathed deeply and centered himself. He needed to trust Cain. If he couldn't, then he'd know it in a moment when he was dead.

Marco had an idea. He couldn't see over the roof, so he had no idea if there were guards on that side, too. He somehow doubted it. Oh, no doubt there were black shirts in that part of the yard, and no doubt some of them were armed. But they wouldn't be expecting him, and he'd have a few seconds of surprise, at least, before they realized what was happening and started firing.

He knelt by another of the panels and tinkered with the connections. Everything seemed in place. *Actually, if I weren't bullshitting them, this would be a good thing to do,* he thought. *It can't hurt to make sure everything is ship-shape topside before rerouting the outgoing power.*

He kept moving toward the front of the house, checking each panel as he went. At the last panel, he glanced over and judged that he was about six feet from the edge of the roof, and it was about a nine foot climb up to the peak where the scrap was fluttering in the wind. He lowered his eyes quickly and felt his pulse rise in his throat until a steady beat-beat-beat-beat pounded in his ears. His hands were sweating. *This could be the last minute of my life,* he thought. He looked up at the sun and did a silent salutation. Then he dropped the bag and sprinted up the sloped roof toward the peak. He threw himself over the top of the roof just as he heard the first gunshot. Gaining his balance on the far side, protected for the moment, he reached toward the peak and snatched at the sigil. It tore free in his hand, but before he could tear it a gust of wind tugged it out of his fingers and he nearly fell lunging for it.

But it was no good. The scrap was buffeted by a sudden and strong wind, wafting high above the yard, well beyond his reach, drifting beyond the yard, beyond anywhere he might potentially set hands upon it. He felt his heart sink and was suddenly sick to his stomach. Then a bullet punched a hole in the roof next to him.

He jumped up and scrambled diagonally across the roof, even though it was no safer over there. He was without a plan and without hope. A scuffle below caught his eye, and he turned his head in time to see Cain swing his rifle like a bat, clobbering a black shirt who was aiming directly at Marco. He saw two other black shirts grab Cain by his arms, wrestling him to the ground.

Marco found himself at the edge of the roof. It was too high to jump and too far to jump to the roof of the next house. He was as trapped as a treed squirrel. Panic and bile rose up in his throat and he felt his fingers begin to shake. His hands went up into the air in a gesture of surrender, hoping that no one would simply shoot him.

That's when he realized that no one was even looking at him. They were all staring to the southeast, across the back yard. He followed their gaze but found that the roof was obscuring his vision. He climbed toward the peak again, and as he cleared it, he clutched at the shingles to steady himself.

He saw a solid rod of fire extending from the ground to the sky. The rod seemed to be about the diameter of a small house, but it was impossibly tall. It was the very image of raw, unimaginable power. It was terrible, Marco realized, but also glorious. His chest expanded until it was nearly bursting with awe, with wonder, with terror. Flame roiled and flared out from it, catching fire to several trees as it neared them.

As it neared...the rod, the pillar, he realized, was *moving*. And it was moving directly toward him.

110

BRIAN WAS BARELY conscious of the pillar of cloud behind him as he walked. He knew it was there, the same way he knew the hunch was on his back. It was behind him, out of sight...but present, and somehow now, a part of him. He didn't know how it worked. Would he summon it, or would it simply appear when it was needed? He didn't know.

And maybe he didn't need to know. So much about this new job seemed to be about trusting, not knowing. It was like stepping off a cliff and trusting that some invisible walkway was there to support him. But the more he stepped, the easier it became to trust that the walkway was there.

So far, it had supported him every step of the way. So far, he hadn't needed to know a thing. He simply felt his connection to HaShem, looked at the person in front of him with compassion, and spoke what he saw. That was it. And it seemed to be enough.

The patchwork dinosaur thundered ahead of him, almost now at the border to Albany. Brian was following in its wake, speed walking, and making some progress on the great, lumbering atrocity. The beast had crushed the walls surrounding Golden Gate Fields—the north Berkeley horse race track—and Brian had followed it through the ruin of the wall. He'd followed it halfway across the race track when he noticed something in his peripheral vision. Following the motion, he turned his head only to discover his sight was blocked by the pillar of cloud. He circumambulated the cloud and saw that a contingent of the Oakland army had been waiting by the wall and had now closed in and blocked it.

Brian felt the hair on the back of his neck prickle. He suddenly felt cold in the marrow of his bones. When he circled back to the north side of the cloud pillar he saw the patchwork dinosaur staring at him, surrounded by thousands of armed people—not even a fraction of the Oakland army, but more than enough to do him in. Everyone was staring at him. No one looked pleased to see him. Some of them, however, smiled with wicked relish, imagining his bloody end, no doubt.

Time seemed suspended, and Brian suddenly felt very alone. He swallowed thickly and turned around, looking for an out. There was none. He was surrounded on every side by the walls of the racetrack, and the smashed wall to the south was amply guarded. "Whoo boy," he said, and it was, in its own way, a prayer.

Brian looked up and saw the demon Duke astride the dinosaur, his great gauntleted legs gripping its meaty neck, reigns held up in one terrible, clawed hand. In his other hand he wielded a long gold scepter, encrusted with jewels and crowned at the tip—an emblem of his authority and might. A larger, proper crown sat upon his head, his sharp, terrible beak snapping open and closed in gleeful anticipation.

It struck Brian as odd that he could see the Duke. Normally, demons were invisible unless they chose to be seen. But Brian realized that his ability to see the Truth of the situation meant that he could also see the Truth of their presence. *It's going to take me a while to get a sense of these abilities,* he thought. *If I survive this, that is.*

One contingent of the army took a step toward him, then another. Another contingent did the same. They were still a couple hundred feet away, but Brian reflexively stepped back, nearly backing into the cloud. His hands started to sweat and then shake.

Okay, panic isn't going to solve anything, he thought to himself. *You don't need to know what to do. You know what to do. Relax. Connect.* He closed his eyes and breathed deeply, clearing his mind and concentrating only on his breath. In the space of those breaths, there was only breathing. There was no danger. There was no fear. There was nothing but the air coming in and the air going out. He felt his muscles loosen their stranglehold. He felt his chest relax. The knot of pain just over his aorta unspooled. He reached out with his heart, with his fingers, with his will, and felt another hand, another heart, another will, reaching out for him. The hands clasped, the hearts entwined, the wills became one. He felt himself utterly embraced by his God. He felt himself become...what? An appendage. A member. An instrument.

His eyes snapped open and he beheld the demonic army now actively closing in on him. The dinosaur, too, was lumbering toward him, the Duke swinging his scepter and emitting an ear-splitting screech from his snapping beak. Brian saw not only the Duke, but his henchmen—legions of demons, hovering above the heads of the Oaklanders, sapping them of their reason and their will and compelling them forward, drunk on chaos and bloodlust that was not their own.

Looking at them as a group, he only saw the collective menace of their demon taskmasters, as the nefarious hosts cackled and cracked their whips, driving them on. But when he looked at them as individuals, he saw the Truth about them. He focused on one woman, advancing toward him with a two-by-four, studded at one end with nails. Her eyes were wild and her mouth was turned up in something halfway between a sneer and a smile.

He looked more deeply and saw the pain of her childhood, the abandonment of her father, the abuse of her mother. He saw how she had sought to escape the horrific stories she was told about herself, stories she believed. He saw the empty sex, the sting of alcohol, the soothing blanket of the heroin. He saw the flicker of hope in her heart nearly extinguished, and he experienced the broken-hearted ache of HaShem's love for her. He felt compassion for her blossom inside him. He longed to rush to her, to take her head in his hands, to tell her the Truth—that she was loved and lovable.

But he knew that the moment he reached her, he would be overwhelmed and overcome. At the momentary thought of his own protection, the light of his awareness shone on himself, and he nearly staggered from the force of it. In the space of what must have been only a few seconds, he saw the way he had always discounted himself. He was, after all, supremely unworthy. He was deformed, for one thing. His mind flashed to images of being shunned in school, even at Temple, for being a "freak." He saw how he had hated himself because of his homosexuality—how he had been expelled from the seminary once his "secret" had become known. How he had been disowned by his father and shunned by his mother. He saw how the tender flower of his soul had recoiled at Terry's betrayal, and how deep down he felt that he somehow deserved it.

He saw that all this was true—he had felt these things. These perceptions had directed his life. But he also saw that they were perceptions only, and not reality. They were the Truth, but seen through the twisted, distorting lens of his own self-hatred, fear, and despair. He saw in that moment how the twisting had happened, how his tender heart had become bruised and tattered. His heart swelled with compassion for the boy he had been and saw the teasing and rejection for the evil it was. He was overcome with pity on his younger self for the endless nights of self-loathing over his sexuality. He saw the tender soul at the heart of him...and he loved it as God loved it.

And in that moment, he was overcome by an elation that felt a lot like freedom. He saw the stories he had told himself and saw how they had been distortions and lies. He saw the way others looked at him and now knew the problem was with them. He saw the whole world and his place within it—and saw that it was both beautiful and twisted, splendid and chronically ill.

Then the physical manifestation of that illness rose up before him and beat the air with its clumsy claws. Brian blinked as he took in the fatal proximity of the dinosaur, but he couldn't tear himself away from the revelations that rocked his soul. He looked within again and saw Terry, and he saw that he loved him. *When I'm done here*, he thought, *I'll go back to Alameda. I'll find him. I'll tell him the Truth about himself. Then he'll be sorry...* Then he stopped. He saw an even deeper Truth about himself. Yes, there was a part of him that was still hurt, that wanted revenge, that wanted to see Terry grovel.

But he saw something deeper. He saw that this was not what he *really* wanted. He saw that he loved Terry not with a hurt, tenuous love, but with his whole heart, with everything that was in him. Not in spite of his betrayal, but embracing it—even, in some way he did not understand, because of it. More than anything he wanted to feel Terry's lips on his own, wanted to feel Terry's arms around his neck, wanted to feel the tiny shudder of Terry's body when his partner came. Love for him welled up within him and threatened to spill out of his eyes. He didn't want revenge, he just wanted Terry. In the worst, best way.

A demonic scream snapped Brian back to the present. The patch-work dinosaur reared up, it's great, awkward feet almost directly above his head. The Oakland hordes were only a few paces away, and still they kept coming, driven by their demonic oppressors into a frantic orgy of senseless, gleeful hate.

Brian shook his head to clear it, the gaze of Truth still focused on himself. And he saw something else. He saw not just who he had been, but who he was. Not just a respected Talmudic scholar, but more. Not just a cook and a caretaker of people he loved. Not just a wounded animal, but a healer. He stepped forward and addressed the demonic Duke.

"Duke Caphalaxus—I see you. I call upon you to dismount and treat with me face-to-face."

The Duke's beak parted and issued forth a scream that sounded like the tortured cries of a thousand damned souls. The dinosaur's great patchwork feet crashed mere inches from Brian, and he knew the next footfall would not be near him but *on* him. He reached out and touched the dead skin of the beast, shuddering as he realized that the portion of the monster he touched was the headless torso of a man, bolted through the collarbone and stitched with twine into the body of the beast.

And yet at his touch, the dinosaur stopped. Brian spoke to the whole of it generally, and to the torso of the man specifically. "I see you and what has become of you. And it is wrong. It is time for you to rest and to reclaim the dignity that is yours. Return now to your rightful place."

As he finished these words, the great beast swayed, and the massive chunks of meat of which it was composed—both human and animal—began to rain down, plummeting to earth as the illusory spells and demon magick that permitted its cohesion gave way to the Truth, and the ropes, bolts, staples, and stitching that seemed to hold everything in place were no longer adequate. Flesh ripped from flesh and the giant mountain of gore gave way, falling and rolling and splaying out onto the earth to claim its right and proper home in the dust.

As it did so, the demon Duke also tumbled to the ground, its noble limbs splayed out in its indignity, it's beak cawing in protest, and its crown cast into the dirt. Uncertain what to make of this spectacle, the Oakland hordes involuntarily took a step back, clearing a way for Brian to make his way to the fallen Duke.

Climbing over the great, cold chunks of fallen flesh that had so recently composed the patchwork dinosaur, Brian stooped and retrieved the crown. He turned and handed it to the Duke, who was drawing himself upright once again, towering now over Brian, and waving his menacing, skeletal limbs in wrathful protest.

From somewhere within him, a calm washed over Brian—a calm born of true knowledge of who he was, from whence he had come, and the real power that resided within him. "I won't let you frighten me," Brian said. "So flap all you want. You cannot hurt me...not anymore. In case you don't recognize me, allow me to introduce myself. I am the Forerunner. I go before the Lord. I tell the Truth. And the Truth is that you're work here is finished. You and your legions have tormented these good...well, these complicated people...for long enough. The Glory will no longer be hid but is shining forth even now, and it is a searching brightness that you cannot bear."

The pillar of cloud was advancing again, just as Brian knew it would, and it was headed straight for the Duke. "So you may face it now...or you may slink back to the shadows, you and all your hosts, and delay the hour of your accounting until judgment. But know this, Duke Caphalaxus, that day is coming—and on that day, the House of the Lie that you serve will no longer stand. So choose."

The Duke shrank back, raising its hands to ward off the pillar of cloud, shrieking like the terror of the newly dead.

A QUARTET OF EPILOGUES

Your light shall break forth like the dawn,
and your healing shall spring up quickly;
your vindicator shall go before you,
the glory of the Lord shall be your rear guard.
Then you shall call, and the Lord will answer;
you shall cry for help, and he will say, "Here I am."
—*Isaiah 58:8-9*

EPILOGUE 1

BRIAN PAUSED when he reached the shore and, stepping around the pillar of cloud to get an unobstructed view, he gazed back over Oakland. The smoke from several fires were still sending plumes into the evening air, but most of the killing had stopped. He had spent the entire day approaching the oppressed and the broken, speaking the Truth to them, watching how it had crushed them and healed them at the same time.

The seeing and speaking came naturally to him now. He didn't even think about it. Long before this interminable day had been done, he had relaxed into it until it had become like the effortless muscle memory of a pianist.

The marrow of his bones felt tired. In the distance he could see the pillar of fire and knew that Maggie was headed in this direction as well. He knew there was more to do, but it would be tomorrow's work. He had seen enough heartbreak, devastation, and salvation for one day.

Now there was only one thing on his mind. One more thing that needed to be made whole. Without even stopping to think how weird it was, he stepped out onto the water and crossed the short distance between Oakland and Alameda.

His friends were waiting. As he approached the docks, Dylan and Susan rushed to him and threw their arms around him. Mikael and Kat had not yet made it over, but Richard had crossed the distance somehow. He was lying on the ground, apparently exhausted, and gave Brian a wave. Tobias had been more enthusiastic, jumping up on him and giving his face a sloppy lick.

"Where's Terry?" Brian asked, pushing Toby down.

In answer, Dylan tossed his head toward one of the low buildings near the dock. Terry edged around the corner, and, head hung low, he avoided Brian's eyes as he slunk over to where he was standing. *If he had a hat, it would be in his hands,* Brian thought.

"Good shabbas, Bucky," Terry said.

"Good shabbas, bunny. I missed you."

Terry looked like he was going to cry. "I missed you, too. Horribly."

An awkward silence passed between them. Then Terry spoke again, so softly Brian could hardly hear it. "I'm sorry I was such a horn dog."

"I'm sorry I shut you out. Can you forgive me?"

Terry's lower lip was trembling as he raised his head. His eyes were brimming with tears as he met Brian's gaze for the first time. "You didn't do anything wrong."

Brian could see into Terry's soul, and as he gazed at his love, he saw true contrition, without even a grain of self-justification held in reserve. He saw how the dynamics of their relationship had led to Terry's transgression, and saw the Truth of his own part in it. "Yes, honey. Yes, I did. And I'm sorry."

Terry rushed to him then, and he felt his heart leap into his throat as he caught his partner up in his arms. He blinked back tears as he smelled Terry's hair and felt the press of his arms as he squeezed him. Then he held his partner as his shoulders shook with sobs.

"I don't have any excuses, and I don't expect you to forgive me. I'm just...I'm so sorry." Terry said, his voice muffled by Brian's shirt and vest.

"Shhh...it's okay, bunny." He lifted Terry's chin so that he was looking up into his eyes. His lower lip was trembling. Brian kissed it and held it still with his own lips. Then he drew back and spoke. "I forgive you. And my entire heart is yours."

Terry buried his face in his shirt again, lost in another round of sobs. When they subsided, Brian said. "I have a promise to make to you. From now on shabbas is *always* nookie night, no matter what."

Terry sniffed and hyperventilated. "You know what, Bucky? *Tonight* is shabbas."

"Why yes," Brian said. "Yes it is."

EPILOGUE 2

Holy Apocrypha Abby, Two Weeks Later

SUSAN POURED herself a cup of tea when Marco entered and set a beautiful wooden box on the kitchen table. His round face was the very picture of satisfaction.

"What's that?" Susan asked.

"It's a gift."

"For who?"

"For Kat."

Kat looked at Marco, startled. Then she looked at Mikael, who was sitting beside her in their regular places. His eyebrows raised. "Okay," she said, leaning over and dragging it toward her. It was large, about a foot-and-a-half square, but only about three-inches deep. The wood was stained a deep, reddish brown and shone from a fresh coat of lacquer.

Susan could still smell the lacquer and half expected it to be tacky to the touch, but if it was, Kat did not mention it. She watched as Kat opened the catch on the box's lid and pushed it back on its hinges. Her face was screwed up in curiosity as she gazed into it.

"It's...broken glass," she said.

"Not just any broken glass," Marco said.

Kat's breath caught. "It's Randy," she said. Susan saw her bite her lips against the emotion rising up in her.

When they had returned to the Abbey from Alameda, the place had been trashed. It was impossible to tell who had broken in or why, but there was not much in the house that had been left unmolested. Furniture had been smashed, along with a good number of dishes. The sacristy cupboard had been looted, leaving only a single pottery chalice with which to say mass. The monstrance and several of the relics and "sacred chochkes," as Marco called them, had been stolen or destroyed. But thankfully there had been no structural damage— nothing that trash bags, Lysol, and a toolkit couldn't put right.

But none of that had mattered much. What had broken Susan's heart had been the sight of Kat approaching what was left of the mirror that had once held her brother. It had been shattered into thousands of shards, scattered from one side of the kitchen to the other.

Kat had been inconsolable. Even though she knew her brother was an unpleasant person, even openly hostile most of the time, she had loved him. She had always struggled with him—with his reclusiveness, his Asperger's, his involvement with the Lodge of the Hawk and Serpent—but she had loved him, too. It had been terrible to watch him fade out, but it had been worse to see the only vehicle for his existence smashed beyond repair, beyond any hope of restoration.

Kat's hand went to her mouth. "What's it for?"

"Uh..." Marco's eyes flitted back and forth between Susan and Mikael, as if entreating them for a little help.

"It's a beautiful memorial, Marco," Susan said. "If we had Randy's ashes, we'd put them in an elegant urn. But we don't have ashes—"

"We have glass," Mikael said, nodding. "It's not a gravestone, honey, but it's something to visit."

Kat swallowed. She nodded. "It's lovely, Marco." Her voice was thick and it cracked as she spoke. "Thank you." She wiped her eyes.

"You're welcome, Catnip."

Kat extricated herself from her bench and caught him in a hug.

"Let's find a good place for that," Mikael said, freeing his legs from the table and pointing toward the staircase. Kat nodded and reverently carried the box upstairs with Mikael close behind.

Just then the screen door slammed open as Mike rushed into the kitchen and out the other side toward the chapel, squealing. Not far behind him was Chicken, wearing a cape and goggles and carrying a plumber's wrench, shouting, "I'll get you with my demon-smasher!" She, too, raced out of the room.

"It's going to be a little different around here," Marco said.

"It already is," Susan smiled, taking another sip of her tea.

"Demon-smasher..." Marco stroked his chin, looking at the ceiling.

Once they had returned to the house, one of the biggest problems they'd faced had been how to house the children. The old farmhouse was large, but the rooms were spoken for. In the end, they'd decided to build an addition, and until that was done Chicken and Sophie would share the guest room, while they moved a cot into Richard's room for Mike.

None of them had expected to have children, but after a couple of weeks it seemed impossible to imagine the place without them. They all knew there would be beaurocratic nonsense to sort out down the line, but it would take months before any of the city agencies actually got around to them, and they'd have their ducks in a row before then.

The screen door banged again as Sophie came through it, carrying herself with a superior air. She rolled her eyes, "Kids."

Susan almost spit her tea back into her cup.

"Hey, that reminds me, I've been working on something I want to show the kids," Marco said, following Sophie out of the kitchen.

"Ah...quiet..." Susan said to herself, and closed her eyes as she took another sip.

"Don't get too used to that," Brian's voice invaded her solitude. He lowered an armful of dishes into the sink.

"I'm just taking my peace where I can find it," Susan sighed.

"Things are almost back to normal," Brian said.

"I'm not sure things will ever be normal. For instance, you're not going to be cooking for us—"

"Sure I will," Brian said. "I'll just be away more. Besides, I don't just cook for you. I do it for my soul." He cocked his head, considering. "You know, I've never thought of it before, but now that I've found my work, it kind of frees me up to enjoy cooking as my art."

"I like that," Susan kissed his cheek.

"But it'll still never be normal. I mean, there's the kids..." He paused and considered. "Do you mind the kids?"

She shook her head. "No. I've never thought of any of us as breeders, but it somehow seems fitting that there should be kids in the Abbey at our age. It's like Martin and Katie filling the Augustinian monastery with their own kids. It was unheard of at the time, but oddly fitting for them. And for us, I think."

Brian smiled. "I think so. Terry's gotten pretty attached to Chicken."

"So have I. We just need to establish some discipline and a new division of labor around here. No thanks to some of us..." she growled.

"Are you talking about Dylan?" Brian asked.

"He spoils them rotten," Susan folded her arms and shook her head.

"You know, you might want to rethink that air of moral superiority," Brian said. "I've seen the can of cream cheese frosting you keep in the back of the fridge. Now that Dylan is...allergic, you're the addict in the family."

Susan went white and looked away. She opened her mouth, then closed it again. Then her face became hard and mean and she looked Brian in the eye. "You don't seriously think you're going to live here and do that...Forerunner stuff on us, do you?"

"Why, because calling bullshit on the rest of us is your job?"

Susan looked away again. "I deserved that," she admitted.

"Look," Brian said, touching her elbow, "don't be afraid. I know very well that little white lies are the lubricant that keep families from utterly imploding on a daily basis. Terry and I have been together too long for me to think otherwise. I'm not going to call out the little stuff. Mikael didn't become insufferable once he got that Talisman of Amitiel, did he?"

"No, but he's Mikael," Susan said.

"And I'm...?"

"A total sweetheart," she rose and kissed him on the cheek. "Most of the time."

Brian chuckled. "A Jewish mother has to set boundaries sometimes."

"She does indeed."

"And it will be useful to have two of us around who know when someone's lying—we often work in two teams."

"We are, you're right. I just...have to live with both of you."

"We all have to live with each other." Brian hugged her. "Thank God."

"Thanks be to God," she rejoined, returning his hug.

The doorbell sounded. "That must be Maggie," Brian said, looking at his watch.

"Do you need any help with dinner?"

"No, everything's prepped. We'll just snag it from the fridge and throw it on the grill when folks get hungry."

"Okay, but you let me know."

"I will. Go see Mags. I'm going to do some cleanup here."

Susan put her cup in the sink and squeezed his elbow briefly. Then she stepped briskly through the door, crossed the chapel, and opened the door.

"Maggie!" she said, throwing open the screen door. "We hoped it was you."

"Thank you, love," she said, handing a bottle of wine to Susan before squirming out of her jacket. Susan shut the door behind her and shouted for all the house to hear, "Maggie!"

Soon, she heard footsteps on the front stairs that could only be Richard. He ducked to avoid hitting his head as he stepped into the living room and gave Maggie a bear hug. "Good to see you, Maggie," he said.

"And you, Dickey."

Susan heard a wail.

"I'd better investigate that..." She took off for the living room.

Richard watched her go, but she was quickly replaced by Dylan.

"No snacks yet?" he asked. "If God is just, there oughta be snacks."

"How's the eye, Captain Bly?" Maggie asked as she hugged him.

"Weird," Dylan said. "Sometimes it hurts an' there's nothin' there *to* hurt," he said.

"Yes, I've heard of that. It's like the phantom limb thingy."

"Ah guess."

"Can I offer you some wine, Maggie?" Richard asked.

There were a couple of bottles and several glasses on the credence table mere steps away.

"Red, please. Something with enough oak and tannin to punch you in the kisser."

"Coming right up, then."

After he handed her a glass, he took Marco's spectacles out of his pocket. "I don't think you've seen these."

"Oh! Joseph Smith's magic spectacles."

"How did you know?"

She narrowed one eye at him but didn't answer. "What about them?"

"These are really helpful at night—you can see anything, as if it were noon. You can even see things that are normally invisible—"

"Like what?" Dylan asked.

"Like demons, for one thing," Richard answered.

"Why would you want to?" Dylan asked.

"Well, it's good to see what you're up against."

Dylan nodded. "Ah suppose. Scary, though."

"During the day, though, it's so bright I can hardly stand to wear them."

Maggie took a sip of her wine and made a face.

"Too much?"

"No...just savoring."

"It looks like it was too much."

"I get to savor any way I want."

"Fair enough," Richard said.

"My guess is that the light that the spectacles reveal is cumulative. Remember that Joe Smith used to only wear them when he had his face buried in a hat. It's dark in a hat."

"That there is the voice of experience," Dylan pointed at her. "She sounds like she's spent some time in a hat."

"You are a silly man."

"Lovable, though."

"Let me see them." Maggie stuck her hand out.

Richard removed them from his pocket and traded them for her wine glass. Taking them up in her deformed hands, she removed her own glasses and put on the spectacles. She squinted. "Oh! Yes, I see what you mean." She turned around, taking in the room. Then she removed them and handed them back to Richard, replacing her own glasses and taking back her wine. "It's a negative filter, is all."

"What does that mean?"

"It means that none of us can take in everything around us, so our brains filter things out. It's why autistic folks have such a hard time—they have faulty filters, and so they are simply assaulted by information. The information is always there, we just have it filtered down to a manageable level. Those specs are a negative filter—they counteract the filter that we naturally employ and shows us what is always there."

"And what's that?" Dylan asked.

"The glory of God, of course," Maggie smiled. "Everything is awash in it. We just don't see it. But it's surrounding and upholding everything all the time. Even when the demons were aprowl the light was undiminished—it upholds and fills them, too, you know."

"God's glory fills the demons, too?" Dylan looked shocked.

"Of course. They would wink out of existence if it didn't." Maggie turned to Richard and as an aside said, "He is a *silly* man."

"Ya have'ta admit it's counter-intuitive."

Brian approached and put a tray of cheese and crackers on the altar.

"But why would God bother with the demons?" Dylan persisted.

"God help us all if God's favor turned on or off like a light switch based on whatever it was we were doing," Maggie answered, reaching for a cracker. "You might think glory is something you can bring on yourself, but it isn't. It is always and only a gift."

"Maggie," Brian cocked his head, "Is that why, up in the sephirot, you said everything was beautiful, even in the midst of all that destruction?"

"It was," she smiled at him warmly. "I was just seeing it as it was, rather than as it seemed. Unlike most of you poor sods, I don't need corrective lenses like those." She pointed at Richard's pocket.

Just then they heard a squeal, the sharp retort of a child's voice, and much urgent "shush"-ing. Richard raised an eyebrow and crossed the foyer into the living room.

"Why does Chicken get to go first?" Sophie crossed her arms defiantly. Mike stood beside her and seemed to be a little in awe of Marco.

"Because Chicken asked first," Marco explained. He was sitting cross-legged on the floor by the window. In front of him, Tobias seemed to be fast asleep in a spot warmed by the late afternoon sun. Richard saw his legs twitch and his lips move in response to some somnambulistic impulse. Susan stood by, hands on her hips, not looking at all sure about what she was hearing.

Marco picked up something that looked like a Victorian blinder for a stereoscopic viewer. Instead of the holder in front of it, however, where the postcards would be, was a mass of electronics that looked to Richard as if they grew cancerously rather than by human design.

"Is that safe?" Susan asked, looking worried.

"Of course it's safe."

"Gimme," Chicken said, reaching for the contraption.

"Wait, let me explain first," Marco swung sideways to avoid her grasping fingers. "If you're quiet and patient, then you can go inside Toby's head and see what he's dreaming." Marco looked up at Susan and gave her a wink.

Richard reached out and squeezed Dylan's arm. "Whoa boy," he said. "It was innocent."

"Like hell," Dylan whispered. "He's after mah woman. An' after mah accident, Ah ain't as pretty as Ah used to be."

"I hate to break it to you, but you were never pretty, Dylan."

"Yore taste just don't run to Melungeons is all. Yore loss."

Marco fitted the viewer onto Chicken's head, adjusting a leather strap to keep it tight.

"It's not fair," Sophie objected.

"It's not not fair," Mike reasoned. "Someone has to go first."

"You just *like* her," Sophie accused.

Mike didn't answer, but his grin said it all.

"Now, Chicken, I want you to go into vision."

"How do I do that?" Chicken's grin was superhumanly wide.

"Imagine you are going into a movie theater. Can you do that?"

Chicken gave her big, loopy nod.

"Woah, less enthusiasm please, or you'll buck off the electronics."

"Sorry," Chicken said, her smile undiminished.

"Can you see the theater?"

Chicken gave a more restrained nod.

"Now, go toward the big screen. As you get closer, you'll see some stairs that will lead you up onto kind of a stage where the screen is. Do you see it?"

Nod.

"Good. Now, go through the little curtain off to the side of the screen. Now you are backstage, and you see the back of the movie screen."

"It's dark..." Chicken breathed. "And dusty."

"You are in exactly the right place then. Look at the back of the screen. Near the bottom you'll see two things. The biggest thing is Toby, sleeping on the floor—"

"What is he doing there?" Chicken asked. She seemed a little concerned.

"Sleeping, of course," Marco answered. "Now, look at the bottom of the screen. There's a cord running from it, and at the end of the cord is a little plug."

"It looks like a black snake," Chicken breathed.

"That's the one. Now pick it up and find the plug at the end. Got it?"

Chicken nodded.

"Okay, now look at Toby's head. At the back of his skull you'll find a port—a little place that you can slide the plug into. It will fit perfectly. Just slide it in there—"

"Oh for crying out loud," Susan looked impatient.

"Just go with it." Marco shot her a warning look.

Susan shook her head. She might be incredulous, Richard noted, but she was not unamused.

"Did it fit?"

Chicken nodded.

"Okay, now I'm going to switch on the viewer. You'll hear a little whine from the electronics, and you'll see a flicker for a moment, but then you should be able to see what Toby sees." Marco reached over and flipped a toggle switch on the side of the viewer.

Chicken's face lit up and her mouth dropped open.

"Okay, Chicken, now tell me what you see."

"I see a lot of green grass—it's a big, big yard."

"Like a park?"

"Yeah, only nice." Marco scowled in non-comprehension, but Susan understood. She had certainly seen her share of Oakland parks. "The sun is out," Chicken continued, "but I can't see everywhere. It's misty—"

"Toby's brain is only generating pictures for the part that he's paying attention to. If you pay attention to something else, it won't be there. Just stick with what Toby is seeing."

"Okie-Dokie," Chicken agreed.

"Now there's lots and lots of other dogs. They're jumping up and down and playing." The smile on her face was precious. Richard wished he had a glass of wine.

"There's this one dog...Toby is sniffing at his butt—"

Susan rolled her eyes.

Chicken looked alarmed. "There's something wrong with his butt! It's really big and puffy and kind of red...and the dog is looking back at Toby and his tail is wagging in a weird way. And now Toby is..." Chicken cocked her head. "Playing leap-frog...or piggie back...I don't know what Toby is doing to that other dog."

"Enough!" Susan snatched the viewer off of Chicken's face.

"Hey!" Marco objected.

Susan ignored him. "No. I don't care if Toby wants to fuck his way through every bitch in the Elysian Fields—Chicken doesn't have to watch it."

"A man's fantasies should be his own," Dylan agreed.

Chicken seemed stunned. "I think it was a lady dog. What was wrong with that lady dog? What was wrong with her butt?"

"Not a damn thing!" Susan shouted. "Ice cream! Now!"

"But ice cream is for after supper—" Sophie objected.

"Don't care! Ice cream!"

EPILOGUE 3

FRATER KHAMS STUCK his head into Larch's room. "What's the racket?" he asked. Frater Eleazar was sitting on the bed, looking confused.

"But where are you going?" Eleazar asked.

A suitcase was open on Larch's bed. Larch was moving in a calm, unhurried way, packing the few belongings he had with him.

"I'm going to see a priest." Larch folded a tweed jacket and placed it on top of his folded shirts. "I realized something about myself during my ascent."

Khams shot Eleazar a worried look. Larch had never been so forthcoming or openly introspective before.

"It was revealed to me that my...anger...was misdirected."

He placed a hat beside the jacket. Then he opened a chest of drawers and drew forth a snub-nosed revolver. He placed the revolver in a shoe.

"Um...this priest...do you mean one of the Blackfriars?" Eleazar asked.

"Tempting as that is...no." Larch withdrew a box of bullets and placed them in the other shoe. Then he neatly put the shoes into the suitcase. "I'm going to Downer's Grove. Illinois. Let's just say I have some...family business to attend to."

EPILOGUE 4

Holy Apocrypha Abbey—One Month Later

RICHARD PINNED the orchid to Brian's lapel and straightened it. "That looks...that's a damn fine flower." He clapped Brian on the shoulder and said, "I'm so glad you're home." He pressed his forehead against Brian's for a moment. "Hell, I'm glad we're all home."

"Amen to that," Brian said.

Richard straightened Brian's tie.

"I never thought we'd do it. I never thought we'd actually get married."

"I thought you'd never get around to asking him."

"After all we've been through...it seemed stupid not to."

"Well, 'bout fucking time, if you ask me. You ready?"

"As ready as I'll ever be."

"Let's do this."

Richard led Brian from the living room through the chapel and into the kitchen where Mother Maggie was waiting. Brian noted that she looked smaller and more wizened than her counterparts in the upper sephirot, but there was no mistaking her soul, which had been vibrant and present in every world he had seen. She was dressed in a white chasuble, with a white, floral-patterned overlay stole. Gilding the lily was an orchid pinned to the stole, a perfect match to Brian's own.

"This will be my last priestly act," Maggie beamed. "Tomorrow, I am retired. From *everything*, dammit."

"No more spiritual direction?" Richard asked.

"Oh, poo, spiritual direction is a fine retirement career. I'll see you when I get back. I mean I'll be retired from being the Forerunner. And from priesting."

"Is priesting even a word?" Brian asked.

"It is to Episcopalians," she said. "We live in our own little world. Normal laws of grammar and physics do not apply."

"I've always suspected," Brain noted.

"You won't need those silly spectacles today, Dicky," Maggie said. She raised a horribly twisted hand and pointed to the back yard. "It's truly glorious out. You won't be able to miss it." Maggie peeked through the curtains. "That's our cue, gentles. Let's go."

Brian reached over Maggie's shoulder and opened the door for her. She clutched her prayer book to her breast and walked regally down the back steps into the yard. Brian followed close behind, and Richard brought up the rear.

The back yard was resplendent with beauty. Spring was truly in full bloom, and the garden looked none the worse for all the damage done to the East Bay over the past several weeks. Several rows of chairs had been set up, all of them full of family and friends—with nearly as many standing wherever they could find a spot. Brian saw Chava and Elsa, Marco, Cain, Chaplain Fran, the Reverends Oberlin and Dunne and their spouses, folks from the Jewish Renewal Center in Berkeley, Terry's parents and siblings, and even some faces he didn't recognize.

Brian stopped at the entrance to the cottage, while Maggie and Richard processed to their spots. Maggie took her place beneath a shower of Bougainvillea, and Richard stood beside her. As Brian waited, Dylan and Susan processed down the aisle, taking up their place on the other side of Maggie. Then Mike walked down, carrying a pillow with the rings tied to the top of it, and took his place beside Richard. Finally, Chicken and Sophie walked down together, casting flowers all along their way. Once at the front, they took the seats reserved for them.

Once everyone was in place, Brian ascended the steps to the cottage and knocked on the door. "Don't keep me waiting," he called, and all who heard him laughed. Then the door opened and Terry was there, wearing a blinding white satin tuxedo over a ruffly white shirt straight out of the French renaissance. "Ready, my love?" Brian asked, offering his arm. Terry was too emotional to answer, but he took his arm and together they walked into the garden, surrounded by the stubborn love of friends, the relentless mercy of God, and the inescapable light of glory.

ALSO BY J.R. MABRY

...please check out

The Worship of Mystery

"If you found God—or if God found you—

would that be a good thing?"

Chaplaincy instructor Jun Battacharya only needs one more tour of duty to retire, and he is determined that his last semester will be quiet and uneventful. But the very day he lands on the planet Skagway, a mining accident forces him to launch his students into action with zero training.

Jun is certain that if they can just get through the crisis, everything will quiet down and go back to normal. Then Jun receives a letter from the native alien species—specifically from their ranking clergy—inviting him and his students to attend their most sacred ritual.

Jun is fascinated to discover that the aliens worship Mystery—whatever is unseen or unknown is sacred to them. He considers this an intriguing but quaint theology, but when the humans arrive for the ritual, each of them—in very different ways—has an encounter with Mystery that brings the world as they know it to an end...

Get your copy of *The Worship of Mystery* today!

www.ingramcontent.com/pod-product-compliance
Lightning Source LLC
Chambersburg PA
CBHW022231020726
47496CB00004B/850